PENGUIN BOOKS
FRONTIERS

Medha Deshmukh Bhaskaran is a microbiologist and has worked for food and pharmaceutical companies in marketing as well as business development in countries like Germany, India and the United Arab Emirates. From a young age, she has dabbled in poetry in Marathi and English. She has written articles on a variety of subjects for leading newspapers in India as well as in the Gulf. She is the author of Shivaji's bestselling biography, *Challenging Destiny*. Her book on the world of pharmaceuticals and medicines, *Prescription of Life*, was published in May 2018. Now a full-time writer, she enjoys long walks, cooking and farming for leisure. *Frontiers* is her first work of fiction.

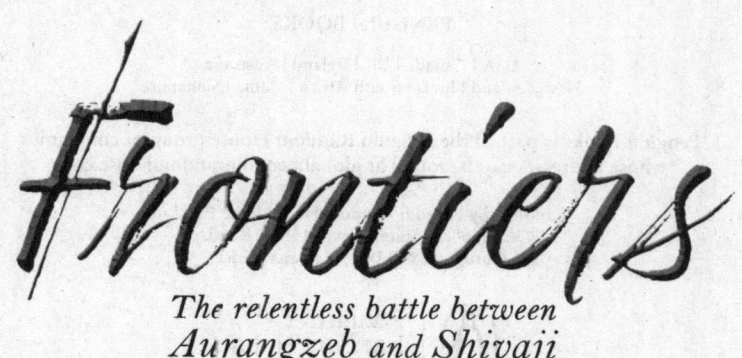

Frontiers

The relentless battle between
Aurangzeb and Shivaji

Medha Deshmukh Bhaskaran

PENGUIN BOOKS

An imprint of Penguin Random House

PENGUIN BOOKS

USA | Canada | UK | Ireland | Australia
New Zealand | India | South Africa | China | Singapore

Penguin Books is part of the Penguin Random House group of companies
whose addresses can be found at global.penguinrandomhouse.com

Published by Penguin Random House India Pvt. Ltd
4th Floor, Capital Tower 1, MG Road,
Gurugram 122 002, Haryana, India

Penguin
Random House
India

First published in Penguin Books by Penguin Random House India 2018

10 9 8 7 6 5 4 3 2

This is a work of fiction. Names, characters, places and incidents are either the
product of the author's imagination or are used fictitiously and any resemblance to
any actual person, living or dead, events or locales is entirely coincidental.

ISBN 9780143441724

Typeset in Minion Pro by Manipal Digital Systems, Manipal

Printed at Manipal Technologies Limited, India

www.penguin.co.in

MIX
Paper | Supporting
responsible forestry
FSC® C043100

This is a legitimate digitally printed version of the book and therefore might not
have certain extra finishing on the cover.

*To my late father-in-law, Air Commodore
M. Bhaskaran, PVSM, one of the pioneers of the Indian Air Force
From him I learnt to be fearless in the face of adversity.*

CONTENTS

CONTENTS

INTRODUCTION

Seventeenth century AD was a turbulent period for the Indian subcontinent. Powerful Hindu kings had turned into vassals of the rapidly growing Mughal empire in the north. The south, or the Deccan, had its own despotic Hindu landlords working for the powerful Muslim kings whose ancestors had long ago arrived from Central Asia and beyond. Coastal Deccan was teeming with European sea traders with high political aspirations, growing fast in their strength and influence due to their technological prowess.

It was during this time that Shivaji Bhosale was born. The son of a *jagirdar*, he was expected to follow in the footsteps of his forefathers and become a nobleman in the court of Adil Shah, as a jagirdar or a landholder. The path laid out for him was easy—to live luxuriously, maintain a well-equipped and strong cavalry, occasionally fight wars and earn grand titles. But when Shivaji looked around him, he saw a world riddled with cruelty, religious conflicts and mindless carnage, the noblemen blind with greed and immorality, the people enslaved, helpless and defeated, and spurned the life he was born into. He picked up his sword and chose to fight for his people's freedom, for a free Maratha nation—the Hindavi Swaraj. Shivaji's dream would soon darken under the shadows of swords and shatter under the heels of the armies of the Mughal empire. Witness the chronicling of momentous intrigues and battles, victories and defeats, triumphs and heartbreaks that sent thunderbolts across the centuries.

Shivaji's dream to free his people was seen as a challenge to Islam, a power that spanned half the globe and was knocking on the doors of Europe. They called him a rebel, a bandit, a guerrilla, a mountain rat. Soon enough, Shivaji and Aurangzeb's histories would get entangled with each other. Shivaji's overarching vision made him great and unstoppable. Armies and cannons cannot still such storms.

But who was Shivaji really? Was he a petty bandit or a brilliant general? Was he merely a power-hungry man or a luminous visionary? Was he really the founder of a new era or is he just a footnote in the numerous pages of history? Shivaji is regarded as a philosopher king by some and a robber baron by some others. In the state of Maharashtra, he is akin to God. My research took me through so many pages of Shivaji's life that I realized that the young India does not really know one of its greatest ancestors. In this historical fiction which is based on a true story, I have called him just Shivaji, without any prefix or suffix since the story starts when he was barely out of his teens. The purpose is to show him to people who always wonder who Chhatrapati Shivaji Maharaj really was.

During my research I came across a foreword written by Narhar Kurundkar for a famous Marathi novel by Ranjit Desai on Shivaji, called *Shriman Yogi*. Kurundkar strongly held that a portrayal of Shivaji could only be completed by showing not just who he was but also who he was up against—his enemies, big and small. And so was formed the idea for this book, and its second protagonist— Aurangzeb. It is based on history but is fiction nevertheless because fiction allowed me the space to take all I had learned over the course of eighteen years and recreate what would have happened, what they would have said, how they would have fought.

Aurangzeb, who goes on to become the Mughal emperor bathing Hindustan in blood in this historical fiction was and has remained one of the most inscrutable men in Indian history. Was he just a jihadist or a supreme war strategist? How did the men of power in Agra plot against him? Why were some Mughal noblemen afraid that Emperor Shah Jahan's first son, Dara Shikoh, would become the next emperor? What compelled Aurangzeb to embrace ideologies and philosophies of his perception of Islam? Was he a senseless aggressor or a literary genius who expressed his philosophies through his poignant poetry? What was his vision and mission? Did he have the power to crush the heart and soul of the Indian subcontinent? Was he just a mindless murderer—of his brothers, of Hindus and of anyone who dared to challenge his beliefs?

Shivaji's war was fought on a much bigger platform than a mere religious conflict. It was a clash of visions, a battle for the inner being of the Indian subcontinent. His unshakeable faith in the inherent decency of humankind is a thread that runs through his life and connects his disparate actions.

History looks different in different books. It was a monumental task to study the history of seventeenth-century India. I visited forts, pored over maps and exchanged ideas with the authors of some books that I have used as references. I do believe I am not the sole custodian of this task of telling this story. During my journey, I met some very dedicated people and without their help it would not have been possible to write this story, but I have persevered with all my heart and soul and hope that I have been able to recreate a bit, if not all, of what once had been.

The English translations of the Persian and Arabic poetry of Shah Jahan and Aurangzeb have been taken from various books by Sir Jadunath Sarkar. I have tweaked some lines of these. The English translations of poetry written by Marathi saint poets are mine.

PART I
1656–59

PART 1

1956–59

PROLOGUE

1648

A chalky moon floats in the inky sky above the huge rock of Kandakada rising above the slopes of Purandar Hill. Shivaji Bhosale narrows his eyes to peer down the cliff. The darkness at the base of the mountain is broken by the distant glow of torches. The Adilshahi sultanate's cavalry squadron has arrived from the east to reach the northern side of the hill. Shivaji knows that their commander, Fatte Khan, is seething with rage. It is quite likely that khan will send his men, two thousand as per the scout's estimate, up the hill. But Shivaji is not worried. The sultanate's heavily armed cavalrymen are not trained to scale even small hillocks. And upon this hill, where even agile horses used to moving across hilly paths are rendered useless, the enemy will be forced to come up on foot.

Besides, Purandar Hill is darker than the rest of the region, with the dense foliage blocking the fragile moonlight from lighting up the forest floor. It is suicidal to climb the mountain to mount an attack when the enemy sits on the top, backed by a hill fort. But Muse Khan has been briefed to do just this by his commander Fatte Khan and is desperate to prove his military prowess.

'Move! Extinguish the torches; we are going up!' Muse Khan shouts his orders. His men leave their horses at the foot of the mountain and start climbing. For Muse Khan, it is worth the risk. Shivaji has illegally taken over some of the hill forts in the region. If Muse Khan can capture Shivaji and present him alive in the court of their king, Mohammed Adil Shah, he will be rewarded with *jagirs* and titles. His life will change.

3

The region belongs to Mohammed Adil Shah, and the hill forts are his kingdom's military strongholds. Muse Khan has come to reclaim his king's territory from a rebel supposed to be serving the king. Initially the campaign was intended to teach Shivaji a lesson and show him his place. Adil Shah had declared in the royal court, 'Show the boy some muscle and he will kneel; he is barely eighteen!' Instead, the lad had bared his fangs. As they set up camp a few *kos* east of Purandar Hill, Shivaji's lightweight cavalry had started harassing them, first assaulting the detachments and then cutting off supplies by sabotaging their lines of communication. Shivaji's men waiting in ambush had killed the Adilshahi's cavalrymen in command of cargo oxen, and then herded the animals deep into the jungles. A week since, they had become even more daring, and started attacking flanks of the main camp and then galloping away into the forests.

Muse Khan knows the odds, but does not allow it to dampen his spirits. He is trained as a heavy cavalry soldier and is protected by armour. But that damned life-saving chain mail and armour suddenly feels heavy! The shield tied to his back is getting heavier. His sandals, suited for the flat plains, slip and make him fall on his knees, not once, not twice, but many times. The climb is riddled with steep slopes; at places they are simply vertical. Behind him, Muse Khan hears his soldiers grunt with fatigue as they struggle to tackle the climb. Suddenly everyone stops in their tracks. The hill has started shuddering with the echo of drumbeats. There are whooshing noises in the air as arrows fly past and he hears some of his men scream. To his horror, many of them fall to the ground, dead already. Just then an arrow whizzes past him, its shaft brushing his turban. Muse Khan winces. The drumbeats stop as suddenly as they had started, throwing the mountain into a strange abyss of silence. The hush is far more unnerving. Stunned, he moves sideways to find a clear view through the branches above him and sees the faint outline of the fort's ramparts. The drums start beating again and Muse Khan notices shadows of men moving swiftly, leaping down from a cliff into the shallow depression of the mountainside.

Shivaji has ordered his archers to stop shooting and start descending the hill to intercept the enemy and finish them off before they reach the fort. He watches from the ramparts as Shivaji's men leave, merging with the forest, dark shadows moving through the trees. Sixty-year-old Pasalkar, one of his oldest soldiers, is among them. The shadows glide through Bini Gate in a file. They resemble a black snake swimming across dark waters, swift and silent. Most of them are peasants, goatherds, barbers, cobblers and blacksmiths, born to work with wooden sticks, nails, razors and hammers.

On the slopes, Kavji, one of Shivaji's ace fighters, readies his spear. He and a few men are lying in wait just beyond Bini Gate, hidden on the trees. The enemy will soon reach Bini Gate and start climbing in the direction of the ramparts where Shivaji stands with just a few men. It is Kavji's charge to kill whoever comes near the gate to prevent him from reaching the top.

Before Muse Khan can recover from the arrow whizzing past his ear and decide between fight and flight, a shadow has emerged from behind a tree. Muse Khan senses a man's presence and begins to remove the shield from his back. But it is too late. He sees the outline of a spear flicker for a fraction in the air, and is thrown by searing pain. The impact makes him lurch back and collapse. The straight blow of the spear, powered by speed, has pierced through the metal links of his armour and fractured his ribs. He scrambles, keeping his shield and sword on the ground. Gritting his teeth to gather courage, he holds the shaft of the spear in both his hands and forces out its sharp iron head from his chest. Warm blood gushes out. He grabs his sword and grapples to get up, trembling. It is getting difficult to breathe and he suspects that one of his lungs is punctured. Cursing, he prepares to parry the enemy's blow. Muse Khan can see the man now—he has pulled out the sword from his scabbard.

Kavji marvels at Muse Khan's strength. He holds the hilt of his sword with both hands. He is at a higher level and has the advantage of position. Muse Khan, standing below and feebly brandishing his sword, looks utterly vulnerable. Kavji's blade comes down with full force to pierce him between his neck and collarbone, the part not protected by armour. Muse Khan collapses. Kavji looks up to see the sultanate's remaining men running away. He hears a familiar voice. Somewhere beyond, through the trees, Pasalkar is roaring, *'Har Har*

Mahadev!' hailing the might of Lord Shiva and sprinting down to hunt the enemy. The words of the sixty-year-old warrior inject a fresh dose of battle energy into Kavji's blood. He wrenches his sword out from the dead man, wields it in the air and runs down the hill to join his comrades.

Abaji Ghadge and his hundred men have been hiding in the trees near Bini Gate, listening to the gasps and yells around them. They do not intend to join their fleeing comrades. Ghadge has decided to fight Shivaji Bhosale till death and has made such a promise to Muse Khan. He watches as Shivaji's men vanish down the slope. It is the right time to take the traitor by surprise. Shivaji Bhosale is an ordinary native, a Hindu like him, but wants to be a sultan. It is a sin to challenge the ancient protocol that says that the Maratha satraps must obey the Muslim kings. He gestures to his men to follow him and starts climbing. They have barely walked a few paces when a rumbling sound makes them look up. Ghadge sees an enormous boulder rolling down towards him. Before he can move out of its way, it strikes him. He buckles and is flung into a ditch. The boulder crashes beside him. There is the metallic taste of blood and a dislodged tooth in his mouth. An excruciating pain runs through Ghadge's body. He opens his eyes to see but there is only darkness . . .

CHAPTER ONE

1

The night sky is clear. A waxing moon throws pale light on the surroundings. Hyderabad, the capital of the Qutbshahi, also called the Golconda Kingdom, has been surrounded by the Mughal army. Shahzaada Muhammad Sultan, Aurangzeb's eldest son, stands with Mir Jumla, looking out to the city, his elephant swaying like a ship in the seas. Despite wearing a woollen sweater below his armour, the prince shivers as cold winds sweep across the flat highlands of the eastern Deccan. Winter is almost over but the cold is cutting through Sultan's bones. But he is busy admiring Hyderabad, its countless minarets, domes and spires shimmering in the moonlight like artefacts of polished silver. He has heard of the wealth hidden beneath the veneer of the city's splendour; he can't wait to see it for himself.

Looking at the city, Sultan thinks about his father, Aurangzeb, who is currently the *subhedar*, or the viceroy, of the Deccan regions under the Mughal empire. He is the third among the four sons of Emperor Shah Jahan. In recent times, Sultan's father is possessed with just one thought: to swallow the sultanates of the south. He does not want the southern kingdoms as just the tributary states of the Mughal empire; he wants them as provinces, *subhas*, of the empire.

'Sunni in Arabic means the one who follows the traditions of the Prophet (peace be upon him). Sunnis are born to rule,' Muhammad Sultan has often heard his father declare with pride, as if being Sunni is a hundred times better than being a mere Muslim. The Prophet's death axed Islam, which stands for peace and submission to the

7

will of God, into two factions filled with intolerance and anger for each other. The Shias hate the Prophet's friend, Abu Bakr, who was declared as the first caliph of Islam, and felt that the leadership should have gone to Ali Bin Abu Talib, the Prophet's cousin. The Sunnis loathe the very idea and call the Shias *Shia-tu-Ali* or 'the gang of Ali'.

'We will destroy the Shia kingdoms of the Deccan for they do not follow the traditions of the Prophet!' Aurangzeb had declared in the open court filled with some of their finest Shia and Hindu military officers, who had stood with downcast eyes and faces red with shame and anger. Sultan has many questions on this issue. But who is he to ask? Sultan's own mother is a Hindu by birth and now a mere convert, just another wife of his staunch Sunni father, a wife who could never be a queen consort to the emperor, if Sultan's father does become one.

For the time being, Sultan is happy to be a part of his father's battles of expansion. Their first target is the Qutbshahi sultanate. The plan of this annexation was hatched at Naukhanda Palace in Aurangabad, their Deccan capital, with the help of Mir Jumla, a Shia and the recently ousted grand wazir of the Qutbshahi Kingdom.

'A desperate man like Mir Jumla, whose family has been thrown in the dungeons by the Qutbshahi king, and who thinks we are the ablest to help him, will give us all he can offer,' Aurangzeb had told Sultan before the meeting.

The first gift Mir Jumla had given to Sultan's father was indeed priceless. It was a seven-hundred-and-fifty-six-carat uncut diamond bigger than a man's fist. 'If this stone is finely cut, it will be a *Koh-i-noor*, a mountain of light!' Mir had told the emperor as he paid obeisance to him.

Muhammad Sultan would never forget the evening when Mir Jumla had arrived on a caparisoned elephant at the high, pillared patio of their palace. The howdah was made of silver and glittered with precious stones. More than a hundred horsemen wearing silk robes and colourful turbans strutted behind the trundling elephant, the trumpeters walked ahead of it. It was as if a king had arrived. The fair Persian sat in the howdah, wearing a *kimoush* turban fixed with a crown band.

Sultan had stood with his father in the balcony and stared awestruck at their glamorous guest dressed in a long black robe with a sash dazzling with diamonds. 'Mir Jumla always wears black; it is his style statement,' someone had whispered. Mir Jumla was his title, meaning the grand wazir, but everyone addressed him as Mir Jumla instead of by his actual name. Sultan was briefed about Mir's status as the wealthiest jagirdar of the Qutbshahi whose land yielded forty lakh rupees of yearly revenue. Sultan had done some quick calculations keeping the most frequently used imperial coins in mind. One could mint two lakh fifty thousand ashrafi mohurs with that money, each made with one *tola* of pure gold! And that was not all. Mir Jumla was also the owner of several diamond mines. He was famous too, and was known the world over as a renowned diamond merchant. His wealth that overshadowed the grandeur of his king's court, his scholarly knowledge of artillery, his capacity to demand loyalty from the Qutbshahi's top military officials, his private, well-equipped cavalry and his networking abilities had made Qutb Shah jealous and sleepless. The king's minions further fanned his insecurity. Now, Mir Jumla's arrogant son Amin had added fuel to the already explosive situation. He had one day arrived drunk in the king's court and urinated on the floor to show off his father's power. In a fit of rage, the king had thrown him and his family in the dungeons of Golconda Fort. Mir Jumla had been away in Bengal then. He did not return. Instead, for a year he had roamed the world, visiting men of might who could help him to get his wife and children out of the dungeons.

Sultan had sensed that Mir Jumla indeed needed them, though the fact was that they needed him more. The Mughal palace at Aurangabad was spruced up for the meeting, with a large new gilded chandelier and new silk curtains adding to the already decorous *baithak*.

Unlike other times, Aurangzeb was waiting for his guest.

Mir Jumla had entered with a swagger and then bowed slightly. After the initial pleasantries he had come straight to the point.

'Shahzaade,' Mir had addressed Sultan's father as prince in chaste Persian. 'I have served the Qutbshahi for the past twenty years, joining them as a military officer, and have risen to become the grand wazir.

You need not worry about the Qutbshahi military commanders; they consider me their leader. I have led them to victory in battles of expansion and have annexed countless temple cities of the south.

'The ruler, Abdullah Qutb Shah is a romantic man and lives in a fantasy world. He is not worthy of being the shah of the state that yields several lakh rupees a year only in land revenue. Taxes collected on the diamond and tobacco trades fetch him a few more lakhs,' the ousted and angry Mir Jumla had put forth his strategy.

Sultan had known what his father was thinking. He wanted money to strengthen his army to fight the impending war of succession with his brothers. The Shia kingdoms of the Deccan had become the empire's vassals twenty years ago but in recent days they had stopped paying the tribute money.

'If Abdullah is a fool as you say he is, call him for a meeting and slaughter him. Lighten the burden of his head on his neck,' Sultan's father had eagerly suggested.

'That may anger his as well as my followers. Instead we will march into Hyderabad. If he is in the city and offers resistance, we will kill him. If he is in the fort, we will besiege the fort later. Once the fort falls, the Qutbshahi sultanate is ours. This land is a gold mine. The villages to the north of Hyderabad are famous for high-quality iron ore that is greatly valued by blacksmiths all over the world. The weavers of the port city of Masulipatnam export chintz to Mecca. The carpet makers of Eluru have been renowned for their skill for centuries.' Mir Jumla knew how to entice; it was one of his skills as a world-renowned diamond merchant. He had rolled his eyes and then, spreading his arms in the air, announced, 'It is not just the diamond mines. Consider the forests teeming with herds of elephants, keenly sought by cavalry commanders, and also the trade of tobacco and toddy that brings in enormous funds in taxes for the ruler.'

Sultan had glanced at his father and noticed, just for the flicker of a moment, a glint of greed creeping into his eyes. He suspected that even Mir Jumla had noticed it.

Mir Jumla had not come alone. He had his own, well-mounted cavalry of six thousand horses, a fully armed infantry of fifteen thousand men, one hundred and fifty war elephants and regiments of modern light artillery of easy mobility that could fire modern explosives that Mir Jumla had himself invented. His army combined with Aurangzeb's army was enough to destroy the Qutbshahi.

'I will be with your son like a shield, my precious shahzaade,' Mir Jumla had promised Aurangzeb.

2

With the help of the Qutbshahi's ousted grand wazir, Sultan's journey to the banks of the river Musi has been hassle-free. He is fascinated by what he has seen. Even in winter, the rambling meadows have retained a part of their post-monsoon lushness, dotted here and there by enormous rocks piled on each other with hues of brown and red. Sometimes they look like unstable hillocks, ready to tumble on to intruders. Sultan encounters man-made lakes, sweeping across the land till they merged with the horizon. The villages are surrounded by patches of cultivated earth with tall stalks of millet grass swaying in the wind. The army camps on the banks of the Hussain Sagar on the northern border of the city.

When Sultan moves into the suburbs with his large military, no one intercepts the army. They move unchallenged, setting fires to the buildings as they go. The fires still rage behind him, as the rising clouds of black smoke make the northern sky pitch dark. Soon, they reach the boundaries of the inner, walled city of Hyderabad without any trouble. To his left, on the western horizon, Sultan can see a faint outline of the Golconda Fort. But that is not his target right now, the city of Hyderabad is. Now, between him and the walls of the city it is only the river Musi flowing peacefully and its dark waters do not seem daunting.

'The inner, walled city and the fort are separated by the Musi. The city is on its southern banks and the fort on its northern banks, four kos upstream. The fort is protected by a half-kos-long outer wall, six to twelve *guj* thick, twenty guj high and fortified with eighty-seven bastions overlooking a deep, water-filled and crocodile-infested moat. Unlike the fort, the city has only an outer wall,' Mir Jumla had said.

Feeling safe with Mir hovering around, Sultan tells his *ankush*-wielding mahout to goad the animal farther towards the river. The high-arched bridge above the waters of the river is deserted, and the massive gate studded with steel spikes at the other end of the bridge is closed shut. The ramparts of the city wall do seem hostile, yet ripe for invasion.

He has been duly warned that in the darkness above the bastions near the bridge are archers waiting for his men to step on to the bridge. He looks around. His ears pick up the sound of splashing from the river. His scouts have slipped into the water to swim across, some of them carrying wooden buckets. He looks down from the howdah and can see a sea of horsemen around him. Mir Jumla has steered his horse towards the scaffolding they have erected to hold their cannons and stands waiting, ready to give his orders. His artillerymen, hanging like spiders on the scaffolding, are quite skilled and quick at loading the cannons with explosives. He has chosen the latest bombards, the European *granados*—iron shells filled with explosives and fitted with a slow-burning fuse. His gunners have already inserted the propellant explosives in the cannons that will soon start exploding one after another.

Mir Jumla knows his men are the best but he is also aware that only he knows how to design the fuse so that it burns at the right time and the shells explode at the right place. He has also added extra saltpetre to the gunpowder to make the explosions stronger and noisier. For him, it is not just about damaging the enemy's property or killing them; the blast must coax their minds to yield to thoughts of surrender.

'Take position!' Mir Jumla barks at the artillerymen minding the cannons. The fire has to hit the gate before the scouts emerge from the waters.

'Fire!' he shouts and his men spring into action.

The earth shudders with each hit. Chunks of debris fly in all directions. The spiked gate catches fire. The explosions add muscle to the inferno. The horses neigh in panic and the elephants trumpet with fear but the explosions continue till the sky is covered with burning specks as dust and smoke billow from the burning ramparts.

Sultan sees a small part of the wall, adjacent to the gate, blow up. The flames rise high and the sky is lit with red and yellow flames. He notices shadows scurrying over the ramparts, the archers running away from the flames rising from the bastions. In the midst of the fire and noise, the scouts jump out of the river. Soaked, shivering in their clothes that have become heavier with the icy river waters, they scuttle and run zigzag to avoid arrows shot by the archers that are holding their ground. The Qutbshahi cannons mounted on the other, intact, bastions now start flinging fire from across the river. They do little damage, as Mir Jumla knows exactly where the cannons will strike, and has cleared away his men from the range of fire. He orders his henchmen to cease fire for the men to attack.

A scout manages to reach a gap in the wall, his soaked clothes protecting him from the still-smouldering slivers of explosives. In the trembling light of flames still rising over the charred gate, he can see the tree-lined avenue going towards the Charminar. He has heard about the monument with the four soaring minarets and arches built at the intersection of the city's four major streets. The king's palace is towards its west. He is aware that the grounds hidden behind the trees are teeming with the enemy's troops. Any moment now they will come marching out. Time is of great essence. He turns to his left and realizes that some of his men are following him. He has been told about the secret staircases leading to the ramparts. Armed with just daggers, the men climb the narrow, poorly lit, spiralling staircase tunnels. Once on the ramparts, they hide in the shadows of the turrets, waiting for the archers to pass by, before attacking stealthily. The archers fall silently, their quivers still holding unused arrows. Leaving behind his comrades, the scout runs further east to look for more archers but finds the ramparts empty. At the north-facing parapet, he pulls out a small trumpet from his belt and blows it hard, till he is gasping for breath.

'Move in!' Sultan orders his men as the trumpet sounds from the ramparts. A few horsemen around him take off to pass on his message to his commanders on their armed elephants a little distance away. Soon, they march over the bridge.

'We will be safe on the bridge. They will not fire explosives there,' Mir Jumla had assured them. 'The bridge is their pride, a reminder of their past glory, built seventy years ago so that the then prince could visit his Hindu beloved who lived on the other side of the river Musi. He later married her and made her his queen.'

Several scouts are busy throwing buckets of water over the gap created by explosives near the city's entrance gate to douse the lingering flames. Sultan's army crosses the bridge; horsemen and foot soldiers jump over the gap and enter the city. Some take the avenue leading to Charminar. Some steer their horses to streets lined with mansions of the ministers and nobles, yelling *'Deen! Deen! Deen!'* hailing the supremacy of Islam. They toss burning torches randomly on to balconies encased in wooden parapets, starting fires that flush out panicked residents. As the Qutbshahi's soldiers watch in horror and the people run to hide, thirty thousand Sultan's men enter the city of Hyderabad.

The Qutbshahi soldiers, distinct with their hair tied tightly in buns over their heads, seem overwhelmed by the waves of the Mughal's men. The war-hardened Mughal soldiers cut through their shocked regiments like a blade through enemy flesh. And Hyderabad watches silently with stunned rage. The city's soldiers are startled to see a fully armoured Mir Jumla, wearing his famous black tunic and golden sash, riding towards the palace. There is no mistaking him; he is *their* Mir Jumla, who had led them to success in so many battles of expansion. He is surrounded by several horsemen holding torches, throwing a bright glow over him, as if the torchbearers want to show him to them. The Qutbshahi archers gaze at him, forgetting to shoot, the commanders no longer sure whether to fight or not.

Mir Jumla kicks his horse and turns to face Sultan's elephant, surrounded by one hundred horsemen protecting their prince who is barely twenty years old. Mir Jumla waves his hand to signal to Sultan. 'Follow me, young shahzaade,' he calls out.

Sultan has decided that this city is even more glorious than Agra. Never mind that its streets are right now littered with limbs, torsos and heads. As they move through a street lined with shopping arcades, he stares ahead in amazement. Four sky-piercing minarets with rings of balconies gleaming in the pale moonlight rise above the enormous arches and appear to be the city's everlasting guardians. Oh! The irony! After crossing the major intersection through its archway, Sultan notices flames rising above the residential areas. The sky has turned dull with smoke. He can hear the faint screams of people when his elephant turns to the left and enters a wide road lined with columns of trees leading to the king's palace. With numerous torches around, the pillared corridors of the palace amplify the darkness lurking across its arches. Its cupolas and domes are shrouded in smoke drifting from the burning city. The courtyard is littered with dead bodies. Small dark pools let crimson streams flow and meander randomly across the marbled floor. He climbs down with the help of a rope ladder as his guards fuss over him. He has to jump over the bodies and avoid stepping in the blood streams to enter the palace.

The court is more like a museum, filled with chandeliers from Europe, carpets from Persia, ceramic from China and many priceless artefacts of gold and silver studded with precious stones. The walls are covered with brass murals of parts of the world he has not even heard of. The windows are covered with fine printed fabric that he has never seen.

Behind the court is an enormous foyer with marble shelves. Sultan's jaw drops as he stares at the opulence around him.

'What must be done, young shahzaade?' Mir Jumla asks with a smirk. His men have marched through the maze of courts and corridors, apartments and underground vaults. Abdullah Qutb Shah is nowhere to be seen.

Sultan looks at Mir Jumla unsurely. 'Lock the palace and guard it,' he orders, not knowing what else has to be done. The treasure is too huge to carry anywhere.

Outside, the plaza covered with polished marble is crowded with quivering dance girls. The Deccan, Turkish, Persian and Armenian courtesans have never seen a battle. The glimpse of the beautiful women makes the lice-ridden soldiers, who stink of sweat and grime, abruptly stop. They start encircling these women with long and lustrous hair and smooth skins, each trying to hide behind the other. The rustle of their silk skirts and the jingle of their anklets make the men laugh as if tickled. Some start whistling and some make lewd comments.

<h1 style="text-align:center">3</h1>

The evening sun has turned into a red orb and the western sky looks like an altar of fire. The waters of the river Mutha reflect the flaming colours in its restless waters. As the sun is swallowed by the hills of Maval, the sunset hills, the colours fade away into darkness. The forest-clad hills in the distance turn shell pink, indigo and then peacock green tinged with scarlet. Soon enough, golden sunbeams melt into a distant gloom and the hills turn dull grey, like heaps of ash.

'What you have just witnessed is the magic of Maya,' Shivaji says without glancing at Raghunath, his hands resting on the parapet. They stand side by side on the balcony of Shivaji's palace, the Lal Mahal.

Fifty-year-old Raghunath Ballal Korde is Shivaji's Brahmin diplomat and soldier. The political negotiator knows his master's habit of being cryptic. He says softly, 'Knowing that the world is an illusion, we still struggle, plan and fight wars . . .'

'Because,' Shivaji interrupts him, 'many times the truth rips open its illusive cover and breaks free like a bee seeking to sting, especially when it comes from pangs of hunger and the pains of injustice. And this truth need not be seen but felt—like the sting that brings tears to the eyes.'

'Raja, you called for me for something?' Raghunath asks hesitatingly, quickly trying to change the subject. He knows there is no point in arguing. The young Maratha has his own definitions of illusion, life, war and dreams that sometimes make the logical diplomat in him disoriented.

'Raghunathji, you are aware that our jagir is small. It is barely fifty kos from east to west and twenty-five kos from north to south, a few hill forts around the region of Pune, Chakan in the north, Maval in the west and Shirwal, Supe, Indapur regions in the south-east. We need to expand.'

How can Raja Shivaji expand his jagir? Raghunath wonders. The very ambition defies the laws of the land.

'With our *watandars*, the agricultural revenue collectors like the *deshmukh*s and *patil*s, tamed and with no subhedar to watch over us, it is time for some action,' Shivaji insists.

Raghunath continues to search for answers. Raja Shivaji's jagir is mainly hilly and secluded. It has never been rich enough to attract the prying eyes of the Adilshahi's court officials. There are other reasons for the neglect. The estate was granted to Raja's father by the Nizam Shah. The Nizamshahi was annexed twenty years ago. The region now belongs to the Adilshahi, and the king, Mohammed Adil Shah, has died just recently. He was bedridden for ten long years, too sick to look after his kingdom's affairs, and his son, Ali Adil Shah, the present king, is too young and still learning. He is not yet thinking about the far-flung and remote regions of his kingdom. His mother, the recently widowed Badi Sahiba, is the de-facto ruler.

'Without freedom, we cannot do what we want to and what we aspire to. Without freedom we die not knowing the very purpose of our life.'

Raghunath has heard it before. Raja Shivaji's father is the Adilshahi's regent and lives three hundred kos away. He has made Bendakaluru at the southern borders of the Adilshahi his home and has not visited his jagir in years. Fate has provided enough liberty to Raja Shivaji since he was just eight, enough to cherish his freedom, enough to hate being under any authority and enough to dream of a sovereign nation, the Hindavi Swaraj.

'Jawali is the key to our dream, our first step to swaraj. If we cannot get the valley amicably, then we shall take it by the sword,' Shivaji says, his eyes shining with inexplicable optimism.

Raghunath has already met the jagirdar of Jawali, Chandrarao Morey, before, with a proposal for an alliance against the Adilshahi king. The at-first-polite proposal was followed by many warning letters. But the man had repeatedly and vehemently refused their offer and snubbed their threats. Raghunath is aware that for a jagirdar like Raja Shivaji, dealing with the defiant deshmukhs of his jagir is an internal matter, but intimidating another jagirdar or seizing another jagir is treason. The Adilshahi rulers already hate Shivaji for grabbing the hill forts that lie within his jagir. The new king, Ali Adil Shah, calls him a traitor, a notorious rebel and a *namak haraam*—one who, after eating their salt, is not loyal to his masters. Ten years ago, before he fell ill, the late Mohammed Adil Shah had wanted Raja Shivaji dead. Who could ever forget the battle of Purandar?

'You have seen the valley. Aren't the hills of Jawali far more hostile than the ones we have in Maval?' Shivaji asks excitedly.

Raghunath nods. The Sahyadri Range runs north to south along the western edge of the Deccan. These mountains separate the plateau called Desh from the narrow coastal strip called the Konkan. At Maval the hills are steep and rocky, girded towards the top by massive basaltic rocks. The lower slopes are riddled with deep, snaking dells that look like enormous elephant trunks. These hills are regarded as the war elephants of the region. Just twenty-five kos southwards, in Jawali, the same mountains take on a more aggressive avatar. The hills become steeper, the valleys deeper and the forests at the foothills denser.

'To invade the valley, one needs hill men who can also ride horses. Heavy, armoured cavalry is the main strength of our king. The valley will make it as redundant as a ship stuck in sand dunes. If Maval is our sword, Jawali will be our shield. Remove Morey for good,' Shivaji says softly.

Raghunath understands in a flash.

'To expand northwards we need to fight the Mughal, to expand eastward or southwards we need to fight the Adilshahi. We are not strong enough, not yet. We want Jawali. Once that is in our hands, it will be easier to take over the western region, the coastal region of Konkan,' Shivaji announces as if his jagir is already an independent territory.

'Konkan is ruled by the Mughal and Adilshahi sultanates in parts, and not to forget the African Siddis holed up in the invincible sea fort Janjira,' Raghunath reminds his raja lest he has forgotten.

'Konkan's western borders are all sea, and eastern borders all hills. It is easier to fight their armies on that strip than anywhere else. Also we need to be stronger in areas where they are weaker,' Shivaji says.

'Meaning?' Raghunath sounds puzzled.

'Konkan will give us opportunities to develop our navy,' Shivaji utters softly, his eyes distant.

'We are trapped between the Mughal empire and the Adilshahi, living in the coils of two hungry pythons, Konkan is the key even if the entire Deccan comes under the Mughal,' Shivaji sighs, looking at Raghunath, resentment evident in his features. 'Aurangzeb has crushed Hyderabad. The entire eastern Deccan may soon turn bloody.'

Raghunath blinks as the revelation hits him. Jawali is Raja Shivaji's first step to prepare for a major, long drawn-out war, not just against his own king, Ali Adil Shah, but against something far bigger and far more powerful.

After Raghunath leaves, Shivaji returns to pacing the corridors of the Lal Mahal. The red palace is not the usual palace with gardens, domes, cupolas or carved parapets and pillared courts. It is actually a large, two-storey building made with red bricks, near the southern boundary of Pune. It has a front yard planted with neem and pipal trees. The backyard has sheds and stables for cattle and horses. The central courtyard is used as a meeting place.

A cold breeze blows in from the north-west. A silky window curtain flutters. Shivaji walks towards the steps leading to the ground floor. The house is unusually quiet, and the prayer room where his mother chanted mantras to evoke the powers of the family deity, Goddess Bhavani, is vacant. Gently rising smoke from the incense sticks is trying to fill the emptiness. His mother, wives and daughters have left for the Purandar Hill Fort as it has become dangerous to live on the flat plateau of the Sahyadri Range. He removes his sandals, walks inside the prayer room and kneels before the statue of Goddess Bhavani. She is the violent avatar of Goddess Parvati, the giver of life. Her kohl-smeared, enormous eyes glare at him.

Swaraj is Lord Shiva's wish, he prays, *and you are his energy. You have brought me here for a purpose. Help me fulfil that purpose, Divine Mother . . .*

Twenty years ago, Shahji Bhosale, Shivaji's father, had been forced to serve the Adilshahi and move three hundred kos away to Bendakaluru, the kingdom's southern borders. Shivaji remembers how his father had taken his elder brother and left, while he and his mother had stayed put on the hill fort of Shivneri near the town of Junnar, a part of his father's jagir. The years that followed saw Emperor Shah Jahan and the king of the Adilshahi rip away portions of the Nizamshahi, like dogs fighting over a dead rabbit. The region to the north of the river Bhima that included the prosperous cities of Ahmednagar, Junnar and Nashik was swallowed up by the Mughals. The region to the south of the Bhima, like north Konkan, Pune, Wangi, Paranda and the cities of Solapur and Pandharpur, was devoured by the Adilshahi. The Bhosale jagir was axed into two.

When the Mughal armies had galloped across Junnar and Ahmednagar to find and slaughter families who had served the Nizamshahi, his mother and he had had to flee to the southern part of their jagir that came under the Adilshahi. His first journey to this terrain was etched on his heart by sharp, cutting memories. Even now, after twenty years, when he recalls them, they bring to the surface the heartbreaking sorrow of those times. He can even hear the sound of pebbles rolling under the hooves of the horses as they crossed the stony riverbeds of the Bhima and Mutha rivers. It takes him back to his past.

One night, he was woken up by cries and screams and had run out to see people running helter-skelter. He caught a few words: 'Mughal', 'armies', 'marching'. Somewhere close by, he heard his mother shout instructions. 'No torches!' she yelled. 'We must cross the river Bhima as soon as possible!' Everything was happening very fast, and before he knew it he had been whisked up behind his mother on her steed as around twenty people raced down the mountainside. It was still dark. It would be a while even before the morning star shone in the eastern sky. The slopes of Shivneri were dark, but they knew the trail so well that they could have descended blindfolded. They had finally reached the river Bhima at dawn. It was almost dry, with a small stream of brownish water trickling on its own meandering path over the vast riverbed. They had kept going on, through fields and forests and unpaved paths. Nobody had said much, and he had been too scared to ask much. It was almost evening by the time they crossed another dry riverbed.

'River Mutha,' someone had said. 'We are almost there'.

Beyond the Mutha, sloping columns of the sun's beams fell over the leafless branches of babul trees that covered every patch of land. Mother had said that they would be living here, but he could see no houses; there were no streets. He held on to his mother with a tight grip as she steered her horse through narrow paths covered with sallow grass blades. The earth had looked broken and caked, as if the soil had not drunk a drop of water for years. He spotted ruins of temples, with crumpled mortar and broken pillars. Occasionally they came across the stinking carcasses of dead animals—cows and goats swollen like billows, with all four legs stiff and stretched. The stench was overbearing. Columns of dust made his throat parched and his eyes teary. He rubbed them against his mother's sari so that he could see. He noticed strange people staring at them. They looked different, large-eyed, faces covered with dust, tangled hair as matted as a bird's nest. He had feared that they would attack them. His wooden sword was slung to his belt. But mother had told him that to face a real enemy he needed a real sword made of steel. It was getting dark. He tried to see as far as he could to search for his kingdom, to see temple spires going high in the air, with saffron flags fluttering above them and pillared palaces behind their walled courtyards.

His kingdom was not waiting for him.

CHAPTER TWO

1

Abdullah Qutb Shah feels safe in Golconda Fort. Sitting in his private theatre on the third floor of his many-arched pavilion called the *balahisaar baradari*, he wants to forget what has happened to his beloved Hyderabad. He does not want to remember how he had left his subjects in the hands of those cold-hearted, lice-ridden, libidinous and uncouth men of Aurangzeb. He reads Aurangzeb's *paigam* again. The Mughal prince has written in chaste Persian:

> The war against you is ordained by Allah, and I must fulfil his wishes, not just as a leader of the Sunnis but also as the destroyer of those who do not conform to His idea of Islam. Twenty years ago, my father, Emperor Shah Jahan, had warned you—you, a Shia Muslim ruler who gladly agreed to be the vassal of the empire and pay a yearly tribute of ten lakh rupees—that if you do not pay the tribute on regular basis we shall annex your sultanate. Let me remind you of the arrears. You owe me twenty lakh rupees, that is, one thousand five hundred ser of pure gold. And it is not just about the money. With great distress, we consider you a *rafizi* and *ghul-i-biyabani*. We have pledged to protect your subjects from following your perceptions of our faith. We want to save them from hell. If we allow you to rule, we will do injustice to the soil of Hindustan. You have left us with no alternative but to destroy you.

The letter has Aurangzeb's palm impression.

Hurriedly he downs a few goblets of wine, and intoxicated, he wanders unsteadily towards the eastern windows and narrows his eyes to stare at his beloved city in the distance. It has been two months since it was captured and torn apart by the savage soldiers of Aurangzeb, backed by his own grand wazir, Mir Jumla. And what had he, the king of the Qutbshahi, done to stop the calamity? *Nothing!*

The city has fallen and once the imperial army is successful in capturing this fort, his kingdom will only be a distant memory—

if he lives, of course. His eyes scan the battlefield between the city
and the fort. The earth looks wounded with freshly dug trenches.
The northern side of the Musi has become a burial ground. He
has lost thousands of his swordsmen, archers and musketeers. The
air is heavy with the stench of decaying bodies and the odour of
spent gunpowder. Beyond the battlefield, he can see the siege. He
is horrified. Hundreds of cannons stand in a semi-circle around
the fort, waiting for orders. Aurangzeb has arrived personally from
Aurangabad with fresh reinforcements. His personal squadron has
the most brutal, remorseless beasts who have not known life outside
killing fields. Aurangzeb's favourite commander and maternal uncle,
Shaista Khan, has also joined him.

'It is all over,' Abdullah says to himself, and nothing else matters to
him any more. The shortage of cannonballs and explosives has rendered
his long-range, high-calibre cannon, mounted on the fort's ramparts,
useless. Behind him, Taramati sings, her body swaying as she personifies
Carnatic music in her mystic dance of Bharatanatyam. A sole musician
seems lost in the *tha-tdhi-thom* rhythms of his mridangam. Her
postures, sometimes gracefully feminine and sometimes aggressively
masculine, kindle the expressions of the element of fire in the world
around her. The air is jolted alive with her melodious voice as she
makes a crisp alaap to explore the Raga Sahana where the verses of
the grand poet Kshetrayya elevate the union of a man and woman to
the celestial order. She is devotion, he is God. Taramati's voice surges
earnestly like a youthful spring from the mountains. Her words rain
from her Muslim master's arched, multi-storey palace and sprinkle the
lush gardens covering the hilltop. A faint trail of her singing manages
to caress the protective ring of walls made of huge blocks of masonry,
fortified by eighty-seven bastions and armed with cannons. Some
residual strains of her magical voice reluctantly dip and vanish into the
muddy waters of the moat infested with crocodiles.

2

'Last year, the Mughal empire collected taxes worth one lakh ser of
gold. The Adilshahi has collected one-fourth of that amount. And

we, the so-called Hindu warriors, fight with each other for scraps of our own land thrown at us by them, the invaders. They treat us as lesser humans and we prove them right by behaving like beasts!' Shivaji thunders.

Raghunath has been summoned again. This time the meeting is being held in a dark, inner room adjacent to the main foyer, lit with a single lamp. The elderly diplomat has well-honed instincts and understands Shivaji well. He has guessed that the jagirdar of Jawali has once again refused to join hands with Raja Shivaji, inciting his fury.

'Time has come to eliminate Morey. Make it happen during negotiations,' Shivaji orders.

'I understand,' Raghunath says gravely as he feels his heart pounding in his ribcage. It is a clear-cut order, without any possibility of debate or justification. A diplomat or a vakeel follows an unwritten rule: he will not kill and nobody will kill him. The diplomatic immunity allows him unhindered access into the homes of the landlords and the courts of Islamic rulers. The time has come to break that law in order to usher in the new world order.

'Even laws are amended for a greater reason,' Shivaji says, regarding his vakeel who stands straight and looks younger than his years.

'How do you think Ali Adil Shah will react?' Raghunath asks.

'The Muslim sultans rule the cities and the jagirdars and watandars rule the villages, while the poor continue to be the bondsmen, the ghulams; everyone in power wants the old order to continue,' Shivaji says, ignoring the question.

Bells have started tolling for the evening worship at the Ganesha temple. So loud are the peals that it seems as if the priests are trying to jolt awake the Vighnaharta, the remover of obstacles. The echoes burn holes in the shallow calm of the region, as if exposing the depth of its violent history. The peace that they enjoy now is so fragile, so brittle, that it is almost a fantasy. Raghunath maintains a solemn expression. He has heard that the Mughals have taken over Hyderabad. It is time to wait and watch. But Raja Shivaji is not one to wait and worry; he has planned his own offensive.

'Ali Adil Shah seeks to eliminate us, and Aurangzeb seeks to swallow the Deccan that includes the Adilshahi. Someday we may come face to face with the mighty Mughal. It is time to look into history to prepare for the future,' Shivaji says softly as he regards the vakeel.

Raghunath nods. History is a quarry of lessons. The serious Mughal incursions had begun more than thirty years ago when Jahangir was the emperor. His empire had stretched from Bengal in the east to Sindh in the west and Kashmir in the north to Gujarat and Khandesh in the south. But further south, in the region of Deccan, it was another story. Unlike the north where the Mughal reigned supreme, the Deccan was ruled by three Muslim shahis. Roughly saying, the Nizamshahi dynasty of Ahmednagar had ruled over the Maratha country, while the Adilshahi of Bijapur ruled over Karnataka and the Qutbshahi of Golconda over Andhra. Physical proximity made the Nizamshahi the first target of Emperor Jahangir's strategy of expansion. He had unleashed his army on Nizam Shah, who was a useless drunkard. His wazir, the African warrior Malik Ambar, had maintained order and fiercely defended the kingdom's northern borders from Daulatabad Fort. Raja Shivaji's father, then a regent of Nizam Shah, had shielded Ahmednagar, the capital of the Nizamshahi thirty-five kos south of Daulatabad. Jahangir had failed, again and again, his addiction to opium responsible for his defeats. Meanwhile, his footloose generals did nothing other than enjoying life.

But times have changed. Aurangzeb is no Jahangir!

Raghunath glances at Raja Shivaji who is now gazing in the direction of the hills of Maval. He wonders if his raja can see something that he cannot. Emperor Jahangir was gone, but the Mughal passion for the Deccan had lived on like an immortal spirit, hovering in the Deccan skies, hungrier and meaner than before. After the death of Jahangir, his son, Emperor Shah Jahan, had marched into the Deccan with more than one lakh cavalrymen. The last king of the Nizamshahi was captured and sent to the prison in Gwalior to be killed by opium overdose. But Shivaji's father had decided to guard the Nizamshahi by using the hills and the hill forts of Maharashtra as his hideouts. He had also formed an alliance with the Adilshahi against the Mughal. Shah Jahan had countered him intelligently by threatening the Deccan kingdoms. Abdullah Qutb Shah had quickly turned the Mughal empire's vassal whereas Mohammed Adil Shah had decided to fight for his kingdom. Shah Jahan's army had entered the kingdom by three different routes, destroying all traces of cultivation, burning down cities, towns and villages. They had driven off cattle and butchered the old people and captured young men and women as slaves. All this had gone on incessantly till the Adilshahi had become the tributary state of the Mughal empire.

'They always form alliances to trap us,' Shivaji says.

Raghunath knows it very well. The defeated Mohammed Adil Shah was forced to form an alliance with the triumphant Shah Jahan. Shahji Bhosale was alienated and forced to surrender. He was given an ultimatum to serve the Adilshahi or die. The allied forces had even tried to flatten his jagir. They wanted to teach him a lesson he would never dare to forget. Raghunath remembers vividly how their cavalrymen had come to Pune screaming, 'Deen! Deen! Deen!' Houses were set on fire and columns of smoke had first spiralled upwards and then swept across the bleak skies. The protective wall and its bastions had turned into mere rubble. The land was ploughed by donkeys to make it ill-fated so that no one dared to till it again. The peasants had fled into the nearby forests. Raja was a little boy of five then, living with his mother in Shivneri Fort near Junnar.

'Do not blame only the Muslim rulers. The men who actively helped them flatten our jagir were the Hindus. It was Jagdev who ploughed Pune with donkeys. And it was Rayarao who ordered his men to set fire to the barns and houses. And our king bestowed him with a lofty title—The Brave One,' Shivaji's words lance through the vakeel's conscience.

On his way home, Raghunath thinks about the vanished Hindu kingdoms. The kings of the Deccan had lived in their mythological world. They followed the war etiquette observed by their gods and god-like people from the Ramayana and the Mahabharata. Even the time to begin the battle was fixed by astrologers and the position of the planets influenced their moves and countermoves. Civilian lives were spared. Three centuries ago, Alauddin Khalji's army had invaded the Deccan, flouting all the rules of war. At the end of the thirteenth century, he had brought his armies into the bedrooms, slaying and slaughtering. Even the newborns were not spared. Soon, the Hindu dynasties of the south—the Cholas, the Cheras, the Pandyans, the Hoysalas and the Kakatiyas—were flattened under the hooves of Alauddin's heavy cavalry. In the fourteenth century, two empires were born in the Deccan. Another Alauddin had arrived from Turkistan. Alauddin Hasan Bahaman Shah had swiftly conquered northern parts of the Deccan. He, the descendent of the Persian king Kai Bahaman, named his new kingdom the Bahamani empire. Deeper in the south, in the regions of Tamil Nadu and south Karnataka, a Hindu empire of Vijayanagara was founded by a Harihara and Bukka of Sangama Dynasty. The new empires clashed over the fertile regions around the Tungabhadra, Krishna and Godavari rivers. The sixteenth century saw the rise of Krishna Deva Rai, one of the greatest Hindu rulers of the Vijayanagara empire. After his untimely death, the last of the Deccan's Hindu empires started shrinking. Even the Bahamani empire had by then broken into many fragments. History was changing in the north. The late sixteenth and early seventeenth century had witnessed the steady and continuous rise of the Mughal empire as it flourished and grew under the rule of Emperor Akbar. In the years that followed, his son Jahangir and then Jahangir's son Shah Jahan expanded the empire in all directions except the south where the Muslim shahis and bits of the Vijayanagara empire had managed to survive. The Nizamshahi was eventually swallowed by the joint armies of the Mughal empire and the Adilshahi, and the remnants of the Vijayanagara empire were devoured by the Qutbshahi. And today, in the middle of the seventeenth century, his master, Raja Shivaji, had asked him to break an unwritten law for a bigger purpose.

Raghunath looks at the clear sky through the window of his palanquin. The stars twinkle in the night sky, charting his future according to his birthdate, time and place. But Raghunath diverts his gaze to his hands; he needs to refresh his moves with daggers and swords. His destiny is his doing, his karma. He has been blind all along; now he longs to see the world hidden inside of Raja Shivaji's vision.

3

Thirty-five kos south of Pune, the village called Jawali seems oblivious to the outside world. Trapped in the mountains and valleys, the jagirdar, Chandrarao Morey, can feel his temper rise to boiling point. Fuming, he looks out of the window of his den on the second storey of his walled fortress. Beyond the small village, cramped between vertical hills, more hills rise to unbelievable heights, thus forming a natural wall around his valley. He does not need to bother about men like Shivaji. Still, when he looks at the crumpled paper in his hand, the message from Shivaji, he has an urge to read it again and again:

Ten years ago we had helped the barren widow of the then legitimate Jawali ruler to adopt you—you, the then thirty-five-year-old man without any worthy achievements. Our word, we being the jagirdars of this region for years, carried weight. All the worthy landlords voted for you. In turn, you had promised your unflinching loyalty to us. The sudden rush of power has made you deliberately forget your promise. You have ignored our hand of friendship. We are aware of your deeds. You call yourself a king and send your revenue collectors into our jurisdiction, our jagir, to fleece our peasants. Merchants from Konkan are forced to use the mountain tracks passing through your valley. You demand unreasonable taxes from the traders. If they refuse, your goons kill them. You are also trying to thwart our policy of bringing the watandars of the region together. We hear that you have gone ahead and made an anti-Bhosale coalition in the king's court. Remember, your duty is to serve us in our struggle to establish a swaraj, a state not ruled by external powers. Decide today, else, tomorrow, we will annex your valley and haul you out in shackles.

The letter has Shivaji Bhosale's seal and the message therein is provocation beyond all fairness.

Chandrarao jerks his head in disgust and something makes him glance back. His brother, Prataprao, stands near the door, his hands resting on his large waist.

'Vakeel Raghunath Korde is coming with armed men,' Prataprao says, his gaze fixed on Chandrarao.

'Not in large numbers though.' Chandrarao frowns and continues, 'Let us see how far they go with their verbal threats.'

'Do you think they can really march in and cut right through the heart of this valley?' Prataprao Morey sounds concerned.

Chandrarao does not nod. This over-aggressive son of Shahji Bhosale has been trying to bully them for years. In the beginning his letters were polite, but later the words turned threatening and then outright mean. First he had ignored the arrogant young man who had forced many big landlords to join him to form a united sovereign Maratha state, a Maratha kingdom!

'I doubt it,' Chandrarao barks.

Prataprao nods pensively and asks, 'Shall we ask Murarbaji to stay till the vakeel and his men are here?'

'No, let him guard his post. Our usual security is enough,' he waves his hand and dismisses his brother's idea. 'Allow only the vakeel and one more man to enter the fortress.'

A hundred years ago, Jawali had belonged to the Wai province of the Adilshahi. It was granted to the then head of the Morey family as jagir. The then king, Ibrahim Adil Shah, had bestowed upon the jagirdar the title of Chandrarao, meaning the ruler of the moon. The first Chandrarao and his men had slaughtered the tribals and flattened their habitats, cleared part of the forests and tilled the land. The valley was very near to the port city of Dabhol in coastal Konkan, a rich trading centre under the Adilshahi. Essentials like salt, spices, textiles and wood came to Dabhol from other ports. The goods were then transported to Bijapur, the capital of the Adilshahi, through the mountains. In the region are several ghats, the tracks skirting the hills. Only two were wide enough for the merchants and both passed through Jawali. Thousands of oxen entered his valley every day. The money from toll taxes had made him rich, very rich.

All this has not come to him easy and free. Born in a poor family remotely related to the Moreys, he had burrowed his way into the heart of the barren widow of the last Chandrarao. He had cleverly outwitted the young men from her family who were vying to be her adopted son and had taken that title, making sure that the adoption was done with all the rituals and protocols. Documents holding his new mother's palm prints were safely locked away in his vaults. Now Shivaji was threatening to take away all that.

Let him try; I'm not a fool, Chandrarao Morey thinks to himself.

'This is the last time I will entertain Shivaji's vakeel,' he looks up and says.

CHAPTER THREE

1

This is Raghunath's second visit. Morey's residence, surrounded by high walls and strengthened with bastions, stands tall. Countless men wielding swords, axes and spears wait in its huge courtyard. The entrance of the house is lit by a number of torches kept in iron brackets nailed to the walls. The assembly chamber is enormous, with divans covered in rugs and carpets spread over the floor. Pillars support the ceiling which has teak beams. Silver chandeliers and glass urns holding oil lamps hang from gilded chains. Around twenty men rest at one end of the room, idly lounging on the divans, their hands resting on the bolsters and listening to their master, occasionally breaking into a collective laugh.

Chandrarao Morey, wearing a large yellow turban, gestures animatedly. He seems comfortable on a high platform with his legs tucked under him. Two men with vacant faces fan him with fluffy feathers fixed to silver sterns. Raghunath, standing at the entrance of the chamber, is surprised by the unhealthy pallor of Morey's skin, usually noted in heavy drinkers. On Morey's right, a wiry scribe sits behind a writing desk and fiddles with his feather nib. On his left, near but not on the platform, a man rests his back on a bolster and sniffs tobacco. Raghunath has seen him before—Hanumanth, the administrator of the jagir. Fortunately, the captain of Morey's army, Murarbaji, is not in the room.

'Come, come, sit,' he hears Chandrarao Morey call out to him. The ruler of Jawali has finally noticed his guests.

Raghunath and his aide bow deep while their host accepts their greetings by nodding lightly and waving his stubby fingers. They choose to be away from the Morey clansmen and sit near the exit. From here Raghunath can see the armed sentries who guard the entrance to the house.

'You are back,' Chandrarao says sarcastically.

'It is my fortune,' Raghunath mumbles.

'And who is the man accompanying you?'

'He is Sambhaji Kavji, captain of the cavalry squadron accompanying us,' Raghunath replies glancing at his aide, a dark-skinned man wearing a fine jacket.

Chandrarao Morey keeps mum, letting the silence grow between them. Raghunath too does not bother to open his mouth. After a while, an obviously irritated Morey asks, 'What happened to Shivaji Bhosale's plan to annex Jawali? Or you have come back for the bangles?'

Raghunath remembers his last visit. After reading Raja's message, Chandrarao in a fitful rage had asked his scribe to write an immediate reply. While dictating the letter, the words had frothed in his mouth as he had changed them repeatedly to make them more and more demeaning:

You are just an ignorant son of a jagirdar. What do you know? We are the hereditary owners of this region, and not just mere jagirdars. A hundred years ago the Adilshahi rulers honoured us with a throne, and gave us the title of Chandrarao. I am the undisputed king of Jawali. You are welcome to annex it but you will die like a hunted beast on the very soil of my valley. I am not one of your *deshmukhs* whom you can tame. Why are you waiting till tomorrow? Come today if you are a real man. If not, wear bangles, I will send you some as a gift.

That was a month ago.

At this very moment Raghunath needs to take stock of things. What had happened yesterday and what would happen today? Last night, after they had arrived, he and his men were not allowed to enter the courtyard. They had spent the night in the barracks built in the midst of animal stables and sheds behind the fortress. The people tending to the animals had given them food and water. The morning was spent in anxiety, and only in the late evening had a grim-looking servant suddenly appeared and rudely announced, 'Only two may come with me, the third will be kept waiting outside the gate.' As Raghunath and Sambhaji Kavji had followed him, darkness had settled in. Outside the barracks, men who had come with him were relaxing around small fires, bantering loudly. Raghunath wonders if they realize that they are in a death trap called Jawali! He also hopes that they manage to enter the Morey house by killing the entrance guards in time.

Reaching this place was an ordeal; escaping might be equally bad. At places, the ghats had narrowed down to slim trails with mountain on one side and ravines on the other. Even in the afternoon it was ominously dark under the teak and jamun trees. The hills loomed over them, blocking the sunlight. The men could barely avoid their horses getting entangled with the woody vines of liana. Twice he had spotted leopards, sitting on the edges of the cliffs. Countless times, their horses had panicked when snakes slithered in their paths. The only thing that had made the place less sinister was the calls of parakeets, bulbuls and slurred whistles of orioles. The air had smelt sharp and pungent with the aroma of wild berries. At places, brooding bamboo forests had replaced the trees. Here only tiny babblers hopped around making a '*churr churr*' sound. What Raja had said was right. Heavy cavalries would be like ships stuck in sand dunes in this valley.

Raghunath gathers himself and says softly, 'I have another letter for you from Raja Shivaji Bhosale.'

'Before I read the letter, explain: why a swaraj?' Chandrarao snaps, thumping his wrists on the wooden platform that he is sitting on. 'I had asked you the last time and you had never bothered to explain. You owe me an answer now.'

Raghunath takes a few deep breaths before he opens his mouth. The answer needs to be diplomatic, the vaguer the better.

'At the end of the thirteenth century, Muslim invaders set foot in the Deccan. The mighty Hindu dynasties, the Yadavas of Devagiri, Kakatiyas of Warangal, Pandyans of Madurai and Hoysalas of Dwarakamudra, vanished. The invaders turned into ruthless rulers, killing innocent people under the name of religion, abducting our women and children as spoils-of-war to feed their slave trade. Now it is time to fight them. And I suppose, to fight them, we need to unite.'

There is a long silence in the chamber. Chandrarao regards the intelligent vakeel for a while and then suddenly throws his hands excitedly in the air and says, 'Brilliant rhetoric! But you have still not answered my question. All these lofty explanations are good to impress a child with milk teeth still hanging on his gums. You tell me, why is your Shivaji interested in my valley?'

Raghunath thinks hard. *Chandrarao might be a drunkard but he is cunning.*

'Raja Shivaji is interested in powerful men like you. Also, we believe that the hills in your valley are the best in the region to build hill forts; they can be the sentinels of the Maratha kingdom.'

'Do you think of us as brainless? Now let me tell you your Shivaji's ulterior motive. The Mughal prince Aurangzeb has taken Hyderabad. I see the entire Deccan being swallowed by him in the near future. Even your master's jagir will soon be *khalisa,* a part of the Mughal empire.' Chandrarao speaks slowly so that the vakeel can decipher his Marathi accent.

'Your Shivaji Bhosale *needs* this valley to hide when the Mughal armies march in—just to buy some more time and keep himself alive. If he had a little dignity, he would come marching to the valley with his army and claim it like a warrior.' Chandrarao winks at his officer and says, 'What say, Hanumanth?'

'I have a letter for you from Raja Shivaji,' Raghunath persists and gets up holding an epistle. Even before he steps forward, a servant comes running from somewhere, seizes it from him and hands it over to his master.

Chandrarao holds the epistle between two fingers as if holding a dead scorpion and shouts, his voice gruff. 'Look at the audacity of the man! His lofty seal reads, "Like a crescent moon grows the kingdom of Shivaji, son of Shahji, always seeking the welfare of the people"!'

Chandrarao stops for a moment to breathe. *Oh! The man's arrogance! When everyone's seal is in Farsi, his is in Sanskrit!*

The silence in the room is interrupted by the new entrant who walks in with a swagger.

'Read, brother, read it,' a man who resembles Chandrarao Morey declares with scorn. Raghunath guesses the man is Prataprao, the younger of the Morey brothers.

Chandrarao throws the epistle on the desk of his scribe, who picks it up, opens it carefully and starts reading loudly:

> We have given you enough time and warnings. This is the last one.
> Remove all your titles, abandon the throne, stop calling yourself
> a king, tie your hands and come to me as a servant. We leave you
> with no option. Join us in our struggle for swaraj or die.

The words resound in the chamber like granados from cannons. A deathly silence fills the air for a few moments before the brothers, red in the face, explode in verbal infernos. Chandrarao again thumps his wrists on the platform while Prataprao grits his teeth and dredges his brain for the right words to express his fury. He turns in fury towards the vakeel, jerks his head in disgust and screams, 'Who does Shivaji think he is? The emperor of Hindustan?'

A flurry of voices filled with scorn rattles the air. Prataprao has started laughing, but he stops abruptly as if blessed with a divine vision and barks, 'The leaves of Shivaji Bhosale's dream will soon be swept away by the gales of the Mughals' might!' The Morey clansmen take cue, and debate among themselves.

'Egregious!' Prataprao screams.

'In uncertain times like these, Shivaji Bhosale must scramble to help our esteemed king, Ali Adil Shah of the Adilshahi. Shivaji's father is the Adilshahi's regent. Their Pune jagir falls in the sultanate's terrain. That makes serving the Adilshahi Shivaji Bhosale's duty his karma. And as you Brahmins say, it is his opportunity to attain moksha if he is killed defending his true masters!' Prataprao rants.

Raghunath smiles bitterly. The four ways that lead to moksha the cosmic freedom from the circle of life, have become ways to either divide or fool others. The word karma, especially, is used like a whip to make weak men do what powerful men want them to do, even if it means dying in the battlefields of the invaders. To die for them is the easiest way to live. At least the servants of the invaders die with titles and their children remain alive and wealthy. The rebels of the land are hunted down like rabid dogs, their heads displayed as trophies, their families captured, wives molested and children sold as slaves.

Chandrarao claps loudly, trying to draw attention towards what he is about to say. His eyes shine with malice. 'Tell him: if he is a warrior, he must stop sending us vakeels. And tell him what I think of the piece of paper on which he has written his letter.'

The scribe takes clue, jumps out from behind the desk and hands his master the letter. The master, his face scrunched up in disgust, crushes the paper into a ball and throws it in the vakeel's direction. Raghunath has not expected this. He misses the catch and turns to pick up the paper fallen behind him. 'I am just a humble vakeel; pardon me if we have hurt your sentiments,' he says after moments of silence, and fingers the hilt of his knife under his clothes.

'You are a Brahmin. You wear your red turban, silk robes, fat gold earrings and that sandalwood paste on your forehead to show your supremacy. But *you* could have done something more, put some sense in your master's head, let him follow his father and serve Adil Shah!' Chandrarao shouts as if he has lost his head.

It is common to drag caste issues into political meetings.

Raghunath keeps cool, and secretly prays that his men are at their job. The timing needs to be perfect. Even if the fortress looks formidable, there are no archers on the ramparts. The watchtowers rising over the bastions are empty. The main gate is guarded only by a few but the courtyard is full of armed men. Raghunath tries to reflect on his men to draw some comfort. These men Raja Shivaji has given him and their captain do look like a squadron with their uniforms—a pair of tight breeches and pleated *angirkha*s of quilted cotton. While on their way to Jawali he had looked at them with admiration, comparing his own troops' uniforms. These men had covered their heads with Turkish turbans with one fold passing tightly under their chins. Their *dhop* swords, fixed to their belts, were not ordinary. Raghunath was told that the blades of these dhops are more than one-and-a-half guj long. They are pointed to pierce, and are lengthy enough to cut a man even from horseback. The lower edge of the blade is sharp all through its length, making the sword an extraordinary chopping machine. The upper edge, called the *pipala*, is the most lethal, jagged to tear the flesh with ease. If the enemy ducked and avoids the swordsman's forward blow, he gets chopped by its backward blow. All this happens in the blink of an eye. The bottom end of the hilt has long nails tapering to make its lower end pointed enough to kill. If the enemy is too close to use the long blade, hilts can be held vertically above the enemy to hit the head to crack the skull or use horizontally as a dagger to tear through the enemy's viscera.

'Have you lost your voice?' Prataprao is shouting.

Raghunath responds reluctantly, 'Raja Shivaji had no choice.'

'But we have a choice! Do you have anything more to say?' Prataprao sounds as if he has reached the edge of his patience.

Raghunath glances at his captain for a brief moment before he turns to Chandrarao Morey and says, 'We, Sambhaji Kavji and I, think you deserve to know the truth.'

'What truth?' Chandrarao demands and glances at his estate manager, Hanumanth, who shrugs and shakes his head helplessly.

'Say it,' Prataprao throws a challenge.

'I need privacy. Some truths are not meant to be revealed in public.' Raghunath is resolute. The vakeels frequently asked for a private talk—it was not unusual.

Chandrarao takes a deep breath and thinks rapidly. It is the first time that the vakeel has been assertive. Years of wealth and authority have made Chandrarao presumptuous. He feels one is assertive only when one is being honest. And the vakeels have always been good sources of information. He nods while the others seem shocked by his affirmation. He ignores them and dredges his brains for answers. 'What can it be?'

'It is important for you to know what we know. Also, we must maintain its confidentiality. Raja Shivaji must never know that we have shared this information with you,' Raghunath says softly.

'Do not play tricks!' Prataprao yells.

'Why would we? What do we have to gain? And if you do not want to know, so be it,' Raghunath says coolly.

'What would you get by telling *us* the truth?' Hanumanth snaps.

'Now stop it. Let's go to my den. I want to know what this truth is.' Chandrarao staggers to his feet.

Four men exit the chamber and head for the staircase. It is well lit with tiny earthen lamps kept in alcoves carved in the wall. Prataprao keeps his right hand on the hilt of his sword and stays close behind Raghunath. Raghunath walks behind the ruler who struggles and pants while climbing. The vakeel notices how obese Chandrarao Morey has become. Sambhaji Kavji remains at the end of the file, his face solemn, his eyes watching Prataprao's hand on his belt.

Chandrarao's den is a small room with arched windows. Pale outlines of hills are seen as an inky blue sky is illuminated with sparkling stars. There are no chandeliers here, only a few tall brass lamps that burn in the corners of the room. Their flames quiver as a gentle breeze blows in from the windows.

'My apologies for the trouble,' Raghunath says, trying to be polite.

'No pretences, out with your truth,' Chandrarao clamours at him; anxiety flickering in his eyes.

'The truth is that my master has formed an alliance with Ali Adil Shah. He has promised the king the valley of Jawali if they offer him protection when and if the forces of Aurangzeb come marching towards his jagir,' says Raghunath without any fuss.

'I will kill you and feed you to the jackals roaming in the valley if you are lying!' Prataprao threatens Raghunath who stays mum.

There is silence for a while. Prataprao caresses his beard and regards Raghunath intently. But the hush is soon broken by yells from the courtyard followed by the clinks of swords clashing.

'I knew it!' Prataprao screams and rushes to the window. He shudders in shock. Chandrarao is left alone for a moment. He notices something sinister in Raghunath's eyes. The vakeel's narrow face has become mean. His jaw is tight and the veins on his forehead look swollen under the horizontal lines of sandalwood paste.

Chandrarao opens his mouth to shout.

There is no time to waste. Raghunath glares at Chandrarao's open mouth and pulls out a *bichwa*, a dagger, hidden in his sash, its long blade shaped like a scorpion's stinger. He has to go for the jugular, as the cut needs to be mortal for a quick and noiseless death. Kavji has slunk behind Morey and is holding the fat man in a tight grip. Raghunath darts forward and slits Chandrarao's throat in one stroke. The cut is clean and precise. The dying man's eyes are filled with astonishment. He tries to say something but his voice is lost to him. Only a guttural sound leaks through his bloody throat. Kavji lets go of his grip allowing the Jawali ruler to fall on the floor, limp, like a rag doll. Blood splutters out from the gash on to the carpet. Prataprao turns back to tell Chandrarao what he has seen. Instead he starts screaming like an animal at the sight of his dead brother. However, before Kavji can catch him, he is gone, and so is Hanumanth.

Raghunath looks at his hand that still holds the dagger: it is bloody right up to the hilt. Kavji has pulled out the dead man's sword from the scabbard. They rush down to Chandrarao's darbar. Morey's clansmen are running around like mad. Hanumanth and Prataprao are missing. Chaos reigns supreme, commotion fills their ears. They rush out. The chamber entrance is littered with twisted bodies of the guards, they have been beheaded, and the place is messy with blood. The main gate is wide open. The courtyard echoes with the sounds of clashing blades and the screams of those dying. In the light of the torches fixed on the outside wall, the vakeel can see shadows of men, some fleeing, some charging. They remain near the entrance till calmness dawns on the scene, then they enter the courtyard. Their men are standing in small groups. The vakeel quickly unties the strings of his angirkha, pulls out a small trumpet and starts blowing; Kavji does the same.

The valley around them vibrates with the calls of their trumpets.

2

The forest between the banks of Koyana and the foothills of the western hills is raven dark. Shivaji strains his eyes to see as one horseman after the other appears from the forest around him. It is impossible for any army to march into this valley. One has to make way through too many narrow passes. It is impractical to form multiple columns as a maze of passes open up in different directions. For a month, all of his two thousand soldiers have roamed Jawali, as goatherds, cattle herds or farm hands. Each one of them had learnt the hideouts of Morey's garrisons. Each one had figured his own way to come to this place, a few kos north of Jawali village. Five smaller squadrons comprising two hundred men each have stationed themselves at various locations in the valley.

Under the canopies of the trees, dirt tracks fill up with Shivaji's horsemen. The forest ahead swarms with tribals who work for him as scouts. He is aware that they, at this very moment, are hacking the wooden vines of liana to clear the way and also scanning the hills to spot human movements. He notes their signals as they hoot like owls and snarl throatily like tigers, their animalistic sounds rising above the never-ending drone of cicadas. The time has come to move on. He signals and the shadows of his horsemen start moving southwards. The earth is uneven. His horse trots like a mountain goat under him, stretching its front legs to climb and raising its haunches to climb down. The gusty wind rattles the upper branches of the trees. Somewhere in the distance, a real tiger growls, its sound echoing through the valley. A lapwing flies over them, screeching 'tcheeit, tcheeit!' The ear-piercing call of the bird pumps energy into his blood. Then there is another sound carried on the wind, the call of the trumpet that has travelled through the woods and the hills. It is time to head directly to Jawali.

Chandrarao Morey is dead.

'Raghunathji and Kavji have done it,' Shivaji hears Tanaji Malusare screaming in sheer excitement. As per the plan, Tanaji has kicked his horse to a canter and has gone ahead. Yesaji Kank follows him.

Their vanishing shadows bring the memories of how he had met his best swordsman and his best wrestler after a night of utter disappointment, a time at the end of his first voyage when he had just discovered that there was no kingdom waiting for him.

Shivaji was eight and had already learnt his lesson. Their long journey from Shivneri Fort had ended. They had reached a village. Icy winds had started blowing, carrying the smell of wood smoke. A few torchbearers had joined them on foot, lighting their way. A Brahmin with a stern face had come on a horse to greet them. 'He is Sonoji Dabir; he used to be your Abba sahib's adviser,' his mother had informed him. The man had smiled and said, 'This is a part of your jagir, your kingdom.' He had seen Bijapur and had thought that kind of city would await him. But there were no streets teeming with trundling elephants, scurrying palanquins or galloping horsemen here; instead, there were gangs of muscular wild dogs, their reddish coats gleaming in the dim light of torches. Their eyes had shone like embers as they had looked for food, waiting for their chance. He gazed at them, their tilted heads, raised hackles, exposed fangs. Their bold grunts had made him hold his mother tighter. But the torchbearers had not been perturbed. They had finally arrived at a small stone house with red tiles on its sloping roof. It had been enclosed in a short fence made of flat stones piled on each other. Beyond, the stars had blinked in the darkened sky, aloof and distant. Someone had lifted him from the horse and carried him inside the compound. He had not protested. There had been something more urgent on his mind. As he had relieved himself behind the house, he noticed a large hole in the fence wall. Looking through, he had caught glimpses of silhouettes of tree trunks at the edge of the dark skyline. The moon had been unusually large and hung over a lone boulder like an orb of silver, a little away from the house. A shadow moved stealthily in the dark. A wild dog again? Narrowing his eyes, he had realized that there were many out there. One had climbed on to the boulder, raised its head and let out a long howl—a deep, reverberating sound. It had certainly been a wolf, its shadow against the moon terrifying to the little boy. He had run to the front yard, his heart beating louder than the howls.

He had stayed put in the front of the house for a while to quieten his fear, watched men tie their horses to the nearby trees and draw water from a well. Another man was busy hammering pegs into the ground to pitch tents in the compound. Finally he went inside the house to find his mother. His mother's maids had lit the firewood to make dinner. The rooms were clean. The floor was covered with soft quilts. He had just wanted to sleep.

In the morning, when he had stepped out, he was jolted by the sight of the barren land and leafless trees. He recalled the sigh of the wolf he had seen last night and shuddered. He had to live here. Instinctively, he had gone to the backyard to see if the wolves were still there. The darkness, the looming moon, the wolf had all vanished. Instead, golden sunrays swept across the parched earth. Even the large boulder had gleamed in its light as two boys ran around its girth laughing and jumping. One of them was Tana and the other Yesa, both older and taller than him.

3

The morning star appears in the east. A few kos south of Jawali, sitting on the charpoy, Murarbaji, Morey's lieutenant, sniffs his tobacco, holding it in his palm. Suddenly, his ears pick up distant sounds. Trumpet calls are coming from the direction of his master's fortress. There can only be one reason.

'Tuzya maila!' he swears under his breath for remaining complacent. He jumps out of his bed and strides out of his barracks built on the banks of the river Koyana. His men, sitting and chatting around small fires, look startled, straining to listen; they too have heard the calls. Never before has anyone blown trumpets in the valley. And tonight, at this late hour, someone blows persistently, as if giving out a signal. He thinks about their garrisons scattered all over the forest and wonders if these calls would jolt awake the men from their drunken trance. Else, it would be only he and his men to face whatever lay ahead. He remembers Shivaji Bhosale's vakeel. The Brahmin was to meet his master tonight. But he had come only with a few horsemen. The trumpets are surely a signal, but to whom. Has Shivaji arrived in the valley with his squadrons?

'Move!' he shouts at his men, and knows that the time has come to unsheathe his sword. The shack is lit only by the silvery moonlight falling in through the open windows. A *pata* sword, kept on a soft cotton cloth on a far shelf, shimmers and smells of the clove oil that is used regularly to polish it. It is more than one-and-a-half guj long. Its straight blade has ridges that taper to sharp, lethal edges on either side, thus making it difficult to break or bend. Its metal arm guard is long enough to protect his arm till the elbow. It also allows the sword to be a part of him, an extension of his hand. Once fixed, he can use the muscles of his arm with full force. He picks up the sword, and eases it into the scabbard. Before exiting, he fetches a leather shield hung on the wall.

Guilt overpowers Murarbaji as he hastens. He should have stayed behind for the meeting with Shivaji's vakeel. It was the question of his master's life. His men are ready to follow him. As they jump over the nettles and sprint through the dirt tracks towards the village, time seems to keep stretching like a never-ending path.

A raucous sound travels on the wind. It is the jackals on their edgy hunt for food. The sound pervades the hanging darkness of the forest. It lingers, dies away, only to rise to a crescendo and then to die again. On a nearby tree, a lark awakes from its slumber, letting out shrill whistles that rattle across the woods. Murarbaji's ears pick up faint sounds of hooves from the direction of the village. He tries to clear his mind; whoever is waiting for them near the village can be handled by his five hundred men.

He looks back and sees his men. In the dim yellow light of their torches, their faces look grim, their hurriedly worn angirkhas balloon behind them, the blades of their swords gleam. He wishes he had wings to fly. The narrow trail has finally ended. Scaling a small hillock to scout the northern expanse, he peers down into the valley. The enormous spiked gate of the fortress is ajar. From inside the courtyard, a dim light filters out to form a long, yellow patch on the dark earth. The village is quiet. The surrounding forest is a mass of moving shadows with moonlight falling over the swaying canopies.

The faint sounds of hooves can no longer be heard; still he senses unusual movement in the forest. He fears that some of them have barged into the fortress. He must rush before they shut the gate. And he must take his men through the narrow lanes of the village, because he is not sure what's hiding in the woods. Even if there is a wee bit chance to save his master, he will grab it.

'To the fortress,' he says in a hushed voice to his men and leaps across the slope to reach the main gate through the village. The gate is closing on them. His heart starts pounding. The enormous doors are inching closer. He grits his teeth and leads his men to punch their way through the closing gate, like water through the falling wall of a dam. The courtyard is well lit by torches hanging in iron baskets near the main house. He spots long shadows of horsemen on the floor—not one, not two, but countless.

'These are the notorious men of Shivaji,' he shouts to warn his men but his words dissolve into the sounds of hooves. Instantly, he knows. The trumpet calls were from the vakeel, a signal for Shivaji Bhosale to advance towards the fortress. It can mean only one thing—Chandrarao Sahib has been killed.

Murarbaji watches helplessly as his men run blindly into the arms of a powerful enemy. The horsemen move ahead swiftly, striking slashing blows of their dhops on Murarbaji's men who have arrived on foot, carrying shorter and curved swords. The courtyard is filled with sounds of whooshing of blades and the splatter of blood. Shivaji's men seem to know how to hit footmen from horseback. Their strikes are so powerful that their blades run deep into his men. The swords are easily wrenched out by holding the hilts with all their might as their horses keep sweeping past.

A little away from Murarbaji, Tanaji Malusare rides through the carnage, brandishing his pata and occasionally slaughtering an enemy who has dared to wander in his path. 'Har Har Mahadev!' he screams the battle cry hailing the might of Lord Shiva, his dark face flush, his muscles bulging under the tight sleeves of his short angirkha, his cries sparking valour in the hearts of his men. Soon the ground is covered with bodies and swords. Yesaji hovers around his master, scanning the fortress and its open windows for archers.

Shivaji watches with interest as his men wipe out their enemies, striking the forward and backward blows with equal ease, chopping off heads and torsos. This battle is their military test. Then he notices a man with a pata sword, his right hand fixed into a gauntlet and his left holding a large leather shield. The blade of the pata is long and moves in slightly elliptical movement as he swirls, leaping over the dead and avoiding the ground that is sodden with blood. The blade moves like a tongue of flame, gleaming and then fading. The man spins in the midst of the horsemen like a wasp. His movements are rhythmic, creating an unbeatable fence with his ridged, killer blade. Soon he starts reaching Shivaji's horsemen who in turn struggle to reach him with their swords. But they are confused and are unable to use their dhops. Instead some get hit by the pata and collapse, dead or writhing in pain.

Shivaji stares at the man whose movements remind him of his own favourite stances. The man moves in perfect circles. His movements are too swift for others to judge his next attack. Handling the pata sword is an art and only few can master it. Shivaji wrenches at his reins and jerks his horse into a trot. Tanaji Malusare too has spurred his horse to start moving towards the man.

'Retreat!' Shivaji screams at his men. The man continues to swirl, moving towards the retreating enemy horsemen. Shivaji directs his horse in a circle around the man who continues to swirl and dance. It is dangerous to handle a pata swordsman. After a while of brandishing their swords, pata swordsmen lose the fear of death, making them fiercer, but also vulnerable to mistakes, almost easy targets for any other skilled pata swordsman. But in the depth of his heart, Shivaji does not want this man to die.

'Halt! That's an order. I know who you are. You are Murarbaji!' Shivaji yells at the man.

Murarbaji seems deaf to the outside world. Shivaji wishes he too had a pata sword. It may have been easier to stop the man then. He plans to move closer, but before he nudges his mount, like a flash, Tanaji jumps down from his horse and moves between him and Murarbaji.

Tanaji has a pata sword in his right hand and a leather shield in his left. When Tanaji is close to the enemy, he swings his pata near the periphery of the enemy's blade, rotating it rapidly. His hand moves in several directions, as if he knows the orbit of the enemy's pata well in advance. Sometimes his blade flies at a tangent and sometimes the blades clash and screech, metal against metal as sparks fly between them like fireflies. Tanaji is warming up. But one wrong move and the enemy's blade can dislodge a chunk of his body. Shivaji brings his horse to a halt, not believing the drama of pata swords unfolding before his very eyes.

Murarbaji is furious but senses that his opponent is not an ordinary swordsman. Both spin wildly. Even before Murarbaji can grasp his moves, Tanaji suddenly stops and steps forward, spreads his hand and glides his blade to strike a horizontal forward blow. The unexpected shift startles Murarbaji and he skips back, swaying his hand that holds the shield. In a flash Tanaji moves his hand backwards in an anti-circular motion. The tip of his blade brushes against Murarbaji, tearing his angirkha over his chest. He loses his balance and tries hard not to trip. Tanaji strikes a forward blow. It lances through the shoulder of Murarbaji's right hand that holds the sword. Blood splutters out. Murarbaji keeps spinning, but feels his energy waning. Tanaji moves closer still. One strike and it will all be over.

'No, Tanaji, don't!' Raja Shivaji stops his commander. Tanaji leaps back, away from the reach of Murarbaji's pata.

Murarbaji slouches in fatigue. Despite the shooting pain that almost makes him clutch his hand and roll on the ground, his eyes rove. The man firing instructions looks like a leader. His face is familiar, someone he has heard of. He is fair, and wears a saffron turban that looks like the spire of a temple. The angirkha is of a pale colour, finely cut. His silvery sash shimmers in the yellow light of the torches. Murarbaji recognizes him, and deep hatred fills his heart, shining through his eyes.

Shivaji dismounts and comes to stand in front of Murarbaji. 'Where is my master?' Murarbaji screams. 'Your vakeel has killed my master, hasn't he? I knew of your plan, the moment I heard the trumpets. Chandrarao Sahib had welcomed your vakeel, but he had an agenda. *Randichya!*' Murarbaji calls Raghunath the son of a prostitute.

Something snaps inside Shivaji.

'Your *great* Chandrarao Sahib,' Shivaji says mockingly, gritting his teeth. 'You are either blind or choose to be so. Don't you see that the people of your valley have become ghulams? He used them, stole from them, tortured them and murdered them at his whim. The people of the valley live like helpless goats in your pens, meek and ready to be slaughtered?' Shivaji pauses. 'And what did you do all your life? You made a show of your valour by terrorizing the helpless peasants, sucking them dry in the seasons of harvest, so that your master could reap benefits. Do not consider yourself a warrior. You are a petty bully, working for a depraved despot.'

Murarbaji is speechless; nobody has talked to him like this before. He breathes heavily in rage. Blood oozes from his shoulder, drenching his clothes.

Shivaji removes his hand from the hilt and starts pacing. This is a man he can use. He just needs him on his side. He suddenly stops and says, 'You have another duty, a very noble one. You and your goons tax the merchants coming from Konkan as per your whim. If they protest, you slaughter them and feed them to the wolves. You do not even spare the Lamani gypsies and their oxen who work for your merchants. The ridges of the cart tracks going down to the coast are covered with the shards of their bones. Is that not true?'

Murarbaji does not reply—in defence or otherwise.

'There is another world beyond the hill to the east, the world of the Adilshahi. And there is another world far away from the northern boundaries of this valley, the world of the Mughal empire. These emperors of the north and kings of the southern sultanates have built forts, palaces, gardens, mausoleums and baths from the sweat and blood of *our* peasants. Their armies are fed by *our* soil. And they don't care if these peasants live the distressed, disdainful life of ghulams, under men like Chandrarao Sahib Morey. And men like Morey don't even care if they live at all!'

Raja Shivaji turns his gaze on Murarbaji and asks, his voice barely a whisper, 'And do you?'

Murarbaji avoids meeting his gaze.

'No, you don't care either. And how does your master dare to perform such vile acts? It is only because he has people like you— you, a noble soul of Jawali!'

The night is almost over. Dawn is seeping over the horizon. The main gate is shut. The watchtowers over the ramparts of the wall teem with Shivaji's archers. The leader of the Marathas looks at Murarbaji who sways with fatigue, his hand fixed into the pata sword that now dangles loose. The pool of blood has swelled, and as the sun throws its first rays over the sky, Murarbaji faints and collapses in a heap.

'Get him out of here, I want him alive,' Shivaji says swinging around, his voice loud and clear.

Shivaji turns to look at Tanaji. 'Let the womenfolk and the children of the house go wherever they want to. Send escorts with them. And remember, the valley is swarming with Morey's men. Clear the nearby forest and hack the branches of large trees that block our view. Keep our best archers at the ramparts day and night. Our squadrons gone deeper in the valley must have attacked the enemy garrisons in the night. Inform all those who surrender that Murarbaji has already joined our military.'

The last sentence brings a smile to everyone's lips.

CHAPTER FOUR

1

It has been just a week since Aurangzeb reached Hyderabad, having travelled one-hundred-and-seventy-five kos south-east from Aurangabad to reach the city. But a *farman* has already arrived for him, as if his father, Emperor Shah Jahan, has been keeping a watch on his son. Aurangzeb waits on the banks of the Musi for the ceremonial camel to arrive. His memories churn. He recalls when his father, then known only as Prince Khurram, had been a mere fugitive.

Aurangzeb was ten. His family had been camping in the northern parts of the Deccan. Shah Jahan had become the target of his stepmother, Nur Jahan's wrath. Emperor Jahangir, always high on opium, had become her royal toy. Aurangzeb, his brothers, sisters and parents had everything that the royalty could have, but all of them were constantly under watch. Nur Jahan wanted to destroy them. It was a night to remember. The forest around had turned pitch dark. They had been waiting for the imperial soldiers to arrive from Agra. Aurangzeb was old enough to understand that it was a matter of life and death.

Nur Jahan was Aurangzeb's mother's aunt. Emperor Jahangir had cast aside all his other wives, declaring her as his empress. It was rumoured that Nur Jahan secretly ground opium and added it into the emperor's food, poisoning his mind against her stepson, Prince Khurram. Her daughter from a previous marriage was wedded to Prince Shahryar, Emperor Jahangir's youngest son from one of his wives. Nur Jahan planned to make him the next emperor. Shah Jahan, the eldest of Emperor Jahangir's sons, had been accused of rebelling against the emperor. The empress had demanded Shah Jahan's two sons as hostages in exchange for sparing his life. Aurangzeb was not afraid of being a hostage, because he was not quite sure what it meant to be one. But something else had nagged him incessantly. While he had been sitting waiting for people to come and fetch Dara bhai and him, he had watched his father fussing over Dara bhai, tousling his hair, kissing his head repeatedly. Aurangzeb's other siblings, fourteen-year-old Jahanara, twelve-year-old Shuja, eleven-year-old Roshanara and three-year-old Murad, had been sitting around their mother, silently gazing at her face. She had looked oblivious of them and had stared into nothing. It was the first time he had felt jealous of Dara bhai. A question had haunted him: Why had the empress chosen Dara bhai and him as hostages? Why not the others? What was so special about them? Much later, when Dara bhai and he were put under house arrest in Nur Jahan's palace at Lahore, he had discovered the truth.

Nur Jahan wanted the two boys dead, but they were protected by Jahangir's grand wazir, their maternal uncle Abu Talib, alias Shaista

Khan, who had always loved his sister's sons. He had watched over them, had inspected the food given to them and had kept his personal guards to keep vigil at nights. Once when they were chatting, Shaista Khan had unwittingly revealed that the empress had demanded Dara bhai and any other child of the family. Uncle had said that it was common knowledge that Dara bhai was the apple of his father's eyes. The words had shattered little Aurangzeb. The truth had hit him like an arrow. He was regarded by his father as an expendable commodity. He was the one his father would throw to the wolves to save the others in the family! Aurangzeb had tucked away this bitter truth in his heart. He had hoped that his father might change. At the age of ten, any disturbing emotion can be turned into hope—or hate.

The memory brings a bitter smile to Aurangzeb's face. All his life he has sought his father's love, and if that was not possible, at least his approval. The forty-year-old Aurangzeb suddenly feels a bit faint. The strong stench of burning human flesh and sandalwood churns his stomach. The northern banks of the Musi have turned into a cremation ground for his dead Rajput soldiers. Under the morning sun, flames of countless pyres look pale and lifeless while the dark columns of smoke rise above them, robust and conspicuous. He might have lost three thousand men, but his army has slaughtered *seventeen* thousand Hyderabadi soldiers. A harsh rattling sound makes him glance to his left.

'My prince, the emperor's farman has arrived,' Aurangzeb hears a slave announce.

He looks northwards as drumbeats echo above the din of the carts. Narrowing his eyes, he sees a camel, surrounded by drummers, appear on the horizon. Soon the procession stops at a distance, waiting for him to make his next move as per imperial protocol. Taking cue, Aurangzeb strides towards the camel, alone. The warm river breeze gently blows eastwards as the morning sun cruises in all its winter glory towards the middle of the sky. The cremation ground, burning pyres, trenches, cannon carts, the fort, its bastions—nothing matters any more. Like a little boy seeking parental approval, he is eager to read what his father has written. It is crucial now, more than ever before, as Shah Jahan is getting old and weak.

A milling crowd gathers at a distance to watch him. He first performs *kurnish*, by placing the palm of his right hand on his forehead and then bending his head forward, as if cradling his head in his palm. It is the way the emperor is saluted, an act of putting one's mind, which is the seat of one's intellect, into the humility of one's hand.

From the rider, Aurangzeb takes the robe-of-honour offered to him and then the epistle. Father has finally recognized his credentials. He holds the epistle as if it is a copy of the Holy Quran, touches it fervently with his forehead and walks away from the camel taking backward steps, all the way to the place from where he had started.

Shaista Khan, meaning the 'cultured one', has deliberately avoided the ceremony. Instead, he waits patiently near his nephew's tent. Shaista Khan is the subhedar of the Khandesh region. The city of Burhanpur on the banks of the river Tapti is his headquarters. He has come to help Aurangzeb take over the Golconda kingdom. After his arrival at Hyderabad, he had noted the celebrations over the conquests. Mir Jumla, Muhammad Sultan and the other officials had let their guard down. After four nights of feasting and revelry, the men had finally got back into their battle spirit. But his nephew, Aurangzeb, had stayed put in his tent in the military camp, praying, reading the Holy Quran and ruminating. Aurangzeb had always been so, even as a young man—always grave, never caught laughing aloud. It was as if his youth had met an untimely death unnoticed by anyone.

Shaista, too, is curious to know the contents of the emperor's decree. The sudden sound of footsteps interrupts his thoughts. It is Aurangzeb, his face flushed, striding towards the tent. He goes in without bothering to look at his uncle. Shaista Khan follows him, apprehensive and worried.

Shaista loves his nephew like his own son, despite the fact that Aurangzeb is a staunch Sunni and he an austere Shia. And despite the fact that Aurangzeb is almost forty and he just ten years older. There are reasons for the affection he feels for his lonely nephew forsaken by his own father. Shaista Khan hates his brother-in-law; hence he loves his sister's son even more. Outside, one thousand cannon carts have taken their allotted positions. The artillerymen wait for orders from Mir Jumla who in turn waits for Aurangzeb. The air is heavy with intangible energy. Thousands of swordsmen crouch in the trenches and brave the scorching sun, eagerly looking forward to explosives smashing the wall of the Golconda Fort.

All depends on what the emperor's farman says.

Shaista Khan gazes out from the window as the wind kicks up the dust from the mounds of earth piled near the trenches. As the dusty clouds rise above the battlefield, his mind flits from the past to the present to the future. Every Mughal emperor's sons have fought for the throne, blinding or murdering their brothers. Even Shah Jahan had either slaughtered or poisoned his brothers. Shaista Khan's late sister's bones may be resting in the Taj Mahal but her sons cannot escape their destiny. Only one of them will become the emperor and the other three will be killed or thrown into the dungeons.

Shaista takes the present into consideration. Dara Shikoh, the forty-two-year-old eldest prince, has been given the viceroyalty of several rich provinces, and all he does is sit in his libraries, translate Hindu scriptures to Persian and hold seminars with Hindu pundits or Sufi saints. Shah Shuja, the second prince, is the subhedar of Bengal and a man of battles. He is into women, hundreds if not thousands, most of them captured from the villages of Bengal; the others have been gifted to him by the kings of Persia and Europe. Aurangzeb, the third prince, the subhedar of the Deccan, is silent and religious. He has spent most of his life in the battlefields, surrounded by death and decay. The emperor regards him as the competition to his favourite son Dara Shikoh. Murad Baksh, the fourth prince, is the subhedar of Gujarat. His senses are blunted by wine, and his mind blinded by flatterers.

'We cannot fight this battle,' says Aurangzeb, his voice cracking. Shaista turns around, walks towards a wooden divan kept near Aurangzeb's charpoy and asks, 'Why, son? What does it say?'

'Read it for yourself.' Aurangzeb hands over the farman. He can trust his maternal uncle, his *mama jaan*; in fact, he is the only one left in the family whom Aurangzeb can trust.

It is a short letter. Shaista frowns as he reads drawing the paper closer to his eyes. The letter reads:

My son, it is proper for the emperors and their sons to have lofty spirits and to display courage and military might to take on new frontiers. Time is of the essence. The Deccan kingdoms had declared their vassalage years ago. They are technically the vassals of the empire, our tributary states and are under our protection. This is not the right time to annex the Qutbshahi. I am in touch with Abdullah Qutb Shah and have promised him cessation of hostilities from our side. They will pay revenue, and that money must directly come to the central treasury at Agra. Retreat immediately and cancel all your future battle plans.

'Strange . . .' murmurs Shaista, wiping his brows with his stole.

'What do you think, Mama Jaan?' Aurangzeb asks anxiously.

Shaista waits before answering. He has lived all his life with the imperial family. His father and grandfather have been the grand wazirs of the empire. His aunt, Nur Jahan, was Emperor Jahangir's queen consort, his sister, Anjuman Banu, Emperor Shah Jahan's queen consort. But what he has been seeing is unbelievable. Dara Shikoh has been given a glorifying yet unprecedented title of Shah Bulund Iqbal, the king of lofty fortunes. Never before had any of the past emperors allowed their sons to sit in their courts on a golden chair, kept only at a small distance away from the throne. For Aurangzeb, the rules are decidedly different. He has been kept away from Agra and Dilli for twenty-two years now, and transferred from one difficult province to another. The emperor has made sure that his third son is always short of reinforcements and funds. Aurangzeb's transfer to the Deccan for the second time too was a deliberate conspiracy. The Mughal-occupied areas of the Deccan give Aurangzeb less than one crore rupees a year as land revenue. Corruption is rampant and the collection a hassle. It is a poor region. In the beginning, Aurangzeb had required support from the central treasury even to sustain his army, leave alone equip them with better arms. The treasurer at Agra had reported to Dara Shikoh who was quick to blame Aurangzeb for arrears. If now Aurangzeb annexes the Golconda kingdom and adds it to the imperial dominations, his income will increase several-fold. The financial autonomy will set Aurangzeb free to develop his army. And with his aptitude for battle and war strategy, he will be able to build the strongest force as compared to all his brothers.

In short, Aurangzeb will then become a *real* threat to Dara Shikoh.

'The Deccan kingdoms may have been the vassals of the empire, but they have stopped paying tribute. The farman does not make sense. This shows that your father does not want you to be more powerful than Dara,' Shaista says truthfully.

'All these years,' Aurangzeb says caustically, 'Dara bhai has been busy with cerebral pursuits and philosophical discussions on infidels with men of theory, while we—you, me, and many others, our military officials and soldiers—have suffered on the battlefields of Multan, Balkh, Gujarat and Deccan, wrestling with dust storms, floods, famines and plagues. We've fought battles of expansion and pushed the borders of the empire, in the north, south and east.'

Shaista nods and wonders, *How can the emperor of Hindustan lack insight? And how can he be so passionate in his love for one son and his hatred for another, both born from the same mother?*

'He has been more vicious towards me after Ammi's death. He loves only the two of them, Jahanara apa and Dara bhai, both of whom look like Ammi.'

Shaista hears his nephew's words and looks at him. Aurangzeb seems to be talking to himself, as if in a trance, oblivious to his presence. He almost looks like a lost little boy without his favourite toy, the heartbreak evident on his face.

Shaista is reminded of a particular incident that happened years ago, just before Shah Jahan's accession to the throne—the only time when Shah Jahan had displayed any affection for Aurangzeb. The winter morning had been bright, and the waters of the Yamuna seemed greenish blue. The city of Agra had gathered in sheer anticipation to watch the sport. A large arena had been set up in front of the mansion occupied by Shah Jahan. The sand was levelled, the arena fenced. The elephants had arrived, trumpeting, their trunks raised in the air. Once the fight had started, the elephants had grappled and shoved and locked their trunks. In the midst of their combat, one elephant, the smaller of the two, had started bleeding. For a moment the animal had stood rooted with terror and the next moment he had fled towards the river. The other, on seeing his opponent vanish, had turned furious, trampled the fence and charged towards the crowd. People had panicked and mayhem ensued. Dara, Shuja and Murad had vanished. Only Aurangzeb had remained calm on his horseback, and drawn his sword when thrown on the ground by the enraged elephant's whipping trunk. That might have been his last breath but for the quick intervention of a mahout. On that day, Shah Jahan had held Aurangzeb close to his chest, calling him *bahadur*, the brave one. The next day, in the celebrated ritual of *tula daan*, the doting father had donated gold bars equivalent to Aurangzeb's weight, and had given him gifts worth two lakh rupees. His bravery was celebrated by court singers in Persian. This had been before the death of Anjuman Banu, Shaista Khan's sister, Shah Jahan's wife and Aurangzeb's mother. Things had changed since then between the father and son.

'What have you decided to do? What about Mir Jumla's family?' Shaista asks softly.

Aurangzeb looks at him, dark shadows of finality fleeting across his pale eyes.

'You will see,' he says calmly and recites:

Who can clasp the arms of a bride called kingship?
Only the man who can plant a kiss
On the lips of an eager sword
And bind its blade with his life
Firm, like in a kinship!

'Did you pen it?' Shaista asks with admiration.

'Yes,' says Aurangzeb and, looking into the eyes of his uncle, asks, 'What are my frontiers? The real frontiers?'

Shaista cannot stand Aurangzeb's piercing gaze. He looks at the floor and answers so very softly, 'For ordinary people, life is a constant struggle, but for you, life *is* frontiers, where you may have to wage wars with your father, brothers and perhaps even your sons. Shaista is surprised by his own answer. He slowly and gingerly lifts his head to see Aurangzeb's reaction.

Aurangzeb is the figure of a lithe man with a trim beard sitting on a metal charpoy. With a posture unusually erect and head slightly thrown back, Shah Jahan's third son looks different from Dara Shikoh. He is much leaner, and his tanned face is covered with sun wrinkles. His embroidered muslin *jama*, a garment lined with green brocade, matches the emerald-studded turban. A few daggers with jewelled hilts hang from the golden sash supported by a narrow leather belt. Aurangzeb's eyes are pale grey. A shiver runs down his spine. The cold stare hints at a molten core of violence boiling in the mind.

2

Aurangzeb sits alone in his tent for the rest of the day counting beads and shifting between his charpoy and prayer mat. Only the eunuch Mutamad is allowed in, that too to bring him food. Mutamad watches intently as his master eats slowly. Mutamad knows what's bothering the prince. *The sorrows of the royals are as pompous as their lives,* he thinks despite his genuine affection for his master.

Aurangzeb is too busy to notice his servant. His mind is pondering something else, something far more important. The question, 'How must I respond to my father's farman?' has become Aurangzeb's present obsession. It is only late in the evening that he decides his course of action. He will entice his father with Mir Jumla's wealth and extract maximum tribute money from the stupid king of Qutbshahi. He summons his scribe and dictates:

What the esteemed emperor has most kindly written with your gracious pen concerning this slave has come like a revelation from the heavens. I shall act according to your wish and retreat. I shall send Mir Jumla of Golconda to you to be employed to serve the empire. As the emperor is aware, he is the richest man of the

Deccan. His jagir fetches him forty lakh rupees in revenue and he owns some of the world's finest diamond mines. He also has five thousand well-mounted and well-equipped cavalry and ten thousand infantrymen. His expertise in the field of artillery will enhance the might of the imperial army. And he, Mir Jumla, wants to present you with a priceless diamond and one thousand one hundred and one ser of pure, high-quality gold worth fifteen lakh rupees.

A second letter is to Abdullah Qutb Shah. It reads:

Be advised. We have already taken Hyderabad, and soon head for Kollur to capture your diamond mines. You could safeguard your kingdom from total ruin if you release Mir Jumla's family. Do not forget that twenty years ago you had declared your kingdom as a tributary state of the empire. Make haste, pay up the arrears. Keeping the current exchange rate in mind, the tribute of twenty lakh rupees, in pure gold, is due from you. The transaction will be carried out between you and me. And when this is done, we will give our consent to the marriage of your daughter to my son Sultan that you have proposed. But again, that will only happen if you cede the Ramgir Fort and the territory around it, yielding the revenue of six lakh rupees a year to me, and this transaction too must remain strictly between you and me.

3

Dark clouds gently slither into the southern sky of Jawali. A flock of herons flies westwards in the direction of *Sindhu Sagar*, the Arabian Ocean. The birds' wings shimmer in the golden hues of the morning sun. Slow-flowing Koyana river cuts through the valley. Its waters look a darker shade of olive green. The river seems to be waiting for the monsoons when it swells with water and its colour changes to bluish brown. From its bank rises a steep and rocky hill, Bhorpya Hill, where Shivaji's dream is slowly taking shape into reality. Bhorpya

Hill is a plateau, girded towards the top which is flat and smooth. It is about forty guj in length and breadth, a perfect place for a citadel or upper fort. A fort is being built here. Shivaji has already named it Pratapgad—the fort of brave deeds. At its centre, the walls of a large court and private apartments have already risen above a large plinth. Around it, labourers busily lay basalt slabs, finely squared at their edges, in lime mortar. Towards the southern edge of the plateau, a few stonecutters hammer away in a frenzy, the deafening sound echoing in the valley. Shivaji strides towards the north-west of the plateau, observing the way the fort is building up and watching the workers. Moroji Pinglay follows him, half-walking and half-running. Behind them, a few of Shivaji's guards march briskly to keep pace.

Some workers notice him. They fall to their knees and slyly regard him from the corner of their eyes. Unlike many other employers, he looks directly at them, and accepts their presence. They catch the glimpse of his face—sun-swept yet fetching. His nose is like an eagle's beak. His large brown eyes are curious and responsive, not aloof or scornful. He has a short beard and a light moustache. They like his saffron turban that seems like a slanting temple spire with the few pearl strings attached to its apex. They admire his silky, pale, knee-length robe worn over tight breeches, and his long woollen stole. His golden sash has been woven with gold. They feel him regarding them as men of flesh and bones, with minds and feelings. It is a strange sensation for them who have lived their lives being treated like oxen, born to trudge, be whipped and breed to produce more resources for men of wealth.

It does not take too long for Shivaji to reach the western edge. He staggers, trying to balance against the blustery wind blowing mercilessly around them. He tries to walk ahead without stumbling, as his robe balloons behind him. He leans over the newly built parapet and peers down. The hillside looks like it has been hacked down by an infinitely huge axe. The vertical rock, black and shining, plunges straight and seems to collide with the land. Far below, the earth unfolds before his eyes, hilly, ridden with ravines, covered with patches of wild bushes. It is a clear day, without the usual mist that gathers around the hills. The ghats skirting the hills look like serpents clinging to the slopes. Many kos away, at the edge, the grey-blue skyline has sunk into a thin blue line—perhaps the waters of the Arabian Ocean. Not a single hill stands so high that it can block his view of the sea.

'This spot lets you look into the horizon and watch all that takes place between Pratapgad and the sea,' Shivaji observes.

'And from this side no one can enter the fort,' Pinglay adds.

'Even if they ride on the waves of their imagination,' Shivaji replies with a smile, turning to look at the stocky Brahmin. 'Unlike our other hill forts around Pune, this one cannot be besieged from all sides.'

Even as he speaks, Shivaji moves towards the south. The lower fort and its extensions suddenly rise into the range of his vision. More than a thousand men labour on the flat expanse of the lower ridge. He notices some women near the limekilns. The bastions of the main entrance facing the south are halfway through. To the east, a long arm of the lower fort extension seems like an enormous war ship suspended above the sea of valleys. At its south-western corner, diggers scoop out the earth to make an artificial lake for harvesting rainwater.

Shivaji nods approvingly and looks at Pinglay who had initially worked along with him on the drawings of the plan of the fort. Ten years ago, the man with the intense black eyes and brooding mouth had knocked at Shivaji's doors. Pinglay always has questions, but over the years, Shivaji had discovered his many talents—a leader in the battlefields, a negotiator who speaks many tongues, a planner who's good with numbers and an architect with a vision.

'It is proving to be an expensive fort,' Shivaji hears Pinglay comment. His dark eyes show fleeting shadows of anxiety and he knows why. Niloji Sondev and Anna Datto, his financial adviser and treasurer, have written to him regarding the burgeoning costs of the construction.

After getting hold of Chandrarao Morey's treasury with one thousand ser of gold and five thousand ser of silver, Raja Shivaji had decided to build a fort. For a month, Pinglay and he had scoured the area till they had come across this plateau in the middle of the valley. Together, they had worked with fort engineers on the structural drawings. On paper, Pratapgad looked like an eagle perched on a large basaltic rock that rises like an enormous column over the valley. The fort had been designed to defend and protect. Raja Shivaji had visualized it clearly: the protective walls meandering over the cliffs and ridges, making approaching them impossible and climbing inconceivable. The ramparts were designed to have umbilical defence—two walls running parallel to each other so that even if the enemy manages to break one and enter, he will be killed instantly by soldiers standing on the ramparts of the other wall. Provisions had been made for toilets too so that archers need not go far from their posts. The main entrance of the fort was planned with intricate details. The approach ran parallel to the ramparts so that the archers would never miss an intruder. The main gate opened into a small area in the front with an abrupt fall into the valley's abyss. This was to make sure that it could never be targeted by enemy cannons.

'I hope this is worth it in the time of need,' says Pinglay, sounding stressed, even though majority of the funds have been drawn from Morey's treasury.

'Moroji,' Shivaji stops and fixes his gaze on the Brahmin's face, 'forts can be built everywhere, on the riverbanks, at the confluence, on the islands in the midst of oceans, in the desert, in the forest and on a hill like this one. Hill forts are the most difficult to reach. But the foothills of most of the hill forts can be accessed by enemy cavalry. Pratapgad is unique. It is an invincible fort in an impassable valley. Only an enemy backed by a strong infantry can reach here. And the kingdoms around us rely mostly on their heavily armoured cavalry. Military strongholds like this one will make our enemy infinitely weaker.'

The Brahmin begins to understand the returns on investment.

Shivaji adds, 'Letting the enemy revel in the perceptions of his power is the first step to victory. Creating a *ranangan*, the battle yard that helps us achieve this, is a strategy neglected by our native kings.'

Pinglay loves Raja Shivaji's definition of ranangan; he has never heard of 'battle-yard creation' before.

'But it is not all about the battles,' Shivaji says softly. 'It is more about making the valley worthy to live for the peasants. Call the watandars of the valley to meet us. Tell them that the valley is now one of our districts.'

Pinglay nods.

'The valley looks red; this kind of laterite soil depends on rain. The peasants will need help if the monsoons fail.'

Pinglay smiles. Unlike many jagirdars his master is interested in the science of agriculture.

'I want to know how much land in the valley is under cultivation. Have you found out what are the important crops that grow here?'

'*Ji,*' Pinglay bows slightly and says, 'when the rainfall is good, which is usually the case, the soil here gives sorghum, pearl millets, wheat, maize, groundnut and *tur.*'

'Keep the records of the entire area under cultivation, the exact proportion of land under the various crops at a given point of time. Tell the deshmukhs and the patils of the valley they will henceforth report to our revenue officials.'

'*Ji,*' Pinglay whispers, following Raja Shivaji down the steps leading to the lower fort, concealing the joy he feels at the new responsibilities he is expected to fulfil. But he has still not received the list of villages in the valley. In Raja's jagir, every village is a small world in itself, with boundaries carefully defined, encroachments avoided. *Paragana*s are divided into tehsils or *taluk*s. The *tehsildar*'s office that keeps land records reports directly to Raja Shivaji. Tillable land is divided into fields and the peasants are given interest-free loans, and when the rainfall is low, the revenue collected from them is reduced accordingly.

Pinglay knows that a thousand odd villages in Raja's jagir generate three lakh rupees per year, with each village on an average giving three hundred rupees in cash or kind. This accounts for barely two hundred and fifty ser of gold per year. With Jawali under them, there will be considerable increase in the state income.

Shivaji leaps lithely over the last steps. He turns to his right and then marches towards the main entrance. To his left, a bunch of women are busy assisting their menfolk, their dusky faces gleaming in sweat in the vicinity of the heated limekiln. Their bodies are barely covered with grubby, frayed saris. Between the kilns and the eastern extension, under the shade of a few banyan trees, Shivaji notices a few hammocks hanging on the lower branches. He sees a toddler yelling, and a bunch of half-naked children playing in the dirt, as cold winds continue to blow.

'Moroji, get some warm clothes for the women and children. Remember, those who work for us are under *our* care, even the labourers who work temporarily. The required funds are to be taken from our treasury,' Shivaji says.

It is only late in the night when Shivaji finally rests. Icy winds bluster with a shrill whistle as the cloth panels of his tent flutter wildly, as if threatening to fly away and leave him exposed to the elements. Through the thin panels, he can see flickering lights of fires lit by his guards and can faintly hear their banter. Between him and the cold earth, there is only a small quilt made out of sheep's wool. Using his hand as pillow he looks at the dark sky through a small slit and notices that the southern clouds have drifted overhead. Before he falls off to sleep, thoughts are swirling in Shivaji's mind:

It is just a matter of time before the Mughal armies flood their borders. And if Aurangzeb annexes the Adilshahi, a large part of the Deccan, south of the river Bhima, including my jagir, will become Mughal terrain. On the other hand, if Aurangzeb renews the old peace treaty with Ali Adil Shah, the allied forces will prove dangerous. History might repeat itself. So, this is the right time to start diplomatic relations with Aurangzeb, the Mughal subhedar of the Deccan. It is the only way to keep the Adilshahi armies at bay. It is the only way to get funds for our campaigns to seize part of Konkan under the Adilshahi.

4

A little over twelve kos south-east of Pune, an enormous mountain rises less than one kos above the Sahyadri Plateau. The hill fort of Purandar is enveloped in darkness. The room is dimly lit by the pale rays of the moon as they sneak in through the chinks of the ventilators above the closed windows. At first Jija bai thinks she is dreaming, but then she hears it clearly—the knocking. She quickly throws off the blankets as frosty air slices through her old bones. Gathering the *pallu* of her sari to cover her head, she moves towards the door, trying not to stumble over anything. A million dark thoughts race through her mind as she pushes the wooden crossbar to a side and opens the door. A gust of icy wind hits her like a whip. A maid stands outside, holding a small lamp covered in a glass bulb, her face ashen with fear. A veil of soot and a strong smell of burning oil lingers.

'Sayee Bai Sahib is in trouble,' the maid whispers, her teeth chattering in the cold.

Without a word, Jija bai follows her to the chamber of her son's first wife. They walk through an open corridor joining the women's quarters, and are almost blown by the wind by the time they reach. It is warmer inside; a few earthen lamps burn in the alcoves of the stone walls. Jija bai is alarmed to see Sayee sitting on her bed with her hands clasped around her stomach even as three little girls wrapped in woollen mufflers fidget at the far end of the room, almost on the verge of crying.

'Your mother is fine, I am here now,' she whispers keeping her voice as calm as possible and signals the maid to take them away.

Sayee moans in pain. Jija bai rushes to her bed.

The young woman raises her head, and looks up as tears roll down her cheeks. 'Ma sahib,' she says sobbing, 'I don't want to lose this baby. I know it is a boy.'

Jija bai sits on the bed facing Sayee who has grown far too thin. It is her fourth pregnancy. The lustre women acquire when heavy with child is distinctly missing. Her eyes have sunk into dark circles and her face looks gaunt as of a starving human. *How playful was she when I brought her home as a bride! And how seamlessly she had grown into a beautiful young woman,* Jija bai thinks with regret and mutters, 'Sayee, the astrologer has told us that you will carry this baby full term. Have faith.'

'These spasms take my breath away. Only when they became unbearable did I ask the maid to call you.'

Jija bai misses her son and feels guilty somewhere deep in her heart. In the past her loneliness had made her jittery. She had sought eight marriage alliances for her Shivaji even before he was fourteen. She had made her home full with eight brides: Sayee, Soyara, Putala, Laxmi, Kashi, Saguna, Gunwanti and Sakwar. This had brought eight politically strong families into her fold: the Nimbalkars, the Mohites, the Palkars, the Vichares, the Jadavs, the Shirkes, the Ingales and the Gaikwads. But she knows that her son loves his first wife, Sayee, and she is his true friend. The others do feel neglected. And now, all of them are compelled to live in the residential quarters of Purandar Hill Fort for their own safety. Despite Jija bai's pleas, Sayee has been fasting, eating only one meal a day as atonement so that a son is born to her. Jija bai sighs. She remembers her home in Pune, the warm, red-stone building surrounded by temples and rice fields.

'Ma sahib, do I worry you too much?'

She gently pats Sayee's stomach and says, 'Worry about him. He is your priority.'

The corners of the room are shrouded in darkness, as the light from the lamp fails to permeate the clinging, enveloping gloom. Jija bai's gaze falls on a lamp and its flame. She wonders if her life has been like its wick—one end dipped in oil and another burning itself away, just a medium to transport volatile fuel. Her son, the light of her life is struggling, fired by the dream she had made him see.

'We will get through this, will we not?' she hears Sayee ask.

Jija bai does not reply. Shivaji is busy at Pratapgad, his military base in Jawali. 'Without military strongholds, you will share the futile destiny of your warrior father,' she had once said to her son.

'My son, he will be fine, won't he?' she hears Sayee repeat her concern.

Jija bai feels anxious and uncertain as she thinks about the destiny of the child growing inside Sayee. Will it be a son as Sayee believes? What has happened to the men of her family in the past—will it happen again in the future? Some have died fighting battles for their Muslim rulers, some have been murdered and some are serving the

Muslim kingdoms. Her father and brother were beheaded in Nizam Shah's court.

Jija bai looks at Sayee who has fallen asleep. The lamp has dimmed and the room has turned darker. She covers her daughter-in-law with a quilt and goes back to her thoughts.

Till today, for the past twenty years, her husband has served the Adilshahi like a loyal warrior. He is responsible for annexing the remaining parts of the Vijayanagara empire for his Muslim master and has become popular in the Bijapur court. His fame has created a political lobby against them. The head of the lobby is Afzal Khan, subhedar of the Wai province. The man has devastated Jija bai's world. His prying eyes had fallen on their son Sambhaji, who had grown into a strapping young man who lived with his father. Afzal Khan had ordered him to annex the kingdom of Kanakgiri. Her firstborn son Sambhaji had led his men to the trenches near the fort and had waited for the reinforcements that had never arrived. During the ensuing battle, her twenty-five-year-old firstborn was killed. A cannonball had struck him, crushing his face to pulp. People say that Afzal Khan did not send help on purpose. Some even say that Afzal had bribed the king of Kanakgiri to kill Sambhaji. Her husband had not dared to ask questions. Who could he approach? The king was on his deathbed. There was no case and no justice.

'Freedom—' she had told Shivaji when he was a young boy, '—serving them means the end of it.'

She would ask young Shivaji to note the hills, pointing to the surrounding mountains while in Pune, and say, 'There are forts up there. You will need several such military strongholds and thousands of men trained in swordfight and archery before you can even lift your eyes to challenge the old order.' Her warnings had rung clear. 'You must change the definition of your karma and fight at frontiers never encountered by your father or his father or even my father. These new frontiers will define you, the frontiers of your karma,' she had told him several times, always deliberately maintaining a steely expression in her eyes, unsure if her young son understood her words or not.

CHAPTER FIVE

1

One hundred and fifty kos east of Pune, the fort city of Bidar that stands on a high plateau is regarded as the north-eastern stronghold of the Adilshahi kingdom. It is surrounded on all sides by a wall that has a circumference of more than half a kos, cut in solid rock and strengthened by bastions loaded with huge cannons. The city boasts of mosques, palaces, Turkish baths and a mint. It is believed to be impregnable to assault. But the Mughals have proved it otherwise. The city is burning and is surrounded by ugly trenches dug by Aurangzeb's diggers. The last of the trenches is wide enough to pitch tents. One of them belongs to the prince himself.

'If only . . .' mourns Shaista Khan, sitting on a wooden platform and studying a map, holding the paper close to his face to see properly.

The map has been clearly drawn. For more than two hundred and fifty kos, the river Bhima flows from the north-west to the south-east. Its roaring waters cut through the Deccan till it meets the river Krishna. The Krishna is the Mughal empire's southern border and regions of Maharashtra and Karnataka, north of Bhima, belong to the empire. The Adilshahi's north-east stronghold, Bidar, has already fallen. Only Gulbarga needs to be axed away from the kingdom.

If only the emperor had allowed them to take Hyderabad as well as the Golconda Fort, the entire Deccan north of Bhima would have been a part of the imperial dominations, Shaista thinks regretfully as he glances at Aurangzeb.

The entrance to the pavilion is wide. Aurangzeb, sitting on a high divan, can see Bidar from his dugout, its protective walls fallen at places and two bastions turned into mere rubble. Inside the fort, some of the buildings still burn with a raging intensity. Enormous clouds of black soot have gathered in the morning sky above the inferno. His job is done, despite his brother's manipulation to prevent him from annexing the Shia kingdoms. Aurangzeb had argued about the illegitimacy of Ali Adil Shah's rule, since Ali is an adopted son of late

Mohammed Adil Shah, and sought permission from the emperor to annex the Adilshahi. Initially his father had refused, but later he had had a change of heart after Mir Jumla had gifted him the priceless Koh-i-noor at Aurangzeb's behest. Funds and reinforcements had arrived in time. Mir Jumla too, who, after the safe release of his family from the clutches of Qutb Shah, had turned an Aurangzeb loyalist, has now returned to the Deccan with the latest artillery recently bought by the imperial army.

'Shiva Bhosale's diplomat is here,' Shaista hears Aurangzeb murmur.

It is rather early in the morning. Winter is long gone but the air has remained cool. Darkness still lingers in the tent. Mutamad pours more oil into the cups of brass lamps. His master has a long day ahead. Local landlords who have assured the third prince of their support have been called for the meeting. Some of Aurangzeb's military officers who nurture new ideas of battle tactics have been called in the afternoon. But before anything else, they need to meet Shivaji Bhosale's vakeel, an elderly Brahmin called Sonoji Dabir.

Shaista follows his nephew's gaze. Outside, a little away from the entrance of the tent, a thin man wearing a red turban emerges from the fog and walks towards them briskly, business-like. Two armed guards follow him. One can never be sure of the Marathas.

Aurangzeb glances at his uncle and smiles mockingly.

Sonoji, Shivaji's *dabir*, the man assigned to look after the external affairs of the budding Maratha kingdom, does not miss the scornful smile. He bows deep, slyly glancing at Aurangzeb. The third prince sits very straight and busily counts the beads of his rosary with eyes half-closed. In the yellow light of oil lamps, Aurangzeb's features appear sharp; he looks virtuous in his white brocade robe and his embroidered *patka* turban. It is hard to imagine that this man is responsible for the Bidar massacre. Dabir is proud of the fact that he can judge people's characters just by looking at them, but until now he has not seen such a contrast—a refined facade masking a dangerous mind! The truth shines through when Aurangzeb opens his eyes. A shiver runs down Dabir's spine. At first he thinks Aurangzeb's eyes are empty, but then he realizes that they have pale grey irises.

For a while, silence reigns.

'I, Sonoji Dabir, the adviser to Raja Shivaji Bhosale, bow to Your Imperial Highness. I stand here with a humble heart,' Dabir says in Urdu tinged with a slight Deccan accent.

Aurangzeb does not respond, filling the silence with invisible yet physically tangible impatience.

He speaks slowly, 'Say what you want to. And don't linger.'

'Raja Shivaji sends his humble greetings and a letter to Your Imperial Highness. Raja looks forward to serving the empire in the capacity of a regent and helping the imperial forces conquer the rest of the Adilshahi sultanate. In return, all he wants is a formal recognition of his right over the land and forts in his possession.' Dabir speaks unhurriedly but emphasizing each word clearly.

Aurangzeb feels an uncontrollable urge to laugh loudly. These uncouth mountain folks! He, the subhedar of the Mughal-occupied Deccan, does not need any Shivaji, and men like Shivaji will not fit in the Mughal system. He wonders if Shivaji knows the rock-solid structure of the empire. The head is the emperor, followed by his sons and the wazir, the prime minister. Decisions regarding the military appointments are taken by the *mir bakshi*, the army chief, and the *mir atish*, the artillery chief. Provincial heads, the subhedars, are assigned military officers called the *mansabdars*. High-ranking mansabdars are given jagirs. But they are liable to be transferred. Every once in a while, their old jagirs are taken away and they are given the new ones. This is to ensure that they do not remain at one place for a long time and develop alliances with the local populace, a sure-fire formula to become a rebel. Rajputs are the only exceptions to the rule. They are allowed to keep their ancient kingdoms but are always kept busy at far-off frontiers, thus preventing rebellion from their end.

'Why doesn't your Raja Shivaji go to Bijapur instead? It is easy to get an assignment as a regent with them,' Shaista says with a serious face. It is his way to deflate the man's price and ego.

Dabir blinks. He cannot think of a proper answer.

Aurangzeb's countenance does not betray his thoughts. Jagirdar Shivaji wants to rebel against his own king Ali Adil Shah! Aurangzeb knows that in the Deccan jagirdars are independent of any king, even when these estates fall into the terrain that officially belongs to a kingdom. These jagirs are also claimed by inheritance, like Shivaji sitting on his father's jagir. They are allowed to have their own little courts and even thrones. The king is regarded as a mere overlord. Some of the jagirdars avoid paying revenue. Some become wealthier and more powerful than their kings. Mir Jumla is an example.

'Say in brief what the letter says,' Shaista demands.

'The letter says that Raja Shivaji wants to help the imperial army as an independent regent. He is already in possession of the districts of Pune, Supe, Chakan, Indapur, the valley of Jawali and the hilly Maval, along with the hill forts of the region. North Konkan is a part of the Adilshahi. If you allow him, he will wrench the region from them.'

Shivaji thinks that we are retarded, intellectually compromised humans! Aurangzeb fumes.

'Shivaji Bhosale has, over the years, mustered more than ten thousand horsemen. He has created a fast-moving light cavalry, a perfect war machine for the hilly regions of the Deccan. He could even offer protection to the empire's Deccan territories,' the Maratha vakeel drags on.

The old man is all business. Aurangzeb searches for the vakeel's hidden motives. Shivaji wants imperial protection to his jagir that, as of now, falls within the Adilshahi's territory. He is securing his jagir's future, when and if the entire region comes under the imperial rule or the old peace treaty is renewed between the Mughal empire and the Adilshahi sultanate. Shivaji also wants to expand his jagir, take the coastal Konkan that as of now is in the Adilshahi's terrain. The region has markets like Kalyan where wealthy merchants operate to feed supplies to sea freight, and salt to the rest of the country. Shivaji wants to collect those taxes as well, all under the imperial protection and with the help of the imperial funds. Not bad at all!

'The benevolent Mughal prince, Your Imperial Highness has recently taken a regent of Hyderabad. That has kindled hopes in the heart of Raja Shivaji.' The fidgeting vakeel persists with an expression of optimism lathered on his face.

Aurangzeb's fingers work furiously on his rosary beads. The clever vakeel is referring to Mir Jumla. What do these dimwits know? Mir Jumla had a weakness. His family was languishing in the dungeons of Golconda Fort. To ensure their release, Mir had been ready to do what Aurangzeb had wished for. Shivaji's case is different; he has no weakness. Shivaji comes with strengths like his hill forts, repaired and strengthened for battles. Once Shivaji garners power under the imperial protection, he will surely bare his fangs. One needs special skills to hunt leopards that have the expertise to climb trees.

'How is Shiva's father?' Aurangzeb asks with blank interest.

'As my esteemed Mughal prince must be aware, Raja Shahji Bhosale is serving the Adilshahi as a regent,' he responds nervously.

'It is a good reason for Shivaji to serve Ali Adil Shah!' Shaista says derisively while Aurangzeb jerks his head to show disgust. The action is involuntary. Petty jagirdars like Shivaji and Shahji call themselves Rajas, the little kings without *real* kingdoms! Even the rulers of the Deccan sultanates are not allowed to call themselves emperors or kings; they are just shahs, that is, overlords. The rulers of the Deccan humour the likes of Shahji who call themselves Rajas because they are at their jagirdars' mercy in times of war. The entire military system of the Deccan kingdoms is in a mess. Men like Shivaji Bhosale must be made to feel like scorpions without their stingers, and tigers without their carnassial. It is easy, if, like his father, Shivaji is removed from the hills of Maval and made to work in the flat regions of the Adilshahi—he will be like an eagle without its talons.

'The old Bhosale has wizened with age. His son must learn from him,' Shaista says while rolling the maps.

Dabir stares at Shaista Khan; he is a handsome man with a white beard wearing a headgear laden with jewels. *Looks like this man has a habit of taunting and inciting people, to make them say what they do not want to say, so he can catch them in words*, he muses. *It is tricky to challenge him.* Shaista was the ex-subhedar of the Deccan, he also belongs to the imperial family and wields considerable power over the Mughal policies of the region. Dabir has never taken such insults laying down and always given a piece of his mind to those who've been cheeky. But the two men standing before him are the two most powerful military men in this part of the world. And he must focus on his mission as has been clearly outlined by Raja Shivaji. 'History may repeat. Our king, Ali Adil Shah, is in the process of losing his north-eastern strongholds like Bidar. He is likely to buckle under the pressure. He may renew the old peace treaty and surrender some regions to the Mughal prince that may include our territory. He may form an alliance with Aurangzeb or declare total defeat. Such situations may prove dangerous for us. But if we get the support from Aurangzeb, we will be safe for a while, till we gather some more strength, some more manpower,' Raja Shivaji had said.

'*Moshekeli, moshekeli!*' Shaista murmurs in Farsi, his eyes shining with glee.

Dabir understands what the khan has whispered and why he is delighted. Moshekeli means 'difficulty or problem' in Farsi. Shaista thinks that they have managed to shut him up. He has heard that the imperial royals always revert to Farsi or Arabic in the Deccan if they do not wish the others to understand them. It is time to beat them in their own game, without hurting his objectives.

'*Maen ra babaekhsh,*' Dabir asks Aurangzeb for forgiveness in fluent Farsi. The vakeel continues to speak the language of the high and mighty with ease. 'I am just a humble vakeel of my master. It is not in my capacity to answer your question, my respected prince. I am here to carry your esteemed message to Raja Shivaji.'

It takes a while for the two men to get over the shock.

'*Aaghel, aaghel,*' an irritated Shaista Khan calls the vakeel wise in throaty Farsi, his tone sounding an insult, and waves his hand in the air to show annoyance. 'Stick to Urdu,' he orders and continues, 'if your Raja wants to serve us, he will have to join our military ranks and become our mansabdar.'

Dabir smiles at the irritated Shaista Khan. Men who like to tease do not take kindly to being teased. But that is the least of his problems. Shaista Khan's proposal has put Dabir in a quandary. A jagirdar in the Deccan is like a lion in the forest, and a mansabdar in the Mughal army is a circus lion. Potentially defiant mansabdars are sent on the most difficult campaigns at perilous frontiers like the extreme north-eastern or north-western borders. Thus, they remain at the empire's mercy for vital supplies. Aurangzeb may do the same with Raja Shivaji.

'And there is another problem. The Jawali massacre is still fresh on everybody's mind. We need time to think,' says Shaista.

Dabir's face turns red. Shaista Khan's comment is utterly shameless. What about the Hyderabad and Bidar massacres? Siddi Marjan, the jagirdar of Bidar, and his sons have been killed by Aurangzeb's artillery attacks. All his family members have been hounded out of their palaces, chased and slaughtered. Thousands of women from the city have already been dragged out of their homes into the Mughal camp. Aurangzeb is known to keep away from women, but his soldiers are granted the lease to please themselves.

'Meanwhile, tell Shivaji Bhosale to behave, and not to leave such an incriminating bloody trail like he has done in Jawali. The Deccan will soon be the empire's terrain. And the rebels and their supporters will soon be dead men. He will be responsible for the deaths of thousands,' Aurangzeb mutters.

Dabir wants to laugh out loud. *Is that a threat?* Men have always died in battles. Does Aurangzeb not hold himself responsible for the deaths of his own soldiers? Or are the rules different for him? When Dabir had entered the Mughal camp just a few hours before, he had seen countless bodies of the soldiers covered with bulky rodents feasting on dead meat.

'We shall let you know further . . .' Aurangzeb says, his eyes half shut as his fingers move over the beads of his *tesbih*. 'Technically, the territories of the Deccan Shia kingdoms are already a part of the empire. And we do not need anyone to protect us from our vassals.'

'Remind Shivaji that in the long history of our empire, no one has dared to cross our borders and attack our terrains,' Shaista lashes out.

The vakeel bows deeply, hands over the letter to one of armed guards and asks, 'What must I tell my master?'

'Tell him that capturing the valley of Jawali and killing its ruler was criminal. From what we have heard, it was an act of premeditated, cold-blooded murder for personal gains—not pardonable since it was not done in self-defence or on an impulse because of a heated argument. How do you think we can take such a criminal into our folds, even as a mansabdar?'

The meeting is dismissed. Sonoji's old frame quivers as he steps out.

Aurangzeb knows what jabs the vakeel's head. The pesky intellectual! He knows how to hit them without warning, and leave them feeling humiliated. When the Mughals kill to annex, it is war of expansions. But when others do it, it is crime! Aurangzeb is not ashamed to tell that to the world.

Aurangzeb has all too soon forgotten about the Maratha vakeel, and is now thinking about his full bladder and empty stomach. But he decides to get over with the meeting that has been arranged with Mir Jumla before taking a break. Shaista Khan, eyes closed in a state of bliss, holds the metal pipe of his hookah in his hands and hurtles rings of smoke in the air. A strong smell of mint envelops the tent.

When Shaista opens his eyes, he notices Mir Jumla standing in front of him, grinning from ear to ear. The Persian seems to be in an exuberant mood. His family is safe in Dilli and he is the new mir atish of the entire imperial army. The new artillery adviser has shown how the latest cannon can be pulled by a single horse on to the field as opposed to the old ones that required at least sixteen horses or oxen. The new weapons-of-fire are changing the war game, especially when enemies, like that of the ones at Bidar Fort, enjoy advantages of many-kos-long ramparts and countless strong static cannons.

'Wallah!' Mir Jumla throws his hands in the air and cries, 'The time has come for my prince to enter Bidar as a victor.'

'The victor' and 'the vanquished' are Aurangzeb's favourite words. He smiles for the first time. There is one more reason. The vaults of Bidar Fort are filled with gold and silver. The throne in the court of Siddi Marjan is made of solid gold and laden with precious stones. The estimated cost of the throne is not less than four crore rupees. With these riches, he can buy thousands of Adilshahi soldiers.

2

It has been just a week since Dabir's return from Bidar and Raja Shivaji has suddenly called for an urgent meeting in the land fort of Chakan, just a few kos away from the river Bhima.

As the summer night descends like a waterfall, the land fort disappears in the darkness. A waning moon appears in the inky sky as ashen shapes of its light cut through the trees. The fort's massive walls look dark and distant. The drawbridges have been raised over the moat and the gates are closed shut. The archers move silently on the ramparts. Scouts, assembled on the surveillance turrets built on the bulging bastions, try hard to scan the surroundings, as the loud droning of countless cicadas sweeps across the forest floor.

Adjacent to the dark, sprawling courtyard is a *sadar*, the official meeting place. It has a room hidden from prying eyes. It is a *khalbatkhana*, a den for secret discussions, and is lit by two torches hung on its walls. Now, men fill its every corner. They sit on a thick *jajum* and watch Raja Shivaji who stands near a wooden platform. Sonoji Dabir, his son Trimbak Dabir, Tanaji, Yesaji and the fort-keeper Firangoji Narsala look puzzled, almost confused. Cavalry captains Minaji and Kashirao prefer to stand near the lone window. Moroji Pinglay has come all the way from Pratapgad. *Where do I begin? The strategy that may shock them,* Raja Shivaji contemplates. *I shall take it forward slowly, step by step,* he finally decides.

'After Jawali we are moving towards Konkan. The campaign requires one thousand warhorses. We also need battlefield allowances and supplies ready. We had hoped that the Mughal would fund our campaigns against the Adilshahi, but Aurangzeb has refused to form an alliance with us.'

Dabir nods in affirmation.

'We can still make the Mughals pay for our campaigns,' Shivaji announces cautiously. There is a flurry as a few straighten up, some lean forward, eager to hear more.

'How?' Dabir is confused.

Shivaji deliberates for a moment before he speaks again. 'Aurangzeb has deployed all his military at the north-east borders of the Adilshahi, leaving his other territories in the Deccan exposed and vulnerable.'

'Who will dare attack their territory?' Yesaji questions, glancing at Dabir for approval.

'We shall!' declares Shivaji.

'It is banditry!' an obviously nervous Pinglay protests.

'Then all of them are bandits!' Dabir retorts. 'The shahis of the Deccan have destroyed the remnants of Vijayanagara empire and looted the temple cities of the south. Twenty years ago, the Mughal had attacked the Deccan kingdoms. The Nizamshahi was destroyed and the other shahis became the tribute states of the empire. Now Aurangzeb has plundered Hyderabad for funds to support his army. And if you had seen the devastation of Bidar, you would never have said what you have just said.'

'The imperial terrain is regarded as sacred,' Moroji Pinglay persists.

'By whom?' Shivaji demands answers. 'Bidar is one hundred and fifty kos east of us. The imperial army is busy invading deeper parts of the Adilshahi. The region around Junnar and Ahmednagar is without sufficient military protection,' he declares and starts pacing. His gaze on the ground he announces, 'Tanaji, Yesaji and I will lead our men to Junnar while Minaji and Kashirao will go further north to Ahmednagar.'

Shivaji persists. 'We need to grow strong to retain our liberty. Ali Adil Shah will attack us eventually. The reason they have not done so is because Mohammed Adil Shah was bedridden for ten long years before his death. His son Ali was too young to take military decisions. In the recent past Ali was too anxious about the imminent Mughal invasions to bother us. At present he is busy battling them.'

'You mean to say we have just been lucky to escape because the Adilshahi has had its own share of problems?' Pinglay asks wryly.

Shivaji watches his men. They know the truth as well as he but no one wants to admit it. It is the right time to put it in words. 'What else then? This kind of luck may not last for long. Politics is like a chameleon, it changes colours to survive, and in the Deccan, it may turn bloody for *us*—in an instant.

'To begin with, I have stopped thinking of myself as a mere jagirdar. And you must stop thinking of *us* as rebels. A rebel is one who defies an authority and undermines an establishment. Against whom or what do we rebel? Against the ghost of Nizam Shah or Ali Adil Shah or Emperor Shah Jahan?' Raja Shivaji asks sardonically. 'They are the invaders, the intruders. We fight for our land, our freedom and our people's freedom from their raids, from their killing us under the name of religion, from their abductions of our women and children, from their deliberate destruction of our homes and farms.'

'The invaders have ruled us for centuries . . .' Dabir utters.

'Only because we have let them. Emperor Shah Jahan has blinded or killed six of his stepsiblings. Our king, late Mohammed Adil Shah, had captured his older brother, Darvesh, and gouged out his eyes. To disqualify his younger brothers from kingship, he had ordered amputation of their ring fingers. I definitely do not want to bow to such men or the sons of such men!' There is a shadow of finality in Shivaji's eyes as he hits his right fist on the palm of his left hand. 'We must now prepare for an offensive before they do.'

Dabir looks worried. It is not as simple as Raja Shivaji makes it sound. All the native Hindu kings have perished while defending their kingdoms. He remembers that the aggressions of Muslim invaders riding high on jihad were opposed tooth and nail by the Rajputs for centuries, but eventually they had to give up. History has repeated itself in the Deccan. The Hindu kings have perished as well, one by one.

'We must beat them at their own game,' Shivaji says and pauses for a few moments to watch the effect of his words on his men.

'Our need of funds is just one reason. The mighty fort of Bidar has fallen. The Adilshahi's north-eastern frontiers may soon lose some more military strongholds. Aurangzeb is arrogant and evasive; he will either swallow the Adilshahi or form an alliance with them. If one situation is death-by-fire for us, the other is a funeral pyre.'

Dabir agrees. Aurangzeb's letter for Raja Shivaji was given to him just before he left the ruins of Bidar. He had written:

For now, we let you retain the territory that is in your possession. This is the time to show your loyalty. As you are aware, Bidar Fort, which was hitherto regarded as impregnable, and which has

opened the path to conquering other parts of the Deccan, has been
reduced within weeks to ruins by us. For any other man, it would
have taken a year to do that. Soon we will blind the Adilshahi rulers
with fear. We will either flatten their kingdom or turn them into
our eternal vassals . . .

'We will be safe only if the Adilshahi forces keep fighting with
Aurangzeb. If they do, they will be too busy to think of us. If we
attack the Mughal terrain it may infuse courage in the minds of
the Adilshahi rulers. But as per our intelligence, Ali Adil Shah is
ready to sign a peace treaty with Aurangzeb, offering him the entire
Nizamshahi territory as well as one-and-a-half crore rupees.'

The men gape.

'That money is equal to more than one thousand ser of gold,'
Shivaji says, shaking his head with dismay. 'But that is not the real
problem. Once the treaty is signed, our terrain will belong to the
Mughals and they are far more powerful for us to handle, so somehow
we must convince Ali Adil Shah to keep fighting with the Mughals.'

'You are playing with fire,' Trimbak speaks for the first time. He
looks like a younger version of his father, Sonoji Dabir—fair, with
sparkling eyes full of wisdom.

Shivaji stares at his childhood friend and says, 'This fire is for
light. In the darkness, only fire shows the light. One must light it,
kindle it, fan it, fuel it, or even play with it to keep it burning.'

'You are opening up dangerous frontiers; they can burn our
world to cinders,' Moroji Pinglay warns.

'As I said before, our people are, till now, living either with death-
by-fire or funeral pyre. Now let them use fire for light. Perhaps the
new frontiers will scoop out dying sparks from within the heaps of
ash,' Shivaji sounds optimistic.

'So you will again cross the waters of the Bhima?' Dabir asks. He
knows that it is just the beginning of a long war.

Outside, the moon has reached the middle of the star-laden sky
and the air has turned frosty. It smells of wood smoke. The midnight
wind blows fiercely across the forest. The howling of the wolves has
stopped.

3

The scorching heat of the summer morning remains trapped between the hills around Junnar. Standing near the western gate, Salim and his men check the oxen carts, horsemen and palanquins entering the town. It is past lunchtime and the last cart has finally gone in. The carts come from the imperial cities of Agra, Dilli, Gwalior, Ujjain, Aurangabad and Ahmednagar. Salim is already tired, but his duty will end only in the evening, after several hours.

'I envy the night guards, bloody *haraamis*,' he grumbles. He is new but has managed to join as the head of the morning watchmen of the western gate who guard the town of Junnar.

The others chuckle, the night guards are indeed bastards. At night, with the market closed, they play cards and smoke their chillums. Most of them drink, and snore the rest of the night. The merchants who illegally smuggle in alcohol into the town at night bribe them with drinks. Salim looks inside—the plaza is teeming with people. The famous market in the Deccan is bustling. Today is a particularly busy day. The horse traders have arrived from the port of Cholamandalam. Loaded carts try to find their way through the moving throng; their drivers shout abuses at the people blocking their way. It is noisy, with children running about, screaming. Beggars yell for alms while some sing praises of a merciful God in throaty voices. Coolies, bending with loads, move behind traders. Richly attired buyers cluster around stalls showcasing carpets, jajums, *shatranjis* and pashmina shawls. Beyond the textile market is the jewellery souk. Behind the souk stand rows of stables, where horse traders gather to sell their animals.

'He is here again,' Salim hears one of his men say.

A beggar, in an oversized grimy robe torn and darned at places walks in slowly. The sores on his face ooze with whitish fluid. His fingers are bandaged. He stinks like a dead rat. A whiff of that smell has already reached them.

'Is he a leper?' Salim has already planted doubt in his men's minds. They remain away from him, too disgusted and terrified to go near and ask questions.

The beggar moves on. He has noticed the reaction of the gatekeepers. He does not bother to look at them and is happy with the alms he gets. For the first few days, he just begged and got enough coins to buy food; it was later that he made friends. The beggars here are a jolly lot. They accepted him when he told them that his wounds are not leprosy. He had removed his bandages and shown them his fingers, whole and healthy, not stubby and fallen. At night, they gather and gossip especially about rich merchants, their daily collections and places they hide their cash. Today, under the scorching sun, he trots from shop to shop, dragging one of his feet. A tiny copper coin or some leftover food from the shopkeeper's lunch or even a piece of a duster will do. He accepts everything with a smile. Some shoo him away, but he still keeps smiling. He moves towards a lane full of Turkish shops, overflowing with carpets hung on wooden stands. Their floral and geometrical designs overshadow the vibrant colours of their wool and silk. He stops in front of a particularly large edifice and stares at a rich-looking customer, an African wearing a long white robe. He wonders whether the man is new, as the owner talks to him about the genuine items and the fakes. His assistant unfurls one carpet after the other, first flinging them in the air with ease and then letting them fall on the floor with flamboyance. The beggar moves his eyes away from the customer and the carpets. He turns to watch the shop accountant shoving pouches filled with coins into a large trunk.

The accountant notices the tramp drooling at his pouches from outside the door. He feels uncomfortable, jumps a step towards the beggar and gesticulates, asking him to vanish, and then spits at him saying, 'Let your eye that casts a spell on our collection go blind!'

The beggar disappears, dissolving in the milling crowd like sugar in water. He is not seen by anybody even as night falls and the shops start closing.

And nobody misses him.

4

Shivaji leads his horse carefully as the waters of Bhima whirl around his feet before flowing downstream. One thousand Maratha cavalrymen follow him. He and his men mount their horses and kick them to a canter. A crescent moon hangs overhead as Raja Shivaji and Tanaji lead their men to Junnar. Within a few hours of riding in the dark, Shivaji finally spots it—the silhouette of a hill rising above the plains. As if eternally waiting for him to come by, it creates an illusion of a massive ship mounted on a steep rock. No one can really guess that Shivneri Fort is perched on the hill's crest. A strange pain cuts through his heart. He was born there. His earliest memories are of his brother's face, mischievous yet smiling.

With a shake of his head he collects his thoughts and concentrates on the present. At the end of the northern skyline, a shadow of Junnar's outer wall is clearly visible. They are already fifteen kos into the Mughal terrain. It is strange that they have faced no resistance yet. No one seems to have heard the hoof beats. But Shivaji is not surprised. His scouts have been roaming the terrain for months. The Mughals have become smug and confident. They fear no invasions and even believe that their region is too sacred to be attacked. At last, Shivaji notices an outline of a wall over the horizon to the north. Beyond the wall, the night sky glows pale yellow. The morning star shines bright in the east when they reach the base of the wall and gallop along its shadow. The outer wall is not fortified with a moat and there are no drawbridges to cross. As his scouts have already informed him, there are no archers or guards on the ramparts. He senses Tanaji slowing down his horse. They halt near a gate facing east. The tired and thirsty horses have started snorting. The animals are quickly taken away by caretakers who have ridden with Shivaji. Men with iron hooks and ropes are already at work. He waits as Yesaji hovers behind him. The ropes are flung. In the light of a single flickering torch held by Tanaji, the shadows of his men look like spiders busy scaling a wall.

'Clear,' Shivaji hears Tanaji call softly as he moves towards the wall. The wall is not high and the ropes are thick, easy to hold and grip. The ramparts are soon crowded with his men. Some of them begin to scale down the wall on the other side to enter the town. Shivaji jumps over the flat terrace of the western bastion to scout; he likes to do that, see for himself even though his men consider it as a security hazard. Below, between the market and the gate, a few men, probably guards, lie flat around the dying fires. They are very still, probably passed out on wine. The plaza is deserted and shops shut but the place is well lit by a number of torches placed in sand-filled iron baskets. Beyond the market, residential buildings stand clustered, dark and aloof. A few minarets and temple spires rise above them and glimmer in the faint moonlight.

The shadows of his men move across the plaza, noiseless, like predators. It is time to enter the wealthy town, now a part of the imperial territory. Tanaji is waiting for Raja Shivaji to descend. Shivaji scales the wall swiftly, facing the wall and taking short backward leaps. A shiver runs through his body as he puts his feet on the ground. Junnar—the town his father loved. His eyes wander eagerly. He notices a beggar standing with Salim at the market entrance. The beggar waves his hand and darts towards him, pointing at the eastern gate. Shivaji wants to know what the beggar implies. He notices gatekeepers scrambling to get up, their minds still in a drunken stupor. Some have started yelling. Tanaji along with a few swordsmen runs towards the unsteady guards. The yells grow louder while the imperial dust gets sodden with the blood of their own guards for the first time in history.

Shivaji waits with the beggar while Salim joins them. He marvels at how his scouts have seamlessly transformed into a beggar and a Muslim guard. The beggar is Bahirji, the master of Shivaji's spy network; his men have performed what was expected of them.

Tanaji and his men return, their swords dripping with blood. The beggar disappears with them. He seems to know the shops of the cash-rich merchants in the market. The men from the Maval region are in their element. They break open the wooden shutters and go straight for the iron vaults. The town seems to have woken up and the air vibrates with screams of the residents. The beggar turns up again, wielding an axe, and gives Raja Shivaji a signal. Shivaji wrenches out his sword from his scabbard and runs behind the beggar as Yesaji follows them. They stop in front of a large shop, its wooden doors closed shut. Before they can kick the door, it is opened from inside as a few men jump out brandishing swords. They are not trained swordsmen and seem to have never fought real fights. It takes only a few moments for them to fall. Shivaji enters the shop that is lit by a small oil lamp. With his axe, the beggar breaks open the trunk to spill across the floor countless ashrafi mohurs of high-quality gold.

Behind the market, two hundred Arabian horses are taken from the stables. Such fine horses are hard to come by. Tonight the fine animals will be used as the carriers of the plunder. Stolen Mughal horses will carry the stolen Mughal wealth to Shivaji's terrain.

CHAPTER SIX

1

'Ma sahib!' Jija bai hears her son call out to her.

Her frail body shivers as he touches her feet. She stares at him— he has become thinner and darker. His face looks more angular. She notices fine lines under his eyes. Her stomach churns. While she lives a comfortable life, mostly within the walls of their hill forts, he stays in the wilderness of enemy terrain, sleeps in the open and spends his days galloping under the sun, with the shadow of death looming over him.

'You have plundered the terrain of the Mughals!' she says with some pride and some trepidation, her eyes welling up.

Shivaji remains silent with his eyes fixed on his mother who had recounted to him the stories of the invaders. He remembers what she had said a long time ago while her eyes had shone with rage and helplessness, 'They have two weapons: one, their mind—pitiless, remorseless and empty of scruples; and the second, our mind— servile and fearful.'

'How could you *not* think of the consequences?' she asks. He had not told her about his plans.

It was easy to tell him about creating new frontiers when he was a small boy, safe under my wings, she thinks.

'You have sowed the seeds of new frontiers in my mind, Ma sahib, and they have turned into golden cobs of fearless dreams. They are steeped in ideas of freedom.' Then, as if he has read her mind, he says, 'Will the armies of the empires and the kingdoms not be aggressive and brutal if I refrain from doing that which I have?' he asks softly.

She fidgets uneasily and wraps her shawl around her shoulders. She knows what he means. Once she had told him the story of eastern Kabul, ruled by Maharaja Jayapala of the Hindu Shahiya dynasty six centuries ago. The Turks had started gnawing at his borders. His cavalry of countless elephants had crushed the marching armies. Then Mohammad Ghaznavi had arrived with his fifty thousand soldiers. Jayapala had declared truce, paying heavy ransom. Within a few years, Ghaznavi had returned. He had stormed, pounded and seized coins worth seven crore rupees and seven lakh carts of gold and silver. The bloods of men, women and children had flown into every stream, river, well and lake. There was not a drop of water to drink.

'If you fight them, they kill you; if you declare truce, they deceive you; if you kneel, they behead you. Now you choose your option,' she had told him a few years ago.

'After Maharaja Jayapala's fall, the dice of destiny was thrown against Hindustan. The invaders had arrived. They did not need provocation to be rabid,' her son whispers.

'I am worried about the present. The Mughal may not waste time. They may soon come—within days,' she replies.

He points at the sky. 'Mother, look at those dark clouds. They are on a mission. It is pouring in the valley. The rivers and streams are flooded. The trails and tracks have disappeared under water. They will have to wait for three long months to enter this region.'

Jija bai smiles nervously. The temple priest seems to have finished his ritualistic prayer. He emerges crouching from the small door of the temple and comes towards them. His salver has a silver lamp, its flame flickers with the wind. She holds her hand above the flame of the lone lamp and then touches her forehead, seeking blessings from the fire used in worship. As the priest turns towards her son to offer blessings, she glances at the sky; the clouds indeed seem ready to pour. She quickly enters the small temple. It is warmer inside, and smells of flowers and incense sticks. The lingam, adorned with freshly plucked mountain flowers, glows in the light of several earthen lamps. The power of God Shiva, of destruction and creation, has turned tangible in that small space. It is almost as if Jija bai can touch it or even take some of it away for later use. Her son has followed her. Raja Shivaji kneels, his hands folded, his eyes closed.

I have done what I had to do. They will do what they have always been doing. And you do what must be done, he prays.

When they step out, he tries to hold her hand to support her on the steps, but she is quick to jerk her hand away. He smiles, and knows that she has always cherished her independence. Her freedom and her self-reliance have been and continue to be her most prized possession. He stares at her—the large pearls in her nose ring and the red kumkum on her forehead makes her face look small, like it has shrunk. The lines around her eyes have become deeper with strain.

She has not finished her talk. 'After the monsoons Aurangzeb will unleash his squadrons. Our small region will soon burn in fires of arson. Peasants will flee. Women and children will be taken as slaves,' her voice cracks and her eyes shine with tears.

'The Mughals think that it is their imperial right to invade under the patriotic title of war of expansions. They do not need any provocation. They would do it anyway,' Shivaji says, his eyes showing shadows of a steely finality she has not seen before.

'Your father left us to serve the Adilshahi twenty years ago. We, you and I remained here to look after the estate. Meanwhile your father's rival in Bijapur court, Afzal Khan, killed your brother by not sending him reinforcements, on purpose. Shiva ba, I cannot lose *you*,' his mother tugs at her last defence.

'Death is final yet fickle. I do not have to be in the Mughal territory to die. I can die here, in the safe confines of Purandar—of snakebite!'

Jija bai winces. She does not like her son's definition of death. 'But offending Aurangzeb is like knowingly stamping on a snake. It is suicidal!'

Shivaji can see his mother losing her temper. 'Do you think that living like a coward will make me immortal? Mother, think, what will happen if Badi Sahiba and Ali Adil Shah renew the old peace treaty with Aurangzeb?'

Jija bai does not say a word. She knows. The alliance between the Mughal empire and the Adilshahi sultanate had once proved disastrous.

'We plundered the Mughal terrain because we needed the money for expanding our military. Also we wanted to kindle the fire of courage in the hearts of the Adilshahi rulers. We wanted to show them that one can fight the Mughals,' he says softly. 'And, despite our efforts, the renewal may take place. Peace at one front promotes war at the others. And if that happens, guess who may march in to get us?'

'Who?' Jija bai asks anxiously.

'Either Khan Mohammed, the general of the Adilshahi, or Afzal Khan. Ali Adil Shah has grown up into a clever man. He will take the enmity between Afzal Khan and Abba sahib into consideration. Afzal Khan is also the subhedar of the Wai province to which Jawali once belonged. Once the peace prevails at their north-eastern frontiers, Afzal Khan is free to war with us.'

Jija bai stares at her son intently.

'But I am prepared, Ma sahib,' Shivaji says and smiles.

And together they walk to the place where the bearers wait with her *mena* and his palanquin.

As the bearers climb another hillock called Rajgaddi, he muses quietly. He has his own laws of war and they say that the imperials are not gods and their terrain not sacred! But some things are forbidden, like mocking the religions of the defeated or slaughtering Muslims just because of their faith. His fight is different; his fight is for the freedom of his people.

'I want you to meet our very special guest. We had sent a message about his arrival when you were in the Mughal terrain,' Raja Shivaji hears his mother's words. They have reached their private apartments on the Rajgad hillock.

Shivaji's heart jumps up to his throat.

It is dark inside the stone buildings, and warm. It smells of burning incense and *ajwain* seeds. Seeing them enter, the maids busy with their morning chores quickly cover their heads. A few disappear into the inner chamber. Two are back within moments, holding a bundle. Excitement runs through his body, and it is divine, akin to seeing thousands of little lamps in a temple. He is scared to move, or even make any sound. The maids move nearer. Jija bai takes the bundle in her hands. She gently shows what she holds to her son.

He stares at the small face of his son, *his first son*. Tiny, as if carved by a sculptor out of fine, alabaster marble, using a toy hammer. A short mop of curly hair grows on his head like a crown. His tiny lips quiver as if he is about to smile or cry. His eyes are closed. There is a big dot of soot on his cheek—to ward off the evil eye. Shivaji gingerly touches the boy's face with his index finger and is shocked by the tenderness of the skin. The twenty-day-old boy starts to smirk and opens his eyes at once; they are not brown like his. The boy has black, limpid eyes, like his mother's.

'Go meet his mother,' Jija bai nudges him.

Shivaji enters the 'birth chamber' and several maids sitting around a bed scramble, bow to him and exit hastily. The yellow light of a few oil lamps fails to reach all the corners of the room. Mercifully, a sudden burst of rain starts pounding on the roof, driving out the stubborn stillness piled up around his wife. Pillars in the middle of the room stand in breathless anticipation, like shameless intruders. In that large foyer meant for women to deliver their babies, his Sayee sits on a huge mahogany bed, wearing a peacock green sari, the colour he likes. He removes his turban and stands in front of her, letting his hair fall on his shoulders. She looks up and stares at him unbelievingly; he looks handsome, his brown eyes, his gently curling tresses and the corded muscles of his shoulders visible through his angirkha. Her heart fills with enormous pride, and she feels scared that it might just burst. It has been months since she last set her eyes on the man she has loved ever since they got married.

'Did you see him?' she asks, smiling.

He looks at her. What he has heard is true. Not only does she look ill but also she *is* very ill indeed. Her doe eyes have dark circles under them and her collarbones jut out from near the hemline of her blouse. To him they look like sharp mountain ridges reeling under an attack. She has not bothered to cover her head. He notices that her long curls are all gone, taken as pillage by her illness. He takes her hands in his own, they have lost their softness. He raises them to inspect them closely; they look as if they belong to an old woman. The skin has shrivelled, making the bluish veins look swollen, like rivers in the valleys seen from the hill forts.

'He is beautiful and he has your eyes,' he whispers, looking into her dark, moist eyes shining with mysterious happiness.

She frowns and says, 'I hope he is born with your vision.'

'And your wit,' he intercepts, and asks, 'Have you and mother decided on his name?' It feels good to talk about their son. It reconfirms his existence.

She hesitates and says, 'I thought Sambhaji will be best. We have lost your brother, respected Dada sahib. Our boy might fill that void in Ma sahib's life.'

Shivaji stares at his young wife. She wants to name her son after his slain brother. He draws her closer. Sayee rests her head on his chest. Her eyes slowly fill with tears. She does not want him to know that during childbirth she had bled excessively. The fort midwife has warned that such bleeding could lead to something far more serious called the 'childbirth malady'. It claims half the women before their baby is two years old. But he knows much more. The fort medic suspects tuberculosis. Shivaji is utterly helpless while trying to hide his knowledge and feels as powerless as a soldier who has lost his sword on a busy battlefield.

'I am glad our son has been born in Purandar. This fort has taught you that you could stop them,' she murmurs.

'It is true,' he says, remembering Muse Khan's defeat.

'You need to go, we shall meet later in the day,' she whispers, trying to push the sobs down her throat.

She is right. Today's meeting is crucial. The pillage from the Mughal territory has been brought to Purandar. They need to plan how to put the funds to use. The construction of Pratapgad has been costly. After Jawali's capture, the number of his horsemen has risen to over ten thousand. They are being directly paid from the state treasury. He also plans to expand his infantry.

'Are you worried about the Mughal attacks?' he asks her softly.

'The Sahyadri Mountains offer divine protection in the monsoons. No one can enter this region. You have time,' Sayee responds. Her words render him speechless. Lying here, while her life is drained out of her slowly, she contemplates his military problems and their solutions.

'Sayee . . .' he whispers holding her close to him, 'you surprise me.'

'I cannot do anything else but think. And I cannot think of anything else but you,' she admits candidly. 'Please do not have doubts. Earnest and truthful karma is pregnant with wonders. Do you remember Mukta bai's poem? Isn't it so relevant even centuries after it was written?' she asks softly, as her lips quiver with memories. 'When we were children, we used to sing it often.' She pauses for a while and starts humming: 'An ant has flown to the sky and swallowed the sun. A wonder has happened; a barren woman has borne a son.'

Her words bring a smile to Shivaji's face and tears to his eyes. Sayee has this habit of saying what she wants to say through verses of famous saints. And she has memorized the writings of Mukta bai, the younger sister of Saint Gyaneshwar who had risen above superstitions and rituals of Hinduism.

'You live in my heart, Sayee,' he says softly.

Pointing upwards, Sayee responds, 'Mukta bai says, *His* spirit lives in our soul and only *He* is the abode of our hearts.'

Shivaji knows. She is preparing him for her death.

He is reluctant to leave; there is so much to say. But men are waiting for him. Today he is to announce the names of his central ministers. Pinglay will be rewarded with the prime ministership, and will henceforth be called the *peshwa* of the Maratha kingdom. Niloji Sondev will continue to be the *muzumdar*, and look after the financial matters of the state. Anna Datto, the scholar of mathematics, will assist Niloji Sondev and be the *surnis*, the man responsible for the revenue collection. Yesaji Kank will be the commander of Maval infantry. Tanaji Malusare will head the infantry garrisons at Konkan.

Sonoji Dabir continues to be the dabir and look after the external affairs. Raghunath Ballal Korde will be elevated to the position of the state *subnis*, the paymaster general who will work with the peshwa. And Netoji Palkar will be the *sarnobat*, the commander-in-chief of the Maratha army. Most of these men will also command Maratha squadrons in battles and defend the state in times of war. Shivaji remembers that Netoji Palkar has to meet Murarbaji, the new fort commander of Purandar, to orient the new *qiledar*.

2

The bastions are made of black stones, one a little bigger than the other. When Murarbaji had approached the bastions for the first time, he was surprised to discover that a gate to enter the fort was hidden between them. The ramparts of the fort wall run above the gate where a few archers march up and down with large quivers on their shoulders. They know that he has come to the fort just the day before and that he might be their new chief. They wave at him, smiling. A few drops of rain fall on him. *It is a good omen*, he thinks, looking at the sky. Dark clouds have gathered. The wind has turned gusty, making it difficult for him to stand still. For a moment, his eyes blink; a streak of lightning flashes across the sky. The clouds thunder, making the hills tremble, as sheets of rain start falling on the steps between the bastions. He runs for cover and stands under the massive stone arch of the gate along with a few gatekeepers stationed there to mind the entrance.

Jawali was his past. The moment he had collapsed unconscious on the battlefield had been the end of his old world. He had woken up with a huge gash on his shoulder and unbearable pain. It was Raja Shivaji who had come with the medic every morning for several days. The young man with brown eyes had watched without showing any revulsion, as the medic washed his wound and smeared it with clarified butter. Every day before they left, Raja had said to him, 'You will stay alive. I can read the invisible lines written on your forehead. I can see you fighting for me, leading my men to success.'

It was not an easy decision to make. He had lost his parents in a pox epidemic. He was small and weak, his brothers even smaller. The Morey family had given them shelter and food. His corded muscles were brimming with the rice, bread of pearl millets, soups of lentil that had come from Morey's kitchen. Someone had once commented about his natural talent and it was Chandrarao Sahib who had put him up for training. He had tried to repay his master by being loyal and obedient, complying with his wishes without ever asking questions. But when he had seen Pratapgad being constructed, his mind had changed. His master Chandrarao Sahib had never thought of building one such fort despite the mountains and the money. A hope had sprouted in his heart: to live for a bigger cause, and die for one.

Murarbaji is brought back to the present as rain lashes him from one side, carried in by the strong winds. The rain turns into a downpour. While he thinks of ways to remain dry, he notices a tall figure standing to his right.

'Scared of the rain? Let's move,' says Netoji Palkar gruffly.

Murarbaji shakes his head, but Palkar is impatient. He has already moved inside the fort and has turned left. Murarbaji's ego is slightly hurt. He runs behind to keep pace with Palkar's long strides. To their left, he can see a hill rising high. A hill above a hill! One can see quarters on its crest, partially blocked by a bastion. Palkar stops abruptly. Murarbaji almost bumps into him.

'This hill is called Rajgaddi, the king's seat, and the large house hidden behind the bastion is Raja Shivaji's home. Let me brief you about the fort first. Less than eight kos south-west of Pune, from the point of Kondana Fort, a branch of the Sahyadri Range turns towards the east. The same extension of the range is known as the mountains of Bhuleshwar. These hills are named after the innocent avatar of God Shiva. This range has many hills, and on one of the hills stands this fort.'

'Which is the nearest town?' Murarbaji asks, stopping Palkar's barrage.

'The fort is barely a few kos south-east of Saswad. It is a famous market in this region,' Palkar replies.

'How far is Purandar from the Adilshahi's borders?'

'Forty kos east is Indapur, our last eastern region. Fifteen kos south of Purandar is the Adilshahi's Wai province. Jawali was once a part of Wai, before it was given to the Moreys a hundred years ago. I hope you know that much,' Palkar is curt. He wants to stick to his agenda.

Murarbaji knows about the Wai province and its subhedar Afzal Khan. His late master was afraid of only one man. Chandrarao Sahib used to say, 'If we can save ourselves from Afzal Khan, even God cannot touch us!'

Palkar has now moved towards the east but waves his hand pointing northwards. 'As you will later see, it is easier for the enemy to enter from the north despite the steep slopes. The cliff drops to a short distance. The wall fortifications are stronger here. Remember, the watchtowers need to be manned at all times.'

Murarbaji listens with keen interest, no longer bothered by the rainwater that rolls down his face. He has heard about Palkar. This tall and middle-aged man with heavy brows, giant whiskers and a grim face loves very large turbans. He has been a military officer of Adilshahi. It is said that he rides a horse as if the animal is his slave and the earth his carpet. His swordfights are legendary, as if the blade of his sword is an extension of his hand, or sometimes, he is an extension of his sword. Palkar, the master of guerrilla tactics, is Raja Shivaji's guru. He and his men cut off the enemy's food and water supply and kill thousands by sheer dehydration and starvation.

According to the recent news, Raja has chosen Palkar as the sarnobat, the commander-in-chief of the Maratha army.

While on the move, Murarbaji is told about the *chowkie*s or the check posts dotting the hill, and about the watchtowers built in stone, called Nishana Burj, Shendri Burj, Hatti Burj and Konknya Burj. The rain's fury is over, it is now content being a drizzle. He is taken to a large stone chamber near the Konknya Burj. It is bare and has just one huge window. The wind barges in through it, strong and shrieking. A dark man armed with a large cleaver guards the window. Murarbaji peers down and immediately feels dizzy. The window opens on to a cliff, smooth and vertical black basalt plunging down into the valley.

He cannot see the valley now as a rain cloud floats between him and the abyss.

'Criminals sentenced to death are thrown from here. They are rolled in blankets, but their heads are not covered, on purpose.' He hears Palkar's chilling words.

'Which crimes are punishable by death?' Murarbaji is curious.

'Mainly treachery, but recently two of our soldiers were thrown down for molesting women,' Palkar answers with a blank face, and before Murarbaji can recover he finds himself running behind the sarnobat-to-be. He is shown some more chambers of granaries, ordinance depots and stockyards.

The rain has completely stopped now. So has Palkar. Murarbaji shivers with cold as mountain winds invade his drenched angirkha. It has been months since the Jawali war, but the wounds, though dried, still hurt with constant rain lashing on them.

'Remember, we have decided to hand over Purandar to you. You are its qiledar, the fort commander. This fort is hardly twenty kos south from the Bhima. Beyond the river is the Mughal terrain.' Palkar's dark eyes, surrounded by webs of wrinkles, bore into his eyes.

Murarbaji's chest swells with pride. Raja has given him a strategic fort!

Palkar notices shadows of pleasure fleeting across the newcomer's eyes. He says tersely, 'You are not the only man in charge of the fort. Three men are assigned to manage each of our forts: a qiledar, a subnis, usually a Brahmin to help the qiledar in clerical work, and the *karkhanees*, primarily a commissary of grain and stores. There will be other officials responsible for gate passes, patrols, watchtowers, stores of ammunition and weaponry. They will report to all three of you.'

'Who guards the foothills?' Murarbaji clears his throat and asks cautiously.

'Tribals are our foothill sentinels. The outcast Balutes, who do village work other than farming, are our foothill guards. Raja calls them *gadkari*s, the garrison men. And remember, under Raja, nobody is allowed to treat them as untouchables; they must be treated with utmost respect. They are on permanent assignments in Raja Shivaji's army. They have been given rent-free lands between the forts to till and make a comfortable living from.'

Murarbaji has never heard anything like this before.

'If you and I are the ramparts and bastions of the fort, they are the foundation. If you and I are the branches of the trees, they form the roots. We are more expendable than them.'

He just nods quietly. Palkar continues, 'There are a number of temples and lakes on this fort. The temple caretakers also have the hereditary right to mind the temples. A fixed amount is given to them. The fort may change hands but they are and remain the oldest inhabitants of the fort. These watandars and their families are directly under the care of the fort commander. This fort is a world in itself, equipped to face months of enemy besiegement.'

Murarbaji starts feeling the pressure of the enormous responsibility. Palkar once again walks towards the east saying, 'We need to climb a hillock. I need to show you something.'

Murarbaji is eager to ask something that is not related to Purandar. He gathers enough courage before they reach the foothills. 'Have you been to Dilli or Agra? Are these cities real?'

Palkar turns back and glares at this rustic man with large eyes who speaks Marathi in a strange accent. *A real idiot from the ghats of Jawali. The man is as stupid as a mule,* he thinks to himself, barely concealing his smile. The hills are full of village idiots like this one.

'I have not been to Dilli and Agra, but I lived in Bijapur for a few years,' he snaps. *What did Raja see in this man? Just the dhop swordsmanship?*

They come to the foothill of a large rock rising above Purandar Hill. Palkar climbs a slushy path holding on to the liana vines hanging down from the cliff like ropes. Murarbaji follows him gingerly, his clothes soaked and heavy. It is very slippery as even the rocks jutting out from the muddy earth are covered with moss. It takes them a while to reach the top of the hillock. At the end of the trail is a watchtower. The wind is at its strongest at this point. He sees a bastion over the hillock and notices a few archers pacing the tower.

'This is the Kandakada. From this watchtower you can see the fort called Vajragad protecting Purandar.' Palkar is shouting to be heard over the shrill wind.

Murarbaji looks down towards the north and notices a ledge. It is hardly four guj wide and is strengthened by two watchtowers at its north-east corner. The towers rise high above the wall. One is painted white and the other black. Between them, on the rampart joining the two, is a large cannon mounted on a platform.

'These towers are vital to launch an attack if the enemy does reach the smaller fort. Below those towers is an underground vault to store cannonballs and explosives.'

Murarbaji glances at another hill beyond the watchtowers. It is separated from Purandar Hill by a shallow ravine.

'If the Mughals come from the north or the Adilshahi cavalry marches in from the east, they will first encounter Vajragad. The hill of Vajragad seems easy to climb so if they reach the top of that hill, they can bring down the black and white watchtowers with explosives. Then it is just a matter of crossing the shallow ravine and reaching one of the gates of Purandar,' Murarbaji rattles.

'That's a remote possibility,' Palkar replies hesitantly. *I guess the idiot is not such a simpleton after all.*

'Vajragad terraces are at a much lower level than the Purandar fortifications that are at a much higher level. It is not easy to bring the towers down,' Palkar wants to have the last word.

'But it is not impossible either, if the enemy is clever enough to put the cannon on scaffolds. Purandar's weapon can turn into its weakness.' Even as Murarbaji muses, an unknown fear grips him. His eyelid has started twitching, and that is not a good omen.

CHAPTER SEVEN

1

The Dilli monsoon has been delayed. Afternoons in the imperial capital have turned unbearably hot. Khus curtains have been taken out from the attics, sprinkled with water for coolness and fragrance. The poor are seen heaving carts on the roads or carrying loads at the city's numerous construction sites with waterskins tied to their backs. The rich prefer to be indoors in the afternoons. The capital wears a deserted look as its lonely streets languish under the listless trees. Above the canopies the gilded minarets and dome pinnacle bear the brutality of the sun. Its reflections hurt the eyes that dare to glance up at the sky. Mirza Raja Jai Singh's mansion in the elitist area of the imperial capital is surrounded by a lush garden. It is hedged with woody shrubs, covered with clusters of white tubular flowers, blooming and verdant as if the long-drawn summer is not allowed to touch it. The sweeping building with arched corridors and a massive, enormous dome stands on the banks of a placid lake. The courtyard seems busy. A rider has arrived from the *Qila-e-mubarak*, the blessed fort. Emperor Shah Jahan wants to see Mirza—*now!*

As the house servants fuss over him, the rider waits in the courtyard sipping sweetened milk laced with crushed almonds. The gardens, the arabesque marble statues, the fountains and the flowerbeds—he has seen it all. But what surprises him is the temple in the courtyard. Its spire rises high over the carved marble patio resting on two gold pillars. Atop of the gilded pinnacle a saffron flag ripples fearlessly with unnerving pride. Mirza Raja Jai Singh is the blue-eyed mansabdar of the emperor. He is even allowed to hoist a saffron-coloured flag, regarded auspicious by the Hindu Rajputs.

Inside, on the second floor, Mirza is in a hurry. The fifty-year-old descends the stairs and into the courtyard with the agility of a young man. A servant appears with a stallion. Leaving behind the wide, tree-lined streets of Jaisingpura, a suburb named after him, he gallops behind the rider. He is concerned; all sorts of rumours about the emperor's illness have been floating in the city—like vultures encircling the sky above a battlefield, sinister yet sure. Agra's social grapevine is buzzing with gossip. Some say the emperor's illness is terminal. Mirza has not seen his master for a while. What worries him is the sure-shot sign that the emperor has not taken out state processions for a long time. Shah Jahan loves to show off his wealth and military might.

The fort's walls are made of red sandstone. Its turrets and bastions gleam in the golden light of the afternoon sun. The arched watchtowers with intricate cupolas rising above the wall look graceful. The gate and the path leading to the courtyards are well-guarded. As they enter, the sight of the many-pillared *diwan-e-khaas* reminds Mirza of the emperor's court in progress where Shah Jahan sits on the peacock throne, in the shade of a pearl-fringed canopy, supported by gold columns glittering with diamonds and rubies. The princes, the grand wazir, the mir bakshi, the mir atish, the clergy, the mansabdars and the ambassadors from far-off countries stand with their eyes downcast, reluctant to look directly at the emperor. But Mirza loves to gaze at his master whom he considers as his father. Emperor Shah Jahan's fair skin shimmers with health and his fetching features gleam with confidence while he bestows titles, promotions honours and awards.

It has been quite some time since the last court was held.

Mirza is intrigued. The rider takes a right turn towards the private apartments of the emperor. Shah Jahan never holds meetings in his quarters. A contingent of tartar women encircles the royal quarters. The muscular women belong to a warrior tribe whose ancestors lived on the banks of the river Volga. The emperor trusts them to guard his forts and palaces. The women soldiers wear armour, trousers and helmets and seem unmindful of the bright sun. Their faces are covered with thin, transparent veils but their hands hold long spears, with sharp steel heads. Their kohl-lined, emotionless eyes dart in Mirza's direction without blinking. These women are trained in hand-to-hand combat and one can easily handle several men at a time. The riders dismount and the horses are taken away. The messenger nods at one of the women, and the circle breaks for the men to enter.

It takes a while for Mirza to adjust to the darkness. It is much cooler in the room. Huge satin sheets sway above them to produce arterial air currents.

He understands the gravity of the situation only when he sees the emperor. A large bed is kept in the middle of the enormous chamber. The curtains are drawn. A chandelier hangs at the far corner of the room. It is the only source of light but it infuses more dullness than brightness into the chamber. The emperor lies flat on his enormous bed; the first prince sits by his father's side with his hands folded in his lap. Two medics whisper to each other in a corner, their eyes occasionally darting towards their patient. The smells of strange herbs pervade the room.

It is been almost eight months since Mirza has seen the emperor. An epidemic had ravaged Dilli and the nearby areas. The air had reeked of rats lying dead on the streets, in the houses and on the steps of the mosques and temples. Even the tanners were afraid to collect them. He had heard that people had died like flies. Some had developed swelling in the groins or armpits before they had breathed their last. The city's avenues had come alive only when the dead were taken for cremation or burial. The rich had fled the city. The emperor had sailed fifty kos in his royal yacht to live in his palace at the base of the hills of Sirmur.

Mirza has also heard of a gala function that was held at Sirmur to mark the three decades of the emperor's reign. The recently polished seven-hundred-and-fifty-six-carat diamond called the Koh-i-noor had been kept on display for dignitaries to admire. Mirza had not attended the function; he had taken his family to Jaipur to avoid the epidemic.

He moves softly towards the emperor and bows deep. '*Jahanpanah . . . Zohr bekheir, Jahanpanah*.' Mirza urges the emperor to accept the greetings from him, and wishes the emperor a good afternoon in Urdu and Farsi. He always addresses Emperor Shah Jahan as *jahanpanah*, meaning 'the sanctuary of the world', as the Iranis call their emperor.

The emperor, who controls an army of five lakh men, painfully strains to see his most trusted Rajput mansabdar, and speaks slowly, 'We need your help . . .' The emperor gasps. Mirza does not remember his master ever *asking* for help—much less in such a pathetic manner.

He keeps a stoic face. The emperor has given his utmost all his life. The entire ritual of 'giving' seems to take place before Mirza's eyes at that very moment. As the diwan-e-khaas shimmers under the massive chandeliers, Muslim mansabdars wait to receive the title of *khan*, or very exclusive titles such as *khan-e-khanan*. The Hindu mansabdars wait, wondering whether their new title will be *raja*, *rao* or *rai*. The beaming emperor distributes *khilat*s, the robes of honour, *serpech*, the ornaments that adorn the turban, rings engraved with titles, jewellery, hunting dogs, race horses, war elephants and even jagirs or mansabs as gifts. The receiver performs kurnish, bowing three times as he approaches the throne, bending down to the ground so that the back of his right hand touches the floor. The man gets up and touches his forehead with the back of his hand, as if offering his mind and body to the emperor.

But now the emperor seems to be losing his mind and body. The grim-looking hakims have started discussing agitatedly. 'Shhhhh,' Dara Shikoh quietens the noisy medics and speaks to him, 'We need all the help we can muster.' Dara, who is in his early forties, looks younger than his age with his child-like skin and oval face. He is undoubtedly the most handsome among his brothers.

'The shadow of war looms over us,' the emperor whispers.

The life of an emperor is such an illusion, like fireworks that dazzle in the sky for a brief moment and are as suddenly gone, Mirza muses.

That brief moment has lasted for over three decades for Shah Jahan. The man lying on the bed, who controls eight thousand mansabdars and their two lakh horses, looks nothing like an emperor. His skin is covered with moles and is hanging listlessly under his chin, his usually henna-dyed hair still a vibrant red but greying at the roots. The king of Jaipur, Mirza has grown up under the care of the emperor. At a very young age, he had walked away from his kingdom to join the imperial army. For the past several years, the emperor had depended on him to head many wars of expansions—from Afghan in the north to Deccan in the south and from Kandahar in the west to Mungir in the east.

'The emperor's illness is supposed to be a state secret. Only these hakims and very few noblemen know about it. Even my sisters at Agra have no clue. But I am not so sure about my brothers,' the first prince speaks gravely, his limpid, *surma*-smeared eyes boring into Mirza's. A large, gold serpech fixed on Dara's turban dazzles in the dim room.

'It is time to be ready. What do you think?'

In what world does Dara Shikoh live? Mirza wonders. The rich and elite of Agra have already started gossiping about the emperor's illness. But the man before him is Dara Shikoh, the first prince, backed by undue privileges. Who can challenge Dara Shikoh, the 'crown prince'?

'What you say is true, my prince,' Mirza murmurs.

'We have consulted astrologers. My father is destined to live long,' Dara Shikoh says with overt confidence, as if he desperately wants to believe in his own words. 'But even the mere news of his illness will drive my brothers to the capital to claim the throne. Battles may rage around us.' Dara comes straight to the point.

Dara knows well that his family history is bleak. The sons of the emperor have only three choices—either to be the next emperor or to be murdered or to spend the rest of their lives being tortured in the dungeons. Humayun had two brothers. One was sent to Mecca where he mysteriously died and the other, who had dared to proclaim himself as the next emperor, was blinded. His eyeballs were wrenched out of their sockets and the empty holes filled with salt water. Humayun's son Akbar mercifully had no brothers to kill or blind. But there was a cousin who had died in the notorious political prison of Gwalior Fort of opium overdose. Emperor Akbar's sons had simply drunk themselves to death. Only Salim, alias Jahangir, had been lucky to survive his drunken orgies and opium bouts. His throne had been threatened by his own son Khusro, skilled in military training. Emperor Akbar doted on his grandson. After his father's death, Jahangir had crushed his own son's uprising, had blinded him and thrown him in the dungeons. And Mirza's master, Shah Jahan, had no alternative but to kill or blind uncles, half-brothers, cousins and their sons till his empire was cleansed of all the men who could or would aspire for the throne. Some were forced to go into exile to Iran. Even the little son of the blind and imprisoned half-brother Khusro was slaughtered in his sleep. But if Mirza's master had not done what he had, he would have been resting in his grave for thirty years now.

'We have decided on a strategy to stop them from coming closer to the capital. It is time to don the armour, Mirza; you will go east to deal with Shuja,' says the emperor softly.

'Shuja bhai seems to know. The news is that he has planned his coronation ceremony, as the next emperor, in his constituency. I had to let father know this shameful news.' Dara Shikoh's words shock Mirza. He looks at the emperor. Shah Jahan's eyes shine with tears. The second prince wants to declare himself the next emperor while the emperor is still alive. There is nothing more agonizing in the world than the realization that your son wishes you dead.

'I will be ready, Jahanpanah,' Mirza says, his face reflecting the pride in his heart. Dara Shikoh's son, Suleiman, the emperor's favourite grandson, is to take an assignment under him. This does justice to his status.

However, Dara Shikoh knows how Mirza's mind works. The truth is that Suleiman will go along with Mirza to keep an eye on him.

The silence in the chamber is chilly. Suddenly it is interrupted by the emperor's bout of cough. The medics take charge.

'Even Murad has been acting strangely,' says Dara Shikoh. Mirza is intrigued.

'Who will deal with Prince Murad Baksh?' he asks softly.

'Murad is not a threat. The real peril is Aurangzeb. He has collected crores of rupees from Deccan sultanates and has not deposited them in the empire's treasury, he has got huge funds from Bidar conquest to support his military,' the emperor snaps, his head now resting comfortably on silky pillows. There is a fleeting shadow of pain in his eyes. His forth and youngest son, Murad, has grown up to be a foolish and a pleasure-seeking drunkard. In the battlefields, when the carnage rages around him, he lets himself drown in the delight of mindless slaughter. Such a man cannot have brains to plan his strategies. But the third prince, Aurangzeb, has the brains, cunning and wherewithal. His most dangerous weapon is his calm and practical mind that remains unfazed. But Aurangzeb hates Dara, and if he becomes the emperor, the first prince will surely be slaughtered. Shah Jahan's stomach churns with anxiety and his mouth fills with bitter acid. He gulps it to curb another bout of cough. 'One is *anntar* and the other a *heyvoon!*' He calls Murad a baboon and Aurangzeb a beast.

'Does Aurangzeb know about the illness?' Mirza asks warily.

'We don't know,' Dara Shikoh admits.

'What has been planned to stop him?' Mirza is curious.

'What do you suggest?' Dara frowns, but avoids answering.

Mirza ponders for a while. It is not an easy question and there cannot be a single solution. He feels uncertainty for the first time in many years. It is a new emotion for him. 'To begin with, it will be advisable to call back the reinforcements.'

'That's done; Nasiri Khan, Rao Chatrasal, Mir Jumla, Kartalab Khan and others have been contacted directly. They will soon get our farmans and return along with their squadrons.'

'Who goes to the south to stop him?' Mirza asks cautiously.

Dara does not want to give away any name. He knows that the Rajputs are strong military men, each supported by thousands of their warrior clansmen. If he fails to handle the one who stands in front of him, he can never be the emperor. But there is also a weakness. These warriors from the sands of Rajasthan can turn insanely jealous of each other. Dara Shikoh has learnt to play one against another. And he will do so when and if the war of succession breaks out.

'Is it Jaswant Singh Rathod?' Mirza asks directly.

'Maybe, but we have not yet decided,' the emperor sounds truthful.

Mirza stands quietly. Jaswant Singh, the king of Jodhpur, is hardly his son's age, but in military ranks he stands higher. They have bestowed him with the title of Maharaja, meaning a great king, while his own title, Mirza, means 'the son of a king'.

'My last wish on this earth is that my first son, my Dara, becomes the emperor after I am gone,' Shah Jahan whispers. The whole world knows it, and the emperor has made it clear over the years. But it is the first time Mirza actually hears it from his master's lips. *When strong men wish, their wish is a command. When weak men wish, their wish is a weak hope. But when strong men gone weak hang on to their old wishes, what happens?* Mirza wonders and looks at his master. Shah Jahan, *the king of the world*, reminds him of a dying sparrow with a fractured wing.

'*Abba jaan*, you are not going anywhere for a long time.' Dara Shikoh cannot bear the thought of his father's death. Future without father is too bleak.

2

The long-awaited monsoons have finally arrived at Bidar, offering relief from the oppressive summer. The walled city that stands on the highest point of the eastern Deccan plateau looms over a shallow valley with gently rolling hills. The slopes have turned brilliantly green. The fort at the eastern face of the city is protected by another high wall and a deep moat. Cut in solid rock, it is twenty-five guj in width. Palaces, mosques, Turkish baths, a mint, weapon stores, courtrooms and many other buildings fill the fort's courtyard. The enormous gates, battlements and palaces are awash with rain and sparkle in the evening light. The open spaces between the red buildings are filled with lush green lawns and manicured flowering shrubs.

The main courtyard has neat piles of red lateritic stones here and there. More than a thousand labourers on the scaffolds repair the bastions and the fortifications that have been damaged in the recent battle. It is still drizzling when Aurangzeb walks out of the sixteen-pillared mosque, his favourite place in the fort. However, his heart is thumping with rage. Within a month of his meeting with Dabir, Shivaji has raided the imperial territories. The first attack had been on Junnar. They had taken away more than ten thousand gold coins, countless sacks of jewels, clothing and two hundred priceless Arabian warhorses. Thereafter, Shivaji's horsemen had spread in all directions, cutting off supplies and ransacking wealthy villages. The entire region had become unsafe for travellers. Merchants had stopped trading in the area. Many shopkeepers had fled. Even the city of Ahmednagar was not spared.

When Aurangzeb faces the main entrance of the fort, he notices a few horsemen entering through the main gate. They are the men from Samarkand. He quickly turns to his left and rushes towards the palace apartments. Mutamad is holding an umbrella over his head. The eunuch starts running to keep up with his master. After crossing the many-arched corridor supported by enormously massive pillars, Aurangzeb steps into a foyer lit by countless tall brass lamps called *shamdans* and a chandelier.

Kartalab Khan wonders about why he has been summoned from the battlefield. The Mughal army is trying to crush Bijapur. They have already taken over parts of the Adilshahi sultanate to the south and west of the capital. When he enters the foyer he finds his employer sitting on a throne made of ebony and gold. Aurangzeb is counting the beads of his rosary with half-closed eyes. Two guards armed with javelins stand behind him. It is rumoured that the third prince changes his personal guards every alternate day, sometimes every day. But that is not Kartalab's business.

'Our terrain has been disturbed by Shivaji and his bandits. I want you to join our other mansabdars, Nasiri and Iraj, to restore order.' Aurangzeb narrows his eyes and continues, 'Slaughter everyone, take captives and drag them to our camps. Teach Shivaji's men a lesson. Make them writhe in such agony that they beg for death.'

If he could, Aurangzeb would have loved to flog the Maratha by a whip made of raw hide, in public, till he would fall at his feet. Instead, a blade of fury cuts through his body. He shudders, as a feeling of violation shakes him. What they have taken is utterly insignificant in terms of money. It is a question of the universal perception of the invincibility of the imperial territories. It is about keeping the flames of fear burning strong. But Shivaji is showing them dangerous possibilities. The lambs of the Deccan may grow a carnassial and turn into tigers.

Karlatab Khan nods rather vigorously. He has heard that Nasiri Khan was successful in driving away the Marathas from the imperial region. But it was also said that the heavy rains, more than the bravery of Nasiri, had made the Marathas retreat. In fact, it was rumoured the plan had been precisely that—to vanish just before the rains.

'Prepare your men to march into the mountains,' were Aurangzeb's orders.

Kartalab wonders how he would march into the hilly region in this season. He has heard that the continuous downpour has lashed the hills and valleys of the region. The hill forts illegally occupied by Shivaji have become more remote to the plains.

'Have no mercy, ruin his jagir, burn his villages, kill, enslave, do what you please,' says Aurangzeb. He wants his squadrons to go berserk with violence.

Life is a djalyab, Kartalab Khan curses softly in Turkish, calling life a bitch. Aurangzeb does not hear his words. Just before he was to meet the third prince, people had warned Kartalab not to promise a monsoon invasion. They had told him that the rains in the western Deccan turn brutal. The rivers in the hilly region become so aggressive that villagers frequently spot elephants flowing downstream like mere twigs.

'Yes, master,' Kartalab Khan says and bows deep.

The man from Samarkand hates to say yes to everything his master says, but he has no alternative. He is an Uzbek. The region beyond Afghanistan and Persia had lost its major source of income when the Europeans had opened up the sea routes. The trade between Hindustan, the Arab lands and Europe had thus moved away from the Silk Route passing through his region. Men from Uzbek, Tajik, Kazak, Turkmen and Kyrgyz ethnic groups had suddenly found themselves out of work. Kartalab had been lucky. Now, Aurangzeb has made him a mansabdar of two thousand horses, and may even offer him a jagir. Life has been comfortable, more so because he, like most from his region, is a Sunni and speaks Farsi. He is also tall, fair and has light eyes.

'I will do all I can, even face death to fulfil the wishes of my imperial prince,' Kartalab mutters, bowing more deeply than usual.

4

Afzal Khan has arrived from the north-eastern frontiers of the Adilshahi sultanate. He has ridden several hours to reach Bijapur after abandoning the battlefields littered with his dead soldiers—for a purpose. The imperial dogs have outnumbered his garrisons, and have slain and captured thousands. He and the Adilshahi's other commanders have lost everything. The Mughal beasts have wrenched their arms, transport cattle, cannon, gunpowder, slave girls and horses. Villages after villages from Gulbarga, south of Bidar, to Kalyan, west of Bidar, have been razed to dust. The once-peaceful habitats dotted with red tiled roofs are now piles of rubble splattered with blood. Not even a trace of tillage has survived the imperial gallopers and their roving eyes. The northern strongholds of the kingdom like the fort city of Bidar have fallen. But that is not the reason Afzal has come all the way to Bijapur. He has come to the capital to remove a thorn from his career path.

He stares at the wall surrounding Bijapur. It is massive and strong, ten to fifteen guj high and seven guj wide. It is fortified with continuous ramparts and ninety-six bastions, not counting ten more at the gates. The ramparts are protected by battlemented curtain walls from the inside, and are designed for artillery and small arms. He smiles wearily, and kicks his stallion to a trot. Sayed Banda, his chief guard, is riding alongside him. Fifty armed guards follow their master silently.

He chews a betel leaf as they move towards the Alipur gate guarded by two circular watchtowers. The enormous doors made of thick wooden beams, fastened together by iron clamps, strengthened by massive bars and bristling with long steel spikes, are quickly thrown open for him. The sentries kneel in his honour. Someone tells Afzal that the Badi Sahiba has been informed and wants to meet him.

Entering Bijapur always makes the khan feel at home. His kohl-lined eyes wander to the eastern edge of the city where enormous timber scaffoldings rise as if to touch the sky. Tiny figures of labourers are seen hanging over them. They have been building a mausoleum for the past fifteen years. It has the largest dome in the entire world. A faint outline of a huge, dark-grey cupola is seen through the scaffolds. The structure is his master's tomb. Afzal's heart aches; he misses the dead king of the sultanate.

'The world was a different place when Mohammed Adil Shah Sahib was alive,' he says to Sayed in Deccan Urdu, his eyes distant, perhaps gazing at the past.

Sayed nods. He knows his master loved the late king and is loyal to the Badi Sahiba. But there is a problem. The Badi Sahiba loves her son Ali more than anything in the world, despite him not being born of her womb. Even the old courtiers do not have a clue regarding the boy's origin. Adoption of a child is not recognized by Islam, so Ali is not their real king. And Ali does not trust Afzal Khan the way his father did, adding insult to injury.

They pass through markets, streets lined with elephant stables, temples and mosques. The shops are opening, getting ready for the morning business. When he was very young and very poor, Afzal loved to walk through these markets admiring the objects displayed on the shop windows. 'They have no clue what's happening at their borders!' Afzal spits with disgust.

Sayed remains alert, scanning every building and its windows like a hawk. His quiver is full, his bow hangs over his left shoulder and his pata sword is safe in his scabbard. Sayed knows his master hates crowds.

'It has taken me half my life to get over this rotting smell of food,' Sayed hears his master say. He has heard this before and knows why. He glances at Afzal Khan, looks straight ahead, his eyes shining, perhaps with tears, or with memories.

Afzal appreciates Sayed's silence. Nothing has come easily to him. Little Afzal had to run and jostle for every bit he had achieved. He had shed tears of blood and sweat for things other boys had taken for granted. His mother had worked at the palace. While she had washed and cut heaps of vegetables, he had run errands to get meat or spices; while she had cleaned a roomful of pots and pans, he had dried them with a cloth till his hands had ached.

'The late king has given me a new life,' he murmurs while Sayed looks at him with reverence.

That was so true. Afzal was going through a phase of severe depression which was abated only by eating. However, that had slowly turned him into a fat lump. This went on until one day Mohammed Adil Shah spotted him and urged his queen to remove him from the kitchen and put him up for military training. Afzal had loved the camp and had enrolled to learn construction and demolition tasks, wrestled with charging bulls, dragged wheels at the oil mills to turn his bulk into hard muscles. When other boys' fathers had come to see their sons' progress, he had scrambled to hone his skills in sword-fighting and archery, seemingly watched by none. The day he was appointed a soldier, he had gone to meet his mother. But she had long since died, and nobody had bothered to inform him.

'The late king used to call me a *farzand*, a son,' he says wistfully, glancing at Sayed.

Mohammed Adil Shah had done more than that. He had asked Ranadulla Khan, the general of the Adilshahi army, to take Afzal under his wings. Afzal had worshipped the general and the general had also liked him. He had honoured Afzal by first making him the subhedar of Karnataka and then of the Wai province in Maharashtra. But the general had also passed away all too soon. Khan Mohammed, an African Muslim, was made the grand wazir and the army general of the sultanate. The new wazir hates Afzal Khan and is a Bhosale supporter. A single stroke of fate changed Afzal Khan's destiny. His dream of going up in the military ranks is shattered. As long as Khan Mohammed lives, Afzal's dream cannot turn into reality. But now the time has come to correct the state of things and put them in the right order.

Afzal dismounts at the entrance and a few men rush to take his horse. He can only go alone and on foot. Briskly moving towards the ruler's court, the khan prays for success. The many-pillared court is well lit. Twenty-year-old Ali Adil Shah sits on the gilded throne, his dark skin gleaming in the yellow light from the twinkling chandeliers. Beyond the translucent curtains, he can make out the silhouette of the Badi Sahiba, Ali's mother. They are waiting for him. He first bows in the direction of the curtain, and then to the young king.

Ali Adil Shah is closely watching the subhedar of Wai. Bidar has fallen and other cities are under threat. What's the reason for Afzal Khan to rush to the capital?

'*Khosh amadid*, Afzal Khan ji, speak,' Ali welcomes his warrior in Farsi.

'I have rushed from the frontiers with news that is far worse than the defeat we have suffered at the hands of the imperialists,' Afzal says softly.

Ali blinks. His head buzzes with doubt.

'Speak your mind,' the Badi Sahiba speaks aristocratically from behind the curtains.

'We had once succeeded in besieging Aurangzeb and his squadron, cutting off their water and food supplies. Soon they would have had to surrender to us ...' The warrior speaks carefully, choosing each word with utmost care.

Ali stares at his enormous commander whose voice is effeminate, a contrast to his appearance. The man wearing a jewel-studded headgear is bull-necked, dark-skinned and abnormally tall and muscular.

'I do not quite understand,' Ali says. There is silence behind the curtains.

'The Mughal prince was in our hands. A message had come from Aurangzeb, I have seen the epistle. I was there when they read it out loud. Aurangzeb had begged for mercy, he had promised to retreat.' Afzal Khan waits for some reaction, perhaps a comment, but the duo seems speechless with shock. Afzal glances around as if uneasy.

'Go on,' Ali is listening very attentively. He is irritated by Afzal Khan's deliberate delay in revealing the information.

'The letter was replied to in a strange manner. It said, "Early tomorrow morning, get your men ready, make a forced escape. We will let you go."'

There is a gasp from Badi Sahiba. An excited Afzal continues, 'Our siege was broken at places. Aurangzeb was allowed to escape. Very few from our camp know the truth.'

'Who signed the order? Who was in command?' Badi Sahiba demands in fury. What a waste of an opportunity! Years of tension, crores spent in keeping the Mughal at bay, Aurangzeb's humiliating letters calling them the Shia rulers, the heretics, the misbelievers ...

'It is not easy for me to spill his name. I have already endangered my life by having a major argument with him on this issue,' he says evenly.

'You have our protection. Spit the name,' Ali retorts, thumping his right hand on the throne's railings.

'Khan Mohammed Sahib, the sultanate's esteemed general and grand wazir. But for him we would have had Aurangzeb in our hands like a lamb,' Afzal says loudly, wiping his forehead with his large hands.

There is a dazed silence in the court. Even the chandeliers look pale and disenchanted.

'*Fetne kardan!*' Ali curses in Farsi, accusing his general of instigating sedition.

Afzal expects a barrage of questions, and one mistake might take him where he does not want to go. He needs to change the subject quickly. He suddenly says confidently, 'Shivaji Bhosale and his men have attacked the Mughal territories.'

'We know of that,' Badi Sahiba snaps. 'He attacks them while they are ruining us.'

'Afzal Khan,' he hears Ali Adil Shah's words laced with scorn. 'Had Shivaji Bhosale been with us, we may not have lost strongholds like Bidar and Kalyan.'

CHAPTER EIGHT

1

The courtyard of Bidar Fort is busy with labourers finishing the repair work. Inside the courtroom, Aurangzeb sits on late Siddi Marjan's throne worth four crore rupees, his fingers counting the beads of his tesbih. He glances at his scribe who sits behind a small wooden desk, surrounded by piles of papers. He winces. All those letters written and received to and from his military officers are as good as autumn leaves. His fierce battles with the Shia kingdoms have been an utter waste of time.

Aurangzeb's mood is as gloomy as the weather outside. Something is seriously wrong. He has received a farman from the emperor telling him to stay put at Bidar. His mansabdars like Mahabat Khan, Rao Chatrasal, Nasiri Khan, Kartalab Khan and his artillery chief Mir Jumla have been contacted directly and have been called back along with their contingents. They are already on their way to Dilli. Shaista Khan has been asked to go back to his province and is already at Burhanpur. The emperor has also played dirty by directly establishing contact with the Adilshahi rulers for the tribute money. *He*, Aurangzeb, the subhedar of the Mughal-occupied Deccan, who has struggled to take over military strongholds of the Adilshahi sultanate like the fort cities of Bidar and Kalyan, has been sidelined, as if he bears no significance. What kind of message will the Adilshahi rulers get? These events will leave him without a work force, respect and funds in an enemy territory! He will be a military destitute—the worst insult for a prince . . .

'There is a rider at the gate. He wants to see you in person, my prince,' Mutamad informs Aurangzeb.

'Let him come, with our guards,' Aurangzeb becomes alert. The message has surely not come with the *daroga-e-daak*, the official imperial postman. An official postman would never insist on delivering the mail personally to him.

Several moments pass before Aurangzeb hears footsteps. A man appears and bows. He seems exhausted by his task.

'My Imperial Highness, the message is from Dilli, given to me at Burhanpur by khan-e-khanan Shaista. It is tied to my chest.'

Aurangzeb glances at the owner of the drained voice. The messenger has fallen on his knees. His turban is filthy and his jacket is soiled. On a signal from him, the guards pull the man up like a rag doll, make him stand and pull out his jacket. The strings run from his shoulder to his back. One of the guards shoves his fingers below the strings and yanks hard. The messenger cries out in pain, as the skin near his neck is pinched. The epistle is free. One guard hands it over to the prince.

'Take him away,' Aurangzeb says curtly. His hands tremble as he reads the letter:

The emperor is shifted to Agra. He is ill, kept in a curtained chamber at his private quarters in Agra Fort. Only two hakims are allowed in. The area is heavily guarded by armed tartar women. Dara Shikoh spends most of his time with the emperor.

The farmans that have the emperor's seal have probably been written by the first prince, Dara Shikoh, who has taken it for granted that he will be the next emperor!

There is the symbol of a crescent moon where the signature should be.

Aurangzeb understands instantly that the letter is from Isa Beg, his trustworthy envoy. He starts shaking in fury and shock.

The epistle becomes an obsession. That evening, Aurangzeb reads the message several times in the privacy of his apartments in the Rangeen Mahal. *What must he do?* Obey the emperor's latest farman and stay put at Bidar? But that may give Dara bhai the time and means to muster an army. It is risky not to obey the official decree. *What if Father has recovered? What if the farman had been really sent by him?*

Aurangzeb tries to calm his mind while he paces like a caged tiger. A few lamps burning in their tiny glass bulbs throw dim light over the walls. Suddenly, his new acquisition, the Bidar Fort, feels like a dungeon, a pit. He needs to get away, go north. He wants to be a bird and fly this very moment to the room where the emperor lies, to know what has happened to his father. *Is the old man really sick or already dead?*

The intricately carved wooden pillars throw long shadows on the mosaic floor. They look mysterious, as if beckoning him to find answers in their bellies. Something flashes in his mind. *What if he finds a legitimate reason to leave Bidar, a reason strong enough to overrule the royal decree? Is it possible?*

'La ilaha illa'llah!' he prays loudly. *There is no God but Allah.* As the chandelier shimmers, walls with exquisite floral designs gleam, and the shadows on the intricately carved wooden pillars keep drawing long beams of darkness over the floor. He is startled to see Mutamad walk in, with another epistle. This time the man with the slight feminine sway in his walk is sobbing. Aurangzeb instinctively knows what the message is. *Father is dead!* He stands below the chandelier to read the letter. His hands feel a slight tremor and his stomach churns as his eyes move from one word to the other. It is about his beloved wife. She is dead. The woman he had gradually fallen in love with is dead. The mother of his three daughters and two sons has become 'beloved of Allah'. His Persian wife Dilras Banu, his only Muslim consort, whom he had married in a grand ceremony twenty-four years ago, when he was barely seventeen, has died of 'childbirth malady' in Aurangabad. His children born by her, including their newborn son who still is unnamed, need him direly. Aurangzeb feels tears streaming down his face. This is not the message he was waiting for, but in his pain his thoughts move in another direction. The woman he loved and who loved him has posthumously offered him possibilities of escape! He has finally found a perfect reason to leave Bidar, so faultless an alibi that even the emperor's farman will fall weak in its wake.

He wants some fresh air and moves towards the pillared corridor of the Rangeen Mahal. Torches flicker in iron baskets mounted over small marble platforms. He hears footsteps. It is Jaffar Khan, his regional mir bakshi. The paymaster general, who is also Aurangzeb's late mother's sister's husband, has probably heard the sad news. Before the man can open his mouth Aurangzeb raises his hand and stops him.

'I will proceed to Aurangabad. We have ten lakh rupees in the vaults of Bidar. You stay put here. Establish contacts with the jagirdars and deshmukhs of the region. Pay them huge amounts and win them over to our side. Whoever agrees to be with us, send them and their armies to Aurangabad. We need the military manpower there.'

Jaffar Khan whose beard is almost turning white, bows and leaves.

Aurangzeb looks towards the sky. The moon, almost full in its circle, hangs over the eastern skyline, its silvery coin afflicted by pale shadows—like past memories that haunt the present. Looking at the moon, he remembers faintly something that Shivaji's vakeel had said: that they had plans to invade the sultanate's region of north Konkan, the region that initially had belonged to the Nizam Shah of Ahmednagar! He strides towards his official chamber, crossing several closed corridors lit by torches. The guards are surprised to see him. They scramble, throwing their chillums away and stamping the burning sticks with their sandals. The prince arrives at the courtroom where his scribe is still at work in the company of a lone shamdan.

The clerk is about to call it a day and is surprised to see his master at this hour. He takes a fresh paper and opens a new inkpot. Aurangzeb starts dictating. The letter is for Badi Sahiba.

> Our association goes back to your late husband Mohammed Adil Shah agreeing to be the vassal of the empire, and pay the yearly tribute, as was agreed upon, to us. That makes the Adilshahi sultanate a tributary state of the empire. Keeping that in mind, we would like to renew the old peace treaty. I, as the imperial subhedar of the Deccan, assure you that my army will stop further invasions on your terrain. If you agree, you must do two things immediately: Clear all the old tribute dues, and cede some of the Nizam Shah's territories occupied by you to us, as you have recently decided to give us the port city of Kalyan and the surrounding territories in the north Konkan. Do not establish contact with the emperor by bypassing me. I have been kind enough to recognize your adopted son as your legitimate king, despite the fact that it is not recognized by Islam. Obey or else.

After finishing the dictation, Aurangzeb ponders over Kalyan, the latest Mughal conquest. The subhedar appointed by the Adilshahi rulers will soon leave Kalyan, but Aurangzeb does not have an able man who can go to the port city and take over. *Kalyan will remain without an administrative head for a while,* he thinks with dismay.

2

The hills of the Sahyadri Range gleam in the receding evening sun. Five hundred men led by Abaji Sondev move gingerly through a narrow trail adjacent to the frightening cliffs of Tailbaila. His eyes scan their surroundings to catch any movement in the thickets, and his ears strain to pick up even the faintest sounds echoing in the hills. All he hears is the whispering streams, shuffling foliage, droning insects, whistling hornbills, screeching parrots, squeaking langur monkeys—the usual jungle sounds.

He has received the information from tribesmen of the village of Tailbaila hidden in the mountains that Kalyan's subhedar, Mullah Ahmed, has planned to take this route to reach Bijapur. His scouts had sneakily followed the caravan from Kalyan till Sudhagad Fort. The caravan is coming from Kalyan and has to cross the mountains to arrive at the plateau. They will then travel more than one hundred kos south-east to reach Bijapur. Abaji has other plans. He has to take the caravan back to Kalyan. Raja Shivaji has given him his first major assignment and he has to do it right. Feeling agitated, he leans back to balance his weight on his steed and lets his horse canter through the steep, grassy, cattle trails. It is then that his ears pick up what he is waiting for: human voices and the rattling of carts. The caravan has arrived somewhere near the temple of Goddess Waghjai, a short distance away from him and his men. His heart pounds with excitement as he stops his horse and dismounts. At his signal, there is a hushed flurry of activity as half his horsemen dismount and quickly tie their horses to the nearby trees. The others, the backup force, remain on their saddles.

Mullah Ahmed, sitting in his palanquin, yawns. Five hundred armed horsemen in metal helmets and chest armour ride ahead of him and about two hundred follow his caravan. It was his idea to use this mountain trail. Most of the mountain trails from Kalyan to Bijapur either pass through the Mughal terrain or through Maval. This one is a less-travelled route, not frequented by the caravans, so the dacoits do not usually wait here in ambush. Plus he has his armed horsemen. He is not worried about the journey; he is worried about the future that he and his family might have to endure. Kalyan has been his home for the past several years. The region is the merchant's paradise and the tax collection is good. Over the years, he has created wealth for the rulers of Adilshahi. Now the same rulers, to save their sultanate from total ruin, have given away his beloved Kalyan to the Mughal. The old peace treaty has already been renewed. The Badi Sahiba has signed the document. A Mughal subhedar is soon to arrive. So his king has ordered Mullah Ahmed to return to Bijapur in a hurry.

'The haraam politics of the royals!' he mutters angrily under his breath. It was not his doing that the Adilshahi army has failed to protect their north-eastern strongholds. Suddenly his ears pick up swooshing and cracking sounds as his slaves whip the oxen carts that follow his covered palanquin. He sticks his head out from the small window to look back. Yoked together with large wooden beams, several pairs of beasts try hard to climb the steep slope and bear the lashing mutely. The cart drivers are unaware of the contents of swollen sacks they are transporting. The sacks contain all the gold, silver and precious stones from his treasury. Several men follow the carts. He can see his son riding parallel to them to watch over the bearers who carry the women of his family. Something makes him glance ahead. Their track ahead has taken a turn only to disappear into a thicket. The subhedar of Kalyan is suddenly filled with a sense of foreboding. The rising hills looming over the trail, the dense woods, the strange jungle sounds and the frighteningly lonely path make him edgy. He notices his son ride ahead, crossing the caravan and catching up with the horsemen riding in the front. He hears some people shouting. He watches as his horsemen stride ahead with caution, removing their swords from their scabbards. Anxious now, he observes some of his horsemen turn left and disappear. But something is seriously wrong. A bunch of strange-looking men emerge from the bushes. Terror makes Mullah Ahmed's bones go rigid. At least two hundred men have suddenly jumped out from the woods like kernels popping out of fire. The short, muscular and dark men wearing folded turbans like Turkish caps scramble like infuriated honeybees. He sees them running after his horsemen. They hop and sprint, taking strange stances with their swords. Mullah Ahmed can hear their cries, rhythmic, almost a battle cry. Their shrieks ride on the wind and echo in the valley. His horsemen return in haste. The enemy has started dancing around them, like tribals around a fire. His Arabian horses start neighing in panic. He watches as the strange footmen hit their swords in vertical blows, striking his horsemen on their knees or ankles, parts of the body that are not covered with armour. His men try hard to reach the footmen by slumping forward, but their curved blades are too short. Some of the enemy footmen wrench out his men's metal helmets in frenzy, hold their swords upside down and strike the hilts of their swords on to their exposed heads. The hilts seem to have spikes. His horsemen fall on the ground, limp. Within minutes there is complete chaos. Those who are trying to crawl away are caught. His palanquin bearers have stopped, frozen with fear. He jumps out, his hand on the hilt of his sword. But before he can pull out the blade a few men pounce on him. He is soon shackled. He trembles as he notices his son surrounded by men brandishing swords with those long, fearsome blades.

It is probably the darkest night in the life of Mullah Ahmed. They have been captured. The captors drag him and his caravan away. It is only at dawn that he realizes that they are taking his caravan back to Kalyan.

Fifteen kos north, from where the subhedar of Kalyan has been taken as a captive, Shivaji has arrived near the edge of Kalyan at dawn. His scouts have already informed him that the last of Adilshahi's garrison have gone with Mullah Ahmed's caravan. Kalyan is awaiting their new Mughal subhedar. He looks at the south-facing gates that are open. His horsemen, standing behind him, make a large semi-circle and advance towards the gate. They move ahead of him through the overgrown shrubs and bushes. He kicks his horse and enters the main gateway. He is a picture of daring and delight with his carefully chosen silk robe with flower motifs ballooning behind him, his saffron turban with a pearl aigrette gleaming in the morning sun, the hilts of daggers girded to his belt sparkling with rubies and emeralds, his brocade scarf flying in the air and his wide sash glittering like gold. A hundred men ride behind him, attired in equally fancy robes. It is a chance and he will take it. It is a chance to capture Kalyan without bloodshed. A few sleepy gatekeepers notice him and his followers. They straighten up, rubbing their eyes in disbelief. The Mughal subhedar seems to have arrived. Flummoxed, they try to undo each other by bowing deeper than the others.

Within an hour, the gate fortified with iron spikes is being manned by his men. The ramparts are crowded with his archers. By the late morning, his men have occupied the fort. At noon, the news reaches the nearby villages that the new governor has arrived, and several local landlords, wealthy fishermen and village headmen from the countryside gallop towards Kalyan.

3

It is late in the afternoon when Shivaji climbs the steps of Kalyan Fort that lead to the official court of Mullah Ahmed. A saffron flag flickers on a high pole over the courtroom. The paths leading to the fort bustle with Maval men with crimson-coloured Turkish turbans. Shivaji is proud; his men look like a regiment in uniform.

He crosses the courtyard and walks towards the courtroom through an open corridor lined with his men. Yesaji Kank follows him. Before Shivaji enters the building, he glances at the open courtyard of the fort that is filling up with people who have come to see their new subhedar. The courtroom too, is full of local men, perhaps local Hindu and Muslim landlords or officials. He walks briskly to the throne, and occupies it as if it is the most natural thing to do. He gazes at the people, eyes wandering from face to face. Yesaji stands behind him. Men look at Shivaji, suspicion and doubt fleeting in their eyes. They whisper into the ears of others standing near them. Whispers slowly grow into a loud murmur that ripples across the courtroom. He watches them and hopes he can capture their hearts too.

Two shackled prisoners, their sweat trickling down their foreheads, their eyes downcast, walk barefoot in the afternoon sun on the crowded streets of Kalyan. It takes a while for the people to recognize them. They have seen those men riding ceremonial horses through the streets of Kalyan. It is their old subhedar and his son, tied in chains! There is something wrong. The news spreads through the town and there is a stampede as women and children run to the safety of their homes. The caravan is back from where it had started, at the fort steps leading to the yard.

Shivaji watches his men entering the already crowded court. He looks at one and all, especially Abaji Sondev. The man has successfully carried out the task assigned to him. The stress of a long journey and of bringing the prisoners as well as the pillage does not tell on him. The men assigned to him move purposefully and seem well adjusted to their captain. Only the path from the entrance to the throne is free of people. Abaji's men have started pouring the contents of their loaded sacks on the ground. Small mounds of gold coins, Mughal ashrafi mohurs and the Adilshahi *hons* grow larger on the carpeted floor.

'Raja, there is something else,' Abaji speaks, diverting his eyes to the entrance.

The patch near the doorway is bathed in the golden light of the western sun as long shadows of high pillars run over the Persian carpets leading to the throne. Shivaji follows Abaji Sondev's gaze. A veiled, handcuffed woman cuts through the crowd and trudges towards him. Two men push and shove others away from her, as if she is made of glass. The tiny mirrors on her long skirt shimmer in the evening sunlight. Behind her, he notices two more shackled prisoners. The men are tall and very fair, probably Arabs or Turks, wearing conical turbans and ankle-length robes. Their footwear is missing. He can make out that they are men of battle and they usually show defiance as prisoners. The terror in their eyes puzzles him.

The men in the courtroom stare at Shivaji to gauge his next move. They now know who the man who has occupied the throne of their subhedar is. There is no mistaking him—some of them have seen him in the past. They have heard about his Jawali conquest and incursions in the Mughal-occupied Deccan terrains. The men are curious. It is not the first time that they are witnessing the ordeal of a woman. It is known to all that the Mughal raiders have attacked villages in the past and continue to do so without any provocation or justification. The main purpose is to carry off women and children as slaves.

They are interested because they have heard that the man from the Maval mountains is different. But some temptations are hard to resist.

The packed courtroom is eerily silent, broken only by the sound of the bells from the woman's anklets. She is now placid, like calm before a storm.

'Let her go,' the younger man in shackles shouts.

The older captive falls to his knees. His shackles make a harsh metallic sound.

Shivaji glances at the captive. 'Stop crying, don't be afraid,' he says loudly. 'Abaji, tell me who this woman is?'

'She is from the subhedar's family,' Abaji rattles. The rage in his master's eyes sends shivers down his spine.

'Be more specific.'

'She is his son's wife,' Abaji stammers.

'And who are they?'

'The subhedar of Kalyan and his son.'

'Why is *she* here?' The voice is soft but his eyes shine with fury.

'She is a part of the pillage.' That is the blatant truth..

The leader of the Maratha keeps a stoic expression. *Who can blame whom, when the emperors and men of power have already set an example?* The Muslim invaders regard women and children as war booty. The Mughals alone have done enough damage.

'Since when have we started considering humans as pillage? Abaji, if *we* behave like them, why dream of a swaraj?' he asks sadly.

Abaji casts down his eyes.

'Unshackle them and take them to their quarters. Abaji, the subhedar and his son are our guests.'

Abaji seems relieved.

'Whenever they wish to leave, send a hundred escorts to take them to Bijapur. Treat the lady as a family member; give her clothes, bangles and enough food to last for the journey.'

The subhedar stands up with a smile on his face. The young woman falls to her knees, quivers and says, *'Shukran,'* thanking him in Arabic.

There are sighs of relief and murmurs of approval all around.

4

Night has fallen over Bijapur. Only the men minding the streetlights scurry with their ladders to light them with torches. A few stray dogs howl in the dark. The avenues leading to Badi Sahiba's palace are deserted. Khan Mohammed, the grand wazir and the general of the sultanate, is worried. *Why would the Badi Sahiba summon me with such urgency?* he wonders. *And why would she send her royal guards to the north-east frontiers just to make sure that I come? Or is there something more?* He wracks his brain as his palanquin moves towards the palace. *She never summons her noblemen at such unearthly hours.* The African warrior is anxious.

He has given his life to the services of the late king and is as loyal to the Badi Sahiba. His wives and children live in Bijapur. The kingdom has given him wealth and fame beyond his imagination. Life has been tough in the recent past. Aurangzeb and his army had been on the rampage. The Mughals have caused colossal damage to the cities, towns and villages of the sultanate's north-east frontiers. But he has put in his best possible effort.

He struggles to fight despair when he picks up the sound of galloping hooves in the distance. His horsemen always trot when approaching him, so he knows it's not them. As understanding dawns on him, he breaks into a cold sweat. His pulse races as he locks out and sees shadows of approaching horsemen. The street is dimly lit and is lined by trees. Khan Mohammed pulls the sword from his scabbard and jumps out. The palanquin tilts with his weight. The bearers buckle and lose balance. The palanquin crashes loudly. The general's horsemen have sensed danger, but it is too late. Before they can gather their wits they are surrounded by fully armoured horsemen. They are heavily outnumbered and the fight lasts only for a brief time.

Khan Mohammed tries to run away but his fear makes him unsteady. His feet slip on the ground, gone wet with the blood of his people. He tries to get up, holding the hilt of his sword, but trips again and falls flat on the ground, eyes gazing at the sky. Within moments someone jumps over him to pin him down to the ground. All he sees is the shadows of men around him. Several swords go up in the air. He struggles but sees the gleaming blades come down on him.

'Allah . . .' he utters his last word as his blood forms streams on the street of his beloved Bijapur.

CHAPTER NINE

1

The early morning prayer of *fajr* is over, and the *muezzins* from the nearby minarets have long gone back into the mosques. The eastern sky beyond the rocky hills turns orange. Aurangabad, the capital of the Mughal-occupied Deccan, shimmers under the early morning sun. It is spring, and the birds have gone berserk with their chirping. When the Nizamshahi was at its glory, Malik Ambar, the grand wazir of the kingdom, had transformed a small village called Kirki into heaven. Like an artist, he had painted its skyline with arches, domes, temple spires and minarets. Like a water god, he had created aqueducts to provide running water to mosques, palaces and gardens. When the Mughals had annexed the Nizamshahi, Aurangzeb, then just twenty, was made the subhedar of the Mughal-occupied Deccan. He gave a new name to Kirki and called it Aurangabad, the city of the throne, and made it his headquarters.

Aurangzeb stands in the balcony of the Naukhanda Palace built on an elevated ground, and stares at his Deccan capital. He loves everything about the walled city of Aurangabad and its surroundings. It reminds him of his youthful days spent climbing the hill of Daulatabad Fort, visiting the caves of Elura or shooting tigers in the nearby forests. The valley of the watershed was his favourite haunt, where serene blue lakes reflected the azure sky covered with white herons. Those herons always reminded him of his pet, Sherbaaz, a tiger hawk.

For a few years Aurangzeb had enjoyed using Sherbaaz to hunt partridges, and the bird had never let his master down. Aurangzeb could never forget the day he lost his pet. The sky was clear and he had flown Sherbaaz once again. Within moments, the hawk had caught a baby crow. Moments later a mob of crows had risen from somewhere like a smoke, as the air trembled with the harsh din of their cries. The black birds had darted forth in the direction of Sherbaaz. To Aurangzeb's horror, some of them had rapidly descended with outstretched wings and pecked and clawed the bird-of-prey that had taken one of their own. As the bird had fallen, the prince had learnt a lesson that there is a thin line between being a victor and a victim. He had penned a verse back then:

The world changes
In a twinkle, in a breath
A moment ago it was life
Now it is death.

The recall of his poem brings thoughts of Shivaji Bhosale. The rebel has entered the north Konkan and gone wild. The *kafir* is becoming a habitual plunderer and needs to be eliminated *in a breath*, before he wreaks havoc over the Deccan. Aurangzeb has dealt with such men before. A Bundela king called Juzhar and how he had chased the kafir fugitive through forests near Deogarh. Juzhar was soon captured and slain, his sons slaughtered . . .

Aurangzeb has the urge to burn Shivaji Bhosale alive, or crush him under the feet of elephants. But this is not the time to hound Shivaji. More urgent things await him in the north. It is actually meaningless to think of the Deccan politics. What happens in the north will decide his future: it is either the throne or the grave!

If Dara bhai becomes the emperor of Hindustan, he, as the new emperor will be symbolized by *awarang* or the throne, *chhatr* or the umbrella, *shamsha* which means the sun, *alam*, that is, the flag and *kawakaba* or the gilded globes. To challenge him, his name, or anything that represents him, would be a crime of sedition, punishable by death. The empire's bureaucratic machinery will be his slave and the mansabdars will lick the floor he walks on. The jury at the Sharia court will twist the law in his favour. Dara bhai's brothers, including Aurangzeb, will be put to death, and their children will breathe their last in the gloomy dungeons infested with rats and lice. They might even be forced to swallow large doses of opium and left to die rolling in their own filth.

A very sullen Aurangzeb leaves his chamber, and as he crosses one cusped arch after another, countless teary-eyed eunuch slaves stand in rows and bow to him as deeply as they can. Aurangzeb does not bother to glance at the slightly feminine, turbaned slaves dressed in sober-coloured robes who have been his late wife's confidants. He enters the opulent chamber of the late Dilras Banu. His wife's bed is empty; a plump elderly woman sitting on the carpet near his wife's bed gets up hastily. The infant she is holding is jolted out of his slumber and starts wailing loudly.

'Allah!' she exclaims and bows as much as her fat body allows, then straightens up and stretches out her arms to show the Mughal prince his fourth son who is yet to be named. The baby is all wrapped up in woollens. The newborn, who is a Sunni from his father's side and a Shia from his mother's side, has suddenly stopped wailing and has opened his eyes. Aurangzeb peers into those two brilliant pools of innocence and feels calm.

'I will name him Mohammad Akbar, after my great-great-grandfather.' *This baby may turn out to be my most suitable successor.* The thought flashes across his mind as his eyes wander beyond the woman who holds his infant son. From behind her, seven-year-old Azam stares at him. Aurangzeb leans forward and tumbles when he tries to touch his first son born to Dilras. The boy jumps with fright and disappears.

There is not much left to do but to meet his second wife, Nawab bai. He crosses a few courtyards to reach the house of Muhammad Sultan's mother. Seeing him at their doorstep, the guards kneel. He has no time to nod and rushes in to face the woman he has not seen for a while. Aurangzeb finds her looking old, her upper lip turned in a slight curl. *Is she snarling?* he wonders, and cannot believe that he once thought she was a beauty. He shakes his head in dismay and moves to sit on a large divan. The foyer is huge, covered with hand-knotted, sapphire-blue Kashmiri rugs and filled with carved furniture made of walnut wood, wrapped in ruby-red tapestry.

Nawab bai stands in front of her husband of twenty-two years who sits awkwardly on her gilded divan as if he is being punished. Bitterness wells up in her heart, filling her with resentment. She tries hard not to show her emotions. It is the irony of life. A man's love for a woman or vice-versa does not always grow with time but hate persists and swells. Just a few years ago, she had pined for his gaze.

'Our Sultan won the battle of Hyderabad,' she says, hoping that that might stir some emotions in him.

'With the help of Mir Jumla,' he comments wryly.

He treats his own boys from her with contempt, his own flesh and blood. Her eyes bore into him. He is visiting her after many years and looks different. Time has changed him without mercy: his face is gaunt, almost vacant, his nose on the verge of resembling a knife blade, his brows starting to beetle. *Life lived in the battlefields,* she thinks, but is overwhelmed with self-pity. This man, her own husband, has avoided her as if she is an unintelligent, emotionless creature, lusted after but never loved. He has reduced her to being just a number who lives in the imperial harem, an old, forgotten hag. She is shunned by the other women in the zenana who are Muslims by birth and who do not consider her a natural member of the royal seraglio. They call her the insignificant wife, making it sound cheaper than a concubine. But she has two sons to prove her legitimacy. It had not bothered her as long as her husband came to her apartments. But things have changed now.

'Now say what you want to,' he says, getting impatient.

Between man and wife, all cannot be put down in words. Dilras's death has nurtured new hopes. She fidgets, her wide and flowing long skirt sways. Is she being penalized for being born a Hindu? But that had not daunted him from spending nights, sometimes even days, in her lap, as her long curls had covered him like the panels of a tent. Her being an infidel did not deter him when she was young, and when he took her like a fervently possessed, never-satiated predator. Her religious infidelity, her being a born kafir, did not bother him when he seeded her with two sons. She feels a new surge of anger rising in her and looks at him, the man responsible for her loneliness and isolation.

'I have heard that you are going north . . .' she says, not knowing what else to talk about.

'Is that why you called me here—where I do not want to be?' he snarls.

She feels humiliated and glances at his hands resting on his lap; they look rough and dark. Those hands had once touched her bare body.

Just the memory gives her goosebumps. Despite her rage, she longs for that to happen again. Like in the past, she longs for that look in his eyes, severe with craving, shining with interest. She has not forgotten how she used to chew betel leaves to redden her lips and suck some musk pastilles to sweeten her breath. For the past months, she has been smearing herself with sandalwood paste to improve her complexion.

'It has been years since you have set foot in my apartment,' she murmurs, walking two steps ahead.

He winces, wondering if there is any sarcasm in her voice, but finds none. This makes him uncomfortable and he almost pities her. He regards her for a moment; she has not tied her hair and let it fall on her hips. He looks at her. This woman is responsible for his Dilras's death. This is the woman who had gossiped about Dilras being cursed and thus bearing only girls. She is the reason why Dilras insisted on having more children, hoping they would be sons. Dilras had already become weak after bearing him three girls. He had decided not to touch Dilras again, not because he did not love her, but because more pregnancies would have proved dangerous. And they eventually did! Dilras insisted on more children and died giving him two sons.

'I will be leaving for the north in the next few days,' he says coldly.

She freezes for a moment, jerks her head back in defiance, as a kind of riposte to her husband. She is the daughter of a king from Kashmir.

'Our boys, Mohammad Sultan and Muazzam, will go with me,' he sounds curt and gets up to leave.

'I am sorry about the Begum,' she says softly.

He stares at her this time, his pale eyes colder than ice.

'You hated her, didn't you?'

She says nothing as she watches him go. He has shattered her illusions. She does not hate Dilras as much as she hates the men in her life. First it was her father who had shamelessly surrendered to Emperor Shah Jahan, then it was her grandfather who had weaved the story of her birth to marry her off into the imperial family, so that the men in her family were showered with titles and rewarded with high military posts.

She shivers with indignation and falls to her knees, closes her eyes and prays fervently. She prays for the victory and welfare of the man she hates the most—her husband! The safety of her two sons depends on his capabilities. She prays to Allah and the long-forgotten Hindu gods of her childhood. *Will God answer her prayers?*

2

'That's decided then, Your Imperial Highness?' Nijabat Khan asks politely.

Aurangzeb eyes the tall and muscular mansabdar who stands before him and nods. It has been ten days since he has shifted to his camp. His tent is roomy but almost empty, with just a wooden couch in the middle and a scribe's writing desk in one corner. The camp brims over with the clamour of the soldiers, yelling of servants, rattling of carts, hammering of weapon-smiths, neighing and trumpeting of animals. The racket makes him feel at home. Sometimes the wind brings in the aroma of meat boiling in large earthen pots kept in the open. Even the smoke of firewood does not bother him.

Mutamad stands behind his master, but his eyes are fixed on Nijabat.

'We have mustered quite a number of horsemen,' Nijabat states, looking at his master who sits on the divan and counts his beads.

Aurangzeb frowns at Nijabat's serious expression. He glances at his scribe, sitting behind a low desk, surrounded by mountains of papers. The man is staid, a stereotype, talks less and never smiles, but is blessed with a sharp memory. Aurangzeb asks, 'How many men have come from Bidar since last week?'

The scribe does some quick calculations with his fingers before replying in a low voice, 'Five thousand, my prince.'

Jaffar Khan, the man managing Bidar after he had left, has been doing his job well and has already lured more than ten thousand Adilshahi soldiers with the tribute money paid by their own Badi Sahiba.

Nijabat scratches his beard to clear his head. Even though reinforcements sent by the emperor have left, they still have a few hundred mansabdars assigned for the Deccan. Combined with the Adilshahi soldiers coming in, they will have twenty-five thousand cavalry troopers.

'You must hear what my youngest brother, my dear Murad Baksh, has written,' Aurangzeb says to Nijabat with a sneer on his face. 'Read the letter from the viceroy of Gujarat,' Aurangzeb orders his scribe.

The scribe finds the paper quickly and reads out:

Bhai, waiting seems so eternal while our enemy is growing stronger. Make haste and move northwards from Aurangabad.

If we delay, our heretic brother, our father's favourite son, Dara bhai will have time to muster more and more men. I want to join you to fight against Dara bhai. I will go with you. My further actions depend on your orders. In the depth of my heart I know it is our beloved Dara bhai who is running the affairs of the empire from behind the throne. I want to see him dead, beheaded, his torso rolling in his own blood, the *mulhid haraamzada*, the bastard atheist pretending to be a Muslim!

Nijabat is amused. To start with, Murad Baksh is a drunkard and has recently murdered his loyal minister. The good-for-nothing prince has already crowned himself the next emperor, and is plundering the empire's treasuries. He has sent his personal army of eunuchs to Surat, the empire's most famous port where the British and the Dutch ships anchor. It is stuffed with imperial treasure, the collection of custom levies. The basement is hired by the local merchants as a safe deposit vault. Murad's eunuchs have blown up the parts of the defending wall and have robbed the treasure that is meant for military expenses. Like a dying atheist who conveniently resorts to God, the same Murad has suddenly remembered that he has a brother in Aurangzeb. Countless mails have arrived from Gujarat, filled with abuses and plans to murder Dara Shikoh.

Aurangzeb knows what his most trustworthy mansabdar thinks. He says softly, 'Dara bhai is on another trip. He tries to be a liberal and wants to be another Akbar; my great-great-grandfather was also a born military general and a gifted administrator. Dara bhai is a military-illiterate bookworm, basking in the reflected glory of his wealth that has come easily to him.'

'Orthodox mansabdars assigned to do court duties are already weary of the prince's love for the kafirs. They hate him for giving importance to Hindu pundits and propagating Sufism among the fellow Sunnis. The mullahs and ulemas fear the loss of their importance if the first prince comes to power. They will not support him in crisis,' Nijabat states blankly.

A mysterious smile appears on the prince's face.

Nijabat smiles too and asks, 'What is the latest?'

Aurangzeb glances at his scribe who knows what his master wants. He picks up a note from the collector of Agra. The man is an orthodox Muslim and hates Dara Shikoh for his liberal views on Islam. The scribe reads aloud,

> As you already know, Dara Shikoh has shifted the emperor to Agra and guards his apartments like a tigress guarding her cubs. Only Begum Jahanara, a few hakims and some eunuch slaves are allowed to enter the chamber of the patient. The emperor himself never appears in public, giving room to speculation. People throng in front of the window of the special court every day to see him but go back disappointed, the jharokha remains empty. Even I have not seen him for weeks.

'Father loves *jharokha-e-darshan*, appearing in the balcony to show himself to his subjects and accepting their salute when they perform kurnish. And now, it is of paramount significance that he shows himself to his people to crush the rumours of him being an invalid and to prove that he is alive and well,' Aurangzeb muses.

'We should go north immediately,' Nijabat suggests. 'I have a request: If and when we do start our northward journey, we must not halt for more than two nights at any place, because if we do, it will only embolden them.'

Aurangzeb raises his brows. Nobody else talks to him the way Nijabat Khan does. And he does not take such comments from anyone else other than his uncle Shaista Khan. But Nijabat is a man of firm loyalty and great daring.

'First tell me how, and then I shall give my views,' Nijabat hears his master's question.

He is quick to respond: 'I have heard that Mirza Raja Jai Singh and Prince Suleiman have gone eastwards with more than twenty thousand men to stop Prince Shuja from advancing towards Agra. They must have thought of blocking our path too. If we halt, we give them time to march southwards.'

'The essence of my strategy is to weaken the enemy army,' Aurangzeb smiles and says. 'I want them to come. Half of Dara bhai's army will be forced to guard Agra and half will march southwards to intercept us. We have better chances to win two battles with two smaller armies than one battle against one massive army. If we halt for a fortnight before crossing the river Narmada, they will have time to advance towards us and stop us.'

'Do you think prince Dara will come personally or send someone else?' Nijabat's eyes shine with interest.

'I hope Dara bhai, who has induced father to recall the reinforcements from the Deccan, comes to meet me in the battlefield. I have got news that the coward, sitting safely in Agra forts, has established direct contact with Ali Adil Shah and offered him peace for a large indemnity. I hope this time he leaves the safe precincts of my father's forts and meets me on the battlefield,' Aurangzeb says tersely and then suddenly breaks into recitation:

A man far from his asylum,
Helpless, needy and forsaken
Stalked by a hungry death
Then he pleads and then he cries and then he rants
While the lions are shredded by fishes
And crocodiles are devoured by ants.

After an overwhelmed Nijabat Khan leaves, Aurangzeb checks if Mutamad is near the entrance, ensuring that his personal guards are out of earshot. He starts dictating to his scribe. The letter is for Murad Baksh:

My devout struggle to rip off the wicked roots of idolatry and infidelity from the realm of our Islamic empire is already designed and in place. And my brother, you, whom I hold dearer than my own heart, wishes to join me in this holy endeavour. Your wish has renewed the confirmation of faith and teamwork, based on promises and oaths. I shall consider our losses and gains as one. I shall favour you more once the mulhid, the idolater, is plucked out and removed from our path. You cannot imagine what I have in mind for you. I crave to see you sitting on our father's peacock throne.

3

Inside Janjira, the sea fort on the Konkan coast, it is business as usual. Siddi Kashim grins, removes his tunic and flings it away before diving into the deeper end of the pool. On the poolside, his smaller children romp around, black, brown and some pale, with heads covered with woolly or straight hair. He tries to remember the number of his children but gives up—just looking at them makes him feel good about himself, his virility, his manhood. He lowers himself in the water, enjoying its coolness, then floats on his back to stare at the faraway ramparts that rise high beyond the wall enclosing the pool. This is his unbeatable sea fort, built by his ancestors, standing on an oval-shaped rock half a kos away from the shores of Konkan.

In the midst of women's laughter and shrieks, he hears a guard calling him from beyond a wall built to maintain the privacy of the pool. No one dares to disturb him unless the reason is a compelling one. He swears and swims to the edge. As he comes out, a eunuch slave, dark as basalt and thin as reed, appears from behind a fern bush and hands him a towel.

He walks across the gardens wiping himself and opens the door brashly. The guard is scared of his master who is a large man, with muscles corded like the bark of a banyan tree and eyes sharp like a blade. He has a habit of flying into a rage. His fury is legendary; when it possesses him, he kills people by blows of his fists, or kicks them to death.

'Chief Yakub has a message for you.'

Siddi Kashim stares at the guard and nods, giving him permission to speak further. The message is from his younger brother. The dark man wearing a black turban and a short tunic rattles, now with some relief:

> The Marathas have taken Ghosal. But when they tried to attack the fort by sailing in small fishing boats, many sunk after our cannonballs hit them. Some of the boats toppled, sending many to their water graves.

Siddi Kashim smiles and slams the door shut.

On his way back to his pool, he laughs at Shivaji Bhosale and his men. The idiots have attacked his fort in fishing dinghies—like frogs getting at a crocodile or turtles attacking a killer shark. If only they knew the strength of Janjira Fort, they would have sunk their pathetic boats themselves. They are also ignorant about his men, with their strain of African blood, trained sailors and soldiers, fit as stallions, one equal to ten natives in strength. As long as these empires and the kingdoms lack naval power, he is safe and at nobody's mercy. In fact, *they* are at his mercy. They need his help to sail to Mecca. They depend on him for good-quality slaves. And he is free to loot and abduct the people from the mainland coast as and when he pleases.

The tightly packed ship must have reached the deep seas, he thinks before he jumps back into the pool. Supplying loads of slaves to the Muslim empires and kingdoms have made him rich. More importantly, they protect him, and turn a blind eye when he robs and abducts local people from the mainland Konkan.

The ship has indeed reached the deep seas. Balaji Avji and the hundreds of men around him can hardly move, as one man's ankle is shackled to another's. Some are chained to the deck by their necks or hands. It has been a full day since their confinement. His body is numb and his stomach rumbles with hunger. The burning pain on his right shoulder is acute. They were branded with red-hot irons before being thrown on the deck like goats or horses. The ship has hit rough seas and is rocking like a swing. His mind goes back to his father, mild-tempered, an eye opaque with cataract, sinewy neck fixed on a prematurely bent spine, working long hours as an accountant and scribe for the masters of the Janjira Fort. It was his karma to work for the Siddis. Only once in his thirty long years of service had he broken the karma protocol and tried to protest against the sinister operations. A sin was committed. The Siddis had suspected him to be the traitor, leaking information to the Marathas. The consequence was that his father lay at the bottom of this ocean, stuffed in a gunny bag made heavy with stones and knotted at both ends.

Balaji's body convulses with sobs. Someone behind him has relieved himself and the stench is unbearable. There is a small tank full of water to wash up but they cannot reach it easily. They are tied down by heavy chains. The man next to him has started vomiting. He closes his eyes and starts weeping. He is just seventeen. His dream of becoming a scribe is over. It is his fate to be a slave. *Or a eunuch*, he thinks and shudders.

The man has stopped vomiting. He glances at him: the man has fallen back and his shackled legs are twisted. He looks like a dead grasshopper. Someone screams that there is a dead man among them.

Two sailors appear from the deck; these huge men with long matted hair do not bother to check if the man is indeed dead. They discuss something, letting strange syllables fly in the air while unshackling him. It is difficult to drag him through the crowd.

The ship starts rocking even more violently as the rain hits the deck. One of them looks at Balaji Avji for a moment before bending and unlocking his shackles with just one click. The sailor signals him to lift the dead man.

He gets up, feeling giddy, his legs numb. Somehow, he manages to pull the limp body over his shoulders. Some more fluids leak out of the dead man's mouth, its stench making him sick. He moves unsteadily through the rows of chained men with the weight on his shoulders, and almost tumbles as the ship rolls over the wild waters. Many have started retching, and the wooden floor has become slippery. He knows about ships and this one is broad-decked. He spots a formidable gun behind her foremast. They drag him near the railings and push the man resting on his shoulders over the board and into the sea.

Balaji stares at the sea mesmerized. He has never seen such giant waves, like mountains of water moving towards him. For a moment he does not know which is the sea and which is the sky. The sailors try to wrench him back to his place and chain him again. As they yank him, he looks at the sea for the last time and notices a mighty wave hitting the deck. The ship shudders, twists violently and then topples over.

Balaji can only think of the gigantic waves, like surging, fluid mountains as he tries to stay afloat. The last of his memories is a dinghy, and a few men shouting to him.

CHAPTER TEN

1

It is winter. A few kos west of Kalyan, Shivaji and his men—Niraji Raoji, Abaji Sondev and Tanaji Malusare—stand in the compound of a shipyard. Niraji is a scholar in subjects like law, history and finance, and has been working for Shivaji as an adviser for several years. His advice is now needed direly. The Maratha navy is being established. The investment is huge and the returns are not immediate. Shivaji slowly shifts his gaze towards the Ulhas river and smiles. He is fascinated by its wide girth—a perfect waterway for sleek, predatory vessels to enter the wide expanse of the open sea, guard the coast and return quickly to safety if need be. It is a moment of triumph.

This river, the surrounding teak forests and the twenty-five hill forts of north Konkan were initially a part of the Nizamshahi. After its annexation more than twenty years ago, in a treaty signed by the Mughal emperor and Adil Shah, the region became a part of the Adilshahi. The Adilshahi rulers recently handed it over to the Mughals hoping for another peace treaty. But there is trouble in the north and Aurangzeb has already reached Aurangabad. Many of his mansabdars have been called back to Agra. Circumstances have given Shivaji the perfect chance to seize north Konkan without any opposition from the mighty Mughal.

'They never did understand the strategic importance of this region,' Niraji says softly. He has been studying the military importance of Konkan for a while now. He has been meeting the local fishermen to know more about the coastline and the pirate ships that prowl the waters. Niraji is surprised by the natural ports in the terrain. Tanaji, who stands behind the scholar, listens to the conversation between Shivaji and Niraji with interest. He nods. He too has been on a mission to search for the remote villages at the foothills of the mountains towards the eastern side of north Konkan. The region is covered with giant teak trees with layered leafy tops. The forest is intersected by rivers plunging down from the mountains. Along with his two thousand footmen, he has been busy laying tracks to improve the transport of fallen teak trunks to Kalyan. He is here to see their first shipyard.

Shivaji starts walking away from the river and towards the lone massive structure that stands in the middle of the open yard. His men and a few guards follow him. Their eyes scan the area, trained to spot troubles—a hiding archer or a spearman. It is stiflingly warm inside the enormous foyer stuffed with shipbuilding material. The roof is made of wood and is held up by broad brick pillars supporting parallel bays to park smaller boats. At the far end, countless logs of wood are neatly piled against the wall and the floor is covered with masts, oars, ribs, mallets, augurs and boat bases. A large wooden table in the middle is piled with paper sheets, compasses, measurements tapes, pencils, rulers, inkpots, penknives and magnifying lenses. A few men are seen working around a short wooden table.

Rue De Guevera, the Portuguese ship engineer, awaits his new master. The firang engineer has recently started working for Shivaji, much against the wishes of the Portuguese viceroy of Goa.

People have started fussing near the entrance. Some of his Indian carpenters talk excitedly, as they always do when Raja Shivaji Bhosale arrives with his men. Guevera's assistants also promptly leave their tools and stand at attention.

'Bomdia!' Guevera bows deep and greets the brown-eyed short man who wears a slanting turban embellished with pearl strings.

Shivaji smiles briefly and starts talking rapidly. The translator, a
native Catholic who had been chatting with Guevera's men, jumps
forward.

'As we have discussed, the frigates must be lightweight, not more
than a hundred and fifty tons—even smaller will do—so that they
can seek refuge under every shelter the land offers, deep or shallow,
and can anchor near every port, big or small. Make sure that they
are driven by sails as well as oars. Make them as manoeuvrable as
possible. Speed is vital. Have a deck or two that will be able to carry
a principle battery of carriage-mounted guns and a hundred sailors
and fighters put together.'

The interpreter, who has taken off his cap to wipe his sweaty
head, is trying to keep pace, fumbling occasionally.

They have discussed the specifications before, but Shivaji wants
to be very sure. Guevera does not mind the continuous hail of
instructions. He likes the repetition as it gives him a clear vision of
what needs to be done.

Shivaji puts forth a new requirement. 'Make them as lightweight
as possible, with not more than two masts. We must be able to tow
them with row boats.'

'We need twenty such ships within a year,' announces a man in
an official manner. Guevera had not noticed him till then—a thin,
immaculately dressed Brahmin wearing a huge red turban, and with
eyes as brown as his master's.

The demand is stiff and the time insufficient, despite his hundred
technicians and countless artisans at work day and night. He quickly
calculates: twenty ships made will cost one hundred and twenty
thousand rupees, which is equal to one hundred ser of gold. He and
his men earn a hefty percentage. He wonders how rich the native
man is. Guevera looks at his assistants who, despite his warnings,
listen in on the conversation. One of the bolder ones whispers, 'We
will be able to submit the designs in four weeks.'

'Make your design both on paper and as models carved in wood
and iron. Send them to us as soon as you finish,' says Shivaji with
an air of finality. The meeting is over. The engineer watches his
employer leave without waiting for his acknowledgement.

Niraji knows what Guevera thinks. Following social etiquettes is not his master's strong point, and especially not when the discussions are about specific tasks. As he follows Shivaji to the exit, Tanaji and his men walk behind them. They walk through the dock cramped with the hulls of two half-built battleships. The workers glance at their new ruler with interest as he inspects the supporting wooden framework around the hull. The scaffoldings are latticed, distinctly foreign in style. Shivaji gazes at the ramp, trying to gauge if he can leap over it. A labourer applying caulking to the fixed panels swiftly moves across and gives him a hand. The leader of the Marathas walks over the ramp built alongside the hull of one of the ships. Fascinated, he looks around at the entire yard laid out before him. At the far end, under the shade of a huge banyan tree, carpenters saw timber as workers carry heavy beams of teak on their shoulders to the workshop.

Niraji and Abaji march alongside the ramp. Tanaji and the guards follow. Shivaji stops abruptly to touch a wood panel and says, 'I believed that only the hilt of a sword or the saddle of a horse talk to you when you touch them, but even these planks of the ship have a lot to say.'

'And what do they planks say?' Niraji asks with a faint smile.

'They whisper that they are the parts of a powerful war galley. Within months, as a battleship, they will sail the waters of the Ulhas to glide into the ocean via the creek of Vasai. Despite fewer masts, once the sails are fully spread, the battleship, loaded with cannon, will cause ripples of terror in the waters of the ocean,' Shivaji grins.

Niraji does not comment. The firangs rule the sea; they have colonies from the Cape-of-Good-Hope to Macau in China. Most of the important ports between Diu in the north of Konkan and Kochi in the south belong to them, with Goa as their capital.

'I know what you are thinking, Niraji,' Shivaji says. 'I don't deny that this is just the beginning for us. We will soon take over the trade, or at least a part of it.'

Niraji nods. He has discussed this issue with Raja Shivaji. It is about the essentials of life. Salt is harvested and spices are grown in Konkan. They need to be transported from one port to another and then carried by the oxen to the cities on the mountain plateaus through the tracks that run through Jawali. The merchants are mostly natives and are compelled to pay hefty fee for passports to the firangs to set sail. Siddi pirates attack their ships. Jagirdars like Morey fleece them when their oxen carrying goods cross the mountains. Raja Shivaji dreams of providing the natives with merchant ships at affordable costs and levying reasonable taxes. He also wants to do away with the passports.

The men have reached the end of the shipyard. They stand under the coconut trees at the edge of the yard. Cool shadows of the enormous leaves dance on the ground. Despite winter, the breeze has turned warm and humid. Somewhere in the nearby bushes a lark repeatedly lets out melodious whistles.

'Ship-building is only the first step; we will have to take over the ports by sword,' Raja Shivaji says.

Niraji looks at him and nods. The dream of swaraj needs funds. The main legitimate sources of money are land revenue, road toll collection and tribute paid by the vassal kings. Konkan is blessed with groves of coconut. It has orchards of banana, mango, jackfruit, papaya, jamun, gooseberry and cashew. Spices grow in abundance and quality salt is processed from the sea. The forests in the east are mostly teak trees. Teakwood from here is transported to different countries in order to build ships.

'Swaraj is His wish, but there are some realities that we must confront, especially to reduce our dependence on the watandars.' Shivaji says and continues.

'That means we pay our military men and our revenue officials every month, directly from our treasury. Our horseman gets five rupees as monthly salary. The horse is owned by the state. Ten thousand horses need sixty thousand ser of grain and fodder every day for survival. Our infantrymen too are on our payroll. The peasants in our regions are provided with farm animals, instruments and quality seeds. If the monsoons fail, we shouldn't charge revenue. From where will we get the funds from?

Niraji clears his throat but keeps mum. The present land revenue is just enough to maintain their *tiny* military. Konkan provides opportunities in terms of taxes on salt, spices and wood. The textile industry has flourished in the natural harbours of Konkan. Its skilled weavers spin silk and cotton fabric. Shiploads of their satin, taffeta and muslin bales leave the moors of Konkan for the rest of the world. They are sold mostly to emperors and kings.

'Another way to raise funds is to provide ships to our sea merchants. The money can be used to build ports, war ships and sea forts,' Shivaji says.

'We have failed to conquer Janjira,' Abaji reminds him gently.

'We will take it one day, or build another equally invincible sea fort in the near future to keep them under control. You have a lot of work to do, Abaji. You will be our subhedar of Kalyan.' There is no hint of sarcasm in Shivaji's words.

Abaji's eyes shine.

'That reminds me,' Tanaji says, 'Raghunathji has rescued a young boy named Balaji Avji of the Prabhu community from the sea. He was on the slave ship of the Siddis. The boy has lofty dreams; he wants to work as a scribe for you.'

'How many could have been rescued, and how many need yet to be rescued from this beautiful coast with an ugly past!' Shivaji says bitterly.

'Where is Raghunathji now?' Niraji inquires.

'He has gone to Aurangabad to meet with Aurangzeb. All sorts of rumours have been floating in the Deccan about the emperor's health. People say that Aurangzeb may go north, to Agra. Without him in the Deccan, the Adilshahi rulers will have time to deal with us. We need the Mughal backing more than ever before,' Shivaji says.

Niraji raises his brows. 'Will Aurangzeb entertain him?' he asks.

'This is politics. We deal with it as it comes.'

2

'Summon Shiva Bhosale's man, with two armed guards on either side, and keep the sentinels posted around the tent. Ask them to be alert,' Aurangzeb says loudly to Mutamad who is standing at the entrance.

Then he gathers himself on his divan and picks up his rosary beads lying on a small table next to him, dropping his eyelids like flags flying at half-mast.

Raghunath is nervous. He has ridden seventy-five kos northwards from Rajgad to reach here. The journey had not been easy. But what he has seen after reaching his destination has made him weak with anxiety. It is a massive military camp, with the green tents of the Muslim squadrons and the saffron tents of the Rajput squadrons, and animal stables at the periphery that seem to extend to the horizon. There are foreigners in the camp too, tall and blue-eyed men hailing from Afghanistan and beyond, and white men from Europe. Raghunath feels overwhelmed on seeing the weapon-smiths and their portable forges, cartloads of cattle and goats that are fed on the camp, and the markets stuffed with all possible kinds of things.

In contrast, he is surprised to see the sparse tent of Aurangzeb, the viceroy of the Mughal-occupied Deccan. Unlike a few Muslim men of importance whom he had met in the past, the third prince, with his long silvery beard, looks genteel. His divan lacks grandeur and he sits wearing a white, full-sleeved robe and a matching turban. His fingers count the beads of his tesbih. His eyes are half-closed, as if he is praying.

'I, the humble vakeel of Raja Shivaji Bhosale, bow to Your Imperial Highness, who is also the esteemed imperial subhedar of the Deccan.'

Aurangzeb feels the visitor's gaze and knows that he is dealing with a cunning and intelligent man. Shiva's vakeel has come for some shameless diplomacy.

'My master, Raja Shivaji Bhosale, asks for your pardon,' Raghunath does not waste time and bows as deep as he can. This is another Maratha trait that Aurangzeb hates. No small talk, no pleasantries, no foreplay with words. The Marathas are cunning, like sly foxes hiding in the shadows of tall grass, not showing themselves to the world but gauging it from afar.

Raghunath tries to look into Aurangzeb's eyes, concealed behind his drooping lids, for a hint of a reaction, hoping the Mughal prince will grace him by locking eyes with him, but it does not happen, not then at least.

'Are you the one who killed Morey?' he hears a voice, deep and resonant.

'It was in self-defence, my prince,' Raghunath says cautiously. He speaks Urdu slowly, with a Deccan accent, as if he first thinks in his tongue, and then translates to Urdu to speak.

'And the robbery in broad daylight ordained by your raja at Kalyan?' Aurangzeb asks harshly, as if he has been waiting to ask this question.

'The wealth of Kalyan belongs to the imperial treasury, my prince. The sultanate rulers had ceded the land to the empire but their governor was a thief fleeing with the treasure,' announces the vakeel without wincing or showing any guilt.

'Is Shiva an imperial regent who must worry about us?'

'He aspires to be, Your Imperial Highness,' Raghunath says. His dark eyes are fixed on Aurangzeb who suddenly raises his eyelids. His pale irises make the vakeel's hair stand on end.

'If he is an aspirant then he is not our enemy, he is our servant-to-be. And so his attack on the imperial terrain is akin to treason, an act of sedition, punishable only by death.'

Raghunath replies, his voice steady, 'That mistake has changed my master's life. Since then he has started protecting the imperial interests as if he already is an imperial regent.'

Aurangzeb stares at the vakeel with disbelief.

'What he did is still punishable by death. He raised his sword against the Islamic empire, plundered our region . . . . . .it is akin to waging war against God!'

Raghunath bites his lip. It is futile to debate. Aurangzeb might bring out a list of all that is punishable by death according to sharia law, the path to be followed. The first crime in the list would possibly be being an infidel, that is, he might say, akin to defying the existence of God.

The vakeel clears his throat, 'If the imperial prince could officially grant him all the villages and forts in Raja Shivaji's possession, he would do everything in his capacity to guard the southern frontiers of the empire in the Deccan.'

'Even depositing all the funds wrenched from Mullah Ahmed into the imperial treasury?' Aurangzeb cuts in.

'Yes, immediately after the official recognition is granted.' Raghunath is quick.

Aurangzeb shudders with rage. He wants to violently shake the vakeel, slap him, slay him and feed him to the wolves. But his priorities have changed. He must deploy his military force to tackle bigger foes. The empire is at stake.

'Mashallah! Tell me what makes Shiva think that we need his help?'

'It is more about serving you than helping you, my esteemed prince.'

Shiva Bhosale's vakeel is a clever scoundrel. And the whole lot of them, the Marathas, are like the mountain rats. Aurangzeb has heard that the rats survive due to their strong sense of smell. It helps them gather information. It is possible that Shiva has smelled the emperor's illness, and has assumed that he, Aurangzeb, will be gone for a long time. In his absence, the Adilshahi army, free from the Mughal aggressions, will turn their military against them. If he, Aurangzeb, yields now, showing solidarity, then the story might be different. Shiva needs him more than he needs Shiva. Smart move. He needs time to grow stronger.

'It is his wish to serve us then. Despite the grave crimes committed by Shiva, we may consider his request. We'll put him and his cavalry to use—someplace somewhere. We shall send him an official letter sometime in the future.' Aurangzeb says in a voice devoid of any emotion while he counts his beads slowly and deliberately. The prince has spoken, the vakeel has been dismissed.

After Raghunath leaves, Aurangzeb starts dictating a letter. The letter is for the Badi Sahiba. She needs proper warning. The woman has been writing to the emperor to gain sympathy and support.

He dictates:

Be advised. You have paid the initial tribute money after you turned our tributary state more than twenty years ago. We have been ignoring the arrears. But now you have established contact with the emperor. You have promised him that you will pay all the arrears directly to him, casting me aside—I, the imperial subhedar of the Deccan! What do you think? The emperor will protect you from me? And that is not all; you have allowed the Deccan to become a breeding ground for the kafir rebels. Do not forget that you have renewed the peace treaty with us and have promised us part of the Nizamshahi territory taken by you twenty years ago. But that region is no longer under your control. And now the region of Kalyan is also lost. Eliminate Shiva. You may take the help from Shiva's enemies or forge an alliance with Siddis of Janjira if need be. You have defied Islam by adopting a son and making him the king. Do what I say, for if you don't, we will take over Bijapur by force. Your city will burn like a kafir's pyre, and your king will die a pathetic death in our dungeons.

3

The horse carrying Shivaji flies like a javelin across the flatlands of north Konkan, followed by his five thousand horsemen. Cool morning air whips past him as the ground thunders under their horses' hooves. His scouts ride before him, leading him to Mahuli Fort, the only hill fort in the region of north Konkan that remains to be captured. It is also the only fort in the region that belongs to the Mughals. Aurangzeb will not help Shivaji; his evasive answer made that much very clear. Hence, taking over the Mahuli Fort is fully justified. Shivaji's eyes search the skies till the cluster of hills rise high over the northern horizons. The forest at the foothills teems with trees of teak and banyan. As planned, it is time to stop. His men slow down and gather around him. He looks at them, his eyes moving from one face to another: Pinglay, Abaji Sondev, Netoji Palkar, Tanaji, Yesaji, Kavji, Murarbaji and Ibrahim Khan. They are of different castes, but are all warriors, ready to bathe their swords in the blood of their enemies in their fight for swaraj.

His eyes slowly move towards Mahuli Hill. It looms a few hundred guj above him. Enormous spurs rise above the mountain, strangely resembling giant humans. Near the hilltop he can faintly see the outer wall of the fort. Twenty years ago, his father had hidden behind this wall before surrendering to the allied forces. Hunted by the imperial and Adilshahi armies, it was here that he had begged the Portuguese to save him, who had instead helped the emperor to track him down.

Shivaji tries to imagine Aurangzeb's reaction to this attack and smiles. To the fort's west is Vasai, a firang settlement around the Arnala Fort, looking towards the ocean. To its east, mountain passes plunge down from the Deccan capital of the Mughals—Aurangabad. From the citadel of the fort one can keep vigil over all the crucial passes from Kasara to Umbraj, usually preferred by the imperial armies to enter the Konkan. It could also be his military stronghold to protect the shipbuilding dockyards scattered around Kalyan.

He looks back at his men. They are waiting for his orders. He announces, 'Tonight, lay siege around the hill.'

Palkar is surprised. Siege craft is an arduous procedure; even a small fort protected by a few unyielding soldiers could hold out for weeks or even months against the massive number of besieging men.

'We neither have the manpower to block the routes nor enough food to last for even two weeks,' the sarnobat addresses his raja.

Shivaji finally shares his strategy. 'The Mughal garrison up there will be anxious to crush us with boulders. Let them think we are laying siege and they are not in immediate danger. On the fifth night, which is a moonless night, we will climb the fort from all sides so that they do not know which end to protect. In the meantime, send our scouts to study the routes going up from villages at the foothills. Ask them to check the slope that climbs from the northwest. It is covered with dense forests of screw pine. The hidden path takes you all the way to the top.'

The five days of wait are uneventful. Sometimes they can see the small figures of the Mughal soldiers on the ramparts of the fort, but it is too high up to note their actions. On the fifth night, four of the five thousand of Shivaji's men start climbing the hill that rises a few hundred guj from all sides. The leader of the Marathas along with Tanaji and Yesaji scales it from the west. The air is filled with the sweet smell of pine. The hill is steep but not blindingly dark as thousands of fireflies appear and disappear at random places. The little creatures light up the surrounding forest, but their glow is not bright enough to expose the intruders.

Shivaji arrives at the base of the fort wall. To his surprise, there are no night guards on the ramparts. The Mughals are too sure of their power. Within moments, they scale the walls. Some men have even reached the ramparts. According to the plan, a hundred of his men blow the trumpets. The ear-splitting calls shake the mountain. The Mughal garrison finally wakes up, utterly confused by the sound. Arrows are showered on the Mughal soldiers clamouring in the fort's courtyard.

Shivaji waits as Tanaji and Yesaji hover around him. It takes only an hour before he hears shouts from the ramparts.

'All clear!' he hears Palkar bellow, 'They are all killed. The fort is now in our hands.'

The main Kalyan gate facing the west is flung open and Shivaji clambers like a possessed soul. He knows it is more than a mere victory as he enters the courtyard strewn with bodies. It was here that his father had to surrender and give up. At this very place, his father's fate as the future servant of the Adilshahi was sealed.

'Remove the Mughal banner!' Shivaji shouts. 'Let the saffron flag fly!'

4

They have shifted to their new home, Rajgad Fort. It has become Jija bai's favourite pastime to be in the watchtower rising above the fort's citadel. The hills of Maval bathe in the beams of the morning sunlight. A sharp, winter breeze blows around the girth of the fort that is more than ten kos in diameter. It rattles across the giant mountain holes swerving around the ridges and then flies through arched, manmade tunnels dug across the mountain's belly. Today she is waiting for her son to return from the battlefields of Konkan.

Someone else is waiting too.

Sayee lies on her bed, trying to bury her sobs. It is difficult to gauge how many hours have passed. The maid has come twice, once to pour some bitter medicine into her mouth and once to feed her lentil soup. But she has lost all appetite. The fever has come and gone three times, making her sweat and shiver. Slimy spit gathers in her mouth. It makes her feel like throwing up. She is terrified. The last time she tried to vomit, she noticed bloody mucus. She does not know if she is drifting to sleep or death. Suddenly, she is woken up by the sound of drums and trumpet calls. He has arrived. Her bed shudders, as though the hill sways beneath her. She can hear shots from the cannon on the ramparts of citadel. It will be a long time before he comes to her. And she is prepared; he may not stay with her and instead go to his chamber. She will not hold him back. She has made up her mind. She will not make him unhappy by whimpering or crying. She will not show her crumpling self to him.

It is late in the night when Shivaji walks past the queens' palaces of Rajgad Fort. In the evening, his other wives had come to receive him at the main entrance of the citadel. Draped in colourful silk saris, they performed *aarti* with eagerness and devotion, to ward off the malefic influences of the evil eye. They had giggled and nudged each other with their elbows covered with embellished bands of gold while impishly throwing glances at each other. In their eagerness, some had scrambled while holding large gilded trays filled with wick lamps, burning camphor, conch shells filled with water, tiny silver containers of vermillion and lit incense sticks. He had waited patiently till all seven of them repeated the same ritual. Their demureness had occasionally been overruled by their youth as they tried to lock their kohl-smeared eyes with him, gazing at him longingly. He had responded to them while trying hard to hide the shadows of guilt.

He reaches Sayee's chamber with a heart heavy with sorrow. She was already succumbing to her illness when he had last seen her. He feels miserable thinking of how she will look, her body ravaged by tuberculosis. The room is lit brightly with several lamps. She lies on the bed, still as a log of wood. He goes near and gazes at her. Her untied hair has fallen over her chest. She stares at him, her limpid eyes large and moist, her nose ring gleaming with pearls and rubies.

He scans her face to gauge the extent of the havoc that her sickness has wrought. Or, perhaps, to unveil the mask of death that shrouds her pretty face. Or to measure the time that remains. Unexpectedly, she flashes a smile. It reminds him of tiny vinca flowers clinging to life even on dry, rocky and barren earth. Her eyes sparkle with joy and then suddenly the room is filled with waves of her girlish laughter.

He stands there, feeling foolish. Has she caught his eyes hunting for the impending doom?

'Was the Kalyan girl really beautiful?' He hears his wife's question, her voice mocking yet stern and her eyes full of mischief.

'I have not seen her,' he fumbles with words, and then bows to his queen.

CHAPTER ELEVEN

1

As the sun rises above the city of Ujjain, summer breeze from the sandy desert of Rajasthan blows eastward and sweeps across the battlefield. A nervous Maharaja Jaswant Singh Rathod waits for Aurangzeb's army to appear at the southern skyline. He has been told that his sole task at Ujjain is to scare off Aurangzeb. He will show off his army of thirty thousand cavalry and flutter thousands of imperial banners in the air.

Just two days before, Jaswant had been told that Aurangzeb had not taken a long halt before crossing the river Narmada as he had previously planned. At Burhanpur, Murad Baksh had joined Aurangzeb from Gujarat. The brothers and their armies had met on the northern banks of the Narmada. People present at the occasion told him that the allied forces looked like an ocean of troopers, their march purposeful and resolute. The enormous cavalcade had arrived a few kos south of Ujjain, a week before it was anticipated. Jaswant had acted fast. His military formation stood cramped between two hillocks, on an island protected by ditches filled with water. For the past two days, a thousand men had been deployed to bring buckets of water from the Shipra river to fill the trenches dug around the battlefield.

The area is muddy and slushy. Jaswant has put his army in a strong defensive position. He plans to unleash his cavalry once the advancing army of Aurangzeb and Murad slows down by the manmade mire.

A few kos south from where Jaswant and his army await, Aurangzeb, sitting in the howdah of his elephant, is wary but not worried. Dara bhai has thrown the dice first. Aurangzeb is cognizant of Dara bhai's trusted warrior, Maharaja Jaswant Singh Rathod, and his thirty thousand men. Aurangzeb calculates that he has two things working in his favour: Jaswant has not commanded such a large army in the recent past, and Qasim Khan, the powerful mansabdar who has come with Jaswant, hates Dara bhai's liberal views. There is more: Jaswant does not know what modern, lightweight artillery can do. Continuous battles have taught Aurangzeb newer tactics and their impacts.

As his elephant sways beneath him, Aurangzeb appraises the military situation. The enemy's battle formation—the core, the advance guard, the left and the right wings—has been done conservatively. Jaswant's army stands on an island, surrounded by a freshly dug ditch filled with water. The core of Jaswant's army is formed by his few thousand Rajput cavalrymen from his own kingdom of Jodhpur. Two thousand of them are around Jaswant's elephant. Ten thousand cavalrymen are placed in the advanced guard to face Aurangzeb's approaching cavalry. Jaswant's left and right wing have just four to five thousand horsemen, making his advance guard the strongest part of his military formation. Aurangzeb calls it heavy-in-the-front tactic. He has faced such situations and knows how to tackle them. Watching the dense mass of horsemen around him, Aurangzeb considers his battle formation. His advance guard has eight thousand horsemen led by his first son Mohammad Sultan, his right wing has five thousand horsemen under his second son Muazzam, his left wing consists of another five thousand horseman led by Murad. The rest of

the cavalry of several thousand stands around him. By buying
over soldiers from the Adilshahi and uniting forces with Murad,
he has outnumbered Jaswant. But the real power lies somewhere
else. His conservative battle formation is infused with extra power
that is beyond Jaswant's knowledge. Several thousand archers and
musketeers back up his advance guard. His scouts have studied the
battlefield and identified a small hillock. His artillery will be fired
from an elevated position. It is also manned by firangs who have
worked for Mir Jumla. Even though Mir has been called away by
the emperor, he has left behind his experts to serve Aurangzeb who
had saved his family.

Maharaja Jaswant Singh Rathod glances at his advance guard.
The horsemen, dressed in ornamental armour, hold huge imperial
banners made of embroidered silk. The moss-green flags flutter and
show off a rising sun partially eclipsed by a couching, angry lion
about to break into a roar. Thousands of those lions and suns make
Jaswant's heart pound with excitement and help him forget the power
of the enemy, albeit for a moment. He narrows his eyes and watches
as Aurangzeb's army slowly appears on the southern horizon. But
when he sees the sea of troopers gliding down the gentle slopes like
evil shadows of ominous rainclouds sweeping across the earth, his
bones turn cold. The mass looks energetic, despite the fact that they
have travelled one hundred and fifty kos north from Aurangabad to
reach the southwestern side of Ujjain.

Jaswant waits for Aurangzeb's advance guard to move ahead and
fall into his trap. Instead, the earth starts shuddering with explosions.
The shots are being fired from an elevated position such that they
land in the midst of Jaswant's advance guard, causing acute infernos.
Aurangzeb's gunners are swift, their shots precise, not wasted, never
going wayward, and never exploding mid-air. Under the cover of
this barrage, Aurangzeb's archers and musketeers move ahead. The
sky turns dark with arrows flying northwards while the projectiles
tear through the chain armour of Jaswant's horsemen. Aurangzeb's
musketeers move like lightning, pulling triggers with their modern
barrel-loading weapons, the flintlocks. Chaos spreads as Aurangzeb's
orders his cavalry to burst forth. The air reverberates with harsh

sounds of trumpets, drumbeats and piercing battle cries of 'Deen! Deen! Deen!'

On the other hand, the Rajputs seem ready to sacrifice their lives for Jaswant. Their deaths would elevate the status of their beloved motherland, Jodhpur. How can one compare that to the vassalage of the Mughal? They break away from their lines and gallop towards Aurangzeb's artillerymen, and start slaughtering the enemy gunners. Unfortunately for them, the firangs are highly trained in sword combat. They slaughter Jaswant's impulsive soldiers and keep firing. Aurangzeb notices that Jaswant's horsemen from his left and right wing desperately flee the battlefield, their horses stumbling and falling while crossing the water-filled ditch. He laughs as Jaswant's men try to escape from their own trap.

There is more to come—shame and humiliation. Jaswant has watched Aurangzeb's men come in waves, quick and forceful, towards the core of his battle formation. The imperial banners have fallen on the ground and enemy horsemen have ridden over the rising suns and couching lions. Jaswant's men ask him to climb down from his elephant for his own safety. He is swift to dismount as the mahout tries to steady the beast. He takes a horse but fails to see a lone enemy horseman break the ring of his guards. Suddenly, an excruciating pain sears through his body. Blood gushes out from his right arm. He has been shot by an arrow. His guards scramble and kill the attacker. Unfazed, Jaswant wants to gallop straight into the ranks of the advancing enemy. He does not want to be so defeated. But someone catches the bridle of his horse and drags him out of the battlefield, overpowered, injured and filled with rage. He remains alive only to be overcome, to witness the enemy grab his artillery, war animals and weapons.

The battle is over in a day.

Qasim Khan has disappeared along with his five thousand men. Jaswant's war animals and weapons are missing. It is only in the evening, after Aurangzeb's army has marched ahead and disappeared beyond the northern horizon, that a vanquished Jaswant comes out of his hideout and visits the battlefield. He watches in horror as countless vultures glide across the orange sky without flapping their wings—kites of death. The twenty-eight-year-old imperial

commander of seven thousand horses is crestfallen. The raja of
Jodhpur walks gingerly, his gaze fixed on the ground littered with
the dead. More than ten thousand of his men have been slaughtered.
The terrain, one hundred and fifty kos south of Agra and a few kos
southwest of Ujjain city, near Dharmat village, is sodden with blood.
His eyes scan the western horizon. The air stinks of rotting flesh. The
smell is bound to attract packs of wild scavengers. Soon they will rip
his soldiers' bodies apart.

2

Aurangzeb breathes in deeply, filling his lungs with a cool breeze.
Thousands of his soldiers frolic in the muddy river Yamuna. They
have not bathed for weeks. Tonight his men will feast and rest. Goats,
cattle, oil, firewood and bags of rice have arrived from villages across
the Yamuna from his sympathizers.

Aurangzeb has a job to get done. He moves to the edge of
his camp where his Muslim officers have started forming a large
semicircle around a wooden platform. His son Sultan, brother
Murad and his uncle Shaista have already arrived. Aurangzeb notices
a few men standing behind his uncle and whispering to each other.
Some gesticulate to draw his son's and his brother's attention. On
seeing him, they stop talking and are all ears for him. He swaggers
unhurriedly, as if deliberately pondering over the decision he has
already made. The battle ahead is not an ordinary one. For the wars
fought to expand the imperial territory, he needed their strength and
skill. For the battle of succession that looms ahead, he needs their
passion. The men bow deeply, once, twice and then thrice.

Aurangzeb swiftly climbs the platform, his eyes sweeping over
his men in a quick glance. His gaze wanders beyond the gathering.
Far beyond, towards the northwest, a bunch of Arjuna trees with
dusty green canopies rise more than twenty guj above the ground.
Beyond those trees he knows that Dara bhai's army has gathered in
large numbers. He starts speaking, in Urdu that is mixed with Farsi
and Arabic for all to understand.

'All of us gathered here are warriors, fearless, dauntless and ready to spill our blood for the Empire. We have done that in the past, many times over. We are born to die as martyrs. But we have a chance to depart this life in a more meaningful, more divine way. A death of a mujahideen beckons us. A death of a holy warrior! We will slay for a higher cause, get slain for a higher reason. We must take our war to another level. We are the chosen ones to breathe in the vicinity of the divine.'

He stops for breath. Men look at him, confused. He ignores their expression.

'Life is a struggle and all of us die. Death as a mujahideen promises unattainable things, like escape from the interrogation by the angels in the grave, the chance to bypass the purgatory uncertainty, to avoid the agonizing wait to be pure before entering paradise. A mujahideen is entitled to the highest ranks in His court.'

Aurangzeb speaks slowly with dramatic voice modulations as if each word is an ocean pearl, to be seen, felt, pined for and sought with hunger.

Many in the crowd nod vigorously, not knowing what lies ahead.

'What is the meaning of a kafir, the Arabic word which is active participle to the root K-F-R, the word that means to cover, to deny, to hide?' he asks. 'Is it a person who rejects Islamic faith and hides from the truth like an ostrich burying its head in the sand? Or is it also a person who is born a Muslim but wanders into the unholy turfs of infidelity, under the pretext of seeking truth? The truth exists in the holy Quran. Revealed by Him to his chosen Prophet; our beloved *Paigambar*, Peace Be Upon Him. To seek truth elsewhere is to dishonour our Prophet.'

He pauses to take a few deep breaths and to let his words sink in the minds of his men.

'A person who rejects Islam may either be blind or ignorant, stupid or mad. But a Muslim who shows interest in the faiths of the infidels is a shaytan, evil to the core.'

He pauses again to see the expressions on the faces of his warriors, who look utterly puzzled.

'Whoever helps a good cause becomes a partner therein and whoever helps an evil cause shares in its burden.'

Silence fills the empty space above the gathering. He knows that this silence can be far more potent than the dust clouds hovering over the north-western skyline.

'Jihad!' he finally screams. 'This is the only way to deal with these evil men. We hereby declare jihad against the infidel Dara Shikoh, the first prince, for disregarding Islam.' Aurangzeb makes the word jihad sound like an explosive that has been just fired. 'A man who encourages *kufr* or kafirdom and hides from the truth cannot be our ruler,' he repeats over and over again till his throat goes sore and starts itching. 'If your men fight for my cause they will become mujahideen, and if they die, they will become shaheed,' he says with elan as if he was doing a favour by offering the men a chance to become holy warriors, the chance they would never get, and they must never let go. 'Jihad is essential to save our empire from a heretic dog who aspires to be our next emperor. How can he—who regards the holy Quran and the scriptures of the infidels as two sides of one coin!'

He strikes still deeper till the sharpness of his words slice the logic of some of his officers. In sheer disbelief, men of war listen to what their master has to say. Somewhere at the back of the crowd, he hears sullen mutterings of disapproval. This infuriates him but he waits, standing still, without removing his gaze from them. This is one moment to lose or win a thousand hearts, to lose or win the world. Eyes filled with cynicism, doubt, confusion, anger and rage look at him. Whether for him or against him, for Dara bhai or against Dara bhai, he is not yet sure.

'*Anta turidwa-howa, yuriidwallaahyafthreeal ma yuriid,*' Aurangzeb says as loudly as possible in chaste Arabic. 'You want what you want, he wants what he wants, but Allah does what He wants.'

Like molten lava that erupts from a dormant volcano, his few hundred men raise their hands and chant, 'Deen! Deen! Deen! Deen!' Within moments, almost all the men raise their hands and echo the battle cry. The collective sound reverberates through his military camp, rattles above the babul twigs blanketing the terrain, shakes the canopies of arjuna trees and hovers over the north-western dust clouds. Its chilling resonance silences the voices of dissent. Hearts that had pounded with cynicism and doubt explode with the hysteria of pride that they collectively feel for their fidelity and brotherhood.

Mohammed Sultan glares at his father with eyes shining with astonishment and hurt. He has never disliked his Sunni father with so much passion. His father is surely not a man to be trusted. He is a man who wants to use religion as a weapon and he, Mohammad Sultan, may also be a potential victim of his father's fanaticism.

Murad Baksh too glares at his brother as jealousy eats into his heart. Aurangzeb has used his idea to instigate their warriors. He cannot accept the fact that his brother receives all the love and admiration of the military officers. It is he who deserves that adulation.

3

Dara Shikoh does not want to think about the defeat of Jaswant Singh Rathod. And yet a hesitant Dara has decided to wait for three long days, despite his military advisers pleading otherwise. He does not want to launch the first offensive but will instead wait for his younger brothers to march in. He has turned a deaf ear to his advisers warning him of the dangers and the pitfalls of the delay.

Dara wipes his face with a small towel. It is insanely hot. In the sweltering sun, blazing sands and the blistering wind around them, his men and animals sweat profusely under their heavy metal armour. It is their third day of waiting for 'start' orders so they can march on. The marshalling of ranks is long over, battle formation has been done with and his army can be set in motion with one order. His gaze rolls over his army, the enormous elephants wrapped in steel plates strengthened with barbwires. Weapons like swords and spears are tied to their trunks. Their steel-coated howdahs soar above the sea of horsemen and footmen, perhaps fifty, perhaps seventy thousand in numbers commanded by the Muslim khans and the Rajput rajas.

The air is filled with dust particles and rattles with the whinnying of restless horses and trumpeting of impatient elephants. Somewhere in the front, drummers standing behind the cannon make a racket. The cannon carts linked to each other by massive iron chains have formed a barrier.

A steel howdah has been specially designed for him. Its metal plates are thick like bricks, to protect him from arrows. It is secured with metal bars that reach up to its roof making the howdah look like a cage. Footmen with javelins march from behind while countless swordsmen guard the beast's legs. Heavy iron chains with dangling steel balls are tied to its trunk. The tusker is trained to swirl them to kill men who come near it and use axes to chop off their legs.

However, the first prince is disconcerted. He now realizes that he has indeed made a mistake by waiting, thereby putting his army in a contingency mode for three successive days. His uncertainty has allowed his brothers' armies to move further eastwards and reach the banks of the Yamuna. He has given them the leave to rest and recover from the long journey across the dry plains—Ujjain to Gwalior and then towards Agra. The blunder has been committed, and he is aware that his men, horses and elephants are tired and drained under the veneer of banners fluttering in the air like rivers of silk. He looks down. Mir Jumla stands before his elephant, clad in chain mail and armour. He looks ahead and another reality starts to sink in slowly. 'Do not worry, Your Imperial Highness, we are prepared.' Mir Jumla first bows and straightens up, his voice rising above the din of the battlefield. Dara Shikoh raises himself, resting his body on his knees and looks through the bars. Mir Jumla's dark eyes are looking up at him but they just twinkle, giving nothing away.

'Our plans are in place. The artillery, in a half-a-kos-long line of cannon carts surrounded by cannoneers and artillerymen, stands right in the front, stuffed, ready to fire,' shouts Mir Jumla.

Dara Shikoh is not comfortable with Mir Jumla and other military officials. They are strangers to him; he does not know them as he has hardly fought any battles. Dara is dogged by a nervous feeling that they are not under his control. He has been gathering mansabdars from far and nearby provinces. Their contingents have been hastily equipped with armour and weapons with the arsenal from Agra Fort and pampered with huge funds from the imperial treasury. He is unable to deal with them decisively and does not know if they truly stand by him or not.

A strange fear nibbles at his innards. The ill will between his personal army and his father's highly paid *ahadi* soldiers is obvious. Ahadi in Arabic means 'standalone' and these soldiers do not report to any mansabdars, they are reserved for the emperor and a pampered lot. They are not used to taking orders, have not fought any battles in the recent times and are good only for parade.

The mutual jealousy between the Hindu and the Muslim military officials suddenly bothers him. Aurangzeb's victory and Jaswant's defeat have created a new equation in the mind of the people. With one single blow, Aurangzeb has brought him down from the position of the crown prince to a prince. But what hurts the most is Dara's suspicion that some even think of him to be lower in position than Aurangzeb. He is no longer sure how to be the general of this war, or of any war for that matter. Suddenly, terror strikes him. The southern horizon is darkened with dust. It seems that his brothers have reached.

He looks down. Mir Jumla is staring back at him, waiting for orders.

'Fire when you see them!' Dara shouts. He cannot decide if his orders will come sooner or later.

Mir Jumla does not comment, but only turns back and disappears.

Dara Shikoh narrows his eyes and stares ahead. The entire southern horizon has come alive with footmen, horsemen and elephants. Banners flutter wildly in the air. It is unbelievable that his younger brothers have gathered such a large force. He feels the ground shudder beneath him. Between his and his brothers' armies, the plain explodes as a thick cloud of smoke rises like a dark curtain. He looks on, aghast. Mir Jumla seems to empty the stock of their explosives even though the enemy has not walked into the firing range. The explosives hit the barren land between the armies. A curtain of smoke rises, blocking his view. He waits as his elephant raises its trunk in fear and trumpets as his mahout struggles to

control his fidgety animal with his ankush. Acrid smoke that rides
on the wind makes him breathless even as the enemy starts emerging
from the wall of soot.

The enemy comes in waves and he is numb with shock as
explosives, arrows and javelins start raining over his men. Some
arrows hit the metal plates of his elephant. One gets stuck into the
barbed wires and he can see its shaft shudder on impact.

He looks down: one of his bodyguards has fallen, impaled by a
javelin.

The war has begun. Dara looks to his left and shouts, 'Attack!'

His left wing is commanded by Rustum Khan. Thousands
of horsemen pull out swords from their scabbards and charge at
European artillerymen protecting Aurangzeb's right wing.

Dara looks to his right but does not say anything. His right wing
is a sea of Rajput squadrons and is commanded by Chatrasal Hada.

Aurangzeb is not worried, but Dara, not being used to battles,
makes the mistake of using the same old tactic. Worse still, his army
is a motley group of hastily put together squadrons. Dara may be
backed by numbers but his army is not at all a cohesive body. To face
such a disorderly enemy, Aurangzeb has divided his artillery into
two units, and put his heavy cavalry, commanded by Mohammad
Sultan, in the middle. The enemy is likely to attack impulsively, and
will be intercepted by two-pronged artillery attack, while Sultan can
advance towards the core of the enemy's battle formation.

Aurangzeb has placed Murad Baksh and his army behind the
left artillery unit, while he is behind Mohammad Sultan's squadrons
and is surrounded by a mass of horsemen. He watches from his
howdah as both the units of his artillery start firing at once, killing
Dara's horsemen in large numbers. Mohammad Sultan's cavalry
advances towards the core of Dara's army. Another mass of cavalry,
commanded by Murad, press forward towards Dara's right wing.
Suddenly, a sea of saffron-clad Rajput horsemen under Chatrasal
Hada move towards Murad's elephant, the archers shooting wildly.
The projectiles miss Murad but get stuck to his howdah and the
tusker's armour. Soon his war beast looks like a giant porcupine. His
mahout is hit, and falls down on the hot sands of the battlefield, dead.

Dara watches too and realizes that Murad's reckless march has blocked Aurangzeb's artillery. Chatrasal Hada and his Rajput horsemen from Gaur, Sisodia and Rathod clans have charged forward, wielding their swords, literally flinging themselves on Murad's contingent. He feels excited for the first time but his excitement is short-lived. When he looks to his left, Rustum Khan is nowhere to be seen, as if he and his elephant have disappeared in thin air. Dara notices Aurangzeb's horsemen wearing green turbans breaking into his domain, their swords cutting his men down as if they are goats. Aurangzeb's artillerymen are busy firing. Dara notices for the first time that his brother's artillery has a line of archers trained to use their composite bows to fire grenade-like rockets. Flames rise from the midst of the dense body of his cavalry. Around him, his men are shot down quickly by arrows and javelins.

'To the left!' he shouts at his mahout. He has to investigate Rustum's disappearance. The mahout hesitates. His general is not supposed to leave his position.

'To the left!' Dara screams again.

As they move towards the left, his elephant lumbers forward through the sea of his army and he can no longer see his right wing, or what his Muslim commander is up to. He searches for Mir Jumla who has vanished. To his right, he sees a long line of cannons on wheels. His artillerymen have abandoned their guns. His elephant keeps moving towards his left and Aurangzeb's right wing. Dara watches with dread. The battleground is already littered with bodies, broken blades, shields and hilts. Enemy horsemen have broken his artillery barrier. To his right, the earth is strewn with corpses, rolling heads and scattered limbs. Horses stand lost and confused near their dead masters. Injured men cry for help. Aurangzeb's frenzied riders move ruthlessly over those on the brink of death. The deafening noise of clashing swords, leaping hooves and the beastly cries of hysteric warriors pound his eardrums.

He was not born to do this. He was born to study theology, discover the real meaning of religions and write books!

'Our advance guard has vanished,' someone shouts. Dara gazes at his right and a cold shiver runs down his spine: he is in the firing range of the enemy's cannon—one that he had never seen before.

'Turn back!' he yells at his mahout, who too has noted the large and small cannon mounted on pivot over the wheels, surrounded by frantic white men. They swirl the guns in his direction. It takes his mahout a while to turn back the cumbersome beast and start moving across the front line towards their core. The cannons start firing violently. Aurangzeb's archers too have gone insane. He looks up and notices long, burning shafts flying above him. He looks down to see some of his guards turning into bright torches, their high-pitched cries rising above the din of the battle. Iron projectiles hit the targets, carrying off heads and limbs of his remaining guards. He is still safe in his howdah, its thick steel plates resisting the crossfire, but he fails to notice a mysterious horseman appearing to his left. He holds a stretched composite bow to its fullest. The arrows are shot in succession, aiming for the eyeholes of his fully armoured beast. He feels his elephant rock violently under him. Perplexed, he watches as his mahout tumbles down. The elephant raises its trunk to screech in agony, and then stands on its hind legs. He holds on to the steel bars of his howdah. Then the animal suddenly slumps as life is snuffed out of its enormous body. The howdah tumbles down and crashes. Dara finds himself flung on the floor as dust starts rising around him. His fall is awkward, he falls face down. His metal body armour hits his jaw, breaking some of his teeth. His mouth fills up with blood. Someone drags him from behind, lifts him by the armpits and hurls him on a horse.

'The first prince is dead, our beloved Dara Shikoh is dead!' a horseman gallops past the fighting men, shouting.

Dara Shikoh's army starts to scramble; there is a stampede crushing men, animals, artillery carts. Panic leads to mayhem and the pandemonium leads to the crumbling of Dara Shikoh's battle formation. Kalil Ullah Khan from Samarkand, one of Dara's mansabdars, watches the fall of Dara Shikoh from a distance. He is least bothered as he was forced to defend Dara whom he hates. The same prince has had him beaten with a shoe for a trivial matter. The Samarkand warrior nurses ambition to work for Aurangzeb as he gazes at Dara ride towards Agra, running away from the battlefield. Dara has noticed Kalil Ullah Khan staring at him with glee, but he is helpless. He spits to show anger and spews out a few of his broken teeth. He kicks his horse to a full gallop in the direction of Agra. His world of books, music, poetry and theological studies seems to evaporate in the heat and dust of his battlefield he has left behind where another drama of brotherly love unfolds. Aurangzeb has rushed to check on the injured Murad. 'Brother, my brother,' he cries while watching the best medic tend to Murad's superficial wounds. 'What will I do if anything happens to you!' he laments and keeps Murad's injured hand on his knee. He touches it tenderly and says, 'The war was fought for you, my brother and the future emperor. You must take care as you are precious to me, much more than anything in the world.'

4

It is rather early for the monsoon but rain clouds float over Agra. It seems like the sky's attempt to wash away the blood of the thousands lying on the battlefield. Eleven days and eleven nights have passed since Agra fell into Aurangzeb's hands. Dara Shikoh, the holder of lofty titles such as *Shah Bulund Iqbal*, the king of lofty fortunes, *Padshahzaada-i-Buzurg Artaba*, the senior son of the emperor, and *Jalal-ul-Kadir*, the superior and the most capable, has run away like a frightened rabbit, first to Agra Fort and then to Dilli. A smile appears on Aurangzeb's face. The emperor has shut the gates of Agra Fort and Aurangzeb has cut off the water supply that the fort enjoys from the Yamuna. The news that many of the fort inhabitants have died of thirst has been making the rounds. He diverts his gaze from the sky to the path before him and walks briskly through his camp at Nur Manzil, a far-off suburb south of Agra, while Shaista Khan runs behind him muttering a request.

'Son, do not get carried away by your father's sudden hail of love, it is a fake show of well-thought-out diplomacy. Sending her is a part of that plan.'

He is probably right, Aurangzeb thinks. *Father has shut the gates of the fort on my face, and now when I have cut off water supplies to the fort, he is trying to be tactful.*

He does not utter a word but rushes towards his *shamiana*, made to befit the victorious prince. The floor is covered with Persian carpets and the panels are made of satin. At the far end, away from the entrance and facing a gilded chair, a woman wearing a long white mantle and a thin veil sits on the ground. At the far end, Mutamad stands like a statue. It is the first time that he is looking at the famous princess, the emperor's favourite person in the world, who refers to her as the *Padishah Begum*, the empress!

The Mughal princess hears her brother's footsteps but avoids looking up, even after he occupies the high-backed, gilded chair before her. The third prince stares down at her, wondering what he must say. His eldest sibling, their father's heartbeat, Padishah Begum, sits near his feet like his ghulam. He watches as she takes off her veil and looks up, her greenish-blue eyes staring at her younger brother. His sister's once beautiful face is covered with fine wrinkles, and her hair has streaks of henna dyed red. He jerks his head backwards, just to show her that he is now in command. She looks like a wretch in a mantle with a high Chinese collar. He knows what she hides behind her clothes—ugly scars of a severe burn. She had tried to burn herself when she was accused of having a relationship with her own father.

She cannot bear the silence any longer and starts crying, her thin frame convulsing with each sob.

Aurangzeb lets her weep. He has always seen her dressed in gowns, made of silk and chintz, wearing the best of what the famous jewellers of Hindustan could offer. She, Jahanara, has always been in control, always in command, always amazing people with her philosophical rhetoric. He and his brothers would hover around her, amazed at her grace. But that was thousands of moons ago; he has not met her for a while and feels like a stranger now.

Still sobbing, she stretches her hand, hands over an epistle to him and whispers, 'It is from father.'

Father is a beaten man now. His letter is no longer a farman.

He rips it open with total disregard and takes the Kashmiri silken paper out to read. Father's Arabic is chaste; he has written a verse in black ink.

My son, you are my champion
I, the emperor, backed by a half a million troopers,
am a beggar
My fate, slapping me hard,
made me a prisoner, a mere ward
Remember, not a leaf falls from a tree without Allah's will
And still
We remain proud of our triumph in this perishable world
Lying in a drain called life
Like a worm eternally curled
I praise the Hindus who put water in the mouth of the dying
You, my son, a chaste Muslim, are starving me of the elixir of life
It is akin to slaughter and slaying.

Aurangzeb wants to laugh. For the first time, his father speaks like
a commoner, without orders, arrogance or accusations. He throws
the paper away. He watches his startled sister and says, 'Now I have
become his champion, huh, now that he is left without a choice.'

'Bhai,' Jahanara speaks, her voice quivering with emotions, 'what
is happening to our family, to us, and why?'

'You mean our dysfunctional family?' he says scornfully and
wags his index finger at her. 'You and your Dara bhai should know
why better than I do, Begum Sahiba; you have lived with father in the
palaces, adorned with riches. For you, far far away has been the world
of battlefields sodden with blood and filled with the stench of rotting
dead. That world has never touched you—that world has been my
home for years.'

'Why did you do what you did?'

'What have I done? I was on my way to seeing my sick father
when Jaswant intercepted me with his army. Is it a sin to come home
when your father is ill?'

'I am talking about your declaration of jihad against Dara bhai.
Why jihad against your own blood?' Her voice is clear.

'Do you not know?'

'Kindly enlighten me,' Jahanara whispers, trying hard not to
sound scornful. He stares at her, searching for even a slight shadow
of a snigger, but she looks sincere and grave.

'Once Dara bhai made his intentions clear by sending Jaswant to stop me, I started to think . . . What must one call a man who draws parallels between the holy Quran and the Upanishads of the kafirs? What must one say about his public statements such as infidelity and Islam are twin sisters? You must agree that his deeds make him an enemy of Islam. Will this enemy of Islam rule our Islamic empire? What must a chaste Muslim like me do when he happens to be my brother? You must agree that it is my duty to fight him. And what must one call this fight against the enemy of Islam? You must agree that it is called jihad.'

For a moment she is speechless. 'The holy Quran talks about tolerance, even towards the followers of other religions. Here we talk about our own brother, a Muslim—a liberal Muslim at that,' she whispers.

'That's your interpretation,' he cuts her off.

'And if your interpretation of jihad is to kill even the liberal Muslim, what happens to your tolerance then?' she asks softly.

'Dear sister, under the circumstances, what kind of jihad should I have followed—by words, or by swords? I would have started this spiritual fight by words, but Dara bhai did not give me such an opportunity; he prepared for war.' Aurangzeb pulls out a tesbih from the pocket of his robe and starts counting the beads.

She listens, her eyes fixed on his beads. Words bubble in her mouth like froth. Spitting them out may mean death. 'Jihad,' she says bitterly, 'and all for the bloody throne.'

'Talk for Dara bhai, you do not know me. I am not interested in your throne,' he says calmly.

'Who then will be the next emperor?' she asks coldly. Her gaze has fallen to the carpet near his feet.

'How is father?' he replies, ignoring her question and her coldness.

'He is recovering,' she says defiantly. In the depth of her heart she knows that father's recovery is politically insignificant. Dara bhai's loyal warriors, like Chatrasal Hada, Ram Singh Rathod, Bhimsing Gaur, and others have been killed. Thousands of mansabdars who had fought for Dara have joined the victor, including Mir Jumla, Maharaja Jaswant Singh Rathod and Diler Khan. The news is that even Mirza Raja Jai Singh has left Suleiman Shikoh, Dara Shikoh's eldest son, and is on his way to Agra from Bengal. The orthodox Muslim warriors have joined Aurangzeb in large numbers.

'If he is well enough and decides to punish the infidels like Dara bhai, he may continue to rule by the dictums of the holy Quran. Otherwise, both Murad and Shuja bhai have already got the *khutba* to read in their names. They have also minted the coins. How can I vouch for their actions? Both of them want to be the emperor.'

'Murad?' Jahanara mutters to herself and falls silent. Murad had always been a difficult child, destructive and unmanageable. His favourite game had been hurting swans with his catapult and rolling on the ground laughing when the birds had screeched and fluttered, bled and sometimes died. The palace servants had been his targets too. He would fling pebbles and even rocks at them, till they begged him to spare them and cried at his feet. She had hoped he would grow out of it, but even at the age of thirty-eight he remained the same. A failed viceroy of Balkh and Gujarat, an alcoholic, wasting his time in the court intrigues of his sycophant noblemen.

Aurangzeb keenly watches his sister's face. His lips curl into a sceptical smile.

'Then, who do you think? Do you think Shah Shuja will be a better choice?' Aurangzeb asks contemptuously.

'Why not Suleiman?' Jahanara blurts and then bites her tongue with deep regret. Twenty-four-year-old Suleiman Shikoh is the pride of her family; Dara bhai's eldest son has been born with beauty and bravery. He is the star of her father's eyes.

'Where is *his* father?' Aurangzeb asks as his eyes bore into her eyes.

She shudders and knows that he knows. The night of the defeat was one of the darkest. The streets of Agra were hushed like a graveyard. Everyone at the fort lay silent, as slaves and servants moved through the corridors and courtyards like lost spirits. The escapees from the battlefields started arriving in the city, the hoof beats shattering the ominous stillness. Dara bhai who had left shouting slogans like 'Victory or the grave!' had returned, vanquished yet alive. He had not come to meet them but she was told that his face had blisters, his eyes were swollen and his clothes were covered with soot. She could hear the wails and cries of his wives from his apartment.

Dara bhai had to leave, vanish before he was captured. Father ordered mules loaded with gold and silver coins to be sent with him. A farman was dispatched to the governor of Dilli to open the fort and treasury for the vanquished prince. She watched from her balcony as the first prince left for Dilli, shadows of horsemen, palanquins, mules and slaves moving westwards. She had run towards her father's apartments, her father had been watching from his balcony. The thin old man, with his long face, grey beard and bleary eyes, stood staring as shadows of his first son and his tiny convoy dissolved into the night.

'I will leave for Dilli tonight,' she hears her brother speak. She is terrified; she must dispatch a message, Dara bhai must know. Aurangzeb watches her face like a cat looking at a trapped mouse.

'Don't bother. The coward has already fled from Dilli.'

She hears Aurangzeb's words filled with derision and exhales in relief but cannot resist speaking further. 'So, chase, bloodbath and death—are these the fate of our family?'

'That,' he says with contempt, not taking his eyes away from his sister, 'you should have asked father before he advised your beloved Dara bhai to wait for me at Samugad with fifty thousand soldiers.'

'I had begged them to consider,' she says feebly.

'Did they pay any heed, your beloved father and your mulhid brother? And now you want me to follow what you say—you, who concurred with Dara bhai's heretical views and exalted his image by preaching his philosophies that were against Islam?' He relaxes his body on the backrest of his gilded chair and counts his beads faster.

'I do not preach his philosophies as I too believe in those ideas. In fact, I had asked to translate Hindu scriptures like the Upanishads into Farsi,' she says without cringing.

'I do not want to argue with you. Just agree to the fact that it was father's and Dara bhai's idea to send Jaswant to intercept me near Ujjain. Even the battle near Samugad was well planned.'

'What could they do? You were advancing towards Agra with your and Murad's armies.'

'Is it a crime for a son to visit his ailing father?' Aurangzeb asks blandly. 'Is the emperor afraid of his own army governed by his own sons?'

Silence lingers for a long time as Jahanara mulls over her victorious brother's words.

'Father begs you to keep your brothers from harm, they are your own flesh and blood,' she whispers softly, her tears falling on the carpet.

'Father is in no position to cast morals. Have you asked our dear father what he had done to his uncles, half-brothers, cousins and nephew? He murdered them, blinded them and expelled them'.

'Had he not done so, we would not be alive. In fact it was done primarily to save you and Dara bhai.'

'Really?' Aurangzeb says and laughs very loudly.

'For his love for Ammi, our Ammi, please spare him the anguish of seeing his first son die,' Jahanara plays her last card.

Aurangzeb can no longer maintain his composure, but bursts out laughing.

'Love for Ammi? That man is a cannonball of lust, ready to explode between his thighs at the sight of any woman. Can you count the number of women he has taken after Ammi was gone? You should know better.'

Mutamad shudders. *What is his master trying to imply?* He has heard the rumours about the emperor and his first daughter. He looks at the princess. He cannot see her face but he knows that she has started to sob.

'And what is the cause of his illness? Is it not the overdose of aphrodisiacs as I have heard? Is the senile old man still hungry for the female flesh?'

She closes her eyes with indignation, as tears stream down her face.

'Entire Hindustan talks about his erotic endeavours . . . Who would know better than you, sister?' he insists mockingly.

Mutamad squirms; he has never heard his master talk so explicitly, not even to him, a lowly eunuch slave.

'Father wants you to come to the fort and meet him . . .' she says dejectedly.

He nods affirmatively knowing that he will never do so. She suddenly gets up. He realizes that she is far too frail, almost like a reed wearing a gown. She looks into his eyes and says evenly, 'The true meaning of jihad is to declare war with our inner demons.'

'La ilaha illa'llah!' he whispers. *There is no God except Allah.*

5

Murad Baksh thinks fondly about Aurangzeb. His big brother has proved his loyalty by sending him a gift of one hundred and fifty thousand ashrafi mohurs and two hundred and fifty Arabian horses. 'We must rejoice our victory, my brother and the future emperor,' Aurangzeb has written.

Murad agrees to have dinner with him. *Why not?* he thinks. *I am surrounded by my ten thousand troopers.*

The shamiana is lit by a hundred polished and shining brass shamdans. The ceremonial tent is covered with colourful Turkish carpets. Smell of roasted gosht kebabs wafts in the air. But Murad looks forward to the several silver ewers filled with wine that beckon him. His brother has managed to get glasses made of rock glass. Murad has decided to drink, and he is not worried about his safety. His guard Niruddin Khawas is with him. Niruddin does not drink and will die for him if need be. As Aurangzeb empties small cups of Turkish coffee, Murad empties glasses of wine. Murad does not remember the rest of the night. When he wakes up, he finds himself shackled in a palanquin. He tries to shout, but his mouth is stuffed with pebbles. They have also taped it shut.

CHAPTER TWELVE

1

Shivaji glances at Moroji Pinglay, whose face is flushed with excitement. They have crossed Mahad, a small town of narrow lanes and huddled houses and are riding along the river Gandhari. The wind howls, sounding eerily like a wailing woman. His *kathiawadi* horse canters through the uneven trail. The land is covered with luxuriant vegetation. Gleams of sunshine sneak through the broken masses of rainclouds. They colour every mountain with countless fleeting hues. He narrows his eyes to focus. They have reached the edge. Stretches of grassland unfold in front of him. Near the skyline, huge hills wait like beasts, their girths gigantic, their peaks shrouded in clouds. One hill is the largest, sitting smug in the midst of others, like a lion bounded by its pride.

'That one, the mother hill, looks like someone has axed it away from the Sahyadri Range,' he mutters.

'That is the hill of Rairi, it is special,' Pinglay responds quickly.

'It is just twenty-five kos away from the Arabian Sea and three to four days by horse from Rajgad Fort,' he comments.

'That's only a part of it,' Pinglay replies.

It does not take much time for them to reach the base of the hill. Pinglay seems to know the path, so there is no need to look for one. As they start climbing, their horses slow down. He notices a large cliff hanging over their heads, like the raised hood of a giant snake. Moving a little ahead, a huge cascade bursts into his vision. It plunges from the cliff into a deep ravine. He wrenches the reins to pause for a brief moment. Water has always fascinated him. Here it is trapped between two giant rocks, jutting out from the crag only to leap down with a roar, forming a foamy torrent in the gap and spraying the path with milky effervescence.

'The real surprise lies ahead,' Pinglay declares as his eyes shine.

He smiles and guides his horse through a slushy patch as a hundred men silently ride behind them. It's getting misty; he looks ahead and sees the trail becoming narrower and steeper. His horse climbs slowly, cautiously taking one step at a time. He grabs the saddle horn to keep his weight forward and notices the earth below, uneven, covered with mud and stones. After a particularly treacherous bend they are suddenly blinded by strong sunlight. The mist has vanished. He looks into the valley; the world below is submerged in the dark clouds as the world above basks in the golden rays of the afternoon sun. The surrounding mountains have risen above the blanket of clouds. They are smeared with several white streaks of rainwater torrents pouring from the sides. His horse has chosen its own path to climb the last stretch before they reach the crest. It is a many-kos-long plateau. An enormous hill looms over him and his men, rising above the mountain table like a horn on the head of a giant. He kicks his horse to a gallop. The boundary of the black basalt against the backdrop of the blue expanse creates an ethereal suspension. Countless eagles fly, drawing circles in that suspended space with serene dignity, carefully guarding the rock from the bending sky.

'The fort is on top of the rocky hill. Prataprao Morey has been driven out. It is yours now, Raja,' Pinglay finally announces.

The horses are left behind with a few men to water and feed them. The upward climb will be on foot. A few local herdsmen are there to guide them. Their leather sandals with flexible soles save them from slipping down each time a stone is dislodged by their weight. They grab ledges and crevices, sometimes tough vines, as they push themselves upwards. He starts feeling a tingling sensation in his knees and looks at the Brahmin who is older than him. His peshwa shows no sign of distress. The air has thinned and the winds are cooler. The men need to breathe deeply to fill their lungs. It takes them a good hour to reach their destination. Shivaji looks on with fascination. A large plateau on the hilltop lies before him. As he walks past small stone structures and ruins of a stone wall, he sees a flat mountain crest, vast and endless. It is less than a kos above the sea and overlooking the coast, with abrupt slopes plunging into Konkan. It is unlike anything that he has seen before.

One can build a city here, he thinks, and turns to look at Pinglay who is watching him, his eyes shining like jewels. 'This place will be the capital of our swaraj, floating in the sky and overlooking the Sindhu Sagar,' Shivaji announces, his eyes dreamy.

The leader of the Maratha feels overwhelmed. He walks ahead and notices men practice with wooden swords. Two of them have strayed away from the others. They are quick, and seem to sense each other's moves. They take stances with their swords, turning offensive or defensive as the game demands. One of them is large and stocky, and the other, small and wiry. Each one tries to push his rival backwards over obstacles like rocks or shallow ditches. They move, shoving each other with their strikes from the flat earth and climb over the rocky mounds. The stocky man starts losing his balance. Shivaji watches them fight, first with interest and then with fascination as their wooden swords bang against each other, especially when they block or parry each other's blows. The wiry man is far more nimble and seems to guess from which direction his opponent will deliver his blow.

'Who is he?' Shivaji asks Pinglay, pointing towards the thin man.

'Jiva Mahale.'

'I want to meet him after their fight is over.'

'He will come by,' Pinglay assures him.

He watches them till they finish their fight as the wiry man finally manages to accomplish the leverage he was seeking, his sword hand moving swiftly as the wooden blade of his opponent can no longer parry the attacks. The fight is over. He notices the winner walk towards them uncertainly, streaks of sweat streaming down his face.

'Give him your sword,' Shivaji orders Pinglay.

'You have just finished a gruelling drill and I have just climbed this steep hill. We are equally drained of energy,' says the man with the brown eyes who has a regal air about him.

Jiva Mahale throws his wooden sword away and takes the dhop sword offered to him by Pinglay. It is shining and straight, real metal. He stares at the raja—he wears a finely cut angirkha made of costly chintz and a saffron turban laden with pearls. Mahale has not seen a man with such fair skin and sparkling eyes before.

He must be Raja Shivaji, Mahale decides. His opponent looks calm, and his blade gleams under the afternoon sun. He holds his ground by keeping a wide distance between his feet and tries to guess the direction and the force of Shivaji's strike. He knows that the ability to think beyond one's mind saves one's life. Sweat dribbles down from Mahale's forehead and into his eyes. It stings, but it is dangerous to blink. He has heard that Raja Shivaji trains every alternate day, and has garnered incredible sword skills. The raja's strong offensive bouts make his enemies lose their ground and crumble. Mahale holds his sword near his body. Only this way can he retain the strength of his arms to parry the strikes of his famous opponent. As the distance between them shortens, Shivaji delivers a forward blow, gliding his sword horizontally. Mahale avoids it by jumping backwards, away from the orbit of the raja's blade. Within a blink, Shivaji's backward strike brings the blade of his sword towards Mahale's right knee. He jumps high, letting the blade slide beneath him, without touching him in the slightest.

An energetic fight explodes between them as the air vibrates with the clang of their blades. Many leave their drills and run towards the fighters and form a large circle around them. To their left Shivaji has seen a small spur with a slope on one side and a drop of two guj on the other. He increases the strengths of his blows and darts forward as Mahale parries his attacks and moves away. Sometimes, unexpectedly, Mahale moves forward, cutting off the power of his opponent's blows, but Raja Shivaji manages to push him unhindered towards the slope of the spur and within moments brings him to its edge. Mahale immediately knows that he cannot retreat. It would probably be best to push the blows of his opponent and move forward, but he hesitates, then buckles and falls back from the spur. A blade is at his throat. Mahale closes his eyes.

'Will you be my guard?' he hears Raja Shivaji ask.

'Ji, ji, ji,' Mahale cries with happiness as he scrambles to get up.

'Put him up for pata training,' Shivaji tells Pinglay.

'He is a lowly Balute from an obscure village on the borders of Jawali,' Pinglay informs Shivaji.

'Moroji, the sword is a great leveller. It kills the enemy and shatters disparity. For the sword is then God, and the holder its disciple. Some of these disciples of the blade live life by their own codes—codes that do not differentiate between life and death, profit and loss, wealth and poverty . . . And our Jiva Mahale is one such disciple. You will see,' Raja Shivaji tells his peshwa. Great men had come into his life in the past; now he will have to create them for the future of his nation. He remembers Dadaji . . .

He was eleven. The great famine was over. The monsoon had arrived in full swing. The denuded forest surrounding his stone house had turned green as leaves burst out from the twigs that had suddenly gone tender. Dust devils did not haunt the region anymore; instead, gushing streams had swirled and rushed over rolling cobblestones and danced around the giant boulders. Flocks of different birds had started frequenting the skies above them as if the lost souls with wings had at last found their sky. The days had gone by as he along with his gang had romped and played about. They jumped in the muddy pools to dirty each other's clothes, rode their ponies standing on the stirrups and followed the shadows of flying eagles. The number of his friends had grown—Tana, Yesa, Tana's brother Surya, Bhima, Bhika, Kavji, Chimna and Bala, some as young as ten and some as old as twenty. The only exception had been Baji Pasalkar, who was an old man of sixty. But all that would change.

A very old man had arrived in a palanquin along with Sonoji Dabir. 'He is Dadaji, the diwan of your father's jagir and the surrounding hill forts,' his mother, sitting on a charpoy in the open veranda, had whispered to him. The men had bowed to her. Dadaji's red silk turban with a wide rim looked like a large umbrella on his head. His eyes were sharp, like a knife with a blade of steel. Shivaji had listened as they discussed something about the peasants who had run away and disappeared in the hills, about the earth that was tilled by donkeys, about the babul trees growing instead of rice and corn saplings, about wolves breeding like lice and snatching away livestock, about hunger despite the rain.

'People without a country and a country without its people,' Dadaji had whispered. This time his deep eyes had cut through Shivaji's soul. 'Raja, you will come with me to find the people of this country. They are yours, and you are their jagirdar, the protector of their children and their women.'

Dadaji had showed him how cultivation could be profitable and how farmers could be soldiers.

2

As the domes and minarets of Bijapur gleam in the morning sun, the palaces in the citadel take one's breath away. The Badi Sahiba bathes

in her private *hamaam* on the second floor of her seven-storey Hawa
Mahal, the wind palace. Her slave girls carefully pour rosewater on
her henna-coloured hair. The water in the enormous marble tub is
lukewarm, just the way she likes it. The girls tending to her fear her
fragility and hence are as nimble as possible. They also know that she
is temperamental and even the slightest mistake in the bathing ritual
can end up in flogging. But again, it is quite understandable that she
is short-tempered. Managing the kingdom after her husband's death
has not been easy. Ali's adoption, his education and the effort to win
his love were hard. Added to that, Aurangzeb's repeated invasions
have left her paranoid. He has seized her north-eastern military
strongholds, including the fort city of Bidar. He would have tried
for Bijapur but he had to go north. The news heralds that he has
conquered Agra and Dilli, which means that he will probably stay
away from the Deccan for a while now. Something flashes in her
mind; she knows that it is time to do that which will eventually keep
her kingdom safe.

'Hurry,' she orders the girls. Soon she's rushing to the seventh
floor. The palace servants look aghast, and bow as she walks past. She
has never done this before; she has always been a strict queen who
has stuck to royal protocols.

'Ali! Ali!' she calls, almost breathless.

Ali is puzzled. Rarely does mother climb to the seventh floor
to meet him. She always sends a messenger. He rushes out to the
main entrance, to his mother who waits for him near the parapet that
overlooks the lush gardens.

'Badi Sahiba,' he exclaims in surprise and bows deeply to his
mother. She is tall and stands upright in a long gown with sleeves
woven with pearls and rubies. Her deep brown eyes have fine wrinkles
around them—dignified and strong even at this age.

She looks at him affectionately. Ali calls her Badi Sahiba and
not Ammi as she longs to hear. He knows that his childless mother
cherishes him more than anything the world can offer. And the
world has offered her everything that she has ever wished for. She is
the sister to the king of Golconda, Abdullah Qutb Shah, and was the
queen consort to the late king of the Adilshahi sultanate, Mohammed

Adil Shah. When Ali had come to know that he had been adopted, he had felt betrayed and disappointed, even though his ammi loved him unconditionally.

'Ali, my son,' she says eagerly, 'Aurangzeb has taken over Agra, he is the emperor-to-be.'

An overweight Ali, wearing a finely cut silk jama with flower motif, looks perplexed. He knows about it.

'This means that he may not come to the Deccan for a long time. Good news for us!' she says.

The Badi Sahiba's excitement is not unfounded. Aurangzeb's second tenure in the Deccan as a subhedar or imperial viceroy had brought her grief and heartbreak. Each night for the past few years, she has stood near the arched window of her bedroom and stared at the protective ring that the walls form around her city. She has inspected the bastions guarded by armed men scanning the vast expanse for advancing enemies. When sleepless nights have given way to lethargic days, the Badi Sahiba has anxiously read Aurangzeb's humiliating letters written to her after the demise of her husband a year ago.

The most recent one is the most dreadful. If they failed to eliminate Shiva, and hand over the regions under him to Aurangzeb, he threatened to burn Bijapur like a funeral pyre of the kafirs. Her beloved Ali would die a pathetic death in the Mughal prison if he has his way.

'We must in this time wrench away our north-eastern frontiers from the clutches of the Mughals,' she says looking at her son.

'Badi Sahiba, we can get back the region either by fighting the Mughals or by eliminating Shiva. Our kingdom has been the tributary state of the empire for long. We have also renewed the old peace treaty with them. Fighting them will be treason. Instead, we will do what the emperor-to-be desires. We shall eliminate Shiva Bhosale.'

She hears Ali, and knows that he is being rational. Their army is also not in a position to face the imperial army. Many of her military officials have joined the imperial army under the third prince. The exodus has weakened her kingdom. But the battle with Shiva is not going to be a walkover either. 'It's not easy. Shiva has the hill forts to

hide, to launch attacks, to be invincible. And who do you think will
hunt him down?' she asks gloomily as she looks around the balcony
in search of eavesdroppers.

He walks closer to her and whispers, 'Consider Afzal Khan for
various reasons. He is the viceroy of our Wai province, the frontiers
of our western borders and is acquainted with the terrain of Jawali
and Maval. Also . . .' Ali lowers his voice further and mutters, 'he has
personal vendetta. He hates Shahji Bhosale. Remember that he has
helped us annex Hindu kingdoms of Karnataka either by sword or
by deceit. Kasturiranga, the chief of Sira, was lured by Afzal Khan to
negotiate a treaty and killed during the meeting.'

'How will Shahji Bhosale react?' the Badi Sahiba questions. She
does not want to offend him. If he decides to revolt, her kingdom will
be in deep trouble.

'I will take care of Shahji Bhosale,' Ali assures his mother.

Finally, she nods, accepting his suggestion.

Ali and his scribe spend their night in the library. A letter is
written to Shahji Bhosale, each word thought over a million times.

Be it known to Maharaja Farzand Shahji Bhosale:

> In the recent past you must have been tormented by the arrogance
> and treason committed by your son, Shivaji Bhosale. You need
> not live with that terrible burden. From the depth of our hearts
> we understand your plight. We know that you are in no way
> responsible for your son Shivaji's deeds. He alone is and will be
> dealt with in our own way. We shall give you your Bendakaluru
> jagir as has been decided. We have also informed all the chieftains
> to assist you in all possible ways. If anyone behaves otherwise, he
> will be severely punished by us.

3

Afzal Khan's caparisoned elephant trundles to enter the city from
the Ali Rauza gate. This western side has its own advantages. The
subhedar of Wai likes to see the fifty-five tonnes of *malik-e-maidan*,

and avoid the crowded streets of the eastern suburbs that stink of rotten food. The giant cannon weighing fifty-five-thousand ser mounted on an enormous stone is the pride of Bijapur. Its muzzle is shaped like a lion's head, whose open jaw crushes an iron elephant to death. While he is busy admiring the gun, he feels the fearful gaze of people on him. He is a huge man, his head touching the roof of his howdah, making the muscular mahout look puny in comparison. Rumours are rife in the city that it is he, Afzal Khan, who instigated the queen to murder Khan Mohammad, the late wazir of the sultanate.

Afzal swaggers with an air of arrogance as he enters the enormous court of the Adilshahi royals. He is careful to keep his kohl-lined eyes expressionless and roving. The court has an unusually high ceiling supported by countless pillars that form overhead arches. The massive windows embellished with carved wooden panels are covered with satin curtains heavily upholstered with gold brocade. Huge chandeliers dressed with rock crystals have been lit. The floor is covered with several Turkish rugs of different colours and designs. At the far end, on the gilded throne, with two lions made of pure gold squatting on either side like domesticated pets, he notices a pensive Ali. The young king's chin rests on the cusp of his right hand. To the right of the throne is another chair, partially blocked by a semi-transparent curtain. He can see the outline of Badi Sahiba. There is nobody else in the court.

Afzal Khan bows deeply first to her and then to her son.

'How is your family? How is Fazal Khan?' She keeps her voice sweet and motherly. She knows he dotes on Fazal Khan, his eldest son.

'By the grace of Allah . . .' he murmurs, again bowing.

'Farzand Afzal Khan . . .' she begins, 'we have renewed the peace treaty with the Mughals. We have offered Aurangzeb our regions that include the Bhosale jagir as well as north Konkan.'

Ali speaks as soon as she falls silent, 'Shiva Bhosale is unlikely to let go of his jagir without a fight, and Aurangzeb has written that if we do not do what we have promised he will burn Bijapur like the pyre of the kafirs. If left alive on the edge of our kingdom, Shiva will destroy us.'

'I understand,' Afzal says after a while, 'but how would Shahji Bhosale react?' His beady eyes watch Ali intently.

'Shahji Bhosale has written a letter to us saying that we are free to deal with Shiva in whatever way we deem fit; the letter has his seal,' Ali replies.

'We must consider our future and not what Shahji Bhosale will make of this matter,' interjects the Badi Sahiba. 'We cannot delay. Shiva, we hear, is on a horse-buying spree.'

'Most of his horsemen are *bargirs*. Shiva selects each one personally. He is not just cunning, but also has military intelligence,' Ali incites.

'Even a *shiledar* is directly paid from Shiva's coffer, which overflows as a result of robbing and plundering. Netoji Palkar who previously worked for us has been made the military chief, their sarnobat. He has helped Shiva gather a few thousand such shiledars,' says the Badi Sahiba, sounding distressed.

Afzal does not reply immediately. Shiva Bhosale is indeed clever. Bargirs are well-mounted, armed horsemen who are paid by the kingdom they work for. Even their horse belongs to the state. Shiledars too are horsemen paid by the kingdom, but they bring their own horses and equipment. Even the Mughals have to depend on their mansabdars for maintaining cavalry. Most of them cheat the empire's military system by keeping less number of horses to save and amass money. It is even worse in his country. The Adilshahi rulers have to threaten, bribe or beg their jagirdars and deshmukhs for military support in times of war. They can never be sure as to who will stand by them and who will join the enemy. But a salaried cavalry, paid by the state, will always be faithful. Its ruler will always be sure of the numbers.

'Shiva's system is against the watandars. Soon he will take away lands from the nearby jagirdars and deshmukhs and bring it under his revenue officials. He has done it in Jawali,' Afzal finally says.

'You can convince the Maval deshmukhs to join you. Tell them they will cease to exist if Shiva Bhosale prevails,' Badi Sahiba insists.

'North Konkan is taken. His men have tried attacking Janjira Fort. He has also started work at shipyards, and tomorrow he may even build sea forts. The man is dynamic. It is easy for him to enter our other regions, for example Wai, the province under your supervision that lies just east of Jawali,' Ali's words sting.

'Shiva is amassing strength by the day. We have heard that our Ibrahim Khan has joined him along with his one thousand African horsemen,' informs the Badi Sahiba.

'After returning to Bijapur, the dumb man Mullah Ahmed is busy singing praises of the kafir,' Afzal whispers to himself.

'After the takeover of the Nizamshahi, we had allowed Shahji Bhosale to keep his old jagir. Who ever knew that his son would turn out to be a traitor and unlawfully seize the hill forts in that jagir? What have we done so far? We have recently lost more than twenty-five forts of north Kalyan to Shiva. And one of our strongest forts, Bidar Fort that guarded our north-eastern borders has been swallowed by the Mughals,' says Ali sullenly.

Afzal raises his eyebrows. Is the king holding him responsible for the loss? He is not the military general of the Adilshahi; he is just a subhedar of the Wai province! After the death of Khan Mohammad, who was the wazir as well as the general, Ali has announced the name of the new wazir. But he is yet to name the new military general. And how can Ali hold him responsible? For the past ten years, he has been trying hard to expand the kingdom by taking over the Hindu kingdoms of Karnataka in the south and dealing with the aggression of Aurangzeb in the north. He has struggled in the battlefields, while his sultan, Mohammed Adil Shah, has remained in bed, paralysed and stricken with bedsores. Ali was just a boy of ten when his father fell ill. Now this juvenile young man is belittling him. What does this adopted son of the late king know?

'If this goes on, son . . .' the Badi Sahiba intervenes, her voice soft enough to make up for Ali's rudeness, 'Shiva Bhosale will make us beg. With Jawali in his hands, he controls the trade route of Dabhol on which our supply of salt, spices, wood, textile, and other such things depends. Shiva can starve our kingdom of those essentials.'

'We feel that you are the most competent to take up the challenge,' Ali's affirms.

Afzal does not want to say anything amiss. There are traps within traps within traps, but no time to unravel them. He has cleverly gotten rid of Khan Mohammad, but there is a new wazir now. Khavas Khan the African warrior, is rather close to Ali Adil Shah. He needs to find out whether Ali is acting on his own or is being incited by Khavas Khan. Perhaps it is Khavas Khan's idea to send him to the peril called Shiva. But Afzal thinks decisively. He will treat this as an opportunity given by Allah. If he eliminates Shiva, his court rivals like the new wazir will collapse inevitably.

'We have kept funds aside to bribe the deshmukhs of Maval,' the Badi Sahiba assures.

'If you can buy off Kanhoji Jedhe, the deshmukh of Bhor Maval, half your job is done. He wields considerable amount of power over the other deshmukhs from Shiva's jagir,' advises Ali.

'Am I the only man in control of this operation or will our wazir also be in command?' asks Afzal, sounding resolute.

'You are now the general of the Adilshahi, Afzal Khan Sahib, and henceforth you will not take orders from anyone,' announces Ali.

Afzal nods trying to conceal his happiness, raises his hands skywards and says gravely, 'My esteemed king, I promise you I will bring Shiva's head to your feet. If I fail, then sever my hands from my body.'

4

On his way home, Afzal cannot help but think about his past, when he had saved the Adilshahi from being wiped out. When the Mughal emperor and his late king had joined hands to annex the Nizamshahi and later to defeat Shahji Bhosale, his master had accepted the vassalage of the empire. He had also agreed to pay two crore rupees as tribute. After a few years, when Mohammed Adil Shah had started ignoring the protocols of the Mughal treaty, he was reprimanded by the emperor for carrying out practices that were the prerogatives of only, well, the emperor. Holding court in lofty places outside the citadel, witnessing elephant combats and using sovereign emblems fixed on a long, gold spike—a sun, a fish, an upraised hand and scales of justice. Over the years, Mohammed Adil Shah had broken the stringent protocols on various occasions and was reprimanded with the serious threat of war.

Afzal still lucidly remembers the night of the festivities. On an event to celebrate a battle victory over parts of Karnataka that was ruled by a few stray Hindu kings, a still robust and beaming Mohammed Adil Shah had thrown a lavish party. On the terrace of his seven-storey palace in the air, the drunken king had been enjoying with his favourite nobles.

'Tell me, what do people in my kingdom talk about me, Afzal Khanji?' he had asked.

'They are singing your praise, what else can they say?' he had replied cautiously.

'What does Shah Jahan think of himself? What will happen if we challenge the protocol of the Mughal treaty, Afzal Khanji?'

'If you do that, my king, instead of the sounds of revelry, we will only hear lamentations of grief. The streets lit by lamps will be drenched in the blood of our men. The Adilshahi will be a part of the Mughal Deccan.'

The master, even in his state of total drunkenness, had heeded his advice and had sent a letter of apology to Shah Jahan and saved his kingdom. Peace had reigned for ten long years until Aurangzeb had started his war against the Shia kingdoms of the south. It was time to protect Bijapur again. He had saved his beloved Adilshahi in the past and he would do so again in the future.

CHAPTER THIRTEEN

1

Yesaji Kank stands inside the wrestler's *akhaada*, barefoot, in a loincloth. The commander of the Maval infantry is a simple wrestler at heart. He intently watches two young men struggle in another mud pit and makes mental notes as their torsos and limbs twist and turn to lock their opponent in a python grip. He notices several flaws. For him, every single move, every single glance, every single movement and even a moment of stillness is a move or a counter-move.

Suddenly, his ears pick up the familiar sound of hoof beats. He jumps out of the wrestling pit, and leaps towards the entrance. He reaches just in time to see Raja Shivaji and his guards dismount from their horses. His instincts tell him that something serious has happened. The visitor is grim and there is that worrisome tightness around his mouth as he looks around cautiously. Barring a few men pulling shafts of wheels near a well to draw water, the place is empty. The tree stump stands still—it was used by them as a base point when they played hide and seek just fifteen years ago. The visitor quickly sits on the stump, not bothering about the dust that has gathered on its surface. Yesaji and some of his wrestlers circle around him.

'The news is true. Afzal Khan has taken up the challenge. He is the new general of the Adilshahi,' Shivaji whispers restlessly.

Yesaji takes a moment to understand. This is the first time that the Adilshahi rulers have considered a man of Afzal Khan's military status. It is disturbing news. The Sultani calamity is about to march in from the east.

Yesaji has turned rigid.

'Many of the Adilshahi subhedars have already reported for duty. Several jagirdars and deshmukhs have agreed to help the new general. They have all gathered at Bijapur along with their men. Afzal Khan has mustered ten thousand well-mounted cavalry and equal number of infantry. We will get the precise numbers of his war elephants, camels and guns-on-wheels within days.'

Yesaji nods.

'We need new swords. Leave immediately and start meeting the blade-makers of the region. Find new swordsmiths if need be. Explain to each one the length, weight, balance and sharpness of blades we need for our dhop swords, patas, daggers and javelins. Specify proportions and the dimensions of the blade. Change the design of the hilts. Add cushioned linings and bigger knuckle guards for a better grip.'

Yesaji already knows all this.

'And yes, make the ridges of the pata blades heavy. Ask them to add more metal to the blade near the hilt. That will bring the centre of gravity closer to the hand that holds the sword.

'A few blade smiths had visited Rajgad last week. They insisted that a little more carbon and chromium in the iron make the blades less bendable, yet they do not break when they hit the bones.'

Yesaji counts his fingers. He must remember the number of instructions.

Shivaji smiles, but soon turns serious. 'The rulers of the sultanate have opened the doors of their treasure in support of Afzal Khan. The number of soldiers deployed to finish us is huge. Soon, our small terrain will turn into a battlefield—a real one.'

Yesaji and his wrestlers remain silent.

'I need to go, sarnobat Palkar is waiting for me. We need to send the letters to the Maval deshmukhs. Afzal Khan has already written to them saying that if they do not join him he will dig them out from their hiding places, slaughter them and their family members to pieces and extrude their body parts through oil mills,' Shivaji relates.

'That's typical of him,' Yesaji murmurs.

He stands near the entrance to watch Shivaji and his guards gallop away, kicking up behind them a small dust storm. He stares till the horsemen become mere specks and then vanish from the range of his vision.

He remembers the past, especially their visit to the ancient temple of Lord Shiva when Raja was barely fifteen.

'Friends . . .' young Raja Shivaji had lowered his voice and bitten his lower lip, 'you call me a raja, a king, because I am the son of a jagirdar. But remember, all the jagir holders in the Deccan call themselves rajas. We, the jagirdars, are mere revenue-collectors who work for the Muslim kingdoms. Our armies are meant to fight their wars. Our blood is meant to irrigate their battlefields.'

The boys had looked on, wide-eyed.

'The real rulers humour us when we call ourselves rajas, like lions that ignore the barks of lowly dogs. The emboldened dogs may perceive that they are kings of the jungle, but it is not true. We too live in such perception.'

Shivaji had stopped for breath.

'We are like the wooden swords used in the drills. They are called swords but they actually are not. They have no blades to cut the enemy.'

There was utter silence. Raja's words rang true in their ears.

'We are even less effective than the wooden swords, as we do not know who our enemy is.'

'In the name of God Shiva, I want to tell you that I dream of a raj, a swaraj—our own state that is ruled by *us*. I want our own military bases, manned by our armed garrisons, in places that will be inaccessible to the Adilshahi or Mughal armies, and we will never have to bow to any of them.'

The raja had spoken unhurriedly. Later, he had turned around to look at each of them to see their reactions: a smile, a snigger or a mocking glance could mean that they had not taken him seriously.

'We have seen the intervening hills of this region, and many have a fort built on their crest. We want them all. They will be our military bases. It is a difficult task, as difficult as touching the moon. Today, in this ancient temple, I take an oath. My first step will be to acquire the dilapidated, neglected hill forts of the Adilshahi standing in my jagir and repair them. These will be our military strongholds, the seeds of our swaraj.'

Yesa had watched as Raja Shiva had wrenched his new, real sword out of his belt, moved further towards the lingam and held his left thumb over it. Before they could guess, he had raised the blade of his sword and made a sharp cut on his own thumb. Crimson droplets had fallen on the lingam.

'I do not want to be a wooden sword. I want to be a blade, sharp and cutting, one made of iron. This is my first offering,' the young jagirdar had concluded.

Each of them had followed him, bathing the lingam with their blood, thus binding their pact with the blood that they had spilled in the ancient temple of God Shiva.

2

Afzal Khan's horse trots through his military camp, half-a-kos east of Bijapur. Sayed Banda and his men follow him vigilantly, holding naked swords in one hand and navigating the horse with the other. The drummers make a deafening racket as they rally before his procession. He is not an ordinary viceroy anymore but the Adilshahi general. Never before has he experienced such public adulation, and never before has he been the cynosure of all eyes. He watches as the soldiers jostle and push, and shamelessly climb on each other's shoulders just to get a glimpse of him. This rise in the social ladder achieved at the age of forty is truly mesmerizing. People who have never seen him before are stunned at his physique. He is indeed a big man, whose fully grown horse looks like a pony. His jama lined with silver brocade dazzles in the afternoon sun and the kimoush turban embellished with emeralds makes him look taller. He waves as some raise their swords to hail their new master and some scream and chant his name and the words written in his seal.

'Afzal Khan, Afzal Khan, *Katil-e-Kafiran* Afzal Khan!'

The chants please him immensely and he caresses his long, henna-dyed beard. The seal that he put on each of his official letters has been the subject of discussion in the Deccan. In fact, some of the Hindu landlords went cold with fear when they received letters with his seal: *Katil-e-Kafiran, Sinkada-Biniyade-Butan*. The killer of the infidels and the destroyer of the deities.

Afzal is proud of his name that in Arabic means superior, most excellent and principal. Impulsively, he turns to Sayed and shouts, 'Send notes of encouragement with my new seal to all my officers, and demand that they read them aloud to their respective contingents.'

Sayed nods with reverence as he is reminded of the words etched on his master's new pledge of assurance.

If you seek higher heavens
Then compare this Afzal, with the Afzal, the supreme, in the best
     of men
And when the beads of the rosary are counted

You will hear only one name,
Afzal, Afzal, and only Afzal.

Afzal has many other things on his mind. He signals Sayed and leaves
alone. For a distance, Afzal rides parallel to the moat infested with
crocodiles and gallops along the outer wall of the fort city of Bijapur.
The archers minding the bastions of Bijapur's outer wall recognize
him and wave. He waves back to them in acceptance of their greetings
while crossing the north-facing Bahamani Gate. Thereafter, he kicks
his horse to fly north-west through vast stretches of open farmlands. It
is evening by the time he arrives near a hillock. From its base he can see
a low yet ornate building enclosed in a compound wall. He dismounts
quietly, and leads his horse uphill. The path is well looked-after,
hedged with flowering shrubs. Afzal quietly tethers his tired animal
to a lone mango tree near the gate and shakes off his sandals before
entering the building. A blind old man sits near the shrine covered
in red and green brocaded velvet cloth, surrounded by heaps of roses
and jasmine. The pleats of the man's long robe fall around him and
his long, silvery beard covers his chest. He seems lost while counting
his sandalwood rosary beads. Another man sitting behind the shrine
chants to evoke the divine powers of the Sufi saint Hazrath Pir Amin
Chisti, who lived during the times of Mohammed Adil Shah's father.

'Is that you? You have come after a long time,' he hears the blind
old man whisper. It is known that the divine light was transmitted
from the famous Hazrath Pir Amin Chisti's heart to the blind man's
almost fifty years ago.

Afzal removes his turban, hunkers down his body and puts his
head on the floor before the old man.

'Son,' the old man finally speaks in a quivering voice, 'do not go
for in my vision your body has been severed from your head.'

For the first time in many years, Afzal's heart misses a beat. Then
he feels the touch of the old man's trembling hand on his head. The
Sufi saint consoles him mutely, urging him to accept Allah's decree.
Afzal says nothing. While heading home he just thinks and thinks.

It is late into the night but sleep eludes Afzal. Should he trust the
blind man or should he just let it go? He curses himself for going to

the dargah to seek his future. But that was a done deed. And a seed
of doubt has already been sown. Even though the chandeliers burn,
throwing golden light over his enormous bed, bleak thoughts flood
his mind. He has to wind up his personal affairs before he leaves for
his western campaign.

His fifteen legitimate wives and their children are to accompany
him. His twenty-year-old son, Fazal, is to be his right hand. His
concubines, picked from different parts of his country, bought
from the slave traders or presented to him by his officers, will be left
behind. A new stock of seventy-seven young women has been left
untouched. The bloody battles with the imperialists and tensions of
court politics have robbed him of both his leisure and his libido. Who
will have them if he dies in the battlefield? The girls will fill someone
else's bed, sire someone else's children. Sheer jealousy overwhelms
him as visions of these virgins in other men's arms hammer his skull
like an iron mallet striking a large metal bell.

'Bring Amina,' he screams as eunuchs scurry outside his door.
His youngest catch is almost thrown into his room as the door is
bolted shut behind her. A slim girl with large eyes, long, lustrous
hair and wearing a transparent skirt with a very short blouse looks
up at him. He waits as she shivers, her hands trying to cover her
breasts. She, the incapable bitch, has failed to stir his manhood. For
a moment he disregards the fact that, in the recent past, all of them
have. A blade of rage slices through his mind. He gets up at once
and rushes towards her, with the confidence of a hyena lunging at an
animal already killed by a jungle cat. Seeing him advance so rashly,
she turns stiff with dread and then falls on the ground like a dry,
broken reed. He lifts her by her hair, holds her in one hand and starts
marching towards his private bath. She hobbles like a dead animal
as he drags her across a long corridor lined with cusped arches. The
main foyer has a large marble tub and a fountain spewing water jets
at its centre. He kneels near the tub and submerges her in the water.
She floats like a petal as he stares at her striking face, translucent skin
and small breasts. Her flimsy clothes flail around her like wings of
a bird dropping dead from the sky. The faint sound of spluttering
echoes in the marble-floored bath. The mild scent of rose and khus

wafts in the air. He watches her as she jerks in his arms and thrashes her limbs about, like a calf on its last spasm before being devoured by a carnivore. He holds her hard with one hand around her waist and uses the other to drown her face. She struggles feebly and within moments is limp, her fourteen-year-life gone too quickly. He lets go of her and marches back to his chamber, breathing heavily.

He has decided to kill the remaining seventy-five women in the next few days. They will drown in the same manner, in the same bathtub. He has also decided to build tombs of precisely the same pattern for each of them, seven in eleven rows. The tombstones will rise over a raised platform at the backyard of this very palace. He intends to name the place *sattkabar*, to let the world know his absolute passion.

3

Standing on the ramparts of the Rajgad citadel, Raja Shivaji glances at the vast expanse and the hills beyond. From the east, night descends like a raven waterfall. As he gazes at the abysmal slopes plunging beyond the western boundaries of Rajgad, he notices the orange sun, half-buried in the earth's horizon. *What will tomorrow witness—carnage or courage?* There is not much time left. The Adilshahi general will soon reach Baramati. From there he plans to proceed thirty kos north-west to reach the foothills of this very fort. The mighty khan will break, slash and burn everything along his path. There is a chance to change the general's mind while he is at Baramati. He must cancel his north-west journey and go fifteen kos south-west towards Wai.

Shivaji gazes at the distant hills of Torana and Lohagad forts and remembers how he had acquired them. He was fifteen, accompanied by the three Maratha friends who would die for him: Tana, Yesa and Baji Pasalkar. His two advisers, Sonoji Dabir and Dadaji Kondev, were by his side too. And then there was Palkar. Moroji Pinglay had just joined them. He had one hill in his possession, the hill of Murumbgad with the ruins of an ancient fort on its table. He longed for Torana, the fort above a steep hill ten kos south-west of Pune, at the source of the river Neera. There were deliberations and discussions. Along with Yesa, Tana and Baji Pasalkar, he had galloped towards Torana. They had scaled the exceedingly difficult hill by foot, dressed in their finest silk angirkhas and pearl-studded turbans. Sixty-year-old Baji with his white moustache was made to look like a military official of the Adilshahi.

They had pretended to be Adilshahi officials and had offered the keeper of Torana, an elderly Muslim, a hundred rupees and ten gold hones to leave the desolate place. The fort was in ruins—its outer walls had fallen, the quarters were damp and the woodwork infested with white ants. Even the courtyard was overgrown with weeds. The granaries were empty, and the ceilings had bats hanging upside down from them. Weather and erosion had turned the fortified bastions into abodes of predators. When Shivaji had ordered the repairing of Torana, there had been a miracle.

The diggers had discovered an old trunk full of ancient gold coins buried below a fallen turret. Some king had perhaps hidden his wealth in times of war. With that treasure, Shivaji could hire labourers working at Torana as well as Murumbgad, now called Rajgad. They had cleared the hilltops of overgrown bushes, rebuilt the walls and bastions, cleaned the mossy water tanks, repaired the inner offices and residential quarters and mounted new cannons on the ramparts. Soon the hill forts had men assigned to hold the fort in times of attack. The foothills were guarded by tribals living in the forests.

The news had soon reached Mohammed Adil Shah's ears. Shivaji's father had written a warning letter to reprimand him.

Dadaji, now old, worn-out and anxious, was on his deathbed. Shivaji had gone to see him and it had turned out to be their last meeting. 'What can I say? I am a mere servant of your father, and your father works for the king. You must be loyal to the king, but whatever you do, look after the cultivators, the real children of this soil. Do not put them all in one basket. Levy taxes according to their soil, availability of water and what they produce. Think of variables like seasons, rains and human errors, and do not rely on permanent land assessments. This soil is *Kali Aai*, our black mother.' The old man had died after giving him the last advice.

Another blow came immediately; Mohammed Adil Shah had sent his army to eliminate him. He could never forget his first battle fought at Purandar. The Adilshahi was defeated, Muse Khan was killed. Shivaji lost his old guard. Baji Pasalkar was killed while chasing the Adilshahi army.

And this is the second battle. *Who will be the victor and who will be the vanquished?*

Shivaji searches the sky as if to decipher God's message. Around him, a strong draught of chill air slithers like the floating spirit of a furious serpent eager to strike. He shivers at the thought of having to meet Sayee, perhaps for the last time. Tomorrow he would be gone to the valley of Jawali. Walking down the stairs, his carefully constructed emotional fortifications collapse in a pile of sorrow.

When he enters Sayee's chamber in Daruni Palace, it is dark. She lies on the bed like someone waiting for death. Hearing his footsteps, she opens her eyes. Moving closer, he notices that her eyes exude grief, deep and longing.

'For Sambhaji,' she whispers, 'you are both his father and his mother from now on. May God bestow upon you a long life, and in the coming battle against the sultanate, may you emerge victorious.'

'I hope so too.'

'Hopes,' she sighs and continues in a quivering voice, 'are the shackles of life, defiant to everything, including death. Death too bows down to these chains.'

'You always confuse me, don't you?'

'This is what you have taught me,' she smiles weakly and continues. 'But it is very simple. You are my God, the owner of my destiny and the master of the vermillion that adorns my forehead. I have always wished that you light my pyre. Women have this habit of making even their deaths a prisoner of their hopes.'

'I shall do all that you hope for.'

'I have no such wish now as I have set my death free from the fetters of hope. It has already granted me my most cherished wish that is longed for and prayed for by every Hindu woman . . .'

'Sayee . . .' he interrupts, his throat tight, 'I haven't done anything for you. I have always been away.'

'It is about being a part of your life,' she says, her eyes shining with tears, 'it is about your life touching mine.'

'Even at a tangent?'

She keeps silent as if she is contemplating the greater purpose of her short existence. The lamp has suddenly dimmed. He looks away in desperation, in hope, that all this is just a nightmare.

'Sayee . . . Don't go. Please don't leave me!' he pleads, swallowing a sob.

'We always wish to control things that are beyond us and we always let go of things that are within our reach.'

'What do you mean?'

'Like my death and your life. It is time for you to take control. This is the first time that they have not dismissed you as a mere rebel but have sent such a huge army. This is the first time that they have regarded you as a proper enemy. Regard that as a tribute to your rising power. I am glad that this has happened before I am gone.'

'What about Sambhaji?'

'He has you,' she quips, her words now barely audible.

He holds her close to his heart as her thin frame shivers with fever and weakness.

'When we married, we were just children. We grew up together. Your ideas initially surprised me. Our fathers worked for the sultanate and you were born to serve the masters of your father—that was your duty, your karma. But you charted a new path, drew new frontiers of swaraj that did not exist,' she says softly but with pride.

He looks down at his dying wife, takes her hands in his and for the first time in eighteen years of their married life declares, 'I love you, Sayee. I love you so much.'

Unexpectedly, the room is filled with Sayee's laughter. 'I have never believed you capable of saying such romantic things.'

He notices the familiar twinge of mischief in her eyes.

Shaken, he too joins her and laughs, holding her hands close to his heart.

A little later, he visits his mother. Jija bai is in her prayer room.

'Ma sahib,' he says softly and she quickly turns around, as if she has been waiting for him all along. He touches her feet and settles near her. She looks at his face as if trying to remember the details. And despite her earlier resolve, she asks, 'Are you sure that there is no possibility of declaring a truce?'

'No, Ma sahib, there is no choice now.' His eyes take in the deity of Tuljapur Bhavani, a replica of the original from the temple in the hills of Tuljapur town on the western borders of the sultanate.

Goddess Bhavani, the destroyer avatar of Goddess Parvati, God Shiva's wife, is known as the Shakti Peetha, a source of primal energy. Her eight hands hold eight weapons, but her eyes inspire dread and fear. They seem to peel off the outer layers of his being and strike his soul. The force of her gaze becomes tangible, crushing all his doubts to pulp.

CHAPTER FOURTEEN

1

Despite a few stray clouds, the sky above Pratapgad is clear. The meandering wall fortified with enormous bastions creates an illusion of a crown of black iron metal fixed on the head of a tribal king. The gigantic fort extensions spread out like his long, muscular arms. Below lie the dense forests of the valley. At the upper fort, several sentinels carrying javelins have formed two semicircles around huge bastions guarding the citadel. Peshwa Moroji Pinglay glances at the guards to be sure. They are smartly attired in their tight breeches and brocaded angirkhas. Their Turkish turbans look like small crimson boats on their heads. Satisfied, he goes back to the sadar, a large assembly chamber built with stones and supported by pillars. A few servants are busy placing tall brass *samayee* lamps in the corners. A short divan has been placed at the northern side of the room, near a large window towards the west. A small desk for the scribe stands facing the open window.

The first to arrive are Sonoji Dabir, his son Trimbak Dabir, and surnis Annaji Datto. A little later, the newly appointed secretary— scribe Balaji Avji, who was rescued from the sea—walks in with an inkpot, a notebook and a long feather with a nib. They have been called to Jawali by Raja Shivaji. They know why. Their faces are flushed with admiration for the newly built fort. They wonder at the pillars rising above the stone pedestals, strings of fresh jasmine and marigold draped around them, the ceiling of polished wooden beams, an enamelled glass chandelier bound to gilded chains, its light falling gracefully on the black basalt floor covered at places with carpets and the bolsters that are draped in silk cases neatly lined up near the walls.

The nervous whispers of the men fill the room. Ibrahim Khan who has quit the service of the Adilshahi to join the Maratha army has come from Konkan dressed in a long, green jama and a shining kimoush turban. Sarnobat Palkar and the infantry commanders Tanaji and Yesaji have arrived from Maval. The drums start beating and as the voices of the guards announcing his arrival wither in the air, Shivaji walks in taking long strides and stands before the board.

'Be seated,' says the leader of the Marathas. His men obey; they either sit cross-legged or on their knees, their gaze fixed on him. It is no longer a matter of plundering an isolated caravan near Kalyan, or fighting a small battle with jagirdars like Morey. It is the matter of an impending confrontation with the Adilshahi general and his army. There is the chance that they will perish, and their families will be killed, abducted and enslaved. Tales of Afzal Khan's strength and merciless nature have reached their ears and filled their hearts with dread.

In the depth of his heart, Shivaji knows that his men may urge him to make peace. He feels their gaze, and knows that they are searching his face for traces of panic.

'The battle is at our door. Afzal Khan is already in our territory and has reached Baramati, a fifty kos north-east from this very fort. Soon his war animals will stamp our terrain turning it into a battlefield, sodden with blood and strewn with limbs. Rumour says that after camping for a week in Baramati he intends to march towards Pune. If he does, his enormous cavalcade will destroy our jagir, the core of our budding nation. His archers have already turned easy with their bows, stretching them and letting the arrows fly at the peasants working in the fields.

'And we have done nothing to stop him,' snaps Dabir.

'What do you want me to do, venture out to oppose him in the open?' Shivaji asks with a sneer that he does not bother to hide. 'That is precisely what Afzal wants.'

'A few things have already been done.' Palkar, who stands near Pinglay, announces in a distinct tone. 'All our forts are well manned. Our intelligence system has been put to work. Bahirji Naik and his men have infiltrated the Adilshahi general's army.'

Shivaji nods. Palkar has been on the move for the past few months, visiting hill forts of Kondana, Purandar, Torana, Lohagad and others. He has briefed each of the fort commanders to keep their granaries stuffed with enough grains, salt, oil as well as medicines and has made sure that they know about the calibre, mobility and range of the cannons mounted on their ramparts. He has personally inspected the garrisons, taken stock of the storehouses and checked the quality of the gunpowder and cast-iron projectiles. During his innumerable meetings with the tribals at the foothills of those forts, he has made sure that they keep a constant vigil on the forest trails leading to the fort.

'Subhedar Abaji Sondev guards our western borders from Kalyan, Murarbaji, our eastern borders from Purandar Fort and Firangoji Narsala our northern borders from Chakan Fort,' Palkar assures the gathering.

'Are we then preparing for war? Is there no possibility of a treaty?' Pinglay asks anxiously.

Shivaji stares at his peshwa and speaks in words loud and clear, 'A treaty with Afzal Khan? Do you not know what happened to Kasturiranga, the king of Sira, when he had gone to Afzal Khan to make his submission, to my brother who had trusted Afzal Khan and waited in the trenches for the reinforcements to arrive or to the Adilshahi's loyal wazir, Khan Mohammad? All killed, brutally and cunningly.'

'Then war is the only option,' Dabir says, his face shrivelled with worry. 'Now when we raise our sword against the king, the doors of any kind of treaty with the Adilshahi will be forever closed. In this world of Islamic empires and the kingdoms, we have no one to turn to, to fall back on.'

Shivaji closes his eyes briefly and says in a steady voice, 'Speculating about the future will only lead to confusion. We must find out what Afzal Khan seeks—a treaty or my head. But while doing so we must also prepare for war.'

Palkar takes over. 'The first step is to choose our battleground for it can turn into a dangerous zone, where people will be killed, houses destroyed, farmlands flattened and barns set on fire.'

'What do you mean?' Pinglay stares at Palkar.

'I shall explain.' Shivaji intervenes as his eyes sparkle. 'In our jagir, the grasses of sorghum, pearl millets, gram and horse gram have already begun to grow. If Afzal takes his army towards Pune, the peasants will be slaughtered and their fields looted. Their morale, their livelihood, their families and their cattle will be trampled under the hooves of the khan's war animals. We must stop him from entering the region around Pune.'

'Do we have a choice?' Dabir asks.

Balaji Avji sitting behind the small desk tries to scribble the essence of the discussions. Shivaji remains silent for a while and says, 'We do.'

Dabir smiles doubtfully.

'What if Afzal Khan cancels his plans to go to Pune and steers his cavalcade towards Wai, the province he governs as a subhedar?' Shivaji suggests. 'He knows I am here. He had sent a few scouts to confirm the news. The scouts were brought here by Bahirji's men who had posed as guides. And the general's men have seen me at the foothills of this fort. To be very precise, it was arranged that they see me here.'

Dabir nods appreciatively. If Afzal wants to extract a treaty on his terms, he will first destroy the region to show his might. But if he wants Raja Shivaji's head, he will steer his army towards Jawali as the valley is just ten kos east of Wai.

'What if he decides to proceed towards Pune? What then is our plan of action?' Pinglay inquires.

'That is unlikely, and to analyse why so, we must look beyond what's obvious,' Shivaji replies. 'The Mughal pose a far greater threat to Adilshahi than we do. With Aurangzeb busy warring with his brothers, logically, Ali Adil Shah should have tried to recover his military strongholds lost to the Mughal. Instead, he has unleashed his army towards us. What does that say?'

Palkar answers, 'There is a sequence. Ali Adil Shah has renewed the old peace treaty with Aurangzeb, reinforcing their status as a tributary state of the empire. It is also well known that Aurangzeb is furious with us. We have plundered his region. He had ordered his army to waste our villages, slay our people without pity and plunder the region. But then he had to go north to fight the war of succession, so he must have commanded the Adilshahi king to deal with Raja Shivaji. Perhaps our Raja's elimination is one of the clauses in their peace treaty.'

Shivaji says softly, 'Aurangzeb is a man on a mission. I can actually see what his vision is. Such a man will not accept the "rise of a kafir". He must have given an ultimatum to Ali: "Kill Shivaji or else".'

'May I say something?' Ibrahim Khan requests permission, his handsome face serious. He hails from Afghanistan and is a Shia Muslim. Previously a cavalry commander in the Adilshahi army, he has witnessed many a court intrigue. He was in the court of Kalyan when Shivaji had shown respect for the captive woman. It was then that he had decided to leave the king's army along with his five hundred Pashtun horsemen to join the leader of the Marathas. This religious zeal is an act. Had they been so spiritually inclined, they would have become avliyas, pirs or fakirs. When politically powerful men talk of religion, they use it as a weapon to gain power. Aurangzeb has incited the empire's military men, especially the orthodox, against his own brother Dara Shikoh, calling him a heretic. He does not want the other powerful kafirs, for that is what he calls them, like the Sikhs, the Rajputs, the Bundelas, the Marathas and others, to take cue and rise against the empire. He wants to destroy the man who has set a dangerous precedent. He plans to achieve his objective through Ali Adil Shah, who is eager to please the emperor-to-be to keep his sultanate safe from further Mughal invasions.'

The others who still have trouble trusting Ibrahim gape at him while Raja Shivaji smiles and says, 'What Ibrahim says is true. That is the reason why Afzal will come to Wai. It is Aurangzeb's wish to capture or kill me, and his wish is the Adilshahi king's command!'

'Afzal will reach Wai in a week or so. The monsoon season is upon us. It is impossible for any army to move in the direction of Jawali from Wai. During the monsoons, this valley turns into a water trap as its rivers are flooded, mountain trails blocked by landslides and slopes covered by wild vegetation. The locals say that even the wings of the flying birds turn mossy,' says Palkar.

'Then this valley will be our ranangan, our battlefield!' Shivaji announces.

Palkar walks near the board and points to the map and explains, his index finger forming a trail. 'Wai may be just ten kos from this fort, but to reach here one has to travel twenty kos across the mountains and valleys, hiking a steady climb to reach the plateau of Mahabaleshwar and then braving the abrupt descent from the ghats of Radatondi. As we know, *radatondi* means crying face, and this trail makes even the mountain men weep.'

Dabir comments, 'If Afzal Khan wants Raja Shivaji, he will come to Wai. But what will make him undertake the perilous expedition to reach the ranangan of our choice? Surely he knows the valley, considering that he has been the subhedar of Wai for the past ten years. He may insist that he meets Raja in his den, at Wai . . .'

'Yes, he will want to do that. But we will invite him to Jawali,' Shivaji says nonchalantly.

'All this happens only if Afzal Khan is a dimwit. It beats all logic,' says Dabir sharply.

Shivaji closes his eyes for a moment. Then he speaks, 'Even psychology takes a different form when battles loom ahead. Wars defy logic. Ali Adil Shah is too young and is a man of finance and not of battles. It has already been months since Afzal Khan has left Bijapur. He must have already spent lakhs of rupees. By the time we invite him to Jawali he would have wasted three more months of monsoon. The king will be impatient for the returns on his investment.'

'Will Afzal Khan's advisers let him jump into our trap?' Dabir challenges.

It is Ibrahim who responds. 'Afzal Khan is an autocrat and does what he wants. Nobody advises him. If someone attempts to, he makes fun of him.'

'How many men do we need and have?' Yesaji asks hesitantly.

'It is not about how many, it is about the kind they are. That is why we want all of you to pick up mountain men and the rock climbers from your forces and bring them to the field. We want numbers from each of you in two weeks,' Palkar dictates.

'Call for woodcutters, grain traders, butchers and cooks from the nearby villages. Let it seem like we are expecting thousands of guests and have to supply the general's army with firewood, grains, meat, spices and even wine. No costs must be spared,' Shivaji slowly unfolds his plan.

'Are you planning to feed his army?' Anna Datto asks, incredulous. Niloji Sondev, whom Anna Datto reports to, is a very strict finance man. The accounts are closed annually and balance payments due by the state are either paid in cash or by bills on the collection of revenue. The deficit caused by this sudden and huge expense will have to be worked out by him.

'Not just the army, even his war animals.'

'It is an enormously expensive gamble,' worries Anna Datto; he knows that the expense may run into thousands of rupees, if not hundreds of thousands.

'You seem to have even planned to provide him with servants, maids and *shikaldar*s to sharpen their blades to chop us swiftly!' Sonoji Dabir says with sarcasm.

'Yes, that's the plan. And if we *win* the battle, Annaji will have no deficit, only surplus. Ideally, spoils of war must foot the bills of our wars,' Shivaji quips, but Annaji does not look impressed. 'Annaji, when we built this very fort, questions were raised regarding the huge funds being invested. The fort's remoteness, its inaccessibility, its location in this perilous valley where enemy armies may not even dare enter were the issues. Remember, if we can win this battle *because* of this fort, just *this* battle, the fort has served its purpose. Military investments are not a gamble; they form the thin lines between victory and defeat.'

'And who will serve as the brilliant vakeel to hold meetings and discussions with the mighty Afzal?' Dabir's interest is piqued.

'I have someone in mind.' Shivaji says and claps his hands.

Two guards enter, bringing a man along.

'For this operation, we have chosen him as our vakeel who will deal with the mighty general. He will tackle Afzal Khan and bring him to Jawali, where the offenders will be forced to become the defenders and the defenders will get a chance to be the offenders,' announces Raja Shivaji as the men sitting before him blink in disbelief.

Gopinath Bokil, the vakeel being entrusted with this crucial task, is a frail old Brahmin who has lost all his teeth, literally and metaphorically.

2

The rambling Shalimar Gardens in the northwest suburb of Dilli look freshly drenched by the recent bout of rains. The ponds and lakes are filled with clean blue waters, partially hidden under blooming lotuses and their large, round leaves. Arches built over the canals are decorated with strings of marigold, while swans with snow-white plumage float in pairs like sail boats. Large numbers of peacocks forage and leap in the shades of enormous fruit trees. The apartment buildings near the central Sheesh Mahal are crowded with personal guests invited by Aurangzeb. They are looked after by well-attired servants who prepare sherbets and black *kahva* as welcome drinks and hookahs to smoke.

The procession starts with the deafening din of drums, tambourines and trumpets. The skirting of the tree-lined avenue running through the sprawling garden is packed with people. A long file of ceremonial elephants adorned with gilded chains and dangling bells trundle from the garden's southern gate to reach the Sheesh Mahal. The mahouts are in red silk tunics and turbans, their javelins resting on their shoulders glittering with diamonds. Their ornately decorated tuskers carry an imperial benchmark of polished balls slung from a pole, the ensigns of the Ottoman empire. The men on other elephants carry the various symbols of a Mughal emperor, made of silver and gold. The emblems are of the sun, an upraised hand, scales of justice, a fish, a tiger's head and a horse's head. Behind them, horsemen ride smartly, carrying silver maces. They are followed by the dense columns of uniformed footmen, musketeers, artillerymen and the scouts. The cavalcade moves through the barricaded path. Throngs of noblemen dressed impeccably in silk robes and colourful headgears walk solemnly behind the footmen. They are followed by others carrying an hourglass, a gong and a hammer to tell the time. At the end trundles a huge, caparisoned elephant, carrying a gilded throne on its back. Aurangzeb sits on the chair as his eyes survey his subjects who jostle and push each other to get a glimpse of their master on his coronation day. Behind him, on a large wooden platform, an elderly man stands holding the backrest of the throne. It is Uncle Abu Talib, alias Shaista Khan.

But the emperor-to-be is not exactly brimming with happiness. His heart is not filled with joy, and his mind is full of worries.

Dara bhai has been seen wandering on the banks of the river Sutlej in Punjab. The vanquished prince might have headed for Bolan Pass, more than five hundred kos north-west of Agra, and may travel across the pass to reach Persia. The Persian emperor likes Dara bhai and they both might form an alliance to attack Dilli. On the other hand, religious men, the sayyids, mullahs, imams and fakirs of Mecca will not recognize him as the new emperor if the former is still alive. He has already sent forty-five thousand ashrafi mohurs to Syed Mir Ibrahim of Mecca. There are some things that need to be taken care of immediately. The liberal Muslims who have helped Dara bhai ought to die. But that has to be done cleverly, within the precincts of sharia law.

The news from the Deccan is not so encouraging either. The Adilshahi general has steered his military cavalcade towards the Wai town in the mountains at the eastern borders of Jawali. The news is that Shivaji Bhosale has been holed up in the valley. Not yet caught or killed.

The royal elephant stops in front of a lofty pavilion with bright coverings. It is decorated with tapestries of embroidered velvet, European screens and gold tissue from Turkey and China. As he alights, all the people kneel, some even fall prostrate. As he enters the pavilion, hush prevails, as if people are afraid to even breathe. The astrologers have declared the time: three hours and fifteen minutes to sunrise. When Aurangzeb finally climbs the steps of the platform, a sea of people has gathered, blocking all the routes to the venue of his coronation. The air vibrates with tangible divinity as clergies recite the holy Quran in their high-pitched voices.

People notice that Aurangzeb's swagger has changed and he walks more like an emperor and less like a soldier. He even sits on the satin cushions of the coronation throne kept in the open courtyard like his father, legs folded under him, and the silk of his jama falling around him. A turban bound around his head glitters with diamonds, rubies and emeralds. An aigrette with a nodding fringe adorning the front part of his headgear is special, worn only by the kings and emperors. His name and titles are publicly proclaimed through the religious sermon. The Muslim clergies do not mind reading the khutba in his name even when the old, dethroned emperor still lives. Coins bearing his name are thrown on the waiting crowd. His titles are announced loudly: Bahadur, the brave, Alamgir, the conqueror of the world, Padishah, the emperor, Ghazi, the holy warrior. The final announcement is made in a verse:

The newly minted coins,
are stamped with his name
They shine like the moon
And he, Aurangzeb
The Alamgir,
will dazzle the world
through day, night and noon.

3

Dara Shikoh looks in the broken mirror and shudders with self-pity. He hates his reflection: it is that of a sick man with dark circles around his eyes and an unruly beard. His front teeth are missing, and his head, wrapped in a soiled turban, is full of greys.

It is a desolate place called Dadur, four-and-a-half kos east of Bolan Pass near the Afghan border, and many hundred kos away from his home, Agra. His wife, Nadira Begum, is dead. The last day of her life was spent gasping for breath, in his arms, asking for water that was not available. She, the mother of his sons Suleiman and Siphir, had been groomed to be the empress. The scorching heat of this region that made the birds drop dead from the sky had put his delicate wife to death.

What has become of his family? This was not the life that he was supposed to lead! His palaces, the gardens, the pavilions, the plush apartments, his retinue of slaves tending to his needs, his wardrobes filled with carefully chosen clothes, his libraries stuffed with rare manuscripts, pundits who came from far and near just to listen to his views, his countless concubines, each one prettier than the other, his guards, his horses, his ceremonial elephants, iron vaults stuffed with jewels and his army of twenty thousand cavalry and equal number of infantry—all have vanished as if they had never existed.

If memories stab him like a dagger, guilt consumes him when he thinks of his father. He has left the emperor at the mercy of the murderous Aurangzeb. The future of his two sons is bleak. His dreams for Suleiman have shattered, the young prince now in his twenties stranded in Kashmir with his army. The last piece of news that he had heard said that Mirza Jai Singh had deserted Suleiman and had run back to Dilli to join Aurangzeb. His second son Siphir is at least with him, sleeping in another room, but his body has been burning with fever due to this oppressive heat. Dara angrily wrenches the turban from his head and throws it away in anguish and walks back to his bed, defeated.

He has tried his best. Having lost the battle with Aurangzeb and realizing that Dilli was too dangerous for him, he had travelled hundreds of kos to reach Lahore and lavished whatever funds he had on whoever was prepared to join him. In a short span of time he had mustered twenty thousand men. But Aurangzeb's murderous army, full of vicious jihadis, had followed him. They chased him across flooded rivers, braving severe monsoons and treading swamped paths. His hastily collected soldiers had been slaughtered or bought over. He and his family had gone into hiding and crossed the frozen waters of the Sutlej in Punjab. With a few remaining guards and eunuch slaves, they had spent an entire day in the open, shivering in their tattered clothes like vagrants. That had been the most dreadful day of his life and it was there that he had received the news of Aurangzeb's impending coronation. Everything was over. He had fled to Sindh, then Rann of Kutch, borrowing money, food and clothes from people who had once kneeled before him for favours. He had wept bitterly over his fate. He had finally fled to the region near to the borders of Afghan and had taken refuge in the camp of Malik Jiuan. The Afghan chief had once been captured and brought to Agra as a fugitive and was condemned to death under the feet of an elephant. Dara Shikoh had intervened and goaded his father to spare the life of Malik Jiuan and set him free.

Dara Shikoh's body shudders with sobs. He hopes that Malik Jiuan can provide secrecy and protection to him for a few days.

'Your Imperial Highness, wake up, please wake up, we must move,' he hears his personal guard. 'Malik Jiuan has turned a traitor.'

How can it be? he thinks as the information hits him. He jerks his head and jumps out of his bed. He rushes out to a small corridor, like a wounded deer chased by a wild cat. The night is dark and not a single torch burns anywhere. He runs to his son's room, kicks open the flimsy door and gathers the young boy in his arms. Siphir is hot, burning with fever.

'Call the others and get our horses!' he orders, carrying his son on his shoulder. It is dangerous not to believe his guard and wait to confront Jiuan. He has decided to go north, towards the province of Kandahar, and then flee to Persia. There is hardly any choice, but the animals look tired and underfed. His horse protests by snorting when he tries to get it to walk and then kicks it hard to a gallop. They move towards the north. Only fifteen guards and eunuch slaves follow him on their horses. It is a difficult ride, holding the feverish Siphir with one hand and managing the bounding horse with another. If he leaves his hand, the boy will slip and fall on the rocky ground.

The faithful horses fly over the hilly region as the waxing moon throws enough light over the hills to form large, dreadful shadows. It is still hot; the wind hits his face like whips of flames. Within a few hours, the morning star appears in the east, and the enormous hills of Bolan become visible on the northern skyline. So colossal, so high are the silhouettes that they look like beasts waiting to swallow the world. As they ride closer, he is able to spot the pass.

The faint silvery light of the moon has cracked the shadows of Bolan hills into two halves. They slow down to enter. The tired horses trot and pant with exhaustion. The pass is wide but feels dingy between the two hills looming on either side. It is like a furnace and a blast of hot air greets them. They cannot breathe. He holds his son tighter, checking to see if the boy is still alive. At places, the passage between the limestone rocks narrows to a tight trail, allowing only two men to ride abreast. The wind suddenly starts blowing through the winding path. He looks at the sky and notices that the stars have disappeared and the moon has turned pale. The first rays of the sun gradually turn the night into day. He slowly diverts his gaze from the sky onto the path unfolding before him. Something makes him turn back. He notices small specks moving up and down at the far end. He narrows his eyes and realizes that they are horses galloping purposefully towards him. His blood turns cold.

Everything happens quickly, in the blink of an eye. The chasers take hold of him in the pass and Siphir is snatched away. He is shackled and put on another horse. His captor is Mirza Raja Jai Singh.

202 Medha Deshmukh Bhaskaran

Dara remembers the extremely long journey back to Dilli with pain and humiliation. He wants to forget the times when he was dragged for many kos tied to a trotting horse while climbing the slopes or when the food was thrown at him as if he was a tramp. All he remembers is being hauled by slaves in the court of the Qila-e-mubarak, hands tied behind his back, feet heavy with iron shackles, along with his son, Siphir Shikoh. He remembers his long, unkempt hair not letting him see properly. He remembers not walking but heaving himself against his will.

His befuddled mind replays Aurangzeb's instructions. 'I want them to be paraded on the back of a female elephant through all the major avenues of this city. And do not forget to smear this elephant with dirt—for that is what they are worthy of.'

Dara wonders if his father is still alive, or aware of what is happening to his eldest son. The sun is harsh and it is extremely hot and humid. As the elephant sways, Dara looks at his beloved capital. He is not on a howdah; he is tied to the back of a small female elephant. The avenues look familiar. Thousands of horrified eyes watch him, some are full of pity. The elephant is not a magnificent male tusker, it is a measurable female smeared with mud. The animal is neither pompously caparisoned nor is it decorated with gilded framework. The first prince is not sitting in a howdah inlaid with gold and covered with a glorious canopy that resembles a silver cupola. The first prince himself does not look like Dara Shikoh, Shah Bulund Iqbal, the king of lofty fortunes who always wears large pearls, an enormous turban with gilded serpech and an embroidered coat.

Once his people had looked up at him with love and worship, now they look at him with shock mixed with fear. Dara Shikoh hates to look up. He sits there like an old man with a bent spine, his matted hair on his face like a veil. He lets his shoulders droop and keeps his hands limp on his lap. He is thirsty and fears for Siphir who is lying still next to him. He sees thousands of people, barricades keeping them off the street. He hears them scream and chant his name. He slowly drifts to sleep and the screams of his people turn faint.

From the watchtower, Aurangzeb too hears people chant Dara bhai's name. He is livid, his subjects love Dara!

There is a danger of a civil war.

'Call all my advisers, whoever is in the fort!' he barks before marching off towards the diwan-e-khaas. Mutamad is shocked; his master has lost his temper after many years.

The meeting takes place in the evening. Tiny oil lamps burn in the chandeliers hung in the patio of the diwan-e-khaas. In that twinkling light, precious stones stuck to the pillars reflect rays in every possible direction, rendering hints of life to their floral patterns. Aurangzeb sits calm, composed and seething. The beauty of his new home fails to kindle any cheer in his heart. Sitting on his father's peacock throne, he glances at the faces of his men from the corner of his eyes. He has to be careful; as per the royal etiquette, even his gaze is now a reward, a *meher-e-nazar*, the gaze of mercy. His uncle Shaista Khan, who was always against Dara bhai; Mirza Raja Jai Singh; Mir Jumla's son, Mohammad Amin Khan, whom he had saved from death in the dungeons of Golconda Fort; Bahadur Khan, who is his loyalist; Danishmand Khan, who was first a Dara loyalist but now has changed his mind; and Hakim Daud, the orthodox noble who considers Dara bhai a heretic, are standing in front of him with sullen faces. Their expensive clothes, embellished with motifs of floral patterns, gold and silver ornaments and colourful turbans have no impact on him.

He does not start a conversation and lets the silence grow, waiting for his men to turn uneasy and then blurt out their thoughts.

'Spare his life,' he hears Danishmand Khan, his face flushed with anxiety.

Shaista Khan seems restless. His favourite nephew has made a big mistake, wanting to make Dara Shikoh look silly in public. But the tables have turned. The avenues of Dilli have formed gossip hovels. They cannot rule out trouble now that the people are fuming in rage. Anything can happen and it is best for all that his eldest nephew, Dara Shikoh the crown prince, is dead.

'Who are we to decide?' Shaista says solemnly, his eyes filled with concern. 'It is up to the theologians of the sharia court to punish him for his heretic ways of life.'

'Kill him; he does not need a trial. His death will be lauded by Islam and the empire,' spits out Hakim Daud.

'The emperor must decide,' Mirza Jai Singh quips. He is the only Rajput in this meeting.

Aurangzeb has closed his eyes and is counting the beads of his rosary. The men vent their opinions and suggestions, discuss, and try to outwit others. Aurangzeb thinks of the reasons why his brother must die. Princess Roshanara has sent him the message that Dara must die. She has stated several reasons, the most important being the fact that the people support him, since they know him more than the other princes who have always been away. But Aurangzeb has other things in mind. It is better to cut off a limb that has turned gangrenous. Public memory is short. In any case, orthodox noblemen fear Dara bhai's liberal views that may lessen their importance if Dara becomes the emperor. He suddenly gets up and climbs down the stairs of the throne platform.

'It is our duty to give my brother a fair trial. Please find the people who have witnessed his love for the infidels' faith.'

That is all he manages to say. Now, he must wait, in silence and hope.

The very next morning, avoiding the diwan-e-khaas, he chooses a barren, curtained room beyond his private quarters for the trial. He stands in a corner, keeping a low profile. The chamber mills with qazis, the judges, imams, the religious leaders, and the muftis who interpret the sharia law. Dara stands to his left, shackled, unkempt, looking like an old man, older than his father. A witness standing in front of him reads what Dara Shikoh, the crown prince, has written.

I love this story that explains the Vedanta. It is simple and easy. A tree has two little birds. The first one is perched on the uppermost branch. It does not hop or swing, but is serene and still. It looks so pleased as if it seeks nothing from the world. The other bird is restless and hops from one branch to the other, pecking at sweet and bitter fruits. When it tastes a bitter fruit it jumps one branch higher. After a while the restless bird finds itself on the same branch as the happy bird. Then a primal truth dawns on its soul. It realizes that the first bird that seeks nothing from the world is, in fact, the real one. Its humble soul is a part of the absolute, the divine. And hence I have in my most modest pursuit written a book called *Majma-ul-Bahrain, The Mingling of Two Oceans*, as I find such similarities in basic truths stated in Hinduism and Sufism. That you are the divine and the divine is you.

The witness has finished reading. Aurangzeb knows what the qazis think. His brother has wandered into the turf of infidelity, first learning Sanskrit and then going to Varanasi, the Mecca of the Hindus, to learn from the pundits. He has gone to Lahore and has become the disciple of Mullah Shah, whose heart, people say, was lit by the divine light sparked in the heart of the famous Sufi saint Mian Mir.

Another witness is called.

Why did I spend years in writing the book *The Mingling of Two Oceans*? It is because of my understanding of *Yoga Vasistha*, the original scriptures where God Rama learns about the truth from Sage Vasistha. It is enchanting when you can see a real snake while only looking at its image. You imagine it rearing its hood and striking like a whip. You see in your mind's eye its fearful fangs, and are scared. The fear thrills you. But once you know it is just an image, it no longer seems terrible. The world is such; it is full of maya, the illusion. Maya brings enlightenment through its own destruction. Once you know what maya is, it is no longer charming. The world becomes flat and dull for some.

The third witness reads out one of Dara Shikoh's poems:

May the world be free from the noise of mullahs . . .
And their fatwa
These 'learned' to the ignorant
And their ignoramus vents
Inflicting torments on true saints . . .

Aurangzeb watches the qazis and the muftis looking aghast. They exchange glances, shrugging helplessly.

Someone reads out the final verdict.

'Dara Shikoh, the accused, has to pay for his association with the pundits. He has to pay for translating the Hindu Vedas into Persian. He has to be punished for writing a book called *The Mingling of Two Oceans* in which he preaches to unite Hinduism and Islam. He has to be punished for translating the book from Persian into Sanskrit. He has to be punished for studying *Talmud*, the New Testament of the Jews, and Sufi writings.'

'The accused is determined to disgrace Islam,' the qazis have declared their unanimous verdict. The muftis demand a death sentence.

They have signed a decree on the ground of infidelity and deviation from Islamic orthodoxy that is punishable only by death. Their verdict clearly states that the criminal should be beheaded.

Aurangzeb walks out. It is risky to delay any further. The royal execution must take place soon. He waits under the arched pavilions till they take Dara away. He knows what is happening in the dungeons nearby.

The door makes a creaking sound; the slaves push their hands under Dara's armpits and pull him up. For a few moments, they wait for their new master's orders while the crown prince hangs between them, limp. Aurangzeb obliges and signals. He follows them to an inner chamber of the prison. It is dark, with a single torch burning on a wall. The slaves scurry around the empty room, make Dara kneel, his hands on his waist. His iron chains jingle sadly. The muscular slaves armed with swords surround him. Aurangzeb raises his right hand and the swords fly. The convict's head rolls on the ground as blood spews forth in torrents.

CHAPTER FIFTEEN

1

Krishnaji Bhaskar is confident of his negotiation skills, but Shivaji Bhosale and his men are dangerous. 'Invite Shiva Bhosale to Wai and

make sure he comes,' his master, Afzal Khan, has ordered. As the
bearers of his palanquin reach the base of the hill, he narrows his eyes
and looks at the newly built Pratapgad. Shivaji has been holed up all
along atop this beastly hill, while Afzal Khan Sahib and his army have
been camping near Wai for months. Krishnaji sighs. His hometown
has been cramped with twenty thousand men and ten thousand
animals. The butchers work continuously, swiftly cutting the throats
of the cattle and goats and leaving them to bleed. The bloodless meat
is halal, lawful to eat by the Muslims. The Brahmin's stomach churns
as his olfactory nerve recalls the stink of bones and skin waiting to be
disposed of. The soldiers defecate on the banks of the river Krishna.
Even the war animals bathe in the same water. Medics of Wai have
been busy treating soldiers suffering from diarrhoea, a disease so
common in the monsoons. Rains are synonymous with immobility,
and this status quo has been unnerving.

Krishnaji looks out as his palanquin bearers cross the narrow
lanes of Par village and climb the hill. This trail twists and turns to
reach the main entrance of the fort. The newly built outer wall is awash
with rain, its basalt stones gleaming in the sunlight. He is amazed at
the massive ramparts and bastions. However, the fort itself is small,
and can accommodate only a few hundred men at a time. The turrets
over the ramparts are manned by archers. How can a mere jagirdar
afford this? Time has come to meet the most infamous rebel of the
Adilshahi sultanate. Shivaji's sentinels, who have gathered around
him to take him to their master, are armed with swords, quivers full
of arrows and bows. Krishnaji is impatient to enter the massive stone
structure built on a high plinth where Shivaji Bhosale awaits him.

The sadar is quiet and cold as the mountain wind circles in
its empty void. Shivaji sits on a divan, his hands folded in his laps.
Gopinath Bokil stands near his master. Afzal's vakeel has come with
the invitation. They watch a tall and muscular Krishnaji walk in.
He has a large moustache, and is dressed in silk dhoti and orange
angirkha. His red turban looks new. An embroidered shawl is thrown
across his shoulders. Shivaji notes a sword tucked in his belt.

Krishnaji regards the two men. One is a short tonsured man, a
Brahmin with a naive face standing next to the divan. He guesses that

it is Shivaji's vakeel, and finds nothing outstanding in him. But the man who sits on the divan is certainly not ordinary. He had heard about Shivaji's remarkable brown eyes. It is almost impossible for anyone to fathom the thoughts and feelings of this man by looking into his eyes. The face is serious, almost resolute, and the forehead is smeared with horizontal lines of sandalwood. Krishnaji admits to himself that the rebel does look like a king in his saffron, pearl-studded turban.

It is when Krishnaji looks into Shivaji's eyes that a shiver runs down his spine. His sharp and piercing gaze bores into him. He feels nervous, clears his throat, adjusts his sash, bows involuntarily and says, 'Afzal Khan Sahib is concerned.'

'I know, so are we,' he hears a humble voice. The gaze of his host is no longer sharp and cold.

Krishnaji is eager to say what he intends to. The rebel needs to know where he stands and what his status is. 'Raja Shivaji, I must tell you that one should know one's limitations. Can we at all compare ourselves with them?'

'The benevolent king, Ali Adil Shah, is the sun of our skies. Our general is a brilliant ray of that sun and we are the lost shadows waiting for resurrection,' Shivaji says slightly, bowing his head.

'That is a brilliant comparison,' admits Krishnaji, wrapping his shawl which has unravelled slightly.

'But *you* are the torch that will guide us through the darkness of night,' says Bokil, while nodding his head.

Krishnaji merely shrugs and declares in a plaintive voice, as if it pains him to see men like Shivaji wasting their time in rebellion, 'Nothing will be gained by rebelling against the king. If I were to advise you, I would tell you to enjoy the lavish life that only the king's court can bestow on you. Come to Wai and surrender to the general.'

'Do you truly feel that we have a chance to bask in Bijapur's glory?' Bokil asks earnestly, looking vulnerable.

'Why did I make such mistakes?' Shivaji laments. 'What had come over me all these years?'

Krishnaji feels pity as he looks at the youthful face and says patronizingly, 'What are you fighting for? You are a wealthy man, born to a jagirdar, and, with our hereditary laws in place, you are already a jagirdar. You have the means to chart your own path to be a nobleman in the king's court.'

Shivaji lowers his eyes, his expression withdrawn and brooding. He plays with the strings of pearls around his throat and says, 'Men make mistakes. One cannot turn back wheels of time and undo what has already been done. One can only forget or forgive to a certain extent. But let me tell you truthfully that I have soulfully resigned to the fact that I am a mere servant of the Adilshahi. The proof lies in the fact that I have not troubled your general's army. I sit here, quietly, repenting and asking God for forgiveness.'

Raja Shivaji's words ring true. Afzal Khan Sahib had tried all the tricks in the book to provoke the holed-up rat. He had even threatened the temple priests of Goddess Bhavani's temple at Tuljapur and extracted large amounts of funds from them. The khan had purposely called the jagirdar of Phultan, brother of Raja Shivaji's wife, Sayee Bai Sahib, and compelled him to convert to Islam. His general had also struck terror by letting his archers take aim at the innocent peasants in Shivaji's territory. But they have all been met with silence.

Bokil clears his throat and says hesitantly, 'Grave mistakes have been committed by us. But we want the general to know that we have rebuilt and repaired the old, dilapidated hill forts and built this one. Our lands are generating revenue of ten lakh rupees a year. All will be surrendered at his feet for the benefit of the king. But we have kept personal gifts for the general: two hundred Arabian horses and one thousand ashrafi mohurs.'

Krishnaji does some quick calculations. A thousand ashrafi mohurs would mean twelve ser of pure gold. 'Khan Sahib hates personal gifts. When do you intend to give them to him?' he asks casually, looking at Shivaji.

'We will give them personally, only when we meet him, like a devotee placing a petal at the feet of his favourite deity,' whispers Shivaji. 'You know, Krishnaji,' he says with dreamy eyes, 'it may wash away some of our sins. To us, the general means more than the Adilshahi king. He is not an outsider, a Turani or an Irani. He is a

Deccani, a native Muslim, a son of this soil. I am eager to kneel before him. He is one of us.'

'He is more than all of us,' Krishnaji's tone turns righteous, but somewhere deep in his heart he is pleased; at least Shivaji wants to meet his master. 'Our Afzal Khan Sahib is a self-made man. His father was neither a subhedar nor a watandar. It is not easy to rise to the coveted position that the general enjoys!'

Shivaji smiles at the Khan's vakeel's taunt guised in the veneer of graciousness.

'You are right. We are among the millions, but the general is indeed a man in a million. And he has chosen you to show us the light. It speaks volumes of your talent, intelligence and capabilities. How do we take things from here?' Bokil asks keeping both his hands on his chest.

Shivaji turns his gaze to his vakeel and says gravely, 'Gopinathji, as we have discussed, we know our goal; our journey ends at the general's feet.'

'I know you are anxious to meet Khan Sahib. I have come here to make your dream come true,' says Krishnaji, his hands locked in a tight fist.

'Let us hear what plans you have for us,' Bokil asks, looking up at Krishnaji, his eyes brimming with hope.

The khan's vakeel needs time. He looks around, eyes moving from pillar to pillar as he flings his shawl over his right shoulder. A lot of money has been spent on this fort. He diverts his gaze back to Shivaji and appeals, 'Afzal Khan Sahib was, at one time, very close to your father. He wishes to maintain the relationship. The general is keen to recommend your name to His Majesty, Ali Adil Shah, for ranks and titles.'

'It is the general's generosity. What is his message for us?' Shivaji asks politely as his eyes shine with optimism.

Krishnaji pulls out an epistle from under his belt and hands it over to Gopinath, who opens it carefully as if it is a gold chest containing precious pearls from the deep ocean.

The letter is in Modi script, in Marathi peppered with Farsi words. He reads it slowly:

Your frequent impertinence has caused anguish to the king. You
have the hereditary right only on your jagir. But you have taken
the forts and seized Jawali. Your men have brutally murdered
Chandrarao Morey. You have plundered our subhedar of Kalyan.
You have harassed the peace-loving, religious Siddis of Janjira.
You have unlawfully taken over the region of north Konkan. We
had ceded some of that territory to the Mughals to maintain peace
in the region. Before I think of waging a war, surrender all your
forts and provinces to me, for that is what the king, Ali Adil Shah,
wishes.

The letter has Afzal Khan's seal that says 'Katil-e-Kafiran, Sinka_a-
Biniyade-Butan', the killer of the infidels and the destroyer of the
deities.

Krishnaji does not look away from Raja Shivaji as the note
is read. Raja Shivaji's brown eyes look like lamps that have been
rudely snuffed out by a storm. Finally the disheartened rebel darts
a questioning look at him and says in a defeated voice, 'What do I
have to do?'

'Come and meet Afzal Khan Sahib at Wai,' says Krishnaji
magnanimously.

Shivaji stares at him, not responding to his proposal. After a long
silence he says, 'This valley lies at the western borders of the Wai
province of which Khan Sahib is the subhedar. In simple words this
valley, including this new fort, are the part of the general's region. He
must come and claim it. The battle is already over; he is the conqueror
and I the vanquished.'

Krishnaji does not want to say something that he might regret
later. The man sitting in front of him is dangerous, but what he says
is not untrue either. His words imply that the general must come to
his conquest as all conquerors do.

'By God Shiva, fear breeds hesitancy. And hesitancy means
indefinite delays,' Gopinath says with a long sigh.

Krishnaji nods. If Shivaji hesitates to meet his master in Wai,
it will be disastrous. Time is slipping away like a thief, snatching
enormous funds with each passing day. Five months have gone by.

The Badi Sahiba is impatient and has been asking for a probable outcome.

'Your master is the brave one, and bravery also means resolve. I am sure the general will decide. But it is not a thing that one can convey through a letter. A confrontation will do,' says Shivaji. Krishnaji is suddenly uncomfortable as a tinge of fear rushes through his mind.

'Please let me come with you to Wai to meet the general,' says Bokil apologetically while pulling the strings of the small satin bag that he holds. He takes out a heavy bracelet of gold embellished with stones, and ten mohurs with imperial engravings.

'It is our humble way of honouring you.'

'That's not necessary,' Krishnaji blurts, but takes the bracelet. The rubies and emeralds encrusted on it shine luminously. The general's vakeel tries to feel its weight in the cusp of his right hand by swinging it up and down. He does not refuse the coins either.

'An Arabian stallion too is a part of our goodwill gift to you. It is waiting at the courtyard of the lower fort,' insists Shivaji.

'When can we leave for Wai?' asks Bokil eagerly.

'Tomorrow should be fine,' says Krishnaji.

'Let me take you to your quarters. You must be tired.'

'When the heart is filled with fear, you fight or flee. It is worse when it is filled with shame, like mine is, as you are then bound with fetters of dishonour,' says Raja Shivaji as Bokil and Krishnaji exit the chamber.

2

Jahanara is numb with sorrow. The red sandstone of Agra Fort shines broodingly in the mild, early morning sunlight. The mighty walls with massive bastions that encase the fort stand mute. The fort's courtyard, pavilions, mosques and gardens are crowded with Aurangzeb's soldiers. His personal slave, eunuch Mutamad, has taken over as their chief. She hears him firing orders. They have been accessing Dara bhai's palaces that are within the Agra Fort and even those outside, she has heard. Countless trunks filled with his wealth are already on their way to Dilli.

The *serdab*, underground vaults built under the pavilion for the royal seraglio, are silent. Her aunts, sisters-in-laws, ladies-in-waiting, slave girls, concubines and courtesans living in the harem mourn. The underground passages that join the quarters of the royal ladies are empty. She walks across them and feels several pairs of eyes watching her through slits of the windows. She knows that the women here are desperately bored and live on hearsay. They pounce on any shred of gossip like jackals on a bloody carcass.

Jahanara ignores their gazes and walks along the garden, the Angoori Bagh. She climbs the stairs of her Mahal to enter the extravagantly decorated foyer of her apartment. Two enormous chandeliers float in mid-air. Hundreds of tiny lamps burn in them, protected by small glass shades. Pale silk curtains billow inwards into her room creating pastel ripples in the air. She looks at a painting hung on the wall. It is a portrait of her mother. The aging daughter goes close to the painting and peers into her beautiful mother's eyes. But her mother does not look at her; she seems to stare out, at her own tomb, the Taj Mahal. Tears flood Jahanara's eyes. She walks mutely towards the balcony that rises above the outer walls. Her eyes wander beyond the luminous Yamuna, beyond the blurring sands, and stop at the Taj Mahal, the mausoleum that houses her mother's remains. Her ammi jaan is luckier than her abba jaan, the dethroned, heartbroken emperor who is now captive at Musamman Burj, the octagonal tower that overlooks the magnificent tomb. Death has spared her mother from being a witness to despairing tragedies. Jahanara glances at the Yamuna. The river drifts gently, as if grieving over the fate of the royal family.

'He will not stop; he will keep flogging the shadows, forever, till they come alive with pain, and he will burn everyone around him till their ashes become mere dust,' Jahanara whispers to herself. She has understood that it is impossible to hate anyone in the world the way Aurangzeb despises anyone who stands between him and the throne, including those he suspects. No one and nothing is spared, even the dead.

The previous day was the darkest day of her life. A coffin engraved with holy text and sealed with wooden bars had arrived from Dilli.

It was taken to the dethroned emperor and opened, while all in the chamber stood weak with dread. They had a faint inkling what the coffin contained and hoped that their guess was wrong. As the slaves dislodged the nails of the bars with hammers and finally opened its lid, the smell of death filled the corridors of Musamman Burj. Her beloved brother, her own flesh and blood, the son of this fort, Dara bhai, lay in the coffin, his matted hair covering his face and shackles still grasping his body. His eyes were wide open and looked glassy. She had glanced at her father. Yellowish green bile had streamed down from the corner of the dethroned emperor's mouth. He had started flapping his hands like the wings of an injured bird and had started choking. At that very moment she had looked at the distant marble mausoleum, the Taj Mahal, the iconic monument of love between her parents! Just a blur at first, it had then broken into millions of fragments. The fragments had flown gradually into the space above and looked like a cloud of marauding locusts. The marble cenotaph of her mother had gone missing, and Jahanara could see her mother's body. It had shuddered violently. The lonely minarets had suddenly appeared like four venomous fangs guarding her mother's mortal remains. Then, it was just darkness. She had fainted and remained so till the evening. When she had awakened and gathered her wits, words of the famous Sufi poet Amir Khusrau who lived centuries ago had sloshed in her mind. 'Even an infidel will not do what you have done. Is it halal to break someone's heart the way you have broken mine? Is it allowed by Islam?'

Late at night she scribbles in her diary,

I have survived the fire, to face something far worse. How many will die a brutal death, how many will turn into miserable spirits and how many will burn in hell under my family's curse?

3

Bokil's sleep is disturbed by the incessant cries of an infant. He is at Krishnaji's house at Wai. Six days and six nights have gone by waiting for Afzal Khan to summon him for a meeting. It is early in the morning and his bath time. He goes to the backyard. Someone has already filled the buckets of water and kept them near the well. A round brass pot floats in one of the buckets. He gingerly pours cold water over his head. It is icy, making him cringe and shiver. What bothers him more is that Raja has chosen *him* to tackle the mighty khan. He goes through his strengths just to feel assured— he can analyse other people's thoughts, and stay calm in situations that infuriate others; he can be firm when pushed to the brink. Also, the Bhosale family has known him for years. He has been in the services of Raja Shivaji's father since even before Raja was born. He is a man who likes to keep a low profile. Almost retired, all he does is to occasionally help muzumdar Niloji Sondev, the financial adviser, and surnis Annaji Datto, the man responsible for revenue and expenditure. But now his master has placed on *his* shoulders the task to deal with Afzal Khan and his snobbish vakeel Krishnaji.

Back in his room he sits on the floor to meditate, placing his right foot on the left thigh and left foot on the right one—the padmasana. He shuts his eyes and tries to clear his head of thoughts, to reach the blank space in his mind where thoughts, reflections, estimates, planning, questions and answers do not intrude. It is his private domain.

An hour later, he descends from his room, with a silk shawl thrown over his shoulders. Seeing no one in the front yard, he decides to take a walk. It is still early, and the streets of Wai are empty. He is determined to do that which he has not done in the past few days: see the camp. After a few hundred guj of brisk walk, the banks of the river Krishna unfold before him. The stone steps leading to the water are polished, flat and wide. The skyline is filled with spires of temples, built with black stones, the reflections of which shimmer in the gentle waters of the river. He walks downstream, and hears horses neighing, elephants trumpeting and men shouting. He quickly climbs a small hill to investigate. The vast ground is covered with rows of elephants, horses, oxen and camels. An army of slaves wash, tether and feed the beasts of war and burden. The stench of the droppings makes the Brahmin cover his nose with his hands. He turns back and notices Krishnaji running towards him.

'The general has granted you an audience—tomorrow at noon.'

Relief surges through Bokil's body. These six days and six nights have finally been rewarded.

The next day, Krishnaji leads Bokil through the lanes of the Brahmin gully floored with irregular stone tiles. Wai is a typical Marathi town. The localities are segregated according to the castes. The houses are huddled together. But one can see only bare walls and the wooden doors embellished with iron spikes or rings. Most of the doors are shut. The vakeels enter a narrow path, a *lohaar* gully lined with small brick houses. A few blacksmiths are busy either hammering iron or pumping their bellows to warm their forges. They enter a path that runs between the river and the sugar cane fields. Beyond the fields, a little away from the river, Bokil notices a large fortress rising in front of him, close to the banks of the river.

'That is Afzal Khan Sahib's residence,' says Krishnaji, speaking for the first time. Despite the fact that he is prepared for the meeting, a shiver runs down Bokil's spine. He tries to calm his mind and continues taking deep breaths till they reach a huge gate. A few guards stand chewing betel leaves, their lips red with the betel paste. They do not glance at the vakeels.

This is where I will meet Afzal Khan face-to-face, guesses Bokil. The entrance is not bolted and Krishnaji pushes it open, inviting his guest into the courtyard. Beyond the door stands a massive stone mansion, and a few steps take one to a many-pillared patio. On either side of the steps, two fountains spray jets of water in circular stone tubs. On the patio, a few swordsmen stand as guards, watching the visitors. The duo first enters an antechamber and then a large, pillared foyer.

At the far end a few people have gathered around a gilded chair taken up by an enormous man, who seated seems as tall as the men standing around him. Someone announces their arrival: 'Khan Sahib, Shiva's vakeel is here.'

The huge man darts a look at Bokil.

Afzal speaks in Urdu that is laced with a Deccani accent. In the quiet room, his voice booms, 'Where is your Shiva hiding?'

At once everybody's attention shifts to Bokil. He moves forward as men around the general make way for him. They watch him as he kneels, untying something from his shawl and placing it near the Khan's feet. When he straightens up, he sees a servant in a black tunic picking the gift and handing it over to the general.

A bejewelled dagger is a mark of the highest regard. It is given to honour a warrior, in recognition of his valour. A dagger can thrust, stab, penetrate and pierce. A gift such as this one inflates someone's ego. The dagger has a sharp and shining blade made of steel. The blade is firmly fixed in a jade hilt embellished with decorative designs. So intricate is the work that a look at the hilt will convince a connoisseur that the dagger is not an ordinary one.

Afzal rises from his seat with the dagger in his hands. He is a keen collector of weapons. Bokil stares at the general in astonishment as his headgear almost touches the wooden beams of the ceiling. He feels like a midget. The general curls his upper lip and scrutinizes his gift. Without removing his eyes from its hilt he says, 'Stolen, huh?'

Some chuckle, while others sneer.

'Maybe ours, taken after seizing our valley,' a fat man standing behind the general suddenly declares, his voice full of hatred.

'Hmm . . . is that so, Prataprao? Did this really belong to your brother, Chandrarao?' asks Afzal absent-mindedly.

'Here is a letter from Raja Shivaji, my esteemed general,' says Bokil, trying to draw Afzal Khan's attention to business.

For the first time, Afzal bothers to, literally, look down at Bokil. He smiles indulgently, takes the letter and hands it over to Krishnaji, who first fumbles and then reads it out like a pupil duly reading out text after being admonished by his teacher:

You, the general of Adilshahi, who has defeated the mighty kings of Karnataka and dealt with the rampaging armies of the Mughals, must know that it is our privilege to meet you. It is our fortune that you have come to bless us. Your bravery can only be compared to fire that has the power to destroy everything. We humbly invite you to the valley, the region that will soon be yours. We do not fear the kings or even the emperors. We fear *you*, for men like you make them. Please come and claim your terrain. Kindly bring your army along, for we have no deceit in our heart. It is our responsibility to look after them. Please enjoy our hospitality that includes food, water, shelter, firewood and servants. After all, those too will soon be yours.

Bokil watches Afzal, who has gone back to his gilded chair, from the corner of his eyes. The vakeel suspects that Afzal is letting the silence grow in the chamber on purpose, waiting for him to say something. The general's minions too wait with bated breath, ready to react according to their master's inclinations.

Afzal is visibly irritated. His vakeel should have managed to bring the rebel to Wai. He clears his throat, shifts his gaze to Shivaji's vakeel and asks harshly, 'Who killed Chandrarao Morey?'

Bokil knows that he must speak the truth.

'Raghunath Korde,' he answers calmly and wants to ask. *Who killed Kasturiranga?*

'Who gave the orders?'

'Raja Shivaji Bhosale.'

'He killed my brother by deceit,' Prataprao shouts, thrashing his right hand in the air.

'And you want me to trust Shiva and come to Jawali?' the general sneers.

Bokil takes some deep breaths. What he will say now will lead to his success or failure. He must, without wavering or blinking, look straight into Afzal's eyes.

'By God Shiva, forgive me for being truthful. For a hundred long years, the Moreys had occupied the valley and amassed wealth through land revenue and road taxes. The benevolent kings of Adilshahi had never asked for any kind of explanation. You, the esteemed general, had been busy either defending or expanding the northern and southern borders of the Adilshahi, while the Moreys had been filling their coffers without paying any revenue to the king. When we opened their vaults, we found trunks stuffed with gold and silver.'

Bokil waits to breathe. Krishnaji is shocked. This ordinary vakeel of Shivaji can twist and turn a story well, very well indeed.

Prataprao Morey fidgets behind the general.

'A man of your years and wisdom should know that Shivaji Bhosale has not paid a dime to us either,' says Afzal, cutting off Bokil's argument with a blank face.

'By God Shiva, the esteemed general knows that Raja Shivaji's jagir was destroyed by the allied forces of the empire and the Adilshahi kingdom. The peasants had fled. Thorny babul had invaded the soil where millets had once grown. During the same period, a famine ravaged the region for three long years. It has taken us years to gather the absconding peasants to till the land. Only recently, after taking over Jawali and parts of north Konkan, have the lands under Raja Shivaji started generating good revenue. He is keen to surrender his terrain at your feet.'

Not a word from Bokil sounds untrue.

'Shiva Bhosale has turned the hill forts of the region into his military strongholds.'

'I am glad that the wise general has brought this up. It is time to speak without fear. The fort commanders appointed by Adilshahi rulers had turned these military strongholds into brothels or gambling dens. While the late king, the benevolent Mohammed Adil Shah, had lain in bed, while you had fought battles at the Adilshahi's north and south borders, the erstwhile wazir Khan Mohammad neglected the sultanate. All we did was to throw those pimps out and repair the forts to prevent structural damage.'

'Well . . .' Afzal regards Bokil for a while. The short, frail, old, toothless and naive looking vakeel is shrewd; he has anticipated these questions and is doling out well-rehearsed answers. He must be thrown off his guard. Afzal suddenly asks, 'Why did Shiva attack Muse Khan at Purandar ten years ago?'

Bokil does not blink but just clears his throat before speaking. 'Muse Khan had come marching to attack. No talks or conciliation were considered. You are the first person who has hinted at the avenues of negotiations.'

'Shiva Bhosale plundered our subhedar's caravan and had taken Kalyan pretending to be the Mughal subhedar. He has even seized all the forts of north Konkan. Now do not give reasons saying that it was done for some greater good.'

Bokil does not wait to answer. 'It was indeed a grave mistake. Then again, we had information that Mullah Ahmed was defecting. He had plans to run away with the treasure and join the Mughal. Where is Mullah Ahmed now?'

Afzal smiles for the first time. Bokil realizes that the bull-necked man with beady eyes does have a charming smile that can disarm the other person.

Mullah Ahmed and his family have recently gone to Aurangabad. Mullah's son is now a Mughal mansabdar of five thousand horses.

Bokil does not give in to the temptation and does not smile back. That would mean that he is just spinning a yarn knowing well that Mullah Ahmed has recently defected. Keeping a worried face, he rattles, 'General, please put an end to this. My young raja is now ready to surrender. He trusts you. Please do not delay your decision. Raja Shivaji is remorseful and depressed. If he gives up the hope of your pardon, he may just become desperate and disappear into one of those hills. It will mean war, a loss of life, property and time. And then you may not find him, ever.'

Afzal knows how perilous the valley is, a perfect hiding place for a rebel.

'Why can't Shiva Bhosale come here, to Wai? What is he so afraid of?' Afzal asks.

'There is a simple answer to that. Raja Shivaji is terrified of you, not because he thinks you will harm him, but because he has no moral courage to face you. We may debate on this for hours, but the truth is that he will not venture out of the valley.' Bokil is resolute.

'He must know that I am like an uncle to him, his chachaji. Since his father and I have fought many battles together, I consider Shiva my nephew.' Afzal's voice is tender and his eyes soft. Some of his men, including Krishnaji, nod vigorously.

Bokil retains his passive expression but allows a shade of regret to float in his eyes. 'My esteemed general, now that I know that you regard the raja as your nephew, let me tell you something. Knowing the path and walking it are two different things.'

'What do you mean?' blurts Krishnaji.

Bokil ignores him and goes on, 'Raja Shivaji believes all that you have said. Even then it terrifies him to act on his beliefs and come to

Wai to pay his respects. He is unable to do what you wish him and what even he wishes to do.'

'What can we do to make Shiva walk the path?' Afzal questions, his eyes losing their softness at an alarming rate.

'By God Shiva, I wish I knew,' Bokil says sadly, shaking his head with regret.

'What are the options?' Krishnaji wants to know, his eyes fixed on Shivaji's vakeel.

'The only option is for you to come to the valley, the region that Raja Shivaji is so eager to surrender to you.'

'How many men are there in Pratapgad?' asks Afzal.

The wary and reluctant fish is taking the bait.

'The lower fort may have a few hundred and the upper fort is guarded by not more than a hundred men,' answers Bokil carefully.

Afzal suddenly throws a question at Bokil as his beady eyes regard the Brahmin.

'Can you take a sacred oath for our safety?'

'If only I could get a leaf of papal and some Gangajal, water of Ganga river . . .' Bokil replies, knowing fully well that an oath of a Brahmin is a line etched by a knife on a rock of black basalt. If they break the oath taken, their seven generations are ordained to burn in hell without any hope of moksha, the cosmic freedom that releases their souls from the vicious circle of life and death. Disregarding an oath is moral treason, and for a Brahmin it is akin to betraying God. A Brahmin has to be sure of what he says before deciding and while taking an oath. If he envisages the opposite while he swears to God, he seals the fate of his soul, the soul that embarks on a sinful, endless voyage from earth to hell and from hell to earth.

Krishnaji looks at his master with admiration. Why couldn't he think of this earlier?

A servant in a black tunic runs to the courtyard. Shivaji's vakeel feels the general's gaze fasten on him, searching his face for clues that will reveal his thoughts.

The servant is back with a leaf and a small brass container of water.

Bokil sits on the floor, his legs once again folded in a padmasana. As Afzal Khan, Krishnaji, Prataprao and others loom over him, he closes his eyes to contemplate. The leaf and the water are kept before him. He takes the leaf in his hand and crushes it as savagely as he can, declaring, 'God will crush me and my forty-two forefathers if I break my oath taken for the general's safety when he comes to the valley of Jawali.' After throwing the crushed leaf on the ground he takes the water container in his left hand and starts reciting a mantra. During the recitation, he pours a bit of water in the cusp of his right hand and swallows it from the base of his thumb. He does it three times, and for the fourth time holds the water in the cusp and declares, 'I embrace the divine water of the Ganga in my hand. I swear by its divinity that I will be truthful to my oath for as long as I live.' Then he pours the water on the floor.

It has started pouring outside. 'Even the Gods agree, even they are pouring the water of my oath,' he says pointing at the rains.

Silence reigns for a long time.

'I will think over it,' declares Afzal finally, wrenching out another dagger from his belt and chafing its blade on the blade of the dagger that has been gifted to him.

The noise of the screeching metal sets Bokil's toothless gums on edge. He mutters, quivering, 'I will never break my oath.'

Being a Brahmin himself, Krishnaji is sure of what his counterpart has muttered. A Brahmin will never even contemplate breaching an oath.

'Betraying you is akin to betraying the emperor now that the peace treaty has been renewed. Raja Shivaji is well aware of this,' assures Bokil and bows deep for one last time. 'Sahib, once you decide to come we will clear the mountain path from Wai to Pratapgad, and that is the promise of a Brahmin.'

CHAPTER SIXTEEN

1

Darkness fills the citadel housing the residential quarters of Pratapgad. The world has shrunk and turned into circles of pale light only around the torches. Despite hundreds of men on the fort, a deathly silence reigns. The fragile hush is occasionally broken by the wailing of jackals or screech of an owl, somewhere in the woods of the lower slopes. Shivaji walks along the western ramparts of the Konkan, the vast expanse of which is an abyss of darkness. It has been days since Bokil has returned from Wai but Afzal Khan has not sent any message. Incidentally, something else bothers Shivaji much more. He feels a strange sense of premonition. He paces in a pensive mood, his ears pick up the sound of footsteps. Alert, his hand touches the hilt of his sword, but he knows who, or what, has come.

The messenger from Rajgad informs him that Sayee has passed away.

Shivaji wants to let out an untamed cry, to weep openly, to sob and let out his emotions, but his eyes are dry. He has been expecting the news, but somewhere deep in his heart he has wished for a miracle to happen. He was told of the diagnosis and the prognosis of the disease by the fort medic. It was a secret that he had never told her but suspected she knew. *Rajayakshma* or tuberculosis, the king of diseases, had devoured her leisurely for two long years. She had already set her death free and now her death had set her free. His heart aches with guilt for not being able to be by her side. The mother of his son has died alone. He wishes her funeral pyre would swallow his memories of her too.

Shivaji was thirteen, wide-eyed. They had just moved into a new home—a large house built with red bricks. He had sprinted through the ground-floor foyer and had climbed the stairs. His friends had followed him in a file. The stairs had opened on to a long corridor, large windows on one side and rooms on the other. They had bounded through the sunlit passage that had a ceiling of massive wooden beams. There was a balcony and he was curious what could be seen from there. He had gazed at the expanse and noticed hills silhouetted against the horizon. Between him and the hills there had flown a winding river, swollen with water.

'Shiva ba!' his mother had called him. There was some strange urgency in her voice.

There were people with Ma sahib—a tall man wearing a colourful turban and a woman who was perhaps his wife. As he had come to know later, the man was the jagirdar of Phultan near Jawali. Behind the couple had stood a wiry, dusky girl, seven or eight years old. She was floating in a sari, head covered with her pallu. She had stared at him with big eyes, shadows of anger fleeting across them. A strange smile on his mother's face had made him uneasy, and what she muttered had embarrassed him. 'She is Sayee; we have arranged your marriage with her.'

His friends had giggled. This could not be true. He had to do or say something.

He had shot back. 'I don't like her, her eyes are like saucers.' His friends had stopped giggling. Some had even looked at him with respect.

'And I don't like him either, his nose is too big,' he heard Sayee's clear and fearless voice for the first time.

The old memories have already started haunting him. He walks back to his quarters leaving the messenger. A few oil lamps burn mutely, and the shadows of flames dance on the ceiling, looking like beasts of sorrow—sorrow that mottles his throat, threatening the choking sobs to break free. Keeping his sword away he slumps on the bed, hides his head in his hands and shudders with sobs. He lies there hurting, waiting for the night to slip away until he can hear the temple bells of the morning worship. As the sky beyond the windows turns pale, he pulls himself out of his bed. He moves towards the entrance and then to the steps that take him to the lower fort. He rubs his eyes that still sting, and glances at the lower fort. He narrows his eyes to focus and notices a fort guard run towards him.

'News has come. Afzal Khan has decided to come to the valley,' says the informer, panting with excitement.

Shivaji buries his sorrow deep in his heart. He is expecting people to arrive from Hirdas Maval. It is only at noontime that the visitors arrive. When Shivaji enters the sadar, he sees an old man with a white beard standing near the door along with his five sons. His eyes shine with tears when he bows deep.

The man and his sons gather around Shivaji as he sits on the divan.

'Raja, we have heard the news,' the old man whispers. Shivaji sadly waves his hand to stop the visitor from talking about Sayee. He does not want to break down. This is no time.

'Kanhoji, you have received a threatening letter from Afzal Khan. But you have come to me. If I lose the battle, you will lose everything too, your watan and your family. There is still time. Go to Afzal Khan, help him.'

The old man's eyes fill with tears. He says in a quivering voice, 'Raja, it is not about my watan or my family; it is about saving my soul. You fight for our freedom. I place my watan at your feet. We are ready to die for your cause.'

'Are you sure?' Shivaji asks bitterly. 'Your neighbours, deshmukhs like Khandoji Khopade, Utravalikar, Kedarji and Jagdale, have gone to Afzal Khan. If he wins, these men will be rewarded with titles, military posts and bigger watans.'

Kanhoji bows deep and whispers, 'They have gone, that is their karma. I have come to you along with the Silimkars, Pasalkars and other deshmukhs. I have told them that Afzal Khan is deceitful; once his objective is accomplished he will ruin us all. While the Maratha kingdom is ours, it is our swaraj.'

2

Something is afoot inside Afzal's fortress in Wai. People have gathered in the main foyer. They are worried; some are angry with their general's decision. His most trusted men, son Fazal, vakeel Krishnaji, the late general's older son Ranadulla, chief guard Sayed Banda, officers Yakut and Mambaji Bhosale, Shivaji's father's first cousin, stand around his chair. When Afzal had left Bijapur he had had strategies and tactics in mind. Those had worked with the Hindu kings of Karnataka. Kafir men of power had a weakness, they could either be subdued with fear or provoked to turn hostile. But Karnataka was a different region. It was not hilly and there Afzal could confront the enemy who refused to meet him.

Shiva could not be provoked.

The mere sight of his enormous cavalcade of ten thousand horsemen, an equal number of footmen, five thousand artillerymen, a thousand camels, a hundred elephants and five hundred cannons on wheels, thousands of beasts of burden, countless slaves, women, traders and hangers-on has already struck terror in the hearts of people. His bards have done the rest. They have gone from village to village and sung hoarsely, exaggerating his and his army's strength. When some of the deshmukhs from Shivaji's jagir had meekly come to him, he had accepted them graciously. He had moved leisurely through the terrain, camped near the famous temples, threatened the priests and forced them to part with wealth from their treasuries. But kafir Shiva had refused to be provoked as he had hoped. Shiva's wife's brother, the jagirdar of Phultan, was captured and circumcised. Even that had failed to infuse rage in Shiva's heart. Raiding some of Shiva's territories, random killings of villagers, nothing had worked to bring the coward out in the open. That is when Afzal Khan was forced to think about new battle tactics.

The new emperor, Aurangzeb, wants Shiva's territories in exchange for peace in the region. Afzal's king is clear: he wants Shiva, dead or alive. And he, Afzal, has decided that the hunter and the beast ought to meet. It has become imperative to seek the alpha wolf, because the beast with his pack cunningly avoids the hunter. The hunter has to seek, even if that means walking into the den of the wolves in the dangerous hills.

Besides, the king and the Badi Sahiba are getting impatient now. It has been six months since he has left Bijapur. More than a million rupees have already been spent on this expedition: the heavy salaries of royal cavalrymen, bribes given to the Maratha landlords, food and fodder needed to feed twenty-five thousand men and thousands of war animals. There is another problem. Kanhoji Jedhe, despite dire threats, has decided to help Shiva Bhosale and has convinced several deshmukhs from Maval to join the rebel. Their infantries are trained to fight in the mountains. It is a great loss indeed. Further delay may mean more deshmukhs joining hands with the enemy, albeit not openly!

'Sahib, isn't there any other way?' Sayed, standing to Afzal's left, leans forward to be properly heard.

'Sayed, you should be the last person to be wary,' thunders Afzal.

'Sahib, you think I am scared?'

'Are you not?' Afzal sounds angry, but the next moment he modulates his voice to the mournful tone of a man who has been sinned against, 'What is wrong with all of you?'

'Father, we are all concerned about your safety,' declares Fazal whose cherubic face has darkened considerably with exposure to the sun.

Afzal regards his twenty-year-old son with dismay. The boy is a good horse rider and has learnt sword fighting from famous masters but has grown up in the safe confines of palaces. He is yet to rise to the harsh realities of life. 'Jawali is not as dangerous as we think,' says Prataprao Morey, speaking for the first time, and waits for a glance or a nod.

'Say what is on your mind,' replies Afzal.

Prataprao curls his moustache nervously and rattles, 'I know every corner of the valley. With our mighty army, what harm can befall us?'

'It is not about Jawali, it is about Shiva Bhosale. My nephew is a dangerous man, just like his father. They say one thing and do the other,' Mambaji Bhosale objects to Prataprao Morey's statement while blotting his face with his shawl.

Afzal looks at the aging Maratha for a while and says, 'Can someone give me a solution? Will Shiva come to Wai?'

'That is unlikely,' Krishnaji declares.

'Shiva has twenty-five of our hill forts. He has repaired and equipped them with garrisons, explosives, food and water. Those military strongholds were once manned by our men who had adorned them with wine jars and nautch girls. Shiva may have removed our imprudent fort-keepers by sweet talk, bribes and threats. It is not easy to face a man in the hills who has some magnificent hill forts, and is unwilling to meet us on a plateau. Ten years ago, we had tried fighting him at Purandar Fort when our warrior Muse Khan was killed.'

The men around Afzal are at a loss.

He waves his hand and continues. 'Months may pass before we seize just one of our own hill forts. We will need massive preparations for laying siege. We have an option to destroy Shiva's terrain and lay bare the villages. But what will we achieve? People will hate our new king. Shiva will still have his hill forts. His garrisons will launch fresh attacks on us. And even if we win, the emperor will be displeased when he receives a ransacked terrain. Now, Shiva has said that he is ready to surrender all he owns at our feet. Tell me what we must do next. How do we deal with such a man without meeting him?'

'We can once again try forcing Shiva to come to Wai. There must be some way we can do it,' says Sayed, sounding enthusiastic.

Krishnaji fidgets, his face turns red. Sayed's words imply that he has not tried earnestly. But Afzal Khan thinks of something else. The face of the blind Sufi saint floats in his mind and his words ring in his ears. 'Son, do not go,' he had said, 'for in my vision your body has been severed from your head.'

'Shiva will not surface, he will drag on. He is not in a hurry, we are,' grunts Afzal, barely suppressing his anger. He has managed to steer his thoughts away from the Sufi saint and towards the court politics of Bijapur. He has heard that the new wazir, Khavas Khan, hovers around the king. Afzal is sure that the wazir wants him to fail. If he dies, Khavas Khan will rule unhindered from behind the throne. If he wins, he, Afzal Khan, will be the wazir, the most powerful amongst the Adilshahi noblemen.

Afzal once again searches his mind to check if he has missed anything. He is going with an army which will not be raided during the difficult journey. Shiva's vakeel has taken an oath. He will be safe till he reaches Pratapgad. A slight smile appears on his grave face. His councillors watch him, tense and anxious. Shiva will come and visit him in his camp. That is the moment for which he will be prepared.

Afzal shuts his eyes, 'Inshallah, everything will go well.' He opens his eyes and speaks tersely, 'As decided, we leave for Jawali within a week.' The old memories and ancient hate have started bubbling in him. He was successful in killing Shahji Bhosale's first son, Sambhaji.

'What if we wait for some more time?' Fazal suggests.

Afzal Khan smiles, a hint of pity in his eyes. What does his son know about court politics? He has promised the king to bring Shiva to the court, dead or alive. Ali Adil Shah already knows that Shiva has agreed to surrender. If he delays further and avoids going to

Jawali, it will look like he is being bribed. Questions will be asked, and rumours will start flying in the court corridors.

'There are ample opportunities to ambush us,' Fazal persists.

'You are scared like a woman. Wear bangles,' Afzal wants to say to his son, but he resists. 'We will do as decided,' he dismisses the meeting. There is no further talk on the subject. The general has decided to take half his army with him and the rest to stay at Wai. Camels will be left behind, but some war elephants will enter the valley.

The day of departure does not bring the usual excitement as many of Afzal Khan's officers remain glum. Their long march through the steady climb to reach the wooded highland of Mahabaleshwar Plateau takes a full day. Afzal sits on a silver howdah on the back of an elephant, but soon takes to a horse. From east to west, they have to travel through ghats in the mountains, some suspended a few hundred guj above the surrounding valley. One small mistake, a slip of a foot or dislodging of a stone is enough for men and animals to disappear into the abyss. It is a steep, upward climb. The elephants struggle ahead in order to clear the way for the rest of the army. As the animals stagger through the dense woods, their bodies scrape against tree trunks, their thick hides are lacerated and they bleed. When they step on softer soil, they dislodge massive boulders. The rocks tumble down the slopes and crash on the slaves plodding along below with the luggage.

After a day's travel, they come to a mountain plateau a few hundred guj above the valley. They camp at the highest point. The night is windy but clear, and the camp shimmers in silvery moonlight. As Afzal sits smoking his hookah in his tent he feels peaceful. He has done the right thing.

The journey resumes as the sun rises above the mountains. The descent starts and it is a terrifying experience.

'It is too dangerous,' Fazal says while riding behind his father's horse, his skin red with mosquito bites.

Afzal keeps his cool. He knows that worrying is more dangerous than what lies ahead. He is sure that his army will not be attacked by Shiva during this journey. The Brahmin vakeel of Shiva is bound by oath, and a Brahmin's oath is a powerful assurance. But he, Afzal Khan, is not bound by any such oath. It is also imperative to take risks—it is an integral part of being a soldier, an occupational hazard. He is not afraid, he never was.

The ghats of Radatondi make some of Afzal's men weep with fear. The mountains rise around them as the valleys disappear in the abyss. Many feel dizzy when they cross very narrow trails. One elephant falls suddenly and is quickly followed by another. The enormous animals slip over the miry edge of the slender path. Villagers from the nearby hamlets hear the heartbreaking trumpets of the falling beasts, and the other tuskers trumpet in fear. Their screams make the mountains shudder. The shocked birds fly away in fear shrieking a blustering orchestra over the hills. Their frantic calls panic the horses. The animals then neigh and rear aimlessly. Men who try to help their confused mounts are dragged along and fall into the abyss.

Afzal remains in control. It is only about a hundred men, fifty horses and two elephants that he has lost. It is his war and his decisions. As his horse canters carefully through the greenish-brown waters of the river Koyana, he glances at the enormous hill of Pratapgad. *Nothing intimidates me*, he reassures himself. The surrounding forest is dark and discouraging. The path that leads them from the river to the camp is riddled with rocks and chasms. His fifteen thousand men and animals move towards the campsite not far from the river. It is an open space and the tents are large and comfortable. The locals have gathered and seem eager to cater to their needs. Most of them fall prostrate when they see him. *Poor folks from the hills*, he thinks. *They are lucky to get a glimpse me in their lifetime.*

The relatively flat region near the banks of Koyana has been cleared, dense thickets uprooted and the uneven earth flattened. Piles of freshly sawed wooden logs and sacks of grains have started arriving from all parts of the valley. Hundreds of helpers have been called from the nearby villages before his military cavalcade starts its final expedition. Huge funds have been invested by Shivaji Bhosale to pitch palatial tents befitting the status of the Adilshahi general. A market with rows of shops has suddenly made its appearance along the banks of the Koyana. The butchers, barbers, merchants, jewellers and even the swordsmiths have come from Pune to cater to the armies of Afzal.

He scans the camp where shops have been built on wooden platforms and stuffed with grain sacks, oil drums and jars filled with salt and spices. Some butchers have skinned animals and let the meat hang on the hooks as display. He has been told that each of the thousands of tents has a pile of firewood, a large earthen pot filled with drinking water and sacks of grain, even some jars of wine. His soldiers are scrambling to grab the tents. Thousands of local men scurry to remove their sandals, start boiling water for their bath or stand behind to fan them with bunched peacock feathers. Some carry large copper containers to water the animals. Shiva Bhosale is indeed trying hard to impress him.

3

After a thorough scrub by his favourite slave, Afzal gets dressed and is ready for the meeting. Krishnaji and Sayed wait at the entrance along with a number of armed men. He stands with them for a while gazing at the fort. The hill looms almost a few hundred guj above him. While the upper portion looks steep, the lower slopes descend relatively gently towards the camp. Krishnaji has told him that the fort has been splendidly built. Its outer walls, bastions, ramparts, terraces, citadels, assembly chambers and private palaces are stone structures. He has an urge to see the fort with his own eyes, see what a mere jagirdar has done. It is then that it strikes him that something is amiss. A man capable of building such a fort cannot be so scared. But it's a momentary thought. Afzal does not want to think too much. He decides to go inside his tent and wait for Bokil. It is a bit warm inside the tent. He sits relaxed against the propped-up pillows on his divan and signals a slave to bring his hookah.

Three men eventually walk into his tent: Krishnaji, Sayed and Bokil. Holding a thin brass cylinder in his hands while exhaling smoke through his mouth, he regards the short vakeel of Shiva. It is the third time that Bokil has come to meet him in the camp. Afzal remembers the first visit. The clever Brahmin had been very sweet, acting as a perfect host. Making a round trip of the camp, he had ensured that everything was in proper order. He had also handed over a cloth bag made of satin to Krishnaji. It had had a thousand ashrafi mohurs, a gift from Shiva to him. Before departing, Bokil had asked for an audience.

He had asked about Shiva in a rasping voice, purposely towering over the puny vakeel. To his surprise, unlike before, Bokil had looked at him in defiance and shot back in a loud voice, 'The meeting will be arranged on a neutral ground. This is the message from Raja Shivaji.' The cunning fellow had then asked for permission to depart before anyone could utter anything.

'Does that mean he will not come to the camp?' an astonished Krishnaji had asked.

'General,' Bokil had ignored Krishnaji and had fixed his eyes on him, 'you are a rich man, used to the splendour of Bijapur. We are poor and yet, Raja Shivaji wants to receive you with protocol that befits you. He has never met anyone of your status in his life.'

Afzal had known at that instant that he had no choice but to accept this condition. He could not go back to Wai safely after rejecting this offer. Further negotiations on this point would mean extending his stay in Jawali, a dangerous proposition.

'This neutral ground,' Afzal had insisted loudly, 'will be approved by my people and that is final.'

Bokil had readily agreed to that. 'I was about to suggest the same. We would not ask you to come to a place unless it is inspected and approved by your trusted advisers.'

Afzal had appointed Sayed Banda, Prataprao Morey and Krishnaji as his team for approving the meeting place.

During his second visit, Bokil had said in a low tone, 'We have finally found an appropriate place for the meeting. It is a flat glade on the slopes of the Pratapgad hill, a golden middle between the fort and the camp. Our people will pitch a palatial shamiana in your honour, my general.'

Afzal had looked at his men and they had nodded in silent agreement. Now for the third time the old fox was standing in front of him with a bowed head.

'Is the meeting place ready or are your men still at it? Are they building a Taj Mahal?' Afzal Khan has long finished his part of the bargain. He has come to Jawali as decided.

'Today, we shall finalize everything, the date, time and other terms and conditions for this meeting,' says Bokil calmly.

After hours of negotiations the terms are finally agreed upon. The meeting will take place in the afternoon of the seventh new moon day, which is a Thursday. The general and Raja Shivaji will come fully armed. Each will be accompanied by his vakeel. Additional ten armed guards from each side will be posted at a distance of an arrow shot from the shamiana. These terms will be written on paper and presented to Afzal for his final approval.

A worried Krishnaji wants to say something. Afzal waves his hand to quieten his vakeel. He thinks for a long time, making Bokil go fidgety with unease. If he declines now, the whole matter may drag on. He assures himself that he is the general of the Adilshahi and Shiva will not dare to do anything foolish at this point of time.

Finally he shrugs and asks, 'I hope that you have not forgotten your oath.'

'Shiva, Shiva,' Bokil mutters in a quivering voice as if to ward off the evil that waits to pounce on him for even brooding over the possibility of breaching his oath. 'How can you even doubt the oath of a Brahmin? If I do so, my forty-two forefathers and I will be confined to infinite imprisonment in Naraka, the hell of the Hindus. We will undergo hellish tortures, they will blind us, flog us with whips, fling us in boiling water, they will make us drink molten iron, and throw us in dungeons filled with hooded serpents.'

Afzal gives Bokil his most charming smile, his beady eyes glinting smugly.

He says, 'Tell my nephew that I will see him personally as agreed. I will forgive him his past and take him to our king. At Bijapur, he will receive riches beyond his dreams.'

'By God Shiva, I must go and give our raja this excellent news!' announces Bokil joyously.

Afzal watches till Shiva's vakeel disappears from his sight and then asks Krishnaji, 'How tall is this Shiva?'

'His head may barely reach your chest.'

The answer brings a strange smile to Afzal's face while he tries to calm his mind.

'Sayed, choose one thousand five hundred of our best infantrymen, armoured and armed with swords, bows and arrows. They will come with us to the meeting place. But keep this a secret.'

4

Two days before the meeting, Shivaji has called all his men for one last meeting. The air in the assembly chamber is throbbing with anxiety. It is a time of uncertain destinies. Men of might may fail, meticulous planning may turn into chaos, hopes may turn into despair and death. It is therefore important that Shivaji and his men go over their plans one last time.

Shivaji stands in their midst, wearing his usual saffron turban and white chintz angirkha. He knows that the morale of his men is not very high. They have seen Afzal's camp and realized that they lack in numbers, equipment and war animals. The Adilshahi army has surrounded the fort. From above, one is bound to feel trapped inside the fort.

He stares at his nervous men and says, 'It surprises me that the general has not objected to the campsite. His entire army is spread out on the banks of Koyana. As you can see from this hill, we are not locked in by them, they are trapped in the bowl of the valley. If I were the general, I would have first thought of the possibility of the enemy squadrons pouncing down from the surrounding hills. I would have demanded strategic hilltops to camp in, places from where I could watch the terrain.'

'He is overestimating his strength,' retorts Dabir.

'And underestimating ours,' says Pinglay while smiling.

'Underestimating your enemy is the basic military blunder,' announces Shivaji, 'and Afzal's estimations are our strengths. All we need to do is to keep his belief intact.'

'Let us again go over our battle positions,' sarnobat Palkar takes over. 'Only a few hundred men are and will remain on this fort. Our squadrons will arrive tomorrow, some from Maval and some from Konkan. They will enter the valley stealthily. At any cost, they must conceal themselves from the eyes of the Adilshahi scouts who have started roaming the nearby forest.'

'We have secured the fort. Of the two approaches to it, we have blocked the one from the north-east, from Kumbroshi village, by felling the trees. One can enter the fort now only from the south, through Sonpar village. The upward trail that leads to the fort is circuitous. A large army cannot use it to charge,' says Shivaji.

'We must block and slay them if they move towards us or intercept and kill them when they run away from us. Our infantrymen will hide at the foothills. They will stop the enemy squadrons from entering the fort. Our cavalrymen will hide in the faraway forests. They will chase and slaughter the enemy running away from the ranangan,' Palkar is ruthless.

The men nod silently. Sarnobat continues.

'The north-west side of this fort needs no security. The rock precipice takes a straight plunge half-a-kos-deep into the abyss. But the foothills ought to be protected from the other sides. Kanhoji Jedhe, Bandal Deshmukh and Yesaji Kank have called their chosen infantrymen, five thousand in number, from Maval. They will wait in ambush at the southern foothills, in the forest surrounding Sonpar. Peshwa Moroji's infantry will arrive from Rairi. One half will wait near Kineshwar village, at the western foothills of the fort, and the other half will be stationed at the ghats of Ambenali, beyond the north-east foothills.'

Palkar bows slightly. Shivaji takes over from where he has left. Everything is planned—who will say what.

'The royal tent or the shamiana is at the south-east, not exactly at the foothills. Afzal's palanquin will have to climb a part of this hill to reach the meeting place. They will enter through Sonpar. If you see from above, you will know that the place is surrounded by natural knolls that run along the slopes. Between the knolls are ravines. It is as if someone has made trenches for people to hide. Raghunathji,

Annaji Datto, Hiroji and their infantrymen will hide in the ravines that surround the shamiana. They will wait in ambush.'

Palkar must go into minute details. His face is hidden in massive greying whiskers, his bushy brows peppered with more greys. But his eyes are sharp, almost lancing his men's souls with stringency.

'Now it is time to talk about the cavalry. I along with my five thousand horsemen shall wait a few kos east of the camp. Babaji Bhosale will block the mountain ghats of Radatondi with another two thousand to block the path to Wai.'

'Any questions, any doubts?' asks Shivaji. There is silence. He goes on. 'Now, for the communication protocol, on the day, two trumpeters will sit near the shamiana. Once I go in for the meeting, anything can happen. The general will try to capture or kill me and I will have to defend myself. If either of us is killed, the trumpeters will blow their trumpets to alert our cannoneers on the upper fort. The alerted guards will fire the cannon mounted on the eastern ramparts three times.'

He stops and looks at his grim-faced men, trying to gauge their comprehension, then looks at Palkar and nods. Palkar takes over.

'Let us go through the remaining plan of action. As soon as the blasts echo in the valley, men hiding in the ravines surrounding the shamiana will rush to the meeting place. Remember, this is very vital, and all ten guards of Afzal must die. They must not live to alert the camp.'

Shivaji says, 'The camp must remain unsuspecting. Once the cannon blasts are heard, Kanhoji, Yesaji and their infantrymen will descend on the camp from the southern foothills. Moroji's infantry will launch an attack from the west and the north-east. Remember, we certainly want victory but we also want their horses, weapons and treasure.'

There is a long silence before Shivaji speaks again.

'In the last meeting Tanaji had asked what we intend to do if we win. I shall answer that now. When the camp is attacked from all three sides, a huge number of enemy troopers will perish. Many of them will try to run away in the direction of Wai. Babaji Bhosale and his men will intercept them in the ghats, while our sarnobat leads his cavalry to Wai. He must destroy the remaining of Afzal's army at Wai before the news reaches Bijapur. We have planned to infiltrate the Adilshahi territory to its core. Unsuspecting enemy is the best enemy! Adilshahi is sure of their general's success.'

'Do you plan to attack their capital, Bijapur?' asks Dabir incredulously.

Shivaji just smiles and says, 'Let's first go back to the shamiana, ground zero of the ground zero. Tanaji Malusare, Sambhaji Kavji, Jiva Mahale, Ibrahim Khan and a few others will accompany me as my personal guards. The meeting will take place at noon with just the four of us in the shamiana: Afzal, his vakeel Krishnaji, our Gopinath Bokil and I.'

The men gathered in the assembly room marvel at the confidence that Raja Shivaji exudes. With an assuring smile on his lips he says softly, as if he is sharing a secret, 'Remember, the entire operation commences at noon and the battle begins in the afternoon. It is early winter and the sun sets early. The valley becomes dark an hour before the actual sunset. That night the moon will rise late. For a couple of hours, our ranangan will be pitch-dark. You are used to the darkness and the place, while they will be blind as bats. The terrain and the time are our military backups.'

'Follow the communication protocol. Do not stir unless needed, do not defy orders unless absolutely crucial and do not execute until the time is right. Follow what's been told to you,' says Palkar. 'Raja's personal cavalry will wait for him at the foothills of Mahabaleshwar hill. After the battle at the foothills, we have planned to meet at Wai, early next day, just as the morning star appears in the eastern sky, at the time when the general's camp will turn in their early morning dreams. This is our war against Adilshahi rulers who are following Aurangzeb's orders. The end of Afzal may just be the beginning. It is not I but the raja who is the sarnobat of this campaign.'

His eyes glistening with tears, Yesaji says, 'Raja, do not forget that the general is a skilled wrestler. Afzal Khan has inquired about your height. Your head will only reach his chest. It will be easy for him to grab your neck under his left armpit and crush it. His right hand will remain free to strike you with a dagger perhaps, while yours will be left dangling and useless. In such a situation you will have only a few moments to defend yourself with your left hand.'

Shivaji can see the worry in everyone's eyes.

There is one last, and the most important, thing that Shivaji needs to share with them. He shifts his gaze from one face to another, slowly and deliberately. Then he says, 'Whatever happens, even if I am captured or killed, Afzal and his men must not reach the fort. It is imperative that we win this battle. Even if I die, please continue to fight for swaraj with my son as your leader.'

The men's faces darken in their gloom, their eyes shy away the shadows of anxiety and their jaws tighten with anticipation. Then they hear something that makes them rouse with optimism. Their leader's words fall like sparks of hope on them. 'I had a celestial vision. She showed her divine self to me . . .'

'Who?' they ask in chorus.

'Tuljapur Bhavani,' says Shivaji, as his eyes stare into the nothingness beyond the assembly. 'It was an experience, outstanding and mesmerizing. It was akin to witnessing a million lamps floating in the sky, or listening to a million bells tolling at once. I felt as if my mind was empty of desires and my soul full of yearning. Bhavani, the giver of life, the source of primal energy, had come with a message. She had shed the tears of red embers. The self-manifested Shiva-lingam in her crown had sparkled like a diamond. Her lion had roared angrily. She, the ferocious avatar of Parvati, had the fire of rage in her eyes, but I could also see shades of compassion in them. Each of her eight hands had held a weapon. A quiver full of arrows was tied to her back, a large bow thrown on her shoulders. "Swaraj is His wish," I heard her say.'

His words have infused valour in their minds and lit their souls. The potential energy has transformed itself into a kinetic power that pounds everyone's hearts.

5

The fort shimmers in the clear sunlight. While the gigantic cliffs and their vertical drops of the western and northern side of the fort seem nonchalant, the eastern and southern slopes, despite being defenced by towers and bastions, look vulnerable. Raja Shivaji is in his private quarters in the upper fort, dressing up for the event. The general has come to Jawali, making his intentions clear. Afzal wants to either take him as a captive to the Bijapur court or present his head as proof and trophy. The very nature of the mission calls for treachery, cunning, slyness and fraudulence.

Shivaji puts on a jacket made of steel mesh and then his usual, long-sleeved silk robe, long enough to reach his knees over a pair of tight breeches. A servant rushes in with a metal helmet and places it on his head; a saffron turban with pearl strings hides the head armour. The servant ties a sash over his robe. Shivaji turns towards a small wooden desk and picks up a metal instrument. It is a concealable weapon called the *baghnach*. This 'tiger's claw' is an iron bar with two rings at the edges, studded with diamonds and rubies to resemble finger rings. He slips his index and the last, small finger of his left hand into them, and opens his palm to look. Four curved, pointed blades affixed to the crossbar unfold before him like an extension of his body. He feels like a tiger with claws, or a bird with talons. He smiles to himself. There is another object on the wooden desk. It is a bichwa, a scorpion dagger with a blade that looks like a large stinger of a scorpion. He gently picks it up and tucks it under his left sleeve. Before leaving his quarters, Shivaji glides the blade of his dhop sword into the scabbard and grits it on his waistband.

'Now everything is in God Shiva's hands. The *rudra tandava* is about to begin.'

At the foothills, Bokil, nervous and irritable, has reached the camp along with several local men. It is a bright and clear day and the recent monsoons have turned the surrounding valley into a lush green carpet. Several carts carrying fruits, vegetables and meat roll down the tracks from the west. A group of tribal women carrying firewood bundles on their heads scamper towards the north end of the camp. Afzal's men look relaxed, some are even busy playing dice. For them the battle is over now that they have reached Jawali. They have won, their general is already a victor. Bokil glances at the stables, the horses are not saddled and the elephants wander around near the edge of the camp, feasting on bamboos.

The vakeel's eyes search for the main guest who is attired in a light-green silk jama with gold brocade and a glittering zari sash. The general's kimoush turban is white in colour, embellished with tiny diamonds and a single topaz. Even his leather sandals sparkle with precious stones. Ten armed guards wait behind him. Bokil recognizes only two of them—one is Sayed Banda and the other is Rahim, Afzal's nephew who he had seen in Wai. Krishnaji stands to the general's right, a large scabbard girded to his belt. Before Bokil can bow, the general slinks into his palanquin. Nobody speaks a word as they move towards Sonpar. But Bokil, who walks along with Krishnaji behind the general's palanquin, feels edgy. Something is amiss and it makes him glance behind him. A squadron of armed men, with swords, shields, quivers and bows follow them, soft-footed and silent.

This was not to be.

Bokil feels cheated but lets it pass. As they move silently, he contemplates that such a number of armed men around the meeting place would breed trouble for them. He looks at the hill where the gold pinnacle at the top of the shamiana dazzles in the morning sunlight. Gentle mountain breeze flutters the textile panels, lending a magical quality to it all. He glances ahead: they are at the edge of Sonpar now. They cross the village and enter into a ditch. The shamiana is not visible from this place. The hill blocks the view. He glances back; the camp too is out of sight. Soon they will climb the hill to reach the shamiana. It will not be safe to allow these soldiers to go ahead. He looks at Krishnaji and says, 'By God Shiva, how many armed men are following us? Is it more than a thousand? They will have to wait here. If you insist, Raja Shivaji will vanish in the labyrinth of this valley for sure.'

Krishnaji is startled, but instead of being apologetic he sniggers.

Bokil points at a few men in loincloths hovering at the foothills and says, 'Look at those men. They may wear just a grubby loincloth, but they are the famous rock-climbers of the area. They will take very little time to reach the fort to warn Raja Shivaji.' His eyes are cold.

Krishnaji jerks his head to spit out betel pulp as a mark of his anger and disregard, and rushes towards Afzal's palanquin. Bokil waits as an excited Krishnaji says something to his master and returns with a grim face, nodding his head in utter disbelief. 'The armed squadron will wait here.'

On his way out, Shivaji looks at the main entrance of the fort flanked by the majestic bastions. The thought that it might be the last time that he sees the gates cuts through his mind. He quickly dismisses it. He travels on his palanquin, his ten guards following him on foot. As they near the shamiana, he notices Bokil walking briskly towards him. There is something serious on Bokil's mind. Shivaji waits inside his palanquin till his vakeel comes near.

Bokil speaks quickly and urgently, 'The bad news is that Afzal's contingent of one thousand armed men waits near Sonpar. The good news is that the general has reached and seems pleased.' He takes a few deep breaths and announces, 'Sayed Banda is still inside.'

Shivaji looks at the shamiana where they have to meet. It looks like destiny's indifferent hand, stern and uncaring. Beyond the shamiana is the impassive valley, deep and deadly. Behind him stands the fort, helpless and mute. To enter the shamiana, one has to cross a natural but narrow mud bridge with a steep drop on either side. There are no escape routes, for anyone. The mountain stands chill and aloof, the atmosphere silent and unmoved.

'Tell him if he wants this meeting to take place, Sayed should leave,' says Shivaji in a low voice without coming out of his palanquin. Bokil nods and leaves.

'As per the agreement, only Krishnaji and I stay,' Bokil declares to the general. 'If Sayed remains inside, the meeting will be cancelled.'

Afzal waves his hand signalling the guard to leave. It is after several months, long journeys, heavy loss of men and animals in the mountains and millions of moments of anguish and anticipation that he has finally managed to make it to his destination. He will not let it go. Plus, he has nothing to fear. His enemies do.

Shivaji watches Sayed leave, his steps heavy and reluctant. The muscular man with a strong jawline wears a metal helmet and vest armour. His eyes bore into Shivaji who watches till the man is outside the tent. Shivaji glances at his two guards: Mahale's eyes are fixed on Sayed, Sambhaji Kavji stares blankly at the sky, Ibrahim seems alert and others have kept their eyes on the shamiana. It is time to go inside. He alights from his palanquin and moves towards the venue. Bokil is back at the entrance. Shivaji removes his sword tucked in his belt and hands it over to his vakeel. Then he climbs the steps into the tent.

Afzal sits on the divan, his back resting on the soft silk cushions, his roving eyes full of admiration and envy as they take in the silk panels embellished with pearls, the large silver urns and the Persian carpets. A dais with steps has been built to honour him. When Shivaji reaches the edge of the dais, he notices the general's sword lying next to him. Krishnaji stands at his master's right with a large scabbard girded to his belt.

Moments slip by stealthily. Then, like a prowling tiger coming out in the open, the general rises to his feet. Only when Afzal stands does Shivaji realize how huge his guest is. He has to throw his head back to look at the general's face. A bulkily coiled kimoush turban makes him look taller. He has a rugged face with beady eyes and an enormous beard that crawls to his chest.

Afzal stares down at the rebel, an impeccably attired young man. His face instantly reminds him of Shahji Bhosale—the same brown eyes, the aquiline nose, the moustache and the trimmed beard. Shiva stands there, with folded hands, an impish, charming smile playing on his lips.

As his temper rises, Afzal thinks, *Shackle them, humiliate them, crush them with cannonballs, but the men of the Bhosale family keep bouncing back. Like stubborn weeds, growing at all places, multiplying, invading anything, not allowing the precious to thrive. First there was Shahji who has taken away the rich jagir of Bendakaluru, and now his brazen traitor son who wants to swallow the western regions.*

A stab of jealousy pierces Afzal's heart, like a hawk dismembering its prey with its talons. He closely scrutinizes Shivaji, his saffron turban laden with pearls, his neat sideburns, the large earrings embellished with rubies, the tear-shaped pearls, his expensive, embroidered clothes and the cashmere shawl. It is Shivaji's lotus-shaped confident eyes that he hates the most. The fear, the guilt, the humility, the apology, the regret, the remorse that he had to see in them is clearly missing. He is overwhelmed with a revelation he does not anticipate at all. He had been looking forward to meeting a coward, immature Shiva, eager to fall prostrate at his feet, begging and pleading, but he now realizes that his assumptions had been wrong.

Afzal suddenly feels an impulse to humiliate his enemy. The emotion overtakes his planned civility. His mind spins with the heat of rage and words pop out like kernels, 'You seem to have looted the sultanate and the empire, you and your criminal banditry. I can see it all over the place.'

'The Almighty alone knows who the bandit is, general. Earlier, the hill forts were occupied by criminals and the land had turned barren. I have brought order to the region. The hill forts are well made up and the land generates revenue,' says Shivaji softly without taking his eyes off Afzal. He is surprised by his guest's effeminate voice. *This is the man who calls himself the slayer of the kafirs, this is the man who is responsible for my brother's tragic death in the trenches, this is the man who had invited Kasturiranga, the king of Shirepattan, for a truce and killed him by deceit.*

'Let bygones be bygones,' Afzal says, 'surrender the region and the forts to me, and come with me to Bijapur.'

'Have you got the king's farman for me?' Shivaji asks with scorn. 'If so, I shall place it on my head and obey you, my general.'

Krishnaji breaks in, 'You have come under the protection of Afzal Khan Sahib. Get your offences be pardoned by the general and *then* expect a king's farman.'

Shivaji regards Afzal with intrepid eyes and says, 'The general and I, we both are the servants of Ali Adil Shah. Who is *he* to pardon me? It should come from the king!'

The words seem to sting Afzal. He has been belittled. But he needs to keep his calm. The enemy is not an ordinary coward as he was made to believe. He needs to be careful, and decides to be his gracious self. He fixes his gaze on his host. His upper lip curves for a moment but he says patronizingly, in a soft voice, 'The king trusts me, and if I pardon you, he too will. I agree with you that we are equal, so we must meet like the equals do. You do not have to be scared.'

'I feel humbled but not scared,' says Shivaji, bowing to show respect. Not showing any surprise at his enemy's sudden change of attitude, he continues, 'I just cannot believe that I am standing here, face-to-face with the Adilshahi general.'

'You seemed eager to wage war with us, you stubborn lad. You are still young and there is enough time for you to redeem yourself. In your youthful arrogance, you have shown disrespect to our king as well as the emperor of Hindustan. I have come to reprimand you as a senior servant of Ali Adil Shah. And you have agreed to surrender your region.'

'I shall certainly surrender all my worldly possessions as agreed before. But do you have the king's farman for me?'

The vakeels freeze. Afzal's face changes rapidly, from rage to disbelief to a smile.

'This element of courage is so rare. The king will be so pleased to meet you. And you can directly surrender to the king. Come, my boy, son of my dear friend Shahji, we are equals and must meet so.' Saying this, Afzal spreads his enormous arms and starts walking towards Shivaji.

Bokil stares at Afzal's agility and notes something sinister in his swagger. Krishnaji too has not expected his master's quick actions. For a moment, time freezes, as if it is seized by a quick bout of stupor. Shivaji remains rooted but soon finds himself in the firm grip of his guest, his face buried in Afzal's chest. He feels suffocated by the strong musk perfume the general wears. Within a fraction of time, he finds his neck under his guest's left armpit. He feels trapped as his right hand dangles aimlessly. The grip is so strong that it is difficult to breathe. Shivaji is sure that if the hold becomes any tighter, he will hear his bones crack. He decides to act with his free left hand. He opens his palm wide and pushes the iron claws inside his enemy's waist with full force. All four steel edges, pointed and jagged, tear through the layers of Afzal's skin and muscles, just below the rib cage. It all happens a lot more easily than Shivaji had imagined. Surprisingly, the general wears no armour. With the blades still stuck in the flesh, he twists his palm, moving the blades in a circular motion. He looks up to see the general raise his right hand that holds a *jambia* dagger, and its shining L-shaped blade comes down on his shoulder. His body shudders with impact, his neck twists, and he sees his headgear fly to the other end of the shamiana. The jambia tears through his jama and slides over his metal armour with a screeching sound.

The excruciating pain in the right abdomen makes Afzal let go off his enemy. With his free right hand, Shivaji takes out the bichwa tucked in his left sleeve, grits his teeth and impales Afzal Khan's stomach repeatedly, once twice, thrice, with full force, as his body jerks forward then backward. Afzal looks at his host, his kohl-lined eyes cold and vacant. He lets out a horrendous shriek as a part of his innards hang out from the gaping wound. Unbalanced and swaying, the general staggers towards the entrance, leaving behind a huge trail of blood.

'Haraamzada! Bloody murderer!' Shivaji hears someone shouting. The trumpets have started blowing as planned, their bellows rising above the screams of the bodyguards. From the corner of his eyes, he sees Sayed bolting into the shamiana, the blade of his pata sword savagely cutting through the air. Shivaji prepares for a lethal blow but notices Mahale leaping in. Mahale's hand holding a dhop sword moves like a whip and chops Sayed's hand in mid-air. Bokil moves forward like the hood of a striking snake and hands over the sword to Shivaji. Krishnaji too pulls out his sword.

'You have broken your oath, the oath of a Brahmin!' screams Afzal's vakeel.

'By God Shiva, my oath did not include self-defence,' shouts back Bokil, looking at the raised blade that is about to attack him.

Shivaji is swift. He strikes at Krishnaji's throat before his sword can harm Bokil. The Adilshahi vakeel crumples in a heap, his sword falling alongside, blocking the entrance of the shamiana. Shivaji looks around to find Sayed lying dead, his head rolling on the carpets like a round boulder and Mahale hovering over his slaughtered enemy. The meeting place has turned into a gruesome battlefield in the matter of a few moments. Shivaji dashes out. Afzal still shouts something guttural. The enormous man manages to cram his body into the palanquin. His bearers are quick, they start racing away. Outside, seventeen men are engaged in a violent battle. Shivaji notes that Kavji has slaughtered his opponent and has leapt towards the palanquin. His sword moves faster than a bird of prey, chopping off the legs of the bearers. They fall one after another, wailing with pain and agony. The palanquin crashes down. As Shivaji looks on, Kavji ruthlessly pulls the bleeding Afzal out. His sword moves in forward motion as the Adilshahi general's head falls on the ground and his body drops on the crashed palanquin, like an uprooted tree.

Kavji lifts Afzal's head like a trophy and grins like an insane man. The fort cannon to signal Shivaji's men who are scattered around have started blasting, its sound infusing an excitement in their blood. Shivaji looks up at the sky and says, 'Swaraj is His wish!'

6

The diwan-e-khaas of the Qila-e-mubarak at Dilli is charged with unseen yet tangible energy. The drums beat to announce the arrival of the new emperor. A hundred eyes are fixed on him, and they are filled with reverence, worship and fear. Aurangzeb does not bother to look at anyone, he fumes when he enters diwan-e-khaas. He looks at the throne before he climbs the platform stairs—he always does that. It feels good, makes him feel powerful. The *takht-e-taus* stands on legs made of solid gold, and is covered with an enamelled canopy. The canopy is supported by twelve emerald pillars, each of which bears two peacocks encrusted with gems. Between those dazzling, stately birds stands a tree so laden with diamonds, emeralds and rubies as if the stones are ready to drop like ripe fruit. The pillars are high, almost about eighteen feet in height. The entire structure has twelve sides made with geometrical precision. Parapets enclose the seat from all sides but from the front for the emperor to enter.

As he makes himself comfortable on the velvety softness of the seat, people in the diwan-e-khaas perform kurnish.

Shaista Khan, Mirza Raja Jai Singh, Mir Jumla, Bahadur Khan, Danishmand Khan, Hakim Daud, Diler Khan, Maharaja Jaswant Singh Rathod, Jaffar Khan and many others stand before him. But the new emperor is seething with rage. The grand clergy of Mecca has refused to recognize him as the emperor of Hindustan. A letter has arrived that says:

Law of the Prophet (Peace Be Upon Him) and the law of nature prevent you from proclaiming yourself as the emperor during the lifetime of your father. Also, you have murdered your brother to whom the empire rightfully belonged after the death of Emperor Shah Jahan.

There is one more letter, far more humiliating than the one from Mecca.

His envoy, Tarbiyat Khan, has returned from Persia after meeting the emperor of Iran, Shah Abbas, who has openly condemned him as the murderer of Dara Shikoh and cursed him for imprisoning his own father. Shah Abbas is a man of power, and if he so wishes, he can invade Dilli with his large army. Aurangzeb had sent valuable presents like diamonds, daggers and swords with gold hilts, all worth seven hundred thousand rupees, or five hundred ser of pure gold. But the Shah has disregarded the gifts by distributing them among his servants. The Persian emperor has offended his messenger, Tarbiyat Khan, by burning his beard in an open court. He has been sent back with a letter, the words of which are embers that burn the new emperor's heart.

We feel that all the landlords of Hindustan have turned insurgents because their new emperor is weak, unskilled and lacking in intelligence. How can such an emperor face Shiva Bhosale? Till now nobody had even known of the existence of the kafir Shiva. Now, people cannot stop talking about him. From what we hear he has taken over hill forts, cities and ports that had belonged to the southern Shia kingdoms. He has even invaded and plundered the imperial terrain. He is about to set an example to other kafirs. You call yourself Alamgir, the conqueror of the world! Your bravery remains limited to imprisoning your father and killing your brothers by deceit. But you cannot tackle Shiva Bhosale, and we know it is beyond your strength. We have been your refuge in the past. Do not forget that we have helped Humayun, your ancestor, to get back the imperial throne of Hindustan. It seems like, you, the descendant of Humayun, too, are in dire need of our help. We will rescue you, by paying you a visit with our vast army. Only we can dowse the fires of kafir rebels in Hindustan.

Aurangzeb's head hurts with wrath. He can no longer control his temper. He direly needs an antidote. The Adilshahi general has been murdered by Shiva Bhosale during a meeting. After the general had been slain, Shiva's foot soldiers had encircled the general's camp and fallen upon it with vehemence. Thousands have been slaughtered and injured, thousands have fled, and the fleeing men were slaughtered by Shiva's horsemen. Shiva Bhosale's victory, in terms of carnage and booty seems glorious—the Marathas have claimed the general's weapons, war animals and all the money. This incidence has stunned the people of Hindustan, and the Deccan is alive with wandering bards singing songs that celebrate the victory of the Marathas. The Portuguese and the English have exchanged letters in frenzy, calling 10 November 1659 a historical landmark, an epoch.

Aurangzeb claps his hands.

Someone brings the sobbing emissary but Aurangzeb does not want to look at his face even though he must hear what the man says. 'Shah Abbas had laughed openly and called my Majesty a hypocrite, a disgrace to Islam.'

There is total silence in the court. The new emperor's face turns red. He surveys the people in his court as they stand mutely, as if they have gone deaf, their eyes focused on the ground, their gaze at their feet.

'Bring in the case,' he orders, startling everyone.

A few slaves gingerly walk in holding a wicker basket. They are followed by a man wearing a long black kaftan. He holds a large, flat, brass container in his hand. He places it in front of the throne.

One of the guards empties the deadly contents of the case into the brass container. A green alert reptile makes a thudding sound as it hits the brass metal. It first moves like a whiplash and then slithers aimlessly, moving its triangular flat head in different directions. The man standing near the container can clearly see its yellow eyeballs with the vertical pupils radiating horror.

He claps his hands again. A few more slaves stumble in and hold the emissary in such a way that the man is not able to move. Then one of them holds his right hand like a wooden log and pulls it near the brass container. Someone takes a stick and starts prodding the deadly reptile to excite it. They seem to know that an enraged snake spews all its venom once the fangs get hold of the flesh, flesh that invariably has very little time to live. People can now hear the irate hissing sounds of the deadliest poisonous serpent—the green Himalayan viper. Tarbiyat Khan's hand is offered to the insanely frightened and enraged snake as a consolation prize. A horrendous, never-ending shriek rattles the pillars of the court. The slaves crop the man on the ground and look on impassively. People stare at their emperor; he is counting the beads of his tesbih, his pale eyes distant.

PART II

1659–66

PROLOGUE

1656

Silhouettes of the Maval hills look like giant waves of a violent ocean, their escarpments, cliffs and gorges drowning into the darkness. Winter is almost over but icy winds still blow across the valleys hidden between the overlapping mountains. The village of Sind at the foothills of Rohida Hill looks deceptively peaceful. Mud houses covered with straw roofs supported by rickety beams of wood stand together on the sides of narrow gullies. The spire of a Shiva temple, rising above the surrounding structures, gleams in the moonlight. At the edge of the village, torches still burn in the courtyard of a small fortress protected by walls fortified with ramparts and a few bastions. The master of the house, Baji Prabhu Deshpande, is fast asleep, his rhythmic snores resonating in the courtyard. His guards are puzzled by something they have seen. Before they rush to warn their master, Baji is jolted out of his slumber by the faint sounds of explosions in the distance. From the ramparts of the wall that protect his home, he can see flames rising above the hill. The sudden bursts of several infernos seem to be originating from grenades. His master's fort is burning, and the high flames erupting from the fort's outer walls make Baji's blood freeze with dread and his mind explode with anger. It must be their jagirdar's son, the arrogant Shivaji and his gang! He and his men will have to leave at once! The horses of Baji's one hundred sentinels are trained to scale steep slopes; the horse-friendly trail hidden in the wooded slopes of the hill is well trodden and there is no enemy waiting in ambush. Baji is disturbed. Shivaji had sent Krishnaji Bandal a message:

Join my national movement against the Adilshahi king or die.

Baji and his master Krishnaji had laughed and had forgotten about the message and its sender, until the day news arrived about how Shivaji and his men had bathed the nearby valley of Jawali in blood, killing jagirdar Morey and his sentinels. After hearing the news, Baji's sentinels had started keeping vigil even during the night. But now Shivaji and his men have bypassed him and gone straight to his master's fort that Baji thought was invincible with its high walls fortified with ramparts and seven strong bastions.

Thought after thought tears through Baji's head. When they get closer to the hilltop they smell smoke and hear some more explosions. The sound gets louder, and by the time they arrive at the entrance, the enemy has blown up parts of the wall and the ground is covered with chunks of rubble. As they ride gingerly, expecting a sudden attack, nobody actually bothers them. They cross a series of gates leading to the inner courtyard, but what they witness makes Baji and his men gape in disbelief. A bastion to their right has caught fire, its flames now licking the adjoining walls. In the glow that comes with the acrid smell, they notice that the courtyard is covered with bodies sprawled on the floor. At the edge, some injured flounder in pain and cry for help, while others are running in wild terror, not bothering to avoid the little crimson pools of blood. Baji is stumped. Where is the enemy?

A loud noise to their left makes his horse rear and start neighing in distress while Baji's ears ring from the explosion. He tries to control the frightened beast but is alarmed by the screams of his men. He turns his horse with difficulty and is shocked to see that their animals have bolted with fear. Most have turned back and are headed for the entrance, taking their riders along and vanishing before Baji's eyes.

Baji does not know what to do. He turns his horse around and looks up at the flames and surveys the still-intact ramparts and bastions. The ramparts are swarming with men in Turkish turbans, all staring at him as if they expect him to be there. Some climb down using the ropes hanging from the ramparts, and in a flash Baji knows how they must have invaded the seemingly impregnable fort while the inmates slept soundly confident of their security.

Catapults!

He pulls out a sword from his right scabbard and wields it in the air, its blade straight and double-edged, swaying in the air like a banner of death.

Within moments a hundred men have climbed down to the courtyard and they come closer still. He feels his nerves tighten; he is ready to die but not without slaughtering many. Strangely, it seems that the men who are in the process of forming a circle around him do not intend to kill him. They are neither wielding their swords nor aiming their spears. To his dismay, they stop advancing and watch him from a distance, their swords still in their scabbards and their shields held in the front to protect themselves if he charges. For a few moments it is status quo while Baji holds his ground occasionally swaying his sword in the air. Then the tight circle of men around him is broken and a man wearing a saffron headgear enters the arena. As the footmen circling them stand like shadows holding their breath and shields, the man draws closer to him, walking with ease, without a swagger. His attitude unnerves Baji as he prepares to swing his sword to stop the enemy from coming too near. But the man stops midway and pushes his sword into his scabbard. He does not want to fight with Baji. Strange! The man whose saffron turban gleams in the light of the flames that still burns the bastions is an easy target.

'We have heard about you, Baji Prabhu Deshpande,' he hears a young voice that is authoritative, yet not arrogant. Baji's mind spins. Is this really who Baji thinks he is?

'We have taken the hill fort,' the man says sharply. His brown eyes reflect the flames that burn the bastions while his gaze sets fire to Baji's mind.

'Not till I am alive, Raja Shivaji!' Baji shouts haughtily. He is the dewan, the estate manager, of the deshmukhs of Hirdas Maval, the area that belongs to the Adilshahi sultanate. Baji is loyal to his master, Krishnaji Bandal, a watandar who lives like a king in his castle-like fort atop Rohida Hill. With fifty-odd villages in their territory, Baji's job is to maintain a small army of sentinels to keep an eye on the patils. Baji's favourite quote has been, 'People are more scared of the sword than the blades of their own destinies!'

'Hmm, you have recognized me,' Baji hears Shivaji's mocking words.

'Who else will attack the unsuspecting?' Baji responds sardonically while Shivaji's men surrounding him shout angrily in response.

Shivaji raises his hand, ordering silence.

'Your master Krishnaji's paragana falls in my jagir, and officially he was my deshmukh who had to report to me. Have you forgotten the chain, Baji—from patil to deshmukh to jagirdar to subhedar and then the king?'

Was? Baji shivers. 'Have you killed my master?' he yells.

'Yes, I have. He had become a tyrant and was not recognizing our authority. It was my duty to tame him, but he was beyond change.'

'Murderer!' Baji yells, his voice cracking with righteous anger.

'Please tell us how many peasants have fled your region because you have tortured them or how many women your master has lifted from the fields? Numbers, Baji, give me the numbers. You are the administrative head of the Bandals.'

'Ha!' Baji snaps. 'You have killed my master. Raja Shivaji, you will have to kill me before you eliminate my master's family and take over this fort and the land.'

'I do not need to take over anything that is already mine, by killing the Bandal family. Let me remind you, lest you have forgotten, Hirdas Maval falls in my jagir.'

'What do you want from me?'

'Krishnaji Bandal is dead and so is the enmity between us. His first son will carry on with the watan, the hereditary right to collect revenue from the patils of this area. He will remain under our supervision and within our rules that have been etched to empower the peasants. You can still be his divan and my warrior. Baji Prabhu, I need you to fight against our real enemies.'

Baji glares unbelievingly at the audacious young man whose eyes bore into him like daggers, cutting across his mind and touching his soul. 'Your words are tricky, Raja Shivaji. I am a sword worshipper, not a traitor.'

'And people are more scared of your sword than the blades of their own destinies . . . Right, Baji Prabhu?' Shivaji asks, smiling.

Baji is surprised.

'That is your take on your strength, but mine is rather different from yours,' says Shivaji mischievously, while playing with the hilt of his sword. 'I think each sword has a character, and each swordsman has the power to change it to transform the destinies of millions.'

Baji laughs, even though there is a possibility of getting killed. In that chaotic moment, Baji thinks of his blessed life. He has it all, with two wives, seven sons and many servants. His vault has enough gold and silver for his wives to adorn themselves with till they stoop under the weight of their jewels. The sheds and stables behind his house have no place for more cattle or horses. He may lose it all. Does this jagirdar's pompous son really think that he can change the destinies of millions?

'When you use your sword against the unarmed and the defenceless, it turns into the devil; when you help the undeserving and the unscrupulous with it, it becomes a traitor; when you use it against the aggressor to protect the weak, it becomes the worshipper of God; and when you empower the helpless, the vulnerable, to defend themselves with it, it becomes God!'

Shivaji's words fall on Baji like embers that sting but not burn.

CHAPTER SEVENTEEN

1

After the death of Afzal Khan in the valley of Jawali, the Marathas act swiftly, pushing their armies deep into the Adilshahi sultanate. The king, who was sure of Afzal Khan's victory, is shocked; his mother, the Badi Sahiba, is crestfallen. There is more to come.

Shivaji and his sarnobat, Netoji Palkar, gallop in the direction of Bijapur, the capital of the kingdom. Above them, a waning moon looks distant in the sky. Behind them, thousands of horsemen fly like javelins. The colossal hill of Panhala shudders in its own shadow, mutely watching its new captor and his cavalry vanish into the forest at its eastern foothills. Palkar is busy calculating the distance travelled by Rustum Khan, Adilshahi's newly appointed general who had left their capital with ten thousand men a few weeks ago to intercept him. Soon it will be dawn and they will face the Adilshahi army in a battle at close quarters.

The western parts of Miraj have turned noisy. Rustum gets up with a start as the warning bugles whine at the edge of his camp. The noise is followed by shrill yells. Rustum takes time to grasp the situation, jumps out of bed and rushes to the entrance of his tent. The enemy is near and advancing and there is no time to waste. He shouts at his guards, snarling orders. The animals are alert and nervous, protesting by neighing or trumpeting. The camp is filled with the sounds of hoof beats and instructions being shouted in haste. The soldiers have no time even for their morning ablutions. Many have a hangover from the arak they gulped down before their late dinner.

260 Medha Deshmukh Bhaskaran

A zestful Venus has already appeared near the eastern horizon as if to watch the encounter. Rustum's battle formation is traditional, with him, the general, seated comfortably in a howdah on the back of his armoured elephant at the centre. Entrusting his 'left flank' to Fazal Khan, he arranges a security cordon behind him. His Hindu and Muslim commanders along with their horsemen form a seemingly invincible ring around him. After a hectic scramble, an acute spell of utter silence fills the battleground-to-be. After an agonizing wait, the first rays of the sun filter through the canopies of trees only to show his location to the enemy.

Palkar is the first to notice a fading cloud of dust floating above Rustum's battle formation. Without much fuss, the Marathas split, and as planned, Palkar and his squadron gallop towards the right edge of the cloud to hit the enemy's left flank, while Shivaji orders his captain, Tanaji Malusare, to move towards the right flank. Shivaji and some of his horsemen gallop straight ahead, to the middle of Rustum's war formation. The battle cries of 'Har Har Mahadev!' shake the terrain of the Adilshahi sultanate for the first time, and their resonance freezes Rustum's blood. Shivaji's soldiers are in their element, slaughtering his horsemen and eroding his ring. Bile rises from Rustum's throat when he notices the enemy using long and straight blades with ease. Some of his men have started running away from the battlefield, and seeing them flee, he suddenly feels suffocated in his heavy armour.

The battle ends with Rustum fleeing the combat zone, leaving weapons and war animals as spoils-of-war for the Marathas.

'Sarnobat, you will leave immediately for Bijapur with a few squadrons,' Shivaji orders Palkar whose face is flush with victory. He is not worried about the seemingly unachievable target his master has set: capturing one Adilshahi fort a day. Most of the soldiers from Afzal Khan's army are either dead and buried in the soil of the valley of Jawali or injured and left to their fate in the forests at the foothills of Pratapgad, while many have surrendered and been taken as captives. Those from the military camp of Wai have been left without weapons or war animals so they are as harmless as scorpions sans their stingers. Now Palkar is to launch attacks on the suburbs of Bijapur to jolt the king and further reduce the morale of the Adilshahi's military men.

After camping for just a few hours in the wilderness to give their animals some rest, Palkar and his men gallop towards the sultanate's capital through a barren landscape. For the first time, the Adilshahi's stony terrain shudders under the hooves of the Maratha warhorses. Palkar has decided to approach Bijapur from the north-west as his scouts have warned that there is a possibility of the enemy waiting in ambush. For many kos so far they have not encountered any village, but soon the stretch of rolling plains gives way to a few tombs and minarets. For the past month, after the death of Afzal Khan, for Palkar life has been a continuous battle, and he does not remember the last time he slept peacefully through the night or had a hot meal. The winter wind has parched his skin and it stings. He forgets the fatigue of riding for hours when Bijapur suddenly bursts into his vision, the enormous dome of the Gol Gumbaz rising above the intervening highlands. He glances at the massive wall, fortified with bastions, of the city he once loved. Some minarets and towers rising above the fortifications bring back old memories when he had lived in the city. That was another time and another world when Mohammed Adil Shah had ruled the kingdom. Palkar gazes at the outer wall and notices tiny figures of men gathering on the ramparts.

The young king, Ali Adil Shah, has rushed to the ramparts of the outer wall. He squints in disbelief to see what his stammering guards had whispered to him when they had jolted him awake him up in the morning. His archers had vouched that they had spotted many horsemen galloping towards the suburb of Shahpur to the north-west of Bijapur. Ali realizes that the Marathas are at his doorstep and all he feels is intense humiliation. This jagirdar's son from the edge of his sultanate has dared to challenge his two-centuries-old kingdom.

'How many?' he demands still gazing in the direction of the horsemen.

No one has an answer.

Ali turns his head to look at the scout and notices that Khawas Khan, his grand wazir, has arrived with many military officials. He focuses his eyes on the tall and wiry African and orders: 'Gather all our horsemen and lead them to Shahpur.'

Khawas Khan nods, but deep within his heart he is wary of the Marathas. He bows to his king and glances at his officers with a serious face who take the cue and follow him. Within an hour, he gallops towards Shahpur as his heavy cavalry of five thousand horsemen follow him. The sun has turned bright but the northern sky is filled with black clouds from the burning houses. Khawas Khan is not sure of the enemy numbers and ignorant about their plan, preparations and what they aspire to achieve. Do they want to enter Bijapur? The Marathas have arrived and they have set fire to many palaces in Shahpur. Then he notices something disturbing. A cloud of dust is rising in the north. It moves ahead and the noise of the hooves slowly fades. Has the enemy fled? He squints his eyes to mere splits at the north-western skyline and notices a line of horses becoming smaller and smaller.

The enemy just wanted to tell them that even Bijapur is no longer invincible!

2

The atmosphere is rather cold in the court as Ali Adil Shah watches the tall African swagger towards him, while the noblemen stare at the dark warrior with interest. Siddi Jauhar, the rebellious jagirdar of Kurnool that lies about one hundred kos south-east of Bijapur has arrived in the capital with a lot of pomp and glamour. Jauhar had long since stopped paying revenue. And there is more. He has refused to recognize Ali Adil Shah as the king of Bijapur. 'Who is Ali? Who are his real parents? Whose blood runs in his veins? I consider him a bastard king!' Jauhar had declared after Ali's coronation. Ali does not have much choice now; his kingdom is on the brink of ruin, and Siddi Jauhar, unlike his other warriors, is not scared of the Marathas. Jauhar also has a strong personal army. While these thoughts fill Ali's mind, Jauhar's eyes remain fixed on Ali who has put on a lot of weight since Jauhar had last seen him a decade ago as a wiry ten-year-old. Jauhar does not bother to look around, purposely ignoring the riches and grandeur of the Bijapur court that belies the

hollowness of the kingdom's military power. A small-time jagirdar
has shaken the foundation of the Adilshahi and Jauhar wants to
laugh out loud. Meanwhile, Ali regards Jauhar whose long beard falls
on his blue tunic. His sash is like a girdle sewn from several pieces
of fine, large, gold coins and is partially covered with the sleeves of
his mantle. Ali is doubtful. Does this man have the power to crush
Shivaji who is trying to break free from the embryonic stage of a
guerrilla warrior clan and emerge as an independent military power
worth reckoning with?

Ali, as a matter of habit, glances to his right, but behind the
curtain his mother's chair is empty. When the news of Afzal Khan's
murder had arrived he had not believed it in the beginning. His
mother, however, had gone mute, her eyes had turned vacant. Since
then, she stopped attending the court and barely spoke. 'I want to go
to Mecca,' she had insisted, when he had met her the day before to
coax her to come to the court.

Several thoughts cross Jauhar's mind as he watches his king. The
unexpected and unbelievable death of the mighty Afzal Khan, the loss
of thousands of soldiers in the sinister valley of Jawali, the crushing
defeat of Rustum and Fazal in the battlefield near Kolhapur—all have
served to dampen the spirit of the kingdom's noblemen who are, to
start with, not decisive enough as it is. Shivaji has captured fourteen
forts that lie on the trade route between Konkan and Bijapur.
Vishalgad has been taken; Panhala Khelna and Rangna have fallen.
Every fort captured is under the control of Maratha garrisons. If this
is not enough insult to the kingdom's financial system, the Marathas
have plundered the kingdom's port town of Dabhol. They had even
reached Shahpur! That has been like slap on Ali's face. The latest
news is more horrifying, the Maratha sarnobat and his squadron
have besieged the fort of Miraz, hardly thirty-five kos west of Bijapur,
just two days journey by horse. If rumours are to be believed, even
Shivaji has planned to join his sarnobat to strengthen the siege.

Ali keeps staring at Jauhar with shadows of regret floating in his
eyes. Nobody from his court has come forward to fight the enemy,
but this outsider, who is considered a criminal, had written him a
letter saying that if the king forgives and forgets the past, he will deal

with Shivaji. Ali had been overwhelmed by the offer and sent enough funds to fill Jauhar's treasury, bestowing him with the title of Salabat Khan, the invincible one.

'Salabat Khan Sahib,' Ali says in a soft voice laced with sarcasm, 'we have some great warriors in our court, but since you have shown such eagerness to deal with Shivaji we have called you to take charge. Succeed and we shall regard you as the ablest nobleman of our court.'

Jauhar gradually shifts his gaze towards the courtiers. The Adilshahi kings have often granted revenue-rich regions as jagirs to some noblemen who are more sycophants than warriors. They never stay in their jagirs; instead, they live in the capital with their families. They indulge in court gossip and vie for positions and titles, while their wives spend their time visiting each other to play cards and dice. These politically inclined noblemen are not interested in developing their territories or building a strong army to defend even their jagirs. They have allowed the Mughals to take over Bidar and invade the north-eastern parts of the sultanate. Bijapur was spared only because Aurangzeb had to go north to claim the Mughal throne.

'You leave immediately. Meet our wazir and he will give you a list of the names of noblemen who will work under you. He will also give you the specifics in terms of the size of the army we intend to deploy,' Ali says decisively, banging his right fist over the armrest of his throne.

Jauhar does not nod. The best of soldiers have perished in Jawali. He will get the leftovers, even if they are in large numbers.

'What do you think Shivaji will do when you march towards him with such a large army? Do you think he will run away to his jagir?' Ali asks with a straight face.

This is indeed a tricky question. Jauhar has also heard that the new Mughal emperor, Aurangzeb, has appointed his maternal uncle, Shaista Khan, as the subhedar of the Mughal-occupied Deccan, and has given him a huge army to deal with Shivaji. Shivaji surely knows this development, and if he runs home, he runs the risk of being pursued by Jauhar from the east and the Mughal from the north. Will he risk multiple invasions?

'I believe,' Jauhar says cautiously, 'that Shivaji will not leave our terrain; instead, he might run and hide in one of the forts he has taken from us.'

Ali raises his brows. When Jauhar marches from the east, the Marathas may move westwards. Panhala Fort is about forty miles west of Miraz, and it is not only the nearest but also big enough to accommodate a few thousand people.

3

A few days after his meeting with Jauhar, Ali Adil Shah, despite his obesity, runs along the ramparts to get a better look from different angles. From the platform above the Mecca Gate, he notices the lush green of Bijapur, its gardens landscaped with ponds and fountains, their edges lined with mango and tamarind trees. The skyline is crammed with mosque minarets, tomb domes, palace arches, temple spires and raised cannon platforms, all carved from rich brown basalt. Gilded crests of some sky-scraping cupolas shimmer as golden shafts in the evening sunlight. The massive wall enclosing his private palaces is visible to him from the ramparts of the city's outer wall. The main avenue running from east to west that cuts the city into two halves is packed with his military cavalcade that is gradually moving towards the Mecca Gate. Thousands of footmen in Turkish coats with diagonally crossing hems over their chests strut around smartly. Their metal helmets gleam and their leather rucksacks, heavy with clothes, water and food, bulge behind their backs. Some have quivers stuffed with arrows. A contingent of footmen, carrying long spikes, wear armour and coifs made of steel chainmail to protect them from the piercing blows of enemy spearmen. The dense mass of footmen is occasionally broken by caparisoned elephants carrying silver howdahs. The men in the howdahs look confident, sitting very straight and with their turbaned heads thrown back in pride. The air above the avenue has turned opaque with a dust cloud. It's been an hour and the march is still not over. Ali's light cavalry has horses from Arabia and Turkey, and his Afghan contingent is rather impressive. The horsemen are well-built and look handsome in their massive headgear. Adilshahi's war banners, yellow with an ensign of a silver crescent moon, flutter in the wind, forming waves of silk in the air. A contingent of the local Marathas passes by, they are muscular riders with grim faces, holding naked swords in one hand. Then artillerymen appear with their camels carrying lightweight cannon and elephants carrying heavier ones. Some of the animals are loaded with sacks of explosives. At the end of the cavalcade, hundreds of *bhishti*s amble on carrying large leather bags swollen with water. The streets are milling with civilians who have come to see off their military men going on a mission, one they might not return from.

Ali feels proud. He has done it—infused courage and confidence in his men who were shattered in spirit after Afzal Khan's death. He has even managed to get Siddi Jauhar, now his chief military general.

The elephant swings gently beneath Siddi Jauhar, as if rocking him to slumber, but he is wide awake, his eyes darting in every direction while crossing the Mecca Gate. Jauhar looks at the doors of the gate and smiles to himself. They are made of thick wooden beams fastened together by iron clamps powered by massive steel bars bristling with long iron spikes. This gate is protected by another curtain of fortified walls flanked by towers furnished with turrets and battlements. There is another gate to pass! *If fortifications alone could win wars . . .* he thinks.

The cavalcade has moved on, disappeared from Ali's sight, while the melodious calls for *isha adha* echo in his ears as the muezzins from the Rauza Masjid call for the last prayer of the day. Ali looks at the sky. He will lose everything—his kingdom, his family and his life—if he does not hand over the regions in Shivaji's control demanded by Aurangzeb. He kneels down on the tarmac of the ramparts. *Help me eliminate Shivaji,* he prays earnestly.

4

It is late in the evening, and despite heavily curtained windows the breeze from the Yamuna sneaks into the corridors of Musamman

Burj of Agra Fort, moves over the low marble parapets and enters into the chambers built over the fort walls. The chilly draughts cut through the bones of the dethroned Emperor Shah Jahan who lies on a large bed in the foyer, with his head propped up on colourful silk pillows.

Jahanara sitting at the edge of the bed looks at her father; his arms lying over the folds of the blanket look like the pale branches of birch trees. The diamond *arsi* that he has always worn on his thumb now looks out of place on his wrinkled hand. What strikes her most is his face, worn with hopelessness and stained with tears. A rush of love mingled with pity overtakes her as she bends forward and lovingly caresses his forehead as if to heal the invisible wound inflicted on his soul by his own son.

'Do not pity me, daughter,' the former emperor has turned pale in shame for he has noticed sympathy in his daughter's eyes.

She flushes and pretends to look at the chandelier at the corners of the large room. It is easy to pity someone but it is hard to be the object of someone's pity, especially for someone who has been an emperor.

'Aurangzeb has emptied the fort's treasury to support his battle against Shuja,' he sighs and whispers.

She sighs sadly and remembers how their hopes had risen when they had heard that Jaswant Singh Rathod and his army had revolted against Aurangzeb on the battlefields near Khajwa. Villagers had spotted Jaswant and his horsemen loaded with sacks galloping towards Agra. It was rumoured that Aurangzeb had been captured. Then more and more horsemen were seen running away from the field. They had said that they had witnessed the horrific death of Aurangzeb when three elephants of Shuja's army brandishing iron chains tied to their trunks had attacked him. Messengers had told Jahanara that one elephant had flung the chain so high that it had dislodged Aurangzeb's howdah from his elephant, making it crash. He had been lying on the ground when the other mammoths had walked over him, again and again. Seeing their leader's body a mass of blood, muscles and bones, Aurangzeb's ninety thousand troopers had run in all directions like frightened hares. Jahanara and her father had waited anxiously for Jaswant to arrive and tell them the real story but he had fled to Jodhpur. Then they had waited for Shuja bhai to come and rescue them, but he never arrived. The previous news was wrong. Aurangzeb had defeated Shuja bhai in a most unbelievable battle.

Jahanara is aware that at this very moment, a daylight robbery is taking place in this very fort, their home that is supposed to be a sanctuary from the perils of the world. Aurangzeb's personal eunuch, Mutamad, has been digging out Dara bhai's jewels and artefacts from the vaults of her late brother's palaces, most of which were gifts given by her father and other royals such as the kings of Persia, Uzbek, Europe and China.

A bout of anger has stimulated a bout of cough. Jahanara pats her father's chest while he coughs, clenching his chest and stomach. Once his anger had the power to shake the world; now his impotent fury is not even powerful enough to flick a bothersome fly.

'Ask Aurangzeb to take my clothes too. Let the world see a naked old man who once possessed the world,' Shah Jahan says with disgust. A medic comes running with a large spittoon. Jahanara props her father up on his bed and massages his back as tears stream down her face. The fort is swarming with Aurangzeb's slaves. The rooms stuffed with royal apparel, miniature paintings, furniture, crockery and jewels are sealed. Several trunks of gold ashrafi mohurs have already been moved into the vaults of the diwan-e-khaas in the custody of Mutamad. As if their father, whom all the treasure truly belongs to, is a criminal from whom the treasure must be protected.

Jahanara looks out from the arched window. In the golden light of the setting sun, her mother's mausoleum looks fragile, as though waiting to crumble once again, just like she had once seen in a nightmare. She shudders with renewed vigour at the memory of the day when Dara bhai's remains had arrived in an engraved coffin, little knowing that an intruder has been listening to their talk.

Mutamad stands motionless behind a pillar that leads to the antechamber and hears every word with care. He has been instructed to write to his master in Dilli and give him every minute detail of what happens at Agra.

Jahanara feels sobs choking her throat. Who will and can stop Aurangzeb? He is now the Mughal emperor, the head of the most powerful empire founded by Zahir-ud-Din Muhammad Babur more than a century ago. Aurangzeb has celebrated his coronation with pompous glamour, showing off the empire's wealth and military strength. He has dazzled the people so much that their logic has ceased to exist. Recent history is forgotten and men of power have developed a razor-sharp survival instinct.

Jahanara has heard from her sources that the *umrah*s and ulemas gathered at Aurangzeb's coronation have kept quiet about her father's plight. Not even a word was heard about the ailing and imprisoned former emperor, even though they were indebted to him for their ranks and riches, some of them had been lifted by him from utter poverty and some from slavery. These very men had now discovered justifications for Dara bhai's murder, had invented reasons for her father's fall and had realized great qualities of leadership and military intelligence in Aurangzeb who now possessed absolute authority. They know that to challenge Aurangzeb or his authority is treason, punishable only by death. The peacock throne is his seat of power and the other emblems, like the golden chhatr, the kawakaba, the *sayaban* which is a badge in the shape of a fan, the alam, the shamsha and many such other royal symbols, are his exclusive imperial right. No one else in the world is allowed to conduct a jharokha-e-darshan to show himself to his subjects. The sign of Islamic legitimacy, the khutba, is read in his name in thousands of mosques across the empire.

CHAPTER EIGHTEEN

1

It is a pleasant winter evening and shimmering beams of the last sunrays cut through the canopies looming over the undergrowth of shrubs. Shaista Khan, the newly appointed subhedar of the Deccan and the military general of war against Shivaji, has been given the responsibility of opening offensives, with a single aim: while Shivaji is chased and either caught or killed in the Adilshahi sultanate, Shaista Khan must take over his terrain.

The animals in his camp have gone quiet and he no longer hears their neighing, trumpeting or mooing. That means that several thousand horses, four hundred elephants, a hundred camels and countless cattle in makeshift stables at the southern edge of the camp near Ahmednagar are busy with their evening feed. The camp has more than a hundred thousand people, including soldiers, servants, family women, maids, eunuchs, courtesans and the children. They too must be settling down for another night in the forest.

Shaista likes the solitude of this hour that has become so hard to come by. Finally, he opens the epistle for the hundredth time, after he received it a month ago and holds it very close to his eyes. The message is short and crisp:

The searcher of the heart is my witness. I trust you above all, as was proved when I nominated you to use my signet ring when and if I am indisposed. I need to be in Dilli. Shuja bhai and Suleiman are still at large, and hence, as the subhedar of the Mughal-occupied Deccan, the responsibility of eliminating Shiva rests on your able shoulders. Start now from Aurangabad and move southwards. The Marathas are busy taking Adilshahi posts and, as you must now be aware, Ali Adil Shah is appointing one African warrior, Siddi Jauhar, to take care of them. You might be able to enter Shiva's region without resistance as Shiva neither has the manpower nor the resources to fight on two fronts. Lay bare his villages, burn every house down to ashes, seize his forts and take his family as captives. You have under your command a cavalry of seventy-seven thousand horses and four hundred elephants, a hundred camels carrying guns and a specially selected quality infantry of thirty thousand footmen. You have sixty-eight senior mansabdars to obey your command and guide the army. Twenty-nine among them are Muslim Turk, Central Asian, African, Afghan and Persian, and the remaining thirty-nine are Hindus.

The letter is not just an ordinary message; it is a farman from the new emperor, his favourite nephew, Aurangzeb. Shaista Khan has a plan, a superb plan, for the tiny country of the infidel. The Pune region is the heart of Shiva's jagir, to its north is Chakan region; to its west is the hilly Maval, to its south-east, the Supe and Indapur regions. The main hill forts of Rajgad, Torana, Kondana and Purandar loom over the south-eastern and south-western horizons of Pune. Shaista Khan's strategy is simple: after crossing the river Bhima, once they enter the Bhosale jagir, he will steer his mile-long military cavalcade to the town of Baramati between Indapur and Supe. Once the villages in those areas are laid bare, he will head for Shirwal, west of Baramati, and then north, taking the path between the hill forts of Rajgad and Purandar that will eventually lead him to Pune. It is akin to digging the entire region with huge ploughshares, dislodging villages and towns as though they are weeds or matted roots. Shivaji, if he does escape the clutches of the African warrior Siddi Jauhar appointed by the Adilshahi king, will have no country to come back to.

That 'if' is, however, a big concern. Shaista Khan does not think highly of Ali Adil Shah. So sure was the king of Afzal Khan's victory that he had not bothered to maintain the forts that protected his kingdom. The forts neither had strong fort commanders nor was there a contingent of fort soldiers. Shaista Khan has heard that after Shivaji's men had surrounded the Panhala Fort, the fort commander had immediately communicated with him and eagerly showed his intentions to surrender without bloodshed. After the fall of Panhala, Shivaji had ordered his men to take over the rest of the hill forts near Kolhapur, thus establishing his control on the upper courses of the river Krishna.

That was indeed a worrying fact.

2

The north-western skies are tinged with violet and orange, and against the backdrop of the colourful sky, the enormous mass of Masai Rock and its tablelands rising over the plains look threatening.

Shivaji needs to think about the future that seems even more rigid than the edges of Masai tablelands and its barren slopes disappearing into the valleys. Before they were trapped at Panhala, Shivaji had received a very disturbing news about Shaista Khan's massive army advancing towards his jagir.

Has he done the right thing by leading his eight thousand men, mostly from the infantry, from Miraj to Panhala Fort? Should he have taken his men and returned home to Rajgad Fort? What would have probably happened had he gone to Rajgad? The answer is simple: Siddi Jauhar and his army would have come chasing after him. It would have been disastrous, what with Jauhar arriving with his army and Shaista Khan with his at the foothills of Rajgad. But there are dangers in the decision he has taken!

'They have started building mud hovels out there,' Baji's words break Shivaji's thoughts. He turns around to face Baji and Trimbak Dabir, the newly appointed commander of Panhala Fort. The men look as if they have guessed their future, their faces darkened with suntan as well as worry.

They know it very well. Within days of them taking refuge at Panhala, Jauhar, the new general of the Adilshahi army, had arrived at the foothills like a man on a hunt. Since then, his besiegement preparations have been going on in full swing. Their leader's decision to take refuge at Panhala was based on the assumption that Jauhar's besiegement would last only till the monsoons arrived, but assumptions are assumptions! If the besiegement is tight enough to prevent supplies from reaching the fort and if it continues till the monsoons and beyond, everyone at the fort faces certain death by starvation.

'What does that mean, Baji?' Shivaji asks.

'Jauhar seems to be preparing for the monsoons,' Baji says wryly, his large moustache failing to hide his anxiety.

'How long will the food last us?' Shivaji asks Trimbak Dabir.

Trimbak Dabir, like his father Sonoji Dabir, is precise when he answers. 'As you know, Raja, the Ambarkhana contains three large granaries and they can hold up to two crore ser of grains. As of now, it is half-full, stuffed with rice, sorghum, *nachni*, and the grains should last us till the end of the monsoon.'

'Hmm,' Shivaji ponders. If Panhala becomes their graveyard, Shaista Khan will systematically destroy his jagir and let thousands die either by the sword or by torture. All the young people will be taken and sold as slaves; and his family will be taken as prisoners. His mother is sixty and his son just three. The Mughals will not have mercy on anyone, and his loved ones will be subjected to unspeakable atrocities in Aurangzeb's imprisonment. His mother might be sent to the gallows, his wives and daughters to someone's harem and his son either converted to Islam or killed by opium overdose.

'What are the chances of them scaling this hill and entering the fort in large numbers?' he asks Baji.

'Very little, unless we sleep soundly all through the night or they get powerful long-range cannon throwing explosives to blast the fort wall. Jauhar does not have such guns.'

Shivaji nods. Just a few months ago, the Adilshahi commander of this fort had surrendered it rather quickly. Shivaji's men had climbed the hill at night and stormed the inner fort early in the morning when the gates were opened. The easy win of such an invincible military stronghold had surprised Shivaji. He at once knew that Panhala was like massive armour. It was difficult to tell whether the fort protected the rocky hill rising a hundred guj above the valley or vice versa. After staying here for months, he now knows that it is impossible for the enemy to scale the fortified outer wall that runs a good five miles along the cliffs that plunge down to the slopes. Even the slopes are cut by natural trenches made by ravines with very few glades. Even those spaces are covered with thick vegetation broken by massive boulders. The mountain is famous for its venomous snakes. The Adilshahi's troopers, unlike Shivaji's men, are not trained in mountain climbing. That is one comforting thought.

'Jauhar is very unpredictable,' Baji declares.

'He is also persistent and does not give up easily. He will go on with his task as if possessed,' Trimbak warns.

'Let us inspect the siege; every day we note some new development,' Shivaji says and starts walking towards the Sajja Kothi. The three men go past the residential quarters, the massive structure of Ambarkhana, and walk through the tents of soldiers. The wind is strong, and apart from a few stray clouds near the southern horizon, the rest of the sky is violet blue. They reach the Kothi, a three-storey structure made of solid stone. The erstwhile pleasure pavilion that was later used as a punishment cell to torture prisoners is set into the ramparts. Shivaji swiftly climbs the steps to reach the second floor and enters the eastern chamber of the Kothi covered with flattish domes and arcaded balconies that hang over the ramparts. He looks out from one of the large windows and notices that the shallow hill of Pavangad is separated from Panhala only by a ravine. His eyes wander over the Waranna Valley as he sees thousands of labourers busy building hovels and digging trenches.

3

Gangadhar, a medium built Brahmin with tonsured head, has been residing on the fort for generations. Ever since Shivaji made his appearance and took over the fort, he has been fired by the raja's dream. The temple caretaker is looking forward to some excitement in his life. He has come running out of the fort temple after he heard the thundering sounds. *Jauhar must have launched another attack*, he thinks, and runs behind the Ambarkhana. The large structure looms over him while the earth shakes with bombardments. He rushes to the stables for his chestnut steed. Hurriedly he saddles and bridles it, jumps on to the restless mount and takes the reins—gently nudging it with his spurs. The horse canters for a few hundred guj north towards the Sajja Kothi. Gangadhar wants to know what the raja and his people are doing to ward off the attack. The thundering sound continues to shake the ground and the bastions swarm with artillerymen and drum beaters. The rampart guards have taken their positions with their bows stretched and arrows ready to fly. Grasping the situation, Gangadhar jumps from his horse and rushes towards the Sajja Kothi.

At its entrance he notices Raja Shivaji and moves ahead where Baji Prabhu is running on the ramparts barking out orders. Gangadhar leaps towards the parapet to see what a group of artillerymen are peering at. Far away from the foothills of Panhala Hill, he can see the outposts of the besieging army blocking all escape routes. The space between the fort and the siege has been dug up for trenches to protect Jauhar's artillery from the fire of the fort's guns. The trenches are dug cleverly with a zigzag pattern so that the arrows from the fort do not sweep down their length killing all the men hiding in them. He can see small figures of men moving in the trenches, their cannon spewing smoke and raising clouds of soot. His eyes wander towards Pavangad. On top of that shallow hill he can see large cannon with poles bearing blue flags with red lines. Gangadhar recognizes them; they are Union Jacks, the flags of those so-called apolitical English traders. The English are helping Jauhar. They have chosen an elevated ground for the cannon.

'Fire!' shouts Baji Prabhu.

'Fire!' shout the artillerymen in chorus.

The cannon mounted on the ramparts start spitting fire, shaking the very walls on which the Kothi rests.

The drummers who stand below the Kothi start beating their drums. Their rhythmic, high-pitched sound reaches a crescendo that starts turning into a powerful source of energy for the fighters. Gangadhar's eardrums ache and his blood gushes faster in his veins. The explosives rain down and start hitting Jauhar's dugouts at places. He hangs on, not bothering about getting caught in the crossfire. It goes on for a few hours and finally the enemy attack is repelled. Not a single fire from the trenches has reached them; it is only the explosives fired from the English cannon that have landed close to the ramparts near the Kothi.

4

Shaista Khan's cavalcade crosses the Bhima river to enter Shivaji's terrain. They have covered the route from Baramati to Shirwal to Saswad, a few miles from the foothills of Purandar Fort, and are heading for Pune. The region left behind is ruined, and his warriors have killed enough villagers and burnt enough barns to strike terror.

The show of his strength has overwhelmed the enemy, but he has not achieved what he had in mind. His idea was to advance into the heart of Shivaji's terrain and fight at least one face-to-face battle with the Marathas. Instead, the Marathas have harassed his cavalcade by unleashing the elusive horsemen, never coming close enough and never leaving the cavalcade out of sight. They had hovered around like flies, and when he had detached a body of his cavalry to strike them, they lured it away to the forests where more Maratha horsemen waited in ambush, like a tiger hiding in bushes, not seen yet ready to strike.

A few times, a group of infantrymen have descended from Purandar Fort, killing his men patrolling at the edges of their camp. Some attackers have waylaid contingents bringing supplies and cut off stragglers. He has been forced to take care by keeping a squadron of three thousand light cavalry headed by a mansabdar named Sharza Khan constantly on the move to stop the enemy from coming too near. He has taken another precaution and protected the flanks of the cavalcade by heavy cavalry of armed horsemen.

Behind Shaista's elephant, sixty-eight elephants trundle carrying the principal mansabdars. One of the mansabdars is Maharaja Jaswant Singh Rathod. The young man is filled with anger and humiliation. Fate has struck a blow upon him, making him a mere mansabdar who is forced to obey the commands of their new general. But on second thought, he feels grateful that Aurangzeb has not taken any severe action against him even when he had backed Dara Shikoh in the war of succession or turned a traitor when they had fought a battle against Shah Shuja. Maharaja Jaswant is eager to show his skills in this campaign as he must regain his respect at any cost. What is life without esteem or self-respect?

Maharaja Jaswant Singh Rathod's cavalry is followed by heavily armoured elephants carrying Namdar Khan and Kamdar Khan, the sons of Jaffar Khan, who is the husband of Aurangzeb's mother's sister. The brothers are related to Shaista Khan as Aurangzeb is related to him—he is their maternal uncle too.

A few miles ahead, thousands of labourers with axes and mattocks clear the passage for the massive procession. The vanguard leading the cavalcade is commanded by Kartalab Khan who is followed by thirty thousand horsemen.

An army of foot soldiers follow the sea of horsemen briskly on the widened trail as armoured war elephants and camels follow. Mules and oxen carrying food, fodder, firewood and water move reluctantly behind the mass of footmen, some dragging trunks filled with swords, shields, spears, daggers, bows and arrows. Behind the animals, innumerable Abyssinian slaves carry on their heads trunks filled with coins.

As they move through Shivaji's territory, the Mughal procession consumes most of the water from the wells and food stored by the poor cultivators, while their animals feast on the foliage; even the bared branches are hacked for firewood, turning the wooded earth barren. The north-easterly winds from the Sahyadri Mountains have turned heavy with the fetid smell of faeces, urine and animal droppings left behind by the monstrous procession.

Murarbaji has come down from Purandar Fort and is hiding behind a large cliff to see what is happening at the foothills. He has not been able do anything other than send small groups of his men to attack the cavalcade at its flanks and kill a few men. The villages at the foothills look vulnerable, like small hatchlings of sparrows trapped between the coils of a large snake. He notices a cloud of dust from behind a settlement. Within moments, he sees a line of dark specks emerge through the dusty cloud and realizes that they are a detachment of raiders from the cavalcade. There is no time to warn the villagers. He watches helplessly from his hideout as the enemy squadron gallops through the dirt track partially hidden under the canopies of trees. For a moment the raiders disappear in the thicket only to emerge at the border of the settlement. He can see the people from the settlement run aimlessly, their faint cries echoing in the shallow valley around the hill of Purandar.

5

The sun has climbed the eastern sky. From a shallow hill, Pałkar, who has returned from Karnataka to counter the Mughal invasion,

watches the massive cavalcade leaving Saswad for Pune. He
has never seen such a large procession of humans and beasts in
his lifetime. He turns his horse to look behind him and sees his
squadron of three thousand horsemen. There is no point in
attacking the labourers clearing the path and the vanguard is a
sea of cavalry while the flanks are protected by horsemen wearing
metal helmets and chainmail. Palkar looks at his men who wait for
his orders; their worn faces and their anguish-filled eyes fill him
with grief he has not known before. 'We shall attack the tail!' he
shouts, nudging his horse to turn again, and gallops in the direction
of the Mughal cavalcade.

Something unexpected happens as they approach the tail of the
convoy: thousands of Mughal foot soldiers start firing muskets from
their shoulders with an ear-splitting sound. The tail is now shrouded
in smoke but Palkar keeps galloping towards the enemy. Another
wave of thunder follows as Palkar's horsemen start falling in large
numbers.

'We must never let our men die just to satisfy our pride. If
dying in the battlefield is considered the ultimate goal by some of
our northern warrior clans, if throwing themselves in the ravine of
death just to be a martyr is the dream of many warriors, sending
our men to a certain death without a certain gain is an utter waste
of our most precious strength,' Raja Shivaji had said in no uncertain
terms.

'Retreat!' shouts Palkar with a heavy heart, but he has already
lost many men. While galloping away from the cavalcade he wonders
what is happening to their most cherished country. He must go to
Panhala, break the siege and set his master free as only Raja Shivaji
can save their swaraj from the Mughals.

6

A few miles from Shaista Khan's cavalcade, Ibrahim Khan gallops
through a narrow trail darkened by the canopy of banyan trees
thinking about his master Raja Shivaji's confinement at Panhala.

Where are the people? he wonders, as he passes through a village on the banks of the river Indrayani. *At this time of the day, the village bazaar ought to be full of people,* he worries as his horse's hooves interrupt the deathly silence. He nudges his mount, slows down and enters a small alley of huddled houses. Regions between Baramati and the Shirwal–Saswad belt lie devastated. The villagers have either fled to the jungles or have been killed by the Mughal raiders. Ibrahim Khan realized that he must reach Rajgad as quickly as possible and inform Jija Bai Sahib about the conditions of her son's territory.

'Ya Allah! How can Shaista Khan's warriors be so brutal? The Mughals are a disgrace to Islam!'

CHAPTER NINETEEN

1

Under the night sky, large and small houses stand huddled together at the edges of the dark streets of Pune. In contrast, the Mughal base camp spread around the town is well lit with innumerable torches. The markets in the camp are milling with soldiers and hangers-on. The air smells of food, as dinner is being cooked for Shaista's one lakh men.

Shivaji's home, the Lal Mahal, has become Shaista's abode. It has a massive courtyard in the middle where many shamdans burn and bathe the red mansion in their golden glow.

All the rooms open into the courtyard, now filled with the smell of the cooked meat biryani that wafts out from the kitchen crowded with royal chefs and their helpers. A staircase in one of the corners goes up to a covered terrace with several rooms opening into it. About a hundred women, including Shaista Khan's wives, his daughters-in-law, daughters, women slaves, eunuchs and courtesans, have occupied those, while he prefers the ground-floor foyer with its large windows draped in silk curtains and the floor covered with Persian carpets.

His abode allows him to be near the inner courtyard that offers him peace, and he can also keep an eye on the gardeners tending to his flowerpots that have travelled with him from place to place. He wears a pale jama with motifs of golden tulips, and green leggings. Some people are joining him for dinner.

He comes to the divan where his chessboard is kept in the middle. It is made of marble, with the tiny figures made of glazed frit lined up on both the sides. He gently sits beside the board and considers playing alone when, one by one, his guests come in. All three of them are his mansabdars with whom he feels at ease: to show off his shatranj skills and discuss real war strategies. Namdar and Kamdar arrive together wearing golden sashes and leather belts laden with embellished daggers, while Kartalab comes alone wearing a finely cut jama. The men first bow to their general and greet him in Farsi, '*Asr bekheir.*' They gather around him, and he makes his first move just as his eldest son, Abul Fath, walks in.

'It is not how we move but where we reach,' Shaista murmurs as others watch him playing both the sides. After a while, servants start bringing glasses of sherbet and wine. Men stand around the divan, sip wine and watch their master play solo, playing moves as well as countermoves. Soon a large straw *chataai* is brought in and spread on the ground and a wooden table supporting an immense silver plate placed on the same. It is time for dinner.

As the dinner progresses, Shaista, his mouth still full with food, says, 'It has been a month since we have arrived in Pune. I have some plans.'

The men nod and continue to eat. Shaista gulps down the food in his mouth, takes a swig of wine and continues, 'The monsoon is approaching and we will face great hardship from scarcity. When the rains arrive, there will be nothing left in the nearby barns to plunder. Also, procuring food from our base at Ahmednagar will be next to impossible because the rivers will be flooded, cutting off all routes between Ahmednagar and Pune.'

The guests raise their eyebrows; the same fear has been nagging them for weeks.

'There is a military solution to this problem,' Shaista announces.

The men have stopped eating; they want to know more.

'Chakan is on the route to Ahmednagar. The rivers between Pune and Chakan are difficult to cross during monsoons. In comparison, the rivers between Chakan and Ahmednagar are shallow. The region too is relatively flat with no difficult mountain passes to cross. We should shift our military base to Chakan, from where it will be easier to get supplies from Ahmednagar.'

'And also kill two birds with one stone,' Namdar quips.

Shaista smiles; he likes Namdar who is intelligent and quick.

'Yes,' the Mughal general agrees as others look on, their interest has been kindled. 'We will besiege the land fort of Chakan and capture it.'

All the men nod, approving the plan. Capturing Chakan is a good military move. Its possession will mean unhindered communication with Ahmednagar, the base of Mughal supplies, even for all future campaigns.

'Father, what if Shivaji comes back?' an agitated Abul Fath asks loudly.

Shaista counter-questions, 'From where will he come back? From Panhala, his potential grave?'

The men chortle.

'While we are at Chakan, Kartalab Khan will stay put at Pune and prepare to take over Shivaji's territories in the Konkan. I want to make him the Mughal subhedar of north Konkan, based in Kalyan,' Shaista Khan concludes.

Kartalab stops eating and stares unbelievingly at his general: it is a big promotion, from a mansabdar to the subhedar of a region! It has been a long journey from being a poor soldier from the suburbs of Samarkand to being a Mughal governor. Namdar and Kamdar smile indulgently while their host looks at them for approval.

'When do we plan to capture the hill forts around Pune?' Namdar asks.

'Once we take over Chakan and Kalyan, the low-hanging fruit!' Shaista says with a smile and reclines on a bolster kept behind him while letting out a loud belch.

2

Panhala Fort stands in the darkness, silent and mute. An owl hoots dismally from somewhere in the wooded slopes. Mhadu perches on the edge of a cliff on the north-western slopes of Panhala Hill, his eyes fixed on the lower slopes to pick out enemy intruders, if any. The thin sickle of the new moon shines. Myriad stars illuminate the expanse, including the slopes, the valley and the mysterious Masai tablelands. Far below, torches flicker at the foothills, in the outposts set up by Jauhar. Mhadu's eyes discern some movement, a human silhouette a few guj below him. He curbs his impulse to jump on the intruder; one wrong move or one erroneous step will make him tumble down to his death, either by hitting his head on the boulders entrenched over the slopes or by falling vertically from another abrupt cliff cutting the slope. Mhadu stands up and keeps his hand on the hilt of his sword tucked in his belt.

'I need a rope to climb,' the words spoken in Marathi come floating over the violent wind; the voice is familiar. Mhadu narrows his eyes to focus. The visitor seems almost naked in a loincloth. His face is buried in his riotous long hair falling across his face and his jaw is covered in an unruly beard. Mhadu is delighted; the man he was waiting for has arrived. Finally, after months, they will get some outside news. All the eight thousand souls trapped on Panhala Fort want to know whatever has happened to their families.

Mhadu removes his headgear, uncoils it and throws one end of it towards the nearly naked ascetic. The weight makes him wince as he pulls the man towards him. While he is at the task, he notices that the black clouds rising above the south-western horizon have quickly spread across the sky. The glow of stars that had spangled the heavens a few moments earlier is gone. The visitor soon stands beside him and by now it has started drizzling.

'Follow me,' Mhadu whispers while tying his headgear, and then whistles shrilly. It is for the guards on the ramparts to know that he is going inside the fort. He has to take the night visitor to the raja as soon as possible. The guards have already informed raja about the man with Mhadu.

'Mhadu, come in. Who is this stranger with you?' Shivaji asks as he heads towards the fireplace and gestures for them to sit. The room is cold and yet it is filled with strange warmth. They do as they are told and sit cross-legged on the durries that cover the floor. Shivaji watches them, his eyes focused on the stranger, and a sparkle of recognition appears in his eyes. His face breaks into a huge smile.

'Bahirji Naik, is that you?' Shivaji almost shouts, delighted to have his chief-of-intelligence with him. Mhadu is stunned; Naik is his master.

The visitor smiles from ear to ear and his eyes shine with tears.

He remembers his childhood spent in jungles at the foothills of Rajgad. He would have been a lost soul of the forest till he died but Raja Shivaji had plucked him out of that life and made him the master spy in the Maratha army.

'What is happening in the outside world?' Shivaji asks eagerly, breaking Naik's reverie.

'Shaista Khan and his sea of army have ploughed our region and have reached Pune.'

'Where are the Mughals camping?' Shivaji questions, his eyes showing no expression.

'Shaista Khan and his family have occupied the Lal Mahal. More than fifty thousand tents have come up on the southern side of the town,' Naik whispers, his eyes downcast.

'Where is our sarnobat?'

'He is fighting on two fronts; he and his men launched many attacks of the Mughal cavalcade but they failed. He had come close to Panhala and struggled to break through the besieging army at night A number of times, our infantrymen under the cover of ravines have tried to spring on Jauhar's besiegers, but it has proved impossible to break Jauhar's ring.'

'The monsoon has just begun. How long could Jauhar remain camping?' Shivaji asks.

'They are getting ready to face the monsoon. Cartloads of straw and palm leaves have arrived. They are replacing the tents with clay houses with roofs of straw. Countless drains are being dug to flush the rain water away.'

'How tight is the siege?' Shivaji asks.

'Panhala is surrounded by flat plains, so the besiegement is tight at the eastern side with hardly any gaps and a number of sentry posts guard. However, towards the west, at the foothills of Masai Rock, where it is hilly, it thins out.

'It is rumoured that Shaista Khan is in touch with Ali Adil Shah,' Naik says.

'What I have always feared has happened. The Mughals have joined hands with Ali Adil Shah,' Shivaji says disappointedly and starts pacing the room like a trapped tiger. The flames in the fireplace slither like snakes as the wind continues to invade the room from the open door.

'How did you manage to break the cordon and come up?'

Naik clears his throat and answers slowly, 'Disguised as a hermit, I joined a group of men who were travelling from Maval to join Jauhar. After spending two weeks as a soothsayer, men started believing that I have a prophetic vision to see their future. They opened their minds and hearts to me. All were anxious to know when the siege would end and when they could head home. A rumour was making the rounds about Rustum guarding the north. People said that he has remained defiant and at night removes his men from some remote posts as he wants Jauhar to lose this battle. Tonight, in this weather, his men had deserted their posts at the north-eastern side of the hill. At midnight, I climbed one of the cliffs, hung on the other side for a while, before crossing the deep gorge that lay between. After climbing a mossy patch with the help of creepers I could reach a narrow path that leads to the fort.'

'What kind of person is this Jauhar?' Shivaji asks. He has stopped pacing.

'They say he is not afraid of anyone, is brutally frank and trusts easily, but his reputation for rage and fierceness is known,' Naik replies.

'Isn't it wise to surrender to Jauhar? Within a month or two the food will be over, the granaries will be empty and all eight thousand of us will face death by starvation.' Shivaji drops a granado.

Naik stares at Shivaji for a long time, and then nods in agreement while Mhadu gapes at them in astonishment. Thunder continues to rule the sky and lightning strikes the edge of horizon.

3

At the foothills, in the camp, Siddi Jauhar's room shakes with thunder. The wooden armed chair he sits on is a present from his new friend, Henry Revington. The tall brass lamps kept in the corners of his room have been sent by the king and the silk curtains are a gift from the king's mother, the Badi Sahiba. Never in his life was so much affection shown to him by anyone from outside his family.

He tries to look at Panhala Hill through a large window and sheets of rain, but all he can see is a heavy shower. With nothing else to do, his mind goes back to his past. Life has not been kind to him. In the beginning, when he was a mere slave of Malik Raihan, the jagirdar of Kurnool, the southern district of the Adilshahi. After the death of Raihan, Jauhar eliminated his son, Malik Wahah, and took over Kurnool. Over the years his cavalry had grown to ten thousand horsemen, more than any of the noblemen in Ali Adil Shah's court. The late king Mohammed Adil Shah had slammed him for murdering the scion of the jagirdar family of Kurnool, but the king could never bother him. The king had his own problems: first, he was bedridden for ten long years with paralysis, and second, the Mughal prince Aurangzeb hovered like an angry dragon over the Adilshahi kingdom.

The time has come to dream, Jauhar thinks, bringing himself back to the present, and relaxes in his large chair. *All depends on whether I can kill or capture Shivaji.* He grunts, caressing his long, henna-dyed beard. It has been months since he and his men have left Kurnool, and the excitement of the first few weeks has been replaced by foreboding and anxiety. His son-in-law, Masud, has turned restless; his wife, Jauhar's daughter, has given birth to their first son back home. Jauhar has noticed that even his soldiers do not sit around the fires at night anymore; instead, they brood in the dark while keeping

vigil at night and secretly yearn to go back home. His officers have
turned edgy while the king has started counting the expenses. Jauhar
wonders if Ali Adil Shah has already started doubting his abilities
and the thought disturbs him. His hopes had risen when the English
gunner had arrived to give him an on-site demonstration of the long-
range cannon, but the artillery bombardments from the English
cannon had eventually failed to dislodge even a single stone of the
Panhala Fort wall.

Jauhar has still not lost hope; he is prepared to wait till the men
trapped in the fort start dying of starvation, but it could be months
before that happens. Meanwhile, one thought has made him an
insomniac: what if Shivaji escapes while he waits for the Marathas on
Panhala to die of starvation?

Jauhar's thoughts are broken by his son-in-law, a visibly excited
and drenched Masud has rushed in, panting, with his right hand on
his heart.

'Raja Shivaji has sent a message. He wants to surrender and is
sending his men to meet you tomorrow.'

4

Naik wearing a Turkish turban and long, silk angirkha looks very
different from his earlier bearded avatar. He has tied a huge basket
covered with a fine velvet cloth to his back and carries a white flag
in his right hand. Gangadhar follows him with a heavy heart. After
all those battles, they are surrendering to Jauhar, and he has to carry
that message!

Naik has no such qualms, as if surrendering to Jauhar is a
small part of a big game. The duo walks through the triple gate—an
elaborate example of military architecture. First passing through the
innermost entrance that displays an arched recess framing a cupola,
moments later they enter a domed chamber that yields access to a
rectangular court lined with arcades. Naik, a spy for several years, has
developed a habit of noticing the smallest details; he marvels at the
imposing stone structures. The entire entrance is at an awkward angle

to slow down and trap the incoming enemy. The western side of the court is overlooked by an elevated guardroom with triple arches, and some guards standing there wave at them, directing them animatedly to the open gate. Below the guardroom is a well, entrenched into a huge bastion. Naik has heard from the old fort residents that if you throw a lemon engraved with secret messages in it, it surfaces in the lake at the foothills.

After emerging from the main entrance of three successive gates, they turn east and walk for a few hundred guj. They wade over the miry trail that at places has gone slippery. Naik holds the white flag high, as visible as possible, lest someone waiting in ambush mistakes them as intruders and kills them. When they enter a very narrow path skirting the hill, with an escarpment on one side and a deep gorge on the other, Gangadhar looks down gingerly and feels dizzy— the ground below looks like a chessboard with small square fields of rice. At places tall trees have gathered in grooves.

It takes them an hour to descend and then cross the valley to reach the trenches which look empty. They are about to enter the enemy camp. They walk across makeshift bridges made of logs. Near a particularly deep trench, an alert Naik pulls Gangadhar towards him and away from a serpent. And before Gangadhar can gather his wits, two men who look like Jauhar's soldiers appear from the opposite direction.

'We have come from the fort. We are messengers of Shivaji; we have a message for Siddi Jauhar Sahib,' Gangadhar tries to sound as calm as possible.

'Check them,' one says without bothering about responding to Gangadhar's explanation.

Meanwhile, it is impossible for Jauhar to sit still. He waits impatiently for the messengers to arrive. He checks his hookah, pulls out his jambia dagger hanging from his belt and starts tapping its blade when he is informed they have arrived. When he lifts his eyes he sees two men rush in carrying gifts. They bow deeply and remain in that position for a while. Jauhar glances at them: one of them is wearing a pagari turban and is surely a Brahmin, and he has heard that Shivaji's Brahmin vakeels are more cunning than foxes, meaner than jackals and capable of sprouting carnassial of a tiger whenever the need be.

Gangadhar knows that the muscular African warrior, while smoking, is staring at him. He smiles sheepishly while Jauhar quickly diverts his gaze and starts blowing smoke rings.

'Salaam to the General of Adilshahi, we are Raja Shivaji's men,' Gangadhar says while straightening courteously. He signals to Naik who comes forward and gently puts the basket covered with velvet cloth on the floor. Jauhar becomes alert. This is what they do, Shivaji's messengers, he has heard—they bring priceless items in gifts to marinate the enemy's heart, so that they can sink their teeth in it with ease. He does not bother to check or even look at the gift and continues to blow smoke rings in the air, narrows his eyes till they are mere slits and says teasingly, 'What does your master think? Are we idiots?'

Gangadhar swallows hard and coughs loudly, holding his fist to his mouth, and rattles, 'On the contrary . . .'

Jauhar's twisted smile lingers on his lips. He raises his hand interrupting him, 'Hold nothing back, and say what you have come here to say.'

Gangadhar bites his tongue, takes out the epistle from his angirkha's inner pocket and holds it out for the general, but Jauhar manages to look disinterested. Gangadhar keeps holding the letter and stares pointedly at his host. Jauhar takes some more time to take the letter, showing a slight reluctance in pushing away the metal pipe from his mouth.

For a long time Jauhar examines the epistle as if it might contain a granado, and then opens it himself without calling his servant or his scribe. He reads it carefully and then keeps the paper on his lap to resume smoking. Gangadhar watches Jauhar's face for a reaction but there is none. Silence grows between them for a while. Several moments later, Jauhar looks into Gangadhar's eyes and says with a charming smile, 'Why does Shivaji want to surrender all of a sudden?'

Gangadhar hesitates but speaks as if he is ashamed to say what he is about to. 'We have no option. Food supplies have dwindled. Imagine eight thousand men dying of starvation. Raja Shivaji would rather surrender than keep holding the fort for pride's sake.'

Jauhar looks at the Brahmin with mild surprise. The men do look thin—too thin, almost starving. He laughs loudly and snaps, 'Thousands of my men will enter the fort with a snap of my fingers. Shivaji is already a vanquished man!'

'That is not true', Naik butts in. 'The entrance is heavily guarded, and if you are aware of the architecture, it is impossible enter the fort in large numbers. Unless, of course, all of us make merry and drink barrels of wine and fall sleep. But drinking is not allowed in our camps.'

Jauhar raises his eyebrows. He knows that the man is taunting him.

'And, as you already know, a few thousand of us always guard the ramparts, our artillerymen are equipped to blast anyone coming near the foothills,' Naik says evenly.

'So why did you come here? Keep fighting,' Jauhar says coldly, waving his hand as if to show nonchalance.

'We were forced to come. We are ready to fight till the end and die of starvation, but our master wants us to live; he wants to surrender for our sake!' Gangadhar says softly.

'Please do not let him; do not accept Raja Shivaji's offer,' Naik pleads. His earlier arrogance has vanished.

'Please refuse the proposal, my great general of the Adilshahi. We do not want Raja Shivaji to surrender for our sake.' Gangadhar's voice quivers.

Jauhar stares at the men in amazement. Whom to believe and whom not to believe?

'You want me to believe you?' Jauhar asks sarcastically.

'That is up to you, my esteemed general,' Naik bows and says. 'If you agree, Raja Shivaji will come down with just twenty-five men to surrender at your feet, and if you reject his proposal, he will not.'

'Shivaji is willing to walk into my camp with just twenty-five men to get captured. Isn't that a bit hard to believe?'

Gangadhar casts his eyes down and says earnestly, 'Even we cannot believe it. The raja is forced to surrender for the sake of eight thousand lives. He is willing to get captured, imprisoned and even tortured for the sake of eight thousand lives.'

Long after they have gone, Jauhar reads the letter again and again.

You, the new general of the kingdom and jagirdar of Kurnool, are
a brave man, fit to be a king indeed. Allow me to surrender at your
feet and I will come down with only twenty-five men, but please,
I beg you, let my eight thousand men go free. Who knows what
tomorrow holds for us. Perhaps you may change your mind and
we may form an alliance. Perhaps together we may prove more
powerful than Ali Adil Shah!

5

Outside Dilli's Qila-e-mubarak, a tormented Yamuna soars and
dives, roars and surges, racing parallel to the meandering wall of
the Red Fort, unconcerned about what is happening within those
walls. Her monsoon annoyance pushes the mighty heavens to the
brink as lightning rampages through the clouds, splitting the sky into
enormous chunks of dark shadows.

In one of the underground vaults used as makeshift prisons,
a shackled Muhammad Sultan, Aurangzeb's first son, sits with
vacant eyes. He has no idea of the nature's fury outside but there
is a bigger and more devastating storm raging in his own heart.
He knows that he has committed a terrible mistake, a mistake that
might cost him his life, but now it is too late to regret. He should
not have underestimated his father, especially after what he had
witnessed on the battlefields near Khajwa in the fierce battle with
the armies of his uncle, Shah Shuja, when his father, Aurangzeb, had
torn through the jaws of death to emerge victorious. Despite Jaswant
Singh Rathod who had surrendered to his father after the debacle
at Ujjain had turned a traitor. The day before the battle with Shuja
uncle who was advancing towards Agra, Jaswant and his men in the
camp had woken up at midnight and started their killing spree. They
had reached Sultan's side of camp too. But he had survived their
slaughter. They had killed hundreds of men before looting and then
fleeing Sultan's father's camp. At dawn the real battle against Shuja
uncle awaited them.

Sultan can remember that battle as if it has happened yesterday. The first day was as uneventful as it could be on a battlefield, with arrows, rockets, granados fired from cannons darkening the sky, with the ear-splitting noise of muskets, yelling of troopers and trumpeting and neighing of war animals. On the second day, Shah Shuja had thrown a wicked surprise when three trained-to-kill war elephants had entered the field brandishing heavy iron chains with their trunks. The mountainous beasts, the weapons of mass destruction, had cut through the ranks of his father's army, leaving behind a bloody trail of injured and dead. From his howdah, Mohammad Sultan had watched as Aurangzeb's cavalrymen had deserted the field. Then he had witnessed the most appalling event. Two of the elephants had swerved away towards the edge but one had marched on, towards his father's elephant, scattering and shaking the squadrons.

The wisest thing for his father was to jump down, take a horse and flee, but he had stayed put in his howdah even when the enemy elephant was a breath away. Then something remarkable had happened! One of his father's musket men shot the mahout who fell from the beastly elephant like a ripe fruit. Within moments, his father's mahout had jumped down and thrown himself on the beast, climbing it as if it were a mountain. Meanwhile, Sultan's father had swung out from his howdah and taken the place of his mahout to direct his elephant. At the same time, his father's mahout had started hitting the beast with his ankush and had been successful in steering it away!

The drama of imminent death had lasted for barely a few moments. But it felt like an eternity. Then the rumours of his father getting crushed by Shuja uncle's rabid elephants started circulating. But that was that. His father, as always, was the victor and his enemy, the vanquished!

Later, Mohammad Sultan had gathered enough courage to ask his father why he had not dismounted from his elephant in the first place and his father had answered, 'Saving one's life is not always the wisest thing for a leader in a battle. Seeing my empty howdah, our troops would have fled, bringing bigger tragedies on us.'

Shuja uncle had fled to Bengal. Father had deputed him and Mir Jumla to chase Shuja uncle and eliminate him.

It was then that the message had arrived from Sultan's uncle:

> You father will never win the war of succession. And even if he does,
> he will never ever think of you as his successor because your mother
> is a mere convert, not a born Muslim. Join me, marry my daughter,
> and when I become the emperor I will make you my successor.

Like a fool, he had married his uncle's daughter and declared war
against his father, till he was caught and brought back to Dilli. From a
prince to a prisoner—the transaction was swift, and he knows this is
what he is, and will always remain: a prisoner. What hurts Sultan more
than anything else is that his father had forgiven Jaswant and again
taken him back. But his own son is not worthy of the emperor's mercy.

Directly above the vaults where Mohammad Sultan is imprisoned
is the *diwan-e-aam*, its pillars and arches made of red sandstone and
painted with gold shimmer under the brightly lit chandeliers.

6

'Alcohol is forbidden—forbidden to you and your mothers, your
daughters, your sisters, your aunts and your brother's wives . . .'
Aurangzeb preaches, his voice filled with divinity so tangible that it
makes his audience gaze at him with beaming love. Aurangzeb knows
the effect he has on his audience. After an hour of preaching, he gets
up, leaving his audience in a state of poignant stupor.

Later that evening, Aurangzeb crosses the heavily guarded gate
to enter the private palaces of the diwan-e-khaas. He walks past the
manicured lawns, the flowerbeds, colourful bougainvillea hedges,
waterways with dancing fountains, lights burning in shades and rows
of neatly cut trees. He is in a hurry to go to his private bedroom. After
moving through arches and corridors illuminated by chandeliers,
Aurangzeb enters a huge chamber surrounded by terraces with
tapering steps leading to the Yamuna. He longingly looks at the
mahogany bed covered with satin sheets. The roof is made of cut
mirror glasses that twinkle in the pale light of a lone chandelier

hanging in the middle. She is lying on the bed, his beautiful eighteen-year-old Udepuri, who was once Dara bhai's favourite concubine. Her auburn hair encircles her delicate face that looks carved from polished alabaster in the diffused moonlight filtering through the painted glass of several windows. Aurangzeb goes near her, bends and caresses her face as his hands shake with tender love. He has broken many a rule for this love of his, he has bedded her even though he is yet to marry her and he has allowed her drinking habit.

She turns away. She is in a drunken stupor and in no condition to respond to his affections. A dejected Aurangzeb lies next to her with his eyes wide open. He rests his head on a soft pillow stuffed with feathers and thinks of the three doomed men: Shuja bhai, Suleiman Shikoh and Shiva Bhosale. Suleiman is still in Kashmir; Aurangzeb has heard that Prithvi Singh, the king of a small kingdom, has given his daughter to Suleiman in marriage in order to be a relative of the most powerful family of Hindustan. Aurangzeb has already contacted the counsellors of the king, and has sent them sacks full of ashrafi mohurs. When the time comes, they will even go against the king, delivering him what he wants: his nephew. There is no point in letting the traitors go free, he consoles himself. Unable to sleep, the emperor keeps awake for a long time, as the words of a verse float in his mind.

> Even after his death
> A tormenter resurrects
> And keeps drawing a harrow
> Over what's dear to you
> Like plumes of a dead eagle
> Turning up as feathers at the end of an arrow.

7

Shaista and his army have reached the northern borders of Shivaji's jagir. The region around Chakan Fort looks bleak, with columns of smoke rising from the burning villages. For the past fifty days the

Mughals have been besieging the small fortress. The besiegement is tight. Shaista, along with ten mansabdars and their contingents, has been camping at the northern side of the fort. At the eastern side, facing the main gate are six other commanders, including the chief of his artillery, Mir Abdul Mabud, and his men trained in artillery warfare. Many others are scattered around the region. It has been raining heavily since the previous day and, despite the sheets of water falling over them, the commander of Chakan Fort, Firangoji Narsala, has given a robust reply to their guns and muskets. Some of the Marathas from inside the fort have dared to sally out and attack the Mughal besiegers in the trenches and kill some of them. Chakan Fort is a small land fortress, with defences of a square wall built in stone fortified with eight towers, four in the corner and four at the centre of each wall. There is only one entrance at the front, with more than five gateways as protection. The fort is encircled by a moat. In the beginning, Shaista had thought that despite the fortifications, it would be a lot easier than capturing a hill fort. He was proved wrong. Every time the Mughals tried to go anywhere near the fort walls, the Marathas standing on the bastions and ramparts threw rockets, grenades and large stones on the attackers. Even the Mughal war elephants wearing head armour have failed to crush open the main gate fitted with spikes, and the few elephants who tried hard died of head injuries.

Shaista has summoned Mir Abdul Mabud, his artillery advisor, for an urgent meeting. He wants answers. His tent looks like a mini-palace with panels made of colourful fabric. It is protected from rain by massive scaffoldings holding a thin iron sheet like an umbrella above the tent. The floor is covered with light-coloured durries and the divan is draped in dark-blue satin sheets. Despite the comforts around him, Shaista feels very uncomfortable. He wants quick solutions for a quicker victory.

'It has been a month and half since we have besieged this small land fort,' Shaista says, examining the gold rings on his fingers, then slowly shifts his gaze in the direction of Abdul and says, 'People in Dilli will soon wonder about our failure to capture even a single fort. The latest news is that our emperor had said in the court that taking over Chakan will be child's play for the new general. He will do so in a week.'

Mir Abdul Mabud, a stocky man with shining eyes, stares at his general who is looking back at him coldly. A shiver runs down Abdul's spine. 'Give me a day to think of a plan,' he whispers as the sound of the crossfire is heard from the southern direction.

'It is time to smoke out the rats. Dig more trenches all around the fort and gain physical proximity. Do something!' Shaista commands, raising his left eyebrow.

Abdul Mabud sends messages to all besieging commanders that night and has several meetings with them. For the next seven days it is relatively dry, but the earth is still wet. For six nights, hundreds of Mughal diggers work relentlessly in miry, slushy trenches and drag a mine of explosives, bringing it near the bastion on the north-eastern side. On the seventh night, they roll back into the trenches with axes, scurry through digging tunnels like expert bandicoots moving in their burrows, and exit the battlefield.

CHAPTER TWENTY

1

The initial drizzle and now the heavy rain have not dampened Jauhar's spirits. It is a remarkable night, a night of conclusion and a night of celebration. He looks out of the window in the direction of Panhala. Despite it being a full moon night, it is pitch dark because of the heavy storm clouds thundering in the sky, but that does not bother him. The sound of rain feels like music and he knows his men are busy having fun after months of hard work and uncertainty. The man they wanted, dead or alive, is finally surrendering.

It is time for Shivaji to die, Jauhar decides. He had once decided someone else's death a long time ago. It is better to kill them than keep them alive even in captivity. For a live enemy can resurrect from incarceration and seek reprisals!

It was the night when he had chased Malik Wahah, the scion of the jagirdar family of Kurnool, through the dark, twenty-kos-long tunnel that connects the Kurnool Fort to the Gadwal Fort. He had patronizingly warned the young and naive Malik that as the young jagirdar he must travel at least once through the long tunnel and know the escape routes in crisis. Jauhar had convinced his young master that their going into the tunnel must remain a secret. The lad's adolescent blood had boiled over, making him adventurous enough to enter the tunnel that crossed the Tungabhadra river from beneath. Malik's personal guards had been bribed. Once inside the tunnel, Jauhar had attacked Malik from behind and stabbed him with a jambia dagger that had pierced his heart. The bats, the only witnesses, had fluttered overhead without a care.

Then it was Malik Wahah; now it is Shivaji Bhosale!

At the northern side of the camp, a large brick house is lit with several earthen lamps. It is also decorated with fresh flowers plucked earlier from the shallow valley that surrounds the hill. Men have gathered and the mood is cheerful. It's warm and cosy inside the house despite the storm that rages around it. It smells of tobacco as many have been smoking chillums. Jauhar's son-in-law, Siddi Masud, has called for a nautch girl from a nearby village and is keen to give his officers a good time. He watches as servants fill the glasses and some of his military officials down their drinks in one go, while he nurses his first peg. He still thinks that his father-in-law has made haste in announcing the submission of their enemy and suspects that something else may happen tonight.

A group of entertainers, consisting of a dancer, a singer and a few musicians, suddenly barge into the room and move towards an empty corner decorated with strings of jasmine. The air is soon filled with the heady smell of burning incense. A voluptuous, dusky dancer bows, holding her pallu like a peacock spreading its feathers. As she sways to the music, countless bells in her anklets make an energetic sound. The dancer knows that her erotic moves will kindle a wild passion and desire in the sex-starved men. The male dancer poses as though he is her stalker, his leering expression bordering on lust. The man with the dhol bangs mallets on the drum hanging from his neck.

The harmonium player too bursts into the scene. A plain-looking female singer stands with an expressionless face and starts her song laden with pathos and the passions of the adulterous love she so badly seeks. Her words are often vulgar and sexually explicit. Her lyrics are drowned in the ravenous sentiments that make the listener feel that the song is meant only for him. Her sighs between the words are caressing enough to make men go weak. Within half an hour, the men are in a trance.

The evening has progressed into a stormy night and the full moon is eclipsed by layers of dark clouds that have unleashed the fury of the rain. A few hundred men have gathered at the mouth of a tunnel near Rajdindi bastion and they seem to be moving inside the tunnel in a file along with two palanquins. Baji Prabhu follows one of the palanquins through the tunnel lit by a few earthen lamps kept in primitive alcoves, barefoot like all others. What he has heard from his scouts worries him. They had warned that at places rain-sodden slopes have collapsed in torrents of mud and rocky debris. He and his six hundred men from Bandal must ensure that Raja Shivaji escapes from Panhala. If they do not escape tonight, they never will.

Baji and his men know that the journey between Panhala and Vishalgad may be their last, but each of them has made peace with death as long as their master reaches the safe confines of Vishalgad. It is dark, and they depend on the frequent lightning to show them the downhill path. Lightning is a double-edged sword today: it will show them the path but it might also help the enemy to spot them.

Too many thoughts and questions buzz in Baji's head. Panhala is surrounded by flat plains, so the besiegement is tight, with hardly any gaps. Countless sentry posts guard it from all sides. Thousands of men are camping around the hill: Jauhar and Fazal are to the east, Rustum Khan to the west, Siddi Masud to the north and Baji Ghorpade to the south. The siege is tight in the east. Towards the north-west, at the foothills of Masai Rock, it thins out, and that is the weakest link of the enemy besiegement, especially in the rain. Once they reach the foothills of Panhala, Baji Prabhu guides one palanquin followed by large number of people carrying bows on their shoulders, backpack quivers full of arrows, catapults hanging from their necks, and scabbards stuffed with swords tied to their waist as they cross a torrential stream and move towards the Masai tablelands. Baji is in command and races along with the palanquin, anxious but alert. A noise has travelled through the sheets of rain and pierced his eardrums. He orders the palanquin he trails to halt. Quickly, the procession stops and turns still. All men freeze into statues, with racing hearts, fearful minds, darting pupils, constricted bellies and goose-pimpled skin. Then again Baji hears the sound: *ta-ga-da-ka ta-ga-da-ka*. The rhythm of the hooves that now have the power to stop Baji's heart is thankfully getting fainter. They start climbing Masai to reach the tablelands. The path is not steep but the darkness and rain has made it slippery. Some fall, some are even injured. They need to cover a distance of six kos on the flat rock and climb down to reach a village called Pandharpani. The stretch is covered with short, coarse grass.

The second palanquin has not crossed the stream but has mutely moved in the direction of a place called Malkapur. It is accompanied by just twenty-five people.

2

Naik has gone with the first palanquin while Mhadu now runs behind the second one that has headed towards Malkapur. After a while it comes into an open area as if it wants to be spotted and captured. It eventually is stopped by Masud and his horsemen. It still pours when Masud's men remove the cloth that covers the palanquin to protect the very important person who sits in it.

'Light!' screams Masud.

The cover is removed and a torch protected by a wooden umbrella is brought by one of Masud's men. The flame flickers wildly as though possessed. Masud and his men are astonished by what they see. A man stares back at them with a blank expression. He wears very fine clothes and a tapering turban embellished with pearls.

'Who are you?' Masud commands. He is still in his party clothes—a long jama with floral motifs and a colourful turban heavy with emeralds. The clothes have lost their lustre and are dripping with rainwater, but Masud is not bothered about his clothes at the moment. He is just stunned by the discovery.

Is this man really Shivaji? he wonders.

The man in the palanquin does not say a word. Some of the infantrymen following the palanquin draw their swords.

'Do not even think of charging. You are surrounded by hundreds of us,' Masud warns. He signals two of his horsemen who jump down as metal chains make a faint clinking sound. The man in the palanquin is shackled. The bearers shudder with fear and Mhadu, standing behind the palanquin, starts sobbing.

'Shut up,' one of the guards snaps at him. His words vanish in the ear-splitting sound of the thunder. The palanquin bearers and its followers are briskly herded by Masud's hooting horsemen, while Masud's horse, like a victor, canters ahead of the palanquin.

The news spreads and the foothills of Panhala become alive with excitement. Drums start beating as the palanquin is carefully brought into the camp while the slaves waiting at the edge start dancing in front of the palanquin, leading it to Jauhar's tent. A drenched Masud proudly presents his trophy to his esteemed father-in-law, titled Salabat Khan, the invincible one. The prisoner falls to his knees but his eyes bore boldly into Jauhar's.

Jauhar looks on unbelievingly. Is the captive the person he thinks he is?

His room, lit by two torches hung on the wall, is now swarming with men stamping on the clean durries with their muddy feet, as Marathi, Deccani and Turkish words float in the air. Several people who have previously seen Shivaji jostle with each other to get a better look. Jauhar watches them as they stare at the shackled man and knows immediately that something is amiss. Blood rushes to his brain and his heart thumps against his ribcage, his muscles go into spasm and the colour drains from his face. Everything becomes clear in a flash, like the lightning that lights up the world for brief moments, and Jauhar feels as if he has been hit by lightning. He knows that all this was done to fool him, but fool him for what? What do they want to achieve—gain time? But gain time to do what?

'Where is Shivaji and who are you?' Jauhar asks, taking out his sword from its scabbard. The ray of hope of Shivaji joining hands with him against the king has become a noose!

'I am Shiva, Shiva Kashid, and I do not know where Raja Shivaji is. I am just a traveller going towards Bijapur,' Shiva the barber is not bothered about his life anymore; he owes his life to Raja Shivaji for rescuing him and his family from the hands of the Adilshahi soldiers a few years before. He looks up to pray to his God and sees the flash of the gleaming blade of Jauhar's sword.

The news of Shivaji's double and his execution spreads faster than the news of his 'capture'. There is huge confusion. First, it is utter disbelief, and then it is sheer anger at being tricked. At the end of it there is only helplessness. In that hour of bewilderment, rage, raging storm and earth-shaking thunder, some of the Maratha men are captured while some slink away. Mhadu has disappeared in the crowd. Jauhar tries to think fast as moments slip by, while dancing slaves have sprung to action. Some of them are busy carrying away the remains of Shiva Kashid, and some wash the carpet with soap and brush to wipe the stains. Their master likes his room squeaky clean. What must be the motive of this circus? Why a decoy? What is the real one up to?

Lightning strikes again, illuminating the camp full of puzzled men. It also lights up Jauhar's mind. Shivaji has escaped and must have gone westwards while the decoy's palanquin was allowed to wander towards the east on purpose. Since Shivaji and his men have no horses to cover long distances, they must be heading for the nearest fort, Vishalgad. They will cross the rock and reach Pandharpani and then head for Vishalgad.

'Pandharpani!' Jauhar cries looking at Masud, 'Chase them, capture them and kill them all. They are all on foot!'

3

Baji is racing with the palanquin. They have climbed down the rock and have crossed Pandharpani village. They enter a wooded area as ten kos of thick forest unfolds before them. At places it is so dense that even the rain has failed to break in—dry pockets swarm with fireflies that look like floating lights. Then comes the dawn and with it a bit of light. The ground below is slushy with knee-deep muck and everyone is barefoot. They cross countless rainwater streams and ponds. At some places, the entire area is covered with thorny babul. Gradually the eastern skyline brightens; the rain has stopped and the clouds are dispersing. It takes a few more hours for them to reach the path that leads to the river valley. Baji hears the dreadful noise of galloping horses again. Soon the noise turns into the thunder of hooves. Jauhar's army is finally catching up and the borrowed time is over. Shiva Kashid is most probably dead. Baji keeps running despite his feet being punctured by long, sharp babul thorns. He and his men have covered several kos within fifteen hours and are heading for the valley of Kasari river.

Baji takes a decision. He rushes to Raja Shivaji's palanquin and says while running, 'Raja you move on and head for Vishalgad with half the men, I shall stay put here with the rest to take care of the enemy.'

'No!' shouts Shivaji.

'Lakhs of men may die but the one who looks after those lakhs must live,' Baji is firm. The plan is already in place; it now remains to be executed without question or doubt. There is no time to decide otherwise. Naik and half of the Bandal men follow Raja Shivaji's palanquin as they cross the stream of Kasari river. Baji and the rest of his men stay put on the other side of the riverbank. Once the palanquin reaches the safety of the fort, its artillery officers will blast the cannon three times. That is the signal that the leader is safe.

'Hide behind bushes,' Baji orders the remaining three hundred. Within no time they can see Jauhar's horsemen galloping towards them. Baji's men take out the bows from their shoulders and arrows from the quivers. Some use catapults. Within moments the arrows and pebbles fly as some of the galloping horsemen fall with devastating effect, their fallen animals acting as hurdles for the other gallopers. Baji looks back to glance at his men from his region, the Bandals—

they look determined and ready for anything. He calculates: Raja needs three hours to reach the safety of Vishalgad; Baji needs to prevent anyone from crossing the river for the next three hours so he stands on the only path in the midst of the thick forest that leads to the river. He does not want to speculate the numbers of the enemy soldiers and stands rooted in the path, focusing only on sounds. His ears catch an echo of gallops getting louder and louder, and within moments he notices a horseman approaching, then another and another, as arrows from the bows and pebbles from the catapults of his men keep flying.

But some enemy horsemen survive and the distance between them and Baji reduces rapidly.

'Har Har Mahadev!' Baji bellows their battle cry, igniting valour in the hearts of his men, instigating them to launch the offensive. He has one sword in each hand, he does not need a shield. If the enemy horsemen miss death from Baji's swords, they have hundreds blades waiting for them. Baji Prabhu is like a rampart of flesh. He stands between the horsemen and the river. His headgear has fallen and his scalp is bleeding, blood trickling down his face and making him look like a man possessed, but his swords move swiftly and it is difficult to dodge the blows.

Two hours pass thus and Baji starts feeling tired. Many of his men are dead but his eyes keep wandering in the direction of Vishalgad and his ears wait for the signal.

It has been almost twenty-one hours since they have left Panhala and Baji knows he might not last long. The enemy's cavalry seems to have been reinforced. The enemy infantrymen are fresh. He glances back for a brief moment to see only a few of his men still fighting. At that very moment, a tall horseman looming over him attacks him from the side. The force is such that the blade cuts through his left biceps, severing his left hand still holding the sword. But Death must wait till he hears the blasts and Baji keeps swinging his right sword even as the stump of his left arms gurgles blood. He stops for a moment to look up at the sky and sees the afternoon sun blinking through the clouds. It is at that moment a loud sound of three blasts brings peace to his mind and calms his soul. He glances at the direction of Vishalgad for one last time, but all he sees is a blur, for his eyes are filled with tears. He falls, still alive, recalling Raja Shivaji's words: *When you use your sword against the unarmed and the defenceless, it turns into a devil; when you help the undeserving and the unscrupulous with it, it becomes a traitor; when you use it against the aggressor to protect the weak, it becomes a worshipper of God; and when you empower the helpless, the vulnerable, to defend themselves with it, it becomes God!*

Baji smiles. As he falls he whispers, 'Today, my sword has become Bhavani, the goddess of every god's energy!'

Now his Raja can escape. Wooded slopes of Vishalgad disappear into Konkan. From there reaching Rajgad is easy.

CHAPTER TWENTY-ONE

1

Padmavati Temple is bedecked with strings of marigold and chrysanthemum. The vibrant yellow and orange colours of the freshly plucked flowers dazzle in the glow of the morning light. In the inner sanctum, well-lit by several earthen lamps, the statue of the goddess shimmers under the cover of blood-red hibiscus. Saffron flags flutter in the wind above the citadel. Drums have started beating, and moments later, cannons placed on the ramparts of Rajgad start blasting to welcome Shivaji. The ear-splitting sound shakes the colossal hill of the fort as the violet-blue sky above the hill gets filled with confused and fearful eagles. The horses in the stables built on the extension of the hill start whinnying and stamping their hooves in fright. Peasants working in the fields at the foothills narrow their eyes and look up at the fort. All fort residents know the reason for the drums but for one person who does not understand what the fuss is all about.

Hardly knee high, the boy runs defiantly between his grandmother, mothers and sisters, brandishing a small wooden dagger. He is wearing new clothes that make him feel stuffy—the angirkha is laden with pearls and is too heavy for his liking His grandmother has forcefully fitted a new turban on his head. He has given up the idea of throwing a tantrum because he knows that his grandmother can be strict too. Out of sheer defiance, when she was not looking, he has managed to pull out some of his curly locks from under the rim of the headgear. The locks have formed a halo around his angelic face. He has noticed that his mothers and sisters have worn new clothes, adorned themselves with jewellery and decked their hair with flowers. Most of them are holding silver trays with burning lamps placed on them. What is disheartening is that that he is not the object of their interest!

He suddenly notices a man whom he does not know but who seems to be the centre of affection. He looks at the others but they are looking at the man. He too diverts his eyes towards the man but his eyes fall on a scabbard hanging from the man's belt. The boy decides that it is far more interesting than its owner.

'Sword,' the boy commands, pointing at the scabbard as if it is his birth right to get whatever catches his fancy.

The stranger kneels, looks into the boy's eyes and asks with a smile, 'Shambhu Sahib, do you want my sword?'

The boy considers the proposal seriously for a moment and offers his wooden toy to the stranger, as if he does not want any obligation. The stranger looks at the toy; it is a small wooden dagger, well-crafted, with a tiny hilt that is painted red.

'Sword,' the boy twists his lips, creases his forehead with impatience to remind the stranger of his offer. It is a fair bargain and he has finished his part of the deal. He does not want a gift; it is a trade-off, clear and simple.

'Don't go by his size; he is unyielding like iron,' Shivaji hears Jija bai's voice and he swings around and faces his mother. She looks frailer and seems to have aged rapidly, with more wrinkles around her eyes. Yet he feels relieved to see her up and about. Her eyes light up with tears as she looks at him. He has come home from Panhala, dodging death.

'Ma, many have not come home. Our Baji Prabhu, hundreds of his men and Shiva Kashid went on a suicidal mission just to keep me alive,' Shivaji says softly as he bends and touches her feet. He does not want to see anyone rejoicing at his safe return, not even his mother.

'Sword!' they hear Shambhu scream. The boy is angry with the delay, as the women and girls giggle looking at the sullen face of the little one who is now looking up at the stranger, tears of determination welling in his eyes. The man in the saffron turban has cheated him, taking Shambhu's dagger but refusing to part with his sword.

Shivaji looks down and even in that heartbreaking moment he starts laughing, picks up the boy and kisses his forehead. For a moment he is stunned. Looking into his son's eyes he realizes that they are so much like Sayee's: large, dark, limpid and intense, with unusually long lashes. The boy meanwhile screws up his nose in anger, throws a tantrum and struggles to wriggle out of his arms.

Shivaji remains preoccupied with Baji's memories.

Baji Prabhu was a large man, but his body had come in a small sack gone crimson black with dried blood. When they had spread him on the floor, all he could see were pieces of a human body, hacked ruthlessly, with sinister force. The soul-less red bits covered with slivers of skin had looked forlorn, lost without the spirit, the fighting spirit of Baji. The only parts that seemed intact were his feet, swollen with soles covered with countless babul thorns. Looking at those feet, a part of Shivaji had died. The entire struggle, the bravery, the sacrifice of Baji was for him so that he could get away alive.

Shivaji wonders earnestly if and whether his dream of freedom is worth the deaths of Baji, Shiva Kashid and others? Are wars and battle really justified, gaining peace and prosperity for some by paying with violent and brutal death of some others? Was he not responsible for their deaths? Hasn't he made their wives widows and their children father-less? Who can advise him? All he could do was to think of Samarth Ramdas, the saint poet who lived in the forests of Jawali, who had said,

> They have let their pyres burn bright
> with everlasting flames to light up the endless night
> only to show us what is wrong and what is right . . .

The words bring some solace, but there is more: Shivaji also worries about the seven thousand men still stuck at Panhala. He has written to Trimbak Dabir, the fort commander of Panhala, to surrender the fort without bloodshed, and hopes that the king will comply.

It is almost midnight and the fort has gone quiet, the fort extensions are deserted. The only sound filling the valley is that of the mountain wind whistling and moaning through the canopies of the enormous trees at the foothills. Shivaji ventures into Sayee's room for the first time after her death and stands in front of her empty bed. A few samayees lit in the corners gleam in their own pale light, and the wooden pillars stand mute, dissolving in their own shadows. It was here that she breathed her last. The room is filled with the memories of her very last days and her very last thoughts.

'Death, death!' he says loudly.

'Who can avoid death?' he hears Soyara's musical voice. He swings around and sees the tall and pretty woman with a face so fetching that one needs some will power to remove one's gaze from her.

'No one, not even you or I,' he replies politely.

'That is so true,' she agrees quickly with her husband and whispers in her silken voice, 'but it is also one's karma how and when one dies.'

It takes Shivaji several moments to understand what Soyara is trying to say. He smiles sadly and retorts, 'A tragedy has struck us. Why do you talk in riddles?'

She looks like an alabaster statue, luminous in her pale-golden sari with her jewels twinkling around her neck, in her ears and on her hands. The white jasmine flowers tied to her hair fill the room with a sweet fragrance but her face has turned ashen. Sayee was her husband's love and her death might not change things; death cannot kill the intangible. She knows all too well that fear and insecurity are making her say what she does not intend to.

'She was a strong woman,' Soyara mutters, trying to lessen the hurt she has inflicted on her husband.

'Will you not ask me about the battles I fought while death circled over my head?' Shivaji asks sardonically.

Before she can reply, a maid comes running with a message, 'A scout has arrived from Chakan and he has news.' Shivaji rushes out without another glance at Soyara and she knows instantly that she has lost her chance. She feels confused and sad.

2

It rains in Chakan too but Abdul Mabud is not worried, he has finished his pre-launch work. His diggers have dug trenches towards the fort wall, his labourers have constructed raised platforms at suitable points and his artillerymen have mounted large cannons on them. The cannons that have been brought from the Mughal forts in the Deccan. He has been pressing the siege vigorously all through the rain, braving the occasional attacks of arrows, stones and grenades fired at him and his men from the ramparts and the bastions, with only one goal in mind: the fort must be captured and every man from the Maratha garrison must be killed. As night falls, Abdul sends messages to all besieging commanders. The trench at the north-eastern side of the fort is fully stuffed with explosives. The plan is sure and simple, once the wick is ignited by Shaista Khan and the explosives blow, the northern side of the gate and wall will turn into rubble, creating a gaping hole for the Mughals to enter.

Inside the fort, it is quiet. Hours before sunset, Firangoji has swallowed his evening meal of a few pieces of dry bread made of sorghum and washed it down with salty well water. He has a terrible premonition that something is about to happen. He comes out of his barracks and looks at the sky covered with dark clouds and then diverts his gaze towards the bastions of the main gate and sees several archers keeping vigil. Everything looks normal but still there is something sinister, intangible yet palpable, in the air. Seeing his expression, a few men from the fort garrison gather around him. He commands everyone to gather in the courtyard. They were in their barracks after their meal.

'Get all the grenades, large stones, muskets, bows and arrows and pile them in the middle of the courtyard,' he shouts at the men who are running to give his message to others. It is time to go into a contingency mode. *The time has come*, he thinks.

War drama is happening outside the fort as planned by the Mughal. The wick is lit by Shaista on time and as planned—three hours before sunset. A series of ear-splitting sounds shake the region, a huge fireball is seen where the bastion stands and then burning debris including massive pieces of stone wall near the bastion are seen flying in the air. As the enormous parts of the rubble fall on earth, they make repeated thudding sounds. The group of Maratha archers standing on that bastion meet a horrific end. A huge cloud rises above the fort as the acrid smell of smoke fills the region. From the courtyard of the fort, Firangoji and his few hundred men watch in horror as they see a part of the strong wall that separates them from the Mughals being blown away. All the archers keeping vigil have vanished in the rubble. The fort commander has been expecting this sort of disaster to happen. He closes his eyes for a brief moment and remembers Raja Shivaji's words: 'Our forts are our best defences. Our northern stronghold, the Chakan Fort, is under your care, and I trust that you will defend it wisely . . .'

Firangoji turns to his men and shouts, 'We shall not stand and watch the fall of this fort! What a shame it would be that we do nothing! Raja Shivaji has entrusted the fort, the northern stronghold of our kingdom, to us and we shall guard it as long as it is humanly possible.'

The bastion is reduced to a high mound of debris. Within hours, the squadrons of Mughal soldiers press forward: the infantrymen, followed by heavy cavalrymen and then the war elephants. Night has fallen and it has started to drizzle. The air vibrates with the Mughal war cry, 'Deen! Deen! Deen!' as Shaista Khan's men raise their torches in the air. The mound of debris is still hot but they move forward only to find a high embankment of earth made by the Marathas. Within a few moments, rockets, musket shots, grenades, arrows and stones start flying from behind the earth mound and land on the marching Mughals. Small infernos rise as hundreds of Shaista Khan's infantry and cavalrymen start falling dead.

'Har Har Mahadev!' The air starts trembling with the battle cry of the Marathas.

The storming Mughals stop as night falls but they are forced to stand in the rain on the slimy, blood-drenched ground all through the night.

By early next morning, the Mughals have changed their strategy. Fifty armoured war elephants charge at the mound followed by thousands of horsemen. The fort garrison is mowed down and some fall back into the tiny citadel in the middle of the courtyard. Firangoji Narsala and some of his men are forced to leave the fort from secret exits. They disappear into the nearby jungle. Raja Shivaji has always insisted that when death is certain and if one is unable to further harm or fight the enemy, one must not die in vain, but flee, remain alive to fight other battles.

On the fifty-seventh day, Shaista captures Shivaji's northern domination at the cost of a thousand men. The saffron flag of the Marathas is quickly replaced by the green, Mughal alam. The moss-green flag, made of silk; embroidered with the motif of the rising sun eclipsed by a crouching tiger, flutters over the fort's citadel in the midst of the ruins of the fort.

3

Salimgad Fort in Dilli, used as a prison by Aurangzeb, is immersed in darkness. Its round bastions made of rubble masonry soar over the waters of the Yamuna that flows between the fort and the Qila-e-mubarak. The winding corridors that join the cells are lit by torches hung on the wall in dire need of repairs. A shackled Suleiman Shikoh sits in one of those cells and thinks about his last day before he had decided to flee to Kashmir.

It was more than a year ago when life's reality had started unfolding for Suleiman; everything was over, his dreams, his family and his life. He had pretended to watch the sunset from the terrace above the Rani Mahal of Allahabad Fort, but his thoughts had been elsewhere. It was winter and the evening breeze from over the Ganga was cold, but that had not bothered him. His eyes had wandered beyond the enormous wall of the fort and gazed at the *sangam* of the Ganga and Yamuna. Despite the orange hues of the reflecting sun, the line dividing the rivers was clear.

His eyes had moved to a collection of shallow boats with decks rigidly pinned together, forming a path over the water to cross the river for his horses and elephants. *Is it the end of the road?* he had thought. A part of him was already dead, the sounds of the wailing of his wives he was forced to leave behind had made him feel impotent, and the memory of the young women he had gifted away to men of power in hope that they would help him escape had made him feel like a pimp. He had to leave everything behind, the trunks containing jewels and weapons hidden in the vaults of the fort, thousands of war animals including elephants left at the mercy of their caretakers. The victor and the vanquished, such misleading words . . . Just a few days ago he had been a victor, when he had pushed back Shah Shuja's army from the battleground near Varanasi, and forced them to flee to Bengal. Within days, he was the vanquished; his father Dara Shikoh's defeat at the hands of Aurangzeb, his father's third brother, had been nothing less than a death sentence. Suleiman's generals, Mirza Raja Jai Singh and Diler Khan, had since disappeared along with their armies, obviously to join Aurangzeb. Suleiman's path to Punjab was blocked. At Haridwar, Sambhal and many other places, the imperial forces were waiting for him in ambush. A massive army led by his grand-uncle Shaista Khan was already marching towards Varanasi. There was only one option—to flee with minimum horsemen, cross the forests and seek refuge in the kingdom of Prithvi Singh, the king of Kashmir. That was a year ago, and just when he had started feeling safe, a revolt had broken out and the king's counsellors took over the reins. The same night they had arrested him and handed him over to Mirza Raja Jai Singh who had personally come to take him to Dilli, as a prisoner of the new emperor!

Suleiman looks out from the small window of his prison cell and notices the waters of the Yamuna shimmer in the pale moonlight. The glittering water reminds him of his happy childhood spent at the palaces of Agra and Dilli, and a bitter smile creases his handsome face. Tomorrow, he will be facing Aurangzeb who is supposed to announce an appropriate punishment for the 'crimes' Suleiman has committed.

It is only the next day that Suleiman actually realizes what is in store for him. He is taken, still shackled, to the diwan-e-khaas, where he sees all his younger cousins, ministers, umrahs and mansabdars.

When he looks at the throne that rightfully belonged to his father, Dara Shikoh, his eyes become moist.

The throne is far from inanimate, and the gold peacocks seem drunk with power. The gold columns of the throne on which the seat of power rests shimmer in the light of innumerable chandeliers burning in the diwan-e-khaas of the Qila-e-mubarak in Dilli. The diamonds and rubies embedded in them glitter like stars in a clear sky. Reluctantly, Suleiman raises his eyes and sees his father's murderer sitting on the throne, eyes half-closed, counting tesbih beads. The assassin wears a gold-coloured turban fitted with an aigrette studded with large diamonds and a huge topaz. It looks familiar, and then it dawns on Suleiman that it was given to his father by his grandfather. Suleiman shudders with rage; the murderer is also a thief!

Finally Aurangzeb opens his eyes and gazes at his handsome nephew standing before him bound in metal chains. The young man does not stoop like his father but walks towards the throne his head held high, looking straight into the new emperor's eyes with complete disregard—as if he has nothing to lose. But he has, he still has his spirit and that needs to be broken.

Jahanara has come all the way from Agra to witness her family's heart-wrenching drama. She sits in a balcony separated from the main court by a latticed wall, and gazes at the twenty-five-year-old Suleiman, her favourite nephew, in shackles, and tears blur her eyes. The diwan-e-khaas is packed with men, all standing according to their rank and position. She can recognize a few whom she has seen before: Jaffar Khan, her mother's sister's husband and now the wazir-e-azam of the empire, Mirza Raja Jai Singh, who has been elevated to the position of a subhedar of Dilli, and Muhammad Amin Khan, son of Mir Jumla, who is now the new mir bakshi of the empire. Maharaja Jaswant Singh Rathod, Diler Khan, Danishmand Khan, previously a Dara loyalist, and a few more are seen in the first few rows in their finery and colourful turbans.

There are others in the court—ulemas, the learned, sayyids, the nobles, and qazis, the men of justice—who stand at the left side of the throne in their ankle-length robes and long beards. She looks back to see the royal women behind her and is shocked to see Roshanara who she hasn't seen for a while. Her younger sister pretends as if she has not noticed Jahanara. Roshanara wears a short-sleeved bodice studded with pearls as if she has come for a ceremony. Behind her are many women from the royal seraglio—Aurangzeb's daughters, Suleiman's sisters, and wives and daughters of ministers. Everyone has tears in their eyes—except Roshanara.

The trial has begun.

'You are a traitor to the empire. You had taken refuge in the kingdom of Garhwal and incited the king to fight with the imperial army. Do you want to say anything in your defence?' A mullah standing to the left of the throne accuses Suleiman. There is utter silence in the court and all eyes are focused on the prince.

Suleiman smiles bitterly and says, 'No, I have not done anything wrong and I have nothing to say to the *honourable* court.'

'Every criminal says so. If you have nothing to say then you will face the consequences of your actions,' the clergy announces.

The silence in the hall of private audiences has turned transparently ominous. Jahanara sighs; the fate of her nephew is sealed. She looks at Aurangzeb, his face is expressionless. She turns her teary gaze towards Suleiman who stands with his head held high, his silky hair falling on his muscular shoulders, his face red, his eyes redder still. She notices that everyone present is gazing at their own feet as if they are busy surveying the floor. Jahanara is aware that for Aurangzeb it is dicey to announce the death verdict since there are no serious charges against Suleiman and those of sedition are hearsay, not proved.

She is curious to know what Aurangzeb has to say.

Aurangzeb opens his eyes and announces, 'Despite whatever you have done I promise that no harm shall befall you. Have faith in Allah, you shall be treated kindly. *Allah hu Akbar!* God is great. Your father was put to death because he went against Islam and became a kafir. You have nothing to fear.' Aurangzeb pauses. 'But we cannot forget that you have tried to go against the emperor and that is a serious crime. You will be under observation and we shall keep you in some place safe, like the Gwalior Fort.'

This seems like an anti-climax. For a moment Suleiman looks puzzled, then performs kurnish. He waits for a few moments, letting the silence choke the audience, and then says, 'If you intend to feed me with *pousht* made of opium seeds that will first make me insane and then kill me slowly, I beg you to please kill me, put me to death in a quick manner, in whichever way the emperor desires.'

The hall echoes with the solemn words when Aurangzeb says loudly, 'This drink will most certainly not be administered.'

Suleiman performs another kurnish.

4

Houses on the outskirts of Kurnool have been set on fire and the evening sky is covered with black smoke that hangs over the Tungabhadra river. Siddi Jauhar, despite having a severe headache, stands all alone on the western burj of the Kurnool Fort and sadly gazes at the destruction of his city. After the Panhala debacle, he had managed to flee and reach his home, but the angry Ali Adil Shah wants him dead. Now the Adilshahi squadrons are gunning for him. Half his army has deserted him to join Ali, thinking that their master has betrayed them by helping Shivaji escape. For the first time in his life, Jauhar feels that life is not worth living any more. He sighs, clutches his head with both hands and thinks that he must do what he intends to do. Ali's troopers will not stop at anything. He knows that after a while they will enter the fort like untamed elephants gone wild, goring anything in their path. They will surely enter his zenana quarters and the rest is too ghastly to brood over.

He moves away from the battlements and runs along the ramparts as archers guarding the fort give him puzzled looks. The news of the impending calamity seems to have reached the women quarters for he can hear some wailing and screaming. He reaches a massive watchtower and looks around. Making sure that there is no one to see what he is doing, he enters a small room that has steps descending to a vault. It is dark and damp in the narrow passage but he knows that there is a small iron door flush to the wall. He takes out a large key tucked in his belt, unlocks the door and kicks it open. The memories of how he had lured the young jagirdar of Kurnool and stabbed him to death here surface, along with a musty smelling draught of chill air. It is the first time he has entered the tunnel after he had left young Malik bleeding to death somewhere in there. In the gloom and darkness of the tunnel, a million images flash before his eyes. His nostrils pick up another stench, like something dead and rotting, as though the body of the boy is still waiting for him after so many years. Then he thinks he has heard something: the last screams of the dying boy echo in the tunnel and pierce his ears. He soldiers on, like a suicidal man, unafraid of the dark, undaunted by the reptiles hiding in the crevices of the rocks he is walking on. It turns darker and he starts to flounder, his hands moving about him like a blind man searching for obstacles in the path. He stops and listens; the sounds of the outside world have faded away and even the echo of the screams has stopped. He stands still for a while, and takes out a jambia dagger tucked in his belt. Holding its hilt with both his hands, he raises it high and brings it down with all the force he can muster, stabbing his stomach one, twice, thrice, till he can no longer repeat it.

Death is merciful, death is the last refuge, death is a blessing from Allah, death is also an escape from tragedies you do not wish to witness, and this physical pain is only a small price to pay, thinks Salabat Khan, the invincible one, before falling down with a thud and closing his eyes. The tunnel suddenly comes alive with the ominous squeaks of eager rats.

CHAPTER TWENTY-TWO

1

It has been six months since Shivaji's escape from Panhala. The month of Poush has arrived but people of Maval and the surrounding areas are too terrified to celebrate Makar Sankranti, the festival of harvesting.

Everything is gone; the farms are empty, eaten away by the Mughal war animals. Some of the villages have turned into mere ash and thousands of people of the region have been taken as slaves, some of the young women are imprisoned in Shaista's camp as sex slaves and will soon be engaged in the breeding of children sired by Mughal soldiers!

It is midnight, and it is dark on the Padmavati extension of Rajgad. Bahirji Naik waits outside the sadar for Raja Shivaji to arrive. He has important news and he must convey that to the raja tonight. There is very little time, he thinks, as his eyes wander around nervously. The hill on which the citadel is built looks like a gloomy pillar against the backdrop of a star-studded sky. Behind the sadar, an enormous banyan tree hides in its own shadow, its aerial roots swaying with the currents of unconstrained mountain winds. The air smells strange—a mix of jungle herbs, night-cestrum flowers and the weird odour of pongamia oil used as torch fuel.

'What news, Naik?' he hears a familiar voice. Raja Shivaji has come with Tanaji Malusare.

'Kartalab is headed for Kurvanda Pass.'

'Strange . . . Why would he do that? I have taken that route once. The pass turns too narrow at places,' Tanaji comments.

'He does not have much choice. It is either Borghat or Kurvanda Pass. The other mountain paths are too steep and difficult to negotiate. We have a few hundred men holding Borghat and Kartalab knows it,' Shivaji comments and then asks Naik, 'How sure are you?'

'Hundred per cent. I am Kartalab Khan's personal masseur. He likes me so much that he is reluctant to share me with his officers,' Naik says with a straight face.

'What is the strength of his army?' Tanaji asks. He is beginning to understand; Borghat is blocked by the Marathas on purpose to steer Kartalab towards Kurvanda.

'Around twenty thousand, I guess, and it is a big cavalcade complete with horses, carts and palanquins. It looks like Kartalab is planning to stay in the Konkan for a long time,' Naik replies.

'If I remember correctly, there is a mountain glade after a few kos of descent. Thereafter, the pass turns too narrow,' Shivaji says raising his eyebrows.

'Ji, ji,' Naik nods affirmatively, 'it is called Chavani, meaning "to camp", for people descending the mountain can rest there. From Chavani, one has to go westwards to a village called Umbare. Here the trail turns frighteningly narrow; the locals call it Umbarkhind and it is like the barrel of a gun.'

'Can this barrel accommodate them all at once?' Tanaji's eyes shine with interest.

'The barrel is about a mile and half in length. A few thousand Mughal infantrymen will enter it first along with a few hundred labourers to clear the way. By the time they near Umbare, the entire army would have entered the barrel.' Naik knows his business.

'So, we must fire the gun called Umbarkhind when the barrel is stuffed with explosives in the form of the Mughal army,' Shivaji comments wryly. His eyes are twinkling—whether with mischief or anticipation, no one can tell.

'If that happens, the Mughals will have no room to retreat, no space to rally and organize to retaliate, and no place to disperse— they will just explode,' Naik reasons.

'Is there any highland that looks over this track?' Shivaji asks.

'Sure,' Naik replies, 'there are many hills rising above the trail and one is at the end of the pass, or shall we say at the mouth of the barrel, near the village of Umbare. There the barrel runs south along the eastern face of the hill. It is here that it gets partially blocked by this hill in the front. One has to negotiate through a very narrow trail to go westwards towards the Konkan,' Naik replies.

'How much time do we have?' Shivaji asks.

'Three days,' Naik answers, then lowers his voice, 'I have heard that a female warrior is accompanying Kartalab.'

2

Three days and three nights later, Kartalab Khan has finally reached Kurvanda along with his twenty thousand infantry and cavalrymen. He is the commanding officer of the military expedition called the 'North Konkan', to get back what is captured by Shivaji. He, for the first time, leads several contingents commanded by military heavyweights like Kachwah, Chauhan, Amar Singh, Mitrasen, Sarjera Ghadege, Kokate and Jadhavrao. Amongst them is one Savitri bai, titled Rai Baghan, the royal tigress, a Maratha woman who, after the death of her husband, was made a mansabdar by Aurangzeb.

Kartalab's horse stands at the edge of the plateau perched above the slopes plunging into ravines. It is the beginning of the Kurvanda Pass, never used by a military cavalcade before. He has spent a lot of time studying the maps of the region, and knows that to reach the coastal Konkan from Desh, the mountain plateau, one has to cross the ghats, the difficult mountain trails. One has to reach the western edge of the Sahyadri Range, roughly half a kos above sea level, and then descend. The entire expanse is craggy and broken, covered with enormous hills, thick forests and riverbeds. The trails going downhill are just narrow paths or defiles and so steep that horses, even the light cavalry warhorses, find it difficult to keep their footing. Sometimes, it is impossible to reach the high point of these passes from where the descent starts because one has to travel through nearly impassable jungle growth on the mountain plateau. Kartalab had considered some options and was left with just two choices— either Borghat or Kurvanda Pass—and he had chosen Kurvanda for many reasons. For one, it is relatively easier to reach the place and it is not riddled with hills. The downhill journey from there is not steep or abrupt, but steady at a thirty-degree angle all through till one reaches a tiny hamlet called Chavani, and there is enough space for his army to camp and rest there. He has first steered his cavalcade in the direction of Borghat to fool the Marathas and then abruptly turned towards Kurvanda.

The Mughal cavalcade led by Kartalab Khan is on the move.

About a hundred or more Mughal slaves have remained busy clearing the path by hacking the nettles and thorny shrubs with saws and machetes. Kartalab steers his horse more towards the edge. The curious animal looks down into the valley and panics; it rears and neighs loudly. Kartalab swiftly leans forward and gently pulls back the reins with one hand and rubs the animal's neck with another.

The good warhorse calms down quickly as its master stares at the peaks that rise far above the emerald slopes covered with woods. In the light of the rising sun, the summits look like rocky snake hoods. Below them, over the slopes, the mountain trails meander across the girth of the hills. The world before Kartalab Khan is alive with cascading waterfalls, languidly grazing cattle, darting monkeys and resonant birdcalls. He whistles cheerfully as the cold winter wind brushes past him. This is a new beginning for him, opening doors of wealth he could have never imagined in the past. Behind him, thousands of armoured infantrymen wearing round metal helmets pass by. They look carefree and fearless, occasionally chuckling over some private gag. A detachment of heavy cavalry follows. More than five thousand Abyssinian slaves in soiled clothes trudge along carrying metal trunks stuffed with grains and weapons over their heads. Before he advances ahead, he looks back and sees a long line of mena-palanquins covered with colourful curtains. These are carrying his and his officers' families. Beyond them are some more oxen carts, heavily guarded by his expert archers and swordsmen. Those carts carry sacks of gold and silver coins, the funds generously granted to him for this operation.

The Mughal army's descent has started and Kartalab is alert. A few thousand of his infantrymen are good archers. They walk watching every cliff and every tree for any suspicious movement, but there is none. The sound of 'hah hah' when the cart drivers guide their oxen, along with the calls of the orioles, mynah, woodpeckers and many other birds has filled the air which smells of strange herbs. The Mughal men not used to the mountains have started feeling tired. As they go downhill, closer to sea level, the weather has gradually turned humid and warm. The Abyssinian slaves carrying large trunks over their heads drenched in their own sweat have already finished their stock of drinking water and there is nothing available on the way.

They arrive at Chavani in the afternoon. The oxen dragging the carts have started panting and the horses are disoriented. The sun is now directly overhead. Kartalab Khan has decided to camp near the village of Umbare; there they have some hope of getting water for the thirsty men and animals. The river Amba does run parallel to the barrel-like path that lies ahead but it is almost dry. The region looks serene.

Within a few hours, Kartalab decides to start the journey through the pass. The cavalcade will go ahead, and he, his guards and Rai Baghan will follow.

The battle formations of the Marathas are planned. After reaching the mountainous region near Umbarkhind, Shivaji, Palkar and a few hundred horsemen wait in ambush hiding in the thicket growing on the slopes of a hill near Umbare, near the mouth of the barrel. A few thousand Maratha archers have climbed the hills hovering over Umbarkhind and are hiding behind boulders or tree trunks. Shivaji's infantrymen armed with muskets and stones have climbed trees. Some of them also have drums and mallets. Further up, Mhadu hides in the bushes covering the slopes. He has waited for the right moment for almost two hours as hyperactive squirrels run around him and noisy monkeys jump on the branches looming above him, their alarm cries echoing in the air. He watches till the entire Mughal cavalcade has entered the barrel.

Mhadu whistles piercingly and repeatedly.

The whistle is heard by the Maratha drummers who have been hiding in the woods growing on the hills looking down on the path. They start beating their drums with heavy mallets. The ominous sound breaks the silence of the forest, declaring someone's doom. Thousands of birds fly skywards, shrieking with fear. Kartalab Khan who along with Rai Baghan is waiting at Chavani to oversee the safe entry of his cavalcade into the narrow path freezes in shock and horror.

Within moments, the branches looming over the chasm come alive with several thousand archers. As the Mughal soldiers look above they can see a cloud of arrows raining from the hills looming over them and the Mughals start dropping dead on the ground like flies. It takes a few moments for Kartalab to realize that he has made a terrible mistake—he has led his men into a trap! A few hundred footmen start stretching their bows to shoot the hiding Maratha archers but fail to see anyone. The forest looming over the slopes looks deceptively lush and peaceful but the arrows keep flying from behind the curtained canopies of trees rising over the hills, targeting their throats and limbs not covered with armour. There is a stampede as the slaves drop their luggage and try to escape. Seeing them run, even the drivers abandon their carts and flee westwards or eastwards and so do the palanquin bearers. Some run on the dry riverbed and each one is shot dead by the arrows dropping from the sky! Hundreds of cannon lie forlorn on the lonely carts along with the drums of explosives, unused and forgotten. Kartalab's horsemen remain trapped in the middle, their armoured horses buckling with panic. The palanquins lie on the ground unattended, with women and children shrieking and howling in fear. From both sides the track is blocked by Shivaji's men.

Rai Baghan watches the battle with her mouth open and realizes that they both too are the targets.

'We need to surrender,' she raises her voice for the first time, 'else everyone will die.'

'Will they spare our lives then?' Kartalab's voice breaks with fear.

'We must try; I have heard Shivaji never harms women,' Rai Baghan says loudly.

Kartalab stares at the fully armoured woman mounted on a white horse, not knowing if she is earnest or sarcastic. He hesitates, but seeing the fear in her eyes he dismounts and runs to order his bodyguards to wave white flags. The guards run around while dodging the hail of arrows, stones and ammunition fired from muskets to find the cloth and find large trunks left unattended by the slaves covered with white cloth used for packaging. They tear the cloth away, tie the pieces to their javelins and hold them high in the air. As the flags flutter, the arrows stop abruptly. The trapped men stand without even an inch to move in any direction. As moments dissolve into hours, night falls over them like a dark and cold miasma from hell. As time goes by, each moment brings more anxiety, more thrust and more hunger. The Mughals spend the night squatting on the uneven ground, sticking to each other, as countless lie dead around them. The injured writhe in pain and some silently bleed to death.

As the first rays of the morning sun hit Chavani, someone shouts for Kartalab Khan, who has closed his eyes with anguish for a few minutes. He opens his eyes to see the drained faces of his guards, and reality falls on him like Destiny's axe.

'We have to go; a message has arrived,' he hears Rai Baghan shouting.

He drags himself, mounts his horse and follows his guards through the pass. When he sees the men lying dead and injured, he realizes the seriousness of the event. As bitter bile froths in his mouth, Kartalab Khan, with his bladder full, rides limb and spiritless till he notices the hill near Umbare. At its foothills he can see a group of men waiting for them. As they draw close, he stares at the man sitting on a white horse, clad in armour and a golden helmet. A scabbard hangs from his belt; he holds a long trident in his right hand and is surrounded by archers holding long bows.

Kartalab does not want to negotiate; he has had enough. He jumps down from his horse and falls to his knees. Rai Baghan who has been following him does the same.

'Mercy, please show mercy,' Rai Baghan shouts kneeling. Shivaji watches the tall Maratha woman dressed as a soldier and smiles. The woman has guts, while Kartalab is using her as his shield.

'If you leave all your luggage, war animals, weapons, money and carts loaded with cannon in the chasm, we will let you, your men, your slaves and your families go alive,' Shivaji replies.

'As you ordain,' Kartalab replies, without bothering to look up.

Soon the Mughal army's return journey begins, this time without the horses, carts and luggage that have been left behind for Shivaji.

3

A sprawling hill looms over Gwalior. Perched on it, the fort of fine palaces, sparkling ponds and lush gardens looks misleadingly graceful. Below these grand palaces is the murky world of circular dungeons stuffed with men awaiting death by opium. The fort is shut in behind a solid, almost unbeatable, yet ornate, wall made of sandstone. It rises solemnly above the steeply hanging cliffs, as if to hide the unspeakable state of the enemies of the empire rotting in its belly. Around the hill rises the city's skyline silhouetted by bulbous domes, temple spires, minarets, watchtowers and cupolas. The structures hover above the dwellings, mosques and the tombs of the famous and rich men. As the sun sets, the city surrenders to the darkness flooding the foothills. Above the hill, inside the fort, numerous courtyards near the palaces and ponds are lit by torches placed in iron baskets hung on the walls. Long shadows of pillars and arches tremble on the floor of the patios covered with coloured tiles. Aurangzeb walks past the prison sentries and then through the dimly lit staircase leading to the underground vaults. Dara bhai is dead, his son Suleiman is imprisoned and is completely addicted to opium, the vanquished Shuja bhai and his son Bulund are being chased by the victorious Mir Jumla, while Murad is imprisoned and is at Aurangzeb's mercy. But everything is not as smooth as it seems. He has just received a message from the Deccan about Kartalab Khan's miserable defeat. The victorious Shivaji has, along with thousands of infantrymen and a few squadrons of cavalrymen, come down to the coast and marched southwards, moving rapidly, capturing city after city. The ferocity and greed of the Marathas has spread terror. Nizampur, a few miles east of Janjira Fort, has been raided, the port of Dabhol captured. The Muslim subhedar of Sangameshwar has fled and the region between Kalyan and Goa is in disorder. The jagirdars and subhedars of the Adilshahi sultanate whom the region belongs to have either fled or have shamelessly offered help and tribute to the bloody rebel! It is time to wipe out the Shia kingdoms of the Deccan who are allowing the rise of a kafir.

A disturbed Aurangzeb has changed his mind. Instead of going straight to see Suleiman Shikoh's cell, he intends to stop by to meet Muhammad Sultan who had been brought here a few months ago.

Sultan gets up hurriedly and leaps towards the bars, staring hard into his father's eyes to see any promise of freedom, but there is none. Aurangzeb stares back at his son with regret.

'Abba jaan . . .' Sultan's young voice quivers with hope.

Aurangzeb looks down at his son with pity. The young man who not so long ago was so charming and confident has now turned into a wreck. His skin has darkened and his eyes have sunk deep into his face. His unkempt tresses have grown wild, and his face is covered with an unkempt beard.

'Abba jaan,' the twenty-something prince tries to say something but the words do not come out; instead, they fill the young man's chest, causing physical pain. 'You have forgiven Maharaja Jaswant Singh Rathod who has committed treason but you have not forgiven me, your own son,' he says resentfully.

'An artist will come to draw your face. Your mother does not believe that you are alive; she wants to see your picture,' Aurangzeb says formally and moves on, followed by the wooden-faced jailers. He takes another staircase down that leads to the underground dungeons and is forced to hold his shawl over his nose, for the stench is nauseating. Only a single torch burns into a tunnel-like corridor that seems to disappear into the darkness. He crosses several barred cells packed with men. At the end of the tunnel he stops and strains his eyes to look into the smallest dungeon that looks more like an animal trap.

There is someone or something in there.

Whoever that is, is just a skeleton, half-naked. His face looks as if vultures have pecked away at the flesh from the bones. Aurangzeb somehow recognizes him; in fact, he had come all the way to make sure that Suleiman Shikoh, the eldest son of Dara Shikoh and the most handsome young man from the first family of Hindustan, is dying. Suleiman's golden mane has been reduced to a few strands of hair stuck together by filth. They look like horns sticking out from the top of his head. His body is covered with his own waste. The place is filled with a stench that burns Aurangzeb's nostrils.

From the depths of darkness, two burning eyes bore into Aurangzeb; there is nothing human about the creature that lies behind the bars. Still, the new emperor feels that those eyes are throwing questions at him: *Uncle, why did you lie when you said that you would not feed me the poppy drink?*

Without warning, Suleiman starts laughing like a deranged man. The sound of his crazy laughter rattles through the dark corridors of Gwalior Fort. Aurangzeb does not want to stay there any longer; the sound of laughter, the stench, the damp darkness and the soot from the torches hung on the blackened walls suffocate him.

4

Shaista Khan has shifted his base back to Pune after taking over Chakan. He regards Jaffar Khan, his sister's husband, the new wazir of the empire, who has travelled all the way from Dilli to meet him, or more correctly, to inquire. *I must deal cleverly with the grand wazir*, Shaista Khan thinks, and relaxes by sliding his body forward on his gilded, carved chair, putting his feet on the cushioned footrest. It is winter, and despite the heavily draped windows it is cold in the assembly chamber of the Lal Mahal. However, more than the cold, the inquiry against him has dampened his spirit. His nephew-turned-emperor, Aurangzeb, has already asked Jaswant Singh and his Rajputs to besiege Kondana Fort, and now Jaffar Khan is here to probe.

'The region is already ours,' Shaista Khan says, holding the hookah with his left hand and waving his right one flashing his rings.

'Khalisa or not, the region has been flattened for sure, but the failed Konkan expedition has cost millions and the hill forts remain untouched,' Jaffar Khan mutters as politely as possible. His sons Namdar Khan and Kamdar Khan have been assigned to help Shaista Khan and he does not want to offend the new master.

'We win some and lose some. We have captured Parinda Fort!' Shaista Khan asserts himself.

Jaffar Khan smiles discreetly. Parinda Fort does not belong to Shivaji. It is in the Adilshahi kingdom. Shaista Khan has neither won the fort by besiegement nor taken it by force but has paid a heavy bribe to the fort commander to vacate and flee.

Shaista Khan knows what the grand wazir is thinking but stares nonchalantly at the immaculately attired man sitting very properly on the chair. Jaffar Khan is a man who always believed in politically correct behaviour and is far from being assertive. The mild gentleman who loves to drink a few pegs every night before retiring is totally clueless about battles and wars.

'I have lost a thousand men in the battle for Chakan and that fort is at ground level. Hill forts in this region are impossible to capture, and if we try, countless lives will be lost,' Shaista Khan says sternly, his voice asserting his status as the Mughal general. Then he claps his hands announcing the end of the discussion.

Jaffar Khan blinks. He has seen enough after he arrived here a few days ago. He had been warned about Shaista Khan's conduct. It is obvious that Shaista is living the life of a king. His letters of promises sent to the emperor are full of lofty lies. His new residence was previously Shivaji's modest residence. Now, with renovations, refurbishing and extra staff at the cost of more than half a million rupees, it has become an opulent palace. Satin curtains are hung over the windows, the glass urns are replaced with elaborate chandeliers, the rooms are furnished with stately couches and larger beds covered with soft linen seen only in the apartments of Agra Fort. Jaffar Khan has already decided that he will not be swayed by anything, *anything*, and his report to the emperor will contain only the truth. His loyal thoughts are broken when two eunuchs bring a young girl into the chamber. Jaffar Khan glances at her—the girl wears a long and flowing skirt with gold brocade and a very finely cut jacket. A sparkling tiara is placed on her head from which falls a soft veil of a translucent muslin cloth. She boldly leaves behind the eunuch accompanying her and moves forward alone. Jaffar Khan gathers his wits as she approaches him; something in her gait says that she is someone special.

Shaista Khan too straightens up and announces, 'She is Pari Begum.'

Jaffar Khan is surprised. He has heard of Pari, the girl born to Shaista's fourth wife from Persia. The girl memorized the holy Quran at the tender age of six. It is said that she has inherited the beauty of her grand-aunt, Nur Jahan. Jaffar Khan caresses his well-groomed beard nervously and wonders why the girl has been presented to him in such an officious manner.

'By the grace of Allah, I intend to offer Pari Begum to your son Namdar in marriage. I want her to be your daughter-in-law,' Shaista Khan says rather loudly while getting up from his chair and throwing both his hands in the air.

Jaffar Khan nods vigorously, barely concealing his smile. It is too good an offer to refuse.

Within days, the royal astrologer springs into action and the date for the wedding ceremony is fixed. On the night of the wedding, Shaista Khan's sons go to Namdar's shamiana and conduct him to the Lal Mahal. He is given a special turban to wear, with strings of pearls, diamonds and rubies falling over his face. In the presence of Shaista Khan and Jaffar Khan, a qazi unites the young pair in wedlock. The bride wears so much jewellery that her slight frame is bent by its weight. For many nights after the wedding, the sky above Pune is lit by fireworks. Jaffar Khan is so overwhelmed that he has nearly forgotten the main purpose of his Deccan visit. When he remembers it, he sends his newly wed son to meet his father-in-law.

'Abba jaan, if you give me ten thousand light cavalry, I will start taking over the surrounding hill forts. Once Rajgad, Kondana, Torana and Purandar fall into our hands, the region will truly be called Mughal territory,' Namdar says earnestly.

Shaista Khan, who stands in the balcony of his bedroom overlooking the Mutha river, ponders for a while and says philosophically, 'There are two ways to fight a war: one is to totally destroy the enemy, annihilate him, and the other is to exhaust the enemy slowly and bring him to his knees.' He pauses, looks at Namdar and continues, 'This terrain makes it difficult to adopt the first strategy. If we eliminate Shivaji and take over his hill forts, what will happen next?'

Namdar looks puzzled.

'You are still new to politics. Consider for a moment that we have indeed succeeded in driving away Shivaji from his hill forts and imagine our fort-keepers and garrisons on those invincible, unreachable military strongholds. What would that mean?' The older man challenges the younger one with a smile.

Namdar is unable to answer.

'The Deccan is crucial. The new emperor is keen to take over nearby kingdoms. Once he has these hill forts, he will bring one of his own sons as a subhedar of the Deccan. Prince Muazzam, Muhammad Sultan's younger brother, is already eyeing the position. Where do you think we will go then?'

Namdar has not thought of such possibilities, buried so deep in the future.

'The climate here is good, not too cold and not too hot. The presence of our large army is enough to ruin the economy of the country. Our raiders are successful in plundering most of the mountainous region. The time will come when Shivaji will have no other alternative but to surrender to us, maybe after a year or two years or even three years. We will win the hill forts without bloodshed.'

'But we will have to wait and wait!' Namdar argues, a part of him ready to go to battle.

'Over-achievement is risky for us,' Shaista Khan is talking in riddles.

'Meaning?'

'Consider . . . If we do take over a couple of hill forts in quick succession and capture Shivaji, what may happen then? There is a possibility that the new emperor will regard us in high esteem in matters of the military and send us where the trouble is. Take, for example, Mir Jumla: he is a fine military general but is chasing Shahzaada Shuja all over the wretched land of Bengal and Arakan. Allah alone knows if he will ever come back alive.'

Namdar is quick to understand and quips, 'Then we may be sent to Peshawar, and get caught between the Persian army and the radical tribals.'

'My boy, sometimes it is better not to win or lose. For now, maintaining status quo is a wise political move,' Shaista Khan's philosophy is new, but his son-in-law understands it.

'Son, the holy month of Ramadan will soon be upon us. You and your young wife start thinking about iftar. You will have to feed your family and friends, who will break their fast with you,' the father-in-law advises indulgently and says, 'Instead of the hill forts, after Ramadan, you can march to the Konkan, but unlike Kartalab, send your army in small batches. Here, around Pune, we will find out ways to hunt for the villagers who have run away into the nearby jungles. Torturing, capturing or killing them may bring Shivaji out in the open.'

Soft targets, Namdar thinks, and admires his father-in-law's intelligence.

CHAPTER TWENTY-THREE

1

The diwan-e-khaas is crowded. Aurangzeb, in a kimoush headgear embellished with emeralds and a serpech made of gold and diamonds, sits on the peacock throne. His sons who have come of age, Muazzam from Nawab bai and Azam from Dilras Banu, stand to his right, while the ulemas, sayyids, mansabdars, mullahs and qazis stand to his left. The umrahs stand in the front rows, their positions strictly as per their ranks. Jaffar Khan, the wazir-e-azam of the empire, is seen near the gold railing that separates the emperor from others and just behind him.

Mir Jumla's son, Mohammad Amin, the new mir bakshi, stands smiling from ear to ear for reasons only known to him. Behind him three orthodox noblemen, Ali Mardan, Sayyid Miran and Sadulla Khan stand along with Mullah Qawi, the chief qazi, or chief justice, of the empire. All of them wear a severe expression as if a calamity has struck the empire. Something is sloshing in their minds; the air is heavy with anticipation.

Qawi speaks first, his voice severe, 'Alamgir, this shameless man calls himself a fakir, roams naked in Dilli and incites poor and pious Muslims.'

'La ilaha illa'llah! Mohammadur rasool'ullah . . .' Aurangzeb murmurs the *kalma* while counting his tesbih beads. There is no God except Allah, and Prophet Mohammad, peace be upon him, is his messenger.

Aurangzeb has his own intelligence network. After proclaiming himself as the emperor, he has been extra cautious. He is keen to know what people say about him and who still sympathize with his dead or imprisoned or absconding brothers. He does not want a civil war to break out and has nipped many a trouble in the bud by sending hundreds of liberal Muslims to the gallows, by killing an equal number of kafirs under the feet of trained elephants, by slaying Dara bhai's sympathizers and making it look like a kill-to-gain robbery and by bribing countless Muslim clergy and Hindu priests to quieten them.

He is surprised to know that people have been gossiping about his recent marriage to Udepuri even though the wedding was a low-key affair. His spies tell him everything and they have told him about this man called Sarmad, born in Persia, or Armenia, to Jewish parents. He studied his ancestral religion and became a rabbi, thereafter went deep into the philosophy of Sufism and converted to Islam to become a Sufi and translated sections of the Hebrew Bible into Farsi. A few years ago, he had travelled to Hindustan and stayed put. Spies tell Aurangzeb that he is also into Hinduism and roams about without clothes and is known as the *nanga fakir*! This naked ascetic has thousands and thousands of followers. He had even reached the precincts of Agra Fort and Dara bhai had regarded him as his guru!

Qawi has heard Aurangzeb recite the kalma. He remembers something, 'The naked man tells people to say only half of what you have said, and insists that it is true that there is no God except Allah, but Prophet Muhammad, peace be upon him, is not the last paigambar.' The chief justice is shaking with anger.

Aurangzeb listens stoically. He had called the people for some other reason but the subject of Sarmad has suddenly become the topic of prime interest.

'What does he want to imply?' Aurangzeb asks with slight irritation, counting his beads.

Qawi caresses his long, peppery beard, hesitates for a moment and drops a granado, 'Sarmad says he too is a prophet.'

A roar breaks out in the diwan-e-khaas; some clergy start shaking their heads in disbelief as others put their hands on their mouths. All eyes dart towards Emperor Aurangzeb. His only reaction is that he has stopped counting his beads and there is amusement in his eyes. This fakir was Dara bhai's guru who made Dara bhai believe in the supernatural powers of Sufism. The guru also encouraged Aurangzeb's father to make the Mughal court a platform for debates on religions, allowing the Hindu pundits, the Sufi saints and the Zoroastrian scholars exchange blasphemous and profane ideas. Aurangzeb has heard that the ignorant fools had even compared

Hindu scriptures and the holy Quran and had spent weeks and months discussing the defunct philosophies of Aristotle and Plato. Their intellectual deliberations were nicknamed as 'intellectual masturbation' by Aurangzeb, since the discussions were as useless, as shameful and as unproductive. Dara bhai had taken Sarmad's blessings before he left to fight Aurangzeb near Agra. Sarmad had pompously declared that Dara Shikoh would win and become the next emperor. So much for his prophetic vision!

Qawi takes the cue, adjusts his skullcap, raises both his hands in the air and says, 'Alamgir, pardon me, but allow me to say something downright repulsive that may break the etiquette of your esteemed court.'

'Say it,' the emperor commands.

'This naked fakir is going about with a beautiful kafir boy,' Qawi hesitates again, swallows hard and marches on with his words, 'These two, the naked Muslim fakir and the beautiful kafir boy, hug and kiss each other in public places. A few days ago, they displayed their perversion in the middle of Chandni Chowk.' Qawi wipes his forehead and continues, 'I do not want to say the word that is given to this sort of a relationship and you are wise, *Parvardigar*.' Qawi has addressed his emperor as Parvardigar, a name metaphorically used for God in Farsi, on purpose.

'Is he a homosexual?' Jaffar Khan blurts and then bites his tongue. He has committed a faux pas, uttered banned words unwittingly and broken the court etiquette!

There is uproar in the court.

Aurangzeb's sharp gaze cuts through the rows of people standing before him. The noise subsides quickly and most cast their eyes down.

'We should have put him behind bars for performing an immoral act in public,' Aurangzeb snaps.

'We have,' Qawi says. 'He is here, in a cell at Salimgad; the matter now rests in your hands, my Padishah.'

'This matter is trivial,' Jaffar Khan butts in while his wrinkled face winces with annoyance, 'this does not require the emperor's attention.'

'I will see him today,' Aurangzeb cuts off a red-faced Jaffar Khan, 'but before that I need to discuss another, more urgent matter.'

Saying this, Aurangzeb starts counting the beads, his lips are moving too. For a few moments the court is utterly silent. Aurangzeb signals Sadulla Khan, who knows what has to be done and will do it as effectively and as humanely as possible. He is forever indebted to Aurangzeb with whom, in childhood, he had studied the holy Quran. They had spent their adolescent years together and he was the one who had consoled Aurangzeb when the young prince had lost his mother. Aurangzeb too was fond of him and recognized his intelligence.

Sadulla clears his throat and starts in an officious manner, 'The case of late Ali Naqi, the previous mir bakshi of Gujarat, who was assassinated in the court of Gujarat in front of fifty witnesses by none other than Shahzaada Murad Baksh, who was then the subhedar of Gujarat, in a state of inebriation, has been re-opened. The late Ali Naqi's son, Aslam Naqi, has filed a petition in sharia court and has demanded justice.'

The men in the courtroom are stunned; the case is to prove that Murad Baksh, the fourth prince, is a murderer, a criminal.

'What kind of punishment does this sort of a crime demand?' Aurangzeb asks, looking at Qawi with a blasé expression.

Qawi is totally unprepared for this question. His face turns pale and his lips quiver.

'You may deliberate later, consider circumstances and motives and weigh your options to come to the final conclusion whether this crime deserves capital punishment or a more lenient sentence, but give me some clue. What does our law say if a sane man kills another man?' Aurangzeb sounds calm and casual.

'While, after death, there is profound punishment waiting at the hands of God, there is also room for retribution on earth,' Qawi says, wetting his lips with his tongue. He has no other option.

Sayyid Miran raises his hand; he wants to say something. He too has been a victim of Dara Shikoh's fury and it was Aurangzeb who shielded him.

'Speak, Miran bhai, speak from the heart.'

'As per the witnesses, the plan was already hatched to kill Ali Naqi, the strict paymaster general of Gujarat, because he always asked Shahzaada Murad Baksh for accounts and put a cap on his vast spending. The sycophants of Gujarat court, who wanted money to feed their luxurious life, had instigated the prince and devised a fool-proof plan. This makes the crime "a deliberate or intentional murder" and demands death either by beheading or by a firing squad or by hanging or stoning till death.'

Everyone in the court turns into a statue, not moving, not batting an eyelid, and some, it seems, have even stopped breathing. They know Murad Baksh had helped Aurangzeb win the battle of Samugad against Dara Shikoh!

Qawi nods vigorously. What else can he do?

'You may bring the fakir now,' Aurangzeb announces for he does not want to waste time. More time, and courtiers will start thinking about Murad. By sheer luck, the fakir is in Salimgad, just a few blocks away.

'He is totally naked,' Qawi mutters.

'Bring him nonetheless!' Aurangzeb orders.

Qawi signals a guard who stands a few feet away. Meanwhile, the usual court proceedings start. Newly appointed mansabdars are called to pay their respects and tributes like silver and gold coins, by first performing kurnish.

When the naked fakir is brought in with two eunuch guards holding his arms, there is much confusion around. All eyes dart towards the new arrival. The man is big, hairy, bull-necked, dusky and stark naked.

He is placed in front of the throne as if he is an object. Fakir Sarmad seems nonchalant.

Aurangzeb has seen enough. He calls out, 'Danishmand Khan, please come forward.'

Danishmand, previously a Dara Shikoh loyalist, is a scholar of religions. A well-read and well-mannered man, he has become Aurangzeb's favourite. Dressed in a brocaded jama and a turban laden with precious stones, he comes forward, his well-trimmed beard a testimony of his slightly liberal views on religion.

'Ask him, Danishmand, why he is naked.'

The question is asked.

'Because I have nothing to hide,' the fakir replies in a childlike manner. Then he counter-questions, 'Does the sky book say that clothes are compulsory for humans?'

Cross-questioning the emperor is not acceptable and is against the protocol of court etiquette. It is a crime. Also, Aurangzeb does not like the way Sarmad has referred to the holy Quran, but he does not say anything about it at least then.

'Danishmand, ask him why does he recite only half the kalma,' Aurangzeb interrogates. The question is put forward to the defender.

'I believe in La ilaha illa'llah, meaning there is no God but Allah. But I do not believe in the suggestion that Prophet Muhammad is the last paigambar because it means the end of the road for any religion, including Islam, making it stagnant with no room to evolve, no new ideas to keep pace with emerging new worlds and no new messengers to show newer paths.'

'Parvardigar, I cannot hear any more heretical words from this profane and ignorant man. He is insulting Islam!' Qawi shouts.

'The fakir is not merely a mad, naked and uncouth man; he is also a vicious and shrewd shaitan, an enemy of Islam. This man claims to be a Muslim, but his heart seems to be full of hatred towards Islam. *Towbaa towbaa!*' Qawi is slapping his cheeks in disgust. 'It is better that I die before I hear any more nonsense. This man should be hanged.'

'Why am I bothering the Qazi? What does it say about a man of justice who quickly forms his opinions without investigating? Can a man of justice afford to be biased? He, the chief Qazi, is a scholar of law and must know that the truth is not always what it seems but in most of the cases it is hidden, like now it hides in my heart! The Qazi is assassinating my character without proof. Isn't that a crime?' The fakir thinks aloud, caressing his head covered with unruly hair.

A faint wave of laughter ripples through the courtroom.

'Qazi Sahib, you have given the matter in my hands and I must thoroughly investigate before I pronounce the punishment. I cannot hang a man just because he roams about naked; there are millions like him out there. The holy places are full of such men,' Aurangzeb says firmly and diverts his gaze toward the fakir and thinks, *I must ask such questions that the answers will be a solid proof of treason and apostasy; everything must be done within the precincts of law.*

After a few moments, Aurangzeb says, 'I will ask you a direct question, so pay attention, think and answer. We believe that the honest, merciful, just, truthful, compassionate, brave, the last and the greatest prophet Muhammad, peace be upon him, has gone straight to heaven. The truth, Fakir Sahib, is that the Prophet Muhammad, may the blessings of Allah be upon him, was also a reformer and a revolutionary. He established Islam and opened the eyes of the world wrapped in defunct ideologies. What do you have to say about our belief and faith?'

'Aurangzeb,' he addresses the emperor by his first name, which itself is a crime as per court etiquette, and continues, 'you are wisest among the wise and you know philosophies of religions and their effects on the minds of people more than most. Your eyes are the sharpest among all the eyes present here and no one can see through the religions as clearly as you do. Since you have asked, your belief that the Prophet Muhammad went straight to the heavens and straight to Allah itself is a childish thought.'

'Etiquette! Mind your tongue, you are talking to the emperor!' Jaffar Khan shouts, his voice rising above the roar of people around who are now roused and angry.

'Wazir-e-azam, do not lose your cool. At least now we can detain him for insulting the emperor,' Aurangzeb says smiling.

'Explain why you call the thought childish,' Aurangzeb asks the fakir softly, giving more importance to the word 'thought'.

Sarmad is quicker than a striking snake, 'Do not be so naïve, Aurangzeb. Why did Prophet Muhammad have to die, go to heaven and then meet Allah when Allah was in his heart, from womb to tomb?'

The mullahs, the sayyids, the ulemas and the qazis have started shivering with rage. Qawi is clenching his teeth, but the emperor does not show any expression of anger; he has some more questions. Answering those will surely open the doors of gallows for Sarmad. He dismisses the argument with the wave of his hand.

'Who are you? What religion do you follow?'

'I am a human first and then a Muslim sayyid, a Sufi saint, a priest, a Jewish rabbi, Zoroastrian fire-keeper, a gurdwara granthi, and am also aspiring to be a Buddhist monk. I have a deeper faith than all the people present here including you, Aurangzeb, and allow me to quote a verse of mine as a parting gift,' the fakir stops, raises both his hands and sings in a sweet voice.

A true lover-of-God
Is misled by religions
And also lack of true faith
What a paradox!
When a moth burns itself
It does not choose from a candle
And it never asks
If it is burning in a mosque or a temple
This proof is ample.

The fakir stops singing. There is pin-drop silence in the court for a while.

'Who is the kafir boy you are going around with and what is your relationship with him?' Aurangzeb questions sardonically, neither praising nor condemning the fakir's verse. There are other important things on his mind. If the fakir admits to homosexuality, he must be stoned to death as per the sharia law.

'If you are talking about Abhaychand, he is one of my students as far as Hebrew and Farsi languages are concerned and he is also my guru as far as philosophies of Hinduism are concerned. Our love is the love between a student and teacher and there is nothing wrong to hug a student with affection or plant a kiss on a teacher's forehead with reverence. I have relationship only with God and I make love only to life, if that is what you are thinking. And if I had a sexual relationship with the boy I would have admitted it. For me, even that love is sacred, as long as it is love and not hate, as long as it gives pleasure, not pain, as long as it is consensual and not rape.'

People in the court do not know what expression they must show. All cast their eyes down.

Aurangzeb does not want to prolong the case any longer, so he asks, 'Before the clergy come to a decision, do you want to say anything in your defence?'

'Why should I defend myself when I have not committed any offence? Remember, Aurangzeb, the idea of true religion is not differentiating between a mosque or a temple, a church, a synagogue, a Buddhist cave or a gurdwara. Finally it is *fanaa*, the end of our egos and recognition of the presence of the Almighty in all living beings including ourselves.'

Aurangzeb smells the true threat then. The man is fearless and has the courage to speak what he thinks is the truth, and if he is left free he may create thousands of followers having potential to think logically, argue fearlessly and rebel against Aurangzeb's ideology. He does not look at Sarmad again; instead, he glances at Qawi and says, 'Qazi Sahib, please discuss the matter with others and give me your verdict here and now.'

The verdict is delivered by Qawi within moments, 'Fakir Sarmad has broken the etiquettes of the court by uttering inappropriate words and he has shown disrespect to the emperor who is next only to God. For these crimes, we announce ten years rigorous imprisonment. Fakir Sarmad has committed apostasy by insisting that Prophet Muhammad, peace be upon him, is not the last prophet, and has admitted that he supports one man's physical love for another man. Both these crimes belong to the category of spreading mischief in the land and demand capital punishment as per the teachings of Hadith and sharia law. Sarmad must be hanged to death.'

Aurangzeb raises his hand that holds the tesbih beads and says, 'La ilaha illa'llah! Mohammadur rasool'ullah!' He then recites a verse from the sky book, 'Take not life that is made sacred by God, except by way of justice and law, so you may learn wisdom.'

Fakir Sarmad laughs aloud.

While getting down from the throne that afternoon, Aurangzeb thinks of the trials of Dara bhai and Suleiman that had taken place in diwan-e-khaas. He just wonders if he will ever meet Shivaji here and see him standing in front of the throne, helpless and vulnerable, and in a flash Aurangzeb knows that it is bound to happen one day.

2

It is the fag end of winter, but the morning mist still lingers on in the air like some reluctant soldier not leaving the battlefield long after the battle is over. Through the thin curtain of mist, the Sahyadri Mountains look like confused war mammoths left behind by their fleeing mahouts. Their cover of green forest broken by bits of barren rocks resembles the lacerations caused by enemy javelins. Unconcerned about the surroundings, Namdar Khan and his ten thousand horsemen gallop in the direction of Kurvanda Pass, leaving behind clouds of smoke emitted from a hundred burning villages set on fire. His squadrons have killed or captured hundreds of villagers, and taken cattle and food grain stuffed in the barns. The spoils of war are on their way to Pune. 'Have no mercy, these people need to be killed, burnt or enslaved, for they have played a major role in the miserable defeat of Kartalab Khan, by giving Shivaji's men crucial information about our movements. Each one of them is a bloody scout and eager to spy on us,' the words of his father-in-law ring in his ears. His next targets are the villages at the foothills of Lohagad.

The sun has moved towards the centre of the sky when Namdar and his horsemen reach Lonavala village. Some of the horsemen have dismounted and are scampering about to inspect homes, drag people out and slay them, but each time they come out empty-handed, looking puzzled. Some of them have torches in their hands and many of the hovels have started burning. Namdar dismounts. He too is confused, because there is no sound of the wailing of women or crying of children. He walks across a small open space in the middle of Lonavala as canopies of pipal and banyan trees sway over a lone well. The hovels are vacant, the sheds have no cattle and the barns have been emptied. Only a few stray dogs howl at the entrances of the narrow lanes cutting through the mud homes as the dusty wind whirls across the empty village.

Namdar feels his sense of glee dwindle and fade as he walks from one hovel to another—nobody to kill or capture, nothing left to plunder. Many of his mansabdars dismount and group together to inspect. They watch him and shift uncomfortably, uncertain of what must be done next. The awkward silence is broken by the sound of hooves. Some scouts have arrived after inspecting the nearby valley. One of them dismounts and runs towards Namdar yelling, 'All the villages ahead are deserted; the villagers have taken their cattle, grain and have fled and are hiding in the hills.'

Namdar remains silent for a while. This operation was a sudden decision. Till about a day before, only his general and he had discussed it, known about it. Then how did they get to know about it? Perhaps the people who had managed to escape from the villages already ruined must have travelled through the forests to alert people living in this area. However, there is no time to think, he wants to beat them at their own game. And who is there to stop him? He knows that even though the nearby forts of Lohagad and Visapur are with Shivaji, the Maratha garrisons on those are small and Shivaji is away in the Konkan. The Maratha garrisons can defend the fort if attacked but cannot afford to come down and face his ten thousand horsemen.

'We shall camp here, get some firewood and catch enough wild fowls from the forest. Fill your waterskins with well water. We have enough grain to feed us for a few days, so start cooking,' Namdar snarls.

Mhadu hides behind a cliff holding the reins of his mare. He cannot hear what Namdar Khan is saying but realizes that the Mughals are preparing to stay overnight. He has been following them since yesterday, has seen the devastation they have left behind. He has travelled across the forest trails on his small mare to warn and alert the villagers in this region; he is the one who has coaxed them to flee with their cattle and grains and hide in the hills. With his heart pounding in his ribcage, Mhadu waits and watches, patting his tired mare and stroking her ears with affection. It looks like he too will be spending the night here, and before nightfall he must get some water for the animal.

The Mughal soldiers have occupied the empty hovels of Lonavala and remained busy cooking all through the afternoon. Their horses are left free in a nearby meadow to feast on the grass.

Mhadu too has discreetly found a small water pond and a patch of grass to water and feed his mare, but he is back to his post behind the cliff. He has collected wild berries and edible roots of some creepers to fill his stomach, and then there is some food he has packed in a cloth bundle. He munches on his meal and watches the camp, leaving his post only to urinate. Thousands like him have been trained to stay alive in the jungle for days without food. His master Naik had told him, 'I chose people for my spy network based on three qualities: survival instinct, sixth sense and a very high emotional quotient.'

The night falls and the air turns cold. Mhadu removes his turban and unfolds it, wrapping the cloth around him to ward off the cold, but his eyes remain focused on the camp. The camp noise subsides gradually and a few torches that were lit earlier are extinguished and it finally looks like they have retired for the night. After a while, he sits leaning on a rock to catch a few winks. Somewhere at the edge of the forest a deer has started making guttural sounds. The scout is alert instantly. It is an alarm call. Mhadu remains still and prays that his mare does not panic and start neighing. In a while, the jungle sounds fade, and tired, he falls into deep sleep thinking about the question that has nagged him all through the day: *Why are thousands of Mughal soldiers camping in an empty village?*

It is only early in the morning that the intentions of the Mughal soldiers become clear to Mhadu. He watches in helplessness and anger as the Mughals climb the nearby hills on foot, hunting for people. He witnesses as they drag away hundreds of men, women and children, their hands tied behind their back with vines. Some stronger men are tied together with ropes.

Mhadu must leave now. He has to inform Bahirji Naik, his chief, of all that has happened.

CHAPTER TWENTY-FOUR

1

Jahanara has been spending days looking after her father, but at nights she sits in her library filled with over a thousand hand-written manuscripts of renowned philosophers and historians. To suppress her grief, she likes to read a few pages from Dara bhai's book *Majma-ul-Bahrain*, in which he has written about the similarities between the philosophies of Hinduism and Islam, and between a mosque and a temple. She also loves his expansive work and analysis of the Hindu epic, the Mahabharata.

Her mind drifts towards thoughts of the futility of war. What does one achieve by waging war? Is seeking peace the goal of war? Many she loved have either died or are dying. Her beloved Dara bhai has died a most tragic death; he was tried in the royal court, humiliated by his brother and then beheaded. As per yesterday's news, Dara bhai's son Suleiman breathed his last in the damp and dark cell in the vault of Gwalior Fort. When they found him, he was drenched in his own filth. Murad Baksh has been found guilty of murdering the paymaster general of Gujarat and has been executed by a firing squad in the courtyard of the same fort. Muhammad Sultan too is rotting in the same place. People say that the prince, Aurangzeb's first son, is slowly going insane due to depression. Mir Jumla, who has been chasing Shuja bhai in Bengal and the Arakan, is on his deathbed due to cholera. Jahanara is sure that by now he is dead, for no one survives that ailment. Shuja bhai and his family have fled to Burma. Some say that during the journey their boat was captured by the cannibals. Some other events are happening in Dilli. A few months ago, after Ramadan, Aurangzeb too had fallen ill due to severe fasting combined with Dilli's brutal summer and overwork. During those days, their younger sister Roshanara suddenly turned into a dictator and took charge of her delirious brother. As per gossip, Roshanara did not allow anyone to see the emperor, once even dragging Nawab bai, Sultan's mother and Aurangzeb's own wife, by her hair from his chamber. Aurangzeb has recovered since then but is planning to eliminate Roshanara, his favourite sister, who manages the seraglio of Dilli, for he fears that she may turn too political and seek power.

Here at Agra Fort, some strange things are taking place. Eunuch Mutamad has become the dictator and has sent thousands of trunks full of jewels and artefacts loaded on armies of mules to Dilli to fill the treasury of Qila-e-mubarak.

Fakir Sarmad, whom Dara bhai loved and she respected, was hanged at Chandni Chowk in front of thousands of his supporters. Jahanara can see the future of the modernizers, atheists and the liberals who have deviated from the path of Aurangzeb's perception of Islam. The kafirs of Hindustan will soon have to fall in line.

Meanwhile, Aurangzeb has married Udepuri and has left for Kashmir to recover from his illness. His daughters, Zebunissa and Zinatunnisa, have come of age and are languishing in Dilli, spending their lives in literary pursuits and looking after their brothers, Azam and Akbar. She, Jahanara, the Padishahi Begum, is condemned to the state of blessed spinsterhood. It is the fate of many Mughal princesses whose fathers and brothers have not approved of any man outside the family. Not many men are born on this planet suitable for glorious princesses.

2

As Shivaji paces up and down in the sadar at Padmavati extension of Rajgad Fort late at night, he ponders over Shaista Khan, who has come to Pune with one lakh men and an almost equal number of war animals. Later, some reinforcements too have arrived. The region is reeling under the voracious hunger of these intruders and the region's economy has collapsed. The revenue collection is at an all-time low. It is becoming difficult to pay the salaries of his infantrymen and cavalrymen. The Mughal raids have become a daily affair while his men, Palkar, Pinglay, Yesaji, Tanaji and others, are trying their best to fight battles on various fronts. As per his estimate, the Mughals have taken away several thousand cattle from the villages, either for milk or meat, while peasants have fled and are hiding in the mountains. Without cattle, the land will not be tilled; without tilling there will be neither food nor revenue.

Shaista has also sent several squadrons to north Konkan from different jungle routes but the Mughal general has avoided besieging the hill forts. Shaista Khan is following a war strategy of attribution, aiming to exhaust the enemy and his resources and then forcing or even coercing him to surrender. If this goes on for one more year, Shaista's war policy will succeed and Shivaji will have no money to pay his army. In other words, he will have to surrender to the imperialists.

Peshwa Moroji Pinglay, who has returned from Pratapgad, looks on and senses impatience in Raja Shivaji's body language. Palkar too has been summoned. Both Pinglay and Palkar stand as if they are in contingency mode, ready to go to battle at any moment.

Shivaji stops pacing and asks, 'Shaista Khan has made himself and his family safe and secure in the cocoon of Lal Mahal that now stands in the midst of his military encampment. He thinks that he is invincible, and after the defeat of Kartalab he has announced that he will never venture out. There must be a way to reach him, the way that is not in his scheme of things, a crack in his armour that has not yet appeared in his wildest dreams, isn't it?'

Pinglay thinks for a long time, smiles and says, 'Like the demon Mahisha, who was blessed with partial immortality—no male, man or God, in the world or heavens could kill him.'

Shivaji has noticed a slight sarcasm in his peshwa's voice but he ignores it and comments with a straight face, 'The time has come to beckon Goddess Bhavani!'

Pinglay's smile broadens. Is his master joking?

Shivaji ignores him. 'I mean, we must look beyond the obvious. What do you say, Sarnobat Sahib? Aren't we strategically challenged at this point of time?' His brown eyes are now fixed on sarnobat Palkar.

'We are, indeed,' Palkar agrees and continues, 'but what we need right now is a strategy that will lead us to do something unconventional, something that has never been done before to defeat the enemy.'

'What do you mean?'

'We need to get to the enemy hiding in an ivory tower. This can be done only by thinking of something that is beyond his thinking!' Palkar announces nonchalantly.

'Like appearing out of thin air,' Shivaji quips.

'And facing Shaista Khan in Lal Mahal,' Pinglay comments wryly.

Shivaji does not waste time. 'Lal Mahal will be our next ranangan then.'

'One needs to be invisible to do so,' Pinglay quips.

'Imperceptible is the right word,' Palkar replies, 'we will be seen but they will not perceive or make out who we are.'

Pinglay smiles knowingly; he is beginning to understand.

'Get four hundred of our best men from the Sajag squadron,' Shivaji orders.

'Ji,' Pinglay accepts the responsibility by bowing slightly. The Sajag force—ready for action over the *sa*, for *sagar*, that is, sea, on *ja* for *jameen*, that is, land, and *ga* for *gaganchumbi*, that is, the sky-high mountains—is their pride. Sajag also means alert in Marathi. When on duty, these trained-to-be-noiseless men do not even sneeze or cough or even breathe with any sound while chasing elusive and dangerous targets.

'Entering someone's home is not our *rana-neeti*, our policy of battles. There will be women and children in there,' Pinglay reminds his master.

Shivaji guffaws and says, 'It is not someone else's home. It is *my* home and Shaista Khan is the intruder! Let me put it in simple words: the enemy is unleashing terror from an invincible location. He is offensive from a defensive position.'

Pinglay smiles feebly; he does not want to start a debate on offensive defence or defensive offence.

'Do we start from here and travel about fifty kos to reach the camp at midnight?' Pinglay wants to get on with the subject.

'We shall soon shift to Kondana Fort which is just about ten kos south-west of Pune.'

'Who will lead this campaign?' Pinglay is unsure of the raja's role.

'I shall,' Shivaji confirms, touching the string of cowries he wears around his neck.

'Why do you have to go? One of us will be enough,' Pinglay protests.

'My people are out there, getting crushed under the hooves of our enemy. Their morale is low. Their trust in me is dwindling and will soon fade away, unless I strengthen that priceless bond by risking my life to save theirs.'

'This is suicidal,' Pinglay shakes his head in disbelief, his forehead creased. For a few moments there is silence. Shivaji remembers what his beloved Sayee had said to him about her death and his life and utters the same words. 'Moroji, we always wish to control things that are beyond us and we always let go of things that are within our reach.'

'Raja, you speak in riddles,' Pinglay reprimands his master.

'Our goal, swaraj, a country for our people, is not easily attainable,' Shivaji explains. 'All our missions are potentially fatal! Death is invariable but time-of-death is a variable. We shall make our mission as infallible as possible but we shall leave the variables to Him. Do not forget that swaraj is *His* wish,' he concludes with a twinkle in his eyes.

'Maharaja Jaswant Singh Rathod and his ten thousand horsemen have their camp near Kondana,' Pinglay warns.

'He is malleable and pliable and has the soul of a rebel struggling to fight against an establishment called Aurangzeb, even though Aurangzeb has forgiven him for treason. Please start sending him gifts of pearls and precious stones. I have heard that he loves his two wives more than he loves himself and is always searching for presents to send them,' Shivaji whispers.

'I need a map of the camp,' Pinglay is slowly warming up to the idea.

'You will get one very soon. It has been months since Naik and his hundred men have infiltrated the camp,' Shivaji announces nonchalantly.

'We will also need entry papers. I have heard that the gatekeepers are strict.' Pinglay is now interested.

'It is mayhem out there; sometimes I wonder why I have waited for so long,' Shivaji says.

Pinglay raises his eyebrows but nods in agreement. The camp is spread across many kos of flatland at the southern side of Lal Mahal and there are about twenty gates to enter the camp. The makeshift fence is made of a short stone wall. There are people from different castes and creeds fighting under the Mughal banner: Abyssinians, Afghans, Rajputs, Persians, Uzbeks and the local Marathas. All the mansabdars live like little kings in the camp commanding their respective armies. Not many people know or recognize each other. Even the gatekeepers find it difficult to keep tabs on who is returning after a patrol or who is returning after a raid. An army of slaves comes carrying goods plundered from nearby villages and then a large number of new slaves are brought in every day.

'Naik's man Mhadu is a barber for Shaista Khan's security officer. He will be applying for the permit papers of a few.' Shivaji drops a surprise, but Pinglay does not show any reaction, so he persists, 'But we may need at least a hundred sajags infiltrating the camp.'

'Naik has become a good friend of the local gardener who takes care of Shaista's mobile garden that has hundreds of rare flowering plants growing in pots. Together they will pay a bribe of ten gold coins and pester the concerned official for an entry for a small wedding party; we have heard that Naik's aunt's distant cousin's daughter is all set to marry his friend's brother's son.'

'God bless the young couple,' Pinglay says excitedly.

'Ibrahim Khan is a frequent visitor to the camp and has acquired new friends. They have not yet asked him to show papers thinking he is on patrol duty. That evening he will bring in some shackled Maratha slaves, flogging them as he enters,' Shivaji volunteers more information.

'When will this midnight visit be planned?

Shivaji is quick to answer, 'During the Ramadan.'

'Any particular night during the Ramadan?' Pinglay wants to be precise; Ramadan is only a month away.

'It will be the night of the sixth moon after the no-moon night. That night they will also be celebrating the anniversary of Aurangzeb's coronation, beating drums every hour.'

Pinglay is amused, his eyes showing surprise that he was carefully trying to conceal all the while.

'What about the armed guards protecting the house?'

'We will kill them,' Shivaji's answer is chilling.

'From where do you intend to enter the house? Surely not from the main gate?'

'From the cooking section, where the khan's chief gardener has a small outhouse,' Shivaji says.

'Who will go with you to the bedroom other than the Sajag men?' Pinglay's eyes shine with curiosity.

'Babaji and Chiman Deshpande who know Lal Mahal like the back of their hand. As children, they had played hide and seek in that house,' Shivaji answers softly.

'How will you know where he sleeps?' Pinglay's questions have not ended.

'That is the weakest link. Sometimes he sleeps in his chamber on the ground floor but sometimes he goes up to the first floor,' Shivaji answers honestly and asks, 'Any more questions?'

'No,' Pinglay says with a smile. He is fascinated by his raja's out-of-the-box idea.

3

The half-kos-long Mughal encampment on the southern banks of the river Mutha fills the fields and covers the woods around Pune like an enormous python lounging after a good feed. There are precisely sixty-eight camps of sixty-eight principal mansabdars, each having two to five thousand cavalrymen, infantrymen, artillerymen and scouts. There are others too, thousands of beasts of war and burden, concubines, slaves, orderlies and others like cooks, cleaners, animal caretakers and merchants. The servants working in the regal green shamianas of twenty-nine Muslim mansabdars are gearing up for iftar parties. Tonight is special! Tonight they will also celebrate the coronation day of their new emperor! The floors of their shamianas are covered with expensive carpets; the best of their silverware, plates, spoons and glasses are taken out from the wooden chests; and hookah pipes are getting cleaned. They have fasted all through the day and are waiting with bated breath for the cry of the muezzin from the minarets proclaiming that they have caught a glimpse of the moon. Arrangements for food are done so zealously and carefully that not a moment is lost between the cry of the muezzins and the

announcement of iftar and then the first swallow of the food. Everyone
has plans about what to do after breaking the fast. Tonight they will
talk about the future, recite poetry, tell stories and reminisce about
their past while eating kebabs and sweetmeats, drinking scented and
colourful sherbets and then devouring the Ramadan pudding glazed
with the whites of eggs. Tonight they will forget about tomorrow.
Tonight they will forgive their past.

4

A few kos south-east of the camp, the isolated hill of Kondana rises
more than half a mile over the Sahyadri Plateau. The sun has set
behind the hills of Maval, and the sky above is turning darker by
the moment. A contingent of four hundred Sajag men leaves Pune
Darwaza, some in silk angirkhas and colourful turbans, while some
have their heads covered with soiled *mundasa* turbans and torn dhotis
tied tightly to their waists. The archers and artillerymen line up on
the ramparts and watch the Sajags scamper and sprint while going
down the steps and disappear. None of them are carrying torches.
The men standing on the ramparts and watchtowers wonder what is
afoot and where their special force is headed. All they know is that
if they are attacked by the Mughals any time during the night they
must shower the aggressors with arrows, cannonballs, explosives and
large stones.

At the foothills, horses wait for the men. They ride in the direction
of Pune as the canopies of rain trees sway with gentle breeze. Above
the canopies, a crescent moon's silvery sparkle puts the twinkle of
blue-green stars to shame. A few light cavalry detachments wait at
various places between Kondana Fort and the Mughal camp to ensure
a safe journey for the horsemen. Palkar waits on the banks of the river
Mula with a few hundred cavalrymen. He also has a hundred oxen
with him for reasons only known to him. Pinglay and his cavalrymen
wait on the bank of the river Mutha for the Sajags to arrive. He has an
oxen cart decorated with bunting and colourful panels with him. He
is also to cover his master's withdrawal after the event! A little ahead,

Ibrahim Khan waits with a few Pashtun horsemen, with a large whip made of rawhide in hand.

The mansabdars are busy celebrating inside their shamianas. The courtyards of these palatial tents are equipped with at least two or three horses and one elephant, saddled and caparisoned, ready for any emergency. Adjacent to the courtyard, the administrative offices of these high military officials seem full with nautch girls brought in for celebrations. Each mansabdar's establishment is surrounded by thousands of tiny tents of his junior officers and soldiers where countless torches burn with large flickering flames. Here, several thousand soldiers move about recklessly, some with naked swords and some with limp rabbits or fowl caught in their traps. Most are followed by their stressed orderlies barking orders to their cooks to hurry up. The air is thick with the smell of meat, spices and tobacco smoke mixed with the fresh smell of burning firewood. At some places, the soot from the *chullah*s has formed enormous clouds, darkening the place and making people partially blind to their surroundings. There is also a market assigned to each mansabdar, with tiny stands brimming with dates, sugar, grain, olive oil, brown sugar and tobacco. The butchers seem busy hacking meat, the sounds of their cleavers hitting the wooden platforms rising above the yells of vegetable vendors.

At the edge of these camps, within the main encampment, are rows of makeshift latrines with huge uncovered soak pits dug near them. Beyond the latrines stand large animal stables, crowded with elephants, camels, warhorses, oxen and mules, the place buzzing with mosquitoes and flies. Slaves run about with buckets of water and large brooms to clean up the animal droppings. It is difficult to enter these places, blocked by dried grass, cut branches of trees and fodder, and it is increasingly difficult to communicate verbally with the constant whinnying of the bored horses and trumpeting of the frustrated elephants.

The campsites of the Hindu, mostly Rajput and Maratha, mansabdars are no different either, with the saffron shamianas of Hindus rising above the green tents of their Muslim counterparts. The encampments also shudder with excitement as musicians near the Lal Mahal blow horns and trumpets, beat drums and sing every hour to rejoice at the anniversary of Aurangzeb's coronation.

At the southern side of the Mughal encampment, a noisy wedding procession has arrived with drum beaters. The groom, in a colourful bullock cart, is followed by a hundred men dancing to the beats, forming clouds of dusts above their heads. The Mughal sentinels guarding the outposts have been informed about the wedding and most of them shake a leg matching the rhythm of the beats. When they arrive at the gate, the gatekeepers welcome them. They are in a hurry to leave the posts for iftar and are excited to see something different from the usual humdrum happenings. The papers are duly submitted, stamped upon without any questions.

Ibrahim Khan and his few Pashtun cavalrymen cross the river Mutha that has been reduced to a small stream. Their horses canter while they hold the ends of the ropes tied around a large number of slaves and drag them along. They arrive at a gate facing west. The gatekeepers are familiar with the regal-looking Ibrahim with his long beard. Today, he looks even more handsome in his jama woven with fine threads of silk and embellished with gold embroidery, flowing down to his ankles like a kaftan. A massive leather belt around his waist is bedecked with a sword and several daggers. The colourful turban is adding more height to his tall frame.

'Ramadan Mubarak!' he greets each and every gatekeeper.

'Allah Kareem!' they greet him return. God is generous.

Ibrahim and his men along with their spoils of war have no problem in gaining entry. It is a matter of pride when the Mughal military men capture and bring slaves to the camp. The gatekeepers have not even asked for papers!

Ibrahim along with his horsemen and train of slaves canters leisurely through the narrow lanes of the encampment and through the markets thronging with people. The slaves cry aloud and curse when flogged. Passersby shout Mubarak to congratulate Ibrahim for his catch of human booty. Finally they enter the old town, a sharp contrast to the encampment. If the encampment is like a python, the town is like its victim about to be crushed in the reptile's grip. Here, the rickety balconies of huddled houses look empty and forlorn.

Not a single window is open but light sneaks out through the slits of the windows like a guilty thief. A few lanterns do burn faintly at the crossroads, while stray dogs howl soulfully at the edge of the gloomy town. Finally, they reach a small patch of overgrown forest at the rear of Lal Mahal.

Ibrahim signals his men; they dismount and tether their horses while the shackled slaves are set free. As the slaves dissolve in the shadows of the woods, Ibrahim and his men walk confidently towards the rear entrance of Lal Mahal. Khalid, holding a torch, is a newly acquired friend of Ibrahim. He is on palace duty patrolling the place adjacent to the backyard and is startled to see Ibrahim and a few Pashtun men there at midnight. He greets Ibrahim followed by a question, 'Assalamu Alaikum, Ibrahim Bhai. Are you supposed to be here at this time?'

'Waalekum Assalaam, wa Rahamatullahi wa barakaatu hu,' Ibrahim reciprocates in Arabic with a trusting smile and continues, 'I have been entrusted to bring some able men.'

Khalid, who has received many a gift from Ibrahim, narrows his eyes and persists, 'Who has asked you?'

'Abdul Azeez, the head of palace security,' comes the quick answer.

'Why at this hour?' Khalid wonders.

'He had said he wants to put the men straight on duty and see their endurance. I have been told to be at the rear of the compound wall of the general's house,' Ibrahim explains patiently.

'No one from the sentinels guarding the house has informed me,' Khalid wonders, but does not sound alarmed.

'Come, let's go together and verify,' Ibrahim sounds terse, his heart pounding in his chest.

'I did not mean to sound suspicious,' Khalid says apologetically.

'Shall we?' Ibrahim insists.

'It is not necessary; we shall meet in the morning,' Khalid says, then shakes his head and continues, 'I must go and check on the musicians and remind them of their last performance of the night.'

Ibrahim sighs quietly with relief. He hopes that the others have managed to reach the backyard. The wedding procession had gone to the Ganesh temple near Lal Mahal to seek blessings; they were supposed to sneak out one by one and reach the rear of the palace. It is dark at the back of Lal Mahal. Ibrahim and his men take a few moments to adjust to the darkness. A few yards away, a cottage stands illuminated by a single torch. Ibrahim walks behind the hut and sees several men, more than hundred, some dressed in finery and some in soiled clothes, sitting under a huge tree, and he knows one of them is Raja Shivaji.

'Is that you, Ibrahim?' This is surely Tanaji.

'Yes,' Ibrahim replies and asks, 'Was there any trouble for the wedding procession?'

'No.'

'Did they search you for weapons?' Ibrahim asks.

'No.'

'Is the groom here?'

'Yes, I am very much here,' Ibrahim hears the familiar voice of Raja Shivaji.

They wait there for about an hour or so. As the moon disappears, the night turns darker and they can see the shadows of the sentinels moving about the house, their sandals making a rhythmic sound. The torches hanging in the baskets attached to the walls of the house are extinguished one by one with only a few meant to be on all through the night. As planned, fifty Sajag men move like noiseless spirits in the direction of the house, scale the compound wall as if they are gliding over it and vanish.

The Sajags have dispersed like drifting mist, only to appear from the shadows of the trees to pounce on Shaista's guards. They go directly for the jugular, giving the enemy no chance. The guards fall one by one, and are dragged into the backyard and hidden behind the trees. One of the kitchen hands suddenly comes out from the back door holding a big pot. The chief of Sajags notices him and stands very close to the wall but he remains directly under the torch that burns overhead. The man holding the pot opens his mouth to let out a scream. The Sajag lurches forward and clamps the man's mouth shut with his hand, letting only a soft groan. The man is pressed against the kitchen wall and his throat slit. The pot falls down, making a loud metallic sound, from the hands of the dying man.

'What is happening?' someone screams from the kitchen and leaps out from the door and falls directly into the Sajag's hands who is still holding the limp body of his victim. He leaves the body and lets it crumple on the ground, takes on the second arrival and silences him within just a moment. Someone else starts shouting from the direction of the main palace in chaste Farsi, 'Is everything all right?'

The chief Sajag takes a chance and shouts, '*Baleh, baleh,*' in Farsi, saying 'yes', and waits, his heart beating in fluttery panic. If the man from inside the kitchen suspects foul play, he will alert the inmates and soon everything will start going downhill, but the much-desired silence prevails. After a while, the lights in the kitchen dim. Heaving a sigh of relief, his eyes dart about. The place is deserted, there are no more sentinels pacing about. He scampers in the direction of men waiting in the dark, well-hidden in the shrubs.

The chief Sajag signals by crowing thrice.

Shivaji jumps to his feet. The time has come to move. Babaji, Chiman, Ibrahim Khan and Tanaji take cue and rise quickly. The three, followed by many more, proceed towards the house and wait for a while under the mango and fig trees before entering the kitchen. It is empty, lit by a lone lantern hanging on the wall darkened by soot. Within an hour, the place will be crowded by men cooking for *sohoor*, the morning meal before sunrise. Shivaji moves cautiously, and is aware that there is a huge granary attached to the kitchen. He enters the granary followed by the others; it was their favourite place to hide in childhood. Chiman, who walks behind Shivaji, knows that from this granary one can enter the main house. He quickly goes to the spot where the door ought to be, but there is no door there.

'It's been sealed,' Shivaji whispers as they face just a wall.

'They have sealed it with just mud, and painted the wall to camouflage it. It is here,' Chiman says while marking the wall with his fingers.

'Break it,' Shivaji orders a Sajag standing on his left. The man takes out a small hammer tucked in his belt, but this is going to be noisy. Just then the music celebrating the anniversary of Aurangzeb's coronation starts in the front yard of the Lal Mahal. The ear-splitting sound of drums disturbs the horses in the stables inside the compound of the house and they start neighing too. This is the last time the musicians will play it, so it is louder and more robust than the previous bouts. After this, their master Shaista Khan will be going to bed. The Sajag has started hammering the mud wall with a vengeance, and before the music stops, the opening to the courtyard is wide enough for the men to step through.

The courtyard is enclosed in an elevated veranda, an enclosed walkway, its wooden canopy supported by stone pillars. It has a main gate as an exit point. As they enter, they notice that the place is dimly lit by just one lantern hanging on the veranda wall. A few rooms at the entrance of the courtyard are perhaps occupied by Shaista's grown sons. The large foyer at the other end is submerged in darkness. Chiman looks at the staircase in one of the corners that goes up to a covered terrace with several rooms opening into it. He starts calculating, what is the probability of Shaista sleeping on the ground floor? There are neither any guards nor is the place lit. He takes the lead and directs a few Sajags in the direction of the foyer while he leaps towards the staircase followed by Shivaji and the others. When they reach the first floor, they are shocked to see a number of women sleeping on the floor of the upstairs' veranda. Shivaji wonders how claustrophobic the place has become with so many curtains hanging from the ceiling and blocking the view of the courtyard. Here too just one lantern burns in the corner, with a candle that is about to die out.

The men tiptoe past, avoiding the limbs and torsos of women sleeping in various positions. But one woman wakes up to see silhouettes of men hovering above her with naked swords. She lets out a wild scream, and mayhem breaks out as the others wake up in hysteria and the screams become louder.

Ibrahim grabs hold of an elderly woman; her thin frame is bent with jewellery, she is probably the khan's first wife. He says to her urgently in Farsi, '*Moshekeli nist*, no problem, I shall help you. Where is your husband? I must save his life.'

The woman's trembling hand points to a room, the door of which is shut. The 'intruders' dart towards the room but are shocked to see the elderly woman sprinting ahead of them. She kicks the door open and shouts, '*Khatar! Khatar!*', warning of danger. Shivaji ducks and, avoiding the woman, he enters the dimly lit room. He sees a very fair man with white beard quickly jump up from his bed; a younger woman sleeping on the other side is jolted awake and starts screaming. Before Shivaji can chase him, the elderly woman who had kicked open the door scampers ahead with amazing agility and blows out the only oil lamp burning in the room.

There is but one option left for him and the men who have entered the room after him to move their swords in forward and backward strokes. Thereafter, all hell breaks loose, as women inside the room start yelling. There is a room behind the khan's bedroom; some more women from there enter the room and come in the range of the blades of the Maratha swords. Shivaji thinks he heard a man groaning. Then, in the pale yellow light streaming in from the doorway, he realizes that some women are lying dead on the ground and the elderly fair man is nowhere to be seen. In the courtyard, the Sajags are busy fighting with men who have come out from the adjacent rooms with swords and daggers. Soon, the khan's flowerpots are covered in blood.

Some servants have broken free and have run towards the camp shouting incomprehensible words. Most of the Sajag men too follow them shouting, *'Ghaneem! Ghaneem! Ghaneem!'* People in the camp watch the exodus of men coming out from the direction of Lal Mahal, some dripping with blood, shouting, 'Enemy! Enemy! Enemy!' Shivaji, Babaji and Chiman too have joined the Sajags, and all of them soon dissolve in the confused mass of people living in the massive encampment, like vapour disappearing into mist.

Shaista, despite excruciating pain, keeps hanging outside the balcony and patiently waits for someone to rescue him. After what seemed like ages, he notices a few men peering down at him from the balcony. When he realizes that they are his servants, he utters some expletives and asks them to pull him up. When he is pulled up the reality falls on him like lightning. He kneels down and starts howling.

His bedroom, the upstairs veranda and the courtyard are covered with dead bodies, and among those dead is his first son, Abul Fath. The bodies of his other two younger sons, three wives, one of his sons-in-law and all fifty sentinels guarding the house are lying about.

It is like a sinister nightmare. Hakims are called to tend to those who are injured; Shaista has lost three fingers of his right hand which are later found near his bed. Dead bodies, some intact and some in pieces, are finally lined up in the courtyard. There are six strangers among those.

Outside, in the camp, a thousand horsemen from different camps have mounted their horses. They gallop in the eastern direction, for some scouts have seen hundreds of men holding torches and moving eastwards near the banks of the river Mula. They let their horses fly, gritting their teeth and wielding their naked swords, occasionally shouting 'Ghaneem! Ghaneem!', cursing the enemy they do not know and chasing the enemy they have not seen. It is a dark night, and the forest on the banks of the river Mula is even darker. The enormous trunks, branches and canopies of giant rain trees cast ominous shadows on the floor covered with shrubs. The gallopers spot the flickering torches in the dark and ride through the narrow trails to reach the enemy, only to find oxen running about with burning torches tied to their horns!

5

It is now a known fact that Shivaji had, in person, come along with his men to kill Shaista Khan.

It is afternoon. Summer has begun and the weather has turned hot. Shaista Khan sits on a reclining chair in the foyer while a hakim sitting near his feet washes the wound with a medicinal solution. The pus has disappeared and tiny brown crusts have started appearing. Shaista curses as a throbbing pain starts, and intensifies within moments. 'It is healing nicely,' the doctor comments to soothe his master's nerves. Shaista feels numb with shame and grief. How could he have been so careless? Why did he underestimate the Maratha? And now what would Aurangzeb think? What was his and his remaining family's future? There is but one logical explanation and that is that Shivaji must be a disciple of a sinister djinn. How else could he do what he did and suddenly appear in his bedroom?

Shaista shakes his head with dismay. He had heard of people catching fire, stones from the sky crushing heads, sand spilling out and blisters exploding from one's body! Stranger and more sinister things have happened under the spell of a tantric. Such black-magicians can make the victim's body parts vanish one by one. His fingers are gone, what next? A shiver runs down the general's spine.

Shaista has decided to leave for Aurangabad early the next morning.

'Maharaja Jaswant Singh Rathod has come to see you, my master,' a servant comes in and informs him. Shaista Khan smiles bitterly. He does not want to see the face of Jaswant who has surely committed treason after taking expensive gifts from Shivaji. In any case, the man is famous for his traitorous nature; he has proved it during the battle of Khajwa.

'Bring him in,' Shaista murmurs. 'Fan faster,' he says to the two men who are fanning him with large fans made of peacock feathers as he wipes his forehead with his left hand.

Tall and handsome Jaswant walks in wearing a white turban and a white jama to show that he is mourning. The young man is stooping, his face is grief-stricken.

Shaista raises his eyes and regards Jaswant. The doctor has finished putting a fresh bandage on his master's hand. He gets up, bows and says, 'Take care, Sahib, do not allow water to touch the bandage.'

Shaista waves his hand, indicating to the doctor to leave them alone.

After the medic is gone, Shaista looks at Jaswant and says sarcastically, 'Have you come to see if I am really alive?'

Jaswant refuses to look into Shaista Khan's eyes.

'You are camping near Kondana Fort and you claim to have seen nothing on that fateful night.'

Maharaja Jaswant Singh Rathod is filled with shame too. He had refused all the presents that were sent by Shivaji and he and his men had truly not seen anything suspicious that night, but the general will never believe him.

'Besiege Kondana Fort and wait for my further instructions!' the Mughal general instructs Jaswant, dismissing him.

6

Aurangzeb's procession of about four lakh people and animals has left Dilli for Kashmir. Aurangzeb has decided to camp at the foothills of the Himalayas. Evening has fallen and a brilliant orange sun lingers on the western horizon. Clusters of pine trees with their straight and tall trunks rising above the velvety green slopes at the foothills of the high mountains look alluring. The snow caps of the mountains reflecting the golden beams resemble the gilded pinnacles of temples and mosques, while gentle yet icy winds from the north flirt with the panels of Aurangzeb's shamiana. Its panels are violet-red and embroidered with hand-painted chintz from Masulipatnam in Golconda. Fringed with gold, silver threads woven in silk, its poles are painted with gild. The entire mobile palace is separated by wooden screens from the rest of the enormous camp that is three kos in circumference. In the front yard of the shamiana, from a mast rising forty guj high hangs a sky lantern, *akashdeep*—an imperial beacon to guide the wanderers to their tents.

Aurangzeb, who has finished his evening prayers, enters the audience chamber adorned with silk and velvet canopies as thoughts buzz in his head. Few messages have come from the Deccan and he is eager to know about his maternal uncle's success stories.

He eagerly goes to his gilded, throne-like chair and asks his scribe to read the messages. In the light of a few oil lamps burning on his desk, the scribe starts reading.

> Shivaji Bhosale with audacity and malignity carried out a midnight attack on *amir-ul-umara*, khan-e-khanan, General Shaista Khan's camp, and killed many. Unfortunately, Shivaji is rewarded by an immense increase in his prestige. Now he is considered an incarnation of Satan. No place is believed to be proof against his entrance and no feat impossible for him. Everyone is talking with respect and terror of his almost superhuman deed. There is no doubt that Shivaji has mastered witchcraft. Amir-ul-umara is humiliated, has lost a part of his family as well as his face, along with his fingers. Some say that Shivaji is wise and dangerous; it was not a shot in the dark but a well-planned military operation.

There is one more letter from Aurangabad, the Mughal capital of the Deccan.

> Soon after the raid of amir-ul-umara Shaista Khan, Shivaji has again marched into south Konkan, taking over important ports and some sea forts and collecting money from rich traders. The rumour is that he is planning to build an enormous sea fort somewhere near Malvan. The news is true because Shivaji's adviser, one Niraji Raoji, has bought several thousand maunds of iron and lead for the same purpose.

As the words of the scribe start making sense, a slight tremor of fury lances through Aurangzeb. Moments ago, he was looking forward to a lovely holiday in the Shalimar gardens of Srinagar in Kashmir with Udepuri, but that happiness vanishes in a moment. Everything he so longs for—the streams, lakes reflecting the azure sky, palaces built on islands of such lakes surrounded by richly canopied trees, trails vanishing into flowerbeds and the gardens filled with bird songs— seems to have lost its meaning.

He dictates a letter addressed to Mohammad Mir Amin, the mir bakshi of the empire:

> Paymaster general, be informed, this unfortunate and shameful incidence has occurred due to the negligence of the current Mughal subhedar of the Deccan who is also the general of the imperial armies in the region. We therefore dismiss him from the subhedari of the Deccan and order him to proceed to Bengal, report at our offices in Raj Mahal, taking over the charge as the subhedar of Bengal. Shahzaada Muazzam will take over as the subhedar of the Deccan and report at Aurangabad with immediate effect.

Aurangzeb dictates another letter addressed to his maternal uncle Shaista too:

> Please proceed to Bengal without delay or further argument. Do not try and meet me in Kashmir for I have no wish to see your face.

CHAPTER TWENTY-FIVE

1

Surat, in the Mughal subha of Gujarat, is shrouded in winter mist even after the sun has risen to a considerable height in the sky. The port town on the southern banks of the Tapi where the river sweeps unexpectedly westward towards the sea is the empire's pride. Shah Jahan had considered it as an important source of wealth. Aurangzeb wants to further enhance the revenue and make use of it to enhance his military power. From the riverside, Surat looks lush with palm trees, canopies of which shimmer in the golden beams of winter sun. The city is almost eight kos inland from the port of Swally where the Tapi meets the ocean.

Naik looks in the small mirror he has brought with him and smiles; his wrinkled eyes framed by his white brows shine with satisfaction. He has let a few white hairs escape from his faded woollen turban on purpose, to look like a tramp. His dhoti and angirkha are soiled to show that he has no one in the world to take care of him. Pleased with his own look, Naik comes out of the shipwreck, a rotting and mangled mass of iron and wood, rusted in parts, beached on the banks of the Tapi, his home since he came to Surat a week ago. He walks further away from the wreck with the help of his walking stick, darting his gaze in all directions, but does not see anything suspicious.

A fleet of vessels float in the blue-green river as Dutch and English flags, rising above their sails, flutter like waves. Naik is sure that the sailors on the decks of those ships can see the city's solitary fortress enclosed between the turrets where the subhedar of Surat, Inayat Khan, resides. Adjacent to Inayat's house is a sprawling garden full of lush trees and flowering scrubs. Naik has visited the market place called the chowk near the garden and was astonished to see how quickly large sums of money changed hands. He had talked to people and they had told him that every day merchants arrive from far and near on horses, camels, elephants and oxen carts.

He was shocked to see unafraid women, perhaps of Armenian or Zoroastrian origin, dressed in long skirts and plaited hair, walk about without a care in the world. Naik has concluded that the retailers and wholesalers of Surat do brisk business with goods brought in from the large hinterland of Gujarat. Shops overflow with pearls, jewellery, precious stones, gold, silver, spices, textile, sandalwood, saffron, perfumes, silk, carpets and such other valuable things. Mountains of elephant tusks, turtle shells to make shields and medicinal rhinoceros horns are kept separately in wholesale outlets. Special shops have displayed rare articles inlaid with ivory, such as bracelets, sword-hilts, dice and chessboards. Customers have no place to stand as Arabs and Armenians shove and push each other to get the best bargains. He had also never seen thousands of oxen lined up around the market either to deliver the goods or dispatch them.

Naik is a shocked man for more reasons than just the market. Surat is not what he had envisioned. It is neither filled only with palatial homes nor has wide avenues like Bijapur. The inner city is filthy; naked children pick their noses and look at him with big curious eyes as he moves through the narrow lanes lined with huddled houses made of reeds and covered with cow dung mixed with clay. Deeper in the city, the overcrowded hovels are made of sheer cane walls roofed with branches of palm trees and the adjacent cattle sheds overflowing with animals and flies. He ignores the stench, making mental notes of some well-built homes of brick, lime and timber. These houses must belong to shopkeepers or exchange dealers who hide their wealth in the pits dug in their homes and cover them with marble tiles.

He comes across a huge banyan tree in the middle of a crossroad. It has an enormous trunk and a round platform built around it. Beyond the banyan tree, Naik notices a few Jain temples, and a little away from the shrines, imposing structures made of better-quality bricks stand aloof from the rest of the town. Naik knows that a Parsi broker to the king of Bantam lives in one of those and so does the head of the Mahajan community of traders, the spice-king Virji Vora, who is the richest of them all. It is rumoured that he has a few thousand ser of gold hidden in the vaults of his home.

One house with large glass windows with bamboo slats interwoven with khus belongs to the second richest Hindu trader, Mohandas Parekh, and unlike Virji, he is a philanthropist and has nothing stored in his underground vaults. Naik heads for the river and passes through narrow alleys of the inner city blocked at some places by peaceful, cud-chewing cows. He walks carefully without disturbing the animals and reaches three stone structures with many arched verandas. A few men with large turbans and long tunics lounge in one corner and smoke hookah, speaking in strange tongues. He has seen similar buildings in Bijapur; they have courtyards in the middle, called *sarais*. These lodges are used by visiting merchants, moneychangers, bankers or petty peddlers from different countries. A narrow road through the sarais goes in the direction of the one and only land fort in Surat built in a square enclosure with four towers in four corners and guns mounted on parapets.

As he moves towards the waterfront where the Muslim merchants live, he realizes that the cityscape has changed drastically. The narrow lanes have been replaced by noisy streets paved with unbroken and flattened stones crammed with horsemen riding towards the noisy market. He walks on the edge of the road for he does not want to get knocked down by rashly driven, two-wheeled oxen carts, or to collide with harried bearers of palanquins heading for the residential area of the rich. The houses lining the street are large, flat-roofed and terraced with plaster, and boast of huge windows, screened with lattices of wood or glass made from oyster shells. The first large house facing the river is that of Ishak Beg, the key player in trading metal oars, while the other villas in the row belong to the leading merchants such as Haji Zahid Baig, Haji Kasim and Khwaja Minas. Naik's men have infiltrated some of the homes of the rich as servants, plumbers or carpenters. They know where the elite of Surat hide their wealth.

By now Naik has seen it all, and that includes the massive establishments of the Europeans—enormous structures with strong walls built around them, they lie beyond the residential area of the rich Muslims. What has surprised Naik is that the walls of those warehouses are stronger than the fort walls and are defended by men armed with muskets all through the day and night. A large number of officers, soldiers, brokers, packers, weavers, dyers, washers, carpenters and blacksmiths live in harmony behind those walls. The Europeans, especially the English and the Dutch, flourish in their business and always fill the holds of countless ships that throng the harbour during the buying season.

That night he scribbles a note to his master, Raja Shivaji. One of his spies will carry the letter to Rajgad.

The fortress is protected by a shallow moat from three sides and the river Tapi from the rear. The Mughal subhedar Inayat Khan who lives in the fort has never fought a battle and has no idea of the outside world. He is required to keep a strong force of cavalrymen to defend the town but the practical reality is different. It is rumoured that Inayat Khan was to build a high wall strengthened with ramparts and watchtowers around Surat and has taken a huge grant from the emperor for this purpose. The money has been swallowed and the old and crumpling wall around the city is proof of the subhedar's corruption. There are no warships guarding the waters of the Tapi and the entire population lives in some kind of safety bubble that can be burst easily. The houses have been identified and in some cases, even places where the vaults are hidden are known to my men.

2

On an early winter morning, people in Nasik had woken up with sounds of hoof beats, only to see squadrons moving through the mist and towards the west. A few days later, the villages in the forests between the coastal Konkan and coastal Gujarat also sighted a large number of horsemen moving in the northern direction. Many wondered if it was a Mughal mansabdar going to Surat for some official business . . .

Only Shivaji, Palkar and Pinglay know where they are heading. Within days they reach their destination. While sitting on a boulder in the midst of his army camp in a garden near the eastern gate of Surat, Shivaji watches the surroundings. The gate fitted with long and pointed spikes looks imposing in the fading lights of the dying evening, but the wall is in ruin, broken at places, as if waiting to be invaded. There is a hidden lesson about the Mughal defence system in this gate as well as the adjacent wall, he thinks, their strength is backed by weakness. The canopies of sal glow yellow in the light of torches burning in the camp while the shadows of their long trunks quiver on the ground. Staring at them, Shivaji contemplates his immediate future and what he must accomplish over the next few days.

His cavalrymen and their mounts are tired, for they have been riding for a week taking only short breaks during the journey of about one hundred and fifty kos from Rajgad to Surat. They have travelled northwards towards Nasik to descend into the Konkan, taking the mountain trails of Waghai, and thereafter have crossed the forests around Navsari town to reach Surat. It has been done with such speed and secrecy that no one had known about their march till yesterday when he had sent two messengers to the subhedar of Surat, Inayat Khan.

Tomorrow might be a crucial day.

'No reply from Inayat Khan; it is time for us to move in,' Palkar who stands behind Shivaji urges as his dark eyes shine with anticipation.

Shivaji nods and agrees with his sarnobat, but his face goes tight with fury. He had sent a message to Inayat that the three wealthiest men of Surat—Zahid Baig, Virji Vora and Haji Kasim—should come to him in person to negotiate terms. If the city gives him tribute money he will leave them alone, or else. Inayat Khan has not replied; instead, he has invited all the rich who are willing to offer him bribe to his fort and has instructed his thousand horsemen to guard his abode, leaving the city to its fate. The poor have fled into the nearby forests or taken small boats and disappeared in panic; only the English and the Dutch have stayed put in their factories and are ready to defend themselves.

'We move in tomorrow afternoon, but remind our men again and again that women and children are not to be touched, places of worship must be left undamaged and the clergy and their books must be treated with respect,' he says with finality.

'Do we attack the European establishments?' Palkar asks.

'No, they have guns. I do not want to risk the lives of our men.'

'Tomorrow then,' Pinglay says.

The city seems to have a premonition. With light from oil lamps seeping out from shut windows and doors all through the night, people seem to be awake. The next day arrives quietly and the usual carnival-like atmosphere of Surat is replaced by a sinister silence, as if the city is struck by an axe of terror. The morning sees people quietly loading their belongings on to oxen carts and some just walking away from their homes carrying goods on their heads. The markets are deserted and only stray dogs are seen or heard near the crossroads. The stillness of the noon is suddenly disrupted by the harsh sound of the hooves of galloping horses, their masters roaring out their battle cry, 'Har Har Mahadev'. They come from all sides, like flies seeking sweetmeat—hundreds and thousands of them, looking identical in their boat-shaped turbans and bushy moustaches, leaving trails of dust behind and filling the narrow lanes of Surat with dread.

Two days have passed since the Marathas have entered the city. It is evening and the winter sun is about to disappear under the horizon. A cold breeze has started blowing from the west. Inayat Khan, the subhedar of Surat, gazes at the city under his protection from the ramparts of his small fort. Haji Baig standing close to Inayat stares at the city that gives their emperor more than ten lakh rupees, equivalent to seven hundred ser of pure gold, each year in taxes. The streets are deserted, but at one corner he can see the horsemen galloping away. The faint sound of their battle cry has travelled on the wind like a falcon swooping down on its prey. At places, columns of smoke rise above the hovels and the market place adjacent to the fort is in total ruin. What is happing is unbelievable. For the last hundred years, no other kingdom has dared to attack the imperial terrain, especially Surat that is a hundred kos away from its southern borders.

'Do you think we should have gone to meet him—Virji, Kasim and I?' Baig asks softly, his dark eyes boring into Inayat.

Inayat holds his gaze and retorts, 'He might have killed all three of you. I could not have taken that big a risk.'

Baig smiles faintly, his thin lips curling into a slight snigger. A few villagers had come to Inayat a few days ago to say that they had spotted a huge contingent of horsemen camping a few miles away from Surat. Inayat Khan had dismissed it saying it must be some mansabdar riding towards Dilli through the coastal region. When Shivaji had sent Inayat a message for tribute money, Baig was there. Inayat had laughed and said, 'Who will displease the emperor and bring on themselves his wrath? It is like challenging Allah.'

'What if we deploy whatever horsemen we have to drive away the Marathas instead of them just guarding this fort?' Baig asks, looking in the direction of the residential area facing the river where his house stands. Its underground vaults are stuffed with gold coins. Inayat shoots a glance at the fair and short man standing close to him and says, 'In that case, we at the fort will be putting ourselves at risk.'

Baig shakes his head in dismay; he knows that his subhedar is scared to unleash his horsemen who have never fought a battle. These men are good only for a parade, to scare the defenceless Hindu traders of Surat. After the massacre of Shaista Khan's family, things have become a bit more complicated; everyone thinks that the Marathas have some evil, supernatural powers. Baig has heard that men from the mountainous parts of Deccan are born warriors; even the lowliest and the poorest are trained to fight and are hardened in battle.

For the first time, Inayat feels a tinge of regret for retaining only a thousand horsemen instead of the five thousand that he has shown on paper for which he gets a grant directly from the imperial treasury. Shah Jahan and Aurangzeb have believed him and have never sent inspectors to check.

'I have heard that the Europeans are holding their establishments with gunmen planted on the roofs and walls of their factories,' Baig comments looking at the city and then blurts, 'How will the emperor react when he knows what has happened here?'

Inayat feels fear slicing through him. Life as the subhedar of Surat has been more than good—expensive wines from Persia or

Spain, horses from Arabia, days spent in nearby jungles hunting
wild game, fortunes spent in celebrating his own as well as his
children's marriages . . . 'What the emperor will think is not the
priority now; I must protect you and the others at the fort,' he
manages to mumble.

Baig shrugs. It is true that those who have managed to bribe
their way to the fort may survive, but their wealth hidden in their
houses will be taken. He feels his anger rising. Inayat will lose
nothing, as his wealth is hidden in the fort—the wealth he has
amassed by having a stake in his brother's textile business through
which he earns handsomely, even though his financial interest
comes into conflict with his official duties. All the rich Muslim
merchants pay him large amounts of money to get permits,
and the wealthiest Hindu merchants like Virji Vora from the
Bania community give him expensive presents on all auspicious
occasions. The poor brokers are dealt with a little differently; they
are either imprisoned or flogged for no apparent reason till they
cough up some money to continue doing business. Inayat loves
his life of a king, but after this disaster, he is no longer sure about
his future.

Baig feels a pang of sadness along with anger. 'Wonder what they
have done to my home!' he whispers sadly, his long robe fluttering
behind his thin frame. The sun has already set. In the twilight he can
see small infernos rising from the residential area where his house
stands.

It has been two days since the Marathas have been plundering
Surat, as if they have known which house has money and even the
place of hiding. A bunch of Marathas has worked for a day and a
night to first demolish and burn Virji Vora's mansion and then to dig
open its foundation where four thousand ser of gold and thirty ser of
large pearls were kept in underground vaults. All this has happened
while Virji and his family were hiding in the fort. Even though they
cannot see Virji's house from the ramparts, he has heard that the
huge pillars that proudly supported the roof are lying supine, like
dead soldiers on a battlefield. At some places it still smoulders with
spiralling columns of soot still swirling heavenwards. Several other

houses have been destroyed, some burnt, and the Marathas have taken away hundreds of people as captives who have refused to show them where the wealth is hidden.

'What if they reach the fort in large numbers?' Baig asks looking at the short-range cannon mounted on the scaffolds.

'We will fire the cannon, do not worry,' Inayat says pompously.

Baig laughs in his mind. For years they have not fired these guns, and even the artillerymen have no clue where the explosives will fall if and when they do fire them. He also doubts if the explosives have ever been inspected for their capacity to explode or they too are like Inayat—big noise and less fire!

'I have a plan,' Inayat declares smilingly as if he has suddenly had prophetic visions. 'I will teach the Maratha a lesson!'

3

The third evening comes bringing more wealth. Shivaji and Pinglay watch the horsemen as they enter the camp, loaded with filled sacks. The men dismount and empty them on the ground, allowing gold coins, diamonds, rubies, jasper, emeralds, pearls and jade to tumble out and make small mounds. Some bags contain only jewellery and some contain silver vessels, while one man has eight bags full of pearls. It is then that Shivaji hears a commotion. A French missionary has come out of the eastern gate with three unarmed men: two are missionaries and one is a translator.

'Allow him,' he says while watching the bookkeeper make note of the valuables.

Tall and wiry Father Ambros walks in wearing a flowing white robe, and while his face is grim, his eyes twinkle with kindness. The other two missionaries are natives, and the third one is a muscular man wearing a Gujarati angirkha tied together with numerous threads. His turban is massive and colourful and the man is muscular and stocky.

Shivaji bows and greets them and ushers them to his tent, which is just a big cloth tied to the branches of a sal tree. Pinglay and Palkar

continue to check the men bringing the booty while a few of his
guards accompany Shivaji and gather behind him while the guests
stand in front in a line. A lone torch fixed in an iron basket filled with
sand is lit and kept in the middle.

'We have come to request you to spare our prayer houses and
chapels,' says the native translator politely; his Marathi is heavy with
a Gujarati accent.

'My men will not touch any prayer house, temple, mosque or
chapel. Do you have any other complaint?' Shivaji asks calmly.

The translator has a small discussion with Father Ambros, then
he says, 'The missionaries want to go around and offer solace to
people who have lost their wealth. Will you give them permission to
do so?'

'They have nothing to fear as long as they do not interfere in our
business.'

Father Ambros looks satisfied and he again says something to the
translator. The translator starts to speak again, 'Father wants to know
what you will achieve by this violence.'

'Aurangzeb has ruined my land; his general Shaista Khan and
his army have killed, abducted and enslaved my people, ruined their
farmlands and devoured their cattle for three long years. I need
funds to build a strong army to defend my own against the Mughal
invasions.'

'The emperor will be infuriated. He may answer your violence
with greater violence,' Father Ambros warns.

'I am well aware of this. My actions will no doubt create a major
reaction in Dilli, but my inaction will create a kind of ruthless
presumption. Aurangzeb must know that he or his actions will
trigger reactions.'

'Your people will be tortured and you may be the reason for it,'
challenges the French missionary.

'With or without me, my people have been tortured since
centuries. My people have been enduring for generations, blaming
their kismet and their karma for their tragedies.'

'But what you are doing here is robbery. Your name may go
down as a bandit in the annals of history,' braves the translator again.

'Agreed, and honestly, I don't care. If I am a bandit then who are the marauding Mughals who have killed millions in the name of wars of expansion? Who are the whites who have tortured and converted hundreds of thousands of poor natives to Christianity in and around Goa?'

An awkward silence prevails.

'This will create a major conflict between the Hindus and the Muslims,' Father Ambros throws an ace.

'It was the Mughal army who marked Hindu houses in my terrain to kill and plunder. I am not discriminating against anyone on the basis of his religion. Look at my captives—you may find more Hindus than Muslims,' assures Shivaji.

'You have no idea of their power. Power is their slave,' cautions Father.

'Power . . . the volatile energy is a death trap for those who think of her as a slave. Power, like a goddess, needs to be kept in a sanctum sanctorum and worshipped.'

'Then you must be having a deity that represents power?' asks Father light-heartedly, perhaps knowing the natives' penchant for idolatry.

'Ji,' answers Shivaji smilingly. 'We have Bhavani, the goddess of *shakti* or power. She has eight hands and each of her hands carries a deadly weapon; each weapon signifies the power of one mighty God.'

'Subhedar Inayat has a message for you,' Father shrugs and says, pointing at the translator, 'he is the messenger; we leave him to you while we must return to the city as my prayer time is approaching.'

After the missionaries leave, the translator's expressions change from polite to assertive.

'Subhedar Inayat Khan wants you to immediately leave this place, and do not forget to leave behind what you have taken from our people,' the translator sounds outright rude. There is something else in his voice; it is either eagerness or anxiety but there is also guilt. The men standing behind Shivaji become alert, their eyes remain fixed on the translator cum messenger.

Shivaji breathes deeply, glancing at the sky; it is aglow with stars. 'Are you talking about the same shameless Inayat who is hiding inside the fort? The same man who is cooped up inside the chamber like a woman?'

The muscular messenger fidgets with anger; his bloodshot eyes look crimson in the yellow light of the torch.

'Emperor Aurangzeb will burn your country and remove its trace from the maps,' the messenger is now aggressive.

'Only *He* knows what will go and what will remain,' Shivaji points his index finger to the sky.

'And I will show you who is wearing a bangle!' the messenger shouts. He swiftly pulls out a jambia dagger hidden in the folds of his angirkha and leaps forward, kicking the torch in the process. The blade shines as his hand comes down on Shivaji. The men behind Shivaji move forward with naked swords, while Shivaji screams in pain. One of Shivaji's guards raises his sword and brings it down on the neck of the messenger whose head rolls to the ground. The headless torso falls on Shivaji, bathing him in blood. At this point no one knows the intensity of Shivaji's injury. Some people think he is dead.

'Raja Shivaji is dead,' someone yells. The words strike Palkar's ears like an arrow. He starts trembling with rage and leaps towards where the captives are held. 'Kill them all; they have hurt Raja Shivaji,' he shouts again and again. The night quivers with the pathetic screams of the dying captives.

Shivaji realizes what has happened. The assassin has managed to injure his left arm. He pushes the torso fallen on him and gets up, drenched in the messenger's blood.

'Wait, do not kill people, nothing has happened to me. I am alive,' he shouts and starts running in the direction of the captives.

The place where the captives are kept has turned into a bloody battleground. The massacre has started. The enraged Marathas let the heads roll and limbs fly—the earth is drenched with blood.

'Stop! Stop it!' screams Shivaji running from one place to another. No one recognizes him in the beginning and they continue with their swords, killing the shackled and the helpless with severe blows.

By the time the Marathas realize that their raja is alive, hundreds have lost their lives.

The news of the massacre reaches Inayat in the dead of the night. He summons his sleepy artillerymen.

'Fire and destroy the enemy camp!' he orders without a clue about the range of fire.

They decide that raising the cannons higher may increase the range of firing. The artillerymen work for hours, first taking the old unused guns higher on makeshift scaffolds and then loading the muzzles with granados, iron shells filled with explosives and a low-burning fuse. Early next morning they start firing, but their granados fall in the town, in the residential areas, exploding and demolishing several buildings, causing raging fires and killing Surat residents.

For the next few days the Marathas continue with their attacks and then there is quiet. The Marathas seem to have left for the Deccan. The poor of the city start looting the houses of the rich who remain hiding in Inayat Khan's fort. A few weeks later, a thousand cavalrymen arrive from Agra, complete with decorated horses, trundling elephants and oxen laden with food and weapons. Their luxurious tents are soon pitched, but no one is impressed. People finally gather around the fort and extract Inayat and his loyalists out by force. Infuriated throngs first fling dung at them and then beat Inayat up.

4

The evenings are still cold in Dilli, but Aurangzeb is feeling hot for he is burning with fury. A kafir has struck them twice and those have been well-planned, decisive attacks. The kafir has shaken the confidence of the Surat merchants, taken away wealth worth one crore rupees that is equal to eight thousand ser of gold. Entire Hindustan is talking about Shiva Bhosale; even his own daughters seem to admire the kafir. The Sikhs, the Bundelas, the defiant Rajputs and even other Hindu communities have been discussing his rebellion. They call it a fight for freedom. If the natives wake up to Shiva's idea of freedom, Aurangzeb's dream will never come true, the dream based on a vision of entire Hindustan under one rule, controlled by sharia law.

In a fit of rage, Aurangzeb has done something he has never done before: he has cancelled his preaching sessions and the people who had gathered at the diwan-e-aam are asked to leave. Standing at the edge of the zenana pavilions, he stares blankly at the extraordinary alabaster fabric of the lotus-shaped fountain as the dancing water jets its cargo into the marble channels. From where he stands, he can see freshly tended lawns, lush hedges and flowerbeds that fill the distance between the bath and the Rang Mahal. The Hayat Baksh Garden is aflame at places with its numerous Gulmohur trees. Behind the pavilions, the usually empty purdah garden running along the banks of river Yamuna is buzzing with activity. The otherwise inhibited royal women are out for a breath of fresh air.

Near a small water pond covered with lotuses, several maids are busy chasing little Kambaksh, his son from Udepuri who is learning to take his first steps. As the little one prods unsteadily, the boy shrieks with joy and waves at his mother who sits on a bench near the bougainvillea hedges. Udepuri is laughing with delight. The world is at her feet. She is his favourite wife; she is the empress! Her son Kambaksh gets more attention from his father as compared to all his other children, including Akbar.

Aurangzeb is not in a mood to admire his young family. Instead, he glances at the sky as if to find answers. Above the high walls of the Qila-e-mubarak, the sky is turning darker with streaks of orange leaping out from the west. A frail and speechless moon floats in the middle of the blue expanse, as if looking down with envy at the heavenly Shahjahanabad. The divine surroundings do not alter Aurangzeb's mood and the rage from within his heart starts taking over his mind. He signals to his bodyguards and walks briskly towards the diwan-e-khaas where Mirza Raja Jai Singh is waiting for him.

Aurangzeb approaches the throne. Mirza and Jaffar Khan are present in the hall; they lurch forward to perform kurnish.

Once Aurangzeb is seated comfortably, Mirza bends to keep a silver container filled with pearls near the throne and then steps back facing Aurangzeb to stand at a respectable distance from the throne. Other than the scribe who sits behind a wooden desk, there is no one else in that huge hall.

Jaffar Khan hands over a paper to Mirza.

Mirza squints and holds the paper very close to his eyes to read it. It is a list and has the names of some of the most powerful cavalry commanders of the imperial army, like Jallauddin Daudzai, Daud Qureshi, Raja Rai Singh Sisodia, Ihtisham Shaikhzada, Qubaed Khan, Sujan Singh Bundela, Mulla Yahia and many others. The number of horsemen and footmen mentioned is fourteen thousand.

'Is this the final list?' he asks Jaffar Khan in Persian, his dialect pure.

The inclusion of Jallauddin Daudzai, alias Diler Khan, in the list has bothered him. The unusually hefty Diler was Mir Jumla's favourite warrior. They had waded in the blood of pirates and the kings of Bengal and the Arakan, pushing the borders of the empire beyond the hills of Naga. Two other factors favoured Diler. He was a Muslim and had won victories in the mountainous regions of the Arakan.

'Diler is second-in-command.' Aurangzeb's tone suggests that he has already decided. It is dangerous to let Mirza handle the Deccan alone. Mirza is a kafir and so is Shiva Bhosale, and there is a possibility of them joining hands under the banner of Hindu brotherhood. Never underestimate the power of religion over the strongest of minds.

'All the mentioned commanders along with fourteen thousand horsemen will be joined by our southern garrisons. Together it adds up to fifty thousand. Niccolau Manucci will travel with you to advise your artillerymen,' Jaffar Khan informs Mirza, glancing at Aurangzeb, who sits still on the throne, his legs crossed, peering into a map spread before him while counting the beads of his tesbih. There is silence for a few moments before Aurangzeb speaks up.

'Make a descent into the Konkan. Annex the western borders of the Marathas.'

'Konkan?' Mirza exclaims, suspecting it is Diler's suggestion. 'I am suggesting the opposite, my Alamgir.'

Aurangzeb raises his eyebrows, his pale stare demanding explanations. Age has changed the disposition of Mirza. During his father's time, Mirza used to lead hundreds and thousands to the wretched lands to fight bloody battles. He never asked questions, only soldiered, dragging victories along and hurling them at Shah Jahan's feet.

Perturbed by the emperor's stare, Mirza tries to keep his face blank and adjusts his woollen shawl. He hesitates, but a few moments later, he is ready to put forth his logic, 'My Alamgir, my presence in the Deccan might throw Adil Shah and Shivaji into each other's arms. Even the Qutbshahi kingdom may join the Deccan brotherhood.'

Aurangzeb throws a sharp glance at Mirza and asks Jaffar Khan, 'What do you think, Wazir-e-azam?'

Jaffar Khan, the man in his seventies, is pickled in politics. Being Aurangzeb's aunt's husband adds to his credibility. He narrows his eyes till they are mere splits and argues, 'Shivaji will never solicit for political alliance with Bijapur, and even if he does they will never agree.'

But Aurangzeb is beginning to understand Mirza's logic. Shivaji's psychological approach to war must not be underestimated. In the beginning, Aurangzeb's ancestors like Babur and Humayun regarded war as a matter of life and death. For the later emperors like his own father Shah Jahan, war was a matter of expanding the empire, enjoying the riches and building monuments to keep their footprint on earth. For the emotional and chivalrous Rajputs, war was, and still is, more like a sport that inflates their esteem, making dying in the battlefields to become martyrs their goal. What is the purpose of Shiva Bhosale's war? Shiva's philosophy of empowering humans, freeing them from bondage and inspiring them may engulf the land and infect the minds of the kafirs. Aurangzeb's blood runs cold as he ponders over the terrible implications of Shivaji's rise. How do you kill an idea? Can he present an alternate compelling vision? The only solution, Aurangzeb concludes, is the complete destruction of Shiva Bhosale, making him an example so that no one will dream this dream again.

'The Maratha will do anything *to win*; he is a puzzle hard to solve,' Aurangzeb concludes.

A small smile appears on Mirza's face, he whispers, 'We need a psychological warfare, but first we must stop them from joining hands.'

Aurangzeb looks at Jaffar Khan who first fidgets, then adjusts his turban before stroking his totally white beard up to its end. Stretching his facial muscles to create a serious expression, he says gravely, 'Out there in the battlefield it is slay or get slain. Pray, explain, how can you prevent an alliance between the Marathas with Bijapur even if you head east?'

The emperor looks at Mirza, demanding a credible answer.

'My Alamgir, as you are well aware, the Deccan is a peculiar region. On its western side the Sahyadri Mountains run north to south forming a formidable wall. Towards the east of this natural fortification, the ridges taper down gently. These slopes merge into the plains of the Adilshahi kingdom. Towards the west, craggy drops stand facing the ocean, rising almost a kos above the sea.'

'Parvardigar is aware,' Jaffar Khan nudges, but Aurangzeb nods in agreement for Mirza to go ahead.

'Between the slopes and the drops lies the secret of the Maratha power. Shivaji's countless hill forts watch over the ravines and the ridges, the ports and the sea forts, the Adilshahi's western borders and our southern borders. The men from the hunting tribes have been trained to defend the foothills. Most of the Maratha soldiers are peasants and the creatures of the mountains and the valleys.' Mirza stops, inhales deeply and quips, 'We cannot fight a crocodile in water, but we may trap the monster on the plains.'

Aurangzeb is once again peering into the map. Mirza waits for his attention.

'I am listening,' Aurangzeb murmurs.

'Unlike the others, I want to fight them from the east. From here, I may not prevent Shivaji from forging an alliance with Adil Shah but I can watch over all our foes and be forewarned if they do try.' Mirza has finished.

'Is that the only advantage?' The emperor's interest is aroused.

'There are many. The earth is relatively even, not hard on our horsemen, who are our core military strength. It is easier to capture some forts guarding Bhosale jagir's eastern borders, especially those with hidden physical faults, just to show that we can and we will capture the forts if need be.' Mirza stops at that, not explaining further.

Aurangzeb is fascinated. Mirza is talking specifics and not rhetoric. He asks softly, 'Targeting the forts with physical faults—is that your war strategy?'

In the depth of his heart, Mirza admires Aurangzeb's intelligence. His eyes narrowed, his voice husky, Mirza starts talking about his war scheme for the first time: 'More than a hundred hill forts will take more than a hundred years to besiege and to win. We must cut the jugular of the forts by hitting at the revenue stream. If Shivaji is a guerrilla, then we too must checkmate him by becoming one. If his squadrons can cut our supplies by attacking our detachments, we will do the same by systematically crushing his peasants and destroying his revenue system. Without revenue, the hill forts will become as harmless as snakes without fangs.'

For the first time in several months, Aurangzeb smiles. He has understood what Mirza is trying to convey. Seeing him smile, Jaffar Khan too grins but persists with a question that has nagged him, 'If so, why go for the forts, even those with physical faults? Why must we invest just to show off?'

Before Mirza opens his mouth the emperor replies, 'Those conquests will merely be symbolic, to show if we want, we can.'

Mirza is elated. He does not want to wait. He says politely, 'If I am leading the campaign, I need complete authority.'

'You already have it. The imperial treasury has opened its vaults wide. Funds, manpower and weapons—you will get what you demand. Our mir bakshi, Mohammad Amin, will be assigned to follow your requirements and he will be briefed about the urgency of supply,' Jaffar Khan says elegantly, waving his right hand and flashing his four diamond rings.

'It is not just about the supplies; what I need goes beyond mere field authority,' Mirza strikes a blow very softly and very courteously.

'Open your heart, Mirza,' Aurangzeb commands, staring at his oldest warrior who with his military skills had sent the maximum number of men from Balkh in Central Asia to Qandahar in the west and to Mungir in the east.

Mirza does not waste time or words.

'Make me the final authority over promotions, punishments and transfer of the mansabdars, the payment of the troops and the regulation of the Deccan mansabs.'

The other two gape at him.

'You want to be the subhedar of the Deccan?' Aurangzeb says, concealing his shock. Mirza is seeking the kingship of the state and is indirectly suggesting to be allowed to bypass the authority of Prince Muazzam, the present subhedar of the Deccan.

'Do you realize the weight of such enormous responsibility? How will you manage both? Think about controlling fifty thousand warriors on the battlefield and also looking after administration,' Jaffar Khan says, his body swaying by a sudden upsurge of anxiety.

'Not exactly,' Mirza says hastily. 'I would prefer to have complete authority over whoever is involved in this war, for I am the man on the spot.'

'What I wished for happened not. What God willed happened to a dot!' Jaffar Khan throws a Farsi proverb in a teasing tone.

Mirza keeps a stoic expression; he knows the old man likes to tease and incite.

Mirza knows the Deccan and he is a man of tact and endurance, has learnt the ceremonious courtesy of the Mughal court, is fluent in Farsi, Turki, Urdu and Rajasthani, and hence is an ideal leader for the not-so-amalgamated and complex imperial army of Turks, Afghans, Persians, Rajputs and Hindustanis. He has prudence, political shrewdness, communication skills and innate intelligence to calculate risk. Even in tricky situations, he does not display recklessness, impulsive behaviour, bluntness and superfluous chivalry. More than all those qualities, Mirza, who commanded the largest number of Hindu horsemen, had deserted Dara bhai's son Suleiman and joined hands with Aurangzeb against Shah Jahan, thus helping him win the war of succession. In turn, Aurangzeb had rewarded Mirza with the jagirdari of some districts with an annual revenue income of two and half lakh rupees.

'The war in the Deccan needs to be fought not merely with swords, spears and cannons, but the region and its powerful men also need to be tackled by playing with their fears and hopes, perceptions and dreams, emotions and esteem,' Mirza says, his eyes shining with mysterious energy.

Immediately after Mirza leaves, Aurangzeb calls his scribe and dictates a letter to Ali Adil Shah:

> After Surat, Shiva Bhosale may enter Konkan with a big force. If that happens, send an army against Shivaji and destroy him. If you succeed, we promise you that we will redeem a large amount of tribute money you are expected to pay us. If you fail, we will lead an army against the Adilshahi in person and will not stop till the sultanate is conquered.

CHAPTER TWENTY-SIX

1

Mirza works day and night, sending letters to jagirdars and deshmukhs, especially the known revenue collectors of Karnataka, to leave the services of Ali Adil Shah and join him in his war against Shivaji. A vakeel of Mirza has reached Bijapur with a message to Ali Adil Shah that the amount of annual tribute the king pays to the Mughal emperor can be reduced or even waived off if he assists the Mughals in their campaign against the Marathas. Mirza makes every effort for defections and has established contacts with Prataprao Morey, Afzal Khan's son Fazal Khan and some Maratha zamindars of the Konkan. He is paying special attention to the Siddis of Janjira by sending swords and shields as gifts. Promises of the posts of mansabdars in the Mughal services are being used as bait to corrupt some of Shivaji's loyalists, but this, unfortunately, has met with little success.

Aurangzeb too has kept his word. While Prince Muazzam remains the de-facto subhedar of the Deccan, Mirza has all the authority—command not just of field operations but also of all administrative work like promotions, punishments, transfers, payment and regulation of jagirs of the mansabdars under him. The commandants of the Mughal forts, like Daulatabad, Ahmednagar and Parinda, have been asked to report to Mirza who keeps sending a letter to his master about his progress and achievements, every day, without fail. He has also appointed experts who are qualified to detect flaws in Shivaji's hill forts and has begun studying the geographical, social and political situation of the Deccan. Two European naval experts will soon join him to negotiate with the Europeans of Surat, Mumbai and Goa. Mirza is a clever general and knows the difference between the imperial and non-imperial powers. It is the poorly organized and weaker military powers that have higher thresholds for the pain and agonies of a long-drawn-out war.

Mirza has constant meetings with the mansabdars under his supervision as with Diler Khan, the second-in-command, and Niccolau Manucci, the Italian artillery expert. In the meetings that sometimes go on till midnight, maps are drawn and discussed and places to construct permanent Mughal outposts are identified. The most important aspect of military leadership is to coax your men into thinking critically, without remorse or guilt, because ruthless, mass killings of the population is the only way to shake the hills of the Deccan and bring down those who perch on the top of those hills.

After several deliberations with his men he has also come to a decision as to where his own base camp will be: it is a town called Saswad a few kos away from Purandar Fort. Saswad lies on the eastern borders of Shivaji's terrain and at the western borders of the Adilshahi kingdom and is just ten kos south-east of Pune. While the flurry of military activity goes on, not a single meeting is attended by the Mughal subhedar of the Deccan, Prince Muazzam, Aurangzeb's son from his Hindu wife, Nawab Bai. The prince is too preoccupied with hashish and alcohol parties as well as his hunting expeditions. This suits Mirza fine.

After spending a week at the foothills of Daulatabad, Mirza's cavalcade moves towards Pune. It is like a city on the move, with a sea of cavalrymen, dense mass of infantrymen, caparisoned elephants with howdahs carrying the mansabdars, followed by covered palanquins carrying their families and surrounded by slaves, servants, orderlies and cooks. There are also strings of oxen, mules and asses loaded with goods, coolies with waterskins and camels carrying cannons. Above the cavalcade, the moss-green imperial banners flutter with the wind, the rising suns and couching lions embroidered on the silken cloth causing ripples in the Deccan air. Mirza does not rest at Pune and keeps busy meeting mansabdars and other officials in charge of the twenty thousand cavalry left behind by Shaista Khan. He has already met with Maharaja Jaswant Singh Rathod and given him Aurangzeb's message, asking him to proceed to Dilli. Perhaps Jaswant be posted at the empire's north-west frontiers famous for murderous hill men from the mountain ranges of Ghazni and Kabul. Mirza shivers just thinking about it. There birds drop dead in summer when the terrain beyond Qandahar turns into a furnace. With scant supply of water that is brackish, it is impossible to maintain a large number of men in the military camps. Vast patches of desolate regions occupied by lawless tribes with men born with predatory instincts are the worst places for encampment. One does not need a battle to die in those regions.

2

On the borders of the western Deccan, rocky drops stand like forlorn sentinels watching over the coast. The spotless white sands seem to have made a truce with the emerald waters of the ocean. The tide is high and the waters choppy. A hundred small boats sail towards the island of Sindudurg Fort, making their way through a narrow canal between a rock and a small island. Later they bounce violently into the open sea as sailors try hard to cut the mountains of surf with their oars. Shivaji scans the skyline while holding on to the hull as his boat bounces on the sea, its bow rising and diving with the waves. He notices a long wall that has started rising above the rocks at the ridges. Tiny figures of men are seen scurrying about on its ramparts.

As the boats near, the thunderous roar of the waves crashing on the rocks lifts the spirit of the sailors navigating the boats. Shivaji jumps out and walks towards the bastions that seem to seal off the island. The gatekeepers bow and the others follow him as he enters the fort through an opening hidden behind the perimeter of two bulging stone structures.

Inside, another world unfolds as hundreds of labourers are busy in the construction work happening over forty-eight acres of rocky earth. Shivaji checks the construction site for a while, his eyes roving and noticing each and every detail. Skilled men have arrived from Gujarat and beyond. The plunder of Surat and Basnur has helped to mint countless sacks of gold, silver and brass coins. *The funds will soon be over,* he thinks regretfully. There is more trouble: the new Mughal general, Mirza Jai Singh, is advancing towards Pune and the region is once again under threat.

Preoccupied, he moves towards the massive furnaces. The Portuguese metallurgy experts shouting instructions fall quiet and remove their hats and bow to him. He stands back, admiring the resilience of the local blacksmiths who stand so close to the furnace, their eyes scanning the piles of slag iron lumps and lead ingots, their dark skins gleaming with sweat. Shivaji walks away glancing proudly at the outer wall fortifications built with square stones, hiding secret dungeons and tunnels in their bellies. Its ramparts and bastions have already swallowed more than five thousand maunds of metal and countless buckets of lime. They will be his warriors against the gangs of pirates, against the ships of war sailing from the other lands, against the mafia of traders. His eyes wander and notice a line of men in soiled clothes carrying huge jute baskets on their heads. The shell-collectors have been hired from nearby villages after they had come in hoards, with the lure of copper coins and a meal that they were offered at the site. The shells will be converted to lime for the construction.

This fort will be Shivaji's answer to Janjira. This fort will enhance the strength of his navy!

The sun is about to set and the western sky is turning golden. The aroma of millet bread has started replacing the metallic smell of the iron broth. The construction noises are gradually abating. Shivaji is about to reach the entrance when he hears Tanaji Malusare's voice, 'Raja, messengers have arrived from the mountains with news. Mirza Raja Jai Singh has reached Pune and plans to march in the direction of Purandar.'

Shivaji knows what is coming.

Mirza's journey towards Saswad begins with the absolute determination to defeat Shivaji. It is the month of Baisakh but cold winds still sweep in from the faraway mountains. The Mughal cavalcade moves through canopies of banyan, pipal and tamarind trees. Stampeding hooves of Mirza's war animals crush the lumps of black soil. The villages they cross are deserted. They pass by Purandar Fort late in the evening. In the bright moonlight, the craggy ridges of Purandar Hill loom over them. From one of the watchtowers built on the rock of Kandakada, Murarbaji watches the Mughal procession go eastwards. He is aware that the new Mughal general has plans to make Saswad his base camp and he knows that war has arrived at his doorstep, at the foothills of his fort.

Two kos away from Purandar, the Mughal base camp is erected within days. Slaves are seen hammering spikes into the layers of earth to pitch tents, coolies cut, carry and fix logs of wood to make strong stables and sheds for the animals, and latrine pits are dug. A waterproof stone structure is erected to store explosives. Mirza continues to work late into the night. On the fourth night everything seems to be in place and functioning. In his brightly lit palatial den, Mirza relaxes on a stately couch covered with satin durries and bolsters filled with soft and fluffy cotton.

3

The Deccan air has turned sweeter with the scent of ripening mangos still on the trees. Around the Mughal base camp, jungle trails have started filling up with men galloping towards Kondana Fort. They race, crouching on their mounts to avoid getting smashed by the low-hanging branches of the enormous banyan trees. The horses' hooves echo across the valley and the raiders seem to seek their enemy's attention.

The tribesmen guarding the foothills of Purandar have heard the booming noise and have felt the earth shaking beneath their nimble feet. Some have even thought that they have seen countless shadows of horsemen scurrying under the moonless sky.

'Clouds of demons are drifting towards the fort; they will rain evil,' the tribesmen want to warn Murarbaji.

Murarbaji has already heard the news and he shouts orders. The artillerymen quickly take positions behind the cannon placed on the ramparts facing the east. The archers climb the fortified wall and stand vigil under the canopies of watchtowers. More than a thousand scouts stand rooted on the ridges overlooking the valley, with boulders piled at the edge.

'Who is leading them?' Murarbaji wants to know from the tribesmen who have just arrived.

The tribesmen do not have the answer.

Few kos away, Daud Qureshi, the leader of the Mughal raiders, likes to keep a low profile and lead his men from the front. Rai Singh, Amar Singh and others try to keep pace as a sea of raiders follow them, wave after wave. It is time for action after many months of a hard, dreary journey.

The forewarned artillerymen of Purandar wait in anticipation, their guns ready to rain explosives on the approaching enemy. The scouts standing at the lower levels have started hooting to warn the others as artillerymen shove explosives in the muzzles of their cannon. However, the efforts seem futile and the scouts watch in helpless horror. The Mughal raiders have avoided them and have dispersed in the valley where villages lie hidden behind the safety of the hills.

Daud Qureshi is leading eight thousand men to the valley that lies beyond Purandar. He has turned fifty but his muscles have not yet aged and his earliest memories are that of bloody fights at the southern borders of Balkh. For the past few months he has lived the insipid life of a mere traveller and is thirsty for the smell of blood, for the feel of palpable flesh under his blade and for the cries of the vanquished. After a long wait, the time has come. Feeling pleased, Daud pulls the reins as his body stretches backwards. The others following him slow down abruptly, making their horses teeter and then slowly come to a halt.

'Split,' he barks.

Rai Singh, Amar Singh, Sharja Khan, Achal Singh and the others have already been briefed. Eight thousand men are divided into eight flying columns, each moving towards different villages. Before nudging his horse into action, Daud looks back at his horsemen who wait impatiently, looking like a mass of staggering shadows, uneasy but thirsty to strike.

His feet firmly lock in the stirrups as he hits the horse hard with his knees. He leads his men to a sleepy village hidden behind the hills, still untouched by invasions. The hooves of his warhorses flatten the surrounding fields dislodging grains from the cobs only to vanish into dust. The raiders charge ruthlessly, their blades sweeping down on the oblivious peasants safeguarding the fields. Within moments the hamlet is encircled, as the attackers pull the reins with full strength to hold back their mounts.

Daud nudges his horse and enters the village. A few horsemen follow him to a poorly lit open courtyard, their horses skittering over the pebbled floor.

'Get them all!' Daud shouts.

'Out! Out!' thunder the raiders galloping through the narrow lanes of huddled houses. The rude sound shakes the mud walls and fills the villagers with dread. A sudden spill of people in the crooked gullies ends in a stampede. Some Mughal horsemen pull out leashes hooked to their saddles and start whipping the crowd at the flanks and screams of agony tear through the valley. People, numb with the premonition of death, shuffle and waddle, push and heave their bodies in the dark. They are shoved towards a tamarind tree that stands in the middle of the pebbled floor courtyard.

'Sort them,' Daud orders hoarsely.

Some of the horsemen dismount, grabbing the lanterns from the open balconies. They push their way through the mass of people, mute with fear. The lantern holders are quick in their selection.

'You, you and you.' The young and healthy are plucked from the crowd and dragged away towards the edge of the yard. Horsemen encircling the hamlet watch the proceedings with fascination, hooting and whistling as the younger women try to cover their faces in the cusp of their hands, shaking with sobs.

Daud waves his hand.

A few raiders from the encircling lot kick their horses and move towards the chosen lot. They leap down as one of them pulls out a huge bundle of rope tied to his back. The new slaves scream and struggle feebly as their hands are tied behind them, with a single rope. The others, who are not chosen, too have started crying and calling the names of their enslaved boys and girls seeing them getting hauled in a file. Some of them stand rooted, refusing to move. One of the raiders pulls out his leash and starts whipping, his body twisting under the savage vigour of his biceps. The yells slice the air, hammering the ridges of the mountains, and echo through the courtyards of the nearby hill forts. Finally the file of the surrendered is hauled away, raiders tugging and jerking the rope.

Daud's duty is not over. He signals to a man who seems like a native Deccani. The man, holding a gunny bag leaps from his horse and rushes to the captured mass of people, shouting raucously in Marathi, raising his voice above their cries.

'Your gold, silver, jewels! Quick, quick!'

Soon his bag is heavy with nose rings, trinkets, anklets, toe rings and bangles.

A young man darts across wielding a long machete and roaring a battle cry, 'Har Har Mahadev! Har Har Mahadev!' His lithe, half-naked body shimmers in the pale yellow lights of the lanterns. Before anyone can wink, the youngster scythes the man with the leash, again and again and then again. Finally he is left hacking just the dead meat. 'I know you. You are one of us, you traitor,' the youngster yells while sobbing and crying and then looks at the crowd as his eyes sparkle with strange passion.

'Say it!' he thunders, raising his hands as his blood streams down from his machete, 'Har Har Mahadev! Har Har Mahadev!'

'Har Har Mahadev!' the villagers cry out the battle cry as loudly as possible. Death is not avoidable but they do not want the Mughal to take their lives; they want to give their lives to the enemy, as alms.

Daud nudges his horse, his sword once again out of his scabbard, its crimson blade swiftly beheading the budding display of courage. 'That's enough. Move!' he shouts as loudly as possible. The night is not yet over; they have to cover one more village.

The encircling men have heard their master. A hundred of them surge forward, brandishing naked swords. The blades look new.

unused, as if fresh from the blacksmith's forge. The men advance slowly, relishing every moment as bearers of death. The villagers close their eyes and keep shouting 'Har Har Mahadev!', in frenzy. The loud chanting of their battle cry seems to make them martyrs. They are no longer the victims; they are courageous and are sacrificing their life for a cause.

Daud feels disappointed. He wants them to fall to their knees, to beg, to cry in horror. He wanted to see their eyes burn with hatred, and their hearts bleed with dread. Watching human weakness has always made him feel potent, but the villagers have denied him his pleasure. 'Dogs from hell!' he curses. Within moments the cries stop and the courtyard falls silent. The pebbled floor is flooded with blood while the tamarind tree stands mute. Even the phantoms subsisting on its branches might not have witnessed carnage such as this before.

'The cattle,' Daud throws a reminder.

A few horsemen break loose from the circle, unfasten the cattle and herd them away to the same place where the slave train is waiting.

At midnight, Daud and his men leave the hamlet. The deathly silence is broken by the crackle of fire that is about to swallow the barns and the fields. The slave carriers have noticed thick billows of smoke rising from the village, forming a cloud over the summer sky. The captives tied to the single rope look at the smoke, mutely, not yelling or crying, as if they have been robbed of all their tears.

A hundred slaves, a bagful of jewels and two hundred cattle. Mirza Jai Singh will be pleased with the first spoils of this Deccan war, Daud thinks as he kicks his horse into a gallop.

CHAPTER TWENTY-SEVEN

1

'The mountain mass rising a few hundred guj above the plains to our south-west is Purandar, Shivaji's eastern stronghold. It has an upper fort with precipitous drops from all sides and is *almost* invincible, but not quite. Purandar has a twin called Vajragad on a ridge running out east of Purandar. Vajragad in Hindustani means "weapon", but I can assure you that this weapon will help us cut Purandar's jugular,' Mirza says peering into the map drawn on a jute paper spread on a teakwood table in the midst of his tent erected for formal meetings.

Diler Khan and many others surround the table to look at the map they find fascinating. Niccolau Manucci, wearing a large tunic and tight leggings, with two pistols attached to his waist belt, remains seated on Mirza's divan. He has already seen the map.

'Look at this rock rising above the hill of Purandar—it is called Kandakada. It is an extension of the upper fort; the lower fort is almost three hundred guj below the peak. The girth of this lower fort is about two kos, protected by a winding wall fortified with ramparts and watchtowers that are always guarded by archers. To the north, the ledge of the lower fort widens and has barracks of the fort garrison.

'This ledge or terrace is bound by a high hill that starts rising from the base of the steep, overhanging, north-eastern watchtower built on Kandakada, and runs about half a kos east in a narrow ridge, ending in a small flatland. That is Vajragad. There is a shallow ravine between the two forts, called Bhairavkhind.'

'The point is clear: Vajragad is very close to the northern terrace of Purandar's lower fort where the garrison resides,' Diler Khan adds.

Mirza raises his eyebrows in appreciation, and glances at the tall Afghan with kohl-lined eyes and a long beard and says, 'Two watchtowers, one painted black and the other white, face the terrace of Vajragad, which is at a lower level.'

'From what I see in this map, if we can blow up these two towers and cross Bhairavkhind, we can reach Purandar's lower fort. Vajragad is on a relatively smaller hill; it will be easy to climb and take our artillery along. My suggestion is to take Vajragad first and use it to conquer the higher and more difficult Purandar,' Diler says with confidence.

Mirza nods. He likes it when his men say what he wants to say because then there is less resistance from the others.

'We have some immediate tasks to tackle,' Mirza gets to the first step of his strategy. 'We have a sufficiently large army to besiege

Purandar. Take over Vajragad while simultaneously sending flying columns to destroy villages to spread terror and also send garrisons to man our outposts.'

'Daud Qureshi will lead eight flying columns of a thousand horsemen each to attack villages; he has already started his assignment with satisfactory results.'

Mirza stops for a few breaths and says coldly, 'This battle must be won at any cost, and the besiegement must be impregnable. Far-flung outposts are vital in this case and those will serve as isolated obstacles. Remember the men who are responsible to defend these outposts must always hold out, even under the most adverse circumstances, with will power and willingness for self-sacrifice. Understand that these outposts are not to delay the enemy but to stop him from coming anywhere near our besiegement.'

The men nod solemnly.

'I want complete quarantine—isolate and protect our outposts, trenches, besiegement and communications from the enemy,' Mirza instructs.

'Syed Abdul Azeez with his three thousand men will be posted at Niral to stop any external help from reaching the nearby forts, especially Purandar,' says Mirza, then murmurs in a husky voice, 'Direct each of our men to kill anything that moves including the mounts of the Marathas, hack even the dead to pieces, splatter their blood over the jungle trails and scatter their limbs around. Let fear reign! Qutbuddin Khan and seven thousand men will cover the area between Junnar in the north and Fort Lohagad in the west. The barricade will stop the Marathas from entering the Mughal territory,' Mirza announces looking at Qutbuddin who stands next to Diler.

'Ihtishm Khan with his four thousand horsemen will guard Pune and its surroundings. A brigade of two thousand cavalrymen has been delegated the task of watching over the narrow pass between Pune and Lohagad,' Mirza looks into Ihtishm's eyes.

'Twenty thousand men will be deployed to besiege the twin forts while Diler Khan will lead six thousand soldiers and artillerymen to Vajragad to capture Purandar.' Mirza returns to his divan and starts smoking his hookah.

'Daud Qureshi has already started the slaughter. Tonight, sixteen more villages are going down,' he murmurs as others watch with respect.

'And the other hill forts?' Diler asks impatiently.

'In the valleys of the Deccan, haste means death by blade. We need to first test the endurance of our siege,' Mirza says, raising his brow. 'Senor Mannuci, we need three long-range cannons, fifty gunners and some of your artillery experts to go with Diler Khan Sahib.'

Niccolau had finished putting a sieve over his hookah bowl. With a pair of tongs in his hand, he was now staring at the pieces of coal smouldering in an iron pot placed on a tripod. He liked to prepare his own shisha.

'Mirza Sahib, it is true that a deep gorge separates the two targeted forts, but the Purandar side is much higher than the terrace of Vajragad. The explosives will hit only the craggy surface of the steep mountain.' Diler Khan has a point.

Mirza glances at Niccolau and smiles, but Niccolau is busy fiddling with his hookah. The wise Italian knows when to open his mouth. In Urdu spoken with a thick Italian accent, he says, 'Diler Khan Sahib, we will mount the cannons on wooden platforms, taking them very, very high to target even the watchtowers of Purandar. When you have Niccolau, you do not worry.'

'Do not underrate the fort-keeper of Purandar, Murarbaji Deshpande. He has a reputation of being an aggressive warrior. Do not underestimate Shivaji's men,' Mirza's words boom in the tent.

Diler glances at Niccolau who takes his first big hit from the pipe to get the coals going. He has plans to linger on after others have gone. His white skin allows him special privileges.

2

The planned devastation of villages begins. Daud Qureshi and his men start bringing hundreds of slaves and cattle into the camp. The besiegement of the twin fort is in place, with Mirza constantly inspecting the entrenchments of the besieging army. The Marathas are not quiet either; their attacks on dark nights, blocking of roads and passes and setting fire to jungles are killing many imperial horsemen and making it hard for the Mughals to move about. At ground zero, Diler and Niccolau Manucci's artillerymen plan continuous shelling of Vajragad from a hill across the fort, and the ceaseless bombardment for fourteen days demolishes a bastion of Vajragad. A hundred Mughal soldiers have died and an equal number have been seriously injured. Diler does not wait and orders his men to climb the hill to plant the Mughal flag while Mirza deploys hundreds of coolies to take three large guns to the top. Within a few days, the Mughals reach the fort enclosure and drive the Maratha garrison away.

It has been more than a month since the Mughal besiegement moved closer to Purandar.

Some shallow-crawl trenches dug on the ridge of Vajragad are very close to the edge of Purandar where the white and black watchtowers stand more than three hundred guj above the trenches. The soil from the excavation is used to make mud parapets for extra protection, but that is not enough because the enemy is still far above them. In the beginning, they had thought that the noose was finally getting tighter, but nothing spectacular has happened since then. Every time the Mughals have tried to get closer, the Marathas have showered them with an array of missiles from above. Many of their soldiers have been gravely injured by lighted naptha balls, crude granado blasts and stones. At least four times in the last month, the Marathas had managed to climb down to Vajragad from the watchtowers with the help of ropes and cross the shallow Bhairavkhind. They had even made sorties to drive away the men hiding in trenches, killing many in the bargain. In one of those attacks, Mirza's officer Bhupat Singh, a middle-ranking mansabdar, was slain, and Mirza's son Kirat Singh was injured.

The besiegement is tight and Mirza has made sure that supplies do not reach the Maratha garrison in Purandar. The summer is almost over but the enemy has survived and that means they must be getting food and water from outside somehow. Mirza wonders if the Marathas are surviving on mountain air!

Late one night, Mirza, Diler and Gaud Qureshi, along with some guides and armed guards, are out on the flat glades at the top of the newly conquered Vajragad to get a closer look at the newly erected wooden scaffoldings. Mirza is impatient. He wants to experiment. He wants to reach for the twin towers. It is dark and it is also dangerous to light a torch because the Marathas on those watchtowers never seem to sleep. The men walk silently till they reach a high wooden platform of logs and planks erected behind the trenches facing the black and white towers. The massive scaffoldings are more than three hundred guj high. Three large guns have been mounted on them and the gunners and musketeers sitting on the scaffolds are excited to see Mirza; they have started whispering loudly.

'Pursue the enemy wisely and blow one or both the watchtowers.'

'Inshallah!' someone replies from the scaffolds.

Mirza looks up. The structure is almost invisible in the dark but its shadow looms above him, rising above the Purandar towers.

If only those towers are demolished . . . If one cannonball lands on one of those towers, can it blow up the storehouse of the explosives? Diler thinks wistfully.

Tonight the guns will be fired, aimed at the white tower.

'I do not think it will ever work. It may take a long time, months perhaps,' Daud Qureshi, who has been called back from the field to watch over the siege for a few days, whispers. Diler Khan is tempted to reply, but thinks otherwise. Sometimes he suspects that Mirza and Daud Qureshi are secretly helping the Marathas.

'Daud Khan,' Mirza says evenly. He does not want a fight to break between the two. 'I think you must go back to what you were doing—destroying villages. This time, you go for the villages at the foothills of Rajgad, home of Shivaji.'

Mirza has noticed that Daud Qureshi is happiest while raiding villages. Saying this, Mirza starts walking away from the scaffolds and towards the forts enclosure. It is an upward climb.

They barely reach the enclosure when they hear a blast. The men look back in astonishment, thinking that their gunmen have started firing in haste, earlier than planned. What they see makes them freeze. The structure of the scaffolds is on fire, with an inferno rising several guj above it. The fire has come from the towers, those pale-looking shadows, benign and harmless. The noise of the explosion is followed by the agonizing screams of the Mughal gunners and musketeers. Mirza, Daud Qureshi and Diler watch human figures on fire, falling down, limbs flailing, as the scaffold collapses.

* * *

Several nights later, Diler, sleeping in the enclosure of Vajragad, is awakened by the sound of hammering. He gets up and the hinges of his rickety charpoy creak and groan. He staggers into the courtyard, dimly lit with a few lanterns. The floor is littered with his sleeping and snoring men.

Following the sound of hammering, Diler walks steadily towards the main doorway, carefully avoiding stepping on the limbs of sleeping men. The entrance opens between the two bastions and there is no security at the gate. Diler takes the gritty stairs to reach an open mountain table where a robust moon rains silvery light on the rocky terraces. At the far end of the western side, in the direction of Purandar, torches flicker behind a high wooden platform where Manucci's men are at work. He marvels at their suicidal persistence. In the last seven days, the Marathas firing from the Purandar watchtowers have destroyed several scaffoldings even before they could mount the cannon. The Italian has also lost some of his men.

In the bright moonlight, craggy ridges of Purandar Hill loom over Diler Khan. The watchtowers from the other side are clearly visible from his position. With those towers teeming with archers and those ramparts loaded with cannon, it is impossible to cross the gorge and reach Purandar. Within twenty days, these clear skies, the mountaintops and the towers will be covered under thunderclouds, Diler thinks with regret and spreads his hands towards the sky praying, *Allah, let the scaffoldings survive and the cannons be mounted, even if for a brief period.*

The artillerymen are surprised when they notice the huge figure coming towards them, for no one has ever visited them in the dead of the night. They take some time to recognize the man who has come barefoot, wearing an ankle-length kaftan. Diler allows them some time for their shock to wane and declares, 'Do not wait. As soon as the scaffolding is restored, mount the cannon and fire the guns. Every moment is precious.'

So just before the first rays of the sun can hit the ground, huge cannons are placed at the highest levels on the scaffolds. Niccolau Manucci's men have made sure that they have the latest bombards and granados fitted with adjustable fuses. The men are quick in loading the muzzles of the cannon with explosives. The Marathas from the watchtowers have realized what has happened. They fire at the scaffolds that collapse yet again, heaving down the cannons, crushing some artillerymen. Their agonizing cries rise above all other sounds. Diler who is watching from a distance feels disheartened and is about to turn to go back into the enclosure to call his men for help when he hears another deafening sound; he swings around and notices an explosion near the twin watchtowers. An inferno rises and the sky is covered with an orange blaze. Diler watches something quite unbelievable. He sees limbs and heads of the enemy archers and scouts from the blown twin towers flying in all directions, one severed leg landing just a few guj away from him.

Some of Diler's guards sitting in trenches run to inform him that perhaps explosives stored by the Marathas in one of the watchtowers caught fire and exploded, taking the twin towers down and killing or seriously injuring the Maratha archers and scouts who were keeping the Mughals away from Purandar. Diler is not aware of how the explosives caught fire and he doesn't care. All he sees is that the towers are gone and so are the Purandar defenders. The way to the lower fort of Purandar is open to the Mughals! They have to just cross the shallow ditch between the hills!

Diler leaps towards the enclosure where his soldiers are. The time has come to lead his men to their next destination!

A few hours later, thousands of Mughal soldiers are ready to cross Bhairavkhind and reach the ruins of the Purandar watchtowers. Diler is ecstatic; this is his victory and soon Purandar will be in his hands. He gazes at his contingent with pride; they are his men. As he inspects them before the attack on Purandar, he wonders how perfect they looked with chain mail hanging from their metal headgear on either side of their faces. Diler quickly concludes his inspection and orders them to start moving. They march—the thousands of swordsmen with their curved scabbards, followed by a contingent of archers with double-curved bows and quivers loaded with arrows. However, surprisingly, the battle energy that usually runs through their veins making them lethal is missing. They feel that asking them to clash with some obscure rebel tribesmen is akin to a farce.

Mirza is in his camp at Saswad. He has received the news and is waiting for some more.

3

Murarbaji has called his men near the watchtower of Kandakada, the extension of the upper fort. In the afternoon sun, they can clearly see the ruins of black and white watchtowers on the lower cliff. They have tried to pull away as many dead bodies as possible, but some still lie in the shallow ravine that separates the forts.

This is no time for bereavement

'The time has come. The towers and the wall guarding the invaders marching in from Vajragad are gone. It is just a matter of time before they reach the lower fort and gather around Pali Gate to enter the upper fort,' Murarbaji tells his men as they watch their leader with squinted eyes, holding their palms near their brows to avoid the sun.

'Despite the tight siege, a few scouts have managed to reach us, and they have told us horrible stories of how the Mughals are on a rampage, burning villages, killing and enslaving our people, taking away cattle, burning down the standing crops near the foothills of most of our hill forts. The damage is most acute near the forts like Lohagad, Visapur, Tung and Tikona—not a single peasant is alive, not a single woman left behind, not a single farm animal spared.' Murarbaji wipes his forehead and swallows hard before speaking what he wants to say as others watch, their hearts raging with fury.

'I have a plan,' Murarbaji says with a never-seen-before spark in his eyes.

4

On Vajragad's extensive terrace, the Mughal soldiers cross Bhairavkhind with ease to enter the courtyard of the lower fort. It is deserted. Diler is stunned to see the walls fortified with ramparts and watchtowers. When they reach their destination, he notices massive bastions surrounding the Dilli Darwaza, above which a saffron flag ripples with buoyancy. Beyond the fortified gate, the hill that houses the upper fort rises to a considerable height. Diler notices a rock on the top of that hill and a watchtower above the rock, which he has seen from Vajragad. That was from a distance, but from up close, the rock looks invincible. *Allah alone knows how many men are up there,* Diler thinks and signals the artillerymen who have started inspecting the outer wall of the lower fort, its ramparts and watchtowers, to place the cannons to target the gate. Fearing a shower of arrows from the ramparts, Diler does not want his men to move forward unless the wooden gate braced with huge spikes is blown up.

'Archers, take positions!' Diler shouts. *The rats are hiding, without making a sound,* he thinks.

Just then, there is the deafening sound of drums and trumpets, as if the Marathas are celebrating victory. The noise numbs the minds of the Mughals for a brief moment and the enormous doors of Dilli Darwaza are thrown open. The Marathas pour out, like water through a broken dam, wearing tight breeches and pleated angirkhas of quilted cotton, their heads covered with boat-shaped turbans. They advance with raised hands, straight blades of long swords shining under the noon sun, roaring their battle cry that rides above the music of the drums and the trumpets: *'Har Har Mahadev!'*

'Charge!' Diler shouts, feeling breathless for a moment. Initially the Mughal men are puzzled and they falter, but soon they gather their wits and surge forward with a throaty battle cry. Diler has climbed a boulder and joined a few archers so he can see the battleground.

Looking at the size of the enemy contingent, Diler calculates six or seven hundred, one-fifth the size compared to the number of his swordsmen. Something strikes him: the Marathas move with speed, as if they want to take the combat away from their entrance. He watches with interest as they sprint and leap, from left and then to right, some holding a sword in each hand. They also duck and jump to spoil the aim of his archers. Short and agile, some fly over the ridges and some even appear on the ramparts and then throw themselves over his swordsmen. Once on their victims they hold the man in the tight grip of their feet, and then slice their throats, holding their swords like cleavers. Diler stares, his interest turning into fascination. The dark and muscular Marathas look like a different human race, from another world, and are without armour or helmets.

Suddenly, the Marathas launch a hostile attack, using one sword to slaughter and another to defend. The Mughal swordsmen have not discussed any strategies; there was no need for such intricate details when they were to fight against rebel tribesmen. They have not even bothered to inquire about the battleground, because there wasn't supposed to be any real battle. They struggle under the weight of their own armour and bulky shields, stumble and lurch on the rock-strewn earth. The Marathas seem to be trained swordfighters and not random rebels hiding in the jungles. They seem to know their weapon and how to use its somewhat-straight, long and double-edged blade for more hits. They take a low stance, thrusting the blades in upward motion, going for the lower abdomens of the Mughals, not covered by their armour. It takes the Mughal warriors a few moments to cope with the stance of their enemy. The lucky survivors waste a few precious moments in just parrying the rain of enemy's strikes.

'Slaughter the bastards!' a man who seems to lead the Marathas screams.

'Mashallah!' Diler exclaims in admiration as the loud sound of metal banging on metal echoes through the hills. Diler's attack is subdued by a clever sortie designed by his enemies. The Marathas have already accepted death, the acceptance turning them into killing machines, and the Mughals, who have already accepted victory, seem to be retreating.

Diler Khan looks back. His archers stand with stretched bows and aimed arrows, their hands moving as if they are busy charming a snake. The Marathas are moving too fast, their nimble feet making their agile bodies fly. In the midst of the bloody mayhem, Diler notices the leader again—a short and stocky man with both hands fixed in gauntlets with long blades, on a rampage, leaving a trail of dead behind him as he advances fearlessly. The blades of his swords move in elliptical movements as he swirls like a top, as if he is performing a rhythmic death dance, as if the blades are his limbs, as if killing several enemy soldiers in one go is a part of his performance. It goes on for a while until the courtyard of the lower fort is strewn with bodies lying in crimson pools.

A dozen armoured Mughals try to encircle him, holding their shields together to make a trap. The man has lost his turban, blood trickling down from his tonsured head over his shoulders. He has managed to push the ring of his opponents to the edge of the battlefield, just a few yards away from where Diler stands on a boulder. It is then he realizes that the man with gauntlet swords must be Murarbaji!

'Halt! Stop!' Diler shouts passionately, again and again, his heart pounding in his ribcage, his fists boxing the air above him. Something in his voice makes everyone stop, including Murarbaji.

Diler jumps down from the boulder and waves his hands signalling to the others to back off. He stands face to face with the fearless warrior.

'Who are you?' Diler asks.

'Murarbaji,' the answer comes in a booming voice.

'The famous fort-keeper of Purandar?'

'Yes.'

'Allah!' exclaims Diler in Deccani Urdu, 'I have not seen a warrior like you.'

Murarbaji is grim; he is breathing shallow.

'Come to us. The emperor will make you an amir or an omrah; people like me will take orders from you. You will be rich,' says Diler earnestly, staring at Murarbaji. The man is not wearing any armour; his clothes are made of hand-woven cotton, while his sandals are worn out. Diler's patience ebbs; he shouts to make his words clear, 'How much does this Shivaji pay you?'

'You will never understand, you—a salaried dog of the emperor,' Murarbaji says in Marathi. An archer standing behind Diler translates.

Diler shivers with indignation but before he can say something Murarbaji raises his swords and shouts raucously, 'You cannot buy me! No one can!' Then without warning he leaps forward to attack Diler. The Mughal has no time to remove his sword from his scabbard; he retreats involuntarily and stumbles, rolling on the ground, and raises his bare hands to parry the blows of Murarbaji.

The Mughal archers standing on the boulders stretch their bows and narrow their eyes. The target is approaching, and there is not much time; the arrows from the full-drawn bows are released with maximum elastic energy. One of the projectiles slice Murarbaji's neck and blood spurts out of the gash, but he keeps advancing as Diler rolls away further and falls into a shallow ditch.

Finally Murarbaji comes to a halt, staggers for a moment and falls, taking both his swords with him.

The Mughal archers climb down from the boulders and help Diler, who looks around in disbelief. The battleground is strewn with corpses, and the remaining Marathas have disappeared; the gates of Purandar's upper fort are closed shut. Diler now understands his enemy's first move: they took the battle away from the entrance. It was done with a purpose and the Mughals failed to decipher the last move. Diler looks at the upper fort—the saffron flag flutters wildly, with intrepid arrogance. The clouds have started gathering, darkening the blue sky above as if to rue over the death of the Deccan's intrepid warrior. The remaining Mughals have lost all their vigour and enthusiasm and have decided to walk away, leaving behind thousands of dead and fatally injured men, while those with minor injuries are carried by the others. The stench of faeces and urine from torn bowels and bladders has started inviting the scavenger birds. Thousands of swords made from crucible steel from Persia are taken back from the battlefield, while their masters are left behind.

5

It is the end of the month of Baisakh that has brought dry and warm days, and reduced the otherwise swollen rivers to puddles of stagnant water. The mountains and their wooded slopes, the enormous ridges and their plunging drops, and even the uphill trails seem to rue the fate of their valley. In the midst of the Mughal calamity, Rajgad stands mute, looking down at its foothills, as columns of smoke rise heavenwards from villages on fire. The people on the fort move about with grim faces, as if they are observing *sutak*, the grieving period after the death of a family member. In the *khalbatkhana*, the room for political discussions, behind the sadar, Raghunath Korde waits for his master. He has been called back from the Konkan where he was given the duty of keeping an eye on the Siddis of Janjira.

Shivaji enters the room and shuts the door. Raghunath bows and glances at his master whose young face looks aged, and those usually cheerful brown eyes have fleeting shadows of heartbreak.

'You need to get through to Mirza Jai Singh at his base camp near Saswad and arrange for a meeting,' Shivaji comes straight to the point without bothering to even sit down.

'Are we surrendering?' The vakeel in Raghunath is suddenly worried.

'We are not sure what will be the outcome of the meeting, but the destruction of villages and mindless killings must stop. Our people are the victims, the pawns of the Mughal political game. Thousands have been taken as slaves and there is little to imagine their fate.'

'Will the Mughal general agree?' Raghunath asks. He has heard that earlier messages from the raja have been ignored by Mirza.

'Tell him we are ready to surrender,' Shivaji says, his voice quivering.

Later, with a heavy heart, Shivaji comes out for a breath of fresh air, and walks towards the shallow pond built to harvest the rain. The Mughal brutalities have made him mentally fatigued. He notices that the water in the lake has turned muddy and dark as it always does during summer. Hundreds of pink and white lotuses float in the water, some blooming and some budding.

The truth of what has happened stings Shivaji's heart. It is clear that he is unable to stop the destruction of life and property of his people, despite best efforts. Even the villages at the foothills of this very fort have gone, burnt down to ashes. The death of Murarbaji and hundreds of soldiers has torn Shivaji and he cannot afford to lose any more men in this unequal fight. The families of his men trapped in Purandar's upper fort must be freed. Mirza Raja Jai Singh is not Afzal or Shaista who had huge egos; he is sober and wise, a thinker.

'Please guide me,' Shivaji closes his eyes and prays to Goddess Bhavani, the origin of power, and walks towards the stables at the edge of the fort's extension. He hears Ibrahim Khan, who has offered to train his son, talking. Shivaji stands at a distance, wanting to see what little Shambhu is up to.

Shambhu jumps with joy. 'Abba sahib!' he shouts. Ibrahim bows to his master.

'You are a seven-year-old young man; today you may select your own mount,' Shivaji beams at his young son.

The boy cannot believe his ears. He stares at his trainer to confirm whether what he heard is true. Ibrahim knows that his ward has developed strong leg muscles to clear the saddle, kick and squeeze a small horse to move. His body has learnt to balance. His hands have gained adequate power to steer a foal or slow it down to a halt.

CHAPTER TWENTY-EIGHT

1

A cockerel with brilliant red waffles jumps on the wooden fence of the Mughal encampment and starts crowing. The security guards at the entrance facing west smile at each other, because whenever the red waffled cockerel crows near the entrance, they receive an unexpected guest from the upper echelons of Mughal nobility.

Half a mile inside the camp, life seems to go by. Mirza has finished bathing after a sesame-oil massage. But something else bothers him.

How will he react to Shivaji? Draped in a silk dhoti, Mirza stands in an enclosed courtyard behind his shamiana meant for official work and meetings. Basking in the early sun, his mind wanders to his past glory. His father's kingdom of Amber floats across his vision, like an enormous ship with countless masts. His ancestral home with beautiful courts, patios, palaces and gardens had made Emperor Jahangir jealous with rage, despite the fact that Jahangir's mother had been from Mirza's family. He feels blessed, his karma from past births has ensured that he be superior by sheer birth. He is a Kachwah, born into a family whose genesis could be traced back to the Sun. He is a Suryavanshi, a descendant of the most worshipped, most radiant, most visible power in the world—the sun dynasty. The lineage means that an infinitesimal part of Mirza has come from God Rama, the seventh avatar of Lord Vishnu.

Mirza can feel the sun burning into his skin and he is about to start his sun salutations, but a noise disturbs him. Udayaraj Munshi is shouting with excitement, his words disappearing into an incomprehensible echo. Only after a moment of confusion can Mirza hear a complete sentence.

'He . . . he is on his way.'

The Mughal general's body stiffens; the time has come to face Shivaji, on his own terms.

'Is it really him?'

'We have called for people who have met him before. They should confirm.'

'How many men accompany him?'

'Six. He is riding on a ceremonial elephant with a gilded howdah. Raghunath Ballal Korde, who had come to us last week, is also sitting with him, and just four armed horsemen canter along holding silver poles with white flags.' Udayaraj eagerly provides the information.

Mirza's mind swings into action. 'Once Shivaji is with me, ask the artillerymen to blast the cannon three times,' he orders, and prays that his plan is successful.

For the past one month Shivaji has been trying hard to begin a dialogue, sending his messengers with letters. In one of the letters he had suggested that he regarded himself as the emperor's humble servant and if the esteemed Mirza Raja needed help to annex the Adilshahi, he would be most willing to deploy his cavalry. Many messages had arrived showing the desperation of the sender. The more villages fell, the more frequent the letters became. But Mirza had replied only once saying that the imperial army was like a sky laden with stars and soon, the 'sultani skies' would descend on the Sahyadri Mountains to flatten them. In the same note, Mirza had not forgotten to mention the emperor as an 'ocean of mercy', and the world could subsist because Aurangzeb was so compassionate and generous.

Shivaji's last message had come with Raghunath who had admitted that his master wanted to surrender and that had made Mirza relent.

Mirza deliberately takes a long time to trim his beard and moustache with utmost care, even though his personal barber has done the same earlier in the morning. Selecting a jama made from fine muslin cloth with a motif of two tigers in combat, he picks up a ruby-studded turban of many folds and opts for a red cashmere shawl. Finally he wears pearl ear studs, a few strands of gold chains, and a ring set either in diamond or rubies in each of his fingers, including his thumbs.

Mirza fires orders before summoning the guest. 'The contingent of Rajput warriors in ceremonial attire will stay around the shamiana—to welcome the guest and to stand as witnesses if any papers need to be signed. Fifty combat slaves must guard the area with machetes strong enough to slice the bark of an old tree—to kill the visitor, who is a famed murderer, if he turns aggressive. Only Shivaji and his vakeel are to be allowed in. And before he enters this room, check for weapons, especially on him, his hands, his feet, his sash—leave nothing.'

Mirza then heads for the couch, craving for a smoke. Soon the shamiana is filled with smoke rings.

'Is that general Mirza Raja Jai Singh?' Hearing the words in chaste Urdu, Mirza throws back his neck and stares. The man who has entered the shamiana wears light-brown clothes made of fine muslin. The jama is impeccably tailored and his orange turban has strings of pearls wrapped around it. The man, with a trim beard and a slight moustache, is barefoot. The visitor moves nearer and Mirza can see his face under the light of the shamdans. Sharp features with slightly high cheekbones; the forehead is huge with a tilak; the complexion is fair, and the mouth firm. The visitor bows lightly, keeping his right hand on his chest where his heart is, without lifting his gaze from Mirza.

'Here comes the notorious guerrilla,' Mirza comments wryly. Shivaji does not react.

'So you are the hit-and-run man, the man waiting in ambush, with an attitude of "retreat when faced with defeat"; you are the man who avoids bold, face-to-face confrontations!'

Shivaji breathes deeply and utters, 'You are the man of battles, Mirza Raja, who will know better than anyone else that every strategy, be it yours or mine, is to win, to annihilate the enemy.'

'You do not follow principles of ethical war!' Mirza makes a strong statement.

'I follow principles of humanity. I neither attack helpless civilians, nor do I take them as slaves.'

Mirza laughs aloud. A slightly surprised Shivaji asks, 'Why do you laugh?'

'You slay those who embrace you in good faith. I have decided to stay away from you.' Mirza speaks in Urdu deliberately peppered with Farsi.

'I have slain only those who have embraced me with sinister intentions, who want to enslave me, to rob my people's freedom.'

'So you defend yourself and your ideals of freedom by glib talk,' Mirza hits back, as the two men make themselves comfortable on the crescent-shaped couch.

'We do not fight to merely defend our ideals; we fight to turn them into reality,' Shivaji quips, and before Mirza can say anything more, Udayaraj rushes in apologetically. He bows deeply before Shivaji and offers him a hookah and a betel leaf from a silver case. Shivaji refuses both, and a dejected Munshi takes his place behind his desk. For a few moments, there is an awkward silence. Mirza stares at his guest and marvels at the sculpted features, then immediately reminds himself that this man is a dangerous murderer, a bandit who has sacked Mughal territories, forcefully acquired the Adilshahi's hill forts, wiped out jagirdars like Morey and maimed Shaista Khan. He is here because he has no choice. He is cunning and will possibly try hard to forge a friendship. Mirza knows how to tackle people when they try to cultivate him. He is never shy of exposing the clout-seekers for their motives when they praise him shamelessly.

'Mirza Raja,' Shivaji takes the lead, 'this land belongs to peasants of the land, but the real power was in the hands of the native jagirdars. The peasants were their slaves, bonded for life, slogging away, till the last drops of their blood irrigated the soil that produced riches that filled the treasuries of the jagirdars and the kings, making them more powerful to enslave more peasants.'

'Raja Shivaji,' the half-listening Mirza waves his hand and continues, 'we can talk later. Let me first be a good host. You have travelled far to reach here; let me offer you something to eat. Our cook makes good meat kebabs, chickpea sambusa and even your puran poli.'

'It is too early. I eat only one meal in the afternoon and I am a vegetarian,' Shivaji says and continues, 'For the past fifteen years, we have tried to free the peasants from their slavery, establishing a soft revenue system, and providing facilities such as loans or free seeds, fertilizers and farm animals.'

Mirza feels irritated and, glancing at Udayaraj who is busy making notes in his register, he says, 'Now why are you giving me an account of your past deeds?'

'What has taken us years to make, the Mughals have demolished in a month.'

Mirza's eyes bore into Shivaji's and he is hit by a revelation. Those brown eyes are the most earnest eyes he has ever seen—not wavering, not blinking and not even diverting. The gaze is sharp and has the power to slice through a person's soul. Mirza shivers faintly, diverting his own eyes to the chessboard, and retorts, 'You have been illegally occupying the territory that rightfully belongs to the Adilshahi. I must admit that you do have some lofty perceptions of yourself. You have a sense of righteousness that blunts your common sense when you commit crimes like slaughtering jagirdar Morey, murdering Afzal Khan, maiming Shaista Khan and injuring the traders of Surat.'

'In that case, one must change the definition of legal and illegal,' Shivaji murmurs, his eyes distant.

'Do not forget you have begged to meet me,' Mirza reminds him. Just then they hear the cannon blasts. Now Diler Khan must fire the explosives at Dilli Darwaza and set the upper fort of Purandar on fire.

Unperturbed by the blasting sound, Shivaji stares at the handsome Rajput in his late fifties whose face reminds him of the ancient kings in the mythological stories his mother had told him when he was a child. He smiles slightly, ignores Mirza's rudeness and puts his thoughts forth, his words barely reaching the ears of Udayaraj, 'Mirza Raja, the invaders are not innocent. They had come from afar, their blood boiling with rage—the Mongols, the Persians, the Turks and the Balkans. They have slaughtered lakhs of natives, a methodical genocide in the name of jihad. The first Mughal emperor, Babur, had beheaded countless, making pillars of the heads of his victims. Your new emperor is not an exception either. Agreed that I have killed, but I have neither murdered brothers nor committed mass genocide of innocent villagers as you have. Try to see the truth, Mirza Raja, only once.'

Mirza's head spins. *Why am I sitting here and listening to this man who has come to surrender?* The words 'only once' stir some old memories hiding deep in his heart, remembering the Rajput martyr Hammir Deo, who had resisted the murderous Alauddin Khalji for years. Centuries later, in the desert, they still sing his praises:

The lioness gives birth to a cub only once
Once alone is the word of a good man given
The plantain bears fruit only once
A woman is anointed only once with oil for marriage and
Hammir only once gave his irrevocable promise . . .

'Your life will be spared if you bow to the jihadists, and the perks are excellent, but it is suicidal to be their enemies, isn't it, Mirza Raja?

You are a Suryavanshi, your lineage connected to the sun, the star of our solar system. You are the son of this soil, and you were born to rule.' Shivaji is no longer whispering, his scathing words are ruthlessly scraping the scabs from the very old wounds afflicting Mirza's mind.

Mirza cannot believe his own ears. The man sitting in front of him is desperate, as if he has nothing left to live for. Those words uttered against the Mughal emperors can put both of them on a death row. It is dangerous to carry on the conversation, and even the panels of this tent have ears.

Just then Niccolau Manucci enters the shamiana.

Shivaji has not seen blonde hair before—the Portuguese working for him have dark-brown heads.

'Who is he?' Shivaji asks admiringly.

'He is a raja from Europe,' Mirza bluffs as Shivaji's eyes shine with interest.

'Do you wage war in your part of the world?' the Maratha wants to know. Niccolau who is staring at Shivaji instead of fiddling with the hookah that is usually kept for him smiles bitterly, his blue eyes clouded with shadows of sadness.

'Where there are humans, there is war.' Niccolau's Urdu has a strange accent. Something compels him to speak further, 'We have suffered catastrophic wars, cities have been besieged and plundered, hundreds of thousands of civilians abused and killed, crops, livestock and money confiscated. Starvation has led to diseases such as plague, typhus and diarrhoea. That has killed hundreds of thousands of people.'

Shivaji listens carefully and asks, 'What are the reasons for such wars?'

'Many, but now it is the competition to take over foreign trade, for overseas trade means money and money means power. Politics in Europe is changing; it is less about religious conflicts and more about naval might, the backbone of the ability to colonize distant parts of the world.'

'What if the natives take over the sea trade of their respective countries?' Shivaji asks.

'*Penso di no*, I do not think the natives have the power to even *think* in that direction, especially the natives of this country!' Manucci scoffs.

Shivaji smiles mysteriously and continues with his questions, 'Do you ever fight on land, or only on seas?'

Niccolau starts laughing but stops abruptly and says, 'Battles are fought for conquests or defence. It is finally for the land or the trade markets; oceans cannot be conquered or occupied.'

Shivaji's goes on, 'Why did you cross the seven seas and come to our lands?'

Niccolau now knows that he is not dealing with an ordinary native; the man is asking clever questions. He replies earnestly, 'Our country is poor, our trade is declining, and only three players are emerging as superpowers: the Portuguese, the Dutch and the English. The merchant navy is a new concept, and companies who own merchant ships as well as battleships to protect their merchant ships are in demand. These companies employ thousands of sailors and marines and bring big money into the country and pay enormous taxes, making the kings rich. The kings in turn bless the shareholders and top officials of these companies by giving them prime estates, financial compensations, influential positions, titles and other perks. Those not connected with these companies find it difficult. I have come to earn money.'

'These companies must be making huge profits here, in Hindustan and in the Deccan, and using them to build their countries. And instead of fighting them by riding the ocean waves with robust naval power, we, the natives, keep fighting territorial wars with each other, destroying our land and killing our own,' Shivaji says looking at Mirza, while Niccolau Manucci nods vigorously.

'Europe is far ahead of us in their plans, thoughts and strategies,' Shivaji quips.

'You are the first native who seems to have understood,' Niccolau blurts and bites his tongue.

Someone walks in and whispers something in Mirza's ears. Mirza gets up and says, 'Please step outside; I want to show you something.'

Outside, Mirza points out in the direction of the southwest; the hill of Purandar rising a few hundred guj above the plains is clearly visible. Its upper fort rising above the hill burns, and despite the bright sun, enormous flames are seen swallowing the crown of the Maratha pride.

'Purandar's upper fort has fallen. I have requested Diler Khan to spare the families, provided we sign a peace treaty,' Mirza says flatly, his eyes cold. The timing is perfect. In anticipation of Shivaji's visit, Mirza had sent messages to Diler Khan and his son, Kirat. Their trenches had reached the walls of the upper fort. Today, after Shivaji's arrival, Mirza had blasted the cannon as a signal, to deliver an assault on the upper fort.

The fire seems to die in Shivaji's eyes as they watch Purandar burn, and he goes silent.

The night strides like a wounded beast, sluggish and immersed in its own pain. It rains intermittently and Mirza has remained awake while Shivaji, who is given the adjacent tent, has put off the lamps and gone off to sleep. The others accompanying him are somewhere else in the camp. It is a strange night. The empire's most-wanted man is trapped in Mirza's base camp, unarmed, alone and vulnerable. In less than three months, since Mirza has opened the campaign, he has already brought Shivaji to his knees. By tomorrow he will make this illusive rebel cede a large part of his dominion and make him a part of the Mughal army. It is indeed a superb victory. It is a moment of triumph, but Mirza is not as ecstatic as he had thought he would be. Shivaji's guileless words have awakened some old regrets in his heart. Why am I murdering thousands, for Aurangzeb, the emperor of the Mughals—the man who wants entire Hindustan under Islamic rule?

Mirza has no choice but to think of Aurangzeb's latest farman. The Mughal emperor wants all the forts that belonged to the Nizam of Ahmednagar, taken by Shivaji, thirty-five in number.

The next day, when Mirza meets Shivaji and Raghunath in his tent, he is all business. Mirza's son Kirat Singh and his scribe-cum-assistant Udayaraj Munshi are present to help him in negotiations. If Shivaji wishes to stop the devastation of his terrain, if he wishes to save people trapped in the upper fort from death, he must pay the price. Mirza puts forth Aurangzeb's demand of thirty-five forts along with the revenue-generating lands at their foothills.

Shivaji has an inkling of what is to come, and has been thinking all through the night. For the past five years, a large part of his terrain has been under Mughal occupation and his people have suffered the most heinous crimes. He knows that Mirza is trying to swallow his domain and has been tempting the Maratha cavalrymen and infantrymen with mansabs and money, and if the Mughals continue to devastate the region like they are, it is just a matter of time before Mirza separates him from his army.

Several moments pass in silence. Thinking that Shivaji is contemplating, finding it difficult to make up his mind, Mirza says impatiently, 'These lands we are asking for are of ambiguous status. As per the imperial treaty of 1636 that was signed twenty-seven years ago with the then king of the Adilshahi, these regions of the conquered Nizamshahi had become a part of Adilshahi, but as per the latest treaty, Adilshahi rulers have agreed to cede the regions to the empire.'

'I am not aware of any such thing,' Shivaji says earnestly.

'Now you know, you are illegally sitting on someone else's property.'

'The Adilshahi rulers have been claiming this region as theirs.'

'The Adilshahi will soon be a subha of the empire,' Mirza minces no words.

'I have, in principle, decided to be the servant of the empire,' Shivaji diverts the topic, speaking each word in a clear tone, his eyes boring into Mirza's without blinking or showing grief, 'but I will give only twenty-three forts, retaining twelve with me.'

'You are not in the position to negotiate.'

'Yes, I am,' Shivaji shoots back, his head straight.

'I will then call off the negotiations.' Mirza sounds livid. Raghunath, who has not yet removed his large-rimmed pagari turban on purpose, is quick to catch on.

'If you call our discussions a "negotiation" and do not allow us to put forth our demands, you may well call it off,' Raghunath asserts, his narrow face tight, his eyes icy.

Mirza forces himself to calm down. He has come so far, binding Shivaji gradually, forcing him to accept servitude. He has achieved within three months what Shaista Khan could not even after three years. If he does not seal the deal now, there is a risk of driving Shivaji into a triple alliance with the Adilshahi and the Qutbshahi. He turns to Kirat and Udayaraj—they talk in whispers in Rajasthani.

For the next several hours, the men haggle about which forts will be retained by Shivaji and which will be surrendered to the Mughal empire. The marathon discussion ends amicably. Twenty-three of the hill forts, the lands of which yield twenty lakh rupees as annual revenue, will be annexed to the empire. The land left to the Marathas yields five lakh rupees as annual revenue.

'The money you talk about in terms of revenue is mostly on paper, on the ground level. With frequent Mughal invasions, the revenue is far lesser than what you think,' Raghunath warns but Mirza is in no mood to listen.

The men break for a meal only in the evening. After the meal they are back in their seats on Mirza's crescent-shaped divan. The meeting starts with Mirza offering a mansabdar's position of five thousand horses to Shivaji, with a suitable jagir. Shivaji and Raghunath are not caught unawares; they knew this offer was coming.

'Raja Shivaji is ready to serve the empire with all his heart and soul, but he cannot accept the mansab, however high the position may be,' Raghunath says keeping his voice officious.

Mirza laughs aloud. The high-pitched laughter further unsettles the men who are already feeling the heat. People die for a mansab of five thousand horses in the Mughal services. Mirza stares at Raghunath whose eyes radiate blank interest. Shivaji's vakeel has shown disrespect by not removing his turban, and now he is dictating terms!

'You will have to serve us in an official position,' Mirza says with fleeting shadows of irritation in his eyes.

'I have taken over Kalyan; I have plundered the cavalcade of Kartalab Khan; I have maimed Emperor Aurangzeb's uncle, Shaista Khan; I have sacked Mughal markets including the prestigious port town of Surat. In the eyes of the emperor and according to his sharia law, I am a criminal and therefore, morally, I cannot accept your gracious offer,' Shivaji says politely, his eyes downcast. 'If you have no objection, you may offer my son, Sambhaji Bhosale, the mansab you are offering to me.'

Mirza is speechless but he gathers his wits and asks, 'How old is he?'

'Seven.'

Mirza takes some time to recover. 'He will have to come to the court whenever required and he is also liable for transfers. Also, since he is too young, you as the father of our mansabdar will have to perform all military duties assigned to him in any Mughal campaigns.'

'Mirza Raja, please understand, I will not be forced to come to the imperial court, and my son will not be compelled to do so either,' Shivaji protests.

'That is the protocol,' Mirza insists.

'In that case, you may have to amend it,' Raghunath butts in. Mirza feels his pulse race. He hits back, 'Imperial protocols are stringent and will not be amended according to the whims and fancies of a mere fief.'

'We will also be helping you in the war against the other Deccan kingdoms,' Raghunath proposes.

Till midnight, the men discuss, argue and bargain, while the shamdans burn bright. Finally, it is time to put it all on the paper, with the palm impressions of Mirza and Shivaji. The deal must be sealed, and the treaty must be made official. Udayaraj has written one paper in Farsi, and one in Devanagari script. First Raghunath and then Shivaji read the paper carefully, going through the list of the twenty-three forts, including Kondana, Purandar, Lohagad and many others in Konkan with a heavy heart, as Mirza watches his enemies' faces for clues.

Mirza has one more demand before they conclude the meeting, 'We shall amend the protocol and not force you or your son to attend the court. You too must keep your word and help us annex the Adilshahi by providing us with ten thousand men, some of them from your light cavalry.'

'With five thousand horsemen, as per the mansabdari protocol,' Raghunath counters.

Mirza laughs and says, 'Make it double. The mansabdari is to honour your master in the imperial court. The emperor would expect a robust help of manpower from you if truce is what you want.'

Shivaji intervenes. 'So be it. I have but one question. I am not a Mughal mansabdar, so I am independent. I should be allowed to expand as a sovereign king without damaging Mughal interests. Will you allow my remaining cavalry and infantry to fight battles of expansion—especially in the coastal regions that still remain under the Adilshahi kingdom? The revenue collection from these will harvest lakhs. We will pay taxes to Emperor Aurangzeb.'

Mirza understands in a flash the reason why Shivaji has not accepted the mansab. He looks at Udayaraj who is staring at Shivaji with his mouth open, only a bit short of drooling. Mirza is tired. He nods and says, 'We could put this on the paper. This will be approved after we win the war against the Adilshahi.'

Shivaji knows he is dealing with an intelligent man. If they win the war, all the territories of Adilshahi kingdom will become a part of the empire.

Shivaji diverts his gaze from Mirza, saying, 'That is agreeable provided you help us take over the sea fort of Janjira from its Abyssinian occupants.'

Mirza knows his limitations. 'That could only be decided by the emperor. And while you hand over the charge of all twenty-three forts as per the treaty, you must keep our new mansabdar, your son, with us, as surety.'

Shivaji thinks for a while and nods in agreement but the matter is not pushed further.

The same night Mirza dispatches an excited letter to the emperor.

Alamgir, Parvardigar, we have succeeded through Allah's help in pressing him hard, and now that we have taken away twenty-three of his forts we have weakened him. If he strays by a hair's breadth from the path of obedience, he can be totally annihilated by us with the slightest exertion. We must overthrow Bijapur with the help of Shivaji and what can be better than this? I humbly hope that Alamgir's kind heart will bless the promises I made while issuing farmans to Shivaji and his son Sambhaji Bhosale who is our mansabdar. Your Majesty's wishes regarding the Adilshahi should be communicated to this old slave of yours.

2

The third day is Shivaji's last day in the base camp of the Mughal. The rain that had drizzled continuously for two days has stopped a while ago, and it is warm around the campfire lit near Mirza's tent. Mirza wants to play a game of chess with Shivaji—it is Mirza's way to measure his enemies and friends. A game of chess shows if the man is an offender or a defender, a true human or a cheater, has the mind of a strategist or a tactician.

Mirza smiles inwardly while entering his tent where his guest is waiting. It is well lit with four shamdans burning in four corners. The shamiana is filled with the fragrance of *dhoop*. Mirza finds Shivaji intriguing, charming and dangerous, but he is trapped, and such men can turn more aggressive and lethal when trapped, like a tortured snake, eager to strike and empty its venom into the flesh of its tormentor. However, something else about him bothers Mirza. Perhaps a game of chess will shed some light on his character different from the personality he portrays.

'How do you find the facilities? Are you and your men being treated well?' Mirza asks, wanting to be a good host.

'My people find the accommodations most satisfactory, probably the most luxurious they have ever seen,' Shivaji replies.

Mirza walks to his divan, asking Shivaji to sit down. Mirza, a keen observer of people, has been unsuccessful in judging his opponent. He still does not know whether Shivaji will abide by the treaty, keep his promises or betray him. He wants to be certain before his guest departs.

'Do you play shatranj, Raja Shivaji?' he abruptly asks.

Shivaji nods and says, 'I do play but perhaps not at your level I have heard stories of your expertise.'

Mirza is pleased. He is not only an excellent player but he can also read his opponent's soul based on the game.

Mirza flicks his fingers and a board is placed between two men. Mirza offers Shivaji the first choice of the colour. Interestingly Shivaji chooses black. Mirza wonders, but says nothing. The game begins in earnest.

Mirza makes his initial moves quickly and confidently. Shivaji counters with a solid defence—the king is tucked in the corner, the centre is under control, the queen is placed on a strong supporting square. Mirza builds his attack slowly but steadily, while Shivaji seems oblivious to the impending storm, though his defences are impregnable. Mirza makes a quick feint to the other side of the board, apparently making a grab for a pawn. Shivaji successfully diverts the attack and Mirza's players seem to be stymied. Mirza enjoys this and knows that he will soon assess Shivaji's strategic capabilities. He makes a brilliant sacrifice on the king side, a double-edged move, very difficult to counter but not without a grave risk. Shivaji thinks for a long time and counters the gambit. Mirza's scattered pieces suddenly come alive as they converge on Shivaji's king from the other side of the board. Shivaji fights valiantly offering blow for a blow, but Mirza's attack becomes intense, the effects of sacrifice apparent a dozen moves later.

Shivaji looks at the board, shakes his head, and offers congratulations to Mirza. The game is over. Mirza wonders why Shivaji is considered such a threat—his thinking is linear, and his strategies are short-sighted. Mirza is ready to dismiss Shivaji, but he must be given one more chance.

'Do you know why you lost?' Mirza asks.

Shivaji nods and says, 'I had the centre but you had the control; my position looked unassailable, but there were hidden weaknesses— my pieces were connected and coordinated but they were no match to an expert gambler like you. Any position that lacks mobility lacks new ideas. It is based on injustice and not on people's aspirations. It can be destroyed by a brilliant sacrifice, or even by a lowly pawn—all that it needs is a gambler who thinks differently.'

Mirza's smugness vanishes; he suddenly becomes alert.

'You see yourself as that brilliant gambler? You will change the flow of history?'

Shivaji is unperturbed. 'Anything is possible,' he replies.

Mirza is furious. He asks, 'Do you know the military and the financial might of the Mughal empire? Do you know strategic acumen of our battle-hardened mansabdars? Do not even think of becoming a traitor! You will die, your sons will die, your wives will be sold as slaves and your people will keep dying. As you know very well, you are never going to be the same after this visit.' The dark menace in his words is meant to break Shivaji.

Shivaji shows no reaction. Mirza cools down quickly and turns suave as he always is.

'Our military machine can do all that you can, but you cannot do all that we do. Your philosophy of war is not as dynamic as you think and it is rather easily adaptable. The enemy soldiers need to be kept awake in the war zone by systematically attacking and liquidating the outposts, by creating an impression in the mind of the enemy that he is constantly watched, by attacking flanks of the enemy cavalcade and forcing them to send detachments that can later be isolated and annihilated. We can do all that, Raja Shivaji.'

Shivaji smiles sadly and says, 'You cannot create that intense desire residing in the hearts of my men. Your hired soldiers from Uzbekistan, Afghanistan, Punjab, Abyssinia, Rajasthan and Maharashtra are not fired by a dream.'

'I can beat that desire,' Mirza announces confidently.

'You do not have the power to beat that desire, but you have the power to fulfil it. You can join us, Mirza.' Shivaji drops a bombshell. Mirza looks shocked.

'I have already beaten it by making you sign the treaty with us.' Mirza recovers quickly and retorts.

'You have won a battle, not the war.'

'Why not join me?' Mirza recovers from another jolt and asks. 'I rule armies, I guide the destinies of many regions and my voice is heard in the highest council.'

'But you are not the highest council. Your culture, your language and you yourself do not count,' Shivaji points out and suddenly leaning forward he asks, 'Join me; we can make the empire tremble. My peasant armies will knock on the doors of Dilli. We can take over entire Hindustan.'

Shivaji's audacity confounds Mirza. He feels the call of his Rajput ancestors who bowed to no one, charged in the war no matter what the odds, the women who walked in the funeral fire chanting 'Jai Har!', hailing their vanquished men and refusing to submit to the enemy. Sweat breaks out on Mirza's head. What if someone hears this and tells Diler Khan?

'I am fiercely loyal to the emperor. Do not forget I have Rajput blood flowing in my veins,' Mirza says rather loudly as if he wants others to hear it.

416 Medha Deshmukh Bhaskaran

'That is the problem, Mirza. You are loyal to the emperor but you are not loyal to yourself, your homeland, your inner inclinations and your potential.'

This conversation is turning dangerous. Mirza must change the subject and the thought of Diler Khan gives rise to some other thoughts. He has heard that Diler Khan, who has spent months to conquer Purandar, is offended by the peace treaty that has taken away the military glory from him. There is only one way to pacify this dangerous man who has the power to fill Aurangzeb's ears with false information.

'Raja Shivaji, I have organized a meeting between you and Diler Khan. He will be arriving at any moment from Purandar,' Mirza announces. As if on cue, there is a commotion outside the tent.

The two men come out and see a small procession in the midst of the base camp. The tall Pashtun warrior wears a long tunic with a sash glittering with precious stones and a kimoush turban studded with emeralds. Behind him two caparisoned elephants trundle carrying gilded howdahs.

Shivaji knows that the tall man with kohl-lined eyes is Diler Khan.

'Raja Shivaji, I welcome you with all my heart, now that you are one of us,' Diler thunders and steps forward to embrace him. Shivaji leaps forward and the men meet.

What follows surprises Mirza. The caparisoned elephants are a present to Shivaji from Diler who also showers the guest with two horses, a sword, a jewelled dagger and two pieces of silk.

CHAPTER TWENTY-NINE

1

Mirza watches as the region is bathed in the golden columns of the evening sun, ready to plunge into the night's darkness. Within a few hours the winter sun will vanish and they will have to camp at some place in the middle of nowhere. But that does not bother Mirza as he is busy inspecting the dense mass of horsemen and footmen that surround his elephant. He looks back and notices a huge dust cloud left behind by his cavalcade. Ahead, he sees a long stretch of treeless land of rolling plains, its monotony broken by short hills rising in the distance. His army has come several kos into the Adilshahi territory, led by Shivaji and his squadrons that are capturing one military post after another. Because of the Marathas, Mirza has had it easy and he does not regret his decision of invading the Adilshahi territory soon after the Purandar treaty.

He looks proudly at the green Mughal banners fluttering above the mass as they move eastwards towards Bijapur, which is just twenty-six kos south-east from where they are. It is only when he accidently glances at the eastern horizon that he notices a small dust cloud. Instinctively his eyes wander in all directions, noticing several such clouds getting bigger by the moment.

They are under attack!

Mirza looks down from his howdah and notices Diler galloping ahead with his horsemen. The Adilshahi soldiers are indeed using highly damaging guerrilla tactics by dividing themselves into several small contingents. Together, they will be like a pack of wild dogs attacking a lone elephant to tear away its flesh in bits. He watches the advancing squadrons of the enemy's light cavalry, apparently gunning for the flanks of his cavalcade. Within moments, before the enemy can reach them, Diler Khan's horsemen have encircled the Mughal army like a wall. Some of the omrahs mounted on the elephants have joined the human wall and to Mirza they look like the bastions.

Before the sun goes down, the battle starts. Mirza's son Kirat joins the fight with his squadrons. The air vibrates with the noise of sword hitting sword, the screams of injured horses and yells of dying men. Around midnight, the attackers retreat. Mirza is pleased that Shivaji and Palkar had come with their men to rescue him, dashing into the enemy ranks, forcing them to retreat. After the enemy attack is thwarted, Mirza decides to camp, avoiding the battlefield that is strewn with dead. His soldiers are tired and they need food and rest.

Mirza has planned to take the city of Bijapur by storm and not by besiegement. His final halt is five kos north of Bijapur.

2

Ali Adil Shah and his mother watch their beloved city from the seventh floor of the Hawa Mahal. For the past century and a half, Bijapur has been known as the jewel of the Deccan. The city looks even more precious with its palaces, mosques, towers and tombs lit with chandeliers, shamdans and torches. Ali's eyes wander to the eastern border of the city, where the Gol Gumbaz dwarfs its surroundings. His father's bones rest in that tomb, but Ali fears that with the combined armies of Mirza Jai Singh and Shivaji advancing towards Bijapur, his father's remains must be twisting and turning with dread and disquiet. When Ali had heard the news of the treaty between the Mughal and the Marathas, something had snapped in his heart. Since he was a small boy he has been living in fear of the Mughal invasions, sometimes getting up in the night dreaming of a sword coming down on him. Many questions have tormented him from childhood: What right does Aurangzeb have to call his father a heretic just because he followed the Shia sect of Islam? Who is Aurangzeb to say that Ali's coronation is against Islam because he is an adopted son of the late king?

The questions have haunted him for a long time but he has decided to answer them himself. He has decided to face the uncertainty and the doubts with a strong military defence. Come what may, he will not allow the combined forces to be the victors, and they will never enter Bijapur. Just a few months ago, Mirza Raja Jai Singh had sent a Brahmin vakeel with the offer that if Ali helped them in their war against Shivaji, they would consider a reduction in the tribute money that the Adilshahi has to pay to Aurangzeb, or they may even waive it off. The Mughals have played a double game, they always do.

'Son, do you think your plan will work?' Badi Sahiba asks, her voice weak.

Ali looks at his mother. She has aged rapidly, especially after Afzal Khan's murder. Her usually straight head is bent over her stooping shoulders and it trembles.

'Ammi, my strategy is simple, yet, it will hit them in the stomach. They are planning to storm the city but they cannot do it in a day or two. They will have to camp somewhere near Bijapur. Without provisions and water sources, within a few days, their men and animals will start dying of hunger and thirst,' Ali replies as he thinks of his strategy: harassing the enemy without a pitched battle, by adopting the scorched-earth policy that will shock Mirza Raja Jai Singh to death!

Badi Sahiba looks at Ali, the young king in his early twenties, with pride. His obesity and his reluctance to lead his men into battlefields had bothered her in the beginning, but now she knows that he is a good military strategist and is putting her beloved Bijapur in a strong posture of defence. Her eyes wander to the city walls that meander for more than three kos, forming an irregular ellipse around Bijapur. The city is lit by torches kept on the ground as well as on the ramparts as hundreds of labourers keep busy renovating the watchtowers, making them stronger and, in some cases, less vulnerable by raising the parapets higher. The cannons mounted on the ramparts have been serviced, their muzzles cleaned. Sacks full of coal powder and saltpetre have been stored in the watchtowers to make explosives. The water from the largest reservoir on the nearby Torvi hills has been emptied into the moat running parallel to the city walls, and a large number of crocodiles have been caught from the nearby rivers and brought in on carts to be put in the moat.

The Mecca gate is still open and there is some incoming traffic at this late hour. Ali senses his mother's concern and says, 'We have asked the nearby peasants to bring all their produce, cattle, fodder and provisions into the city. They will be provided accommodation within Bijapur.'

'Good,' Badi Sahiba says. 'Are the water wells outside the city walls filled with earth?'

'They are at it, Ammi. The workers are also destroying or draining the water reservoirs. The Mughal must not get even a drop to drink. Once their animals start dying like flies, they will dance like monkeys.'

Badi Sahiba sighs with relief, feeling happy that her Ali nowadays addresses her as 'Ammi' and not Badi Sahiba, as he previously did.

'We have also reinforced thirty thousand foot soldiers to strengthen the usual garrison within the city, and help is also arriving from Hyderabad. It is an all-out war; it is either kill or be killed,' Ali says softly, preparing his mother for any eventuality.

'You are right, son,' Badi Sahiba comments and thinks fondly of her younger brother, Abdullah Qutb Shah.

Ali lowers his tone, bends towards his mother and says, 'Mother, the time has come to kill many birds with one stone. The Maratha sarnobat, Palkar, has sent messages through his underground messengers that he wants to come back to us.'

3

The Mughal cavalcade advances unhindered, crossing desolate country, treeless landscapes and uplands covered with stony soil. The only relief is that it is winter and nights are pleasant, but the days are warm and the afternoon sun still scorching. As they move towards Bijapur, Mirza is disturbed by the news that his scouts have brought: the villages ahead are not just deserted but the barns are either empty or have been burnt down. The wells are filled with earth, the water reservoirs lie either destroyed or drained, the cattle has either been taken away or killed and their carcasses left to rot.

When Bijapur is just five kos away, Mirza decides to set up his base camp, making everyone busy in pitching their tents, watering and feeding their animals and setting up chullahs to cook food. Mirza has realized that he does not have a sufficiently large force to besiege the walled capital of Adilshahi and simultaneously chase away the enemy garrisons attacking his camp. After looking at the colossal walls of Bijapur when he had ventured near the capital with his scouts, he has also understood that it is nearly impossible to take the city by storm, even if he deploys every man in his camp to do so.

On the third evening, when a large moon hangs over the shallow hills north of Bijapur, Diler comes to meet Mirza who sits on a charpoy with Niccolau, Kirat and Udayaraj.

'We have water and food that will last for two more days, and the surrounding country is laid waste by the enemy on purpose. It is drained of its water supply so that not a drop is left for us, and denuded of its trees to kill our animals by starvation.' He comes straight to the point, his kohl-lined eyes fixed on Mirza. This is the first time Diler has spoken without bowing.

Mirza trembles with indignation and asks sardonically, 'What do you suggest?'

'You have planned to storm it; then do it quickly,' Diler replies. 'The city wall is more than three kos long and we cannot fill up such a long stretch with our men.'

'Give me a solution, Khan Sahib.'

'I had sent a few scouts to get the sense of the archers and artillerymen on the ramparts of the city wall. And some of them had gone as close as possible, but soon arrows started whipping overhead, some hitting the targets as many scouts started falling dead from their horses. The latest news is that the walls are protected by about thirty thousand footmen who have formed a ring around Bijapur,' Diler says in a flat tone, his eyes flickering from one man to another. He asks Niccolau Manucci, 'Do we have long-range cannons with us?'

Manucci keeps mum, his eyes pale with guilt. After a few moments he shakes his head.

'We can send a few hundred of our men in the night to cross the moat, climb the wall and capture a bastion,' Kirat says.

Diler looks at the young man more with pity and less with anger. Kirat Singh enjoys his position because of his father, and without a father like Mirza the boy is not even fit to be an orderly. He snaps, 'Are you eager to feed the crocodiles?'

'The fear of dying without water is mounting in the camp. I fail to understand—why have we come so far just to go back with hunger burning our stomachs and thirst parching our throats?' Diler is curt. 'I am sure that Shivaji is responsible for this. All along he was aware of Bijapur's strength but he did not bother to warn us.' This thought has been bothering him for a long time. Then suddenly slapping his right fist into his left palm he says slowly, his each word clear and precise, 'Take my advice and eliminate Shivaji, if possible tonight. If you cannot do it, I will.'

A few moments after Diler leaves, Shivaji comes to meet Mirza, and senses the awkward silence. He has seen Diler leaving the tent in a huff and pass by him without greeting him. He bows to Mirza and sits next to him, saying, 'My spy has news. The cannons on the city's ramparts are ready to rain explosives and they have large stocks of saltpetre to last for a month of heavy artillery firing.'

'What do you advise?' Mirza asks Niccolau.

'We must retreat before men and animals start dying without food and water.'

Mirza nods. The Mughal detachments sent a few days ago to bring supplies have not arrived.

'Let me and my men take Panhala. We know its ins and outs; we have lived there for months,' Shivaji offers.

Mirza lets the silence grow in the tent to do some thinking. Detaching Shivaji and his men from the Mughal army means giving him independence and that may prove dangerous. Keeping him in the camp may end up in getting him killed by Diler that will make every Maratha soldier go berserk in the camp. If Shivaji does capture Panhala, the Mughals will have Bijapur's western stronghold in their hands and it will be easier for them to come back to annex Bijapur. Mirza is ready to take chances. He also has something new to tell Aurangzeb and divert the emperor's mind from his failure to take over Bijapur, even before the battle could take place.

That night Mirza despatches a letter to the emperor:

I have asked Shivaji to proceed towards the fort of Panhala with his men. Once the fort is conquered, it can be our base to launch attacks on Bijapur. The Marathas know secrets of the fort, the strength of its fortifications and the trails hidden under the wooded forest at its foothills.

The next morning, when Diler comes to know about Mirza's decision, he laughs out loud, in front of Mirza's messenger who has come officially to tell him about the developments. He knows that the strength of Shivaji's rapidly moving light infantry lies in its speed, and his hill forts are a perfect refuge. If you ask him to strike at remote places, inflict damage, cut off enemy lines and run back to the safety of a hill fort, it is perfect, but if you ask Shivaji to besiege, dig trenches or storm a massive hill fort like Panhala, then that is a disastrous military decision. Shivaji can take the hill forts when the fort-keepers and the garrisons are weak, unprepared, but that is not the case now. Only the Mughal army has the strength to take the forts by storm, sapping or mining for trenches, and even they have failed to storm Bijapur. No doubt that Shivaji had captured Panhala before, but that time Adilshahi's fort-keepers were not alert and had not expected the defeat of Afzal Khan at the hands of a rebel. Times have changed now; Ali Adil Shah has woken up to save his kingdom.

'And how is Shivaji planning to take Panhala? By climbing the hill with his men at midnight?' Diler asks the messenger mockingly.

4

A few hours before the morning star appears in the sky, a thousand of Shivaji's infantrymen reach the north-western foothills of Panhala. Some of them know the slopes that will take them to the Rajdindi bastion close to the hidden tunnel that enters the fort. At the south-eastern foothills, Shivaji arrives with a squadron of horsemen. He has planned a surprise attack on the fort garrison and he will be successful only if the Adilshahi garrison is not alert and awake, but this is the chance he has to take.

The forest is denser here and it is easy for them to tether their horses to the trunks of the trees and, thankfully, the neighing of the tired horses dissolves into the rustle of leafy branches swinging with the gust of wind. Shivaji constantly scans the surroundings, keeping an eye on the faint outline of the fort wall through the rustling canopies. He and a few of his men wait at the foothills while the rest start climbing the hill. Shivaji watches as his men brave the steep slopes and difficult ridges of the hill, fearing the sudden appearance of rampart guards waiting in ambush or a shower of large stones rolling down to kill them, but that does not happen. Something else worries him: Palkar has not arrived with his squadron and his sarnobat has never been late before.

A little less than a thousand Marathas arrive at the fort early in the morning, some from the tunnel near Rajdindi Gate and some after climbing the wall rear Sajjakothi with catapults and ropes. In the beginning it is all quiet, but before they start dispersing, hundreds of Adilshahi soldiers waiting in ambush behind the walls of Ambarkhana leap out, killing and scattering the Marathas.

Shivaji waits for his men to give him a signal of their victory by blasting the cannon mounted on the ramparts near Sajjakothi, but even as the sun rises there is no sound. The plan is in place, his men must have climbed the slopes to reach Rajdindi Gate as well as Sajjakothi, and then dispersed on the fort to kill the sleeping garrison of a few hundred men. This is the easiest and fastest way to conquer Panhala. However, it is only when the sun rises to a considerable height in the sky that a bleeding man manages to come down where Shivaji stands. 'They . . . the Adilshahi soldiers, have killed all our men,' he mumbles and falls at his master's feet. 'Palkar never arrived. He has defected to the Adilshahi.'

5

Shah Jahan breathes laboriously, struggling to get some air into his lungs as he writhes in pain. For the past few weeks he has been down with fever and bowel problems and he is constantly in an urgent need to urinate. A Hindu medic has been summoned to give him opiate painkillers, but it is not working. The former emperor whose treasury was once filled with unthinkable wealth, the man who has created the Taj Mahal, is on his deathbed with just a few women sobbing around him. Eunuch Mutamad watches the dying man from a distance with a blank face. He has been told that he must begin renovating Agra Fort once the old man dies.

Jahanara is numb with sorrow. The words of Mir Sayyid Muhammad Qanauji sitting in a corner reciting the holy Quran float in the air:

Allah, give us good in this world,
and the world thereafter,
defending us from the torment of the fire.

The words have no impact on Jahanara who has started sobbing. She stares at her father whose breathing is now shallower and gaze emptier. She remembers his titles: Father of Victory, Star of the Faith, Muhammad the Second and Lord of the Conjunction, Warrior of Islam, Refuge of the Caliphate and Shadow of God on Earth. After a few moments, Shah Jahan stops breathing. The women in the chamber start wailing and beating their chests. Jahanara collapses on the ground.

When she comes by and looks at her father's bed, it is empty.

'Where is my father?' she screams and catches hold of one of her maids and shakes her violently for answers.

'They have taken him away,' the maid manages to utter.

Jahanara runs to the parapet of the burj like a woman possessed. She looks down and sees something she will never forget in her life. Her father is being taken out by four bearers from a small gate on a wooden bier. The bearers are led by two holding torches, one of them is Mutamad for sure and the other looks like the eunuch Phul. They seem to be in a terrible hurry to dispose of the body of her father whose pale face looks ghostly in the yellow light. Did they know he was to die today?

'Stop! Stop!' she screams, but within moments the small procession disappears from her vision.

A verse starts forming in her mind:

O sun of mine,
you have vanished from my eyes.
When will there be a dawn that will stop my cries?

Oh, the emperor of the universe,
the axis of the world and the king of its fate,
open the eyes of kindness to see my state,
I cry insanely,
with only wind to grasp,
I burn like a candle,
with only smoke to rasp.

In the middle of the night, Mutamad washes Shah Jahan's body in the cold waters of the Yamuna and then the mortal remains are taken to the marble mausoleum, the Taj Mahal. The dethroned emperor is buried next to his wife. When his corpse is lowered into the white stone enclosure, only one teardrop falls on him, and it is Mutamad's. The heart of the eunuch, who has hated Shah Jahan all his life, melts.

Early next morning, Aurangzeb gets the news at Dilli and sighs with relief. The sick old man who was refusing to die all these years, seven to be precise, is finally dead, forced to be dead, setting Aurangzeb free to be a legal emperor. The holy men of Mecca will no longer be able to question him about the legitimacy of his throne.

6

It has been a month since Shah Jahan passed away. Aurangzeb has come to Agra after seven years. Was her father's death planned by her only surviving brother?

Jahanara cries softly, standing on the open gallery that is framed with pillars and a low marble parapet, where precious and semi-precious stones create inlaid stonework elements of some vanished dreams. Behind her are airy chambers built on fort walls, and before her is the Taj Mahal. Between her and the mausoleum, eagles circle with serenity, unconcerned about the terrible misfortunes that have fallen on the fort inmates.

She stands there watching the Taj Mahal for a long time till the shadows of a vanishing day slide down on the mausoleum. A question haunts her: why had her father, who had started recovering, his face, less sunken and skin regaining its original colour, suddenly taken ill and died? After the new massage therapist sent from Dilli had replaced their old one, father's health had started deteriorating at an alarming speed. She did have her reservations about the masseur with his big hands and the strange-smelling massage oil. She has wondered many times whether that oil had anything to do with her father's death. She had questioned the masseur and he had said that the new European physician appointed to treat royals in Dilli suggested some herbs to strengthen her father's bones. Within weeks, Jahanara had noticed clots of dried blood stuck at the rim of her father's nostrils. After a few days, his nose had started bleeding so profusely that it had scared her. His hands and feet trembled and he developed high fever and stomach spasms. A few days later, he could hardly breathe, his chest swelling and then deflating like bellows of a blacksmith and then, in the end, he died of fever, dysentery and urinary trouble. Something nagged Jahanara in that moment of grief—the order from Dilli for the burial had arrived even more quickly. She had fainted, but her maids had told her the details of what had happened.

The women from the royal seraglio and Jahanara's father's other wives had gathered around her father's bed, some wailing violently and some beating their chests. Just then, *khoja* Phul and *khoja* Mutamad had come rushing in, dressed in funeral white. They had barked orders, directing the four bearers who had come with them carrying a stretcher, and told them that the burial had been planned that night as per the emperor's orders. The women, tearful and devastated, had pleaded with him to wait, and begged for a fair burial. Her father, the former emperor, had had a funeral procession akin to that of a destitute, led by a slave, two eunuchs and four carriers through the Mori Gate to the mausoleum. Her father, who had loved fabulous processions with thousands of spectators watching him, had been buried quietly, without any fuss. She had envisioned a totally different funeral procession for her beloved father: high-ranking mansabdars carrying the coffin through main avenues of Agra, with all ministers and councils walking beside the bier, with tens and thousands of people following to say adieu to their emperor, with palace servants throwing gold and silver coins to

428   Medha Deshmukh Bhaskaran

people waiting at the edge of the road to have a last glimpse of Shah Jahan. Nothing of the sort had taken place; instead, many questions had remained unanswered. How did the news of her father's death reach Dilli so soon? How did they get the orders from Aurangzeb within an hour? Where did the masseur with large hands disappear? Whom will she pose these questions to?

7

Somewhere else in the Agra Fort, the atmosphere is festive as everyone is looking forward to their emperor's fiftieth birthday that will be celebrated at the fort. Aurangzeb has finished inspecting the recently done-up diwan-e-khaas and has given his approval before marching towards the Musamman Burj, as his personal guards try hard to match his speed. The courtyard has a contingent of armed tartar women who stand at attention, their eyes downcast, their faces veiled. Abyssinian slaves prostrate in submission. Aurangzeb's eyes dart across the courtyard. On the other side, hundreds have climbed stepladders, their long brooms moving in circular motion over the surrounding walls to sweep off the cobwebs. A few plumbers engrossed in repairing a fountain pipeline notice the emperor and fall to their knees, their faces pressed to the ground. The guards at the entrance of the Burj bow to the point that they can bend no more.

Inside, where her father has breathed his last, Jahanara hears the commotion. She knows that within moments she will face her brother, in the very chamber where her father had died a thousand deaths thinking about his slain sons and grandson. Her father's chamber is empty and spotless as though wiped clean even of its memories. Her father's bed, too, has been removed.

Aurangzeb walks in and finds his sister standing near the arched window. He shows no surprise and asks his guards to leave. He looks at her: she has lost some more weight, her face is swollen and her eyes are red.

'Apa,' he says softly. Hearing his voice, she starts crying loudly. Dara bhai is dead, Shuja bhai is probably dead in Bengal, Murad is gone, Roshanara has died under mysterious circumstances. Aurangzeb is her only surviving sibling. He was a sickly child and Jahanara had to take great care of him as he would always fall ill with fever, cough and cold. In winters, when the palace went cold and windy, she used to wrap him up in a blanket and carry him around, never trusting the servants, but he wouldn't remember that now. This is her darkest moment. She has to face the man who has wiped out her family and yet her mind seeks emotional comfort from him. Fate has put her in an extraordinary situation. She wipes her tears, swings around and faces her brother evenly, standing straight, refusing to lower her eyes. Aurangzeb's pale glare is firm, without an iota of remorse. Her own reaction surprises her as her stomach clenches with fear under her brother's searching gaze, but she has made up her mind about how to handle her emperor brother for she needs to survive to look after her orphaned nephews and nieces. Trying to sound clear to assert her genuineness she says softly, 'Forgive me, brother. I think in retrospect, I have misjudged.'

Aurangzeb keeps a blasé expression, unsure of what she is getting at. In his father's days she had ruled from behind the throne, taking major political decisions and charting the fate of lakhs; now her destiny hangs on his decision. He notices that his sister's eyes are bleary, surrounded by huge dark circles. He says nothing, waiting for her to continue.

'I have realized my blunder, albeit late. I want to rectify. Let us start being a family again.'

There is silence. Jahanara does not remove her eyes from her brother who wears his prayer cap and holds his tesbih beads in his right hand. She feels as if she is like one of the beads, rolling, falling and being counted, utterly at his finger's mercy.

'What is on your mind?' Aurangzeb sounds edgy as if he wants to get done with the conversation. Jahanara's heart gallops when she replies, each word chosen with utmost care and spoken as if she is sixteen and her brother a little boy of eleven.

'Our family has gone through such upheavals in the recent past. I was blinded by my love for Dara bhai.'

Aurangzeb glances incredulously at his sister who is saying something he never expected she would. He regards her for a while—she seems earnest.

'Our ancestors consolidated north Hindustan, and an empire was born. Your austere rule is necessary to respect our ancestors' bequest and to break the spines of those who dare challenge it,' she says evenly as her heart pounds in her ribcage with fury and hate. She controls her emotions and throws a glance at the mausoleum before settling her gaze on her brother, hoping they do not give away shadows of personal reprisal.

'You have been venting your anger in words. You are holding me responsible for father's death,' Aurangzeb cuts his sister's avalanche of praises.

Her face turns ashen; her brother's spies are keeping a tab on each word that has fallen from her mouth. Her response is crucial. 'Father was like a broken bow after Dara bhai was beheaded,' she murmurs.

'He was punished by the sharia court, not by me.'

Did the court ask you to send his sutured body to father? she wants to say but does not. Instead, she sighs defeatedly, 'I have lost them all and I do not want to lose you too.'

Aurangzeb nods half-heartedly and turns back without saying anything. The inspection of private palaces must be done before going to the mosque.

There is another reason why Aurangzeb is not interested in prolonging this conversation—his mind is in the Deccan. With all those promising letters from Mirza, he has failed miserably in annexing the Adilshahi kingdom and that is a setback. Aurangzeb's vision of Islamic Hindustan calls for a mission of taking over the Deccan, but he has no one who could shoulder such a huge responsibility. Even his ace warrior, Mirza Raja Jai Singh has failed. Aurangzeb has been thinking of going to the Deccan himself to annex the Shia kingdoms but he is the emperor now and there are other responsibilities. The Turks, Iranian clans, the Pashtuns, the Yusufzais and the Afridis are raising their swords in the valleys around Kashmir and Afghanistan and it is dangerous to the empire. Aurangzeb knows that the leaders of those clans have served the Mughal armies and know the strategies and the tactics of the imperialists.

There is something else sloshing in Aurangzeb's mind, an out-of-the-box idea. He has realized that taking over the Deccan will need years of warring and even that may not be enough because one will need to destabilize the Shia kingdoms by resorting to politics before physically striking them. Such a humungous and lengthy task can only be accomplished by someone who is born there, someone who has thousands of native followers, someone who knows the Deccan like the back of his hand and someone who has been successful in subduing the Adilshahi. What if Shivaji turns a loyalist of the Mughal in a true sense, a loyalist who is ready to give his life for Aurangzeb's vision and mission? The Deccan charge is so heavy, so difficult and most of the generals have just wasted imperial resources. Shivaji is known for his frugal resources and big achievements. To understand the man from the mountains, Aurangzeb wants to see him in person. Also, the meeting has to happen in Agra or Dilli, preferably during a grand function when Shivaji will know what a Mughal emperor is and how Aurangzeb is regarded as supreme sovereign in this part of the world and how the mighty Hindu kings, the Rathods, the Chauhans, the Kachwahs and the Ranas fall prostrate in front of him.

That night Aurangzeb sends a farman to Mirza:

Send Shiva Bhosale and his son Sambhaji Bhosale, the Mughal mansabdar, to Agra to attend the celebrations of my fiftieth birthday. Use every ruse in the book, even promise him the subhedari of the Deccan if required.

CHAPTER THIRTY

1

Shivaji has summoned his ministers. His chief advisor, Peshwa Moroji Pinglay, financial controller, Muzumdar Niloji Sondev, revenue chief, Surnis Anna Datto, commander of infantry, Yesaji Kank, commander of infantry garrisons, Tanaji Malusare, external affairs advisor, Trimbak Dabir, law scholar, Niraji Raoji, political negotiator, Raghunath Ballal Korde, and the head of his spy network, Bahirji Naik, have come to Rajgad.

Balaji Avji, Shivaji's scribe, sits behind his desk to take notes.

The morning is bright, and yet the air hangs heavy in the sadar. Years of struggle, the loss of countless men, the bloody battles fought to tame despotic deshmukhs and patils, the sacking of Mughal cities for the want of funds and the constant war with neighbouring kingdoms all seem meaningless now. Shivaji has to convince his men of his and their future and make them understand their responsibilities. He asks them to sit and murmurs, 'What you have heard is true. I have decided to go to Agra with my son.'

Pinglay looks grim and his eyes are red. He asks incredulously, 'Why?'

'I have received a letter from Mirza. He writes that Aurangzeb is keen to make me the subhedar of the Deccan.' Shivaji says with eyes fixed on his chief advisor.

Pinglay is visibly surprised. As the Mughal subhedar of the Deccan, Shivaji will be in control of the provinces of Birar, Khandesh and more than half of the previous Nizamshahi. It also means having hundreds of mansabdars and their squadrons reporting to his master. Pinglay remembers their own terrain, with empty stretches of fields filled with black soil, its harvest of sorghum and millets finished to feed the Mughal armies. If Raja Shivaji becomes the subhedar of the Deccan, his people will never face Mughal invasions and he can also build his private army as well as open offensives in the Konkan and take over the entire coastal strip—all at the expense of the Mughal.

Shivaji knows what is going on in Pinglay's mind and says, 'We could then control the region around Balaghat in Konkan that gives ten lakh rupees in revenue to the Adilshahi.'

'If that is true, the entire region south of Narmada river will be with us,' Niraji Raoji says wistfully.

'Going north to meet the emperor is like entering the jaws of a starving tiger with the sharpest carnassial,' Pinglay dampens the enthusiasm.

'And staying here, fighting battles for the Mughal against the Adilshahi will take us nowhere. Taking no risk is the biggest peril,' Shivaji quips and continues, 'Many things can be achieved. Mirza has promised me an audience with the emperor, and I shall request for his support to conquer the invincible Janjira Fort which we have failed to capture time and again.'

'It is surprising that Mirza has failed at the gates of Bijapur,' Niraji Raoji comments.

Shivaji laughs and says, 'Not surprising at all! Being with them in the recent past, I have seen the weakness of the Mughal armies. Their need for the large amounts of cash to maintain the lavish lifestyle of their officials makes their general totally at the mercy of the emperor during campaigns. The fragility of their supply lines and the strife in the command are some of the reasons that take the sheen away from the halo around the Mughal might.'

'Has Mirza assured your safety?' Pinglay wants to know.

'In his letters he has taken solemn oaths and terms them the *promises of a Rajput*. His elder son, Kunwar Ram Singh, will be my man in the north. He is a mansabdar and has palace duties. His three thousand Rajput men from Mirza's clan will be briefed about my safety.'

'When have you planned to leave?' Pinglay asks for he knows that Raja has made up his mind.

'By spring.'

'Any news of Palkar?' Pinglay asks, keeping his voice low.

'The Adilshahi has given him lands generating rich revenue, but as per the latest news Mirza is trying to buy him off,' Shivaji says impassively and continues, 'Remember, I will need more than two months to cover the distance of over three hundred kos to the north, minimum one month in the city and two months for the return journey. I will be away for six months. In that period, our peshwa, Moroji Pinglay will oversee the functioning of our remaining forts, deciding where our cavalry and infantry will stay. Under no circumstances should the forts be handed over to the Mughals, even if they threaten you with my death.'

An edgy silence fills the sadar.

'Anna Datto will keep a tight control on our treasury; he will also find new places to hide our treasure. The places will only be known to our peshwa and our muzumdar. It is to make sure that even if I am tortured for information I will not be able to give them the whereabouts of our garrisons as well as our treasure,' Shivaji says.

The men are shocked at his words.

Shivaji continues, 'Trimbak Dabir and Raghunathji will leave immediately for Agra and meet Mirza's son Kunwar Ram Singh to plan our stay. Niraji Raoji, Tanaji Malusare, Yesaji Kank, Bahirji Naik and Balaji Avji will accompany me to Agra. My personal guards, Jiva Mahale, Hiroji Farzad and others will come too. Prataprao Gujar, who has been with Palkar in all the battles, will lead the contingent of five hundred horsemen and eight war elephants of the Maratha cavalcade.'

'It will be an expensive journey,' Anna Datto is already calculating.

'Yes, some provision needs to be made, but Aurangzeb has sent a hundred thousand rupees for us to cover the cost of the journey. The travel papers should arrive soon. Without those it is impossible to cross the Narmada and enter the imperial terrain. With the papers we will be able to buy food, fodder or water and cross the rivers.'

'How about the papers that will allow you to come back?' Pinglay questions.

'Those will be issued at Agra.'

'Does this mean that you will be at the mercy of Aurangzeb?' Shivaji nods.

For the next two weeks, Shivaji travels through his tiny kingdom and makes surprise visits to a few hill forts to check the discipline of the fort-keeper, guards at the gate, archers watching the ramparts, artillerymen controlling stores of explosives, and hill men watching the foothills.

2

The Agra-bound contingent of the Marathas is on the move, first arriving at Aurangabad, the Mughal capital of the Deccan, where people wait on the roadside to gaze at the famous Shivaji and his son sitting in a silver howdah mounted on a caparisoned elephant followed by splendidly dressed cavalrymen. After meeting high-ranking mansabdars and halting in the capital for a few days, the Marathas take the main road to Agra armed with necessary papers they need to show at all the Mughal posts, sarais and when they cross the rivers by ferry. They travel by day and spend nights at sarais built for the travellers, keeping a strict schedule as they have to cover hundreds of kos within fifty days to reach Agra the day before Aurangzeb's birthday celebrations. After reaching Burhanpur, they camp one extra night to give their horses and elephants some rest and then cross the Narmada to reach the eastern edge of Bhopal city. From here they move northwards, crossing Narwar to reach Gwalior, braving minor dust storms and a considerable rise in temperatures. While camping at the foothills of the fort where hundreds of political prisoners languish in the vaults, including Aurangzeb's eldest son, Muhammad Sultan, a letter from the emperor arrives for Shivaji.

> Come without delay, with full confidence in my grace, and come
> with a perfect composure of mind. After you have obtained
> audience with me, you will be glorified with my royal favours and
> given permission to return home. I am herewith sending you a
> khilat as a mark of respect.

Each halt is hard work. The elephants need to be unhooked and herded by mahouts towards a patch of open ground. The horses need to be taken out for grazing. Reluctant oxen must once again be fastened to the carts. The minders must pour tiny quantities of lubricant oil on the bearings and axles of the wheels. Defiant mules must be dealt with as they always try to step back to object to the heavy load being piled up on them.

The last major halt is at Dholpur sarai, on the banks of the river Chambal, surrounded by dense forest, adjacent to ravines famous for their gangs of bandits. People warn them to be careful, especially at nights. The sarai is too small to accommodate them, so they have planned to set up their camp behind it. Here the passport papers sent by Aurangzeb mean getting new horses and permission to proceed to Agra.

Inside the encampment, archers and swordsmen sleep, keeping their weapons and uniforms within easy reach. Their military mantra, in any case, is 'When on the move, eat light and sleep light'. Tanaji Malusare is wide awake under the starlit sky, as he cannot sleep when everyone sleeps. He first hears the faint growl of a tiger. He listens carefully and picks up yet another sound that nags him more than the growl. Gallopers are approaching from the north—not one, not two but many.

It is quiet at the sarai, as the pale light of the stars filters through enormous branches making dim patterns on the dung-smeared floor of the open courtyard. The courtyard has two entrances. One door is closed shut with heavy iron bars. Outside that door are the stables and sheds crammed with mules and oxen of the travellers. A row of mud structures next to the stables, which serves as a small market, is deserted. The other, bigger gate is the main entrance. It is bolted from inside and is supposed to be guarded by armed men. They are indeed on duty, sleeping soundly, their bellies bursting with meat stew and spicy rice.

Outside the sarai, shadows move stealthily, carefully stepping on the ground covered with dry leaves. Dacoits from the ravines have ridden several kos to reach the sarai south of Dholpur on the banks of Chambal river. Some of them have started pounding the main entrance with massive logs of wood. Within moments the door gives away and collapses backwards, finally waking up the guards who are heavily under the influence of bhaang. The leader of the dacoit takes one look at them, smiles behind his mask and signals his men to attack. The axes and machetes fly and soon the guards fall, blocking the entrance with their bodies, their swords resting near them, safely tucked in the scabbards. A single iron torch fixed on a pillar at the middle of the courtyard flickers weakly, adding more gloom to the darkness around.

The night raiders are a tall bunch of masked men, wearing rough, dark-coloured sleeveless tunics and leggings. The leader nods and signals to his men to enter, and kicks the bodies with his coarse sandals fitted with hard iron nails to make way. The others follow as one of them takes the lone torch from its niche on the pillar, moving towards the rooms filled with travellers.

There is a commotion in the rooms as the raiders disperse, each heading in different direction. The resting travellers are jolted out from their slumber and struggle aimlessly in the dark. The man holding the torch comes out and stays put in the courtyard, to show the light to his colleagues. The horrified occupants want to avoid bloodshed and hand over their belongings to the masked men. The stars have barely moved a distance of a man's palm and the dacoits are ready to move out with sacks filled with silver and gold. One last aggressor hesitates before getting out from a room. In the dim yellow light he has seen something he had not seen for a long time that makes lust rise under his leggings. He turns back, grabs the young woman and throws her over his shoulders and runs crouching into the open courtyard. For a moment there is grim silence but then the woman starts screaming, calling for help. A lone figure, probably the husband, canters out and clasps the abductor from behind. The dacoit swings around swiftly, twisting the body of his captor as the woman kicks her feet in the air. The leader stops just before exiting the courtyard and signals one of his men. The woman's husband is hacked from behind and collapses into a heap of his own limbs. The sound of his crushing bones turns the woman's screams into loud wails. The man with the torch leaps towards the entrance, giving a hint to others to exit.

Within moments, the dacoits pour out, avoiding the puddles of blood around the entrance littered with wrecked bodies. As they march towards their mounts something makes them stop—all of them. Their path is blocked by a bunch of armed men holding straight, long swords, their double-edged blades shining in the pale yellow light of the lone torch.

The puzzled dacoits look at them, wondering from where the contingent of short but muscular warriors has emerged. The leader knows in a flash that the armed men wearing boat-shaped turbans are certainly a part of a squadron.

'Leave the woman,' orders a man who seems to be in charge; his Urdu sounds heavily accented. The leader of the raiders stares at the man with a big black face that is partially covered with a large moustache. The dacoit leader's heart races a thousand kos because for the first time someone has challenged his gang. He glances at his men; they are stroking and patting their machetes and axes with impatience, waiting for his orders. He is their leader, and they look up to him. He needs to remain on the pedestal and calculates: he has twenty-five men and the unknown squadron has only ten or twelve.

'Kill,' he barks.

All from the opposition unlock their shields tied behind them and take positions and the dacoits have no shields as they have never had to defend themselves. Grinding their teeth with fury, half of them lope forward with their axes and machetes, still wet with the guards' blood. To counter, each from the squadron duck, then rise and swing around, making the dacoits miss their targets and bounce ahead loosely, wielding their weapons cutting the air to pieces. The short and sturdy warriors move their hands with blinding speed, their swords slicing through the dacoits from behind, felling most of them in moments. Meanwhile, the remaining dacoits launch an angry attack, wanting to smash the skulls of the men with orange turbans, but end up hitting them on their shields. Under their shields, the crouched warriors thrust their already crimson blades into the bellies of the axemen. The last one alive is still holding the woman; he throws his catch on the ground and disappears in the dark.

3

Jahanara wipes her tears discreetly. People call Aurangzeb *Zinda Pir*, a living saint, but they do not know that he had taken the hereditary treasure from Agra in one thousand four hundred carts and deposited it in the vaults of the Qila-e-mubarak in Dilli. Now it is back in Agra to be displayed in the court during the ceremony to dazzle visitors and intimidate them with the Mughal wealth.

It is time for Jahanara to attend a meeting to discuss the final arrangements. Partially covering her face with her translucent veil, she strides towards the quarters of her brother. She walks towards the private assembly room where imperial women can sit behind curtains and participate. It is dark in the room; the floor is covered with mats and some bolsters. She sits quietly, listening and watching, the darkness in the room allowing her to see them through the translucent panels. The meeting has already begun.

Aurangzeb sits on a chair, sporting a turban studded with oriental topaz that dazzles like a planet in the night sky. Jaffar Khan stands at a distance with folded hands, his henna-dyed beard covering his chest. Kunwar Ram Singh, Mirza Jai Singh's first son, stands opposite Aurangzeb, his slight body bent with reverence as he updates his master regarding the preparations, a perennial smile plastered on his face.

'People have arrived from Mecca, Balkh, Bokhara, Abyssinia, Kashgar, Basra, Yemen, Mocha, Hadramaut and from all our twenty-two provinces. Nobles have gathered. The clergy have arrived in several groups. We too are prepared, with selected sarais ready for the guests. The borders are lined with people to receive the visitors. The community kitchens are stocked with grain, meat, spices and fruits. Feasts are being cooked. Security arrangements are in order.'

'Where have the Marathas reached?' Aurangzeb asks casually. If Shiva is to serve the empire, he must be humbled and shown his place before he starts thinking of himself as indispensable. To start with, there will not be any special treatment for him. After all he is just a landholder and father of the empire's newest mansabdar.

'They must have entered the city by now. They will be guided towards Mulukchand's sarai. Do you want me to find out the details?'

'Never mind,' the emperor whispers, thinking about the private audience he has ordered with Shivaji a few days later.

'Who has gone to receive them?' Jahanara throws her question from behind the curtain. Aurangzeb is startled; he had not anticipated his sister's presence behind the curtain.

'Kunwar Ram Singh will take care of it. Kunwar's father and Shiva Bhosale know each other. I have also asked Fidai Khan to look into the matter.' The reply is somewhat evasive and Aurangzeb has dipped his voice low so Jahanara has to strain to hear him. Before anybody can ask anything further, Aurangzeb gets up to leave, closes his eyes and prays aloud, 'La ilaha illa'llah!'

'Why are you still here? You should have been camping someplace on the Gwalior–Agra road to meet the Marathas at a day's distance. Where is Fidai Khan?' Jahanara demands to know after her brother is gone, directing her questions at Kunwar through the curtains. He faces the curtains, and bows with an apologetic smile before glancing at Jaffar Khan hoping that he will reply for him, but the suave wazir-e-azam, as usual, keeps mum.

'We have some other commitments, Begum Sahiba. We have asked Giridhar Lal to look into the matter,' Kunwar replies, fidgeting nervously.

'And where is Giridhar Lal?' she asks.

'He is still at the fort; there are some major mistakes in his accounts and he has to redo the counting,' Kunwar says, his voice breaking into palpable guilt. His smile has gone.

'What is the confusion, wazir-e-azam?' The question is directed towards the prime minister who always speaks sparingly when cornered.

'We will sort it out, Begum Sahiba,' he says flatly, bowing deep.

Jahanara is thinking hard but is unable to understand why a lowly mansabdar like Kunwar has been chosen to receive the Marathas. If Kunwar and Fidai Khan are supposed to welcome the Marathas, why have they been kept busy at the fort? Why has Giridhar Lal, a mere book-keeper, now been asked to meet them? Even Mulukchand's sarai is an odd choice. It is meant for destitute travellers and is almost two kos away from the fort.

4

While Jahanara ponders about the Marathas and the arrangements made for them at Agra, Prataprao Gujjar, Tanaji Malusare and Ghazi Beg, Mirza's man who has travelled with them from the Deccan, lead the Marathas to the sarai. No one has yet come to welcome them and guide them to the sarai, and if Ghazi Beg, who has lived in Agra for years, had not been with them, they would have been lost. Under the blindingly bright afternoon sun, the men feel the summer heat and stifling hot winds as if they have walked straight into a furnace.

Shivaji's eyes scan the abode of the Mughals from the howdah mounted on his caparisoned elephant's back. This is not what he had envisioned. He had expected a city wall strengthened by ramparts and fortified with watchtowers teeming with archers, looking down on visitors entering the magnificent gates fitted with pointed iron spikes to injure or kill even armoured elephants in times of war. To his utter surprise, Agra has no proper wall. Its roads are narrow and crooked, flanked by clusters of shanty habitats boasting hovels made of mud and thatched with leaves or some other wretched material. Some of those slums, he suspects, are the encampments of the Mughal soldiers.

A day may come when we can take over this vulnerable city! he thinks.

As they move towards the city, the roads become less narrow but are extremely crowded because of the flat-roofed, single-storey shopping arcades on both sides. At places, the road is blocked with pedestrians, horsemen, cattle, carts and palanquins. There are Muslims and Hindus, some dressed in fine clothes but most of them poor, ragged and miserable and just hanging around on the streets because they have nothing else to do. His horsemen clear the way for Shivaji's elephant to trundle through the crowded streets. After a while, they enter a large avenue paved with stones and lined with trees, their barks partially covered by arabesque boundary walls. Some walls run along the length of the roads and end only at the roundabouts with ponds covered with lilies and hedged with flowering shrubs at the centre. This area is a contrast to the suburbs they have just crossed. Oxen carts rumble past, hastily making space for Agra's rich cruising in gilded chariots drawn by oxen with gold-sheathed horns. Every horseman is dressed in a long tunic and tight leggings, and every horse is of a quality breed. Sometimes elephants with golden howdahs covered with curtains pass by, perhaps carrying royal women. Shivaji notices Agra's wealthy men sitting cross-legged in cushioned palanquins, smoking hookahs while the bearers sweat and run through the crowd.

This street leads to the Agra Fort.

Their cavalcade abruptly leaves the beautiful avenue and joins a desolate road flanked by fields and clusters of slums. After a mile, the Marathas stop at a huge building with a grimy roof and broken tiles, a structure with mortar crumbling at places. It is a rude shock and Shivaji cannot believe that he and his men will be staying here.

'This is Mulukchand's sarai,' someone informs him. Only two men greet the Marathas who have travelled more than three hundred kos to reach Agra: Raghunath and Trimbak Dabir. They were informed about Raja Shivaji's accommodation just the day before.

They all walk in. Some start pitching tents around the sarai.

Thankfully, the sarai is clean from the inside. There is a sweet-water well in the backyard, the servants of the house are polite and the rooms are large. There is a huge courtyard in the middle. Even then, this is not what Shivaji had expected. He had thought Mirza's son Kunwar would welcome him with his retinue and at least provide him with a decent accommodation near the Agra Fort, from the balcony of which he would be able to see the Taj Mahal.

That night, long after Shambhu has gone to sleep, Shivaji stares at his son's translucent face, partially covered with wild curls. He gingerly pushes the curls back from his forehead that has gone moist with sweat and wipes it dry with his handkerchief and then rests his back on a pillow. He closes his eyes and tries to recall Mirza's words: 'The emperor, our ocean of mercy, will grant you a grand welcome and a grander audience. You will meet the wealthiest yet the simplest man on this planet. He, the Zinda Pir, is truly a living saint. You may even discuss the issue of the Janjira Fort. Perhaps the emperor will ask the Siddis to vacate the fort for you. And who knows? You may come back as the Mughal subhedar of the Deccan!'

The oppressive heat does not allow Shivaji to fall asleep. He ventures out into a balcony adjacent to his room. Kunwar Ram Singh has neither established contact nor has he sent anyone else despite the fact that the grand function at the fort is the very next day.

Two kos away from Mulukchand's sarai, Aurangzeb lies on his bed in the private apartments of Agra Fort. The walls are vacuous and filled with water to keep the chambers cool. Outside, palace servants pull on ropes silently to keep huge satin sheaths of the fan swaying and sweeping the trapped ceiling air around the chamber. The water streams jingle through *nahr-e-bahisht* and cool the surroundings. All over the city, lodges for the guests are curtained with khus mats, while jets of water from the fountains in the outside gardens keep sprinkling water on those. Only the Maratha camp at Mulukchand's sarai is devoid of any cooling system. It remains a hot furnace all through the night.

CHAPTER THIRTY-ONE

1

From the minarets rising above the pavilions, muezzins call Muslims to fajr, the early morning prayers. It is still dark, but Agra Fort is already awake, and the torches supported in sconces by brackets high up on walls throw a pale light over the courtyard. The corridors of the structures within the fort are draped in satin durries while the floor is already covered with Turkish and Persian carpets. Slaves scatter rubies and tiny jasmine flowers made of gold on the red carpets leading to the diwan-e-aam and diwan-e-khaas. Eunuchs specially trained in aroma science sprinkle rosewater over the walls and some put smouldering sandalwood sticks into the nooks to freshen up the staleness of the air. Behind the private quarters of the royals, in a small storeroom, men remain busy verifying bequests reserved for the honourable guests. Beauticians and hairdressers check make-up jars, oils, designer clothes and scents again and again to service the royal ladies who have been invited for the function.

The morning star has already appeared in the sky, paling all others, and the city is stirring awake, eagerly looking forward to celebrating their emperor's birthday when sweetmeats and clothes will be distributed. A major event is taking place after years of battles, deaths and mourning. People, starved of happiness, need some reprieve, and even galloping buggies taking visitors to public baths make children squeal with excitement. Small gullies are filling with families walking towards the fort. People hope to grab places on terraces, balconies and rooftops of the houses of their more privileged friends living in the heart of the city, just to catch a glimpse of guests entering the fort.

Two kos away, at Mulukchand's sarai, Shivaji sits inside his chamber on a wooden plank facing a small idol of Goddess Bhavani. The deity holds eight weapons in eight hands. The demon Mahishasura lies crumpled at her feet, impaled by her trident. In the fluttering light of an oil lamp, the goddess seems to have fixed her gaze on Shivaji, her enlarged, kohl-smeared eyes staring down at him.

'Today bears many possibilities of what could and would happen. Mother, you seem adamant to know my reaction. I understand the reasons behind your demand. The sword of "or else" hangs in the skies of our swaraj, its blades sharpened by the emperor, who expects my servitude. It is a vicious circle, Mother, and you know that Aurangzeb's sword is not only thirsty for blood, but it also seeks something far more priceless and far less tangible for its survival—it needs to feed on people's fears and hopes; it seeks elimination of religions and thrives on a strange perception that it is invincible. A refusal to surrender to it has resulted in hundreds of deaths. Show me the way, Mother, make me do something that will not make me a servant of the emperor's sword and let things happen in such a way that I move nearer to my goal!'

The morning winds are humid, promising a long and hot day ahead. Small processions, caparisoned elephants with howdahs, decorated horses and palanquins move towards the fort as invitees pour into the courtyard. Soon, the diwan-e-aam is full. The royal orchestra has started playing, indicating that the time is ripe for the grand entry of the master. The palace announcers alert the assemblage, 'Hoshiyar, hoshiyar! Shehenshah Abul Muzaffar Muhy-ud-Din Muhammad Aurangzeb Bahadur Alamgir, ocean of mercy, shadow of the almighty, the only link between mankind and the divine, makes his august presence . . .'

Then there is silence, followed by the dramatic entry of Emperor Aurangzeb, followed by his sons in all their finery, Muazzam from Nawab Bai, Azam and Akbar from late Dilras, and Kam Baksh from Udepuri. The last prince is still too young to walk on his own and is carried by Aurangzeb's personal eunuch, khoja Mutamad. The emperor walks purposefully as the jewels on him sparkle, making many eyes blink to counter their brilliance. A few ceremonial guards follow him, each carrying separate emblems fixed on a long, gold spike, a sun, a fish, an upraised hand and scales of justice. The sun symbol is enormous; its countless sapphires shine in zest to confirm the direct connection between the divine and the emperor.

The assemblage performs kurnish as a public declaration of total obedience to the royal command and many sigh in hushed veneration. Those who have never seen him before stare from the corner of their eyes and the very thought that they stand under the same roof with the emperor make many feeble with panic, while those who have fallen from his grace pray in silence. The emperor is finally on his throne; the official function has started.

Once their names are called, dignitaries walk forward along with fort attendants carrying gifts. They fall to their knees or prostrate in front of the throne and some bow again and again till they are asked to stop. Aurangzeb's eyes remain half-closed as he counts his prayer beads, only opening them when an announcement is made to shower his meher-e-nazar, the gaze of kindness, on the chosen dignitary. The beneficiary of his gaze at once touches the steps that lead to the throne and kiss the same hand again and again, because it is an achievement to be worthy of the emperor's gaze of kindness. The receiver of such respect will later go back and tell the story of his triumph to his children and then to his children's children.

Kunwar Ram Singh is feeling uneasy. He has finished his duty—the security around the fort is tight, the gates and the courtyard are swarming with guards. Making his way to the diwan-e-aam, Kunwar pushes himself through the human blockade and enters the court. Once inside, he tiptoes and squirms through the rows of dignitaries, advancing towards the throne. There, he stares at his master, hoping to catch his slippery gaze. It is getting late; if he does not leave now to get them, Shivaji will never reach on time. He prays that the guards at the Mansingh Gate have found out about the Marathas and where they have reached.

In the diwan-e-aam, the main part of the function starts. Two muscular Abyssinians rush in carrying a massive gold stand and enormous weighing scales. They fix the central pivot in front of the throne. The jewel-studded arms of the scales hold two huge pans lined with velvet cushions. The audience watches in rapt attention.

Aurangzeb, who completes his fiftieth year at this very moment, rises from his throne, steps down and walks towards the scales. One of the men pulls one side of the scales down till the pan touches the ground. The fulcrum springs into action and the beam tilts abruptly, raising the other empty pan high in the air. Its diameter is greater than the height of a man. Aurangzeb climbs into the lower pan holding the chains, sits down and starts counting his beads while several servants rush in, each loaded with bulging sacks. They swarm around the other side of the scales and start emptying their cargo on to the other pan. Gold, silver and precious stones tumble out, filling the empty pan. The emperor starts rising high, feeling exhilarated under the gaze of hundreds of eyes exploding with admiration.

The scales are finally balanced. Aurangzeb has donated that entire wealth equal to his weight to the poor.

The function at the diwan-e-aam is almost over and most of the civilian guests are politely guided out of the fort. Others—the princes, the ministers, the mansabdars, the clergy and the ambassadors—start moving to the diwan-e-khaas. The emperor moves first, followed dutifully by his richly attired emblem holders. Kunwar looks hassled; he is asked to show the guests their positions, strictly according to their status. What bothers Kunwar is how some nobles show their displeasure to him by frowning at him as if he decides their status. He wishes at least one of them has the courage to ask the decision-maker, the emperor. At last Kunwar's duty is over and all have been given their right positions. The ulemas, the imams and the muezzins stand on one side of the throne and the ministers, including wazir-e-azam Jaffar Khan, on the other. The first row, enclosed by a fence made of gold bars, is crowded with the *amir*s who are the sons, nephews, uncles and some other close relatives of the emperor. Ambassadors from Iran, Uzbekistan, Afghanistan and Mecca stand behind the royals, and after them the nobles according to their military ranks. Kunwar makes a quick exit, this time without bothering to ask for permission. While exiting he glances at Maharaja Jaswant Singh Rathod and wonders why the man looks angry.

Jaswant Singh Rathod is fuming. He has been made to stand in the last row. The distance between the emperor and the standing position of a noble is the most important, and every inch counts. He has surrendered his life in the services of the imperial armies, fighting battles first for Shah Jahan, then for Dara Shikoh and now for Aurangzeb. Despite being the king of Marwar, the largest province of Rajasthan, and despite the late Shah Jahan giving him the highest title of Maharaja, the great king, he is made to stand far away from the throne. He has heard that Shivaji has arrived in Agra and wonders where he is standing.

2

The Marathas have entered the elite area of Agra where the street is lined with mansions of umrahs, rajas and high-ranking mansabdars, surrounded by luxuriant gardens. The sun has risen, making the shadows of men shorter and shorter till they are no longer seen, when the cavalcade crosses the Dahar Gardens and reaches the Noorganj Gardens. The road is cordoned off, as people beyond the barricades shove each other to catch a glimpse of a man who had maimed their emperor's uncle. Slaves in grubby tunics trying to sprinkle water on the road to prevent dust from blowing up, throwing shy glances to see the last cavalcade as their nimble bodies crouch under the weight of enormous waterskins.

From the opposite direction, Kunwar is riding along with Giridhar Lal. Kunwar is drenched in sweat; his head throbs as if someone is drumming inside his skull. With new responsibilities thrown at him and time limits turning unreasonable, Kunwar is driven close to the edge of endurance. He narrows his eyes and looks ahead on the empty road, feebly protecting his eyes with the shade of his hand, and notices, a rippling, blurred image of a lone cavalcade. He nudges his horse with his knees and rides faster. Within moments he is facing the Marathas. He gapes as he notices two palanquins followed by a big line of trundling elephants.

'Please get down, the fort is packed, there is no place for the elephants,' Malusare hears someone shout. The man who looks like a younger Mirza is trying hard to be heard. The cavalcade stops abruptly, and the mahouts try to seat the tuskers trudging anxiously and getting mad because of the heat. Shivaji and Sambhaji are helped down from the back of the seated elephants. Some of the horsemen dismount to make the mounts available to their leader and his officials.

'Ram Ram! I am Kunwar Ram Singh,' Mirza's son introduces himself without getting down from his horse, looking at the man wearing a pale silk tunic and a slivery sash, who has just got down from an elephant and mounted a horse. Shivaji returns his greeting, thinking, *Does Mirza's son not have the courtesy or manners of his father, or is it a part of a bigger conspiracy to humiliate me?*

Kunwar announces abruptly, 'We have to hurry or the function might soon be over.'

Kunwar, Shivaji and Sambhaji ride their horses through the mass of people gathered around Amarsingh Gate, while the rest of the cavalcade is herded off to Firoza Gardens. The fort suddenly appears, its sandstone battlements looming over the mansions of important courtiers stretching along the banks of Yamuna river. The father and son finally enter the Agra Fort and Shivaji is amazed at the massive fortification that meanders beyond the range of his sight. The two men and the boy cross the diwan-e-aam and dismount, giving their horses to the caretakers, and proceed on foot to diwan-e-khaas. Shivaji is astonished to see the grandeur of the fort: the entrance is draped by embroidered velvet, balls of silver and gold laden with precious stones hang down from the arches and the floor is covered with carpets. They are greeted by a grim-faced man who ushers them inside the court.

Aurangzeb, who has been discreetly alert throughout, notices Kunwar coming towards the throne. His jaw tightens. Finally the mighty emperor of the Mughals will be face to face with the man who has dared to challenge the empire.

Sambhaji tries to keep pace with the long strides of Kunwar. For months it was drilled into him that he is the mansabdar of the emperor. Feeling proud, he glances behind and sees his father. Reassured, he smiles to himself as his eyes wander playfully around the arches and pillars inlaid with gold and studded with sparkling stones. His gaze moves beyond the pillars and stops at an enormous chair, almost touching the ceiling. Above the high marble platform is a small temple with large windows made of gold. Inside the golden shrine sits a strange-looking man wearing a huge turban laden with sparkling stones. He is counting beads with sleepy eyes. At that very moment, Aurangzeb opens his eyes and finds himself peering into a pair of eyes beaming with joy. The boy smiles, but he, the emperor, quickly looks away.

Shivaji scans the grandeur that surrounds him. In the massive court, the chandeliers hang low, each with numerous candles. Distinguished-looking men stand, in row after row, in front of the throne at attention, as if they are army recruits. The golden throne with a marble base rises high like a heavenly sanctum floating in the air. In that citadel of power sits the bejewelled, bedecked, beads-counting 'living saint' whose half-closed eyes never seem to open. Behind the throne, Shivaji notices benches of gold, where crown weapons like jewelled swords, daggers, shields and spears are displayed.

Kunwar rushes towards the emperor and whispers anxiously, 'We got delayed, my Alamgir. May I take the opportunity to present Raja Shivaji?'

Aurangzeb, through the slits of his half-closed eyes, has noticed that the Maratha is wearing a silk tunic embroidered with gold thread. His sash dazzles with jewels, while his belt is made of fine leather.

The headgear is saffron and is laden with pearls. Aurangzeb has seen more handsome men in his life, but he has not seen anyone radiating so much courage, so much pride and so much confidence. Shivaji's swagger disturbs Aurangzeb who has started getting annoyed. Shivaji must bow. Hasn't Kunwar briefed him about kurnish? Kunwar notices his master's reaction and leaps towards Shivaji and whispers, 'Kurnish.'

Shivaji touches the string of cowries tied around his neck and begins by first placing the palm of his right hand on his forehead and then bending his head forward, as if cradling it in his palm, as if to admit that he will obey without questions. While saluting the emperor, the vision of Goddess Bhavani floats in his mind, her eight hands holding weapons and a demon impaled by her trident.

Sambhaji emulates his father. Their orange turbans with pearl strings touch the throne's last step as the silver plates filled with freshwater pearls are offered to the emperor as a gift from the Deccan.

After straightening up in a hurry, Shivaji throws back his head to stare at the emperor, hoping he will look at him and smile.

Aurangzeb's eyes are closed but he has seen enough. Not in his living memory does he remember anyone walking so proudly in his presence. Aurangzeb realizes in a flash that Shiva Bhosale will never be his loyalist. This man will never fit in a chain-of-command. This man is not meant to take orders. He is born to give orders. Aurangzeb thinks of his vision and mission, that is, to take over the Deccan to bring entire Hindustan under Sunni rule, where kafirs will not be considered as citizens of the empire. They will be regarded as *zimmi*s, as burdens, and their properties as well as their positions will remain under the strict watch of the Muslim clergy. It will be easy to manipulate zimmis by playing with their hopes and fears, and systematically repressing them with taxes, debarring them from positions in public offices, thus pushing them to convert to Islam. Aurangzeb knows the bitter truth now: between him and the Deccan stands the man who stands before him!

Kunwar makes an announcement.

'Raja Shivaji, the father of our mansabdar of five thousand horses from the Deccan, has offered one thousand gold coins and two thousand rupees as *nazar*—a kind gift—and five thousand rupees as *nisaar*—proprietary alms. Sambhaji Raja, our mansabdar, has offered five hundred gold coins and one thousand rupees as nazar and two thousand rupees as nisaar.'

There is no further announcement, the silence indicating that the time allocated for Shivaji is over. Aurangzeb speaks no word of welcome, has not smiled in recognition and not even looked at his guest to acknowledge the invitee who has travelled more than three hundred kos, braving thick forests, long stretches of deserts and the oppressive summer of north Hindustan.

This is not what Shivaji had envisioned. He too has realized the bitter truth. To serve the emperor means giving up on dignity.

In a 'viewing' balcony made for the royal seraglio, Jahanara sits surrounded by her women relatives, besieged by strong fragrances of wild flowers, sandalwood and jasmine. Udepuri is just behind her, wearing the most magnificent turban heavy with diamond bands. The newly fashioned headgear allows just a teasing glimpse of her auburn hair. Jahanara notices her necklace with a large diamond as a pendant. It sparkles, infusing its rays in the surrounding areas, looking as dominant as the sun in the small universe of the curtained balcony. Aurangzeb has gifted her father's most prized possession, the Koh-i-noor, to his youngest wife.

What is happening in the court is more intriguing. Her eyes dart and remain fixed on the man who has come with Kunwar—he is the Shivaji! Kunwar says something to the handsome Maratha and without showing his back to the emperor guides him through the rows of people. They move silently with the little boy.

Shivaji can feel the gaze of the people trying to catch a glimpse of his face, perhaps searching for the impact of humiliation. Some gazes pierce deep, as if prying on his bleeding heart, and some pour their sympathy through their eyes and that burn holes in his soul. Something snaps in him, bitterness rising in his heart.

Jahanara's eyes follow Shivaji's footsteps. Nobody whispers, nobody even breathes loudly, but everyone stares wide-eyed at the fair man with the saffron turban who tumbles once while walking backwards. Perhaps he had never walked that way before. They reach the last row, and Shivaji is shown his place, *behind* Maharaja Jaswant Singh Rathod!

The court proceedings go on as more dignitaries are called, who kneel, fall prostrate, showering the emperor with more gifts and praise. Shivaji and Sambhaji stand in the last row, lonely and forgotten as if discarded, while Kunwar has disappeared somewhere into the front rows. Shivaji looks around and notices the nobles, looking tall and striking in their traditional silk tunics and brilliantly coloured turbans. Some look at the emperor with devotion in their eyes while others stand with their heads down, with the obedience of a slave, not moving an inch away from the places assigned to them. It is at this point that the name of Maharaja Jaswant Singh Rathod is announced and the man standing in front of Shivaji moves from his place and advances towards the throne.

Shivaji feels anger lance through his brain and cut through his bones. He closes his eyes and envisions Goddess Bhavani. He peers into her rage-filled eyes and feels a strange calm. His anger abruptly vanishes and he is swept by a storm of fearlessness bordering on audacity and is ready to excavate the layers of pretences and expose a lie called Aurangzeb. The Mughal court is not what Mirza has made him believe, and the reality is far from the grand reception Mirza had promised he would get. It is time to show Aurangzeb and his spineless minions that he is not one of them.

Shivaji's face is flushed with anger. Aurangzeb had noticed it. He calls Kunwar and whispers, 'What is bothering Shiva?'

Kunwar runs, making his way through the rows of the courtiers, and reaches Shivaji, panting, but before he can ask Shivaji Aurangzeb's question, Shivaji shouts at him, his words cutting through the cobwebs of the centuries-old reverential silence gathered in the hall. He is not bothered about etiquette any more—his language is Deccani Urdu.

'You, your father and the emperor know what kind of man I am and yet you make me stand behind Maharaja Jaswant Singh Rathod whom we have defeated in battles fought at the foothills of Kondana Fort? If you wanted me to stand, you should have done so according to the right order of precedence.'

Jahanara watches, her mouth open, while everyone in the hall searches for the origin of those loud words, sharper than the blade of a newly honed sword and precise like an arrow flying from a trained archer's bow. Jahanara quickly looks at her brother who has stopped counting his beads and is staring at Shivaji with his eyes wide open, devaluing the significance of his meher-e-nazar, the gaze of mercy! She wants to laugh, viciously and loudly. Someone has finally shaken her brother, whose mind, body and soul are supposed to be invincible!

Aurangzeb cannot believe what is happening and a bolt of embarrassment tears through his body. He tries to calm down and looks at his court, only to discover that no one is looking at him. Their eyes shine in awe and admiration of the brave man who has defied the emperor, ransacked the imperial terrain, defeated Kartalab Khan, maimed Shaista Khan and let go a beautiful captive in Kalyan with honour. Not knowing what to do or how to react to a situation he has never faced before, Aurangzeb simply starts counting the beads again.

Kunwar feels crippled with dread while Shivaji shoves him away and starts exiting the hall, his back to the emperor. Sambhaji runs to follow. Aurangzeb looks on. Never before have any of the Mughal emperors seen anyone's back.

Kunwar rushes to the emperor. He trembles while his voice quivers apologetically, 'Raja Shivaji seems to have annoyed my Alamgir.'

Aurangzeb is forced to break his mystical silence he has created around him. He orders, 'Call him back to the court and ask him to behave. Perhaps the summer of north Hindustan has made him go crazy. Pour some water on his head and see if he cools down.'

Kunwar rushes out only to find Shivaji sitting quietly on the steps of diwan-e-khaas, and little Sambhaji standing next to him. Kunwar goes near them with folded hands and before he opens his mouth Shivaji hollers, 'With such humiliation I cast off your mansab!'

'By breaking the etiquette of the court, you have put yourself in a perilous situation,' Kunwar says softly and continues, 'Please come back to the court as the emperor orders.'

'Do you mean the day of my death has arrived? In that case either you kill me or I will kill myself. But I am not going back to see the emperor again, not now, not later, not again. I will never be his servant, ever!'

Kunwar goes back to Aurangzeb and repeats his conversation with Shivaji. Kunwar's heart is racing.

'La ilaha illa'llah! Mohammadur rasool'ullah . . .' Aurangzeb murmurs the kalma while counting his tesbih beads.

3

The previous day's incident has not shaken Aurangzeb's routine. Overtly calm and peaceful, he moves from his private quarters to the mosque and then to the family court and to his private office at the edge of the court palace, with his prayer beads moving at a steady pace between his fingers. An hour before noon, he has an important meeting with tribal chiefs from the southern borders of Balkh. Outside, Jaswant Singh Rathod waits impatiently in the palace courtyard for the assembly to finish, sweating at the collar in the suffocating heat. After what seems like an eternal wait, he is called in after the Balkhans leave. Their massive turbans with enormous folds have added several inches to their already big frames, forcing the relatively tall Jaswant to look up to see their faces. When they notice Jaswant, they stare at him as glints of recognition flash across their eyes. They mutter to each other with their faces straight and unsmiling.

Jaswant ignores them and enters Aurangzeb's office that has just one table, one chair and a desk for the scribe. The emperor is in his usual attire sans jewels and turban, clad in his muslin jama and a prayer cap, perhaps made with his own hands. He is busy reading, while Jaffar Khan stands next to him. Several moments pass and finally Aurangzeb murmurs without removing his eyes from the papers, 'What is it that you need to discuss, Jaswant?'

Jaswant clears his throat softly, bows deeply and broaches the subject, 'My Alamgir, kindly accept humble salutations from this *nacheez*, this worthless man. It is my honour to stand before you and utter my views. I believe that there is a deeper meaning to whatever happened yesterday in the court. It's a forewarning.'

'Yesterday was a busy day and many things happened in the court; which one in particular are you talking about?' Aurangzeb asks with ease, his face calm.

Jaswant shudders with powerless rage; the emperor is snubbing him blatantly. Shivaji had openly condemned him before challenging the emperor. Everyone in the city is discussing Shivaji's outburst; it is being gossiped about in homes, in the markets, at sarais and even in the emperor's own courtyards.

Jaswant decides to ignore the question, points his forefinger to himself and says regretfully, 'Alamgir, kindly forgive this worthless man for speaking from the depth of his heart. I believe there was some motive in allowing a dangerous man like Shivaji to Agra. Mirza Raja should have warned you.'

Aurangzeb has no appetite to discuss this subject and he does not want or need anyone's advice, especially Jaswant's, who, according to the reports, might have forged a discrete alliance with Shiva in the past.

'Who are you blaming?' Jaffar Khan demands without moving his eyes from Aurangzeb who is still engrossed in reading.

Jaswant hesitates; the young, tall and debonair maharaja of Marwar feels a spasm of fear slither down his spine.

'Raja Jaswant?' Jaffar Khan sounds impatient.

'Mirza Jai Singh should have thought before sending this treacherous creature to Agra. Or, as I suspect, did he have some motive in doing so?'

Aurangzeb smiles. The old Kachwah–Rathod rivalry is rearing its head again! These so-called proud kings pompously wear the crowns of Mughal vassalage and fight among themselves. Mirza's brilliant success in the past has created an anti-Mirza lobby headed by Jaswant who is smarting under Shiva's remarks, Shiva who is a protégée of Mirza.

Jaswant gathers enough courage and persists, 'Allow this nacheez to suggest something of vital importance. I believe that Shivaji must face public death by hanging to teach others a lesson. He has dared to break the protocol of the court and his arrogance is certainly powered by something far more evil.'

Aurangzeb shakes his head with dismay; Jaswant has forgotten how he had intercepted Aurangzeb's forces near Ujjain to defend

Dara bhai, what he had done during the battle at Khajwa when they had fought Shah Shuja. And now this traitor wants the emperor to trust him. *I would rather trust men like Shiva Bhosale than Jaswant Singh Rathod!* Aurangzeb fumes.

'We shall give you the date when you will leave for our north-western frontiers with your men,' Aurangzeb says with finality. The conversation is over.

Jaswant nods with shadows of despair in his eyes.

Aurangzeb and Jaffar Khan do not say anything further, and their impatience for him to leave fills the air. Jaswant has no option but retreat with quiet indignation. After he is gone, Jaffar Khan asks the attendants standing outside the door to summon Kunwar Ram Singh.

Kunwar comes in, his face drained of colour. He bends till his spine aches and stands with folded hands, his shoulders stooping.

'Is Shiva Bhosale coming to meet me today?'

'Raja Shivaji has fever, he will not come today,' Kunwar says while bending his body as much as possible.

Jaffar Khan hands over a paper to him; it is for Shivaji.

We, the imperial power, have rightfully acquired your forts. You, from the depth of your heart, have acknowledged us as your rulers. I, the emperor, tell you to hand over the remaining forts to us in the interest of the empire. You claim to serve with your heart which is supposedly loyal and if that is so, prove it with your actions. Write to your ministers to hand over the forts to Mirza Raja Jai Singh.

The letter has Aurangzeb's palm impression.

While Kunwar exits he hears the emperor say, 'Send our guest from the mountains for a boat ride. Let him see the grandeur of Agra.'

4

After several days, Shivaji hands over his reply to Kunwar who has become a postman carrying letters and delivering them.

I have handed over the forts to Mirza Raja Jai Singh, the forts mentioned in the treaty. Now if you are asking me to hand over the remaining forts to you, in the interest of the empire, let me tell you the bitter truth. I have no control over those as I have declared my prime minister as an independent caretaker. He is not obliged to obey me and he will not.

Kunwar Ram Singh is worried. *Why did things happen the way they did? Was my lack of foresight and sloth responsible for the turn of events? What if I had briefed Raja Shivaji about court etiquette? What if I had informed him that the emperor had asked me to organize a private meeting between them after the function? What if I had informed Raja Shivaji that the emperor was planning to give him a hundred warhorses, two elephants, several robes of honour, head bands, daggers with hilts embellished with jewels, and one lakh rupees? Or did the emperor change his mind and deliberately play the game that led to this mess?* Kunwar fails to understand what had gone wrong. Either he had taken things lightly or the emperor had orchestrated the delay. Kunwar has also heard from a very reliable source that the emperor has had a private meeting with Rad Andaz Khan, the commander of Agra Fort, who has a palatial home with several small cottages that are used as sort of service apartments. When the emperor wants someone to vanish from this planet without lawful trial, that person is sent to Rad Andaz's palace as the guest of honour. The unsuspecting guest is happy with the luxurious dwellings but he will never be seen again, ever, because he has been killed in the dungeons of Rad Andaz's house! Kunwar wonders what is happening in the dungeons at this very moment.

The palace is supported by high marble pillars that gleam in the sun, but beneath its courtyards and gardens is another world, as dark as it is bright above. Rad Andaz Khan, a man of ruthlessness and ferocious intolerance, has become a favourite of Aurangzeb when he wants to eliminate people and throw state prisoners in his dungeons.

Rad Andaz makes his constitutional rounds through the winding passages of his underground prison. Men with hardened faces follow him, some of them experts in ripping out teeth, nails, tongues and eyeballs. They are trained to be deliberately cruel and systematic and have learnt to force the captives to yield information.

The way is lit by torches, and the air filled with the appalling stench of urine and faeces. The walls are of dark, undressed stones and seem resistant to the noxious life around them. The ceiling hangs low like a prying evil, as if to crush anyone who tries to stand tall. The tunnels are lined with tiny cages on either side, each filled with ten or more men. Some of them have been incarcerated for months, their only crime being the fact that they are the suspects in the eyes of the emperor. Rad Andaz likes the way his prisoners look at him, sticking their faces to the bars, their vengeful eyes following him as he moves on. Sometimes he surprises the new ones by spitting at them or shoving iron bars into their eyes or mouths leaving them crying with agony.

At the end of that claustrophobic tunnel is a large chamber. The doorkeeper is an Abyssinian in a loincloth holding a cleaver that looks larger than a sword. He notices his master and his men marching towards him. A chill runs down his spine as he quickly unlocks the massive lock of the iron door and picks up a lit torch from the corridor and leaps inside the chamber to show light. Before the men can barge in, the torch is fixed on a large counter attached to a wall. In the dim light of that single torch one can see an elongated table made of ordinary wood. There are strange-looking objects on it: ropes, tongs, handcuffs, padlocks and leg shackles fastened to heavy iron balls, leashes with thin steel chains, twisted screws, rusted cleavers, small cages filled with live mice and tiny bottles labelled poison. Two massive glass jars with a few slender snakes slithering agitatedly at the bottom are kept in the middle of the table.

The men gather around the table. Rad Andaz loves this room and holds his meetings here.

'We are getting one more facility within a month,' Rad Andaz whispers, opening the mice cage with relish. He whisks out a squeaking mouse by its tail and tosses it in the jar of snakes. 'It is very close to the fort; you might have even seen its compound wall, it is rather high. It has an enormous crypt beneath it. It will have three torture chambers equipped with tools that you have never seen. The tunnels are bigger and are lined with a hundred cells. We can house more than a thousand men in there.'

'Our work will be easier then,' a man says softly.

'The emperor has sent a message. He might send a very special man as our first guest: a haraamzada kafir who has misbehaved in the emperor's court,' Rad Andaz says, his eyes gleaming with hate.

'Be assured we will look after him,' someone replies and others chuckle.

'Now move on, there is work to be done,' Rad Andaz orders.

His men pick up various tools and exit from the chamber.

CHAPTER THIRTY-TWO

1

Oarsmen dressed in finery for the occasion lean as much as they can towards the boat's bow to sweep as much water as they can towards the stern. The men throw glances at their guest and his son sitting in their boat that belongs to the fleet of recreational yachts for the Mughal royals. They have heard that this man from the Deccan has insulted the emperor, the conqueror of the world, in the sacred diwan-e-khaas of the Agra Fort, that too at the time of his birthday celebrations! Some of them wonder what he, the man who has committed an unspeakable crime, is doing here. The oarsmen have seen a lot and know the whims and fancies of their Mughal masters. They know the bloody history, where brothers have slaughtered, tortured or maimed brothers. They are sure of the fate of their guest whose eyes are filled with astonishment.

Shivaji and Sambhaji have not seen anything like this before. The banks of the Yamuna are illuminated by enormous lanterns and torches, making the water surface look like a garden of lights. He has also not heard music like this before. The bands gathered on the either side of the river create pleasing music with their sitars, sarods, tamburas, sarangis and tablas. The magical sound drifts over the river that looks like a heavenly city with hundreds of boats cruising like swans, their planks covered with rows of lanterns, their canopies crowded with nobles who have come to attend the function from far-off lands. Just then, something brightens the sky that compels Shivaji and his son to look up to the lit-up sky in amazement to see fireworks exploding energetically and expanding into designs in dazzling patterns. The people in the other boats jump and dance, their jovial screaming fills the air. Their shouts are accompanied by the bangs, booms, whooshes and fizzles from the sky.

The imperial artillery has been provided with an unlimited supply of recreational explosives, releasing thousands of glittery, twinkly, bright and colourful sparks for more than an hour. Finally, the magic in the sky stops with the largest explosion as a showstopper, creating a figure of a lion and the sun rising behind it, the emblem of the Mughal. Shivaji's boat moves in the direction of Agra Fort and within moments something bursts into his vision, something that is far more beautiful, something that is far more unbelievable than the fireworks that have taken the lustre away from the moon and the stars. What he sees now has the power to belittle even the sun, the god of the sky. It has emerged like a celestial body beyond the waters of the Yamuna, its divine reflection in the river trembling with waves, like its injured alter ego. As the boat moves, the Taj Mahal comes in the full view and looms large over the river, the sky, the gardens and even the horizons, as if nothing else matters. Shivaji's eyes dart in the direction of the water. The reflection of the marble mausoleum that shimmers in thousands of lanterns lit in the garden has a strange, inexplicable power.

The music played by the bands is no longer audible. He hears a distant chant from somewhere within the mysterious tomb. Someone is reciting verses and the sound resonates only to glide out and ride the air. He shudders, feeling an uncanny presence in the vast expanse around him. It is one of nervous energy, deliberately lurking with patience. Despite the summer, a draught of chill air from the Yamuna engulfs him, ushering in a strange sense of melancholy.

His eyes have remained fixed on the reflection of the monument of love, as if by a paranormal force. The trembling minarets look like four limbs of a beast with claws emerging from sheaths of marble to hold him in their grip. The Taj Mahal on the banks of the Yamuna is what the Mughals want to show the world and its reflection in the water is what the mausoleum is trying to expose to the world—the sinister, hollow and deceitful world of the Mughals. *What an irony!* Shivaji feels. *The real monument portrays a lie and its reflection unfolds the truth!* He shakes his head in dismay to get rid of the illusion he has seen in the water. The fantasy disappears like dispersing clouds, but another truth flashes in his mind like lightning. Aurangzeb will not allow him to go home alive. He instinctively touches the string of cowries tied around his neck and feels their vibration. Is it because the boat is swaying beneath him or are the cowries trying to warn him?

After coming back to the sarai that night, Shivaji can barely sleep. It is unusually hot and humid. Sometimes after midnight the windowpanes start making a noise as if someone is banging on them. Shivaji tries to fiddle with the bolt chain of a window of his room to get some fresh air and it flies open with a devilish force. A fierce wind carrying dust particles whips Shivaji's face before barging into the room. An *aandhi*, the blinding dust storm, has just begun to roll through the city. Somehow Shivaji pushes the window shut and bolts it. The room is now filled with darkness, the dust and smell of burning human flesh. Maybe a body is being burnt in the nearby Hindu cremation ground. The night ages slowly, from darkness to darkness as the aandhi rages outside, sounding like a harsh whistle. Inside, the trapped air turns oppressive, its dryness stinging each pore of Shivaji's parched skin, making him feel thirsty. He gulps down two large goblets of water. Thankfully, the earthen pot kept on a tripod near the bed has retained its coolness despite the surroundings.

After a fretful sleep in the night, Shivaji ventures out in the balcony of his room in the morning light. The storm has receded and the morning is bright. The trees in the courtyard, withering due to summer heat, boast of more parrots than leaves. He watches them, squawking, whistling and screeching. His eyes move beyond the walls of the sarai, his gaze piercing the foliage to reach the empty place below them. To his shock, it is no longer empty but is crowded with armed men in red uniforms. Astonished, he looks beyond the men and what he sees makes his heart race in his chest. There is the sudden appearance of an encampment; the tents are pitched randomly. They have besieged his residence!

Yesterday's illusion was not an illusion; it was a message!

2

Not even in his wildest dreams had Kunwar Ram Singh thought that things would turn out the way they have. Under Alamgir's orders, they have besieged Mulukchand's sarai as if it were a hill fort. More than five thousand policemen and soldiers reporting to the police chief of Agra have been deployed around the sarai, with proper military outposts and heavily guarded entry and exit points. Kunwar has not seen anything like this before. Barring a few men from Raja Shivaji's cavalcade, most of the men have been asked to leave the sarai and camp near Kunwar's mansion. Kunwar's backyard is crowded with Raja Shivaji's palanquins, elephants, horses and howdahs. His mansion is surrounded by the encampment of Raja Shivaji's men.

In the upper echelons of Agra's political circles, a lobby has been formed against Kunwar's father, headed by Maharaja Jaswant Singh Rathod and Shaista Khan's family, all pretending to be worried about the emperor's prestige and demanding immediate execution of Raja Shivaji. If that does happen, it will reduce Kunwar's family's prestige to dust. In the Deccan, the Marathas will revolt and may even kill his father. The mere thought of his father's death sends shivers down Kunwar's spine. If Mirza dies, Kunwar, at the age of thirty-five, will become an orphan. The emperor will not hesitate to remove him from his present duty at the palace and send him to the empire's dangerous borders. He will have to leave his wives and children behind at Agra and they will be at the mercy of the emperor.

Kunwar had met the imperial mir bakshi, Mohammad Amin, several times in the recent past. The first paymaster general had told him that the emperor was planning to send Kunwar and Raja Shivaji on a campaign headed by Rad Andaz Khan to Afghanistan to fight Yusufzai and Afridi rebels. Knowing the reputation of Rad Andaz, Kunwar had instantly known the strategy. Once in Kabul, Rad Andaz

Khan would assassinate Raja Shivaji and make it look like an enemy ambush. Kunwar did not mince words; he had told Amin that the emperor must kill him first and then do what he wanted with Raja Shivaji. With repeated visits to the palace and putting up his case in front of wazir-e-azam Jaffar Khan, Kunwar has managed a nod from the emperor to keep some of his trusted Rajputs around Raja Shivaji just to make sure that the police chief and his men do not kill him by deceit. His father has given his word for Raja Shivaji's safety and the Rajput promise has to be kept. The emperor has also agreed that men accompanying Raja Shivaji are allowed in and out of the sarai and that Sambhaji can stay with Kunwar's family and visit his father whenever he feels like.

It is only when Kunwar visits Shivaji for the first time after the besiegement that he realizes how serious the situation is. He has to cross several check posts, each time explaining who he is and why he is there.

Kotwal Fulad Khan and his men stand in the passage of the sarai that leads to the inner courtyard. The chief of the Agra Police has handled hundreds of criminals and caught thousands of fugitives in his life, so this is not something new. He has been told that his latest captive is a dangerous man and has killed and maimed many mighty men in the Deccan. Some have vouched that Shivaji has supernatural powers and can appear at different places at the same time or can just disappear in thin air. Fulad Khan is not scared of such rumours, but has decided to be extra careful. He was born here to his African parents who worked for Shah Jahan. He has grown up playing with catapults and pebbles in the narrow lanes of modest southern habitats of Agra.

He watches Kunwar entering the passage.

'Assalamu Alaikum, Kunwar Bhai, you do not trust us with the captive? You have your own men planted in the sarai?' Fulad asks with a tone of slight disappointment.

'Waalekum Assalaam,' Kunwar reciprocates the greeting and says, 'It is more to make sure that the bird does not fly away.'

'Not even a draught of wind can escape when we are here,' Fulad quips.

Kunwar does not comment but smiles and moves on. The courtyard of the sarai that was covered with tents is now empty since most of the Marathas have shifted near Kunwar's house. The kitchen at the other end is busy with servants of the sarai having their evening meal and the air is filled with the aroma of cooked rice. Kunwar walks along the corridors where he meets his men whose job is to watch over Fulad Khan and his men and make sure that they do not harm Raja Shivaji. They bow to him, he bows back and moves towards Raja Shivaji's chamber, the entrance of which is guarded by a skinny and dark man whom Kunwar does not know. The chamber is lit by just one lamp and in that semi-darkness four men with grave faces sit near the sick man's bed along with the young medic, Niraji Raoji, Hiroji Farzad and Raghunath Korde. Kunwar kneels near the bed and stares at Raja Shivaji who looks ill. His vibrant skin has lost its lustre, and his piercing eyes are only a listless stare.

'What is wrong with him?' Kunwar asks the medic.

'Raja's lungs are giving way. There are some elements in the air of Agra that do not agree with him. He is a mountain man,' the medic answers softly.

'He wishes to send some pearls and diamonds to the esteemed grand wazir, Jaffar Khan Sahib, and the esteemed mir bakshi, Mohammad Amin Sahib.'

Within days of getting gifts, Jaffar Khan presents Shivaji's petition for pardon to Aurangzeb after making Mohammad Amin as his mediator in which Shivaji is ready to give huge sums of money to Aurangzeb to spare him from going to Kabul and let him go home. In that petition, Shivaji asks for the lost forts and asserts that if he is given those forts he will fight for Aurangzeb's cause all his life.

Aurangzeb suspects Jaffar Khan of taking a bribe from Shivaji.

He makes Kunwar sign a security bond for Shivaji's conduct at Agra and see that he does not escape or play any mischief. Kunwar knows what the bond means. If Raja Shivaji escapes, he will be sent to the gallows. There is one more problem. The monsoons have arrived in Agra and Raja Shivaji has remained ill. The fever is not receding and some from the Maratha camp say that their master is dying. Raja Shivaji wants to do charity, a dying man's wish. He also wants to send back most of the men who have come with him from the Deccan, including Malusare, Yesaji Kank, Jiva Mahale and Kavji. They will return under the leadership of Prataprao Gujjar.

3

Mir Bakshi Mohammad Amin has come a long way, from being the spoilt son of the rich and famous Mir Jumla to a responsible paymaster general of the Mughal court. Gone are the days when he used to get drunk and show off his father's riches. So arrogant was he that he had not hesitated to urinate in Qutb Shah's court in Hyderabad to show his contempt. Amin has sobered down and is doing a fine job, shuttling between Agra and Dilli to look after transfers and payments of mansabdars and their travel papers when they are on a campaign.

For the past few weeks, life has been hectic with so many people coming to Agra. A new message has come from the emperor's office to grant permission to some people who have come with Shivaji to return home. It is a routine job. He already has the list and their palm impressions. He has to make new papers and match the new palm impressions with the old ones, but there is a deadline: he must finish the work in one week.

As he gets busy with his scribes, a message arrives from the zenana headquarters. Begum Sahiba Jahanara has summoned him. She has a special place in Mohammad Amin's heart. Unlike most rich Agra residents, he has married only once and loves his wife. But their first three babies had turned out to be stillborn. In the fourth pregnancy, Begum Sahiba had instructed the royal midwife to take care of his wife's health and Mohammad was blessed with a pretty daughter!

He would do anything for Begum Sahiba Jahanara.

With his heart brimming with warmth, Mohammad walks briskly towards the Jahangiri Palace along with tartar women guards who have come to take him. The men can go only up to the library, a small structure topped with domes. There is a strange silence in there and Amin feels a presence behind a curtain hung in one of the corners and hears the rustle of clothes.

He bows deep in front of the curtain and is greeted with kind words. 'Khosh Amadid,' the Begum says in chaste Farsi, 'I have heard from your wife that you spend less time at home.'

'Work keeps me away; you are aware, Begum Sahiba,' Mohammad tries to clear his name.

'Listen carefully; Allah is merciful. Listen to your wife, I do not want excuses.' The voice has suddenly turned cold and steely.

Mohammad is speechless. Begum Sahiba has never sounded like this before and he has not hurt his wife for as long as he remembers. Mumbling a few lame words in his defence he shakes his head in agreement as if saying that he will never ignore his wife again.

'You may go now.' There is urgency in her order.

A eunuch working for khoja Mutamad is eavesdropping, but he is disappointed. The emperor wants news, real news of conspiracies and strategies being hatched in the royal seraglio. He seeks private conversations, gossips that may expose the malicious minds of the enemies of the empire. The eunuch had hoped that something interesting might unfold in the library when he heard that the princess had summoned the mir bakshi, but it has turned out to be a simple homely conversation and a waste of his precious time.

That night when Amin protests to his wife, she tells him something that sends chills down his spine.

'Begum Sahiba wants you to help Kunwar and Raja Shivaji in whichever way you can, even if they need extra travel papers, and for that you will be given new palm impressions. Begum Sahiba will put her seal. Also, she wants you to convince the emperor to free Kunwar Ram Singh from the bond that holds him responsible for Shivaji.'

Mohammad Amin is surprised. He was under the impression that Begum Sahiba Jahanara is a part of the anti-Jai Singh lobby that wants Shivaji's execution.

4

Most people who had come with Shivaji are already on their way to the Deccan, galloping away on their horses. They have left behind palanquins and elephants that are parked in the backyard of Kunwar's house. Only a few people are left behind at Mulukchand's sarai, one can count them on one's fingers: Raghunath Korde, Trimbak Dabir, Niraji Raoji, Hiroji Farzad, the young medic and the skinny man whose name is still a mystery. Sambhaji is still with Kunwar's family.

Shivaji still suffers from fever and Niraji Raoji and the young medic have been busy soaking a cotton cloth in cold water, wringing it out and applying it on Shivaji's forehead. At times, Niraji Raoji and the medic are seen leaving the sarai to collect medicinal herbs from the nearby forests, and Fulad Khan is sympathetic to them. He visits the chamber every now and then to make sure that his captive is in his room. Raghunath and Trimbak visit the sarai rarely since they are busy meeting politically influential people of Agra to get more funds. Their master is dying in an alien land, and wants to donate a considerable sum to attain moksha, salvation from the circle of birth and death. The news has reached Aurangzeb, who has sent a new message to Shivaji through Kunwar.

If you think you are dying why don't you hand over the remaining of your forts to us? We shall allow your son to return home after your death.

Kunwar had to bring this message to Shivaji.

The ailing man asked a scathing question to Kunwar, 'Your father gave Aurangzeb twenty-three of my forts and got the rich paragana of Tonk in Rajasthan as jagir. For the rest of my forts, what are you getting from the emperor? Tell your emperor that I have no control over my men, and they will never listen to me. Please tell your emperor that I am sick, and my death wish is to become a monk and stay at Varanasi.'

To this Aurangzeb sarcastically replies, 'Well, well, let him turn a monk and stay at Prayag instead. Subhedar Bahadur Khan will take care of his death wish.' Bahadur Khan is known for his murderous nature, which is far worse than Rad Andaz Khan.

When Kunwar brings the message, Shivaji, without getting up from his bed, says in a feeble voice, 'I do not think I will leave this bed. I do not blame your father or you, but do me just one last favour: forward my loan application to your emperor. I want to give in charity, and perform a yagna to attain moksha and release my soul from the viscous cycle of birth and death. I want to invite Kavindra, the king of poets, Paramanand from Varanasi to Agra to perform the same. I have made sure that the emperor will release you from my bond. I cannot run away anywhere; only death will take me away from here.'

Shivaji's loan application for sixty-six thousand rupees is approved by Aurangzeb after Shivaji signs the papers of Hundi. The demand draft is quickly sent to Mirza Raja Jai Singh to encash it from Shivaji's men who will take the money out from Shivaji's personal wealth. Kunwar is released from his guarantee, to respect a dying man's wish. The dying man has already started his charity. Fruit, dry fruit and sweetmeat merchants, basket-makers and coolies have started frequenting the sarai, dispatching huge baskets filled with food to Brahmins, religious mendicants and homeless beggars as alms, and to ministers, courtiers and the besieging police, including Fulad Khan, as gifts. Each basket, carried by two bearers, is custom-checked at least at three different check posts by Fulad Khan's men.

Special presents of precious stones and diamonds are sent to Jaffar Khan and Mohammad Amin.

Fulad Khan continues to visit his ward's room several times a day and sometimes even in the night. The purpose of visit has changed though. The man on the deathbed cannot run away but he is destined to escape for sure, with the help of death. The police chief is in fact worried about his ward, who has lost a considerable amount of weight and who has developed dark circles around his eyes. Fulad Khan can recognize him only by the colour of his eyes—brown, and a large gold bracelet he wears on his right hand. He also knows the men who sit around Shivaji: the medic, sharp-featured Niraji Raoji and an emaciated, dark-skinned man whose name Fulad Khan does not know. Sometimes, when Niraji Raoji is not seen, Hiroji Farzad, Raja Shivaji's distant cousin, is seen keeping a vigil on their leader.

5

A scholar of *adhyatma* from Varanasi who is also a renowned poet has arrived at Mulukchand's sarai with many of his disciples. The news has spread and Brahmins of Agra who have never met him before are eager to see him in person.

'Now that I have come, do not worry,' short and fair Paramanand, whom everyone addresses as Kavindra, an unassuming and smiling man wearing a simple white cloth and red headgear, announces and disappears into Shivaji's room. He has known the Bhosale family for a long time and has met Shivaji several times when he had visited Pune.

When Fulad Khan visits Raja Shivaji's chamber, he is pleased to see Kavindra who reads aloud from a fat book in a language Fulad does not understand. In the evening, Kavindra comes out looking exhausted and sad. He looks at Kunwar, Raghunath, Trimbak and Fulad gathered outside the room and says softly, 'It is just a matter of days now.'

Fulad shows no emotion.

Kavindra continues, 'Raja wants me to give a talk on spirituality.' There is silence.

Kavindra persists, 'The talk will be followed by a yagna, where oblations will be offered. Raja wishes to invite all the Brahmins of Agra. It is his last wish.'

That evening, Fulad contemplates on the poet's words and the state of things. Kunwar makes his move the very next day. Since the emperor is on a hunt, the application for permission to fulfil the dying man's last wish is submitted to the wazir-e-azam. Jaffar Khan signs it without any fuss. Kunwar swings into action, and appoints his trusted men to visit the renowned Brahmins of Agra to invite them.

Everything is planned in a day. Hand-drawn maps are given to each of the invitees. A dress code has already been decided. There is an excitement in the Brahmin community of Agra and everyone prays that it does not rain the next day.

Fulad Khan is not happy, but what can he do when the wazir-e-azam has given permission? He decides to take an interpreter along, wanting to know what the poet talks about.

An hour before the appointed time, more than a hundred Brahmins have gathered at the sarai, each wearing a long white tunic, red pagari turban and silk dhoti. Fulad Khan has been generous and has lent a number of wooden benches for the function.

It is quiet in the front yard. Kavindra starts his speech. The renowned poet who has earned the title of *Kavindra Kavishwar*, the king of poetry, speaks rather well, his words wise and poetic. Kavindra talks in chaste Sanskrit: 'We seek the knowledge of "self" with the help of this world we live in and the senses we are born with. The world and our senses are "other than" *atman*, non-self. The real me is not my body or my senses. Could we ever seek self through non-self? The spirit, the atman, when sought through un-atman is reduced to mere material. It has to be considered through itself, by itself. Otherwise it ceases to be what it truly is.'

It has been an hour since all the Brahmins have been listening to the famous man, hauling all their life energies into their ears.

Fulad Khan's muscles ache with boredom and he is beginning to have a headache. Cursing his luck he asks his interpreter to explain the meaning of the long lecture in three simple sentences. The interpreter explains—much to Fulad Khan's chagrin; he finds it absurd! He wants to get away from the congregation of lunatics.

Kunwar holds Sambhaji's hand and listens to the lecture, but his mind is somewhere else. He is not sure if he has made a mistake by helping Raja Shivaji. He realizes that this is the wrong time to hold such ceremonies. It may irritate the emperor and who may order Raja Shivaji to be sent to Rad Andaz Khan's palace. Kunwar has heard that his new palace is already commissioned and its 'new underground prison' has been opened for political prisoners the day before. He has learnt from Agra's grapevine that the new place is fitted with many machines to torture and then kill the inmates.

The venue is filling up with more Brahmins, all chattering in Sanskrit and looking like a contingent in uniform. Some have removed their turbans and with their heads tonsured and their foreheads smeared with vermillion Kunwar finds it tough to recognize even those whom he is acquainted with, unless they come forward and greet him. Fulad Khan is even more confused—his interpreter too is in the same attire and has left his side to talk to others and has vanished in the crowd.

Kunwar holding Sambhaji's hand walks into the courtyard and notices a platform with a pit in which the yagna fire is already lit. A few Brahmins including Kavindra have begun the yagna rituals. Before he can think of going to Raja Shivaji's room, he notices a few men bringing Raja Shivaji on a sedan chair. Raja is all wrapped up in a woollen shawl, his face, half-hidden by a new monkey cap, lamely resting on his right shoulder. Terror cuts through Kunwar's stomach and he starts moving through the crowd towards Raja Shivaji to get a closer look, but someone tugs at his clothes. He looks down and sees Sambhaji weeping. Kunwar lifts the boy up in his arms and watches the rituals instead.

'Is my father dying?' Sambhaji's feeble words are downed by the loud chanting of mantras.

The Brahmin priests have raised their voice and are robustly chanting, while wood, ghee and auspicious herbs are tossed in the fire that emits billows of smoke, making everyone's eyes burn and water. Hiroji Farzad and the medic stand behind the sedan chair, their eyes darting in every direction. Kunwar wonders why. The chanting goes on for a while, and Kunwar notices a Brahmin standing very close to Shivaji whom he has seen somewhere but cannot recollect.

He has seen this man before. Where?

Kunwar's eyes wander in search of Niraji Raoji and others but they are nowhere to be seen. He wants to see the familiar-looking Brahmin from up close, but before he can move towards Raja Shivaji, the Brahmin has vanished.

For a while the soot fills the courtyard. After some time the chants stop and the yagna seems to be over. All of a sudden, the bearers take the sedan chair towards Shivaji's room and at once all the Brahmins follow them.

'What are they doing?' Kunwar hears Fulad Khan scream; he is now standing next to Kunwar. A Brahmin stops to inform him. 'We will chant a mantra and pray for Raja Shivaji's moksha.'

'Let Raja Sambhaji be with me, I must take him to his father,' Raghunath shouts into Kunwar's ears and takes Sambhaji away.

When Fulad and his policemen reach the entrance of Shivaji's room they realize that it is impossible to enter because the place is packed and the chanting has started, the chorus slowly reaching a crescendo. 'What are they saying?' Fulad Khan hisses a question in one of the Brahmins' ears. He does not bother to figure out who the Brahmin is—they all look the same!

'It's a very sacred mantra called the *mahamrityunjaya*, meaning victory over death. They are hailing the three-eyed God Shiva. They are asking him to pluck the life of the dying one away like a farmer who lets a ripe cucumber gently free from its bondage from the vine of life. They are worshipping Shiva to liberate the mortal one so that he becomes immortal.'

Fulad does not understand any bit of that weird explanation but he has, by now, got used to such meaningless blabber. The chanting goes on for a long time, trying his patience till he wants to scream and cry. After a while, the Brahmins start coming out of the room, one by one, some wiping their tears, some shaking their heads in dismay. Fulad Khan shoves men around him and pushes his way into the room, while Kunwar's men, watching Fulad Khan, rush in behind him.

Shivaji is lying on the bed with his eyes closed. Raghunath is busy covering the patient with layers of sheets whose head is partially veiled with a cold compress. Sambhaji watches his father sullenly.

'We have to count the breaths now, the end is near,' Raghunath declares, wiping his tears, offering Raja Shivaji's gold bracelet to Fulad Khan.

'He wants you to have it; it's his last wish and it is an auspicious day,' Raghunath says, sobbing.

Fulad Khan has never taken a bribe in his life, but this is different—it is the dying man's wish. He accepts the bracelet and moves away to join his men guarding the door. Kunwar's men see Fulad Khan taking the gold ornament.

'Where is Niraji Raoji?' Fulad Khan asks.

'He is looking after the guests; the food will soon be ready.'

'The feast is ready,' someone keeps shouting loudly, as everyone, including some of Fulad Khan's men, disappears. It is already late and the aroma of the food has seduced the hungry gathering. Fulad Khan waits stubbornly at the door watching over Raja Shivaji who has gone off to sleep. The medic is busy reading the patient's pulse; his face is serious, his eyes moist. Kunwar's Rajput guards keep hovering around outside the door—they have become an irritant to Fulad Khan.

It is only after his men come back after their meal that Fulad leaves the door. When he comes out, he notices hundreds of sweetmeat baskets ready for dispatch at the entrance of the sarai, with hundreds of bearers hovering around them.

'Open and check each one before the goods leave the premises,' Fulad Khan orders some of his men who have returned after the lunch.

Clean carpets and durries are spread in the courtyard and some in the front yard to accommodate everyone. Water is served in the silver goblets given by Kunwar. The food is delicious and served with dollops of love, reverence and excess, till the visitors belch with satisfaction. Extra attention is paid to Fulad Khan.

After the meal, the guests have started leaving the venue, and each one is greeted by Fulad Khan's men at the exit point. Several Brahmins wearing similar attire accompany Kavindra. As they cross Fulad's check posts under the watchful eyes of the guards, Kavindra explains about the essence of adhyatma in Sanskrit and the Brahmins listen intently, ignoring Fulad's men as they walk on. Once they come out of the police siege they bid farewell to each other and vanish into the waiting palanquins.

Kunwar walks towards Raja Shivaji's chamber. Fulad's guards standing at the entrance move a bit so that Kunwar can squeeze in. Raja is fast asleep, his breathing has become shallower. The chamber is quiet and morose, as death hangs heavy in the air. The medic sits quietly; Sambhaji stands near the bed looking forlorn. Behind Sambhaji stands Niraji Raoji. Kunwar is shocked.

'Where were you?' Kunwar asks. He had not seen the man even during lunch.

'Here and there,' Niraji says and smiles.

'Where is Hiroji?' Kunwar wants to know.

'Must be looking after the guests,' the medic replies, his eyes fixed on his patient.

'I shall wait,' Kunwar says as a sob chokes his throat. Surprisingly, Sambhaji quietly stares at his father's face covered with cold compress. The boy for some reason looks puzzled.

'Kavindra and his men will come to your home. You must go and help them to take the palanquins, elephants and horses kept in your backyard donated to him by Raja Shivaji,' the medic informs Kunwar Singh. 'You may come back here later if you please.'

Kunwar nods and asks Sambhaji to come along. His Rajputs deployed to keep a watch on Raja Shivaji are sitting in the courtyard, some of them smoking. They quickly extinguish their chillums and stand up to bow. Kunwar hardly notices them; his heart is heavy with grief.

Unknown to the world, under the patient's bed, skinny and dark-skinned Naik, the master of guise and make-up, crouches in a foetal position with a makeup box, containing jars filled with coloured powders, tongs, shaving blades, false beards and more.

Kunwar rides home with Sambhaji in a palanquin, thinking about the very fair Brahmin standing next to Raja Shivaji. He looked so familiar! Kunwar is sure he has seen the man before.

Where?

6

Kavindra's entourage, consisting of his disciples, a few Brahmins from Agra, along with a palanquin, elephants and horses, exits Agra from the west and moves towards Fatehpur Sikri. They cover a few kos and camp a little away from the main road. In the dark of the night, a few Brahmins change their attire and become cavalrymen. They mount the horses and ride on south, bypassing Agra. One of the cavalrymen is Shivaji. As they ride on, Shivaji thinks of the past months of planning and of feigning illness, and how Kavindra planned today's yagna rituals when Aurangzeb was away from Agra on a hunting expedition. When the emperor is away, even the security at the city's gates is slack. That is why no one asked the questions they should have asked while the entourage exited. Shivaji smiles at how Fulad's men feasted on milk desert rich with crushed poppy seeds. The impact was immediate. At the check posts around the sarai, most of them were a bit intoxicated.

Niraji Raoji, Hiroji Farzad and the medic have been left behind. Niraji and Hiroji will impersonate him alternatively while the medic will sit by their side with a grave face. The drama must go on.

As they ride on, Shivaji turns back to take a last look at Agra. In the pale moonlight, the domes and minarets washed clean by the rains gleam zestfully. Somewhere in there his Shambhu sleeps peacefully thinking that his father is around to save him in case of any eventuality. That thought wrenches Shivaji's heart, but Shambhu had to stay to create the illusion of his father being there. There is no guarantee that Shivaji will ever see his son again. It is a dangerous strategy, but for the sake of swaraj . . . and swaraj comes first, before anyone Shivaji loves more than his life, but swaraj needs him. If this was not done, he and Shambhu had to, in any case, die a horrific death. Also, Shambhu is too young to withstand the rough, non-stop journey that lies ahead like a death trap. There was also a greater chance of arousing suspicion if he had taken Shambhu along. Shivaji hopes fervently that one day Shambhu will understand his father's actions. Shivaji just hopes against hope.

But if Aurangzeb suspects that they have left Shambhu behind, he will do anything to find the boy. What will happen then? So Aurangzeb must think Shambhu is with his father and have died on the way.

Another strategy starts forming in Shivaji's mind.

Now everything depends on when Aurangzeb discovers the truth—how many days and nights Shivaji gets as leverage to move away from Agra. More the days, better the hope of escape to Rajgad, which is a journey of about five hundred kos through dense forests, rivers, hills and mountain tracks.

Two days later, Aurangzeb arrives at Agra Fort from his hunting expedition from the borders of Gujarat after killing two lions. He is of the opinion that when an emperor kills a lion, it is a good omen. He also likes to count and measure their claws and keep records to boast about it later. What he will never talk about is the amount of opium emptied into the throat of the ass used as bait, and the fact that the lion that devoured the poor animal was already sleepy and weak. He also does not tell people a huntsman's secret that it is much easier to kill a lion than a tiger. What he tells them is that the lions are more dangerous than the tigers because when a tiger jumps on you it is not a devastating blow but when a lion holds you in his mouth, the animal shakes you like a rag doll, with his claws embedded in your flesh.

Courtiers tell their emperor about what took place in Raja Shivaji's sarai, but the emperor just smiles mysteriously.

CHAPTER THIRTY-THREE

1

Three weeks have passed after the yagna, and for everyone in Agra, Shivaji seems still alive, but still sinking. Kunwar Ram Singh and Sambhaji visit regularly. Sambhaji is sad; his abba sahib seems to have changed, and has stopped talking to him and even looking at him. Even his voice is feeble and the words so incomprehensible.

Fulad comes every hour during the day as well as night. He senses that the end is near and has started praying for his ward.

In the citadel of Agra, a sombre Jahanara has come to Musamman Burj in the evening. She always does—to look at the marble mausoleum where her parents' remains are buried gradually fading into the night. None of her other brothers would have or could have treated their father the way Aurangzeb has. White serpent is what she calls Aurangzeb—white because he portrays such a pure, fair and God-fearing personality that hides his venomous character.

She glances at the gradually darkening sky that is getting darker, but her mind is somewhere else.

'Shahzaadi, there is some news,' she hears her personal eunuch, Chameli, speak to her, panting, his eyes dilated in fear.

'What is it?'

'The white serpent has decided to send the man from the Deccan to Rad Andaz's palace tomorrow.'

Jahanara swings into action. There is a mysterious smile on her face. She has to inform Kunwar.

After getting the news, Kunwar visits the sarai at once and tells the comatose Raja Shivaji about Aurangzeb's order while the medic, Trimbak Dabir, Hiroji Farzad and Raghunath stand solemnly near the bed. The skinny, dark man stands behind the medic with an expressionless face. Niraji Raoji is nowhere to be seen.

'Where is Niraji Raoji?' Kunwar asks. He has not seen the Brahmin since three weeks.

'He is always roaming the forests in fond hope of finding some life-saving herbs and returns very late in the night,' the medic says, trying to suppress a sob.

'I shall pick up Raja Sambhaji from your house. The boy must be with his father now,' Raghunath says, his voice heavy.

2

Fulad Khan had gone to meet Rad Andaz Khan to discuss the time when he could bring Shivaji to Rad Andaz's palace. When he returns, someone informs him that Niraji Raoji and the medic have left the sarai. Raghunath had left earlier.

Fulad asks, 'Who is with Raja Shivaji?'

'When I last visited him, he was sleeping, all wrapped up in a sheet. We have been guarding the door ever since,' someone rattles.

'Hiroji Farzad went out just a few minutes ago,' one of Fulad's men minding the last check post informs him.

'You did not stop him?'

His men are puzzled. Other than Raja Shivaji, everyone was free to enter and exit.

A shocking thought crosses Fulad's mind. Raja Shivaji must have died and his men must have left fearing for their own life. He runs towards the sarai followed by a train of policemen. Kunwar's Rajput guards are chatting away in the courtyard.

Something is not right.

Fulad runs to the sick man's chamber and kicks open the door.

What he sees stops his heart.

The room is empty—stark empty. Just an hour ago when he had visited this place, the patient was on his bed, with others hovering around him. Where is his ward? Fulad runs like a mad man around the empty room, prostrating on the ground and looking below the bed, banging the wall and stamping the floor. Finally he kneels, covers his face with his hands and lets out a hoarse cry. His life is over, his job is gone; perhaps he, instead of Raja Shivaji, will be sent to Rad Andaz Khan's new facility as their first guest!

In that moment of shock, something nags him. He does not remember having seen Niraji Raoji when he visited the room an hour ago. In fact none of them have seen Niraji Raoji for a while, but his man had seen Niraji leaving the sarai. Something has gone wrong, terribly wrong!

Fulad does not announce the disappearance of Raja Shivaji for a long time; he has lost his nerve.

When Kunwar comes home from his palace duty, he is informed that Raghunath has taken Sambhaji away. That night, Sambhaji does not come home. Kunwar finds this strange. For some reason he cannot sleep that night and keeps getting an ominous feeling of impending doom. It is then, while twisting and turning on his bed, that he remembers where he had seen the Brahmin who was standing next to Raja Shivaji the day when the yagna was performed. His heart starts racing. That Brahmin looked like Raja Shivaji . . . No! He was indeed Raja Shivaji! Who was the sick man sitting on the sedan chair then? Was he Niraji Raoji? But he had seen Niraji in Raja Shivaji's chamber thereafter, but then Hiroji was missing. Were they taking turns impersonating Raja Shivaji?

This means Raja Shivaji had escaped a few weeks ago! Three weeks to be precise.

3

Next morning, when Aurangzeb enters the courtyard of Agra Fort to go to his private office at the edge of the zenana quarters he feels the eerie silence, with everyone kneeling with grim faces as if a disaster has struck the empire. To his surprise, he notices the police chief of Agra, Fulad Khan, kneeling along with his slaves.

'What is the matter?' he asks Fulad.

'Raja Shivaji is gone.' The police chief is on the verge of crying, his voice cracking with fear.

'Is he dead?' Aurangzeb feels somewhat sad; he wanted Shiva to suffer at the hands of Rad Andaz. He is also puzzled. Why is his police chief so upset over the death of Shiva Bhosale?

'No, he is not dead, he has disappeared.' Fulad is sobbing, his dark face darker in grief and guilt.

Aurangzeb thinks, *Today they were supposed to send Shiva to Rad Andaz Khan's palace and he was supposed to disappear forever.* He has still not caught on when eunuch Mutamad comes running from the entrance of the private palace, bows deep and then whispers something in his master's ears.

'How?' Aurangzeb screams at Fulad.

Fulad gets up. He is shaking, but he manages to utter, Raja Shivaji was in his room, I had visited it just one hour earlier, but he vanished all of a sudden from my sight, he either flew into the sky or went into the earth. He knows witchcraft.'

Yes, right! Aurangzeb thinks and walks towards his private offices, asking Mutamad to call all the mansabdars from Agra and Dilli. They must go on a massive manhunt, but before that he needs to know the story in detail from Kunwar Ram Singh and Fulad Khan.

Till midnight the men go through the chronology of the event as it happened. Aurangzeb asks many questions about the yagna ceremony and what happened thereafter. He also asks them to draw sketches of check posts around the sarai.

Kunwar tells him everything but keeps quiet about the fair Brahmin who looked like Raja Shivaji.

'Where is Shiva's son?' Aurangzeb questions Kunwar.

'He was with me till yesterday. He was taken by one of Raja Shivaji's men in the evening and he has not returned yet.' Kunwar quivers with fright.

'And he will never return,' Aurangzeb comments drily.

'Did any of you ever touch Shiva's forehead to see if he had fever?' Aurangzeb asks narrowing his eyes.

The men cast their eyes down.

'Did anyone see his face or talk to him in the last three to four weeks?'

'He was too sick to talk,' they tell him.

'Were you sure that the man sleeping on the bed was Shiva Bhosale when, as you say, he used to always cover his face with sheets and cold compresses?' he questions Fulad in particular.

Fulad does not look up.

'Have you seen Hiroji Farzad and Niraji Raoji together recently?' The men just look on.

'I have heard that Shiva Bhosale had a skinny and dark-skinned man with him. He must have been Naik, the master of disguise,' Aurangzeb comments wryly.

'Raja Shivaji and his son might have hidden himself in one of the sweetmeat boxes,' Jaffar Khan offers explanations. Hearing this, Aurangzeb's mind explodes. *How can his wazir-e-azam be such a dimwit?*

'That man is too clever to do something like what you say, wazir-e-azam. He will never put himself in such a vulnerable position. If he was found sitting in one of those baskets, he would have been cut to pieces, without a chance to defend himself. And why would his son be sitting in a sweetmeat box to escape? He was free to go in and out of sarai,' Aurangzeb controls his voice and dismisses his prime minister.

Aurangzeb stays awake that night, sitting alone in his private office at the edge of his palace at Agra Fort. He comes to some conclusions, the first of which is that Shiva was never sick, he was only pretending to be sick to reduce the tension among the police force and make them his sympathizers. A bedridden man cannot escape, can he?

It is likely that Shiva quietly left the sarai, disguised as a Brahmin, along with hundreds of others who gathered for the lecture, rituals and the feast three weeks ago. If he covered at least fifteen kos a day by horse, he must be at least three hundred kos away from Agra by now. Shiva had a strategy and *time was of the essence*. He had three weeks to escape without anyone chasing him. It is now difficult to catch up with him.

This thought stops Aurangzeb's heart.

Aurangzeb suddenly knows the truth. The mayhem was purposely created by inviting all those Brahmins for a kafir ritual. Shiva and his men had known that after a heavy meal, which Aurangzeb suspects was mildly laced with opium, Fulad and his men would find it difficult to distinguish between the Brahmins who wore similar attires. It was then easy to escape as a Brahmin while someone else acted as terminally ill on Shiva's bed. Someone was impersonating him during the function, and then thereafter for three weeks till today. Niraji and Hiroji must be taking turns since they both have brown eyes like Shiva! Another fact strikes Aurangzeb that after he has come back from the hunt, there has not been any exchange of messages between him and Shiva.

Aurangzeb also wonders how Shiva and his men would travel through the empire without *dastak* papers. No sooner has he asked himself that question than he gets the answer: Shiva is too shrewd to leave without the papers, because without papers he would not get food, fodder and horses from the sarais and no ferrymen will take him across the rivers that are swollen after the monsoons.

Someone has helped him with dastak papers! The papers must have been procured when most of Shiva's men left for the Deccan. Mohammad Amin cannot do it all by himself—he needs a royal seal for approval and only Aurangzeb's sons and his sister can use it when he is away. But she can feign innocence citing whatever was submitted by Amin was taken with trust since Aurangzeb had given the order about letting Shiva's men go south. The more Aurangzeb thinks, the more furious he becomes. This is not the time to lose his mind; he must act as if he is on the war path.

Aurangzeb decides to do all he can to catch the man who has outwitted him. Kunwar must have played some role in this political drama. He and his father need to be severely punished. Mirza must die. Udayaraj Munshi must poison his master! Shivaji's son must be found so that Aurangzeb can teach Shambhu's father a lesson he will never forget in his life and even in his death!

Where is Sambhaji now? That was the cleverest part of the drama. Shivaji left his son behind to put the Mughals in total complacency. His son acted as an optical illusion for everyone. Even the boy may not know the man on the bed is not his father!

Within days, the entire imperial machinery is activated. Farmans are dispatched to the subhedars of twenty-two Mughal provinces, and also to thousands of mansabdars from the regions between Agra and Aurangabad. Meetings are held, maps are drawn, the smallest forest trails that lead to the Deccan are noted, astrologers and soothsayers are consulted. Fifty thousand horsemen are deployed in the manhunt. They comb the area between Agra and Varanasi, raiding the temples, sarais, mosques, Hindu schools, cremation grounds, burial grounds and even madrassas. Hundreds and thousands of mendicants, ascetics, swamis, priests, fakirs and pirs are arrested, flogged and imprisoned. A contingent of Rajput soldiers is sent to search the regions between the Narmada and Tapi rivers that divide Hindustan into north Hindustan and the Deccan. Every group, Hindu or Muslim, with a small boy is taken into custody and kept under watch for a few days before letting go. Meanwhile, entire Hindustan has started talking that Raja Shivaji escaped by hiding in a sweetmeat container!

Only Aurangzeb knows what could have really happened. The hunt for Kavindra is on. Finally he is found wandering the forty kos away from Agra in the desert of Rajasthan without the elephants, palanquin and the horses. How did he reach there, where are his elephants and horses? He says he has given everything away to the poor! Without any proof he is allowed to go free.

Kunwar Ram Singh is put under house arrest. Someone has told Aurangzeb that Fulad was seen taking a gold bracelet from Shiva's men. Fulad and some of his officers are fired. Mohammed Amin has fallen from Aurangzeb's eyes and his future as the imperial mir bakshi is at stake . . .

It is the beginning of Aurangzeb's true jihad, the war is on. He has decided that the Deccan will be his final frontiers and he will bathe the Deccan with Bhosale blood.

4

It is the end of the rainy season when a contingent of tired horsemen arrives at the gates of Raigad. They say they have come to see Jija Bai Sahib with a message from Agra. Jija bai is very anxious to hear from her son and if he is indeed alive, but she knows the danger of letting the contingent in. Finally, after much deliberation, she allows them to enter as an armed fort garrison surrounds them.

One cavalryman comes forward, touches Jija baji feet and looks up at her.

She stares at him and says in a quivering voice, 'You are my Shiva ba.' She is about to collapse but holds on, looks around desperately and asks, 'Where is my Shambhu?'

Shivaji gets up slowly and says softly, 'Shambhu is no more, Ma sahib.'

Jija bai swoons. Shivaji holds her in his hands and says loudly for everyone to hear, 'Send messages to all our relatives that a death ceremony will be performed for Shambhu for his moksha.'

At the same time he wonders if Aurangzeb, on hearing about the news of Shambhu's death, will give up the search.

About twenty kos north of Agra, in the ancient town of Mathura where Lord Krishna was born and escaped from the clutches of his murderous maternal uncle, a tonsured boy is trying to learn the ancient Hindu scriptures in Sanskrit. His mind, however, is far far away, in and around the hills of the Deccan. He misses his friends and grandmother. He misses his pony rides and swordfights. He wants to go home, but the thought of meeting his father furrows his brow and clouds his face.

Betrayal is difficult to figure, and even more difficult to forgive.

BIBLIOGRAPHY

Asher, C., and C. Talbot. *India before Europe*. Cambridge: Cambridge University Press, 2006.

Bahadur, H.K. *Anecdotes of Aurangzeb*. Translated by J. Sarkar. Kolkata: M.C. Sarkar & Sons, 1925.

Bhosle, Varsha. 'First Blood', Commentary, RediffOnTheNet, 1997. Retrieved from http://www.rediff.com/news/may/23varsha.htm

Boston, A. *The Legacy of Jihad*. New York: Prometheus Books, 2005.

Cardona, G. and D. Jain. *The Indo-Aryan Languages*. London: Routledge, 2003.

Cheema, G.S. *The Forgotten Mughals: A History of the Later Emperors of the House of Babar, 1707–1857*. New Delhi: Manohar, 2002.

Duff, James Grant. *A History of the Mahrattas*. Printed for Longman, Rees, Orme, Brown, and Green by Paternoster-Row, 1826.

Durant, W. *The Story of Civilization, Part I: Our Oriental Heritage*. New York: Simon and Schuster, 1942.

Eaton, Richard M. *A Social History of the Deccan, 1300–1761: Eight Indian Lives, Volume 1*. Cambridge: Cambridge University Press, 2005.

Edwards, S.M. and H.L. Garrett. *Mughal Rule in India*. New Delhi: Atlantic, 1995.

Elliot, H.M. and J. Dowson. *The History of India: As Told by Its Own Historians Vol. VII*. London: Trubner, 1877.

Eraly, A. *The Mughal World: Life in India's Last Golden Age*. New Delhi: Penguin Books India, 2007.

Farooqui, S.A. *A Comprehensive History of Medieval India*. New Delhi: Pearson Education India, 2011.

Godbole, R. *Aurangzeb: Shakyata Aani Shokantika*. Pune: Deshmukh & Co., 2010.

Gokhale, B.G. *Surat in the Seventeenth Century.* Mumbai: Popular Prakashan, 1979.

Gribble, J.D. *History of the Deccan.* London: Luzac & Co., 1896.

Hansen, W. *The Peacock Throne: The Drama of Mogul India.* New Delhi: Motilal Banarsidass, 1972.

———. *The Peacock Throne: The Drama of Mogul India.* New York: Holt, Rinehart and Winston, 1996.

Joshi, A. *Agryahun Sutka.* Pune: Shivapratap Prakashan, 2016.

Khan, M.A. *Islamic Jihad: A Legacy of Forced Conversions, Imperialism, and Slavery.* New York: iUniverse, 2009.

Khare, G.H. *Persian Sources of Indian History (Aitihasik Farsi Sahitya), I–V.* Pune: Bharat Itihas Samshodak Mandal, 1934–61.

Knapp, S. *Crimes against India and the Need to Protect Its Vedic Traditions: 1000 Years of Attacks against Hinduism and What to Do about It.* New York: iUniverse, 2009.

Krishna, B. *Shivaji the Great.* Kolhapur: Arya Book Depot, 1940.

Kulkarni, A.R. *Medieval Deccan History.* Mumbai: Popular Prakashan, 1996.

———. *Shivkalin Maharashtra.* Pune: Rajhans Prakashan, 1997.

———. *Ashi Hoti Shivashahi.* Pune: Ranjhans Prakashan, 1999.

———. *Maharashtra in the Age of Shivaji.* Pune: Diamond Publications, 2008.

Kulkarni, N. *Chhatrapati Shivaji Maharaj Jivan Rahasya.* Pune: Indrayani Sahitya Prakashan, 2003.

Mahajan, V.D. *History of Medieval India.* Mumbai: S. Chand, 1991.

Martin, F. *India in the 17th Century: Social, Economic and Political (Memoirs of Francois Martin): Volume II Part II: 1670–1694.* Translated by L. Varadarajan. New Delhi: Manohar, 1985.

Maskiell, M., and A. Mayor. 'Killer Khilats, Part 2: Imperial Collecting of Poison Dress Legends in India'. *Folklore,* Vol. 112, Issue 1 (2001): 163–82.

Mehendale, G.B. *Shivaji: His Life and Times.* Thane: Param Mitra Publications, 2011.

More, S. 'Rajyay Namah', *Sakal,* 30 August 2015. Retrieved from http://www.esakal.com

Padmanābha. *Kānhaḍade Prabandha, India's Greatest Patriotic Saga of Medieval Times: Padmanabha's Epic Account of Kānhaḍade.* Translated by V.S. Bhatnagar. New Delhi: Aditya Prakashan, 1991.

Palsokar, R.D. *Shivaji: The Great Guerrilla.* Dehradun: Natraj Publishers, 2003.

Purandare, B. *Maharaj*. Pune: Purandare Prakashan, 2016.

Ranade, M.G. *Rise of the Maratha Power*. New Delhi: Ministry of Information and Broadcasting, Government of India, 1974.

Samant, S. *Vedh Mahamanavacha*. Pune: Deshmukh & Co., 2009.

Sardesai, H.S. *Shivaji: The Great Maratha, Volume I*. New Delhi: Cosmo Publications, 2002.

———. *Shivaji: The Great Maratha, Volume III*. New Delhi: Cosmo Publications, 2002.

Sardesai, G.S. *Marathi Riyasat, Volume I*. Mumbai: Popular Prakashan, 1988.

Sarkar, J. *Anecdotes of Aurangzib (English translation of 'Ahkam-i-Alamgiri' Ascribed to Hamid-ud-din-Khan Bahadur) with a Life of Aurangzib and Historical Notes*. Calcutta: M.C. Sarkar & Sons, 1925.

———. *History of Aurangzib*. Mumbai: Maharashtra Rajya Sahitya Sanskruti Mandal, 1978.

———. *House of Shivaji: Studies and Documents on Maratha History, Royal Period*. Calcutta: M.C. Sarkar & Sons, 1955.

———. *Reign of Shah Jehan, History of Aurangzib (Mainly Based on Persian Sources) Vol. I*. Calcutta: M.C. Sarkar and Sons, 1912.

———. *Shivaji and His Times*. Calcutta: M.C. Sarkar & Sons, 1948.

———. *Shivaji and His Times*. London: Longmans, Green and Company, 2007.

Sarkar, J. And R. Sinh. *Rajasthani Records: Shivaji's Visit to Aurangzib at Agra; a Collection of Contemporary Rajasthani Letters from the Jaipur State Archives*. Calcutta: University of Calcutta, 1963.

Sen, S.N. *Administrative System of the Marathas*. Kolkata: KP Bagchi & Co., 1925.

Shiva Charitra Karyalaya. *English Records on Shivaji (1659–1682)*. Contributed by Narasimha Cintāmaṇi Keḷkar. Pune: Shiva Charitra Karyalaya, 1931.

Shivram, B. *The Authority of the Padshahs in Sixteenth Century Mughal India, SACS* [Online], 2(2). Retrieved from https://blogs.edgehill.ac.uk/sacs/files/2012/07/Document4-Shiv%C5%95am-B-The-Authority-of-the-Padshahs-inSixteenthCentury-Mughal-India.pdf

ACKNOWLEDGEMENTS

I thank my family, especially my mother, Leela, for being with me while writing this book. Eighteen years of research work has taken away some precious moments I could have spent with my two sons. I apologize to them and thank them for loving me dearly despite the neglect that might have happened due to this novel. I am indebted to my brother, Dr Ashutosh, and husband, Arun, for remaining enthusiastic even as I received at least a hundred emails of refusals from literary agents and publishers. I depended on friends like Dr Ajit Joshi and late Ravindra Godbole who guided me through history.

I specially thank Vaishali Mathur of Penguin Random House for taking up *Frontiers* and literally sculpting the story. How will I forget my copy editor, Mriga Maithel Negi, who scrutinized every sentence and every word of *Frontiers*?